The Siege

The Siege

A NOVEL

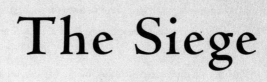

ARTURO PÉREZ-REVERTE

Translated from the Spanish
by Frank Wynne

RANDOM HOUSE

NEW YORK

English translation copyright © 2013 by Frank Wynne

Published in the United States by Random House, an imprint and division of Random House LLC, a Penguin Random House Company, New York.

RANDOM HOUSE and the HOUSE colophon are registered trademarks of Random House LLC.

Originally published in Spanish in Spain by Alfaguara, a division of Santanilla Ediciones Generales, S.L., in 2010, as *El Asedio*. Copyright © 2010 by Arturo Pérez-Reverte. This English translation was originally published in the United Kingdom by Weidenfeld & Nicolson, an imprint of the Orion Publishing Group, London, in 2013.

Library of Congress Cataloging-in-Publication Data
Pérez-Reverte, Arturo.
[Asedio. English]
The siege: a novel/Arturo Pérez-Reverte; translated from the Spanish by Frank Wynne.
pages   cm.
ISBN 978-1-4000-6968-2
eBook ISBN 978-0-8129-9472-8
1. Murder—Investigation—Fiction. 2. Cádiz (Spain)—History—Siege, 1810–1812—Fiction. I. Wynne, Frank, translator. II. Title. PQ6666.E765A7413   2014
863'.64—dc23   2014004597

Printed in the United States of America on acid-free paper

www.atrandom.com

2 4 6 8 9 7 3 1

First U.S. Edition

Title-page image: copyright © iStock.com / © Marcus Lindström

Book design by Victoria Wong

For José Manuel Sánchez Ron
amicus usque ad ara
A friend to the end

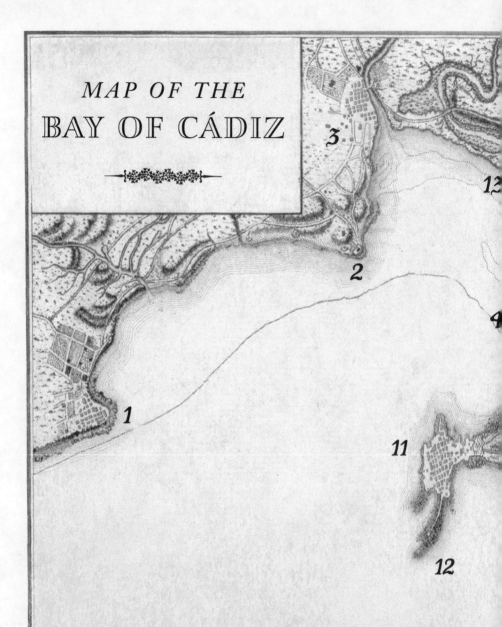

MAP OF THE
BAY OF CÁDIZ

1. Rota
2. Santa Catalina
3. El Puerto de Santa María
4. La Cabezuela
5. Puerto Real
6. La Carraca
7. La Isla
8. Chiclana
9. Sancti Petri
10. Puntales
11. Cádiz
12. San Sebastián
13. Río San Pedro

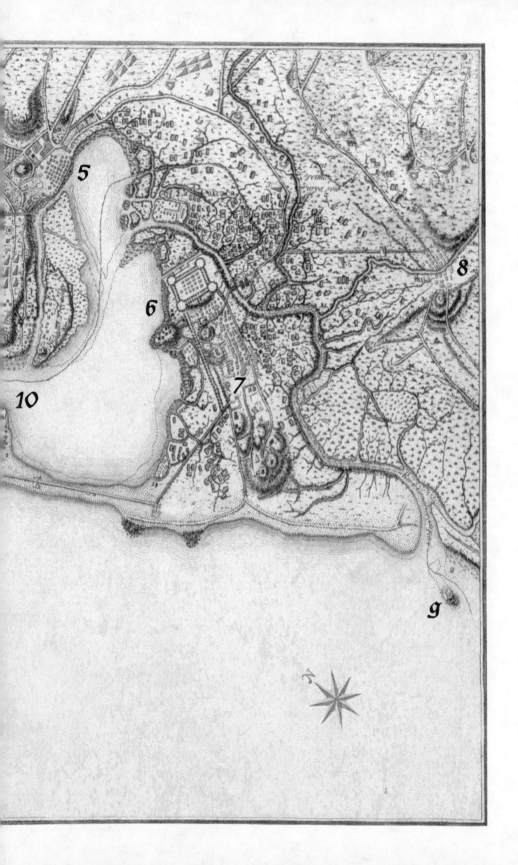

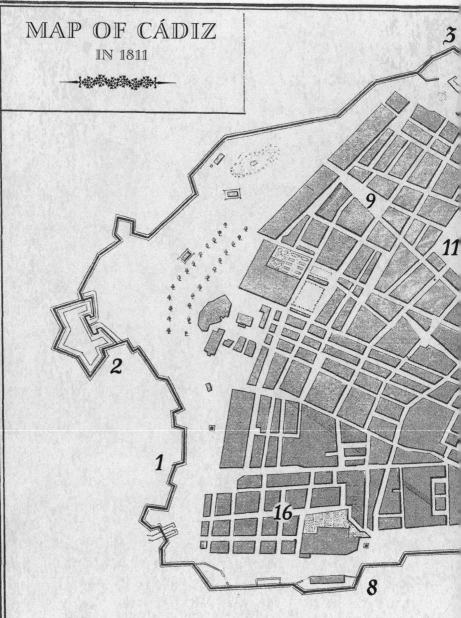

MAP OF CÁDIZ
IN 1811

1. *La Caleta*
2. *Santa Catalina*
3. *La Candelaria*
4. *San Felipe*
5. *Puerta de Mar*
6. *Muelle*
7. *Puerta de Tierra*
8. *Capuchinos*
9. *Mentidero*
10. *Alameda*
11. *San Antonio*
12. *San Francisco*
13. *Aduana*
14. *San Juan de Dios*
15. *Cárcel Real*
16. *La Viña*

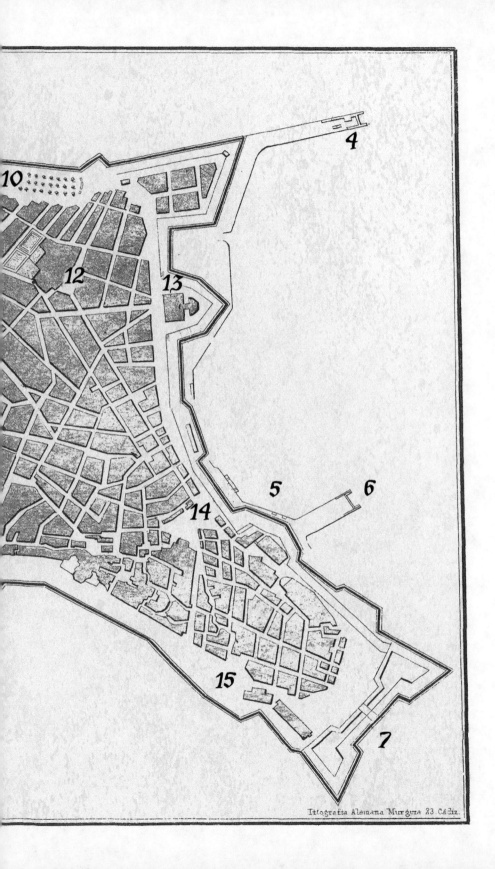

In attempting to dive into the mysteries of nature, it is of importance to know, if the heavenly bodies act upon each other by impulsion or by attraction; if a certain subtle invisible matter impels them toward each other, of it they are endowed with a secret or occult quality by which they are mutually attracted.

Leonard Euler, Letters to a German Princess, 1772

All is possible, when 'tis a god contrives.

Sophocles, Ajax

LIST OF CURRENCY, WEIGHTS, AND MEASUREMENTS

Curtillos—half-liter bottle

Fanega—55.5 liters. There is no English equivalent—the nearest is a bushel at 35 liters.

Napoleon—a gold twenty-franc coin

Onza (de oro)—a coin worth 8 escudos, originally known as a double doubloon but later known as a Spanish doubloon

Toesa—*toise*, old French measurement equivalent to about 6 feet

Vara—unit of distance roughly equivalent to a yard

The Siege

CHAPTER ONE

At the sixteenth lash, the man strapped to the table loses consciousness. His skin is yellowish, almost translucent now; his head hangs limply over the edge of the table. The glow from the oil lamp on the wall reveals the tracks of tears down his filthy cheeks and a thread of blood drips from his nose. The man whipping him stands in silence for a moment, uncertain, one hand gripping the pizzle, the other mopping from his brow the sweat that also soaks his shirt. Then he turns to a third man leaning against the door in the shadows behind him. The face of the man with the whip bears the hangdog look of a hound cowering before its master. A brutish, lumbering mastiff.

In the silence comes the sound of the Atlantic pounding against the shore beyond the shuttered window. No one has said a word since the screaming stopped. Twice, the dark face of the man in the doorway is illuminated by the glowing ember of a cigar.

"It wasn't him," he says finally.

Every man has a breaking point, he thinks, though he does not say as much aloud. Not before his dull-witted companion. Every man will break at a precise point if only he can be brought to it. It is simply a matter of delicacy, of finesse. Of knowing when and how to stop. One more gram on the scales and everything goes to hell. Comes to nothing. Becomes, in short, a fruitless waste of energy. Of time and effort. Blows struck blindly while the true target is making good his escape. Useless sweat, like that of the torturer now mopping his brow, bullwhip in hand, waiting for the order to continue.

"There's nothing more to be done here."

The other man looks at him, slow, uncomprehending. His name is

Cadalso—the word means a gibbet—an apt name given his office. Cigar clenched between his teeth, the man in the doorway moves to the table and, stooping slightly, peers at the unconscious body: unshaven, dirt crusted on his neck, on his hands and between the violet weals crisscrossing his torso. Three more lashes, he calculates; perhaps four. By the twelfth blow, he knew all he needed to know, but it was important to be sure. Besides, in this case no one will ask awkward questions. This man was a vagrant wandering the docks. One of the countless human wrecks washed up in Cádiz by the war and the French siege, just as the sea washes flotsam onto its shores.

"He didn't do it."

The man with the bullwhip blinks, struggling to take in this news. It is almost possible to see the information trickling through the narrow winding pathways of his brain.

"If you let me, I can—"

"Don't be a fool. I'm telling you it wasn't him."

He continues to study the unconscious man closely. The eyes are half-open, fixed and glassy, though the man is not dead. In his professional career Rogelio Tizón has seen enough corpses to recognize the symptoms. The beggar is breathing shallowly and a vein, bloated by the awkward position of his neck, is pulsing weakly. Leaning down, the comisario becomes aware of the acrid stench of damp, dirty skin, of urine spilled on the ground under the force of the lash. The sweat caused by fear—colder now as the unconscious man grows pale—is very different from the other sweat, the animal reek of the man standing nearby holding the whip. With a rictus of disgust, Tizón takes a deep pull on his cigar, exhales a long plume of smoke that fills his nostrils, obliterating the stench. Then, he stands up and walks back to the door.

"When he comes round, give him a couple of coins and warn him that if he breathes a word of complaint hereabouts, we will skin him alive. Like a rabbit."

He drops his cigar stub, crushes it with the toe of his boot then takes his broad-brimmed hat, his cane and his gray redingote from the chair, opens the door and steps out into the blinding sunlight; in the distance, beyond the Puerta de Tierra, the city of Cádiz unfurls, white as the sails of a ship perched upon stone walls that seem to rise from the sea.

Flies buzz. They have come early this year, in search of carrion. The body of the girl still lies on the Atlantic shore of the reef, at the foot of a sand dune whipped by the east wind. Kneeling next to the body, the woman Tizón has had brought from the city works busily between the girl's thighs. The woman is a respected midwife and one of Tizón's regular informants. They call her Tía Perejil. She once worked as a whore around La Merced. Tizón trusts her instincts—and his own—more than he trusts the doctor the police habitually call on, a drunken, mercenary butcher. This is why he calls on this woman for his cases. Twice now in the space of three months. Or four times, if he includes the alewife stabbed by her husband and the innkeeper murdered by a student in a fit of jealous rage. But those were very different cases: it was clear from the outset that they were crimes of passion. Routine. The two murdered girls are a different matter, a strange and much more sinister affair.

"Nothing," says Tía Perejil as Tizón's shadow alerts her to his presence. "Her maidenhood is intact, she's as pure as she was when her mother brought her into this world."

The comisario looks down at the gagged face of the dead girl, her tangle of hair fouled with sand. Fourteen, fifteen perhaps; a scrawny little thing, hardly more than a child. Her skin has been blackened, her features bloated by the heat of the morning sun, but this is nothing compared to the horror of her back, which has been whipped and flayed down to the stark white bones that contrast with the mutilated flesh and congealed blood.

"Just like the other one," adds the midwife.

She rearranges the girl's dress to cover her legs, then stands up, brushing sand from her clothes. She picks up the shawl that is lying nearby and uses it to cover the dead girl's back, swatting the swarm of flies away from the wounds. The shawl is made of thick brown flannel, as plain as the rest of her clothes. The victim has been identified as a maid who worked at a cheap lodging house outside the city, midway between the Puerta de Tierra and the fortifications at La Cortadura. She had set off on foot to visit her frail mother yesterday afternoon while it was still light.

"So what about the beggar, Señor Comisario?"

Tizón shrugs as Tía Perejil looks at him inquisitively. She is a tall, stout woman, sapped by life rather than age. She is almost toothless and gray roots are visible beneath the dye that tints her greasy mane of hair, which is tied up with a kerchief. Around her throat she wears a necklet of holy medals and devotional scapulars, a rosary hangs from a cord at her waist.

"So it wasn't him, then? . . . From the way he screamed, it sounded like he was guilty."

The comisario glares at the midwife until she looks away.

"Hold your tongue, or you'll find yourself screaming too."

Tía Perejil is an inveterate scandalmonger but she has known Tizón for a long time, long enough to know when he is not in the mood for confidences. And today is such a day.

"Forgive me, Don Rogelio, I spoke in jest."

"Save your jests for your sow of a mother should you meet her in hell." Tizón slips two fingers into his jacket pocket, extracts a silver *duro* and tosses it to her. "Now get out of here."

As the woman walks away, the comisario surveys the scene again, as he has a dozen times already. The east wind has long since erased any footprints from the previous night. Besides, ever since the body was discovered by a muleteer who went to a neighboring inn to give the alarm, the countless comings and goings have obliterated any clues there might have been. Tizón stands motionless for a moment, alert to anything that might have escaped his notice, then gives up, disheartened. One long track catches his eyes, a broad groove in the side of the dune, and he crouches down to inspect it. As he squats there, he has the fleeting impression that this has happened before, that he has seen himself crouching, studying traces in the sand. But his mind cannot bring the memory into focus. Perhaps it is nothing more than one of those strange dreams that later seem so real, or perhaps that brief, inexplicable feeling that what is happening has happened before. The comisario gets to his feet having reached no conclusions: the furrow could have been caused by an animal, by a body being dragged, by the wind.

As he passes the corpse he notices that the wind has lifted the girl's skirt, baring her leg to the knee. Tizón is not a tender-hearted man. His profession is brutal and certain rough edges particular to his character have long since led him to think of a corpse—whether in sun or shade—as simply a piece of rotting flesh. As a chore that will entail complications, formalities, investigation, reports to his superiors. Nothing that is likely to trouble the sleep of Rogelio Tizón Peñasco, Commissioner for Districts, Vagrants and Transients, who has spent thirty-two of his fifty-three years working as a policeman, making him a wily old dog. But on this occasion even the hard-nosed comisario cannot help but feel vaguely uncomfortable. And so, with the tip of his cane, he moves the skirt back into place and piles a little heap of sand on it so it will not fly up again. As he does so, he spots a half-buried shard of metal, twisted like a corkscrew. He bends down and picks it up, weighing it in his hand. He immediately recognizes it as a piece of shrapnel created when the French shells explode. There are shards of metal like this all over Cádiz. This one probably came from the yard outside Lame Paco's Tavern where a bomb recently exploded.

He drops the piece of metal and walks back towards the whitewashed wall of the tavern where a group of onlookers is being kept at bay by two soldiers and a corporal sent by the duty officer at San José at the request of Tizón, who felt confident that a few uniforms would command some respect. The crowd is made up of menials, serving wenches from neighboring taverns, muleteers, local mothers and their tykes. Standing at the front, by virtue of his status both as the innkeeper and the person who informed the authorities when the body was discovered, is Lame Paco.

"They say it wasn't the beggar what done it," Paco says as Tizón draws level with him.

"They speak the truth."

The beggar had been skulking around for several days and the local innkeepers were quick to point the finger when the murdered girl was discovered. In fact it was Paco who had arrested the beggar, kept a hunting rifle trained on him until the police arrived and made sure he wasn't roughed up too badly: just a few kicks and punches. The disappointment is visible on the faces of the crowd—especially the boys, who now will have no one at whom they can hurl the stones they've stuffed in their pockets.

"Are you sure, Señor Comisario?"

Tizón does not trouble himself to answer. He looks thoughtfully at the section of wall destroyed by the French shell.

"When did the bomb fall, my friend?"

Thumbs hooked into his belt, Lame Paco comes and stands next to Tizón, respectful and a little cautious. He knows the comisario of old and knows that *"friend"* is simply a turn of phrase and one that, coming from Tizón, could just as easily be a threat. Because Lame Paco is not lame, he has never had a limp, but his grandfather did and in Cádiz nicknames are inherited more surely than money. As are professions. Lame Paco has a face framed by gray whiskers and it is common knowledge that he was a sailor and a smuggler in the past, not to mention the present. Tizón knows that Paco's cellars are full of merchandise from Gibraltar, he knows that on nights when the sea is calm and the wind temperate, the beach is alive with the dark shapes of boats and shadowy figures hauling contraband. Sometimes they even smuggle cattle. But for as long as Lame Paco continues to bribe Customs officers, soldiers and policemen—including Tizón—to look the other way, no one is going to ask questions about whatever is hauled up on this beach. It would be a very different matter if the innkeeper were to become greedy and attempt to shirk his obligations, or if—as some in the city and elsewhere have done—he were to traffic with the enemy. But of that there is no evidence. In the end the people of Cádiz, from the Castillo de San Sebastián to Zuazo Bridge, know each other of old and in spite of the war and the siege, they are content to live and let live. This includes the French, who have not launched a serious attack on the city for some time, shelling it from a distance as though simply observing the formalities.

"The bomb fell yesterday morning, just after eight," the innkeeper explains, gesturing to the east of the bay. "It came from over there, from La Cabezuela. The wife was hanging out the washing and saw the flash. Then *boom*, it exploded over there."

"Any damage?"

"Not much—that bit of wall, the pigeon loft, a few dead chickens . . . The shock was the worst of it. The wife nearly passed out. Thirty paces closer and it would have been a different story."

Tizón digs a fingernail between his teeth—he has a gold canine on the left—as he gazes across the mile-wide inlet of sea that separates the reef—Cádiz is on a peninsula, on one side are the shores of the Atlantic, on the other the bay, the harbor, the salt marshes and the Isla de Léon—from the mainland occupied by the French. The east wind has swept away the clouds so it is possible to see the French fortifications at the Trocadero: to the right the Fort San Louis, to the left the half-ruined walls of the Matagorda and slightly farther away the fortified cannonry of the Cabezuela.

"Have any other shells fallen around here?"

Lame Paco shakes his head, then gestures toward the Reef on either side of his tavern.

"They get a few up near Aguada, and down near Puntales they rain down all day—the people round there have to live like moles . . . This is the first time one has fallen here."

Tizón nods distractedly, still looking toward the French lines, blinking against the dazzling sunlight reflected off the whitewashed wall, the water and the dunes. He is calculating a trajectory, comparing it to others. Something has just occurred to him. It is a hunch, a vague feeling. A nagging sense of foreboding coupled with the conviction that he has somehow experienced this before. Like a line of attack on a chessboard—in this case, the city—made before Tizón could notice it. Two pawns, including the one today. Two pieces captured; two girls.

There might be some connection, he thinks. He has witnessed more complex chess strategies while sitting outside the Café del Correo. Has played them himself, devised them, or used them to counter an adversary's attack. Like a lightning flash, he has an unexpected vision: chess pieces laid out, an unremarkable game, and suddenly, an ambush from behind the knight, a bishop or a pawn, the Attack—and its Capture; a corpse lying at the foot of the dune, dusted with sand carried by the wind. And hovering over all this like a dark shadow, the inkling of something he has experienced before, something he has seen, kneeling as he was then before the traces in the sand and thinking. If only he could remember, everything would be fine. Suddenly, he feels an urgent need to retreat behind the safety of the city walls and begin the necessary investigations. The need to castle, while he considers his strategy. But before he does so, he walks back to the body and, without a word, fumbles in the sand for the twisted hunk of metal and slips it into his pocket.

MEANWHILE, THREE-QUARTERS OF a league east of Lame Paco's Tavern, unshaven and half-asleep, Simon Desfosseux, Imperial Artillery Captain attached to the general staff of the Premier Corps, 2nd Division, is cursing under his breath as he numbers and files the letter he has just received from the Seville Foundry. According to Colonel Fronchard, overseeing the manufacture of Andalusian howitzers, the three defective 9-inch howitzers received by the troops laying siege to Cádiz—flaws which caused the metal to crack after only a few firings—are the result of sabotage during the casting process: a deliberate mistake in the alloy that causes cracks and craters to form in the barrel—*pipes* and *blowholes*, in artillerymen's terms. Two workers and a foreman—all Spaniards—were shot on Fronchard's orders four days ago, but this is cold comfort to Captain Desfosseux. He had high hopes for these new field guns, which have now proved useless. Hopes that he foolishly shared with Marshal Victor and the superior officers who are constantly pressing him to find a solution to a problem that now seems intractable.

"Scout!"

"Yes, Captain."

"Inform Lieutenant Bertoldi I will be upstairs on the observation deck."

Pulling aside the old blanket covering the doorway of his hut, Captain Desfosseux steps outside, climbs the wooden ladder leading to the upper part of the observation post and peers through an embrasure at the city in the distance. Hatless beneath the blazing sun, hands clasped behind his back over the tails of his uniform frockcoat—dark blue with red cuffs. It is not by chance that the observation deck, equipped with several telescopes and an ultramodern Rochon micrometer telescope with a double rock-crystal prism, is situated on the low hill between the fortified gun batteries of the Cabezuela and the fort at the Trocadero. Desfosseux himself chose the location after a careful study of the terrain. From here, it is possible to survey the vast sweep of Cádiz and the bay all the way to the Isla de Léon and, using the spyglasses, to the Zuazo Bridge and the road to Chiclana. All this is his domain. At least in theory: this sweeping expanse of land and water has been placed under his authority by the gods of war and the Imperial Command. An area in which even the word of marshals and generals must sometimes defer to his. A battlefield composed of singular challenges, trials and uncertainties—and indeed insomnia—in which war is not waged through trenches, tactical maneuvers and bayonet charges but using intricate calculations carefully worked out on paper, parabolas, trajectories, angles and mathematical formulae. One of the many paradoxes of the complex war with Spain is that this strange battle in the bay of Cádiz—where the precise mixture of a pound of gunpowder or the combustion speed of fuse matter more than the bravery of a dozen regiments—has been entrusted to an obscure artillery captain.

By land, Cádiz is unassailable. Even Simon Desfosseux knows this, and though no one dares say the word to the Emperor Napoleon, it is accurate. The city is connected to the mainland only by a narrow reef of stone and sand some two leagues in length. The reef road is heavily fortified at a number of points with strategically placed bastions and gun batteries, defenses further reinforced at two key points: the entrance to the city itself, the Puerta de Tierra, equipped with 150 cannons, and, midway along the reef, the Cortadura, a defensive trench still in the process of being dug. Further off, where the peninsula meets the mainland, is the Isla de Léon, protected by a maze of salt marshes, channels and tidal creeks. Such obstacles to any attack are further complicated by the English and Spanish warships anchored in the bay, and by the *Fuerzas Sutiles*—the fleet of gunboats that patrols the bay and the inlets. This formidable array of forces would turn a French assault on land into mass suicide; consequently Desfosseux and his compatriots confine themselves to waging a war of positions along the front line while waiting for better times or some reversal of fortune in the Peninsula. And as they wait, the orders are to tighten the stranglehold on the city, to intensify the shelling of military and civilian targets. It is a strategy about which the French authorities and the government of King Joseph harbor few illusions since it is impossible to blockade the principal access to Cádiz, which is by sea. Ships flying under the flags of various nations come and go and the Imperial Artillery is powerless to stop them. The city still trades with the rebel Spanish ports and half the world besides, resulting in the cruel irony that the besieged are better provisioned than the besiegers.

To Captain Desfosseux, however, this is all relative. Or rather, it matters little. The outcome of the siege of Cádiz, or indeed of the war with Spain, weighs less heavily on his mind than the work that engages all his imagination and his skill. As far as he is concerned, war—something he has only recently experienced, having previously been professor of physics at the School of Applied Artillery in Metz—is a matter of the practical application of the scientific theories to which he has devoted his entire life. His weapon is a slide rule, he likes to say, and his gunpowder trigonometry. The sweeping panorama of the city and the bay is not a target but a technical challenge. He does not say this aloud—to do so would earn him a court-martial—but it is what he believes. Simon Desfosseux's private war is not about national insurrection but a problem of ballistics, and his enemy is not the Spanish but the challenges imposed by the laws of gravity, by friction, air temperature, the nature of elastic fluids, initial velocity and the parabola described by a moving object—in this case a bomb—before it reaches (or fails to reach) the intended point with adequate efficiency. On the orders of his superiors, Desfosseux reluctantly attempted to explain this two days ago to a visiting delegation of French and Spanish officials who had come from Madrid to assess the progress of the siege.

He smiles mischievously as he remembers. The delegates arrived in carriages by the road that runs along the San Pedro River: four Spaniards and two Frenchmen, thirsty, tired, eager for their trip to be over and fearful that the enemy might welcome them with a cannonade from the fortress at Puntales. They clambered down from the coaches, shaking the dust from their frockcoats, waistcoats and hats and all the while looking around apprehensively, trying to pretend they were at ease and composed. The Spaniards were officials in Joseph Bonaparte's government; the French included a secretary to the Royal Household and a squadron leader named Orsini, aide-de-camp to Marshal Victor, who was acting as a guide for the visitors. It was Orsini who suggested a succinct explanation of the matter, so that the gentlemen might understand the importance of artillery to the siege and advise Madrid that, to be done well, things had to be done slowly. "*Chi va piano, va lontano,*" he added—Orsini, in addition to being Corsican was something of a buffoon—"*Chi va forte va a la morte.*"* Et cetera. Desfosseux, who understood the implication, fell into line. "The problem," he explained, calling on his inner professor, still very much alive beneath his uniform, "is not unlike that of throwing a stone. If it were not for gravity, the stone would travel in a straight line. But gravity exists. This is why the trajectory of a projectile propelled by the expanding force of a gunpowder blast is not a straight line but a parabola determined by the uniform acceleration imparted as it leaves the cannon barrel and the vertical pull of free fall which increases in direct proportion to the time the projectile remains in the air. Are you following?" It was clear that they were having trouble following his logic, but seeing one member of the delegation nod, Desfosseux decided to proceed. "The problem, gentlemen, lies in determining the force required to maximize the distance traveled by the stone while minimizing the time it spends in the air. Because the difficulty, gentlemen, is that the 'stones' we are throwing are bombs with timed fuses which explode whether or not they have reached their target. Then there are additional factors: air resis-

* "He who moves slowly goes far; he who goes quickly goes to his death."

tance, divergence caused by crosswinds, not to mention vertical axes which, in accordance with the laws of free fall, determine that distance traveled will be proportional to the square of the time elapsed. Do you still follow me?" He was keenly aware that no one now was following him. "But, obviously, you know all this . . ."

"That's all very well, but what I want to know is do these bombs reach Cádiz or not?" asked one of the Spaniards, summing up the general feeling of the group.

"We're working on it, gentlemen"—Desfosseux glanced at Orsini, who had taken a watch from his pocket and was checking the time— "We're working on it."

One eye pressed to the viewfinder of the micrometer, the artillery captain surveys Cádiz, walled and white, resplendent amid the blue-green waters of the bay. Close yet unattainable—*like a beautiful woman*, another man might say, but Simon Desfosseux is not such a man. In fact the French bombs hit various points inside enemy lines, including the city itself—at the absolute limit of their range, although often they do not explode. However, despite the captain's theoretical work and the dedication and skill of the Imperial Artillery veterans, they have not yet succeeded in extending their range beyond 2,250 *toises*, making it possible to reach the eastern walls of the city and the surrounding area, but no further. Even these bombs are usually ineffective by the time they land since the fuses snuff out during the long flight—an average of 25 seconds between discharge and impact. Desfosseux's cherished ideal—what troubles his sleep and fills his days with a nightmare of logarithms—is a bomb with a fuse that will burn for 45 seconds fired from a field gun capable of attaining more than 3,000 *toises*. On one wall of his hut, pinned up next to the maps, the diagrams and tables, the captain has a map of Cádiz with the location of every bomb: those that exploded are marked with a red dot, those that did not by a black dot. The red dots are discouragingly meager and they, like the black dots, are all grouped around the eastern sector of the city.

"At your service, Captain."

Lieutenant Bertoldi has just climbed the ladder to the observation deck. Desfosseux, who is still looking through the micrometer, turning the copper wheel in order to calculate the height and distance of the towers of the Iglesia del Carmen church, turns away from the eyepiece and looks at his aide.

"Bad news from Seville," Desfosseux says. "Someone added a little too much tin to the brass alloy when they were casting the 9-inch howitzers."

Bertoldi wrinkles his nose. He is a short, potbellied Italian from Piedmont with red whiskers and a cheerful face. He has spent five years with the Imperial Artillery. Those laying siege to Cádiz are not all French: there are also Italians, Poles and Germans. Not to mention the Spanish troops offered by King Joseph.

"Accident or sabotage?"

"Colonel Fronchard claims sabotage. But you know the man . . . I don't trust him."

Bertoldi half smiles, something which always makes him look sweet and youthful. Desfosseux likes his assistant, in spite of his weakness for the sherry and *señoritas* at El Puerto de Santa Maria. They have been working together since crossing the Pyrenees a year earlier after the rout at the Battle of Bailén. Sometimes, when Bertoldi has had too much to drink, he can be a little too familiar, too friendly. It is an infraction for which Desfosseux has never reproached him.

"Nor do I, Captain. The Spanish manager of the foundry, Colonel Sánchez, isn't allowed anywhere near the furnaces . . . Fronchard supervises everything personally."

"Well, he was quick to find a scapegoat. He had three Spanish workmen shot on Monday."

Bertoldi's smile broadens and he makes a gesture as though washing his hands.

"Case closed, then."

"Exactly," Desfosseux says scathingly. "But we still have no howitzers."

Bertoldi raises a finger in protest.

"We have Fanfan."

"Yes. But it's not enough." As he says this, he peers through an em-brasure at a nearby redoubt protected by gabions and mounds of earth where, covered with a canvas tarpaulin and angled at 45 degrees, stands an enormous bronze cylinder—a *grand mortar*—known to its friends as Fanfan. It was Bertoldi who named it. In fact it is a prototype Villantroys-Ruty 10-inch howitzer, capable of firing an 80-pound bomb at the east-ern wall of Cádiz but, as yet, not one *toise* further. And this is only possible when the wind is favorable. With a west wind blowing, the only things being scared by these bombs are the fish in the bay. The howitzers cast in Seville should have been a marked improvement, having bene-fited from calculations and tests done using Fanfan, but there is no way to verify them now, at least not for some time.

"We need to trust in Fanfan," says Bertoldi resignedly.

Desfosseux shakes his head.

"I do trust him, you know I do. But Fanfan has his limits . . . as do I."

The lieutenant is staring at him, and Desfosseux knows he is look-ing at the dark circles under his eyes. The fact he has not shaved does little, he fears, for his military bearing.

"You need to get more sleep."

"And you"—a complicit smile tempers Desfosseux's harsh tone—"should mind your own business."

"This *is* my business, Captain. If you were to fall ill, I would have to deal with Colonel Fronchard and I'd defect to the enemy before I al-lowed that to happen. I'd swim over. They have a better life in Cádiz than we do here."

"I intend to have him shot. Personally. And afterward I plan to dance on his grave."

In his heart, Desfosseux knows that the setback in Seville changes little. He has spent long enough here in Cádiz to know that neither conventional cannons nor howitzers will be enough to raze the city to the ground. Having studied similar situations, like the siege of Gibral-tar in 1782, Desfosseux would be inclined to use large-caliber mortars, but none of his superior officers shares his opinion. The one person he succeeded in convincing—after much effort—Alexandre Hureau, Baron of Sénarmont, artillery general and commander, is no longer here to support him. Having distinguished himself at the battles of Marengo, Friedland and Somosierra, the general became so overconfident, so dismissive of the Spanish—whom he disparagingly referred to as *manolos*—as did all the French, that during a routine inspection of the Villatte gun battery on the Isla de Léon near Chiclana with Colonel Dejermon, Captain Pinondelle, the battery commander and Simon Desfosseux, who had been assigned to the cortège, the Baron of Sénarmont insisted on testing the new gun limbers. The general insisted that all seven cannons be fired at the Spanish lines, specifically at the Gallineras battery. When Pinondelle argued that this would simply draw greater enemy fire, the general, playing the role of the brave artilleryman to the hilt, took off his hat and quipped that he intended to catch every *manolo* grenade.

"Now stop arguing and fire, at once," he ordered.

Pinondelle duly gave the order. And when the Spaniards returned fire, it transpired that Hureau, to his credit, had misjudged the position of his hat by only a few inches. The grenade landed between him, Pinondelle and Colonel Dejermon, the resulting explosion killing all three. Desfosseux was spared because he was somewhat further back looking for a place where he might discreetly urinate behind some earth-filled gabions which took the brunt of the impact. The three men were buried in the Chiclana hermitage of Santa Ana, and with the Baron of Sénarmont was buried any hopes Desfosseux had of leveling Cádiz by mortar fire. Though at least he had the consolation that he lived to tell the tale.

"A pigeon," says Lieutenant Bertoldi, pointing at the sky.

Desfosseux looks up in the direction indicated by his aide. It is true. Coming from Cádiz, the bird flies straight across the bay and past the inconspicuous pigeon loft located next to the artillery barracks and along the coast toward Puerto Real.

"It's not one of ours."

The two soldiers exchange a glance then Bertoldi looks away. He is the only person with whom Desfosseux shares his professional secrets. One of which is that without carrier pigeons, there would be no red or black dots on his map of Cádiz.

THE PAINTED SHIPS hanging on the walls and the scale models in the display cases seem to sail through the gloom of the little mahogany-furnished office, circling the woman writing at her desk in the patch of sunlight that filters between the half-drawn curtains of one window. The woman is Lolita Palma, thirty-two years old, an age by which any tolerably intelligent woman of Cádiz has given up all hope of marriage. But marriage has not been among her chief concerns for some time now; indeed it does not concern her at all. She has more important matters to worry about: the time of the next high tide, for example, the movements of the French corsair felucca that regularly plies the waters of the bay between the headland at Rota and the cove of Sanlúcar. Today, she is worried about the imminent arrival of a ship. From the watchtower on the terrace an elderly manservant has been following the ship's progress with a spyglass ever since the tower at Tavira signaled a sighting to the west: a ship at full sail two miles south of the sunken reefs at Rota. It could be the *Marco Bruto*, a 280-ton brigantine equipped with four cannons, two weeks late coming back from Veracruz and Havana with a declared cargo of coffee, cocoa, dyewood and currency to the value of 15,300 *pesos*. For some days the *Marco Bruto* has been listed in the worrying fourth column of the register that charts the fate of every ship linked to the trade of the city: *delayed, no news, disappeared, lost*. Sometimes, in this last column, are inscribed the fatal words: *lost, with all her crew*.

   Lolita Palma is bent over the piece of paper on which she is writing a letter in English, pausing now and then to consult the figures inscribed in the thick volume of exchange rates, weights and measures that lies open on the desk next to the inkstand containing a silver box of sharpened quills, a sandbox, seals and sealing wax. She writes on a leather desk blotter that belonged to her father and bears the initials *TP*: Tomás Palma. The letter, bearing the family letterhead—*Palma y Hijos, established in Cádiz in the year of our Lord 1754*—is addressed to a correspondent in the United States of America and details a number of irregularities in a cargo comprising 1,210 *fanegas* of flour which arrived in port a week ago after forty-five days in the hold of the schooner *Nueva Soledad* arriving in Cádiz from Baltimore. The cargo has since been reshipped to Valencia and Murcia where food is scarce and flour more prized than gold dust.

Each of the model ships that decorate the office bears a name and Lolita Palma is familiar with every one: some ships she has only heard of, since they were sold, laid up or lost at sea before she was born. Some, she trod the decks of with her brothers as a girl, watching their sails unfurl against the bay as they set out or returned, heard their ringing, hallowed, often enigmatic names—*El Birroño, Bella Mercedes, Amor de Dios*—in countless family conversations: how this one was late putting in to port, how that one was caught up in a nor'easterly gale, how another was pursued by a pirate ship between the Azores and San Vicente. All with detailed references to ports and their cargoes: copper from Veracruz, tobacco from Philadelphia, leather from Montevideo, cotton from La Guaira . . . far-off places as familiar in her house as Calle Nueva, the church of San Francisco or the Alameda. Letters from correspondents, consignees and partners are filed away in thick folders in the ground-floor office next to the warehouse. Ports and ships: two words that have been intimately entwined with expectation and uncertainty for as long as Lolita Palma can remember. She knows that for three generations the fortunes of the Palma family have depended on these ships, on the fortunes made on a day's run, on how they face down calm seas and heavy swells, on the bravery and the skill of their crews in eluding the dangers on sea and land. One of the ships—*Joven Dolores*—even bears her name, or did so until recently. A fortunate ship, the *Joven Dolores;* having spent a profitable career ferrying cargo, first for a British coal merchant and later for the Palma family, she is now spending her old age, nameless and flagless, moored peacefully off the Punta de la Clica near Carraca creek. A ship that never fell victim to the ocean's fury, to pirates, corsairs or to enemy flags; a ship that never brought the shadow of death into a house, left no widows or orphans.

An English burr-walnut barometer clock by the office door sounds three deep peals which are echoed, almost immediately, more silvery and distant, by the other clocks throughout the house. Lolita Palma, who has just finished her letter, sprinkles sand on the fresh ink of the last sentence and leaves it to dry. Then, using a paperknife, she carefully folds the sheet of paper—white, heavy paper of exceptional quality from Valencia—and having written the address on the back, strikes a phosphorus match and carefully seals the folds with wax. She does this as she does everything in life—slowly and meticulously. Then, placing the letter on a wooden tray inlaid with whalebone ivory, she gets to her feet in a rustle of silk from the dark, delicately embroidered Chinese *peignoir* shipped from the Philippines which falls to her satin slippers. As she gets up, she steps on a copy of the *Diario Mercantil* which has fallen onto the Chiclana rug. Picking it up she places it with the others—*El Redactor General, El Conciso*, some old newspapers in English and Portuguese—on a low table.

Downstairs, one of the young maidservants is singing as she waters the ferns and the geraniums around the marble coping of the pool. She has a beautiful voice. The song—a ballad popular in Cádiz about a romance between a marchioness and a patriotic smuggler—rings out more clearly as Lolita Palma leaves the office, walks around two of the four sides of the glassed-in gallery on the main floor and climbs the white marble staircase leading to the terraced roof two floors above. Outside, the dazzling sunlight is in stark contrast to the gloom within, the low whitewashed walls of the terrace shimmer in the afternoon sun, the terra-cotta tiles are warm underfoot while all around the city bustles like a beehive set into the sea. The door to the watchtower in one corner of the terrace is open and, climbing a narrower flight of steps—a spiral staircase with wooden treads—Lolita Palma arrives in a mirador similar to those found in many houses in Cádiz, especially among those families—charterers, shipowners, merchants—who have businesses related to the harbor and the sea. From these watchtowers, a careful observer can recognize a vessel coming into port and, with the aid of a spyglass, can read the signals hoisted on the yardarm: private codes by which each captain lets the shipowner or his agent know how the crossing has gone and what cargo he is carrying. In a merchant city like Cádiz, where the sea is the principal thoroughfare, an umbilical cord in times of war and peace, fortunes can be made through a stroke of luck or an opportunity seized, and for rivals, knowing a half hour earlier or later whose ship it is and what the signals convey, could mean the difference between bankruptcy and riches.

"She doesn't look like the *Marco Bruto*," says Santos.

The elderly manservant has worked for the Palma family since the days of her grandfather Enrique, having signed up as a cabin boy on one of his ships at the age of nine. One hand is crippled now, but he still has a seaman's eye and can identify a ship's captain by the way each one unfurls his sails to avoid the sunken reefs of Las Puercas. Lolita Palma takes the spyglass from him—a fine English gilded brass Dixey with a draw tube—rests it on the lip of the embrasure and looks out at the ship in the distance: square-rigged, with two masts sailing under full canvas to make the most of the fresh westerly wind blowing from starboard, and also to outdistance another ship—rigged with two lateens and a jib—approaching from the headland at Rota, hugging the wind, intent on cutting her off.

"The corsair felucca?" she asks, pointing toward it.

Santos nods, shielding his eyes with a hand that is missing both ring and little finger. On his wrist, at one end of an old scar, is a faint tattoo, faded by sun and time.

"They saw her coming and set more sail, but I don't think they will catch her. She's too close to land."

"The wind might shift."

"It might but, if I may be so bold, Doña Lolita, at worst she would get the wind on her quarter. Enough to make it safely into the bay. The felucca would get the worst of it being head to wind . . . Give her half an hour and I'd reckon she'll leave that French felucca standing."

Lolita Palma gazes at the reefs at the entrance to Cádiz, visible even at high tide. To the right, further in, English and Spanish warships, sails furled and topmasts lowered, lie at anchor between the stronghold of San Felipe and the Puerta de Mar.

"And you say she's not our brigantine?"

"I don't think so." Santos shakes his head without taking his eyes off the sea. "Looks more like a polacca to me."

Lolita Palma peers through the spyglass again. Despite the excellent visibility afforded by the west wind, she cannot see any signal flags. But it's true that though the ship is square-rigged like the *Marco Bruto*, her masts, which from this distance seem to have no crow's nests and no crosstrees, look nothing like those of a standard brigantine. Disappointed and irritated, she looks away. The *Marco Bruto* is already late and there is too much at stake. To lose this ship and her cargo would be a severe blow—the second in the space of three months, and all the more severe since there is no insurance to cover any losses. Because of the French siege, all goods and property are shipped solely at the risk of individuals and shipowners.

"I'd like you to stay up here in any case. Until you're sure it's not her."

"As you wish, Doña Lolita."

Santos still calls her Lolita, as do all the old retainers and servants in the house. The younger ones call her Doña Dolores or señorita. But within Cádiz society, whose members watched her grow up, she is still Lolita Palma, granddaughter of old Don Enrico. The daughter of Tomás Palma. This is how those who know her still refer to her at social gatherings, at meetings and soirées, and it is how she is referred to on the Paseo de la Alameda, on the Calle Ancha or at midday mass on Sundays and holy days at the church of San Francisco—the doffing of hats by the men, the slight bow of the head by the ladies in mantillas, the curiosity of aristocratic refugees who have just been told her story: a young woman from the best family with every advantage who, because of tragic circumstances, has had to take over the running of the family business. She had a modern education, obviously, like many young women in Cádiz. She is modest, never ostentatious, nothing like the frivolous young ladies of the fusty aristocracy, capable only of writing their suitors' names on dance cards and titivating themselves while they wait for *papá* to marry them, and their title, off to the highest bidder. Because in this city, it is not the august, ancient families who have money, but the merchants. In Cádiz, the only nobility respected is hard work and here young ladies are educated as God intended: as girls they are taught to look after their brothers, to be pious but not sanctimonious, and they are tutored in practical subjects and perhaps a foreign language. One never knows when they might have to help out with the family business, deal with the correspondence or something of the sort; nor indeed whether, having been married or widowed, they might have to deal with the problems that afflict many families with mouths to feed, regardless of their wealth. It is common knowledge that, thanks to her father, Lolita—whose grandfather was an eminent syndic—was taught arithmetic, international exchange, weights and measures, foreign currencies and double-entry bookkeeping. She reads and writes English fluently and has an excellent command of French. People say she knows a lot about botany—plants, flowers and suchlike. Such a pity she is still a spinster . . .

This parting comment, *"such a pity she's still a spinster,"* is the petty-minded revenge—malicious, but acceptable—of Cádiz society on the domestic, commercial and civil virtues of Lolita Palma, whose exalted position in the world of commerce is not, as everyone knows, conducive to private pleasures. She has only recently come out of mourning after a family tragedy: two years before her father was carried off by the last epidemic of yellow fever, her only brother, the natural heir of the family, died fighting at Bailén. There is a sister some years her junior who was married off at a young age to a city merchant while their father was still alive. And the mother, of course. What a mother.

Lolita Palma leaves the terrace and goes down to the second floor. On the landing, above the frieze of Portuguese tiles, hangs a portrait of a handsome young man in a high-collared jacket and a broad black tie; he gazes out at her with a friendly, faintly mocking smile. A friend of her father's and the shipping agent in Cádiz for an important French company, he was drowned in 1807 when his ship foundered on the rocks of Bajo Aceitera off Cape Trafalgar.

Looking at the portrait as she comes down the stairs, Lolita Palma runs her fingers along the balustrade of delicately veined white marble.

Though years past, she still remembers him. Perfectly. The young man's name was Miguel Manfredi, and the painting exactly captures his smile.

Downstairs, the servant—her name is Mari Paz and she works as lady's maid to Lolita—has finished watering the plants. The silence of the afternoon pervades the house on the Calle del Baluarte, a short step from the heart of the city. The three-story house is built of local sandstone, and the stout double front door, with gilded bronze studs and door knockers in the form of ships, is invariably left open. A cool, spacious vestibule in white marble leads to a gate and the courtyard around which are the storehouses for perishable goods and the offices used by employees during working hours. The house itself has a staff of seven: old Santos, a maidservant, a black slave, a cook, young Mari Paz, a steward and a coachman.

"How are you today, *mamá*?"

"Same as always."

A softly lit bedroom, cool in summer and warm in winter. An ivory crucifix above a white lacquered iron bedstead, a French window leading on to a balcony with a railing and shutters that overlooks the street and on the balcony, ferns and geraniums, and pots of basil. There is a dressing table with a mirror, another full-length mirror and a mirrored wardrobe. Lots of mirrors and lots of mahogany, very much the style of Cádiz. Very classical. A painting of Our Lady of the Rosary on a low bookshelf—also mahogany—on which there are also seventeen octavo volumes containing the complete collection of the fashion pamphlet *Correo de las Damas*. Sixteen, in fact, since volume seventeen is lying open on the lap of the woman, propped up on pillows, who now tilts her head slightly so her daughter can kiss her cheek. She smells of the Macassar oil she constantly rubs into her hands and the Frangipani powder she uses to give herself a pale complexion.

"You took your time coming to see me. I've been awake for some while."

"I had work to do, *mamá*."

"You always have work to do."

After first plumping the pillows, Lolita Palma draws up a chair and sits next to her mother. Patient. For an instant, she remembers her childhood, when she dreamed of traveling the world aboard those ships with their white sails that glided slowly across the bay. Then she thinks again of the brigantine, the polacca or whatever it was—the mysterious ship which at this very moment is coming out of the west, rigging taut, sails set, fleeing the hunting corsair.

CLINGING TO A shroud line on the mizzenmast, Pépé Lobo watches the maneuvers of the felucca attempting to cut off their route into the bay. His crew of nineteen men watch too, some crowded at the foot of the mast, others in the bow, shaded by the expanse of unfurled sail. The captain of the polacca—which left Lisbon five days ago with a cargo of salt cod, cheese and butter—would feel much calmer were it not for the fact that he knows only too well how capricious the sea can be in her whims and favors. The French felucca is still some way off, the *Risueña* is sailing swiftly on a starboard tack, the swell and the fresh wind are in her favor and, if nothing goes wrong, she will round Las Puercas protected by the guns of the Spanish forts at Santa Catalina and Candelaria.

"We'll make it with time to spare, Captain," says the first mate.

A sallow-faced man with greasy skin, he wears a woolen cap and one week's beard. From time to time, he turns suspiciously to check on the two helmsmen manning the tiller.

"We'll make it," he whispers again under his breath as though in prayer.

Pépé Lobo half-raises his hand, cautious.

"Don't be so sure, Lieutenant. It's not over until it's over."

The other man spits viciously into the sea. Surly.

"I'm not superstitious."

"Well, I am. So keep your filthy mouth shut."

There is a brief, tense silence broken only by the rush of water along the length of the hull, the whistle of the wind in the rigging, the creak of the masts and the shrouds as the ship pitches and rolls. The captain stares across the bows at the corsair while the first mate stares at the captain.

"That is an insult, I will not abide it . . ."

"I told you to shut your mouth. Or I'll shut it for you."

"Are you threatening me, Captain?"

"Indeed I am."

Though he speaks in his accustomed tone, and never takes his eyes off the other ship, Pépé Lobo is undoing the gold buttons of his blue broadcloth coat. He knows some of the sailors are jostling, eyes peeled, ears pricked, missing nothing.

"This is intolerable," protests the first mate. "I shall file a report the moment we land. These men are my witnesses."

The captain lets his shoulders droop.

"In which case they will be able to witness that I blew out your brains for insubordination while we had a corsair in hot pursuit."

The sash band about his waist is now visible, together with the glitter of a pistol butt of brass and wood. The weapon is not intended to be used on the enemy, but to maintain order on his ship. It would not be the first time a crew member lost his head during a difficult maneuver. Nor, if it comes to that, would it be the first time he had resolved the problem in such a brutal fashion. This first mate is a nervous, bloody-minded, sharp-tongued individual who finds it difficult to accept that he is not captain of the polacca. He has spent the past four voyages shrilly inviting a punishment few naval tribunals would censure if the captain were to mete it out, as now, in full view of the enemy. With the prospect of losing the ship and its cargo, and of being taken prisoner, this is no time for squabbles.

The shroud line to which Pépé Lobo is clinging suddenly begins to shudder erratically. There is a rustle of loose canvas from above.

"Now, get to work, Mate! Brail that mizzen-topgallant."

At no time while he is speaking does Pépé Lobo take his eyes off the felucca: a hundred long tons with a narrow hull sailing close hauled with the wind at northeast by east, one mast raked forward, the other raked aft, lateen sails and jib hard and taut as blades. The halyards are bare, it flies no national ensign—nor does the *Risueña*—but there can be little doubt that she is French. No one else would come from land with such obvious intentions but this dog. If it is the same French corsair that prowls the waters of the bay, lying in wait behind the headland

at Rota, its cannons and crew will be well equipped to capture the polacca if she should come within firing range. The polacca, a 170-ton
merchant ship, is armed only with two 4-pound demi-culverins, a few
muskets and some swords; not enough to ward off the two 12-pounder
carronades and the six 6-pounders with which the felucca is said to be
armed. And the felucca's prowess is the stuff of legend. When the *Risueña* left port for Lisbon three weeks ago, the felucca had already captured a Spanish xebec carrying a cargo of 900 quintals of gunpowder
and a North American brigantine blown off-course, captured thirty-
two days after leaving Rhode Island for Cádiz carrying tobacco and
rice. So far, all protests by the merchants of Cádiz about the impunity
of the French corsair have been to no avail. Pépé Lobo knows that the
few English and Spanish warships are of no use, since their orders are
to protect the harbor and the defensive lines, escort convoys and ferry
mail and troops. As for the gunboats of the *fuerzas sutiles*, they are useless in a headwind or against a rising tide, and besides, they spend their
time patrolling the straits at the Trocadero, guarding the bay by night
or ferrying convoys to Huelva, Ayamonte, Tarifa and Algeciras. This
leaves only a Spanish *místico*, number 38, which patrols the waters between the Broa de Sanlúcar and the city of Cádiz to little effect. As a
result, it is easy for the corsair, having spied its prey in the morning
from a position a league from the mouth of the bay or from its hiding
place in the inlet, to give rapid chase and, should it catch its prey, bring
it back to its lair on a coastline entirely controlled by the French. Like
a spider at the center of its web.

Pépé Lobo looks across the bows toward Cádiz: the red-brown city
walls, the countless watchtowers rising above the whitewashed houses,
the fortress of San Sebastián and the lighthouse, the city looks like a
ship foundered on the reef.

Four miles to Las Puecas and the Diamante, Lobo quickly calculates, taking the city and the Rota headland as his markers. The entry
into Cádiz is tricky, with dangerous rocks and a treacherous ebb current at low tide; but the wind today is favorable and the tide will be
high when the polacca, without changing tack, sails between the sunken
reefs and luffs toward the bay and the harbor under the protection of

the gun batteries and the anchored Spanish warships and those of their English allies whose masts will soon be visible in the distance.

English allies. Though this is the fourth year of Napoleon's war on Spain, the word *allies* brings a grim smile to the captain of the *Risueña.* He respects the English as a seafaring nation, but despises them as a people. Were he English himself, he would have no cause for complaint: he would be as knavish and arrogant as they, nor would he lose a moment's sleep. But chance, which decides such things, has meant he was born a Spaniard in the military port of Havana to a Galician father—a bo'sun in the Spanish Navy—and a Creole mother and, from earliest childhood, the sea has been a constant presence, before his eyes, beneath his feet. He first went to sea at the age of eleven and has spent the better part of his thirty-one years on the oceans—cabin boy, a deckhand aboard a whaling ship, topman, first mate, winning his captain's license through hard work and sacrifice—years in which he has seen ample evidence of the treason and treachery of the British fleet. He has never sailed a sea where they were not a constant menace. He feels he knows the English now: he considers them avaricious, arrogant, cynical, ever ready to find a convenient excuse to disregard a pact or break their word. It is something he has experienced personally. The fact that the fickle whims of war and politics now mean that Britain is an ally in Spain's war against Napoleon changes nothing. For Pépé Lobo, whether in time of peace or war, the English have always been the enemy. In some sense, they still are. Twice he has been their prisoner, once in a prison hulk in Portsmouth, the second time in Gibraltar. It is not something he will soon forget.

"The corsair is rounding the headland, Captain."

"I can see it."

The first mate seems more worried than angry. His tone is almost conciliatory. Out of the corner of his eye, Pépé Lobo sees the man glancing nervously at the wind pennant, staring at it. Waiting.

"I think we should—" the first mate begins.

"Shut up."

The captain looks at the sails and then turns to the helmsmen.

"Hard to windward . . . that's it . . . Now hold her steady . . . First Mate, are you blind or deaf? . . . Haul that jib."

In fact Pépé Lobo's present ill-humor has nothing to do with the English. Nor with the felucca which, in a last ditch attempt, is tacking east-southeast to try and intercept them, trusting that a providential cannon shot, a shift in the wind or some injudicious maneuver on their part will cause the rigging of the *Risueña* to snap. No, this is not what is worrying Pépé Lobo. He is so sure they will leave the corsair standing that he has not even ordered the crew to ready the ship's two small guns—which in any case would be useless against an enemy who could blast their deck to kingdom come with a single shot from a carronade. The prospect of a confrontation has unsettled an already surly crew: with the exception of a dozen or so expert sailors, the rest are harbor rats who signed up for little more than their bed and board. Nor would it be the first time Lobo has seen a crew take cover belowdecks during a skirmish. In '97 it cost him a ship and left him bankrupt, to say nothing of the time he spent rotting in that Portsmouth prison hulk. But today all will be well if every sailor holds his nerve and does his job. As for the men under his command, Pépé Lobo's only wish is to drop anchor in Cádiz as soon as possible and never set eyes on them again.

Because the captain of the *Risueña* already knows this will be his last voyage with this crew. When they put out nineteen days ago, relations between him and Ignacio Ussel, a shipowner on the Calle de la Consulado, had already soured; and they will surely get worse when Ussel, or his client, sees the cargo manifest. It has been an ill-starred voyage marred by poor winds and heavy seas off San Vicente, a damaged sternpost that forced them to drop anchor for a day and a half at Cabo de Sines, and administrative problems in Lisbon. All these things have contributed to the polacca arriving late with only half the expected cargo. This will be the last straw. Ussel's company which, like many others in Cádiz, is merely a front for various French merchant houses—until very recently, no foreign power was allowed to trade directly with Spanish ports in the Americas—has been in trouble ever since the war began. Determined to make the most of the opportunities the war afforded to a merchant with few scruples, Señor Ussel extracts maximum profit for minimum cost at the expense of his employees, using any excuse to pay late and badly. For some time now relations between the ship owner and the captain of the *Risueña* have been strained. And Pépé Lobo knows that, as soon as he has dropped the anchor over four or five fathoms in the harbor, he will need to look for another ship on which to make his living. No easy task these days in Cádiz. The city has seen its population swell because of the siege and, although any moldering hulk of wood that can float still sails, ships and crews are in short supply while captains are two a penny. And in the alehouses around the harbor, where forced conscription is commonplace, the only men to be found are rabble prepared to sign up for a few coins.

"The French ship is turning . . . it's turning back!"

A cheer goes up from stem to stern along the polacca. A scattering of applause and shouts of relief. The first mate takes off his cap and wipes the sweat from his brow. Crowding over to the port side of the deck, the crew watch as the corsair goes about and abandons the chase. Its jib shivers for a moment over the long bowsprit as the vessel lists to starboard and heads back toward Rota. As it tacks, the shifting light gives a better view of the long lateen yard and the slim, black hull of the felucca with its stern counter beneath the boom. Swift and dangerous. Some say it is a Portuguese merchant ship seized by the French last year near Chipiona.

"Bear down," Pépé Lobo barks to the helmsmen, "east by south."

Some of the crewmen smile at the captain, nodding and waving their approval. *Like I give a tinker's cuss for their opinion*, he thinks. Climbing down from the shroud lines, he rebuttons his frockcoat over the pistol tucked into his belt then turns to the first mate, who has not taken his eyes off the captain.

"Hoist the flag and trim that sail . . . In half an hour I want the whole crew ready to take in the topgallants."

While the crew trim the sheets and adjust the sails to the new bearing, and a washed-out merchant ensign—two red and three yellow stripes—is hoisted to the top of the mizzen, Pépé Lobo looks toward the corsair felucca, now showing her stern as she heads back to the coast. The *Risueña* is making good headway, the wind is favorable so they will not need to change tack to clear Las Puercas. This means they should make it into the bay without having to brave the dangerous reefs, or the cannons at the other Santa Catalina fortress, the one near El Puerto de Santa María which is wont to fire on ships that stray too far from land. The fortress, half a league to the west off the polacca's larboard bow, is on the far side of Rota inlet and the sandbar of the San Pedro River; nor does Lobo need his spyglass to see the Trocadero peninsula, where more French guns are trained on Cádiz. Pépé Lobo takes the telescope from a drawer in the binnacle, opens it out, and scans the coastline from north to south, pausing when he comes to the three strongholds: the derelict Matagorda fort on the shore and, set further back, Fort Luis and La Cabezuela, their cannons peeping through the embrasures. As he watches he sees a soundless flash and for a second he thinks he can even see the French bomb, a black speck tracing a parabola across the sky toward the city.

Sitting in the courtyard of the Café del Correo, chair tilted back against the wall, long legs stretched out beneath the table—his favorite way of getting comfortable—Rogelio Tizón, Commissioner for Districts, Vagrants and Transients, studies the chessboard in front of him. His right hand holds a cup of coffee while his left strokes his whiskers where they merge with his mustache. The customers who stepped out onto the Calle del Rosario when they heard the bang are beginning to trickle back with news of what happened. Billiard players return to their queues and their ivory balls, customers pick up the newspapers they abandoned in the reading room or on courtyard tables and go back to their seats, groups re-form and there is a murmur of conversation as the waiters begin to circulate again, coffeepots in hand.

"The bomb came down just past San Agustín," says Professor Barrull, taking his seat again. "It didn't explode, they rarely do. Just the shock of the impact."

"Your move, Don Hipólito."

Barrull studies the policeman, who has not looked up from the chessboard, then studies the position of the pieces.

"I admire your equanimity, Comisario. You're as cool as a cucumber."

Tizón drains his coffee and sets the cup by the chessboard amid the captured pieces: six are his, six belong to his opponent. In fact the parity is illusory. This game is not looking good for him.

"My rook is threatened by your bishop and that pawn . . . I've no time to waste worrying about bombs."

Barrull makes an appreciative grunt. He has a mane of thick gray hair, a long, equine face, his teeth are stained yellow with tobacco and his melancholy eyes are framed by steel-rimmed spectacles. A connoisseur of ocher snuff, invariably dressed in breeches, rumpled black socks and old-style frockcoats, Barrull runs the Cádiz Scientific Society and teaches the rudiments of Latin and Greek to young men of good breeding. He is also a fearsome chess player, whose usual calm, genial temperament is utterly transformed when he sits down at a chessboard. As a player, he is ruthless, plotting his strategies with almost murderous fury. In the heat of battle, he has been known to insult his opponents, including Rogelio Tizón: *May hell itself yawn open and swallow you, confound you, you mangy cur. I'll have you drawn and quartered before sunup, 'pon my word. I'll flay the skin from you strip by strip.* Bombastic curses of this kind: Barrull is not an educated man for nothing. But the comisario takes such insults in good part. The two men have known each other and played chess together for more than ten years. They are friends . . . or almost. It is perhaps more accurate to say *almost*, given the imprecise sense the word *friendship* has for the comisario.

"I see you've moved that deuced knight."

"I had no choice."

"Ah, but you had," the professor cackles under his breath, "but I'll not be the one to tell you what it was."

Tizón signals to the café owner, Paco Celis, standing in the kitchen doorway and he dispatches a waiter who refills the comisario's coffee and sets a glass of chilled water next to it. Intent on the game, Barrull shakes his head, waving away the waiter.

"Have at you!" he says, advancing an unexpected pawn.

The comisario studies the board in astonishment. Barrull drums his fingers on the table, glaring at his opponent as though prepared to shoot him in the chest at the first opportunity.

"Check in one," Tizón admits grudgingly.

"And mate in two."

The vanquished player sighs and begins to put away the pieces. The victor, with a malicious smile, looks on. *"Vae Victis,"* he says. In the face of his enemy's triumphalism, the comisario's demeanor is fatalistic. He has become stoic by force of habit; his opponent invariably trounces him in three games out of five.

"You are a scurvy knave, Professor."

"Cry if you must, weep like a weak woman incapable of defending herself."

Tizón lays the remaining black and white pieces in the box, like corpses in a mass grave awaiting the first shovelful of quicklime. The chessboard stands empty, desolate as a beach at low tide. The image of the murdered girl comes back to him. Slipping a hand into his pocket, he fingers the twisted shard of lead he found next to the body.

"Professor . . ."

"Yes?"

Tizón hesitates a moment. It is difficult, he realizes, to put into words the feeling that has been troubling him since his visit to Lame Paco's Tavern. The strange impression he had kneeling next to the dead girl, amid the murmur of the sea, the traces in the sand.

"Footsteps in the sand," he says aloud.

Barrull's cruel smile vanishes; he is himself again. He looks at the policeman in astonishment.

"I beg your pardon?"

His hand still in his pocket, touching the sliver of metal, Tizón makes a vague, helpless gesture.

"I'm sorry, I don't know how else to explain it . . . Something to do with a chess player staring at an empty chessboard. And traces in the sand."

"Is this some jest?" Barrull laughs and adjusts his spectacles. "A puzzle? A riddle?"

"Not at all: just a chessboard, traces in the sand, as I said."

"And what else?"

"Nothing else."

"Is it somehow related to science?"

"I don't know."

The professor, who has taken an enamel snuffbox from his jacket, pauses as he opens it.

"When you say a chessboard, to what exactly are you referring?"

"That is something else I do not know. Cádiz, I suppose. The dead girl on the beach."

"Damn it all, my friend!" Barrull takes a pinch of snuff. "You are exceptionally mysterious this afternoon. So Cádiz is a chessboard?"

"Yes. No . . . I don't know. In a sense, perhaps."

"What then are the chess pieces?"

Tizón glances around him at this perfect microcosm of life in the besieged city: the courtyard and the café are teeming with citizens, merchants, ne'er-do-wells, refugees, students, clerics, workers, journalists, soldiers and members of the Cádiz Cortes—the Spanish parliament—which has recently relocated to Cádiz from the Isla de León. There are marble counters, wood and wicker tables, cane chairs, ashtrays, copper spittoons, some jugs of hot chocolate and many more of coffee as is the custom here: bushels and bushels of ground coffee in the kitchen, served scalding hot, the air is suffused with the smell of it, it even masks the pervasive aroma of tobacco smoke that paints everything in shades of gray. The Café del Correo is the preserve of men—women are admitted only during Carnaval—who come from all walks of life: here, a penniless immigrant's threadbare rags sit cheek by jowl with fashionable suits and discreetly patched frockcoats, new boots with well-worn soles, the garish uniforms of the local volunteer force with the tattered, darned uniforms of Navy officers who have not been paid in more than a year. These men greet each other, ignore each other, gather in groups according to their affinities, their dislikes or interests; they chat between the tables, discuss the contents of the newspapers, play billiards or chess, kill time alone or in groups talking about the war, about politics or women, about the price of dyewood, tobacco or cotton or about the latest libel published—thanks to a newly emancipated press which many applaud and many more deplore—against Fulano, Mengano, Zutano or anyone under the sun.

"I don't know what the pieces are," says Tizón. "Them, I suppose. Us."

"The French?"

"Perhaps. I'm not ruling out the idea that they may have something to do with it."

Professor Barrull is still bewildered.

"With what?"

"I don't know how to explain it. With what is going on."

"Of course they have something to do with it, they have us under siege."

"But that's not what I'm talking about."

Barrull looks at the comisario attentively now, leaning across the table. Eventually, he picks up the glass of water Tizón has not touched and drinks it slowly. When he has finished, he wipes his lips with a kerchief he has taken from a pocket of his frockcoat, glances down at the empty chessboard, then up again. The two men know each other well enough to know when things are serious.

"Traces in the sand," he says gravely.

"Exactly."

"Can you give me any other details . . . It might help."

Tizón shakes his head uncertainly.

"It somehow feels related to you . . . to something you did or said a long time ago. That's why I'm telling you."

"And yet, my dear friend, you are not actually telling me *anything*."

Another bomb, further off this time, interrupts the hum of conversation. The impact, muffled by the distance and the intervening buildings, still makes the panes in the café windows shudder.

"That one was a long way off," says one man. "Must have come down near the port, and it exploded."

"French pigs," says another.

This time fewer people go out to see what is going on. After a moment, someone wanders back and explains that the bomb fell next to La Cruz, just outside the city walls. There were no victims, and no damage.

"I'll see if I can remember anything," says Barrull doubtfully.

Rogelio Tizón takes his leave of the professor, picks up his hat and his cane and steps outside into the waning afternoon where the sun on the horizon is painting the white towers and terraces red. There are still some people on their balconies, looking toward the place where the latest bomb fell. A bedraggled woman reeking of cheap wine steps aside muttering curses as Tizón passes by; she clearly knows him. Old grievances. Pretending not to hear her, the comisario walks off down the street.

Black pawns, white pawns, he thinks. *That is what this is about. And Cádiz as the chessboard.*

TAXIDERMY IS NOT simply a matter of dissection, it involves re-creating the illusion of life. Keenly aware of this fact, the man in the gray smock and the oilskin apron, his measuring tape in hand, takes the necessary precautions, those prescribed by science and by art. In small, neat, careful handwriting he jots down each measurement in a notepad: distance from ear to ear and from head to tail. Then, with a pair of compasses, he measures the internal and external angles of each eye, notes their color, dark brown. Closing the notebook, he looks around and notices that the light streaming through the colored panes of the half-open door that leads on to the terrace is beginning to fade. He lights a paraffin lamp, slots the glass tulip into place and turns up the flame so that it illuminates the body of the dead dog splayed on the marble table.

It is a delicate moment. Very delicate. A false start now might ruin everything. Animal hair can be shed over time; an insect larva or egg in the wadding or seagrass stuffing might destroy his work. These are the limits of his art. Some of the specimens in the workshop now lit up by the oil lamp have been marred by the passage of time: mistakes in re-creating a lifelike pose, damage caused by sunlight, by dust or damp, colors distorted by the use of too much tartar and lime or some inferior varnish. These are the limits of science. And yet these failed works, these sins of youth and inexperience are still here: proof, perhaps, or reminders of how dangerous mistakes can be, in taxidermy as in so many things: contracted muscles distorting the natural form of the animals, poses that are less than lifelike, poorly finished mouths or beaks, errors in the positioning of the internal framework, crude suturing . . . Every detail matters in this workshop where the war and the state of affairs in the city make it difficult to do serious work. It is increasingly difficult to obtain worthwhile animal specimens and he has to make do with what he can find. Make do and mend. Improvising tools and equipment.

The taxidermist goes over to the black woodstove that sits between the door and the stairs leading to the terrace. Next to it is a display cabinet from which a lynx, an owl and a squirrel monkey peer down with lifeless glass eyes. From among the tools, he selects a pair of steel tweezers and an ivory-handled scalpel, brings them back to the table and bends over the animal: a young dog of medium size with a white patch on its belly and another on its forehead. Beautiful canine teeth. A fine specimen, the animal's pelt unmarked by the poison used to kill it. By the lamplight, with great care and skill, the taxidermist extracts the eyes with the tweezers, severs the optic nerve with the scalpel, cleans the empty sockets and sprinkles them with the mixture of alum, tannin and mineral soap he has prepared in a mortar. Then he stuffs the sockets with cotton wool. Finally, having checked that all is well, he turns the animal on to its back, stops its orifices with wadding, spreads the paws and makes an incision from the sternum over the abdomen and begins to skin it.

To one side of the workshop, beneath perches fixed to the wall on which sit a pheasant, a hawk and a bearded vulture, is a desk on which a map of the city is spread out, a large, printed map with a double scale at the bottom indicating both French *toises* and Spanish *varas*. On it lies a pair of dividers, assorted rulers and set squares. The map is crisscrossed by curious penciled lines which fan out from the east, and dotted with crosses and circles that resemble the symptoms of some malignant pox. It looks like a spider's web spread across the city, each dot an insect that has been caught and devoured.

Slowly, night draws in. While the taxidermist flays the dog by the lamplight, carefully easing the skin away from flesh and bones, he hears the sound of pigeons cooing from the stairs leading to the terrace.

CHAPTER TWO

୨୦୧

*B*uenos días. How are you today? Good morning. Give my regards to your wife. Goodbye, so nice to see you. My best to the family. Countless fleeting, friendly exchanges, smiles from acquaintances, brief conversations inquiring about a wife's health, a child's studies, a son-in-law's business. Lolita Palma moves between the groups of people chatting or gazes in the windows of the shops. It is mid-morning on Calle Ancha in Cádiz. The beating heart of the city. Offices, agencies, consulates, ship brokers. It is easy to distinguish the natives of Cádiz from recently arrived foreigners through their manner and their conversation: the latter, who have temporarily taken up residence in hostelries on the Calle Nueva, *posadas* on the Calle Flamencos Borrachos and private houses in the Avemaría district, peer into the windows of the expensive shops and cafés while the natives of the city go about their business, clutching attaché cases, documents and newspapers. Some discuss military campaigns and strategies, defeats and improbable victories while others worry about the price of nankeen cloth, of indigo or cocoa and whether the price of Cuban cigars might rise above 48 *reales* a pound. As for the members of the Cortes, they are not to be found in the streets at this hour. Parliament is in session a few short steps from here at the Oratorio de San Francisco, the galleries filled with an idle public many of whom have been left unemployed by the French siege, and with diplomats eager for news of the Cortes' machinations—the British ambassador sends dispatches to London with every ship leaving port. Shortly after 2 p.m. when the session breaks, the parliamentary deputies will go in search of inns and cafés, discussing points raised during the morning session and, as always, castigating other deputies based on their ideology, affinity and antipathy: clerical, secular, communal, liberal and royalists, from reactionary old stick-in-the-muds to angry young radicals and all shades in between, each with their own cliques and newspapers. A microcosm of Spain and her overseas colonies—many of which are taking advantage of the chaos created by the war to foment revolution.

Lolita Palma has just stepped out of the boutique opposite the Café Apolo on the Plaza de San Antonio. Formerly known as La Mode de Paris, now aptly renamed La Moda Española, it is the most elegant shop in the city, its fabrics and designs prized by the cream of Cádiz society. Despite this fact, the proprietor of Palma e Hijos does not buy her dresses here; instead she has them run up by a dressmaker and an embroideress working from patterns she herself sketches based on ideas from French and English magazines. She visits La Moda Española to keep abreast of fashion and to buy fabrics and accessories; the maid-servant walking three paces behind her is carrying two carefully wrapped boxes containing six pairs of gloves, as many pairs of stockings and some lace for trimming underclothes.

"God be with you, Lolita."

"*Buenos días.* My respects to your lady wife."

The main street in Cádiz is a bustle of faces, mostly familiar, mostly men who doff their hats to her as they pass. This is the Calle Ancha after all. That there are few women about at this early hour earns Lolita more admiring glances from the men. Pleasantries, hats doffed, polite nods of the head. Anyone who is anyone recognizes this woman who, though she is of the weaker sex, prudently and skillfully manages the company that belonged to her late father and her grandfather before him. All life in Cádiz is here: trade with the Indies, shipping, investments, maritime insurance. Lolita is utterly unlike the other women in business, widows for the most part who are content to be mere moneylenders, charging commission and interest. Lolita Palma takes risks, she gambles, sometimes she wins, sometimes she loses. She works hard and makes money. Unencumbered assets, an irreproachable life. Respectable. Solvent, in credit and held in high esteem. Capital amounting to a million and a half *pesos*. At least. She is clearly one of us. One of the twelve or fifteen families that matter. A good head on what people say are rather pretty shoulders; though this is something no one can know for certain. Still a spinster at the age of thirty-two, she has been left on the shelf.

"*Adíos*. Lovely to see you."

Chin up, high heels clacking, Lolita strolls coolly down the middle of the Calle Ancha. This is her street, her city. She is dressed in dark gray, with a dash of color provided by a cotton mantilla trimmed in pale blue ribbon. She carries a small matching handbag. Her mantilla, the hair swept back from her temples into a bun at the nape of her neck, and linen pumps trimmed with silver are her only concessions to this outing; her dress is the simple, comfortable, rather formal one she wears when working or receiving clients in her office. Usually she is in her office at this hour, but has come out because she has a delicate financial matter to deal with: some questionable letters of exchange she acquired three weeks ago but which, fortunately, she successfully negotiated an hour ago at the San Carlos Exchange for a reasonable commission. The gloves, stockings and lace she bought at La Moda Española are by way of a celebration. Restrained. As she is in all her thoughts and deeds.

"Congratulations on the *Marco Bruto*. I read in *El Vigía* that she arrived safely."

It is Alfonso, her brother-in-law, of Solé y Asociados, wholesalers of English fabric and merchandise from Gibraltar. He is cold and aloof as usual, dressed in brown with a mauve jacket, silk stockings and carrying a walking stick from the Indies. He does not doff his hat, merely touches the brim with two fingers, raising it an inch or so. Lolita Palma still finds him as disagreeable as she did six years ago when he married her sister Caridad. Their relationship with the family is strained. Visits to her mother once a week but little more. Alfonso Solé has never been truly satisfied with the dowry of 90,000 *pesos* settled on him by his late father-in-law; for their part, the Palma family are far from happy about the incompetent manner in which the money has been invested for little return. Aside from commercial disagreements, there is the matter of the Puerto Real estate which Alfonso believes is rightfully his by marriage. He has contested the last will and testament of Tomás Palma, which is now in the hands of lawyers and notaries, though any resolution is in abeyance as a result of the war.

"The vessel did arrive, thank the Lord. We had given the cargo up for lost."

She knows that Alfonso cares little about the fate of the *Marco Bruto*, it would not matter to him if the ship were at the bottom of the sea or in a French port. But this is Cádiz, and appearances matter. When in-laws meet on the Calle Ancha, they have to talk about something, however briefly, since the whole city is watching. No business can survive here without the respect and trust of the citizens; even they must observe the proprieties or lose that trust.

"How is Cari?"

"Well, thank you. We shall see you on Friday."

Alfonso touches the brim of his hat again and, taking his leave, walks on down the street. Ramrod straight to the tip of his walking stick. Lolita Palma's relationship with her sister Caridad is also less than cordial. They were never close, even as children. Lolita considers her sister frivolous and selfish, all too happy to live off the hard work of others. Even the death of their father and their brother, Francisco de Paula, has done nothing to bring them closer: they grieved, they mourned, each in private. Their mother is now the only link between them, though even this is a formality; a weekly visit to the family home on the Calle del Baluarte, chocolate, coffee and pastries, a conversation that does not stray beyond the weather, the French bombs and the plants decorating the patio. Visits enlivened only by the arrival of their cousin Toño, a cheerful, affable bachelor.

Caridad's marriage to Alfonso Solé—ambitious, unscrupulous, his father an importer of textiles for the local volunteer corps, his mother haughty and foolish—has only served to increase the distance between the two sisters. Neither Caridad nor her husband will ever forgive Tomás Palma for refusing to take his son-in-law into the family business, nor for limiting his younger daughter's expectations to a simple dowry and the house on the Calle Guanteros where the Solés now live:

a magnificent three-story residence valued at 350,000 *reales.* With that, her father said, they'll have money to burn. As for my daughter Lolita, she has all the qualities necessary to make her own way in the world. Look at her. She's clever, determined. She can stand on her own two feet, and I trust her more than I trust anyone; she knows more than anyone about how to make money, or how not to lose it. Even as a girl. If one day she decides to marry, she is not the kind of woman who will spend her time reading novels or gossiping in the teahouses while her husband breaks his back, take my word for it. She is made of sterner stuff.

"Beautiful as ever, Lolita. Such a pleasure to see you . . . And how is your mother?"

Emilio Sánchez Guinea is holding his hat in one hand and a thick sheaf of letters and documents in the other: he is a plump man of sixty, with thinning white hair. His eyes are wise. He dresses in the English style, with a double watch chain looped through the buttons of his waistcoat, and he has the almost imperceptible, slightly rumpled appearance of merchants of a certain age and standing. In Cádiz, where there is no greater social sin than idleness, to appear a little disheveled— tie or cravat loose, suit a little wrinkled—is considered evidence of having done a hard and honorable day's work.

"I heard your ship finally arrived. A relief for all concerned."

Emilio is an old and dear friend, someone she trusts implicitly. Having attended school with the late Tomás Palma, he has had many dealings with the family firm and indeed continues to share risky schemes and business opportunities with Lolita. In fact there was a time when he hoped she might become his daughter-in-law, might marry his son Miguel, who now works with him and is happily married to another young woman. However, the lack of a marital tie will never alter the excellent relations between the houses of Palma and Sánchez Guinea. It was Don Emilio who advised Lolita in her first business dealings after her father died. He still does so, when she seeks his opinion and experience.

"Are you heading home?"

"No, I'm going to Salcedo's bookshop. I want to see if some books I ordered have arrived."

"I'll walk with you."

"I'm sure you have more important things to do."

The elderly merchant gives a cheerful laugh.

"Whenever I see you, I forget everything else. Shall we go?"

He offers her his arm. On the way, they discuss the general state of affairs and also matters of particular interest to them both. The revolutions in the American colonies are causing serious problems; much more so, in fact, than the French siege. Exports of textiles across the Atlantic have plummeted alarmingly, revenues are minimal, there is a shortage of precious metals which has led to a scarcity of currency, leading some businessmen to rashly invest in *vales reales*—Royal bonds—which have proved difficult to convert into hard cash. Lolita Palma, however, has successfully compensated for the liquidity problem by opening up new markets: importing flour and cotton from the United States, exporting to Russia, promoting Cádiz as an ideally positioned repository for goods in transit. All these things have added to the steady revenue from prudent investments in Letters of Exchange and in marine insurance. The house of Sánchez Guinea specializes in marine insurance and Palma e Hijos regularly works with them, providing capital to finance commercial voyages against premiums and interest. It is a financial arrangement which Don Emilio's blend of experience and common sense has made hugely profitable in a city constantly in need of hard currency.

"You have to accept it, Lolita: one day the war will be over, and then our real problems will begin. By the time the freedom of the seas is restored, it will be too late. Our American colonies are already trading directly with the Yankees and the English. Meanwhile, we in Cádiz want them to go on paying us for something they can get for themselves. The current upheaval in Spain has taught them that they do not need us."

Her arm in his, Lolita Palma walks down the Calle Ancha. Imposing porticos, elegant shops and businesses. As always, Bonalto's silversmiths is crowded with customers. Tight knots of people chatting, greetings from strangers and acquaintances. Following some paces behind, carrying the packages, comes the young Mari Paz, the maid who sings snatches of songs in her bell-like voice as she waters the plants.

"We will survive, Don Emilio . . . America is a big place and the ties of language and culture are not so easily broken. We will always have a presence there. Besides, there are new markets. Think about the Russians . . . If the Czar declares war on France, they will need everything we can supply."

Don Emilio shakes his head skeptically. "Too many years have passed," he says, "too many gray hairs. Besides," he adds, "this city has lost its authority, its raison d'être. The death knell was sounded when the monopoly on overseas trade ended in 1778. Whatever anyone might say, the independence of the American ports cannot be repealed. No one will be able to impose their authority on the Creoles now. Each new turn in this war has been another nail in the coffin for Cádiz."

"Don't be so pessimistic, Don Emilio."

"Pessimistic? How many catastrophes has the city suffered? England's colonial war did us a great deal of harm. Then came our war with revolutionary France followed by the war with England . . . that was where we finally foundered. The Treaty of Amiens brought with it more risk than trade: remember the French houses that had been trading here since time immemorial that went bankrupt overnight? Since then, there's been another war with the English, then the blockade and now the war with France . . . You think I'm being pessimistic, *hija*? For twenty-five years now, the city has been caught between the devil and the deep blue sea."

Lolita Palma smiles and gently squeezes his arm.

"I didn't mean to offend you, my friend."

"You could never offend me, *hija*."

On the corner of the Calle de la Amargura next to the British embassy is a small shipping office and a café frequented by foreigners and naval officers. It is far from the eastern walls where bombs have been falling; none has yet reached this far. Relaxed, making the most of the balmy weather, a number of Englishmen with blond whiskers and gaudy waistcoats are standing in the doorway reading old issues of British newspapers. Several are wearing red military frockcoats.

"Then there are our *allies*," Sánchez Guinea lowers his voice, "pressurizing the Regency and the Cortes to lift restrictions on free trade with the Americas. Constantly seeking an advantage, faithful to their policy of never allowing a stable government to exist anywhere in Europe . . . With Wellington here in the Peninsula, they can kill three birds with one stone: they get Portugal on side, they undermine Napoleon and in doing so they ensure we are in their debt—a debt they will make us pay for later. This alliance is going to cost us dearly."

Lolita Palma indicates the thrum of people all around: the cliques, the passersby. The new edition of the *Diario Mercantil* has just been delivered to the newsstand in the middle of the street and people are milling about, snatching copies from the newsagent.

"Perhaps. But just look at the city . . . it's bubbling with life, with business."

"That's just an illusion, *hija*. The foreigners will leave the moment the blockade is lifted and we will go back to being the city of sixty thousand souls we have always been. What will become of those currently doubling the price of rent and tripling the price of a steak? Those making a living exploiting the suffering of others? The crumbs you see before you today will be nothing compared to tomorrow's famine."

"But the Cortes . . ."

"The Cortes lives in another world," the elderly merchant growls, making no attempt to disguise his contempt. "Constitution, monarchy, Fernando VII. Such things have nothing to do with us. What the people of Cádiz want is freedom, progress. That, in the end, is the foundation of all commerce. Whether or not the Cortes passes laws, whether they decide the king rules by divine right or is the repository of national sovereignty will change nothing: the American ports will still be beyond our control and Cádiz will be bankrupt. When the pox of Constitution comes, the lean cows will low."

Lolita Palma laughs affectionately. Hers is a deep, resonant laugh. One that is young and healthy.

"I always took you for a liberal . . ."

Without letting go of her arm, Sánchez Guinea stops in the middle of the street.

"And by God so I am," he says glaring around him as if anyone might doubt the fact. "But I believe in a liberalism that offers work and prosperity . . . Political hot air will not put food on my family's table or anyone else's. The Cortes demands much but offers little. Just think of the million *pesos* they have demanded the merchants of this city pay toward the war effort. After everything they've already taken from us! Meanwhile, every state counselor is earning forty thousand *reales* a month, and every minister is pocketing eighty thousand."

They walk on. Just ahead, among the scattering of bookshops on the little plazas of San Agustín and El Correo, is Salcedo's bookshop. Don Emilio and Lolita linger for a moment before the bookcases and the shop windows. In the window of Navarro's are a number of soft-cover editions, their pages still uncut, and two large, handsomely bound volumes, one open at the title page: *A History of the Conquest of Mexico* by Antonio de Solis.

"In the current climate," continues Sánchez Guinea, "best to invest in something secure: houses, property, land . . . Keep cash reserves for those things that will still have value when the war is over. Trade as it existed back in the days of your grandfather, or of your father, will never return . . . Without America, Cádiz has no purpose."

Lolita Palma gazes at the shop window. *Too much talk*, she thinks, *on subjects they have discussed a hundred times before. Don Emilio is not a man to waste his time on words. As far as he is concerned, five minutes with no resulting profit is five minutes wasted. And they have been chatting now for fifteen.*

"Come to the point, Don Emilio."

For a moment she fears he is about to suggest some venture involving contraband of the kind she has rejected three times in the past months. Nothing out of the ordinary. Nothing serious. Trading contraband has been a way of life in the city ever since the first galleons set sail from the Indies. It would be a very different matter were he to suggest trading with the occupied French territories, as a number of unscrupulous merchants have been doing since the beginning of the blockade. The house of Sánchez Guinea would never tarnish its reputation with such vile practices; but sometimes, in the gray area that exists between the exigencies of war and the laws in force, some merchandise passes through the Puerta de Mar without customs and excise duties being paid. Among the respectable businessmen of Cádiz, this is known as "working with the left hand."

"Come now, tell me what is on your mind."

The merchant stares at the bookshop window, although Lolita Palma knows that he cares little about the conquest of Mexico. He takes his time. "I think you are managing things very well, Lolita," he says after a moment, "reducing costs, cutting back on luxuries. That's intelligent. You know that this boom will not last forever. You have managed to retain that most precious commodity in this city: reputation. Your grandfather and your father would have been proud of you. What am I saying? They *are* proud, looking down on you from heaven . . ."

"Don't sugar the pill, Don Emilio." Lolita Palma laughs again, her arm still linked in his. "Please, come to the point."

Emilio stares at the ground between the tips of his impeccably polished shoes. Glances again at the books. Eventually he turns and looks at her, determined.

"I'm arming a corsair ship . . . I've purchased a blank Letter of Marque and Reprisal."*

As he says this, he gives her a wink as though he expects her to be shocked. Then he looks at her inquisitively. She nods. She saw this coming; it is a subject they have discussed many times. And she has heard rumors about the Letter of Marque. The cunning old fox. The expression on her face says, "As you know very well I have no taste for such investments. I do not wish to be involved with that. With the war, with those people."

* A Letter of Marque and Reprisal was a government license authorizing a person (known as a privateer) to attack and capture enemy vessels and bring them before admiralty courts for condemnation and sale.

Sánchez Guinea raises a hand, half in apology, half in good-natured protest.

"It's just business, *hija*. These are the same people merchant ships deal with every day . . . and the war affects you just as it affects everyone."

"I despise piracy." She has let go of his arm and is clutching her bag with both hands. "We have suffered from it all too often, and it has cost us dearly."

Don Emilio reasons with her, puts forward his arguments. With genuine affection. A wise counselor.

"A corsair is not a pirate, Lolita, they operate according to strict laws, as you know. Your father, if you remember, had a very different opinion on the subject. In 1806 we shared the cost of arming a corsair and made a handsome profit. Now is the moment. There are incentives, bounties to be earned for captured ships. Enemy cargoes to be seized. It's all perfectly legal. It is merely a matter of putting up the capital, as I am doing. Simply business. Another form of marine insurance."

Lolita Palma gazes at their reflection in the shop window. She knows Don Emilio does not need her money. Or not urgently, in any case. The offer is a generous one, an opportunity to participate in a profitable business venture. There are many people in Cádiz who would be willing to invest in such a business, but Sánchez Guinea has chosen her. A clever, serious girl. Someone who inspires trust and respect. Someone with a reputation. The daughter of his friend Tomás.

"Let me think it over, Don Emilio."

"Of course. Think about it."

CAPTAIN SIMON DESFOSSEUX is feeling awkward. Generals are not his preferred company and today they are all over him. On top of him. Every one hanging on his every word—a fact that does little to calm his spirit: Marshal Victor, Chief of Staff Semellé, generals Villatt and Laval from the Ruffin division, and General Lesueur, Desfosseux's direct superior, commander of the Premier Corps artillery and successor to the late Baron de Senarmont. They landed on him mid-morning when the Duc de Belluno suddenly decided to make an impromptu inspection of the Trocadero, leaving his headquarters at Chiclana under a heavy escort of hussars from the 4th Regiment.

"The idea is to be able to reach the whole of the city," Desfosseux is explaining. "Until now this has proved impossible, we are working at our absolute limit and we're faced with two difficulties: the range, on the one hand, and the fuses on the other . . . The latter are a particular problem since my orders are to launch bombs on the city that actually explode, like grenades. This is why we use a delayed trigger; but the distances involved are so great that many of the bombs explode before they reach their target . . . We have been working on a new fuse, one that burns more slowly and does not snuff out en route."

"And is it available now?" inquires General Leval, head of the 2nd Division quartered in Puerto Real.

"It will be in a few days. Theoretically it should burn for more than thirty seconds, but the timing is not always precise. Sometimes friction with the air accelerates the combustion rate . . . or blows out the fuse."

A pause. The generals, their frockcoats bedecked with medals, regard him attentively, waiting. The marshal is seated, the others, like Desfosseux, standing. On an easel is a large map of the city and another of the bay of Cádiz. Through the open windows come the voices of the sappers working on the foundations for the new gun battery. In a patch of sunlight, flies are swarming around a crushed cockroach. Flies and cockroaches in their thousands teem the barracks and the trenches of the Trocadero. And there are enough rats, bedbugs, lice and mosquitoes to infest the whole Imperial Army.

"This brings us to the second problem: range. I am being asked to cover a range of 3,000 *toises*. With the current means at my disposal, the best I can guarantee is a range of 2,300 *toises*. And even then, we must factor in the crosswinds in the bay which can have a pronounced effect on both distance and trajectory . . . Currently, our range allows us to shell an area extending from here to here."

He indicates several points in the eastern sector of the city: Puerta de Mar, the area around the Customs House. He does not trouble to name them since everyone here has spent the past year poring over this map. Desfosseux's index finger traces a line just inside the city walls that barely encroaches on the city proper aside from a few streets in the Pópulo district next to the Puerta de Tierra. This is all there is, the moving finger seems to say. Desfosseux takes his hand away and looks over at his direct superior, General Lesueur. Implying *the rest, sir, is down to you*, and wordlessly requesting permission to leave. To get out of this place and go back to his slide rule, his telescope and his carrier pigeons. To his work. But of course he does not leave. The worst, he knows, is yet to come.

"The enemy ships anchored in the bay are within this range, are they not?" asks General Ruffin. "Why not launch an attack on them?"

François Amable Ruffin, commander of the 1st Division, is a lean, serious individual with expressionless eyes; a veteran of the battles of Austerlitz and Friedland to name but two. A sensible man, respected by his men. Barely forty, he has risen quickly through the ranks. A firebrand. He is the sort of soldier who dies young and whose name is inscribed on a memorial somewhere.

"We do not bomb the ships," explains Desfosseux, "because they are not within range—the English warships are slightly too far out, the Spanish ships too close. They cleave close to the city, if I may put it so. It is difficult to be accurate at such a distance. Artillery fire is imprecise. It is in the lap of the gods. It is one thing to drop bombs on a city, but to hit a precise target is a very different matter, impossible to guarantee. Take the Customs House, for example, the headquarters of the insurrectionist Regency. Not a single hit.

"Simply put," he concludes, "with the means at our disposal, greater range and greater precision are impossible."

He is about to add something, but hesitates and General Lesueur, who, like the others, has been listening in silence, raises a warning eyebrow. The artillery commander's warning is clear: do not make trouble. Do not make your life or mine any more difficult than it already is. This is just a routine inspection. Tell them what they want to hear, I'll deal with the rest.

"But leaving aside the problem of accuracy, let's concentrate on range; I believe we could obtain better results if we used mortars rather than howitzers."

There, the words have been said. And he does not regret them, even if Lesueur is now glaring at him furiously.

"Out of the question," Lesueur says curtly. "The tests carried out last November using the 12-inch Dedon mortar cast in the foundry in Seville were disastrous . . . The shells fired did not even attain a range of 2,000 *toises*."

Marshal Victor leans back in his chair and gives Lesueur an imperious look. Victor is an experienced artilleryman, well versed in such matters, meticulous and disciplined; he is the sort of man who dives into something only when he knows how he will get out of it. He and Lesueur have known each other since the siege of Toulon when the marshal was still the humble Claude Perrin and they were shelling royalist redoubts and Spanish and British warships with another comrade-in-arms, the young Captain Bonaparte. Let the professional explain himself, the wordless scowl implies. I can speak to you any day, whereas this man is an expert, or so I am told. This is why we are here: so he can tell us what he needs to say. Lesueur slowly closes his mouth and the Duc de Belluno turns back to Desfosseux and invites him to continue.

"At the time I warned that the Dedon mortar was not equal to the task," continues the captain. "It was a plate mortar with a spherical chamber. Extremely difficult to aim and dangerous to operate. The 30-pound charge required was too much: the gunpowder did not combust simultaneously and the substandard thrust resulted in a shorter range . . . Even conventional cannons were more effective."

"A botched job—typical of Dedon," comments the marshal.

Everyone laughs politely except for Desfosseux and Ruffin, who is staring out of the window as though expecting some omen. General Dedon is despised within the Imperial Army. An intelligent theorist and consummate artilleryman, Dedon's noble birth and aristocratic manner rankle with the hard-bitten soldiers who rose from the ranks after the Revolution, as Victor did, starting out as a drummer boy thirty years ago at Grenoble, earning his *saber d'honneur* at Marengo and re-

lieving Marshal Bernadotte at Friedland. They all do their utmost to discredit Dedon's projects and consign his mortars to oblivion.

"The basic concept, however, was a good one," says Desfosseux with the confidence of an expert.

The silence that descends is so charged that even General Ruffin turns to stare at the captain, now vaguely interested. Meanwhile Lesueur, no longer content to raise a single admonishing eyebrow at his subordinate, raises both, his eyes boring into Desfosseux, heavy with menace.

"The problem of partial powder combustion is common to a number of larger field guns," Desfosseux carries on, imperturbable. "The Villantroys howitzers, for example, or the Rutys."

The silence continues. The Duc de Belluno studies Desfosseux thoughtfully, running a hand over his leonine brow and through the thick mane of gray hair whose care he entrusts to a Spanish barber in Chiclana. The captain knows that to speak disrespectfully of the howitzers is to pour scorn on the favored weapons of the siege. Lesueur, his superior, has long vaunted the technical merits of these weapons. And, in doing so, has foolishly fueled expectations among senior personnel which Desfosseux considers unwarranted.

"There is a fundamental difference," says the marshal. "The Emperor is of the opinion that the appropriate field gun for shelling Cádiz is the howitzer . . . The Emperor personally dispatched Colonel Villantroys's designs to us."

A buzzing of flies. All eyes turn to Desfosseux, who swallows hard. *What am I doing here?* he thinks. *Squeezed into this uncomfortable uniform with its itchy collar, holding absurd conversations when I could be back in Metz teaching physics. Instead, here I am in the back of beyond, playing soldiers with bigwigs decked out in medals who only want to hear what suits them. Or what they think suits them. And that pig Lesueur knows it as well as I do, but he's happy to throw me to the wolves.*

"With all due respect to the Emperor, I believe the assault on Cádiz should be carried out using mortars rather than howitzers."

"With all due respect," echoes the marshal, smiling.

His pensive smile would send a shiver down the spine of any soldier. But Captain Desfosseux is a civilian in uniform. A reluctant soldier for the duration of his posting. Which, for the moment, is Cádiz. They put him in a uniform and sent him here from France for this.

"Your Excellency, even the flaws in the fuses have a bearing on this . . . The shells fired by the howitzers require fuses that have proved ineffective whereas larger bombs of greater diameter fired from a mortar would make it possible to use larger fuses. Furthermore, the increased gravity would result in the full combustion of the powder charge when fired thereby affording greater range."

The Chief Marshal of the Premier Corps is still smiling, but his expression now betrays a certain curiosity—a dangerous trait in marshals, generals and their like.

"The Emperor is of a rather different opinion. Don't forget, Napoleon himself was an artilleryman, and prides himself that he is still one. As indeed am I."

Desfosseux nods, but they can't stop him now. He feels uncomfortably hot under his frockcoat, with a pressing need to unbutton the high, stiff collar. But it hardly matters; he has nothing to lose: he will never have a better opportunity to explain himself. Certainly not if he is languishing in a military prison or facing a firing squad. So he takes a deep breath and replies that he is not calling into question the competence of His Imperial Majesty, nor that of His Excellency the Duc de Belluno. Indeed it is precisely because of their knowledge of artillery that he dares to say what he is saying, trusting only to his science and his conscience. His loyalty to the Artillery Corps . . . To France above all things. To his homeland. With regard to the howitzers, he goes on, Marshal Victor was present at the Trocadero when the tests were conducted and must surely remember that of the eight howitzers fired at an angle of 45 degrees, not a single one achieved a range greater than 2,000 *toises*. And many of the shells exploded in midair.

"The result of errors in the mixture used for the fuses," General Lesueur slyly interjects.

"That hardly matters since none of the missiles actually reached the city. The distances attained decreased each time the howitzers were fired. And the bush pins did not help."

"In what sense?" inquires Marshal Victor.

"Every time the cannon was fired the vent was weakened thereby decreasing the thrust."

The silence this time is longer. The marshal studies the map for a moment. General Ruffin has turned back toward the window. From outside comes the clang of the sappers' picks and shovels. After a while, the marshal turns away from the map.

"Let me put it another way, Captain . . . I'm sorry, could you remind me of your name?"

"Simon Desfosseux, Excellency."

"Listen, Captain Desfosseux . . . I have three hundred large-caliber field guns trained on Cádiz and a foundry in Seville working around the clock. I have my senior artillery staff, and I have you who, according to poor Senarmont, may he rest in peace, are a brilliant theorist. I have given you the technical means and the authority . . . What more do you need to bomb the bloody *manolos*?"

"Mortars, Excellency."

A fly lands on the Duc de Belluno's nose.

"Mortars, you say?"

"Yes. Mortars of greater caliber than the Dedon model: fourteen inches."

Victor shoos the fly, with a gesture that, for an instant, reveals the boorish, uncouth soldier beneath the medals and ribbons pinned to his uniform.

"Forget the damned mortars, do you hear me?"

"Perfectly, Your Excellency."

"If the Emperor says we must use howitzers, then we will use howitzers and keep our opinions to ourselves."

Captain Desfosseux raises a hand in supplication. Just one more minute. Because if this is the case, there is something he needs to ask the marshal. Does His Excellency want the bombs to explode, or is it enough for them to drop in Cádiz? Then he falls silent and waits. After a moment's hesitation in which he exchanges glances with his generals, Marshal Victor retorts that he does not understand the captain's question. Desfosseux once again gestures toward the map and explains that he needs to know whether he is required to inflict serious damage on the city or whether it is enough to simply drop bombs, thereby sapping the morale of the inhabitants. Whether the shells are required to explode or whether minor damage is sufficient.

The marshal's consternation is clear. He scratches the spot on his nose where the fly landed.

"What do you mean by minor damage?"

"The damage caused by eighty pounds of inert bomb, which would certainly smash objects and make some noise."

"Listen to me, Captain." Victor no longer seems angry. "What I really want is for the city to be bombed to rubble and then have my grenadiers march in with fixed bayonets and occupy it . . . However, since this has proved impossible, what I want is an article in *Le Moniteur* back in Paris stating—truthfully—that we are pulverizing the city of Cádiz. From one end to the other."

It is Desfosseux's turn to smile. For the first time. Not an insolent smirk, nor anything unbecoming to his rank and station. Merely a faint smile, a hint of things to come.

"I have run tests using a ten-inch howitzer firing special shells. In fact they are very simple: they contain no powder. No fuse, no charge. Some are solid iron, others are filled with lead and sand. They may prove interesting as regards the range if I can resolve a secondary problem."

"And what damage do they inflict?"

"They break things. With any luck, they might damage a building, kill or injure someone. They make a lot of noise. And they may extend our range by a hundred or even two hundred *toises*."

"Tactical efficacy?"

"Negligible."

Victor exchanges a look with General Lesueur, who nods vigorously as though to confirm this, although Desfosseux knows Lesueur is utterly ignorant in the matter. The results of the latest tests with Fan-fan are known only to him and to Lieutenant Bertoldi.

"Very well. At least it is something. It will be enough to satisfy *Le Moniteur* for the time being. But do not give up on the standard weapons. I want you to carry on using conventional shells with fuses and so forth. It's always worthwhile lighting a candle to Christ and another to the devil."

The Duc de Belluno gets to his feet and everyone automatically stands. Hearing the chair scrape across the floor, General Ruffin turns back from the window.

"One more thing, Captain. Should you manage to get a bomb to hit the church of San Felipe Neri—I don't care whether or not the shell explodes—where those outlaws who call themselves the Cortes meet, I will promote you to Commandant. Do you understand? You have my word on it . . ."

General Lesueur makes a face and Marshal Victor glares at him.

"What?" he snaps. "Do you have a problem with my decision?"

"It's not that, sir," Lesueur apologizes. "Captain Desfosseux has twice refused a promotion such as the one your Excellency is suggesting."

As he says this, Lesueur glares at Desfosseux with a palpable mixture of jealousy and animosity. To a professional soldier, any man who refuses a promotion is suspect—to do so is a blatant repudiation of the career path common among veterans in the Imperial Army, those who rise through the ranks, winning honors, being promoted from ordinary foot soldier until, like the Duc de Belluno or indeed General Lesueur himself, they are in a position to pillage the lands, villages and towns under their command and send the spoils back to their mansions in France. Three decades of glory in the service of the Republic, the Consul and the Empire, of stoically facing death, are not inimical to dying a rich man, preferably in one's own bed. All the more reason to mistrust a man like Desfosseux, who insists on marching to the beat of his own drum. Were it not for his undisputed technical abilities, General Lesueur would long since have had the man posted to some remote stronghold, or left him to rot in the squalid trenches dotted around the Isla de León.

"Well, well," says Victor, "I see we are dealing with an individualist. Perhaps he looks down his nose at those of us who accept promotion."

There is an awkward silence which is finally broken by a roar of laughter from the marshal himself.

"Very well, Captain. Keep up the good work and remember what I said about bombing San Felipe. My offer of a promotion still stands . . . Unless there is something you would rather have?"

"A fourteen-inch mortar, Excellency."

"*Get out of here,*" the hero of the battle of Marengo splutters, jerking his head toward the door. "Get out of my sight, you pig-headed bastard!"

THE TAXIDERMIST ARRIVES early at Frasquito Sanlúcar's soap emporium on the Calle Bendición de Dios next to the Plaza Mentidero. It is a cool, narrow, dimly lit shop with a window overlooking an interior courtyard; at the back of the shop stands a display case in front of a curtain leading to the stockroom. Piles of boxes and glass-topped drawers displaying goods. Small bottles intended for expensive products. Colors and scents, the smell of soap and incense. On the wall, a tinted engraving of King Fernando VII and an antique mercury-column ship's barometer.

"Good morning, Frasquito."

The soap merchant, a redhead dressed in gray overalls, looks more English than Spanish despite his surname. He wears spectacles and his face is covered with freckles that disappear into his curly thinning hair.

"Good morning, Don Gregorio, what can I do for you today?"

Gregorio Fumagal—for this is the taxidermist's name—smiles. He is a regular customer here, because Frasquito Sanlúcar's emporium offers the finest range of products in Cádiz, from pomades and translucent, high-quality toilet soaps imported from abroad to the commonplace Spanish soaps used for laundry.

"I'd like some hair dye. And two pounds of the white soap I bought last time."

"What did you think of it?"

"First-rate. You were right, it is perfect for cleaning animal pelts."

"I told you so. Much better than the soap you used to buy. And less expensive."

Two young women come into the shop. "I'm in no hurry," says the taxidermist, stepping away from the display counter while Sanlúcar serves them. They live in the neighborhood and are clearly lower class: they wear thick woolen shawls over serge skirts, their hair is pinned up with clips, and shopping baskets are slung over their arms. They are offhand, in the way only women of Cádiz can be. One of the girls is slim and pretty, with a fine complexion and slender hands. Gregorio Fumagal watches as they rummage through boxes and sacks of merchandise.

"Give me half a pound of this yellow soap, Frasquito."

"Absolutely not. I could not possibly recommend it for you. Too much tallow, *niña*."

"What's wrong with that?"

"It means it contains a lot of fat. Pork fat, mostly. It leaves a faint smell on washing . . . I'll give you some of this one here, it's made of sesame oil. Luxuriously indulgent."

"More expensive too, I've no doubt. I know you."

Frasquito Sanlúcar adopts an innocent expression. "A fraction more expensive, perhaps. But you deserve a soap worthy of a Moorish queen. Exceptional quality. Opulent. For a beauty such as yourself. This very soap is used by the Empress Josephine herself."

"Really? But I don't want to smell like some *gabacho* whore."

"Just a moment, *niña*, I hadn't finished. It was also used by the Queen of England. And the Infanta Carlotta of Portugal. And the Countess—"

"A pretty fairy tale, Frasquito, but I don't believe you."

The soap merchant picks up a box which he is about to wrap in colored paper. With his female customers, he always packs his wares in fancy boxes with expensive paper and labels so they serve as an advertisement for the shop.

"How many pounds did you say you wanted, my dove?"

As he bids the young women goodbye, Gregorio Fumagal steps aside to let them pass, studying them as they leave.

"My apologies, Don Gregorio." The soap merchant turns to him. "Thank you for your patience."

"I see you still have a wide range of stock in spite of the war."

"I can't complain. As long as the port remains free, we have everything we need. I even manage to get goods from France, which is just as well, since Cádiz is accustomed to imported goods, and Spanish soap is not very highly regarded . . . it's said to be grossly adulterated."

"And do you adulterate your soap?"

Sanlúcar now adopts his most haughty expression. "With soaps, there is a difference between *adulteration* and *blending*. Look here," he says indicating a box of soap cakes that are immaculately white. "German soap. Like our own it contains a lot of animal fat, because they have no oils there, but they purify it until it is odorless. No one would want a Spanish toilet soap. The merchandise is poor quality, people simply do not trust it. In the end the innocent"—he pauses, modifying his thought—"in the end *we* the innocent always suffer because of the guilty."

There is a muffled rumble in the distance. Barely enough to shake the wooden floor and the glass in the window frames. Both men listen intently for a moment.

"Do people around here worry much about the bombs?"

"Not much." Sanlúcar casually carries on wrapping the two pounds of soap and the bottle of hair dye in brown paper. "We're too far away. The bombs don't even reach San Agustín."

"How much do I owe you?"

"Seven *reales*."

The taxidermist puts a silver *duro* on the counter and, half-turned toward the direction of the explosion, waits for his change.

"At any event, they are gradually coming closer."

"But not too close, thank the Lord. One landed in the Calle del Rosario this morning. That is as close as they've come, and that's a thousand yards from here. That's why so many people come here at night; people have started coming to this part of the city to sleep."

"In the open air? . . . That must be a queer sight."

"Indeed it is. Every night there are more of them, the plaza is a sea of mattresses, blankets, nightcaps; they sleep in the doorways or anywhere they can find . . . The authorities say they plan to move them on, to build shelters on the waste ground next to Santa Catalina. Behind the barracks."

When Gregorio Fumagal steps out of the soap merchant's emporium, package tucked under his arm, the two girls are up ahead, gazing in shop windows. The taxidermist casts a glance at them, then walks away from the Plaza Mentidero toward the eastern sector of the city through the orderly grid of streets that were designed to temper winds from both east and west. Along the way, he stops at a little shop on the Calle del Tinte where he buys three grains of mercuric chloride, six ounces of camphor and eight of white arsenic. Then he walks on as far as the corner of Amoladores and Rosario where various parishioners are sitting in the doorway of a tavern uncorking a bottle as they stare at the building hit by a bomb at nine o'clock that morning. A section of the facade has been destroyed, ripped open to reveal three floors and a vertical trail of destruction: broken joists, doors open onto the void, prints and paintings askew on the walls, a bed and other furniture perched miraculously over the ruins. Domestic intimacy laid bare in a manner that is almost obscene. Neighbors, soldiers and members of the nightwatch are shoring up the walls and picking through the debris.

"Was anyone hurt?" Fumagal asks the innkeeper.

"Nothing serious, thank God. There was no one in the section of the building that collapsed . . . The landlady and a maid were the only people injured . . . The blast did a lot of damage, but it could have been much worse."

The taxidermist walks over to the spot where a group of bystanders are staring at the remains of the shell case: fragments of iron and lead amid the rubble, twisted shards like corkscrews half a palm's length. Fumagal overhears someone say that the house once belonged to a French merchant who has been incarcerated for the past three years in one of the prison ships anchored in the bay. The new owners converted it into a boardinghouse. The landlady, having been rescued from the rubble, is in the hospital with two broken legs. The chambermaid sustained only minor bruising.

"It was a narrow escape," comments one woman, making the sign of the cross.

The taxidermist's keen eye takes in everything. The direction from which the bomb came, the angle of incidence, the damage caused. The wind is coming from the east today. A light breeze. Doing his best not to attract attention, he walks from the spot where the missile fell to the church—the Iglesia del Rosario—counting his paces, calculating the distance: about twenty-five *toises*. Discreetly, he takes out a lead pencil and jots the figure on a notepad he takes from his coat pocket; from here he will transfer it to the map spread out on the desk in his workshop. Lines and curves. Points of impact on a grid like a spider's web slowly spreading across the city. As he writes, he sees the girls from the soap merchant's who have come to witness the damage caused by the bomb. So intent is he on watching them that the taxidermist bumps into a man of bronzed complexion coming in the other direction, wearing a black tricorne and a blue frockcoat with gilt buttons. After a curt apology from Fumagal, the men go their separate ways.

Pépé Lobo pays no heed to the man in dark clothes shuffling away with two packages clutched in his slim, pale hands. The sailor has other things to think about. Chief among them the realization that misfortune is dogging his every step. His trunk and all his belongings are buried beneath the rubble of the boardinghouse where he lives—or lived in until today. Not that he possesses much, three shirts and some white linen, a jacket, breeches, underwear, a frockcoat, an English spyglass and sextant, a longitude watch, nautical charts, two pistols and a number of crucial items, among them his captain's license. No money; what little money he has he carries with him. Barely enough to jingle in his pocket. As for the money he is owed for his most recent voyage—he doesn't know when he will be paid. His last visit to the owner of the *Risueña* half an hour ago was hardly promising.

"Come back in a couple of days, Captain. When we've taken an inventory of this disastrous voyage and everything is sorted. Our first priority must be to compensate the creditors for the delay in the ship's arrival. *Your* delay, Captain. I hope you are prepared to accept responsibility. Excuse me? Oh, yes. I'm sorry we have no other command positions available. We will of course be in touch should one arise. Never fear. And now, if you'll forgive me . . ."

Crossing the street, the sailor comes upon a group of people gathered outside the house. Angry comments, insults directed at the French. Nothing new. He pushes his way through the crowd of bystanders until a sergeant in the Volunteer Force hails him and tells him in no uncertain terms that he can go no further.

"I live in this house. My name is Captain Lobo."

The sergeant looks him up and down.

"Captain?"

"Indeed."

Titles do not seem to impress the man in the blue and white uniform worn by officers of the urban forces, but being a native of Cádiz, as soon as he realizes that Lobo works for the merchant navy, he tempers his attitude. When the captain tells him about the trunk, the sergeant offers to have a soldier help him search the ruins. Lobo thanks him, removes his frockcoat, rolls up his shirtsleeves and sets about the task. *Finding somewhere else to live will be no easy task*, he thinks worriedly as he shifts stones, bricks and broken planks. The recent influx of foreigners has led to a scarcity in lodgings. The number of inhabitants in Cádiz has doubled: the inns and boardinghouses are full, even rooms and terraces in private houses are being let or sublet at exorbitant rates. It is impossible to find anything for less than 25 *reales* a day, and the annual rent for a modest living space now runs to 10,000 *reales*—a sum few people can afford to pay. Some of the refugees belong to the landed gentry, who receive monies from America, rents from properties in the occupied territories or from businesses in Paris and London; but for the most part they are bankrupt landowners, patriots who refuse to swear allegiance to the royal interloper, unemployed civil servants from the previous administration washed up in Cádiz by the ebb and flow of war. A tide of refugees trailing families who have followed the fleeing Spanish Regency since the French first marched into Madrid and Seville. Countless immigrants have thronged into the city without the means to live with dignity, their number swelled by those who daily flee those parts of Spain already under French occupation and those in danger of being so. There is thankfully no shortage of food, and people muddle by as best they can.

"Is this your trunk, señor?"

"A pox on it . . . Yes, that's it."

Two hours later, filthy, sweaty and resigned, Pépé Lobo—this is not the first time he has been left with little more than the clothes on his back—is walking down by the Puerta de Mar, shouldering a canvas knapsack containing what remains of his personal shipwreck: the handful of belongings he managed to rescue from the flattened trunk. The sextant, spyglass and nautical charts did not survive the fall; the rest of his belongings did, though only just. Then again, had he not taken his time before visiting the *Risueña's* owner, things might have been much worse. He might have been buried beneath the rubble. An explosion and he might have found himself among the heavenly choir, or wherever he is destined to go when eight bells toll. In short, he is in an awkward situation. Delicate. In a city like Cádiz, however, there is always room for maneuver; this is some small comfort to him as he visits the streets and taverns around El Boquete and La Merced, filled with sailors, fishermen, whores and port rats, foreigners and refugees in dire straits. Here, on thoroughfares that bear eloquent names such as Coffin Street and Scabies Alley, he knows places where a sailor can find a mattress for the night for a few coins, though it means sleeping next to a woman with one eye open and a knife beneath the folded jacket he sometimes uses as a pillow.

TIME SEEMS TO be suspended in the silence of the lifeless creatures that line the walls of the workshop. The light streaming through the door glimmers on the glass eyes of the stuffed birds and mammals, on the large crystal jars in which motionless creatures float, chemically suspended in a fetal position. The only sound is the soft, hurried rasp of a pencil. At the center of this curious world, Gregorio Fumagal is writing on a scrap of gossamer paper in his tiny, cramped hand. Wearing a woolen housecoat and nightcap, the taxidermist bends over the tall lectern that serves as a writing desk. From time to time he glances over at the map of Cádiz spread out on the desk and twice he takes a magnifying glass to scrutinize it more closely before returning to the lectern and picking up where he left off.

The bells ring out at the Iglesia de Santiago. Fumagal looks over at the gilt bronze clock on the bureau, dashes off the last few lines and, without rereading what he has written, rolls the slip of paper into a short tight tube which he slips into a sheath made of feathers he takes from the drawer, sealing both ends with wax. He opens the glass door and climbs the few steps to the terrace. Unlike the subdued light of the workshop, the harsh glare up here hurts his eyes. Less than two hundred paces away the unfinished cupola and half-built spires of the new cathedral, still ringed with scaffolding, are framed against the skyline, the expanse of sea, the sandbar, white and shimmering in the sunlight, that extends beyond the reef, curving toward Sancti Petri and the heights of Chiclana like a dyke whose banks are about to be burst by the deep blue of the Atlantic.

Fumagal opens the door to the pigeon loft and steps inside. His is a familiar presence, and the birds barely react. A brief fluttering of wings. The cooing of the pigeons, the customary smell of hempseed and dried peas, of warm air and bird droppings enfolds the taxidermist as he chooses a strong cock pigeon with bluish-gray plumage, a white breast and a collar of iridescent green and violet feathers, a veteran of several flights to the far shore of the bay. A fine specimen whose extraordinary sense of direction has made him a reliable messenger in the service of the Emperor, this pigeon has survived sun, rain and wind, and proved invulnerable to the claws of raptors and the mistrustful gunshots of flightless bipeds. Many pigeons have vanished on their perilous missions, but this one always reaches his destination: a flight of some two and a half minutes depending on wind and weather, flying courageously in a straight line across the bay and later secretly brought back in a cage hidden aboard a smuggler's boat, his fare paid in French gold. Once free, the bird fights his own little war with Spain at three hundred feet.

He holds the pigeon belly up, checking it is healthy, that its flight feathers are intact. Then, taking waxed silk thread, he ties the message to one of the strong tail feathers, closes the pigeon loft and walks over to the east wall of the terrace where the nearby watchtowers rising above the city blot out the bay and the land beyond. Very carefully, having first checked that no one is watching from a neighboring terrace, the taxidermist releases the bird, which gives a joyful coo and flutters in circles for half a minute, rising in the air, getting its bearings. Eventually, its keen homing instinct pinpoints its precise destination and with a rhythmic beating of wings, it quickly sets off for the French fort at the Trocadero, a speck in the sky growing steadily smaller until finally it disappears.

Hands in the pockets of his gray housecoat, Gregorio Fumagal gazes out for a long time at the rooftops and towers of the city. Eventually, he turns and goes back down the steps to his workshop, which seems impossibly dark after the bright glare outside. As he does each time he sends a pigeon east, the taxidermist feels a curious exhilaration. A feeling of great power, a spiritual connection to the ineffable magnetic forces unleashed from the far side of the bay by his will and direction. Nothing could be less ordinary, less innocent, he concludes, than the pigeon, by now far away, which blindly carries the key to complex relationships between living beings, between his life and his death.

This last word hangs in the air among the lifeless animals. The half-dissected dog still lies splayed on the marble table, covered with a white sheet. Like his other work, it is a task that requires patience. Some parts of the body have already been fitted with a wire framework to support the bones and joints, and natural cavities stuffed with wadding. The empty eye sockets are still packed with cotton wool. The animal reeks of the chemicals preserving it from decomposition. Having chopped the soap he bought from Fransquito Sanlúcar and ground it in a mortar with arsenic, mercuric chloride and spirit of wine, the taxidermist has begun painting on the animal's skin with a horsehair brush, carefully following the nap of the hair, dabbing away any foam with a sponge.

The clock on the bureau chimes and, without pausing, Fumagal quickly glances at it. *The pigeon will have arrived by now*, he thinks. With the message that will dictate new lines and curves, new dots marking points of impact and explosions. Once again powerful forces will be set in motion, further extending the spider's web traced over the map, where the most recent bomb to fall is marked with a cross.

When night draws in, he will go out for a walk. A long walk. At this time of year, evening in Cádiz is delightful.

ROGELIO TIZÓN RARELY drinks wine; at most he may have a piece of bread soaked in wine at mid-morning. This evening, as always, he washes down his dinner with water. Soup, a chicken drumstick. A little bread. He is still gnawing on the drumstick when there is a knock at the door. The maid, a morose, elderly woman, answers and returns to announce Hipólito Barrull, who comes in carrying a folder of papers.

"I didn't know whether I should disturb you at such a late hour, Comisario. But you seemed particularly interested . . . traces in the sand, remember?"

"Of course." Tizón gets to his feet, wiping his hands and his mouth with a napkin. "And you could never disturb me, Professor. Would you care for something?"

"No, thank you. I dined a little while ago."

The policeman glances at his wife sitting at the other end of the table: she is painfully thin, her lifeless eyes ringed with dark circles that make her seem older. Her thin lips seem harsh. Everyone in the city knows that this dour, melancholy woman was once a great beauty. And happy too, perhaps, once upon a time. Before she lost her only child, some say. Before she married, the scandalmongers say. But this is Cádiz. Being Comisario Tizón's wife is akin to a life sentence. Is it true that he hits her? That's the least of it, *compadre*. I mean. If all he did was beat her.

"We'll retire to the drawing room, Amparo."

His wife does not respond but simply gives the professor a distracted smile, sitting stiffly in front of her untouched meal, her left hand—the hand that bears her wedding ring—idly rolling crumbs of bread into little balls.

"Make yourself comfortable, Professor." Tizón picks up a paraffin lamp, turning the wheel to adjust the flame. "Would you care for some coffee?"

"No, thank you. I wouldn't sleep."

"It has no effect on me. Coffee or no coffee, I haven't been able to sleep a wink recently. But you'll smoke a cigar with me. Forget your snuff for a while."

"I wouldn't say no."

The drawing room is cozy, with shuttered windows that overlook the Alameda, carved wood chairs and sofas upholstered in damask, a *mesa camilla*—a table with a small brazier underneath—and, set against one wall, a piano no one has played for eleven years. A few crude paintings and a handful of engravings hang on the papered walls and there is a walnut bookcase with some three dozen books: some on the history of Spain, a couple of essays about urban sanitation, booklets of royal ordinances, a dictionary, a five-volume edition of *Don Quixote* published by Sancha, *Romances de Germania* by Juan Hidalgo, and two volumes about Cádiz and Andalucía from the *Chronicles of Spain and Portugal* by Juan Álvarez de Colmenar.

"Try one of these." Tizón opens a cigar case. "They arrived a couple of days ago from Havana."

The cigars, it goes without saying, were free. The comisario accepted eight cases of fine cigars as part-payment—the balance of 200 *reales* in silver *duros*—for authorizing a questionable passport for an immigrant family. The two men sit smoking around a large metal ashtray shaped like the head of a hunting dog. Setting down his recently lit cigar, Hipólito Barrull adjusts his spectacles, opens the folder and sets a sheaf of manuscript pages in front of Tizón. Then he picks up the cigar again, takes a deep draw and settles back in his armchair with a satisfied air.

"Traces in the sand," he says again, slowly exhaling. "I think this is what you were referring to."

Tizón looks at the papers. They seem vaguely familiar, and he recognizes Barrull's handwriting.

Oft have I seen thee, son of Laertes,
Intent on some surprisal of thy foes.

He knows he has read this before. A long time ago. The pages are numbered but bear neither title nor heading. The text takes the form of a dialogue: Athena, Odysseus. *"Right well thy sense hath led thee forth, like some keen hound of Sparta."* Cigar clenched between his teeth, Tizón looks up for some explanation.

"You don't remember?" asks Barrull.

"Vaguely . . ."

"I gave you those pages to read a long time ago. My pitiful attempt at a translation of Sophocles' *Ajax*."

The professor briefly refreshes his memory. For a time in his youth, Barrull devoted himself to the task—never completed—of translating into Spanish the tragedies of Sophocles as collected in the first published edition of the works made in Italy in the sixteenth century. And some three years ago, before war broke out with the French, as they talked about his work over a game of chess in the Café del Correo, Tizón's curiosity had been piqued by *Ajax* when the professor explained to him that the play opens with a police investigation of sorts conducted by Odysseus—Ulysses to his friends.

"Of course. How stupid of me."

Rogelio Tizón taps the papers with a finger and sucks on his cigar. He remembers it all now. Barrull lent him the translation of Sophocles' tragedy, which he read with some interest, though the plot seemed thin. What he remembered was the image of Ulysses, during the siege of Troy, investigating Ajax's slaughter of sheep and oxen in a Greek camp. Enraged by his companions' snub in refusing to award him the armor of the dead Achilles and unable to avenge himself, Ajax vented his anger on the dumb beasts, torturing and killing them in his tent.

"You were right about the beach, the footsteps in the sand . . . Go on, read . . ."

Tizón is already reading, intent on every word:

Now I find thee by the seaward camp,
Where Ajax holds the last place in your line,
Lingering in quest, and scanning the fresh print
Of his late footsteps in the sand . . .

So this is what I have been remembering, he thinks, puzzled. *A sheaf of papers I read years ago. A Greek tragedy.* Hipólito Barrull seems to sense the policeman's disappointment.

"You were hoping for something more, weren't you?"

"No, Professor, I'm sure it will prove useful . . . All I need now is to discover the connection between my memory of *Ajax* and the present events."

"When we spoke the other day, you didn't tell me much about the nature of these events . . . Is it something to do with the French siege or with the murder of those poor girls?"

Tizón stares at the glowing tip of his cigar, groping for an answer. After a moment he shrugs. "That's the problem," he says, "I feel as though both things are somehow connected."

Barrull shakes his head, his expression skeptical.

"Are you relying on your policeman's nose? *'The nose'*—my apologies, I am merely citing the classics—*'of some keen hound of Sparta'*? If you'll forgive my frankness, that seems absurd."

A flicker of irritation. "I know that," murmurs Tizón leafing through the pages, reading lines at random. Still they shed no light. Barrull, with evident curiosity, studies him in silence.

"Damn it, Don Rogelio," he says eventually, "you are a box of surprises."

"What makes you say that?"

"I would never have expected a man like you to drag Sophocles into this."

"What do you mean, 'a man like me'?"

"You know . . . somewhat rough-hewn."

He blows smoke rings. Silence. "You're a police commissioner," says Barrull after a moment, "you're accustomed to dealing with real tragedies, not fictions. Besides, I know you: you're a level-headed man. So I have to wonder whether there can really be any serious connection between the two things. On one hand, you have a murderer—perhaps several murderers—on the other, a siege imposed on us by the French. And how many of them are there?"

From the corner of his mouth, the comisario gives a brusque laugh, flashing his gold canine tooth.

"Then, just to complicate matters, I've got your friend Ajax. The siege of Troy, the siege of Cádiz."

"With Ulysses as detective." Barrull grins, baring his yellow teeth. "As your colleague, in a sense. Though to judge from your expression, the papers I brought have shed no light on the matter."

Tizón makes a vague gesture.

"I'll need to read through them some other time. More carefully."

The flicker of the lamp glints in the professor's spectacles.

"Take all the time you need . . . Meanwhile, I shall be waiting for you tomorrow morning at the café with my chessboard. Ready to crush you pitilessly."

"As always."

"As always. Unless you have some more pressing business to attend to, naturally."

Tizón's wife is standing in the doorway of the drawing room. They did not hear her come in. Sensing her presence, Rogelio Tizón turns and scowls as though he has caught her eavesdropping. It would not be the first time. But she steps into the room and, as her face catches the light, the comisario realizes she comes bearing news, and from her expression it is not good.

"There is a nightwatchman here for you. They've found another dead girl."

CHAPTER THREE

༄

Dawn finds Rogelio Tizón half-illuminated by an oil lamp planted in the ground. The girl—or what remains of her—is young, no more than sixteen or seventeen. Light-brown hair, a delicate frame. She is gagged, lying facedown, her hands tied low on her naked back which has been flayed so viciously that bones are visible through the congealed blood of the purple-black flesh. There are no other visible wounds. It seems clear that, like the others, she was lashed to death.

No one—neither neighbors nor passersby—saw or heard anything. The gag, the isolated location and the time at which the crime occurred all contributed to the murder going unnoticed. The body was found on a patch of waste ground off the Calle de Amoladores where locals dump their rubbish for it to be collected every morning by the cart. The girl is still fully clothed below the waist; Tizón lifts her skirt to check. Her underskirts and unmentionables are intact, which in theory rules out the most depraved forms of assault, if *most* is a word that can be used in such circumstances.

"Tía Perejil has arrived, Señor Comisario."

"Tell her to wait."

The midwife, whom he sent for some time ago, is waiting at the far end of the alley with the nightwatchmen, who are keeping back the few curious neighbors awake at this hour. She is ready to give her professional opinion when the comisario calls on her, but Tizón is in no hurry. For some time now he has been sitting stock-still on a pile of rubble, hat tilted down over his eyes, overcoat around his shoulders, hands resting on the brass head of his walking stick. Staring. His doubts as to whether the girl was murdered here or killed elsewhere and brought here seem to melt with the dawn, which reveals blood spatters on the ground and the rocks nearby. Clearly it was here that the girl was bound, gagged to muffle her screams, and whipped to death.

Rogelio Tizón—as Barrull pointed out last night with caustic candor—is not a man for finer feelings. The routine horrors he has witnessed during his professional career have hardened his gaze and his conscience, and he has played a part in some of those horrors himself. All of Cádiz knows him to be a brutal, dangerous man. Yet in spite of his reputation for violence, the mutilated body next to him stirs a singular unease—not the vague compassion he might feel for any victim, but a curious feeling of reticence or modesty. He feels it more keenly now than he did five months ago when he saw the corpse of the first girl murdered in this way, and more intensely than when he was faced with the body of the girl on the reef. A frightening abyss seems to have opened up before him, a bottomless void that echoes with the sad, haunting notes of the piano in his drawing room that no one plays anymore. The long-ago, never-forgotten scent of a child's skin, the malignant fever growing cold in the mute pain of an empty room. The solitude of silences without tears that drip like the cruel ticking of a clock. In short, the hollow eyes of the woman who now wanders aimlessly through Rogelio Tizón's home, through his life, like a reproach or a witness, a ghost or a shadow.

The policeman gets to his feet, blinking as though he has just returned from somewhere far away. It is time for Tía Perejil to inspect the body. With a wave, he orders his men to bring her through. Without waiting for any greeting or acknowledgment from the midwife, Tizón walks away from the body and spends some time questioning the neighbors who have congregated around the waste ground with blankets, capes and shawls thrown over their nightclothes. No one saw or heard anything. No one knows if the girl is local. No one has heard of any missing girls. Tizón orders Lieutenant Cadalso to have the body removed as soon as the midwife has finished her examination without allowing the neighbors to see it.

"Understood?"

"Yes."

"What the hell do you mean 'yes' . . . Do you understand?"

"I understand, Señor Comisario. The body is to be covered and no one is to be allowed to see it."

"And keep your mouth shut. Don't say anything to anyone. Is that clear?"

"Crystal clear, Señor Comisario."

"Because the first person to open their mouth will have their tongue ripped out," he nods toward Tía Perejil. "And you can tell the old whore that too."

With matters now under control Rogelio Tizón, cane in hand, wanders off to explore the surrounding area. Daylight is beginning to creep over the sea wall and along the Calle Amoladores, painting the facades of the houses in a gray wash. There are no clear outlines yet, only the shadows of doorways and railings, of nooks and crannies. The comisario's footsteps echo on the cobbles as he walks, searching for some clue, some sign. He feels like a chess player faced with a difficult situation and no immediate strategy, blankly staring at the pieces waiting for some sudden revelation, some hitherto unnoticed possibility to inspire his next move. It is not a random impression. The memory of his conversation with Hipólito Barrull is still fresh in his mind. The nose of the keen hound of Sparta. Footprints. The professor came with him last night and briefly surveyed the scene of the crime before tactfully taking his leave. "Let's postpone our chess game," he said on leaving. "It's too late to postpone anything now," Tizón was about to say, his mind on other things. For some time now he has been playing a darker, more complex game. Three pawns lost, an unseen opponent and a city under siege. What the comisario wants to do now is to go home and read the translation of *Ajax* lying next to his armchair, if only to dismiss the connection as absurd or mistaken. He knows how dangerous it can be to get hung up on intriguing ideas, false leads, dead ends and traps. In criminal investigations, where appearances are rarely deceptive, the most obvious path is usually the correct one. To stray from it is to wander into scenarios that are fruitless or dangerous. But this morning he cannot help but think and worry, and this makes him uneasy. The few short lines he read of *Ajax* last night echo to the rhythm of his footfalls in the gray dawn of the city. Tock, tock, tock. *Now I find thee by the seaward camp.* Tock, tock, tock. *Scanning the fresh print of his late footsteps.* Tock, tock, tock. Footprints and tracks. Cádiz is teeming with them. More numerous in the city than on the shore. Footsteps overlaying each other. Thousands of appearances that cloak or conceal the thousands of realities of complex, inconstant, iniquitous human beings. And everything further complicated by the siege the city must endure. By this strange war.

On the corner of the Calle de Amoladores and Calle del Rosario, the ruins of a bombed-out building hit him like a slap in the face. Bitter evidence. The comisario stands frozen for a moment, struck dumb by this surprising—or as he concludes a moment later, this singularly unsurprising—discovery. The French shell landed less than twenty-four hours ago, a mere twenty paces from where the dead girl's body now lies. Carefully, as though afraid he might contaminate the evidence by some ill-judged movement, Tizón studies the ruins, the yawning vertical slash that lays bare three floors of the building, the interior walls shored up with wooden buttresses. Then he turns and looks eastward, across the bay, toward the point from which the shot was fired, calculating the trajectory to the point of impact.

A man steps out into the street. Despite the dawn chill he is wearing shirtsleeves and a long white apron. It is a baker removing timbers from the doorway to his bakery. Tizón walks over and, as he approaches the doorway, he catches the smell of freshly baked loaves. The man looks at him suspiciously, surprised to see a man in a redingote, a tricorne and a cane walking abroad so early.

"What happened to the fragments of the bomb?"

They were taken away, the baker tells him, surprised at being questioned about bombs so early in the morning. Tizón asks for details and the man obliges. "Some of the bombs explode," he says, "others don't. This one did. Hit the top of the building on the corner. There were fragments of lead strewn everywhere."

"Are you sure it was lead, my friend?"

"Yes, señor. Slivers of lead about the length of your finger. The kind that get all twisted when the bomb explodes."

"Like corkscrews?" says Tizón.

"Exactly. My daughter brought home four . . . You want to see them?"

"No."

Tizón turns and heads back down the Calle de Amoladores. Walking faster now, thinking quickly. Two bombs, two girls found dead almost in the same location less than twenty-four hours after each of the bombs fell. It seems too neat to be a coincidence. And there is more, since there have been not two murders, but three. The first girl, also flogged to death, was found in an alley between Santo Domingo and La Merced, in the eastern sector of the city by the docks. At the time no one thought to ask whether there had been any bombs in the area, and this is what Tizón is about to check. Or rather confirm, since he knows in his heart that there must have been an explosion in the area shortly beforehand. That these bombs are killing people in a manner very different to that intended by the French. That on a chessboard, there is no such thing as chance.

The policeman gives a faint smile—"smile" is perhaps excessive to describe the sullen, angular snarl that reveals his gold incisor—as he walks, amid the echoing footsteps and the gray dawn, swinging his cane. Tock, tock, tock. Thinking. It has been a long time—he has forgotten how long—since he felt the prickle of gooseflesh beneath his clothes. The cold shudder of fear.

THE DUCK FLIES low across the salt flats only to be picked off by a bullet. The gunshot sets other birds squawking and flapping in terror. Then silence. A moment later, three figures appear against the leaden dawn wearing the gray cloaks and black shakos of French soldiers. They move cautiously, bodies stooped, rifles in hand. Two of the men remain in the background, standing on a sandbank, weapons raised to provide cover for the third, who is searching in the undergrowth for the bird.

"Don't move," whispers Felipe Mojarra.

He is lying next to a narrow tidal creek, his bare feet and legs dangling into the salty mud, his gun pressed close to his face. Watching the

Frenchmen. Next to him Lorenzo Virués, Captain of Engineers, lies quietly, head down, clutching the leather shoulder bag in which he carries his spyglass, notepads and all his other sketching materials.

"They're just hungry. Soon as they find that duck they'll be gone."

"But what if they come this way?" whispers the other officer.

Mojarra runs his finger around the trigger guard of his flintlock: a fine Charleville musket captured from the enemy some time ago near Zuazo Bridge, it fires spherical lead bullets almost an inch in diameter. In the cartridge belt around his waist, next to his water gourd, he has nineteen more rounds wrapped in wax paper.

"If they come much closer, I'll kill one of them and that should keep the others at bay."

Out of the corner of his eye, he sees Captain Virués take out the pistol he carries in his belt and set it down on the sand within easy reach, just in case. He is an experienced soldier, so Mojarra does not feel the need to remind him to cock his weapon only at the last minute since, in the silence of the salt flats, the slightest sound will carry. Besides, Mojarra would much rather the French soldiers find their duck and head back to the trenches. When it comes to a shooting match, everyone knows how it starts but no one knows how it will end and the salter doesn't much like the idea of having to make it back to the Spanish lines half a league away from this no-man's-land of swamps, canals and quagmire with the *gabachos* on his tail. He has spent four hours guiding his companion through the San Fernando canal to arrive at dawn at the perfect spot: an observation point where the officer can make sketches of the fortifications of the enemy stronghold known as Los Granaderos. Later, when they are safely back behind their own lines, these sketches can be transformed into the detailed plans and charts in which Captain Virués—or at least this is what was said to Mojarra, whose skills are limited to negotiating his way through the swampland—is a master.

"They're leaving. They found the duck."

The three Frenchmen depart as cautiously as they came, rifles cocked, on the alert. From the careful way they move, Mojarra can tell they are veterans—fusiliers from the 9th Line Infantry Regiment which holds the nearest line of trenches—accustomed to being ambushed by the gangs of *guerrilleros* that operate along the fortified line of the Isla de Léon, beyond the meandering course of the Sancti Petri canal and the tidal creek of Santa Cruz. He knows about the 9th Regiment because a month ago, spotting the shako of a French soldier who was squatting in the undergrowth to relieve himself, Mojarra had crept up and slit his throat.

"Come on. Stay six or seven paces behind me."

"Is it far?"

"We're nearly there."

Felipe Mojarra gets to his feet, carefully crouching so he can survey the territory then, knee-deep in water, he wades slowly through the creek clutching his musket. The water in the marshes is so thick with saltpeter that in a few short hours it would flay the skin off any man foolish enough to walk through it barefoot. But Mojarra was born on the salt flats. Weathered by a life spent hunting, the soles of his feet are yellow and callused, tough as old leather, impervious to stones and thorns. As he moves, Mojarra hears the soft squelch of his companion's boots behind him. Unlike Mojarra, who is wearing knee-length shorts, a coarse canvas shirt, a short flannel jacket and a jackknife with a four-inch blade tucked into his belt, the captain is dressed in a blue uniform whose purple collar and lapels bear the insignia of the engineering corps. He is a handsome man, about six foot tall by Mojarra's reckoning, and long past thirty, with dark blond hair and mustaches and impeccable manners. This is their fifth reconnaissance mission together, and the salter is no longer surprised to see the captain wearing full uniform—excepting the regulation tie. Few Spanish soldiers are prepared to venture abroad without their uniform on irregular maneuvers. Should they be captured, their uniform is a guarantee that the French will treat them as equals, as prisoners of war; a very different fate from that which awaits local men like Mojarra. It does not matter what they wear. Should they fall into French hands, they would be greeted with a noose around their necks and the nearest tree branch. Or a bullet through the back of the head.

"Careful, Captain. Go round the other side . . . That's it . . . If you go that way, you'll sink. The mud here would swallow a jockey and his horse with him."

Felipe Mojarra Galeote, forty-six and a native of the Isla de Léon, has never ventured farther than Chiclana, the Puerto Real and the city of Cádiz where his daughter, Mari Paz, works as a lady's maid for a family of wealthy merchants. He has raised his daughter and his three other children—all girls, his only son died before the boy was four years old—and provided for his wife and his elderly half-crippled mother-in-law by working as a salter supplemented with a little illicit poaching along the creeks and salt marshes whose twists and turns he knows better than his own thoughts. Like all those who made their living here in peacetime, a year ago Mojarra signed up with the Salt Marsh Fusiliers, a troop of irregulars set up by his neighbor Don Cristóbal Sánchez de la Campa. The troop brings a little pay from time to time and gives them food. Besides, the salter has no love for the French, they steal bread from the mouths of the poor, string people up, rape women, they are enemies of God and the king.

"The *gabacho* stronghold is over there, Captain."

"That's Los Granaderos? You're sure?"

"It's the only one around here . . . about two hundred feet away."

Lying on a narrow sandbar, musket laid between his legs, Mojarra watches as the officer takes his drawing tools from his knapsack, opens his telescope and smears mud on the barrel and the lens, leaving only a small clean circle in the center. He then crawls to the crest of the ridge and trains his lens on the enemy position. He is wise to be cautious: the dawn sky is clear and cloudless and the sun glimmering on the horizon will soon rise between Medina Sidonia and the pine groves of Chiclana. This is the perfect time of day for sketching, as Captain Virués once explained to Mojarra, because the horizontal light emphasizes shape and detail.

"I'm going to check whether there are *mosíus* on the coast," whispers the salter.

He grabs his rifle and crawls on all fours through the salt marshes and the wild asparagus growing along the ridge. Around him are small sand dunes, shrubs, reed beds, flat stretches of mud dotted with flashes of white where the salt crust crackles underfoot. There are no French soldiers outside the fort. By the time he returns, Virués has set down his spyglass, picked up a pencil and is sketching. Not for the first time, Mojarra admires the man's skill, the deft, precise manner in which he draws the lines of the fortifications on the paper, the mud ramparts, the gabions, the fascines, the cannons poking through the embrasures. A scene repeated, with little variation, from trench to trench along an arc that spans some twelve miles encircling the Isla de Léon and the city of Cádiz from the Trocadero to the fortress of Sancti Petri. This offensive arc is mirrored by a Spanish line running parallel, a dense network of gun emplacements, cannons crisscrossing all approaches, making a direct assault by the Imperial troops impossible.

At the fortress, a trumpet sounds. Mojarra pops his head above the undergrowth and watches as a limp red, white and blue flag is hoisted up the flagpole. Time for breakfast. He slips a hand into his bag-cum-cartridge-belt and takes out a hunk of stale bread, soaks it in a few drops of water from his gourd, and nibbles on it.

"How is it going, Captain?"

"Excellent," the officer replies, not looking up, concentrating on his drawing. "Anything happening?"

"All quiet as a millpond."

"Good. Another half an hour and then we can head back."

Mojarra notices that the water level in the nearby creek has begun to ebb, a sure sign that in the bay the tide is beginning to go out. The flat-bottomed boat they left half a mile back will soon be grounded in the mud. Some hours from now, on the last leg of their journey back to La Caracca, the current will be against them, making headway more difficult. This is an aspect of the curious war being fought in the salt marshes. The rhythmic ebb and flow of the Atlantic tides adds to the singular nature of this military campaign: guerrilla sorties, counter-attacks, gunboats that draw little water moving stealthily through the labyrinth of marshes, tidal creeks and channels.

The sun's first rays, red-gold and almost horizontal, pierce the undergrowth, illuminating the face of Captain Virués, intent on his sketches. Sometimes, in quieter moments—and the early morning sorties of Felipe Mojarra and his companion are filled with prudent pauses and cautious delays—the salter has seen the soldier sketch items from nature: a plant, an eel, a salt-flat crab. Always with the same swift dexterity. Once, at New Year, when they had to spend a whole day hiding out in the ruins of a salt mill, shivering with cold, waiting for nightfall so they could leave unnoticed by the French gun emplacements in the inlet at San Diego, the captain made a sketch of Mojarra himself. It was quite faithful: the thick muttonchop whiskers vying with his bushy eyebrows, the deep furrows of his brow, the laconic, obstinate expression of this man born into a country of sun and wind, of the coarse salt of the marshes. When they had safely arrived back behind Spanish lines, Captain Virués gave Mojarra the portrait as a gift. Satisfied with the likeness, Mojarra now keeps the portrait in a tattered frame with no glass in his humble home on the Isla de Léon.

Three French field guns boom in the distance—half a league away, somewhere in the upper stretch of the Zurraque canal. The shots are immediately answered by the Spanish cannons on the other side. This duel continues for a time while a flock of startled avocets wheel above the salt flats, then silence descends again. Pencil clenched between his teeth, Captain Virués has taken out his spyglass and is once again studying the enemy position, reciting details in a low voice as though committing them to memory. Then he returns to his sketchpad. Mojarra half-stands, glancing around to check that all is still quiet.

"How's it going, Captain?"

"Ten more minutes."

Satisfied, Mojarra nods. Depending on the when, where and how, ten minutes can seem a lifetime so, crouching down, he unfastens his fly and urinates into the canal. Then he lies back, takes from his pocket the faded green kerchief he usually wears knotted around his head and lays it across his face, sets his musket between his legs and falls asleep. Like a baby.

IT IS A small, shabby office with a narrow, barred window that looks out on to the Calle del Mirador and the corner of the Royal Jail. On the wall hangs a portrait—a crude painting, artist unknown—of His Youth-

ful Majesty Fernando VII. There are two chairs upholstered in tattered
leather and a desk with an inkstand equipped with quills and pencils, a
wooden box filled with documents, and a map of Cádiz over which
Rogelio Tizón is currently poring. For some time now the comisario
has been studying the three points ringed in pencil: Lame Paco's Tavern by the reef, the corner of the Calle de Amoladores and Rosario and
the place where the first murdered girl was found—a narrow alley at
the junction of the Calle Sopranis and the Calle de la Gloria, near the
church of Santo Domingo, barely fifty paces from the spot where a
French bomb fell the day before. On the map, it is immediately evident
that all three crimes were committed within an arc to the east of the
city that circumscribes the range of the French guns shelling from La
Cabezuela on the Trocadero some two miles away.

It is simply not possible, he thinks again. Everything he has learned
in his long years as a policeman tells him he should dismiss this intui-
tive connection between the murders and the locations where the
bombs exploded. It is little more than a fanciful, improbable theory,
one of many possibilities. A vague intuition devoid of any serious foundation. And yet this absurd idea seems to have undermined all of
Tizón's other convictions, leaving him inexplicably bewildered. He has
questioned neighbors in the area where the first shell fell six months
ago, and confirmed that, like the others, this bomb also exploded. And
that there were fragments of shrapnel scattered everywhere: slivers of
lead just like the one that lies in his desk drawer, half a palm in length,
slender and twisted, like the hot irons ladies use to curl their hair.

He traces the line of streets and the ramparts with one finger, picturing these places he knows like the back of his hand: the squares, the
alleys, the corners that are pitch dark when night falls, those places
within range of the French bombs and those safely without. Tizón
knows little of the military arts, still less about artillery. He knows no
more than any man in Cádiz who has grown up cheek by jowl with the
Army and the Royal Armada, with the cannons mounted on the ramparts and the ships. And so, some days ago, he consulted an expert.

"I want to know everything there is to know about the French bombs," he explained. "Why some explode and others do not. Where they fall and why."

The expert, an artillery captain named Viñals, who was a regular at the Café del Correo, patiently explained as he drew with a pencil on the marble tabletop: the positions of the enemy gun batteries, the role of the Trocadero and the Cabezuela in the siege, the trajectories of the bombs, the areas of the city within range of the French artillery and those beyond it.

"Tell me about that"—Tizón raised a hand—"about the range . . ."

The soldier smiled; this was his pet subject. A middle-aged man with graying whiskers and a bushy mustache, he was wearing the blue frockcoat trimmed with a red collar befitting his rank. He would spend three out of every four weeks under constant fire, manning the front lines at Puntales less than a mile from the enemy.

"It's tough for the French," he said. "So far, they haven't succeeded in crossing an imaginary line that divides our city. Though it's not for want of trying."

"Where exactly is this line?"

"From top to bottom," explained the officer, "from the Alameda to the old cathedral. More than two-thirds of the city currently lies on the far side of this line, so you can see why the French have been trying to extend their range. Without much success. That's why, until now, the bombs have all fallen in the eastern part of the city. Some three dozen, so far, most of which did not explode."

"Thirty-two," Tizón corrected him, having investigated the matter. "Eleven of which have exploded."

"It's hardly surprising. The distance is considerable so many of the fuses burn out. Sometimes the bombs fall short, or explode in midair. And Lord knows they have tried every possible type of fuse . . . I've personally examined the ones we've managed to recover: they've tried every possible combination of metal and wood and at least a dozen different primers to ignite the charge."

"Are there technical differences between the bombs?"

"You have to understand, this is not just about the shells," the officer explained, "it's about the field guns used to fire them. They fall into three general categories: straight-shot cannons, howitzers and mortars. From the Cabezuela to the city walls is almost half a league, so straight-shot cannons are useless. They simply haven't got the range, the shells just drop into the bay. So the French have been using guns such as mortars and howitzers that fire at an angle. This way the shells follow a curved trajectory." The artilleryman's hand described a parabola in the air.

"From what we've been able to find out, the first tests using eight-inch, nine-inch and ten-inch howitzers brought from France were conducted late last year, but the shells didn't even make it across the bay. After that, they commissioned new howitzers from a man named Pere Ros . . . Does that name mean anything to you, Comisario?"

Tizón nodded. From his reports and informants he knew that Ros, formerly of the Barcelona Royal Foundries and the Academía de Sevogia, was a Spaniard, a Catalan from Urgel who had sworn allegiance to King Joseph Bonaparte. Now in the pay of the French, Ros was the man who oversaw the armaments factory in Seville.

"The *gabachos* ordered seven twelve-inch mortars from Pere Ros based on a design by Dedon—plate mortars with spherical chambers. But Dedon mortars are difficult to cast and very imprecise. When the first prototype shipped from Seville proved useless, production was suspended . . . So they went back to using Villantroys' design—I'm sure you've heard of that, there was a lot of talk last December when they started firing from the Cabezuela—eight-inch howitzers that failed to exceed a range of two thousand *toises* . . . What was worse, every time those guns were fired their range diminished."

"Why so?"

"From what we've heard, the inordinately large powder charge required to fire them damages the bush pins. A disaster . . . Our men have composed ballads about it."

"So what are they using now?"

Viñals shrugged then fished a packet of tobacco and some papers from the pocket of his jacket and began to roll a cigarette.

"We're not quite sure yet. Old news is easy to come by from deserters and spies, but finding out what's happening now is a different matter . . . All we know for sure is that the Catalan turncoat Pere Ros is now casting a new type of howitzer under the supervision of General Ruty. A ten-incher, from what we can tell, that's the caliber of the bombs reaching Cádiz."

"Why do they contain lead?"

Viñals struck a match and exhaled a puff of smoke.

"Not all of them. The bomb that fell on the docks three weeks ago was solid iron. Others contain a standard gunpowder charge—they have the shortest range and the greatest chance of failing. As for the ones containing lead, they're a mystery . . . though there are various theories."

"Tell me yours."

The artilleryman, having drained his cup, called the waiter over. "Another coffee," he said, "and put a shot of brandy in it. Aids the digestion. Over at Puntales we've all got bellyache." He turns back to Tizón.

"The French," he goes on, "have the finest artillery in the world. They have years of testing and experience in the field. And don't forget Napoleon himself is an artilleryman. They have the finest technicians in the field. My theory is that they are using lead as an experiment. They're trying to increase their range."

"So, why lead? I don't understand . . ."

"Because lead is the heaviest metal. The increased specific gravity of the shell makes it possible to extend the trajectory curve. You see, the distance a bomb travels is dependent on its weight and density, though there are other factors—the thrust provided by the initial powder charge and the weather conditions. All these things have a bearing."

"What about the corkscrew shape?"

"The slivers are twisted by the force of the explosion itself. Molten lead is poured into the bomb in thin layers such that, when it explodes, they break apart and coil . . . But don't let yourself be taken in by the results—it can't be easy working at such a distance. No Spanish artilleryman could do what they're doing. Not for want of talent or ideas . . . We have men with the necessary knowledge and experience, what we lack are the *means*. The French must be spending a king's ransom . . . Every bomb they manage to land in the city must be costing them a fortune."

ALONE IN HIS office, thinking back over his conversation with the artillery captain, Rogelio Tizón stares at the map of Cádiz as though interrogating the sphinx. He has too little information, he realizes. None, in fact. He is groping in the dark. Cannons, mortars, howitzers. Bombs. Lead, like the twisted corkscrew he takes from his desk drawer and weighs gravely in his palm. What he is looking for is too nebulous, too vague. What he *thinks* he is looking for. This hunch he has that there is some hidden connection between the bombs and the murdered girls is unsubstantiated and perhaps unfounded. Though he has racked his brains, he still does not have a single clue, a single piece of evidence. Nothing but twisted lumps of lead. Specific gravity, those were Captain Viñal's words. The feeling that he is standing, pockets filled with lead, peering into an abyss. Nothing more. Nothing of any use. Nothing but this map of the city spread out on his desk, this strange chessboard where the hand of some improbable opponent is moving pieces whose very nature Tizón cannot begin to grasp. He has never felt like this before. At his age, the uncertainty frightens him a little. It also angers him. A lot.

Furious, he drops the shard of lead into the drawer and slams it shut. He pounds his fist on the desk so hard that ink sprays from the inkstand, spattering one corner of the map. *A pox on God*, he growls, *and on his Holy Mother.* Hearing the noise, his secretary, working in the next room, pops his head around the door.

"Is something wrong, Señor Comisario?"

"Mind your own business!"

The secretary retreats like a terrified mouse. He recognizes the signs. Tizón stares at the hands gripping the edge of his desk. Broad, hard, callused hands capable of causing pain. And when necessary, they have been known to do just that.

One day he *will* get to the bottom of this, he concludes, and someone will pay dearly.

WITH INFINITE CARE, Lolita Palma places the three amaranth leaves in the herbarium next to a color illustration of the plant she drew herself. Each leaf is two inches long with a tiny, translucent thorn identifying it as *Amarantus spinosus*. It is a plant she has never seen before; the specimens arrived three days ago from Guayaquil in a package with other leaves and dried plants sent by someone she knows there. She feels the thrill of a collector at a recent acquisition. Hers is a modest pleasure. Restrained. When the drop of gum attaching the specimens to the card has dried, she covers them with a sheet of onionskin paper, closes the herbarium and slides it back onto one of the shelves in the large, glass-fronted case next to others bearing the names of extraordinary natural treasures: *Chrysanthemum, Oeil de Boeuf, Centaury, Pascalia*. The study containing her botanical collection, next to her office on the first floor, is small but sufficient to the needs of an amateur collector: cozy, well lit by a window overlooking the Calle del Baluarte and a second that opens onto the interior courtyard. In the study are four large chests with drawers carefully labeled according to their contents, a worktable with a microscope, magnifying glasses and various other tools, and a library of reference books including Linnaeus, copies of Cavanilles' *Description of Plants*, Rabel's *Theatrum Florae, Icones Plantarum Rariorum* by Nikolaus Joseph von Jacquin and a large, color folio of Merian's *The Plants of Europe*. Growing in pots on the glassed balcony are nine different species of fern shipped back from the Americas, the Southern Isles and the East Indies. A further fifteen varieties adorn the ground-floor courtyard, the shaded balconies and other dappled areas of the house. The fern, what the ancients called *filice*, has always been Lolita Palma's favorite plant, perhaps because neither classical scholars nor modern students of botany have succeeded in identifying the male of the species—its very existence is pure conjecture.

Mari Paz, the chambermaid, appears in the doorway.

"If you please, señorita. Don Emilio Sánchez Guinea is downstairs with another gentleman."

"Ask Rosas to have them wait. I shall be down presently."

Fifteen minutes later, having returned to her dressing room to freshen her *toilette*, she goes downstairs, buttoning a gray satin spencer over a white blouse and dark green basque, and crosses the courtyard to that part of the building that houses the offices and storerooms.

"Good morning, Don Emilio. What a pleasant surprise."

The drawing room next to the main study and the ground floor offices is old and comfortable, paneled in dark, varnished wood and hung with framed nautical engravings—scenes of French, English and Spanish ports—and furnished with armchairs, a sofa, a High & Evans pendulum clock and a narrow bookcase, its four shelves filled with works about commerce. Sitting on the sofa are Sánchez Guinea and a younger man with dark, burnished skin. As she enters, they get to their feet, setting down the delicate Chinese porcelain cups in which Rosas, the steward, has just served them coffee. Lolita takes her usual seat, an old leather armchair that once belonged to her father, and gestures for the men to sit.

"What brings you to see me?"

The question is directed at the old family friend, though it is the other man she is studying: he is about forty years old, with black hair and whiskers and bright, sparkling eyes. Intelligent, perhaps. He is not particularly tall, but broad-shouldered beneath a blue frockcoat—somewhat threadbare at the elbows and frayed at the cuffs, she notices—with gilt brass buttons. Strong, firm hands. Clearly a seaman. She has spent too much time in close contact with this world not to recognize a sailor at first glance.

"I wanted to introduce you to this gentleman."

Don Emilio's introduction is brief, pragmatic, to the point. "Captain Don José Lobo, an old acquaintance, is currently staying in Cádiz and has found himself, for various reasons, without work. The firm of Sánchez Guinea intends to engage him in respect of a pending business matter. The venture we spoke about some days ago on the Calle Ancha."

"Would you excuse us a moment?"

Both men get to their feet as Lolita Palma rises and beckons Don Emilio into her private office. As she closes the door, she glances again at the sailor standing in the middle of the drawing room: he seems guarded, but his expression is relaxed, affable. He seems almost amused by the situation. Here, she thinks fleetingly, is a man who smiles with his eyes.

"What is the meaning of this ambush, Don Emilio?"

The elderly merchant protests. "It's nothing of the sort, *hija*, I simply wanted you to meet this gentleman. Pépé Lobo is an experienced captain. A worthy chap, highly competent. It seems an ideal moment to employ him, given he is currently without a vessel and prepared to sail on any piece of wood that will float. We have a cutter almost ready and the Letter of Marque I mentioned the other day. By the end of the month we'll be ready to ship out."

"As I told you before, I will have no dealings with corsairs."

"You need have no dealings with them. It is merely an investment. I will take care of everything else. I plan to post the ship's bond the day after tomorrow."

"Which ship is this?"

Sánchez Guinea describes the vessel with a satisfied air: a 180-ton French cutter captured by a corsair from Algeciras and auctioned off three weeks ago. Old, but in excellent condition. It can take eight 6-pound cannons. Formerly the *Colbert*, it has been renamed the *Culebra*. Bought for twenty thousand *reales*. The equipment—new sails and rigging, light arms, gunpowder and ammunition—will come to a further ten thousand.

"It will do short campaigns: from San Vicente to Gata, certainly no further than Los Palos. With little risk and excellent prospects for a substantial profit. It is, as they say, money for old rope . . . You and I will receive two-thirds, the remaining third goes to the captain and the crew. All strictly aboveboard."

Lolita Palma glances at the closed door.

"What else do you know about this man?"

"He has had a run of bad luck on recent voyages, but he's a fine seaman. He captained a six-gun schooner in the Straits during the last war and made a healthy profit. I should know; I was part-owner of the venture . . . Eventually, he had a stroke of bad luck, he was captured by an English corvette off the cape at Tres Forcas."

"I think I may have heard of him . . . Is he the man who escaped from Gibraltar?"

Sánchez Guinea lets out a sly, approving laugh. The memory clearly amuses him.

"The very one. He was held prisoner and he and a number of others stole a tartane and escaped. For the past four years he has been working on merchant ships . . . He had something of a disagreement with his employer recently."

"Who was the shipowner?"

"Ignacio Ussel."

The old merchant raises an eyebrow as he says the name. Everyone in Cádiz knows that there is bad blood between Ussel and the firm of Palma e Hijos. During the crisis of 1796, Ignacio Ussel's treachery all but bankrupted Tomás Palma, costing him three sizable cargoes. It is a betrayal his daughter has not forgotten.

"We have a two-year Letter of Marque signed by the Regency," Sánchez Guinea continues, "a ship almost ready to sail, a captain capable of assembling an able crew, and a stretch of enemy coastline plied by ships owned either by the French or coming from the occupied territories. What more could we ask for? And over and above the value of any captured ships and their cargoes, there are the bounties paid for the capture of enemy prisoners."

"You make it sound like a patriotic duty, Don Emilio."

The old merchant laughs good-naturedly. "And so it is, *hija*," he responds. "And if there is some personal profit, so much the better. Running a corsair brings no dishonor on a respectable business. Remember your father did so without turning a hair. Though it infuriated the English. We are not talking about the slave trade.

"You know that I would have no problem raising the money," he goes on, "and I could easily find other partners. The fact is, this is a sound business proposition and, as I have done many times, I feel it my duty to offer it to you."

Silence. Lolita Palma is still staring at the closed door.

"Why not sound him out a little?" Sánchez Guinea encourages her. "He is an interesting man. Plain-speaking. I find him very personable."

"You seem to place great confidence in this man . . . How well do you know him?"

"My son Miguel sailed with him once, to Valencia and back. It was just before the evacuation of Seville, everything was in chaos. And they weathered a terrible storm. When he got back, Miguel could not speak highly enough of the man's ability and his composure . . . In fact it was Miguel's idea to put him in command of the *Culebra* as soon as he heard Lobo was in Cádiz and without a vessel."

"Is he from Cádiz?"

"No. I think he was born in Cuba. Havana, or somewhere near there."

Lolita Palma stares at her hands. They are still pretty: she has long, elegant fingers and her nails, though not manicured, are neat. Sánchez Guinea looks at her, his smile pensive. At length, he nods good-naturedly.

"There's something about this man . . . He has spirit, and he is a fascinating character. A little rough around the edges when ashore, perhaps, and you could hardly use the term *gentleman*. In his dealings with women, for example, he is reputed to be less than scrupulous."

"Good Lord, what a dashing portrait you paint of him!"

The old merchant raises his hands in protest.

"I am simply telling you the truth. I know men who despise him and others who worship him. But, as my son says, there are men who would give the shirt off their backs for him."

"And the women? What would they give?"

"That you will have to judge for yourself."

They look at each other and smile. Her smile is vague, a little sad; his is surprised, almost curious.

"It hardly matters," Sánchez Guinea concludes. "We are hiring a captain for a corsair, not organizing a society ball."

GUITARS. THE FLICKERING glow of oil lamps. The dancer's bronzed skin glistens with sweat, her hair is plastered to her forehead. She moves like a lubricious animal, thinks Simon Desfosseux. A filthy Spaniard with coal-black eyes. A gypsy, he imagines. They all look like gypsies.

"From now on, we will use only lead," he says to Lieutenant Bertoldi.

The place is heaving: dragoons, artillerymen, sailors, infantry. Only men. Only officers. They are gathered around tables stained with wine, sitting on benches, chairs and stools.

"Do you ever stop thinking about work, Captain?"

"Never. As you can tell."

With a shrug, Bertoldi drains his glass and pours more wine from the pitcher in front of him. The place is shrouded in a gray fog of tobacco smoke, the air thick with the stench of sweat from frockcoats unbuttoned to reveal waistcoats and shirtsleeves. Even the wine—coarse and acrid, the sort that numbs rather than stimulates—has a pungent smell and is as cloudy as the dozens of eyes turned to watch the woman as she writhes and sways, slapping her hips provocatively to the rhythm of the guitars.

"Pig . . ." mutters Bertoldi, who cannot take his eyes off her.

He watches her for a moment. Finally he turns back to Desfosseux.

"Lead, you say?"

The captain nods. "It's the only solution," he explains. "Using bombs of eighty to ninety pounds packed with lead—no powder charge, no fuse—we could increase our range by at least a hundred *toises*. More if the wind is with us."

"The damage would be minimal," protests Bertoldi.

"We can worry about damage later. What's important now is getting the bombs to hit the center of the city . . . To hit Plaza de San Antonio or somewhere near there."

"Then it's decided?"

"Absolutely."

Bertoldi raises his glass, shrugs his shoulders.

"In that case, a toast to Fanfan."

"Yes, indeed." Desfosseux gently clinks his assistant's glass. "To Fanfan."

The guitars fall silent and the men erupt into thunderous applause, with lewd comments in every conceivable European language. Standing frozen, back arched, hand still raised, the dancer moves her coal-black eyes over the audience. She looks defiant. Confident. Having whipped up their desire she knows that she could have any man she wishes. Her instinct, or her experience—she is very young, but age has little to do with such things—tell her that any man here would toss money at her feet merely to get her to notice him. These are good times for her: the right men in the right place. War does not have to mean poverty, at least not for everyone. Not for a woman with a body as beautiful and eyes as dark as hers. Simon Desfosseux is thinking this as his eyes linger on the dancer's bronzed arms, the beads of sweat glittering in the plunging neckline that shamelessly reveals the tops of her breasts. This woman may well die of starvation in another war when she is wizened and old, but she will not die in this one. That much is obvious from the lustful eyes all staring at her, from the greedy calculations being made behind the apparent modesty of the two guitarists— father, brother, cousin, lover, pimp—sitting on stools, guitars on their knees, looking around smiling at the applause as they hungrily try to work out the location of the pocket jingling loudest this evening. Wondering how much the French gentlemen in this flamenco show in Puerto Real might be prepared to bid—in the current market where fresh meat is in short supply—for the spurious "honor" of their daughter, sister, cousin, lover, protégée . . . Though patriotism and King Fernando are all very well for those who care about such things, a man still has to earn a living.

Simon Desfosseux and Lieutenant Bertoldi step out into the street, feel the relief of the cool breeze. Everything is in darkness. Most of the town's inhabitants fled when the Imperial Army marched in and the abandoned houses have been converted into barracks and billets for soldiers and officers, the courtyards and gardens into stables. The imposing church was quickly looted, the altarpiece turned into kindling, and now it serves as a storehouse for weapons and gunpowder.

"That gypsy whore has got me all worked up," says Bertoldi.

Walking farther down the street, they come to the shore. There is no moon, and the vault of the heavens above the flat roofs of the houses is strewn with stars. Half a league east, on the far side of the black expanse of the bay, they can see scattered lights near the enemy arsenal at La Carraca and the village on the Isla de Léon. As usual, the besieged seem more relaxed than their besiegers.

"It's nearly three months since I last had a bloody letter," Bertoldi says after a while.

In the darkness Desfosseux makes a wry face. He has no trouble following his companion's line of thought. He has also been thinking about the wife waiting for him back in Metz. About the son he barely knows. It has been almost two years now. And there may be many more to come.

"Those bastard *manolos*," mutters the lieutenant bitterly. "Mean bastards."

Bertoldi's habitual good humor seems to have soured in recent weeks. Like the lieutenant, like most of the 23,000 men holed up between Sancti Petri and Chipiona, Captain Desfosseux has no idea what is happening back in France or in the rest of Europe. All he has are speculations, suppositions, rumors. Smoke and mirrors. There have been no recent newspapers, no pamphlets, no letters; such things do not make it this far. The men have had no news of their families, nor their families of them. The guerrilla gang operating along all their lines of communication make it impossible. Traveling in Spain is like travelling in Arabia: couriers are ambushed in the mountains and the forests, captured and brutally slaughtered. Only those under heavy escort can travel about without risking some deadly encounter. The roads leading to Jerez and Seville are lined with blockhouses where small, demoralized garrisons, constantly on the alert, muskets primed, live in permanent fear of the enemy all around them and of the villagers nearby. And after dark, the roads and the fields become the province of the rebels, a deathtrap, and those foolhardy enough to venture abroad without adequate protection are likely to be found at dawn on the edges of the forests of holm oak and pine, having been tortured like brute animals. This is the reality of war in Spain, in Andalucía. The troops of the Premier Corps laying siege to Cádiz are an occupying force in name only, feared more for their reputation than their deeds; they are cut off from everything and everyone, their future uncertain, exiled in this hostile terrain where the narcotics of apathy and boredom can carry off even the best soldiers and where disease and homesickness can claim as many victims as enemy fire.

"They buried Bouvier yesterday," says Bertoldi gloomily.

Desfosseux says nothing. Bertoldi is not relaying news, he is simply thinking aloud. Louis Bouvier, an artillery lieutenant they traveled with from Bayona to Madrid, and met again at the San Diego artillery unit in Chiclana, had been suffering from a nervous condition that plunged him into a profound melancholy. Two days ago, just as he was finishing his duty, Bouvier seized another soldier's musket, holed up in the bunkhouse, jammed the barrel in his mouth, put his big toe on the trigger and blew his brains out.

"God. This is the asshole of the universe."

Still Desfosseux says nothing. The gentle breeze coming off the sea smells of low tide, of silt and seaweed. At the edge of the town, where the last houses peter out, rise the dark shapes of the camp tents and the fortifications protecting the beach against a possible enemy landing. Desfosseux hears the voices of sentries, the soft whinnying of horses in courtyards that have been converted into stables, a vague rumor made up of the countless unidentifiable noises of thousands of men, some sleeping, others wide awake and staring into the darkness, an army run aground before a city.

"It sounds like a good idea, using lead," Bertoldi says, but his tone is that of a drowning man clutching at straws.

Desfosseux takes a few steps then stops, gazing at the city lights in the distance. Mentally working out new trajectories, perfect curves, beautiful, flawless parabolas.

"It's the only way . . . Tomorrow, we'll start work on shifting the center of gravity. Giving it a little rotation by sanding down the bore should do it."

There is a long silence.

"You know what I'm thinking, Captain?"

"No."

"I'm thinking you'll never put a bullet in your brain like that poor bastard Bouvier."

Desfosseux smiles in the darkness, knowing that his assistant is right. Never—not at least while there are still problems to solve. Not for him the perils of boredom or despair. The steel thread that binds Desfosseux to life is braided with concepts not emotions. Words such as *duty, patriotism, solidarity*, the concepts Bertoldi and the other men cling to, are irrelevant to him. He cares only about mass, volume, longitude, elevation, specific gravity, air resistance, spin. The slate and the slide rule. It is these things that make it possible for the artillery captain to remain untroubled by any uncertainty that is not strictly mathematical. Obsession can be the ruin of a man, but it can also be his salvation. Desfosseux's obsession is increasing his range by 750 *toises*.

THREE MEN IN an office beneath another portrait of Fernando VII. Early morning sunlight streaming diagonally through lace curtains, shimmering on the gold collar, cuffs and the lapels of the frockcoat worn by Lieutenant General Juan María Villavicencio of the Royal Armada, Commander of the Fleet and political and military governor of Cádiz.

"Is that all?"

"For the moment."

The governor carefully sets down the report on the green Morocco leather of his desk, allows his spectacles to fall and dangle from the chain threaded through the buttonhole of his lapel and stares at Comisario Rogelio Tizón.

"It doesn't seem to amount to much."

Tizón gives a sidelong glance to his direct superior, Eusebio García Pico, General Intendant and Judge overseeing Crime and Policing who is sitting a little to one side, legs crossed, right thumb hooked into his waistcoat pocket. His face is impassive, as though he is thinking about distant matters: the face of someone who is merely passing through. Tizón, who has spent twenty minutes waiting in the vestibule outside the office, is now wondering what the two men were discussing before he was shown in.

"It is a difficult case, General," says the policeman warily.

Villavicencio continues to stare at him. He is a seaman of fifty-six with gray hair, a man of the old school and veteran of numerous naval campaigns. Forceful, but with a keen sense of diplomacy, despite being a staunch conservative and fiercely loyal to the young king now being held prisoner by the French. Artful, manipulative and wielding the prestige he has earned in military life, the Governor of Cádiz—the beating heart, one might say, of patriotic, revolutionary Spain—gets along with everyone, even the bishops and the British. His name is writ large among those destined to play a role in the new Regency when it comes. A powerful man, as Tizón knows only too well. A man with a future.

"Difficult," echoes Villavicencio pensively.

"That's precisely the word, señor."

A lengthy silence. Tizón would like to smoke but no one indicates that he may do so. Toying with his spectacles, the governor peers again at the report—four scant pages—then sets it down again, carefully aligning it two inches from the edge of the desk.

"And you're certain that all three cases are related to the same murderer?"

The policeman briefly explains himself. Certain, no, one can never be certain of anything, but the method in each case is identical. As is the choice of victim: very young, from humble background. As it says in the report, two servants and another girl it has not been possible to identify. Probably a refugee with no family and no known employment.

"There was no . . . eh . . . physical violence?"

Another sidelong glance. Brief this time. The General Intendant remains mute and still as a statue. As though he were not here.

"All three were lashed to death with a whip, señor. If that does not constitute violence, let Christ himself come down from heaven and say otherwise."

This last comment does not please the governor, whose religious convictions are well known. He sucks in his cheeks, knits his brows and studies his pale, slender hands. Aristocratic hands, notes Tizón, of the sort common among naval officers. Riffraff do not become officers in the Royal Armada. On his left hand is a ring set with a magnificent emerald, a personal gift from the Emperor Napoleon when Villavicencio served with the Franco-Spanish fleet in Brest . . . before everything went to hell, before the battle of Trafalgar, the imprisonment of Fernando VII and the war against France.

"I was referring . . . you understand . . . to a different kind of violence."

"They were not raped—at least there is no evidence that they were."

Villavicencio remains silent, his eyes fixed on Tizón. Waiting. The policeman feels obliged to give a more detailed explanation, though he is not sure that this is what the governor wants. It was the Intendant who brought him here. "Don Juan María," García Pico had said as they climbed the stairs—his use of the governor's first name seemed to be a stern reminder of their respective positions—"has requested a direct, verbal account in addition to the written report. A broader picture. He wants to know whether there is any danger of this business slipping out of his control. Or of yours."

Tizón steels himself and begins again. "It might be said that the last victim was a stroke of luck—no one has claimed her body, no one has reported her missing . . . which means we have been able to hush things up. To avoid panic."

An imperceptible nod from the governor tells him he is on the right track. *So that is what this is about,* Tizón thinks, quickly suppressing a smile. It all makes sense now, García Pico's remarks, his oblique comment on the stairs.

As if to confirm this, Villavicencio gestures casually to Tizón's report with the hand that bears the emerald.

"Three girls murdered in such a manner is not merely a . . . difficult case. It is an outrage. One that would cause a public scandal if news of the matter should leak . . ."

Finally we get to the crux of the matter, thinks Tizón. *I could see you coming, you son of a bitch.*

"I must admit that it has leaked to a certain extent," he says tactfully, "though only a little. There are rumors, gossip, old women prattling . . . Inevitable, as I'm sure you know. The city is small and overcrowded."

He pauses to gauge the effect. The governor looks at him questioningly and García Pico's attitude of studied indifference shifts.

"Even so," says the policeman, "we have everything under control. We've put pressure on neighbors and witnesses. Denied everything . . . And the newspapers haven't printed so much as a word about it."

Now it is finally the Intendant's turn to intervene. Tizón cannot help but notice the alarmed look he exchanges with the governor as he speaks.

"Not yet. But this is an extraordinary story. If the newspapers were to get their teeth into it, they would not let go. This new freedom of the press has already led to terrible abuses. Nothing will stop them—"

Villavicencio raises a peremptory hand, clearly in the habit of interrupting when the mood takes him. In Cádiz, a general in the Royal Armada is a god; in time of war, he is God the Father.

"I've heard something about this case. I know rumors of it have reached the editor of *La Patriota*. The very man who, only last Thursday, had the temerity to question the divine right of kings . . ."

The governor pauses for a moment and allows his words to hang in the air. He is staring at Tizón as though inviting him to consider the foundations of the monarchy.

"Journalists," he eventually mutters scornfully. "What can I say? You know the kind of people we have to deal with here. I denied everything, of course. Fortunately, I have other bones I can toss them. The people of Cádiz are interested only in politics; even the war is of secondary importance to them. The newspapers are using all their ink covering the parliamentary sessions at San Felipe Neri."

An adjutant wearing a uniform of the Royal Guard appears from a side door, crosses to the desk and whispers to Villavicencio. The governor nods and gets to his feet. Tizón and the Intendant immediately do likewise.

"Excuse me, gentlemen, I have to leave you for a moment."

Villavicencio and the adjutant step out of the office leaving the two men gazing out the window at the city walls and the bay beyond. The governor's residence has always enjoyed magnificent views; the self-same views enjoyed three years ago by Villavicencio's predecessor, General Solano, Marquis of Socorro, before a baying mob dragged him through the streets accusing him of being a French sympathizer. Solano had contended that the English were the true enemy and insisted that attacking Admiral Rosily's squadron which was blockaded in the bay, would put the city at risk. The hotheaded citizenry, in the heat of an insurrection led by port rabble, bootleggers, whores and other low life, took this badly. They attacked the governor's residence and Solano was led to the gallows without the officers of the local garrison lifting a finger to save him. Tizón saw him die, run through by sword on the Calle de la Aduana; he made no attempt to intervene. To get involved would have been madness, and the fate of the Marquis of Socorro mattered little to him. Nor does it matter now. He would feel the same supreme indifference today if the mob were to haul away Villavicencio. Or indeed the Intendant García Pico, who is looking at him thoughtfully.

"I assume," García Pico says, "that you accept full responsibility for this situation."

Of course I do, thinks Tizón, jolted back to the present. *Why do you think I'm here, meeting with our illustrious governor* in camera?

"If there are any more murders, we will not be able to keep it quiet," he says.

García Pico frowns at this. "God's blood, man, we have no reason to think there will be anymore . . . How long has it been since the last murder?"

"Four weeks."

"And you still haven't found any solid evidence?"

The phrasing *you still* does not go unremarked by Tizón. He shakes his head.

"Nothing. The murderer always operates in the same manner. He attacks young girls in isolated locations. He gags them and whips them to death."

For a brief instant Tizón is tempted to mention the bombs, the points of impact, but he holds his tongue. Raising the subject now would entail too many explanations. Something he is in no mood to provide. Besides, he has no evidence. Yet.

"It's been a month," says the Intendant. "Maybe the murderer has grown tired of this."

"Anything is possible," Tizón says, looking at him doubtfully. "Then again, he may simply be waiting for the right opportunity."

"You believe that he will kill again?"

"Maybe, maybe not."

"Whatever happens, this is your case. Your responsibility."

"It won't be easy. I'll need—"

The judge interrupts him with an irritable wave of his hand.

"Listen. We all have our problems. Don Juan María has his, I have mine and you have yours . . . Your job is to make sure that *your* problems do not become *mine*."

As he says these words, he stares at the door through which Villavicencio disappeared. After a moment, he turns back to Tizón.

"It can hardly be difficult to find a murderer who kills in this manner. You said it yourself, the city is small."

". . . and overcrowded."

"Dealing with these people is your problem. You have your spies— sound out your informants. Earn your keep." García Pico gestures toward the closed door and lowers his voice. "If there's another death we will need a culprit, someone we can parade in public, understand? Someone to be punished."

Things are becoming much clearer, thinks Tizón almost gleefully.

"Such a thing would be very difficult to prove without a confession," he argues.

He says no more, but looks pointedly at the judge. Both men know that torture is about to be officially outlawed by the Cortes; even judges, courts or tribunals will have no power to sanction it.

"In that case you will have to take responsibility," snaps García Pico. "Full responsibility."

Villavicencio comes back to the office. He seems worried. Distracted. He stares at the two men as though he has forgotten why they are there.

"You'll have to excuse me . . . I've just had word that General Lapeña's troops have landed at Tarifa."

Tizón knows—or believes he knows—what this means. Some days ago, 6,000 Spanish soldiers and as many English, under the command of General Lapeña and General Graham, left Cádiz in two convoys heading west. Landing in Tarifa means military actions near Cádiz, probably centered on the communications post at Medina Sidonia. It might even turn into a major battle, the sort whose outcome—*lurching from defeat to defeat and on to victory*, as locals wits would have it—will be eagerly discussed for weeks by the citizens of Cádiz, in the press, in cafés and at social gatherings, while the generals—who are fiercely jealous and unable to abide one another—and their supporters hurl abuse at each other.

"I'm afraid I must ask you to leave now," says Villavicencio. "I have urgent matters to attend to."

Tizón and García Pico take their leave, the latter with the customary obeisance which the governor acknowledges with a distracted air. Just as they are about to step out, Villavicencio seems to remember something.

"Let me be frank, gentlemen. We are dealing with an extraordinary and tragic state of affairs. As political and military leader, it is my duty to work not only with the Regency and with the Cortes but with our English allies and the people of Cádiz. In addition to dealing with the French siege and the war. To say nothing of the fact that I am expected to govern a city whose population has doubled, which is utterly dependent on the sea for its provisions, not to mention the risk of epidemics and other problems . . . So, although it is appalling that a vicious lunatic is committing atrocities against young girls, it is not—as perhaps you can understand—my foremost priority. Not unless it should become public. Do I make myself clear, Comisario?"

"Crystal clear, señor."

"The days ahead are crucial, because General Lapeña's campaign may change the course of the war in Andalucía. But for now, it is important that these crimes remain confidential. Because if there should be another murder, or if news of the story gets out and the public start clamoring for a culprit, I will expect you to provide one, immediately . . . Do I make myself understood?"

Absolutely, thinks the policeman but he holds his tongue and simply nods. Villavicencio turns and walks back to his desk.

"One more thing," he says as he sits down. "If I were responsible for such a delicate situation, I would ensure that I had something up my sleeve . . . Something that, should it come to that, might expedite matters."

"Are you referring to a scapegoat?"

Ignoring García Pico, who flinches and glares at him, Tizón remains in the doorway waiting for a response. When it comes, it is curt and peremptory.

"I am referring to the murderer, nothing more. With all the foreign rabble roaming the city, it could be anyone."

SPACIOUS AND MAJESTIC, the Palma mansion is one of the finest in Cádiz. Felipe Mojarra gazes at it in satisfaction, happy that his daughter Mari Paz is in service here. Situated a block from the Plaza de San Francisco, the four-story house occupies the whole corner with five balconies and the main entrance opening onto the Calle del Baluarte and a further four balconies overlooking the Calle de los Doblones. Leaning on the corner post opposite the house, wearing a Zamora blanket around his shoulders and a wide-brimmed hat over the kerchief tied about his head, Mojarra smokes a cigar made of tobacco freshly cut with his pocketknife as he waits for his daughter to come out. The salter is a proud man with very clear ideas about a man's station in life which is why he refused the invitation to wait for his daughter in the courtyard with its wrought-iron railings, its marble flagstones, the three columned arches framing the main staircase and the shrine to the Virgin of the Rosary in an alcove in the wall. It is too grand and imposing; his place is in the canals and the marshlands. Besides, his feet, which are swollen and callused from the salt, are unused to the rope sandals he put on to come to Cádiz and which he would dearly like to take off. He left very early, with a safe-conduct issued in due form. Captain Virués is attending an officers' meeting at La Carraca—

something to do with the military campaign at Tarifa—and does not need him so, at his wife's insistence, Mojarra has come to Cádiz to visit his little girl. What with the siege and the war with France, father and daughter have not seen one another for five months, not since—on the parish priest's recommendation—Mari Paz took up her post at the Palma house.

When she finally emerges from the door on the Calle de los Doblones, the salter feels a surge of affection as he sees her coming toward him wearing a white muslin apron over her brown skirt, and a shawl covering her head and shoulders. She looks well. Healthy. She has clearly been eating properly, thank God. The people in Cádiz are better off than those on the Isla de Léon.

"Good morning, Father."

There are no kisses, no displays of affection. People are passing in the street, neighbors are on their balconies, and the Mojarras are respectable folk, not the kind to set tongues wagging. The salter simply smiles tenderly, his thumbs hooked into the belt where he has tucked the horn-handled Albacete knife, and gazes at Mari Paz contentedly. She seems very grown up. Almost a woman. She smiles too, emphasizing the dimple she has had since she was a little girl. She was always more graceful than pretty, with large, gentle eyes. Sixteen. Pure and good.

"How is Mother?"

"She's well. And so are your little sisters and your grandmother. They all send their regards."

The girl nods toward the door leading to the storerooms.

"Don't you want to come inside? Rosas the steward said to invite you in for a cup of coffee or hot chocolate in the kitchen."

"I'm fine here in the street. Why don't we go for a little walk?"

They walk down to the Customs House where soldiers from the Walloon Guards,* bayonets fixed, pace up and down by the sentry boxes along the wharf. A flag flutters gently on its pole. It is inside the Customs House that the gentlemen of the Regency meet, those who

* An elite regiment of the Spanish Royal Guard.

claim to be governing Spain—or what remains of it—in the name of the king held prisoner in France. On the far side of the wall, beneath a clear, almost cloudless sky, the azure bay shimmers.

"How are you, *niña*?"

"I am well, Father. Truly."

"Do you like the house?"

"Very much."

The salter fumbles for words, running a hand over his whiskers and a chin that has not seen a razor in three days.

"I saw the steward . . . He seemed . . . well, you know . . ."

His daughter smiles warmly. "A little soft?"

"Exactly."

"There are a lot of men like that," explains the girl, "some of the best houses employ them. They're neat and methodical. It seems to be the custom here in Cádiz. Rosas is a decent man and he runs the house well. And he gets on with everyone. They respect him."

"Has anyone been courting you?"

Mari Paz blushes, and instinctively pulls the shawl covering her head about her face.

"Don't be foolish, Father, who would be courting me?"

Father and daughter follow the sea wall toward the Plaza de los Pozos de la Nieve and the Alameda, moving away from it only when their path is blocked by the ramparts or the cannons trained on the bay. Below them, the sea crashes against the rocks while above a flock of gulls wheels. Higher still, flying purposefully and directly, is a pigeon heading for the far shore of the bay, rising in the air until it disappears over the sea.

"How have the people upstairs been treating you?"

"Very well. The lady of the house is very gracious. She does not confide in me, but she is friendly."

"An old maid, they say."

"I don't think she would be short of suitors if she were so inclined. And she is an extraordinary woman. Since her father and her brother died, she has been managing everything, the business, the ships . . ."

everything. She likes books and plants. They're her hobby. She collects rare plants she has shipped from the Americas. She has books about them and herbariums and she grows them in pots."

"I suppose it takes all sorts . . ."

"You are right, Father, it does take all sorts, because *la señora*, her widowed mother, is much more difficult. And so rude. She spends most of her time in bed claiming she's ill, but it's not true. She just likes to have people wait on her, especially her daughter. Downstairs, they say she resents her daughter for being alive, running the family business, while her favorite son, Francisco de Paula, died in Bailén . . . But Doña Dolores is very patient with her mother. She is a good daughter."

"Is there no one else in the family?"

"Oh yes, cousin Toño, a bachelor. He is very witty, always in a good mood, and he's very kind to me. Of course, he doesn't live there, but he comes by every afternoon to visit . . . And the señorita has a married sister, but she is very different—very arrogant and snobbish. A disagreeable woman."

Now it is Felipe Mojarra's turn to give his daughter news. He tells her about the situation on the Isla de Léon: the French cordon, the militarization of the area, the men being conscripted, the privations suffered by the local people with the war on their doorstep. The bombs, he tells her, rain down day after day and most of the food goes to feed the soldiers and the Navy. Oil, wine and firewood are scarce; sometimes there is not even enough flour to bake bread. It is nothing like the privileged life here in Cádiz. Fortunately, since he enlisted in the Salt Marsh Fusiliers, he gets a ration of meat two or three times a week to take home to the family stockpot, and he can still fish in the canals or hunt for shellfish in the mud at low tide. Things are much worse in the enemy camp, from what he has heard from soldiers who have defected. Food supplies in the towns and villages have been exhausted and everyone—including the French soldiers—have been reduced to misery. In some areas, they don't even have any wine, despite the fact that Jerez and El Puerto are occupied by the French.

"Are there many deserters?"

"A few. Out of sheer starvation, mostly, or because they have problems with their superiors. They swim through the creeks and surrender to our advance parties. Sometimes they're little more than boys, and most are in a pitiful state when they arrive . . . But don't get the wrong idea—some of our lads desert too. Mostly those with families in the occupied territories. Obviously, if we catch them, we have to shoot them. As an example . . . You used to know one of them . . . Nicolás Sánchez."

Mari Paz looks at her father, eyes wide. "Nico? From the flour mill up at Santa Cristo?"

"The very same. His wife and children were in Chipiona and he wanted to be with them. He was caught one night rowing a dinghy across the Zurraque channel."

The girl makes the sign of the cross. "It seems so cruel, Father."

"The *gabachos* shoot their deserters too, when they catch them."

"It's not the same. Last Sunday, the priest at San Francisco said the French are the servants of the devil and that it is God's will that the Spanish exterminate them like lice."

Mojarra walks a few more paces then stops and stares at the ground. Finally he shakes his head gravely. "I don't pretend to know God's will . . ."

He walks a little further, stops again but does not look up. Though she looks like a woman, Mari Paz is still a child, he thinks. There are things he cannot explain to her, not here, not like this. Things that, in truth, he barely understands himself.

"The French are men just like us," he says at length, "like me . . . At least those I've seen."

"Have you killed many of them?"

Another silence as father gazes at daughter. For a moment, Mojarra is about to say no, but in the end he simply shrugs. *Why deny what I have done*, he thinks, *since I have done it? Out of some blind obedience to God's will—a god whose mysterious ways are of little interest to Felipe Mojarra? Out of duty to his country and King Fernando?* The one thing the salter knows is that, however much he loathes the French, he believes they are no more servants of the devil than many Spaniards he has met. The French also bleed, they howl in fear and pain just as he does. As every man does.

"Yes, I've killed a few."

"Good," the girl crosses herself again. "Since they're French, it's not a sin."

PÉPÉ LOBO PUSHES away the drunk begging for a *cuarto* to buy wine. He is not rough but patient, simply trying to stop this sailor in filthy rags from blocking his path. The drunk reels then stumbles into the shadows beyond the pool of yellow light cast by the lantern on the corner of the Calle de la Sarna.

"We have a problem," says Ricardo Maraña.

The first mate on the *Culebra* has just stepped out of the darkness where he has been standing, motionless, his presence revealed only by the red glow of his cigar. He is tall and pale, dressed all in black, wearing a handsome pair of English-style turndown boots, and no hat. The light from the street lamp directly above makes his eyes seem more sunken in his gaunt face.

"Serious?"

"That depends on you."

The two men are now walking down the street, Maraña limping slightly. In doorways and alleys groups of men and women have gathered and there is the murmur of conversation in Spanish and other languages. From tavern doors or open windows come voices, laughter, insults. Sometimes the sound of a guitar.

"The nightwatch came by half an hour ago," Maraña explains. "An American sailor has been stabbed and they're looking for the culprit. Brasero is a suspect."

"Did he do it?"

"I've no idea."

"Any other suspects?"

"They picked up six or seven men, but none of the others are ours. They're holding them for questioning at the tavern where it happened."

Pépé Lobo shakes his head angrily. He has known the bo'sun—
nostromo in seamen's slang—for fifteen years and knows that when he is
in drink Brasero is not only capable of stabbing an American sailor, he
could even stab his own father. But the bo'sun is a key member of the
crew he has spent days recruiting here in Cádiz; to lose him a week and
a half before they put to sea would be disastrous.

"They're still at the tavern?"

"I assume so. I left orders that I was to be informed if he was arrested."

"Do you know the officer in charge?"

"Only by sight. He's a young lieutenant with the 'macaws.'"

Pépé Lobo smiles to hear the word "young" from his first mate,
since Maraña is himself not yet twenty-one. The youngest son of a
noble family from Málaga, Maraña is nicknamed "the little Marquis"
for his aristocratic manner and his distinguished appearance. A former
midshipman—his limp was acquired when his knee was shattered
aboard the *Bahama* at the battle of Trafalgar—he was dishonorably dis-
charged from the Royal Armada at the tender age of fifteen after a duel
in which he wounded a fellow officer. Since then, he has sailed on corsairs, initially under French and Spanish flags, and more recently with
the English allies. This is the first time he will sail with Captain Lobo,
but the two men are well acquainted. Maraña's most recent ship was
the *Corazón de Jesús*, a four-gun místico out of Algeciras whose Letter
of Marque expired four months ago.

The tavern in question is just one of the many seedy dives around
the port frequented by soldiers and sailors, both Spanish and foreign:
the ceilings are grimy with soot from candles and oil lamps, there are
huge casks of wine, and low stools with upended barrels serving as tables, everything as black and filthy as the floor. The locals and whores
have been sent packing, leaving only seven thuggish men guarded by
half a dozen "macaws" with bayonets fixed.

"Good evening," Lobo addresses the lieutenant. He quickly intro-
duces himself and his companion: Captain so-and-so and first officer
such-and-such of the corsair cutter *Culebra*. Some of his men are being
held here. Apparently suspected of something.

"Of murder," the lieutenant confirms.

"If that is the case"—Lobo gestures toward Brasero, a man of fifty with a shock of graying curly hair, thick mustaches and hands like shovels—"I can assure you this man had nothing to do with it. He has been with me all evening. I sent him here on an errand a short while ago . . . There has clearly been some mistake."

The lieutenant blinks. He is very young, as Maraña said. A well-bred lad. He is hesitating, a little cowed by the title "corsair captain." An officer in the Army or the Armada would not be so impressed, but the macaws are local militia, not *real* soldiers.

"Are you sure, señor?"

Pépé Lobo is still staring at Brasero, who is standing, poker-faced, with the other prisoners, hands stuffed into the pockets of his overcoat, looking down at his shoes. The words *corsair* and *bootlegger* almost seem tattooed on that weather-beaten face, fretted with scars and wrinkles as deep as hatchet blows. A gold stud in each ear, he is tight-lipped and calm. And as dangerous now as when he and Lobo plied the Straits, before being caught in '06 and sharing the same miserable fate in Gibraltar. *Cretinous fool probably did stab the American*, Lobo thinks. *He never could abide anyone who speaks English. I wonder where he's put that vicious knife he usually keeps tucked in his belt. I'll wager it's on the floor, buried in the wine-soaked sawdust under the tables. I'll bet he stashed it the moment the macaws showed up. Son of a bitch!*

"I give you my word of honor."

The macaw hesitates for a moment, more worried about his authority than anything else. Local wits nicknamed the militia "macaws" because of their garish uniform—red frockcoat, bright green collar and cuffs, white belting—worn by the two thousand citizens from the upper classes who are enlisted in the Distinguished Volunteer Corps. In war as in everything, the citizens of Cádiz do not stray from their social class. They may share a fierce patriotic fervor, but it is the only thing they share. The aristocrats, the merchant class and the lower class each have separate militias. And there is no shortage of volunteers since those enlisting in the militia are exempt from being conscripted in the real army and facing the dangers and privations of the front line. For the most part, the military posturing of the militia simply entails wearing a gaudy uniform and parading with a military swagger through the streets, the squares and cafés of the city.

"You are prepared to vouch for him personally?"

"Of course."

Pépé Lobo leaves the tavern with Maraña and Brasero in tow and the three men walk along the walls of Santa María towards El Boquete and the Puerta de Mar. For a long time no one speaks. The streets are dark and the bo'sun shuffles behind the officers like a meek shadow. Aboard ship, Brasero is the most peaceable and trustworthy of men, with a particular talent for managing a crew in difficult circumstances, a good-natured old salt. But when he sets foot on terra firma, he sometimes loses control to the point of going completely berserk.

"Curse you to hell, *nostromo*," Lobo says finally, without turning to look at the man.

There is a tense silence from behind. Next to him he hears a stifled laugh from his first mate. A laugh that dies out in a cough and a ragged hiss of breath. As they pass beneath a street lamp, the corsair glances at the thin figure of Ricardo Maraña as he casually pulls a kerchief from his sleeve and presses it to his thin, bloodless lips. The first mate of the *Culebra* is a man who burns the candle at both ends: a libertine, dissolute to the point of recklessness, cynical to the point of cruelty, courageous to the point of despair, he is paying his debt to life in advance in a somber race against time. He has a confidence unusual for his age and squanders his money with no thought for the future, since his future has long been decided by a diagnosis of incurable tuberculosis.

The three men are stopped by sentries as they arrive at the double gates of the Puerta de Mar, which, given the hour, is closed. Comings and goings to the city are strictly regulated between sunset and sunrise—the Puerta de Tierra closes every morning at Lauds, the Puerta de Mar every evening at Vespers—but an official permit or a few coins in the right palm is sufficient to expedite matters. Identifying themselves as the crew of the cutter *Culebra* and showing permits stamped by the Captaincy, the three sailors pass beneath the stout gate of stone and brick ringed by watchtowers and lit on either side by a street lamp. To the left, beneath the cannons set into the embrasures of the Baluarte de los Negros, is the broad spur of the jetty, flanked by columns bearing the statues of San Servando and San Germán, the patron saints of Cádiz. Beyond, on the dark waters of the bay, huddled like a flock of sheep sheltering from the wolves on the far shore, the dark shapes of vessels of every kind and tonnage bob gently at anchor, bows facing west, anchor lights snuffed out to frustrate the attempts of the French artillery to fire on them from across the narrow strip of water.

"I want you aboard in fifteen minutes, *nostromo*. And I don't want you to set foot ashore again without permission from me or from the first mate, understood?"

Brasero grunts his agreement. Compliant. Pépé Lobo approaches a group of figures dozing among the merchandise piled up on the quay and wakes one of the boatmen. As the man is readying his boat, slotting oars into rowlocks, a group of drunken English sailors pass by, the crew of a warship, coming back from a tour of the bars around the port. The three corsairs watch as the Englishmen board their launch singing and laughing, and row off clumsily, probably in the direction of the 44-gun frigate anchored off Los Corrales.

"Allies my ass," mutters Brasero bitterly.

Lobo smiles to himself. Neither man has forgotten Gibraltar.

"Shut your trap, *nostromo*. I've heard enough out of you today."

Standing next to his first mate, Lobo watches the boat carrying Brasero disappear into the darkness with the slow slap of oars. The *Culebra* is somewhere out in the inky blackness east of the pier, moored over four fathoms of mud, its lone mast bare, the sails and rigging still to come. She is still twelve men short—two artillerymen, a ship's clerk, eight sailors and a trustworthy shipwright—of the forty-eight men needed to sail the ship and fight.

"The Navy has supplied the gunpowder," says Lobo, "fifty-five pounds of it, twenty-two powder horns and eleven and a half pounds of fuse. We had to move heaven and earth to get it shipped here from Tarifa, but we've got it. The governor signed off the chit this morning."

"What about the sixty rifle flints and forty pistol flints?"

"Those too. As soon as we bring the cutter in, you'll need to deal with that; but don't load anything until I'm aboard. I have to pay a visit to the shipowners first."

There is a brief flash from the Trocadero. The two men stop and stare across the bay while Pépé Lobo mentally counts off the seconds. As he reaches ten, they hear the boom of the cannon and seventeen seconds later, a plume of spray lights up the darkness between the black shapes of the anchored ships off the quay.

"They're firing short tonight," Maraña says coolly.

The two men stroll back toward the Puerta de Mar. In the glow of a lantern a sentry peers down at them from his watchtower. Maraña stops before they reach the gate, glancing quickly toward a small jetty under the city walls that run toward the Plataforma de la Cruz and the Puerta de Sevilla.

"How are we set with the paperwork?" he asks.

"Everything is in order. The shipowners have posted their bonds, the contract will be signed on Monday."

The first officer of the *Culebra* is only half-listening. In the lamplight, Pépé Lobo sees him glance again toward the end of the pier, toward Puerto Piojo and the flight of steps leading down to a beach hidden in the shadows of the city walls and exposed only at low tide.

"I'll walk a little way with you," he says.

The other man looks at him grimly. Suspiciously. Finally, he gives a little smile which in the darkness looks more like a sinister scowl.

"How many have invested in the venture?" Maraña asks.

They walk on, their shadows stretching out before them, the sound of their footsteps mixing with the water lapping against the stone pier, whipped by a fresh westerly breeze.

"Two, as I told you," says Lobo. "Both very wealthy. Emilio Sánchez Guinea and Señora Palma . . . *Señorita* rather."

"What is she like?"

"A little dry. Don Emilio says she was difficult to persuade. She has rather a low opinion of corsairs."

He hears a hoarse, wet laugh then a cough being stifled by a kerchief.

"I tend to share her opinion," Maraña mutters.

"Well, it's part of her character I suppose. Playing the respectable merchant. At the end of the day, she's the boss."

"Pretty?"

"An old maid. But she's a handsome woman. Still handsome."

They have come to the steps that lead down to the beach. Below, on the shore, Lobo thinks he can make out a sailboat and two men waiting in the darkness. Bootleggers, probably. They regularly ply these waters, delivering supplies to the enemy shore where hardship has quadrupled the value of everything.

"Good night, Captain," says Maraña.

"Good night."

After the first officer has gone down the steps and disappeared into the shadows, Pépé Lobo stands for a moment, listening to the rustle of rope and canvas as the boatman hoists his sail and casts off. Rumor has it that there is a woman; that Ricardo Maraña has a sweetheart or a mistress in the occupied zone near the Puerto de Santa María. And that some nights, with a following wind and the help of some bootlegger, he crosses the bay to visit her in secret, risking his liberty or even his life.

CHAPTER FOUR

✿

The pine forests surrounding Chiclana are ablaze. A gray-brown pall of smoke, punctuated here and there by cannonfire, hangs between earth and heaven while from the distance comes the muffled crack of rifle shots. The path that rises from the coast toward Chiclana and Puerto Real is teeming with French troops beating a retreat, a tide of fugitives, of carts carrying equipment and injured men, of soldiers trying to make it to safety. It is pandemonium: the news, such as it is, is vague and contradictory. They say there is heavy fighting up on the Cerro del Puerco, where the forces of generals Leval and Ruffin have been caught in a pincer movement, or have already been defeated by the Anglo-Spanish troops who landed at Tarifa and are advancing towards Sancti Petri and Cádiz, trying to break the stranglehold on the city. There are also rumors that the villages of Vejer and Casas Viejas have fallen to the enemy and that Medina Sidonia is under threat, meaning that the entire southern section of the French front line around the Isla de Léon might crumble within a matter of hours. Fearing they will be stranded on the coast, cut off from the interior, the Imperial forces between the sea and the Alcornocal canal are retreating northward.

Simon Desfosseux is swept along by a stream of men, carts and pack animals that stretches back as far as the eye can see. He has lost his hat and is dressed in waistcoat and shirtsleeves, frockcoat over one arm, sword in hand, the sword-knot wrapped around the hilt and scabbard. Like the hundreds of bewildered men, the captain has just waded waist deep through the creeks that ring the small island on which the Almansa mill stands. His breeches and jacket are soaked with muddy water which trickles into his boots at every step. The dirt track is narrow, flanked to the left by swamps and salt marshes, and to the right by a bank that rises steeply to a hill covered in mastic trees and brushwood, beyond which is a pine forest. Shots ring out from behind the hill and everyone turns fearfully, expecting the enemy to appear at any moment, panicked at the thought of falling into the hands of ruthless Spaniards. And if they should think of the vicious guerrillas, that panic turns to terror.

Desfosseux has been unlucky. The enemy attack took him by surprise four leagues from his usual post in the Torre Bermeja camp, where he and General Lesueur, commander of the Premier Corps artillery, spent the night under an escort of six dragoons. Dissatisfied with the firepower of the Las Flechas battery against the Spanish bastion at the mouth of the Sancti Petri channel, the general insisted that Desfosseux come along to help resolve the problem. Or to confirm it. Despite the skirmishes along the front lines in the past week, the landing at Tarifa and the enemy's attempt to throw a pontoon across the lower part of the channel two days ago, Lesueur had decided not to retreat.

"At ease, gentlemen," he said over a dinner washed down perhaps a little too liberally with *manzanilla*. "The Spanish have dismantled their pontoon and scuttled off like rats. Besides, a little action is good for troop morale, don't you think? Those seditious peasants turned tail and fled tonight when three of our regiments advanced along the beach under cover of the dunes. They made it to the far bank and gave them what for. Fine soldiers, General Villatte's men, brave lads. So we have nothing to fear. Pass me a little more wine, Desfosseux, if you would be so kind. Thank you. We'll carry on with our work tomorrow. In the meantime, get some rest."

The rest was short-lived. In the early hours advance enemy parties attacked the French from the rear on the Cerro de Puerco and pushed along the Conil road and across the hard sand laid bare at low tide toward Torre Berjema, while on the far side of Las Flechas, the Spanish once again threw a pontoon bridge over the channel and began to cross. By midday, caught between the enemy forces, the four thousand men of General Villatte's division were retreating chaotically toward Chiclana, and General Lesueur had set off at a gallop with his escort of dragoons leaving Desfosseux, whose horse had been stolen by some unscrupulous individual, wearing out his boot leather.

The gunfire is closer now, almost on the hill abutting the pine forest. There are shouts that the enemy are just on the other side of the hill. The fleeing masses scrabble and jostle, pushing aside any stragglers blocking their path. A cart with a broken wheel is pushed off the road and its occupants straddle their mules and whip them on, riding roughshod over those on foot. Panic quickly spreads and Simon Desfosseux, scrambling forward, his face a mask of fear, peers anxiously up at the hill that looms on his right. He has no desire to get a close view of the sharp blades of the Spanish knives. Or the regimental English bayonets.

From among the mastic trees comes the crack of gunfire, bullets whistle above the marching column. People start to scream. Some men fall out of step, throw themselves to the ground or hunker down, aiming their rifles at the hilltop.

"*Guerrilleros! Guerrilleros!*"

Word goes round that it is not the Spanish but the British planning to cut them off at the little wooden bridge that spans the next canal. Madness begins to set in, men pushing and jostling on the narrow path and those who can begin to run. A crackle of gunfire yet still no enemy has been spotted, and no one has been injured.

"Run for your lives! They're trying to cut off the road to Chiclana!"

Some soldiers try to hack a path through the mastic trees, but the muddy creeks and salt marshes make it impossible. A lieutenant—who Desfosseux identifies from the insignia on his shako as belonging to the 94th Regiment—tries to marshal a team to secure the hill and protect the flank of the fleeing column, but no one is prepared to listen. Some threaten him with their rifles when he grabs their arm, trying to persuade them to join him, but finally the lieutenant abandons his attempt and allows himself to be swept along by the sea of bodies.

"Soldiers—up there among the trees," someone says.

Desfosseux looks up and feels his skin crawl. On the brow of the hill, a dozen riders appear out of the burning pine forest. A wave of terror passes through the retreating column, who assume them to be an enemy scouting party. There is scattered gunfire and Desfosseux, panic-stricken, imagines himself fleeing beneath a rain of saber blows. But the guns quickly fall silent when the riders on the hill are recognized as belonging to Desagne's cavalrymen, escorting a convoy of light artillery retreating to the fort at Santa Ana.

If this is not a rout, thinks Simon Desfosseux, it looks very much like one. Few would dare use the word "rout" when speaking of the Imperial Army; but this would not be the first. The memory of Bailén still smarts, and there have been other, minor incidents in the war against Spain. Napoleonic France is not invincible. But for Desfosseux, this is his first experience of the dark side of military glory: soldiers running amok, mass panic; a world that only yesterday was impeccably regulated, disciplined and orderly has degenerated into every man for himself. And yet, in spite of the panic, the desperate flight to find safety in Chiclana or beyond, the captain has the curious sensation of being two different people; as though Simon Desfosseux has a twin who can dispassionately, methodically survey what is happening around him. The scientific part of his brain is fascinated by the spectacle—new to him and enormously instructive—of how human beings behave when left to themselves, when military and social hierarchies crumble, when the ominous murmur of dishonor or death is all around. Even in these dire circumstances, his natural instinct, his unique way of seeing the world does not desert him. As Lieutenant Bertoldi might say if he were here—fortunately he is watching the scene from the safe distance of the Trocadero—like a leopard, Desfosseux never changes his spots. It is a matter of reflex. Every gunshot he hears, every shudder that runs through these terrified men scrabbling to shelter behind one another, makes Desfosseux think about impacts, probabilities and aleatory systems, of straight lines of fire and the curves described by projectiles, of ounces of lead acted on by thrust at the limit of their range. New ideas, and unfamiliar ways of considering the subject. There are, he feels, two men heading for Chiclana: one, stumbling, running, panting, consumed with dread, a member of a panicked throng; the other, serene and impassive, a shrewd observer of a fascinating world governed by complex universal laws.

"They're behind us," yell the soldiers.

Terror ripples through the crowd once more. Men push and jostle. Reports are circulating that General Ruffin has been killed or captured. Desfosseux is growing weary of the rumors and outbreaks of panic. In the name of God, he thinks, slowing his pace and resisting the temptation to step off the path and sit down. The sheer misery of the retreat is compounded by a terrible sense of absurdity, of personal humiliation. Here he is, a professor of physics from the University of Metz, hatless and in shirtsleeves, being swept along by hundreds of men as fearful as himself.

"Don't lag behind, Captain," advises a mustachioed corporal.

"Leave me in peace."

There is a small building up ahead. One of the many flour mills whose wheel is turned by the ebb and flow of the tides. Next to it is a small house. As he approaches, the captain sees that it has been looted. The door is completely smashed, the floor littered with broken tools and rubble. As he comes closer, he can make out four bodies sprawled on the floor next to a chained dog that is barking furiously at the passing soldiers.

"*Guerrilleros,*" says the corporal, indifferently.

This is not Desfosseux's opinion. The corpses—three men and a woman—are clearly the miller and his family to judge from their appearance. The bodies have been run through with bayonets, the earthen floor is stained with pools of dark, congealing blood. Obviously some retreating French soldiers have vented their anger and frustration. Another act of vengeance, Desfosseux thinks uneasily as he turns away. Just one of many.

The dog goes on barking at the soldiers, jerking wildly on the chain attaching it to the wall. Without pausing, the corporal marching next to Desfosseux draws his pistol, aims and, with a single shot, kills the animal.

GREGORIO FUMAGAL IS dyeing his hair and sideburns with the dye he bought in Frasquito Sanlúcar's soap emporium. The preparation, which the taxidermist applies with a small brush, produces a dark, somewhat auburn color, covering the gray hairs. He works slowly to ensure everything is evenly coated. When he is finished, he dries his face and examines the results in a looking glass. Satisfactory. Then he goes up to the terrace and looks out at the cityscape and the bay beyond. For some time he stands in the sunshine, listening to the rumble of distant cannonfire from the reef between Sancti Petri and the hills of Chiclana. From what he heard while out buying bread at the bakery near Empedradores, Generals Lapeña and Graham broke through the French lines yesterday and are waging a bloody battle between the Cerro de Puerco and the beach at La Barrosa; but misunderstandings between the generals, rivalries and matters of coordination and competency have meant that now the state of affairs is as it was before. The front line, stable once more, is a question of a duel between artillery forces, leaving Cádiz on the margins.

Once his hair is dry, Gregorio Fumagal goes back downstairs and looks at himself in the mirror. His is a peculiar vanity which has little to do with his nonexistent social life. In truth everything is born and dies in him, discreetly: in his daily routine, including the pigeon loft, in the bodies of the dead animals that the taxidermist eviscerates and reconstructs. Unlike a fop or a dandy, Gregorio Fumagal's dyed hair and fastidious personal hygiene are not born of some desire to look youthful or attractive. They are merely a matter of routine. Of healthy discipline. The taxidermist is a man who takes great care over his personal appearance; his exacting regimen ranges from shaving daily to cleaning his fingernails, to the clothes he irons himself or has laundered in a washroom on the Calle del Campillo. He cannot imagine life any other way. For a man of his class, who has neither family nor friends, who is beyond the censure of those who might sit in judgment over his virtues or his weaknesses, this personal, private, inflexible routine has, over time, become a means of survival. Having no faith in the present, nor allegiance to any flag—his loyalty to the flag that flies on the far side of the bay is merely a convenient alliance—his routine, his personal habits, these strict codes that have nothing to do with the vain and venal laws of ordinary men, provide a foxhole in which Gregorio Fumagal shelters in order to survive in hostile territory. For there is no reprieve here, where the prospects for the future are scant and his only comfort lies in re-creating Nature using stuffing and straw, a saddler's needle and eyes fashioned from glass paste.

THEY ARE HIS footsteps and not another's that I stalk; for he hath wrought on us tonight a deed past thought—if he it was, for everything is doubtful and uncertain. Here and there have I found traces I can identify, but there are others that perplex me and I know not whose they be.

This paragraph mesmerizes Rogelio Tizón. It is as though some twenty centuries ago, Sophocles wrote these words thinking of him. Thinking about what he is feeling now. Carefully, the policeman leafs again through the manuscript pages covered in the large, neat hand—almost like that of a scribe—of Professor Barrull. After a moment he pauses at another of the passages he has marked, like the previous one, with a penciled cross in the margin.

And now, his hunger unsated, thirst unslaked, he sits transfixed among the oxen slaughtered by his sword. Clearly plotting some baleful deed.

Unsettled, Tizón sets down the manuscript on the table. The image of the slaughtered oxen corresponds with the images he remembers: the flayed backs of the murdered girls, the bones poking through the flesh. Some time has passed since the last killing, but still Tizón can think of nothing else. A surgeon from the Royal Armada, an old acquaintance whose discretion he values and whom he trusts more than those who usually work with the police, confirmed his suspicion that the whip used is no ordinary riding crop made of rope or leather, nor even a vicious bull's pizzle. It has been specially made, probably using braided wire. An evil contrivance. An instrument designed to inflict damage. To flay the victim to death, ripping away the flesh with every stroke. This means that these crimes were not committed in hot blood, they are not the result of some sudden excess of fury. Whoever he may be, the murderer does not act on impulse. Having meticulously prepared, he deliberately sets out in search of his prey. He revels in the deed. He goes armed to inflict as much pain as he can while he kills.

It is an impossible task, thinks Tizón. At least with the material at his disposal. Like looking for a needle in a haystack, in a city where the war and the French siege have almost doubled the population to more than 100,000 people. To whittle down such a number would be impossible even using the vast network of informants he has patiently built up: harlots, beggars and every manner of agent and spy. Among them, he even counts a man of the cloth, a popular parish priest at the church of San Antonio who is happy to feed him information in exchange for Tizón turning a blind eye to his rather particular manner of ministering to fallen women. Some betray in return for money, impunity or privileges, others to settle a score with peers, politics, or with a world they envy or despise. Given his age and his profession, Rogelio Tizón believes he knows everything there is to know about the dark corners of the human heart; the precise point at which a man will break, crumble, collaborate or be lost forever, the boundless wickedness anyone is capable of when they find, or are offered, the right opportunity.

The comisario abruptly gets to his feet and paces the room, absentmindedly glancing at the spines of the books on the shelves above his desk. He knows he may find some of the answers he seeks in these volumes, but he will not find all of them. Nor will he find them in the manuscript lying on his desk, the ink slightly faded, small penciled crosses in the margins marking out passages that trouble more than they illuminate. Questions that give rise to other questions, to doubt, to helplessness. This last word rings in his head as Tizón runs his fingers over the closed lid of the piano that no one has played in years. The depth and breadth of Tizón's knowledge is extremely useful in his job as a policeman, but it does not cover all that is required now that

Cádiz is filled with immigrants, soldiers and civilians. In theory, all new arrivals must go before the Audiencia Territorial for their case to be assessed and, if approved, be issued with a residence permit. For those in possession of sufficient funds—the requisite bribe is not within everyone's means, and no authority is prepared to certify false papers for less than 150 *duros*—the difficulties are enormous. This has meant that the traffic in people, with all the bureaucracy that it entails, has become a thriving industry involving ships' captains, civil servants, soldiers and smugglers. Even Tizón himself, as Commissioner for Districts, Vagrants and Transients, is not immune. For a family with children, the official fine for attempted illegal entry amounts to a thousand *reales*, plus a further two hundred if they are traveling with a servant— something Tizón is prepared to take care of for a quarter of that sum. Sometimes half. Sometimes he can charge the whole amount if it means turning a blind eye to an expulsion order signed by the Regency. After all, business is business. And life is life.

He walks to the door leading to the rest of the house and listens. Silence is absolute, although he knows his wife is in her bedroom, lips pursed, eyes cast down, sewing or perhaps gazing out at the street through the shutters. Like a statue, as always; expressionless as a sphinx, silent as a reproachful specter. The rosary, which once upon a time never left her hands, now lies forgotten in a drawer of her sewing basket. Nor does she light votives anymore on the shrine of the Nazarene in the hallway. It has been years since anyone in the house prayed.

The comisario goes over to the window that overlooks the Alameda and the bay beyond. Far out, some two miles from Cádiz, facing the Puerto de Santa María, two English warships escorted by Spanish gunboats are firing on the enemy fort at Santa Catalina. He can see the plumes of smoke carried on the breeze, the tiny white triangles of the fluttering sails of ships and boats as they tack and come about. There are sails off the cape at Rota too. If he listens carefully, Tizón can hear the boom of the cannons and the counter fire from the French artillery on the far shore. From this window, he cannot see the southeast of the city. He does not know how matters stand there, aside from having heard that some days ago a bloody battle was fought on the Cerro del

Puerco. Rumor has it that there is still fighting all along the front line, and that Spanish guerrillas have landed at various points along the coast, intent on destroying enemy positions. This morning, coming back from escorting prisoners to the Royal Jail, the comisario was able to scale the fort at Los Mártires and see that, beyond the Isla de Léon, the pine forests of Chiclana were still burning.

But this battle does not concern him. At least he does not feel it should. Rogelio Tizón has never deluded himself. He is keenly aware that if the circumstances were different, he would cheerfully have served the usurper king in Madrid—as have many of his colleagues in the French-occupied zones. Not for ideological reasons but simply because that is the way of the world. He is a government official: his only ideology is support for the established order. A policeman is first and foremost a policeman and every constitutional power needs his services and his experience. No government could survive without the police. It is his job to do his job, regardless of the ideology or the flag he serves. Tizón loves his job. And he is good at it. He knows he possesses the precise combination of ruthlessness, mercenary indifference and apparent loyalty required by the role. He was born a policeman and has climbed the greasy pole, from lowly henchman to the heights of comisario where he has power over life, property and liberty. It was not easy, and his success came at a price. But he is satisfied. His battlefield is the city that extends all about him, ancient and cunning, thronging with human beings. They are the materials of his work. The field of his experimentation and progress. The source of his power.

Moving away from the window, he returns to the desk. Anxious. Prowling like an animal in a cage, he realizes. And this does not please him. This is not his way. Within him he feels a fury, slender and exact, sharp as a dagger. Professor Barrull's manuscript still lies on the desk, as though mocking him: *"here and there have I found traces I can identify, but there are others that perplex me,"* he reads again. The phrase buries itself in Tizón's pride like a jagged splinter. In his professional peace of mind. Three girls murdered in the same way within six months. Fortunately for him, as Governor Villavicencio cuttingly pointed out some weeks ago, the war and the French siege have meant that such crimes have been relegated to the background. But this does little to assuage the comisario's unease; the curious shame that eats away at him each time he thinks about the case. Each time he sees the mute piano and realizes that the murdered girls are almost the same age as the girl who once touched the keys would have been today.

He feels a dull throb of anger. Helplessness, that is the word. A bitterness unlike anything he has ever known, a private hatred that grows with each passing day, belying his dispassionate, impersonal approach to his job. Meanwhile somewhere close at hand, among the crowd—*he sits transfixed among the oxen slaughtered*—is the faceless man, or the man of a thousand faces, who tortured these three unfortunate wretches to death. Every time he steps out into the street, the comisario glances left and right, his eyes following random figures as they move through the crowd, and each time he is forced to conclude that it could be anyone. He has visited the sites where every French bomb fell, studied every detail, questioned the neighbors in a futile attempt to force this vague feeling, this absurd hunch he cannot get out of his mind, to coalesce into some clue, some theory that might make it possible to correlate his intuition with real facts, real people; a face in which he can see some hint of the crime. But from long experience Tizón knows that there are no outward signs to mark out the criminal, that atrocities such as those perpetrated on the girls could be committed by anyone. The truth is that the world is not filled with innocents; quite the reverse, it is filled with people who, without exception, are capable of the vilest crimes. The essential problem for any good policeman is to attribute to each fellow citizen the exact degree of wickedness or blame that corresponds to them for any crimes committed. This is what justice means, what Rogelio Tizón understands it to mean. Assigning to each human being his share of blame and, if possible, bringing him to account. Ruthlessly.

"LET'S GO . . . Move back, slowly . . . Come on, move your asses."

Felipe Mojarra, who has just charged his rifle when he hears this voice, clips the ramrod into place beneath the long barrel and glances left and right. *Time to get the hell out of here*, he thinks. On all fours, the salters and the soldiers posted around the Montecorto mill begin to retreat, pausing now and then to fire at the plumes of smoke made by the muskets along the French line.

"Move back to the boats in an orderly manner . . . Easy does it . . ."

Whup. A bullet raises a cloud of sand among the wild asparagus on the bank. Mojarra does not pause to work out where it came from, but reckons that the enemy fusiliers are no more than fifty paces away. To keep them from showing their faces, he draws himself up a little, aims and squeezes the trigger. Then he fumbles for another round in his cartridge belt, rips the wax paper with his teeth, and tips the powder and bullet into his musket and tamps it again with the ramrod as he continues to retreat, squelching through the mud that oozes between the toes of his bare feet. Another shot, poorly aimed this time, whizzes over his head. The sun is already high, and everywhere crystals of salt—forming thin crusts over the pools, ringing the swamps, the tidal creeks and the runnels—glitter like tiny diamonds. Next to one of the creeks, sprawled on the muddy bank, are the bodies of two French soldiers he noticed when they first landed at dawn. He passed them when he and his comrades were ordered to form an advance party and guard the position they had just captured against an enemy counterattack while the sappers tore down the mud fortifications and the shelters of Montecorto, spiked the French cannons and torched everything that would burn.

The raid today is the third Felipe Mojarra has been involved in since the battle for Chiclana. From what he knows, although the French recovered their positions, Spanish and English incursions have continued all along the front line. Raids and landings in the tidal creeks and all along the coast from Sancti Petri to the Trocadero up to the cape at Rota, which was captured three days ago by Spanish forces. They destroyed the fortifications, tossed the field guns into the bay and harangued the local populace about King Fernando VII, before retreating safely to their boats. Rumor has it that the battle at the Cerro del Puerco was not as successful as first claimed, though the English fought valiantly as always, and that General Graham, incensed by the behavior of General Lapeña during the battle, refused the title which the Cortes wanted to confer on him: Count or Duke or perhaps Marqués de Pueco—Mojarra knows little about aristocratic titles. Some say he refused because of his quarrel with Lapeña, others because someone foolishly mistranslated the title as *Count of Pig*. At all events, there has been much friction between the allies: the Spanish accusing the English of arrogance and they in turn accusing the Spanish of being ill-disciplined. And both parties have a point as Felipe Mojarra himself discovered a week ago during a raid on the French gun emplacement. Half a company of English marines led by eight salters acting as guides came ashore at El Coto where they were forced to fight for almost three hours in hand-to-hand combat because the Spanish reinforcement—seventy men from the Málaga regiment—did not show up until midday, by which time the raiding party was already leaving. Even Mojarra was cursing his compatriots as he trudged back to the boats, half-carrying an English officer whose arm had been blown off by a shell. Mojarra had risked his life to save this man because, before the raid, the "red mullet"—as islanders have nicknamed the British because of their red frockcoats—had made disparaging comments about the guides. In English, obviously, though his remarks required no translation. And Mojarra was determined that, if the English officer survived, every time he looked at his stump he would be reminded of the filthy *dago* to whom he owed his pink skin.

The two French corpses lie almost one on top of the other, their blood staining the salt-crusted edges of the creek. Mojarra does not know who killed them. He assumes that they were advance guards who fell during the first minutes of the fighting when fifty-four sailors and Spanish marines, twelve sappers and twenty-two volunteer salters sailed across the Borriquera channel and landed on the enemy shore under cover of darkness. One of the dead men is gray haired, his face half-pressed into the mud; the other, dark haired with mustaches in the French style, is sprawled on his back, eyes wide, mouth open, half his face blown off by the bullet that killed him. The salter notices that someone has already stolen their rifles, swords and cartridge belts, but not the gold earrings the *gabacho* soldiers always wear. Felipe Mojarra respects the dead. In other circumstances, he would carefully remove the earrings, not rip them out or hack them off with a knife like some men would do. He is not a brute, he is a Christian. But in the heat of the moment, with troops retreating to the channel and the *gabachos* closing in, there is no time for fine sentiments. So he deals with the matter in a few hard tugs, wraps the earrings in his kerchief and is tucking it into his belt when a sweaty marine grenadier rushes up, bent double and gasping for breath.

"A pox on't," says the marine, "you got there before me."

Mojarra says nothing, simply picks up his rifle and walks off leaving the other man to rummage through the dead men's pockets and check their mouths for any gold teeth he might knock out with a rifle butt. Meanwhile, in the undergrowth along the salt marshes, the Spanish troops are still retreating, following the narrow creeks that wind through the swamp and the floodland that surrounds Montecorto toward the main channel. Reaching the shore, the salter sees smoke rising from the shacks and huts around the mill which have been set ablaze. Most of the Spanish boats have already pushed off, protected by two gunboats from Gallineras harbor that are shelling the French positions at regular intervals. Mojarra feels the shudder of the blasts in his eardrums and chest. There appear to be no Spanish fatalities, only walking wounded. They have taken two French prisoners.

"Watch out!" someone yells.

A French grenade drones past and explodes in the air, sending shrapnel slicing across the water. Hearing the blast, most of the men, Mojarra among them, immediately drop to the ground or huddle in the boats. Only a small group of officers remain standing—out of military decorum—next to the mud and stone wall of the sluice gate. Among them, Mojarra recognizes Lorenzo Virués, wearing his blue frockcoat and red collar, the broad hat with the red cockade, his leather bag slung over his shoulder. The Captain of Engineers landed early with the raiding party to get a look at the enemy fortifications. Mojarra assumes he took the opportunity to sketch them before the sappers razed them to the ground.

"Felipe!" Virués seems genuinely pleased to see the salter. "Good to see you in one piece. What's been going on here?"

Mojarra picks at his teeth. He has been chewing wild fennel to ward off thirst—they were put ashore without food or water—and has a stem lodged in his gums.

"Not much, Don Lorenzo. The *mosíus* are gaining ground again, but slowly. Our lads are retreating in an orderly fashion . . . Did you need me for something?"

"No, I'm about to leave with these men. Go with your comrades. We're finished here."

Mojarra gives him a frank smile.

"Get any good sketches, Captain?"

"A few . . ." Virués returns the smile. "I managed to dash off one or two."

The salter brings one finger up to his brow, a casual but respectful version of the military salute, then spits out the piece of fennel and coolly heads back to the boats. Mission accomplished: another one chalked up. King Fernando, in his prison cell in France or wherever he is, would be proud. Mojarra does not care. Just at that moment someone runs past him. A naval officer wearing a threadbare frockcoat darned at the elbows with two pistols tucked in his belt. He is clearly in a hurry.

"Move it! Let's go! The whole place is about to blow."

Before the salter can work out what he means, there is a thunderous explosion behind him and the force of the blast hits him like a fist in the back. Bewildered and terrified, he turns and sees a vast mushroom cloud of black smoke rising into the sky, showering everything with splintered beams and burning brushwood. The sappers have just blown up the Montecorto arsenal.

The easterly breeze blows the smoke across the channel as the last men scramble into boats. Huddled with his comrades in one launch, Mojarra smells a sulfurous reek acrid enough to make a man vomit. But it has been a long time since Mojarra last vomited.

IT IS SUNDAY and the cracked bell of San Antonio tolls the end of midday mass. Sitting at a table in the doorway of Burnel's teashop, beneath the green wrought-iron balconies, the taxidermist Gregorio Fumagal sips a glass of warm milk and watches as the faithful emerge from the church and disperse, some to the marble benches among the orange trees, others to the wide area next to the square where a number of caleches and sedan chairs are waiting. These are for the ladies and the elderly, since in such balmy weather most people prefer to take the customary stroll toward the Calle Ancha or the Alameda. As on any Sunday at this hour, everyone who is anyone—or claims to be—is here: noblemen, eminent merchants, the cream of Cádiz society, distinguished immigrants, officers from the Army, the Navy and the local militias. The square is a pageant of brightly colored uniforms, stars, ribbons and medals, silk stockings, frockcoats and tailcoats, top hats and broad-brimmed hats, traditional redingotes, capes, bicorn hats, even a tricorne or two, since some of the more elderly parishioners prefer to dress in the old style. The times being what they are, even the little boys march in step, dressed in officer's uniforms fashioned according to the whims or the professions of their parents, wearing frockcoats and dress swords and hats with red cockades emblazoned with the letters FVII, in honor of King Fernando.

The taxidermist has his own opinion of the spectacle he is witnessing. He is a man of science, of learning, and considers himself as such. His gaze—analytical and as cold as that of the stuffed animals in his display cases—is devoid of all compassion. As far as Gregorio Fumagal is concerned, the pigeons on his terrace that weave—or help to weave—the tracery of lines and curves across the map of the city are the antithesis of these pheasants, these peacocks strutting and flaunting their plumage, wallowing in a cesspit of depravity and corruption, in this antiquated world that is doomed by the inexorable tide of nature and of history. Gregorio Fumagal firmly believes that this is a tide which even the Cortes in its sessions at San Felipe Neri cannot stop. For the hand that will sweep all of this away will not come from some future Magna Carta, drawn up by priests—the clergy account for half of the deputies in the Cortes—and aristocrats still clinging to the Ancien Régime. If things continue as they are then with or without a new Constitution, and regardless of the trappings used to dress it up, the Spaniard will become a worthless slave, devoid of soul, of reason, of virtue; forbidden by his inhuman jailers from ever seeing the light. An unfortunate wretch subjugated by men who are his equals but who, in his stupidity, his laziness, his superstition, he believes to be anointed by some higher power: these gods among men, wearing ermine and purple, black capes and cassocks, who under every sun and at every latitude will always exploit a man's foolishness in order to enslave him, to make him brutish and miserable, to sap his valor and his courage. Fumagal, whose taste in books tends toward the foreign and the revolutionary—Baron Holbach, known as "Mirabaud," has been his spiritual mentor ever since he first laid hands on a French edition of *System of Nature* some twenty years ago—is of the opinion that Spain has missed the perfect opportunity to adopt the guillotine: a river of blood that, in accordance with universal laws, would have swept clean the Stygian stables of this miserable, ignorant country, eternally in thrall to fanatical clerics, corrupt aristocrats and ineffectual, dissolute monarchs. But he believes it is still possible to throw the windows open, to allow light and air to flood in. The solution, he believes, lies half a league away on the far shore of the bay, in the form of the Imperial eagle, whose magnificent claws are even now crushing the forces of darkness that hold parts of Europe enchained.

Fumagal sips absentmindedly from his glass of goat's milk. A group of ladies, each carrying a rosary and a missal bound in calfskin or mother-of-pearl, stop in front of the teashop. While their husbands remain standing, lighting cigars and toying with their watch chains, greeting passersby and ogling women, the ladies sit, order cold drinks and little cakes and talk about the things that interest them: weddings, births, baptisms, funerals. In short, domestic or social matters. They do not talk about the war except perhaps to complain about its effect on the price of this or that, and the fact it means they have no ice—before the French occupation, ice was brought in by the cartload from Ronda—to cool their drinks. Gregorio Fumagal watches them disdainfully out of the corner of his eye. His contempt is long-standing, one that irrevocably cuts him off from the lives of ordinary men, a physical malaise that even now is making him squirm in his seat. The ladies wear black or dark tones, with bright accent colors provided by gloves and handbags and fans; mantillas of fine lace cover hair piled up in chignons, topknots and corkscrew curls. The fashion is for women to wear rows of buttons that run from wrist to elbow. Lower-class women have buttons of gilded brass; but the ladies here have buttons of solid gold studded with diamonds like those their husbands wear on their waistcoats. Each button, Fumagal calculates, costing no less than two hundred *pesos*.

"What was that?" asks one of the ladies, gesturing for her friends to be silent.

"I don't hear anything, Piedita," says another.

"Hush and listen. In the distance."

A far-off rumble shakes the tables of the tearoom. The ladies and their husbands, and various passersby, glance worriedly toward the Café Apolo on the corner of the Calle Murguía. For a moment, the conversations die away as people try to decide whether this is simply the daily exchange of cannonfire between Puntales and the Trocadero or whether the French artillery—battle lines having been reestablished after Chiclana, their howitzers are once again trained on Cádiz—are attempting to hit the city center.

"It's nothing." Doña Piedita dismisses the matter and returns to her cakes.

With icy contempt, the taxidermist gazes toward the far shore. One day, he thinks, a blistering wind will come out of the east and restore order: the flaming sword of science is steadily advancing, growing stronger, spattering red stain across this city which stubbornly remains on the margins of history. That same sword will one day reach this plaza. He is certain it will come, indeed the work that might cost him his life is in the service of this sword. It is the key to the future. Sooner or later the sword will rule over this dreamlike space peopled by creatures that have long since ceased to be real. This whole pus-filled boil that cries out to be lanced by the surgeon's scalpel. This obdurate, suicidal spoke that jams the wheel of reason and of progress.

The ladies carry on chattering, using their fans to shield their eyes from the sun. Still watching them furtively, Fumagal gives a savage smile. Realizing what he has done, he immediately hides his smile with another sip of milk. Bombs will rain down on their gold and diamond buttons, he gloats, on their silk shawls, their fans, their satin slippers. On their corkscrew curls.

Foolish animals, he thinks, the sick, worthless dross of the earth, condemned from birth to the contagion of error. How he would like to take one of these ladies home, what a singular trophy she would make among the more pedestrian examples of his art that decorate his studio, including the stray dog, his latest effort, which now stands, staring into the void with glittering glass eyes. There, in the warm, welcoming gloom of his workshop, he would dissect this naked lady on the marble table.

As he thinks this, the taxidermist experiences an ill-timed erection—he is wearing knitted breeches, an open frockcoat and a round hat—and to disguise it he is forced to shift in his seat and cross his legs. After all, he thinks, a man's freedom is nothing more than the need he has within him.

A MURMUR OF conversations. No music, since this is Lent. For the rest, the mansion rented by the English ambassador for his party—*reception* is the more discreet term used, given the time of year—shimmers with the light of silver and crystal candelabras set between bouquets of flowers beneath chandeliers that hang from the ceilings. The event is to celebrate the English victory at Cerro del Puerco, though some say it is a diplomatic gesture intended to alleviate tensions between the allies after the spat between generals Graham and Lapeña. This might perhaps explain why Ambassador Wellesley is not hosting the party at his residence on the Calle de la Amargura but on neutral territory. He has rented this mansion for the night—such details fascinate the people of Cádiz—at a cost of 15,000 *reales*, paid into the coffers of the Regency since the building, once owned by the Marqués de Mazatlán, was seized when he pledged allegiance to Joseph Bonaparte. There is little in the way of refreshments: some Spanish and Portuguese wines, an English punch which no one but the British will touch, seafood canapés, fruit and soft drinks. The whole budget was spent on candles and lamps, which is why every salon and every stairwell is a blaze of light. On the street, lit by burning torches, liveried footmen greet the guests while the terrace, hung with lanterns, overlooks the city walls, the dark bay and the distant twinkle of lights from El Puerto de Santa María, the Puerto Real and the Trocadero.

"Here comes Colonel Ortega's widow."

"She looks less like a colonel's widow than a sergeant's bit of fancy."

The assembled company laughs, the ladies discreetly behind their fans. The quip, as usual, came from cousin Toño. He is sitting on a sofa surrounded by armchairs and stools, next to the glass-fronted terrace; next to him are Lolita Palma and several other ladies of Cádiz, married and single. A dozen *señoras* and *señoritas* in total. They are accompanied by a number of gentlemen, holding glasses and cigars, wearing dress coats, white ties or lace ruffs and flamboyant waistcoats in the modern style. There are two Spanish officers in full-dress uniform and a young deputy from the Cortes, Jorge Fernández Cuchillero, the delegate for Buenos Aires and a friend of the Palma family.

"Don't be cruel," Lolita Palma affectionately chides cousin Toño, tugging on his sleeve.

"But that's the only reason you ladies sit with me," says Toño with cheerful frankness. "Because I can say anything."

Cousin Toño—Antonio Cardenal Ugarte—a bachelor, has always maintained excellent relations with the Palma family and every afternoon for years he has visited Lolita and her mother at home where he is the life and soul of the party, and can sink a bottle of *manzanilla* below the waterline. A familiar face in Cádiz café society, Toño is tall and lanky, a little short-sighted, and over the years has developed a slight paunch. He dresses with studied carelessness, a pair of crooked spectacles perched on his nose, a poorly knotted tie, his jacket flecked with ash from his Havana cigars. He is comfortably off, though he has never worked a day in his life; he never rises before midday and he lives off a private income from securities in Havana. The flow of money has not been cut off by the war. For the rest, Toño is staunchly apolitical

and a friend to everyone. Always witty, always scintillating, his unfailing good humor means he is always the center of attention. He has an
extraordinary facility for surrounding himself with young, pretty girls
and the most amusing ladies, and at even the most formal gathering,
Toño's group is always marked out by its gaiety and high spirits.

"Don't even think about tasting the canapés on those trays, *niña*.
They're truly vile. Our ally Wellesley has spent all his money on candles. He's all flash and no substance."

Shocked, Lolita Palma quickly presses a finger to his lips and
glances toward the English ambassador. Dressed in a purple velvet
jacket, black silk stockings and shoes with large silver buckles, General
Wellington's brother is greeting guests by the door of the drawing
room flanked by two redcoats and some others in the elaborate blue
uniforms of the Royal Navy. Among their number, haughty and forbid-
ding, and looking flushed as a cooked lobster, is General Graham. The
hero of Cerro de Puerco.

"Don't talk so loud, he might hear."

"Let him hear, by Gad! The English are starving us to death."

"I thought that was the job of the French?" quips a gentlemen in
the group, a striking officer stationed on the Isla de Léon. Lolita recognizes him from one of the few social gatherings she frequents, hosted
by her godmother Doña Conchita Solís. The officer is her nephew and
his name is Lorenzo Virués. He is from Huesca. A Captain of Engineers.

"Never mind the French," jokes cousin Toño, "I've tasted those
seafood savories, and I can tell you, the enemy is within!"

More laughter. Cousin Toño rattles off one quip after another and
his laugh—uninhibited as a child's—booms around this corner of the
room. Aside from Toño, the person laughing loudest, shaking her ring-
lets, is Curra Vilches, Lolita Palma's closest friend: small, pretty, her
fine, slightly ample figure elegantly set off this evening by a Turkish
shawl tied about the bust of her crêpe de Chine dress. She is married to
a merchant of excellent position who travels constantly but allows her
a considerable degree of social freedom, and her mischievous high-

spiritedness makes her a perfect foil for cousin Toño. She and Lolita have known each other since they attended classes at Doña Rita's Academy for Young Ladies and spent summer holidays in Chiclana between the pine groves and the sea. They also share confidences, loyalty and boundless affection.

"Another drink, Lolita?" offers Captain Virués.

"Please. A lemonade, if you would be so kind."

The officer heads off in search of a waiter while cousin Toño explains to the ladies that the Holy Office*—whose abolition is even now being debated at San Felipe Neri—is opposed to fly fronts in men's breeches, preferring square panels with two sets of buttons.

"A precept which I strictly observe myself. As you can see, ladies, I am not about to brave the fires of hell for a little matter of four buttons."

The comment, delivered with his usual flair, sets off more laughter and fluttering fans. Smiling, Lolita Palma glances around the room. There are a number of cassocks. A group of gentlemen, with no ladies present, are sitting chatting at a table. Lolita Palma knows almost all of them. Most of them are young, members of the reformist group who have acquired a reputation as free-thinkers or liberals, among them a number of members of the Cortes: the eminent Agustín Argüelles, the leader of the group, and José María Quiepo de Llano, Count of Toreno, who, though still little more than a boy, is the delegate for Asturias. Next to them is the eminent man of letters Quintana, the poet Francisco Martínez de la Rosa—a handsome youth with large eyes and something of the gypsy about him—young Antoñete Alcalá Galiano, the son of a brigadier who died at Trafalgar and whom Lolita has known since she was a girl, and Ángel Saavedra, Duque de Rivas, a captain who turns the heads of ladies not merely with his rugged good looks, his officer's stripes and his Suvorov boots, but because, having been injured at the battle of Ocaña, he sports a scar on his forehead where he was slashed by a bayonet. Further away, surrounded by offi-

---

* The Spanish Inquisition.

cers and adjutants are Governor Villavicencio, Lieutenant General
Cayetano Valdés, commander of the *Fuerzas Sútiles*—the coastal surveillance in the bay, and Generals Blake and Castellanos. General Lapeña, still incensed with the English, is nowhere to be seen. Among the
sea of uniforms those of the Volunteer Officers stand out, being gar-
ishly colored with elaborate piping, the number of medals and ribbons
they wear seemingly in inverse proportion to their proximity to the
front lines. As for the women, it is easy to distinguish the ladies of
Cádiz from the wealthy or aristocratic immigrants: the latter still wear
high-waisted dresses in the French style whereas the former favor discreet necklines and muted colors in the English fashion. Some of the
older *émigrées* still wear their hair short at the back with a fringe of
kiss-curls, a style known as "the guillotine" that no one in Cádiz has
worn for some time.

Lolita Palma, for her part, is dressed soberly as always. Tonight she
has eschewed her usual black and gray in favor of a low-waisted light-
blue dress with a fitted bodice and a mantilla of gold lace over her
shoulders. Her hair is swept back and held in place by two small silver
combs. As for jewelry, she is wearing only a family cameo pendant set
in gold. She rarely attends receptions of this kind unless she has some
pressing business reason. As indeed she does this evening. The English
ambassador's invitation arrived just as Palma e Hijos were bidding to
secure the contract to ship beef from Morocco for the British troops.
In such circumstances, it seemed sensible to show her face, even if she
plans to leave early.

Captain Virués comes back, followed by a servant bearing a glass of
lemonade on a tray. Fernández Cuchillero, who has just received a letter from his family in Buenos Aires, is talking about events in Argentina, where the revolutionary Junta has just refused to recognize the
authority of the Regency. As Lolita takes the glass and thanks the officer for his kindness, she is shocked to see Don Emilio Sánchez Guinea
arriving with his son Miguel, both wearing black tailcoats, together
with the sailor Lobo, dressed in a blue jacket with gold buttons and a
corsair's white breeches. She feels vaguely unsettled by the presence of

this man, and not for the first time. She does not know why the Sánchez Guineas have brought him here tonight. He is, after all, merely a junior partner, an underling. Little more than a hired hand.

"Well, well," says Captain Virués, who has followed her gaze. "Look who we have here . . . the man from Gibraltar."

Lolita turns to the officer, surprised.

"Do you know him?"

"A little."

"Why do you say Gibraltar?"

Virués pauses a moment and when he finally replies, there is a curious smile on his lips.

"We were both imprisoned there in 1806."

"Together?"

"We were not what you might call friends."

Lolita Palma cannot fail to notice the cutting tone of this remark, but she has no wish to seem indiscreet or unusually interested. Virués has rejoined the general conversation. From the sofa, Lolita watches as Sánchez Guinea greets the ambassador and a number of the guests and then, seeing her, starts across the room, his son Miguel and the corsair following two steps behind. Driven by an impulse she does not quite understand, she gets to her feet and goes to meet him. The fact is, she does not wish their encounter to be witnessed by her companions, by Captain Virués with his curious smile.

"You look magnificent, Lolita. If only your father were here to see you."

They exchange affectionate pleasantries. Miguel Sánchez Guinea, polite and handsome, though a little short, and the image of his father, comes to greet her. Captain Lobo hangs back, watching the scene, and when Lolita finally looks at him, he greets her with a curt nod, without stepping forward or uttering a word. Taking Don Emilio by the arm, Lolita draws him aside, and drops her voice to a whisper.

"How could you even think of bringing that man here?"

The old merchant attempts to explain himself. Pépé Lobo works for him and indeed her. This is a perfect opportunity to introduce him to a number of English and Spanish contacts who might prove useful in the task at hand. It is always a good idea to oil the hinges of a few doors to ensure they do not squeak. That is how business is done in Cádiz.

"For the love of God, Don Emilio, the man is a corsair."

"Indeed he is. One in whom you have invested just as I have. You have as much of an interest in this venture as I do."

"But bringing him to this reception . . . Be reasonable. There is a time and a place for everything."

She glances around uneasily as she says this. Sánchez Guinea stares at her.

"You're worried about what people will say?"

"Of course."

"I can't say I understand your reservations. He is a sailor like any other. Though I'll grant you he is willing to take greater risks than most."

"Yes . . . for money."

"Just like you, *hija*. Or me. Money is as honorable a motive as any in this city."

Lolita Palma glances over Don Emilio's shoulder. A few feet away, standing next to Miguel Sánchez Guinea, the captain of the corsair is studying the tray of drinks offered by a liveried manservant. After a moment he shakes his head. When he looks up, his eyes meet hers and she turns away.

"You like this man. You told me as much."

"Yes, I do. And Miguel likes him. He is honest and capable. His job requires trust. That is how you should see him."

"Well, I do not like him at all."

The merchant looks at her quizzically. "Truly? At all?"

"I have said so."

"Yet you still invested with us."

"That is a different matter. I invested with *you*, as I've often done in the past."

"Then trust me as you did in the past. I have never steered you wrong before." Sánchez Guinea takes her hand and pats it gently. "It's not as though I'm suggesting you invite him home for hot chocolate."

Lolita gently but firmly removes her hand.

"This is an impertinence, Don Emilio."

"No, *hija*. I only say it because I am fond of you. That's why I don't understand your reaction."

When Miguel Sánchez Guinea comes over to join the conversation, they change the subject. Still the corsair keeps his distance. From time to time, Lolita Palma glances at him as he moves around the room, hands clasped behind his back, looking relaxed and vaguely distant. A little out of place, perhaps . . . Though this, Lolita quickly realizes, is simply her imagination, for when she looks back he is chatting easily with people he did not know a moment earlier.

"Your Captain Lobo is quick to make friends," she says to Miguel Sánchez Guinea.

He smiles as he lights a cigar.

"That's why he came. He's not one to feel like a fish out of water here, or anywhere for that matter. If he fell overboard, he would probably sprout gills and fins."

"Your father tells me he's won you over."

Miguel exhales a plume of smoke and laughs. He and Lolita have known each other since they were children. They played together among the pine trees of Chiclana, in the grounds of their parents' summer houses. She is godmother to his eldest son.

"He is a man through and through," Miguel says, "like men were in the old days."

"And a good sailor?"

"The best I know." Miguel stops sucking on his cigar for a moment and jabs it in the direction of the corsair, who is now chatting to one of General Valdés's adjutants. "He's a confident so-and-so who would remain calm in the middle of a thunderstorm with the coast to leeward and the masts in danger of being swept overboard . . . If luck favors him, he'll make a fine corsair."

"I believe he spent time in Gibraltar."

"He has been there many times. Once, years ago, as a prisoner of the English."

"What happened?"

"He escaped. Right under their noses. Stole a boat."

Around them people come and go, greeting one another, talking about the state of the war and of business—two subjects that seem inextricably linked. Lolita Palma is one of the few women who is happy to join in such conversations—something that invariably intrigues foreigners. Though, as is her way, she is circumspect: listening attentively and reserving her judgment even when it is sought. She and the Sánchez Guineas spend some time chatting to acquaintances about business, listening as they express their concern over the insurrection in the Americas, the revolution and the blockade in Buenos Aires, the loyalty of Cuba, the confusion created by the situation in Spain which has left the coast clear for fortune hunters to fish in troubled waters. The price that, sooner or later, the English will have to pay for their alliance in the war in Spain.

"Excuse me, gentlemen, I am a little tired, I think perhaps it is time I thought about leaving."

She withdraws to the powder room for a moment to freshen up. When she comes back, she discovers Captain Lobo standing directly in her path as she makes her way back to the group from which she can hear the booming laugh of cousin Toño. By an association of ideas, Lolita assumes that the corsair has moved—there is no such thing as chance in such maneuvers—in the way a ship might change tack to intercept another: reckoning its position at a given moment and carefully, patiently, lying in wait. He looks like a man skilled in such calculations.

"I wanted to thank you."

"For what?"

"For investing in the venture."

It is the first time she has seen him up close, spoken to him. A month ago, in her office on the Calle del Baluarte, they saw each other only for a moment, and Sánchez Guinea was present. Suspicious, Lolita Palma wonders if the old merchant or his son has suggested the sailor engineer this meeting.

"I don't know whether you're aware," he adds, "that we ship out in a week."

"I know. Don Emilio told me."

"And he told me that you have a low opinion of corsairs."

Candid, with a soft smile. Faintly impudent without being unseemly or rude. Gills, as Miguel said earlier; if he fell overboard he'd sprout gills and fins.

"Señor Sánchez Guinea talks too much sometimes. But I don't see how this would affect your duties."

"It does not affect them. But it would perhaps be useful for me to explain to you precisely what my duties are."

Close up, his face is not disagreeable though it lacks grace. The nose is large, the profile rough-hewn. Lolita notices a diagonal scar, half-hidden by his whiskers and his collar, that runs across his left ear into the hairline. His eyes are a brilliant green, like a freshly washed grape.

"I am perfectly aware of your responsibilities," she answers. "I was raised in a family that dealt with ships and with cargo, and more than once my family's business was put at risk by men of your ilk."

"Spanish, I assume?"

"Spanish or English, what difference does it make? In my opinion a corsair is little more than a pirate with a Letter of Marque from the king."

He does not rise to the bait, she notes. Nothing. His pale green eyes gaze at her coolly. In this light, she thinks, he looks like a cat.

"But surely the reason you invested was to make a profit?" His smile tempers the objection.

The sailor's speech is careful rather than well educated. It betokens a certain basic but limited level of schooling. Lolita detects a humble family origin in that voice, and in the singularly virile traits of this man. *Virile*, she thinks, is the apposite word. He looks like a strapping peasant farmer, the sort who spends his days laboring in the fields, or a tavern brawler, all cigar smoke, sweat and knives. Indeed, she thinks uneasily, he could well be the latter. It is not difficult to imagine him in one of the seedy bars between the Puerta de Tierra and the Puerta de Mar, or the bawdy houses near La Caleta. This, at least, Emilio Sánchez Guinea warned her about. Even his forthright gaze is not that of a gentleman, nor anyone who might claim to be a gentleman.

"My reasons are my affair, Captain. I would rather not discuss them with you."

The corsair falls silent for a moment, but still he continues to stare at her. His face is serious. "Listen, señora . . . Or would you prefer me to call you señorita?"

"Señora, if you would be so kind."

"Listen. You and Don Emilio have invested money in our cutter, money you could have invested elsewhere. I have invested as much as I have. If anything should go wrong, you will lose only your investment."

"You are forgetting our reputation as shipowners . . ."

"Perhaps. But reputations can be recovered. You are well placed should it come to that. I, however, would be lost with the ship."

Lolita shakes her head slowly, holding the man's gaze.

"I fail to see the point of this conversation. This need you have to explain things to me."

For the first time the man seems uncomfortable. Only for a moment. Only slightly; he wears his discomfort like a badly tailored suit. A well-tailored suit, in his case, Lolita thinks unkindly. Pépé Lobo looks at his hands—broad, powerful, the nails clipped short—and then turns and quickly glances around the room. Lolita Palma suddenly realizes that, though it has been carefully brushed and the lapels pressed, the jacket he is wearing is the one with the frayed sleeves he wore to her office on the Calle del Baluarte. The shirt, too, though freshly laundered and starched, is raveling a little at the collar over the black silk tie. For some inexplicable reason, this makes her think of him more kindly. Though perhaps "kindly" is excessive, maybe even dangerous. She racks her brain for the right word. She *softens* toward him—that will do. She feels more relaxed.

"To be honest, I'm not entirely sure," the sailor replies. "I've always been a man of few words . . . But for some reason I don't understand, I feel compelled to explain things."

"To me?"

"To you."

Lolita, who is still feeling a little embarrassed, is almost relieved to find herself irritated once more. "You feel the need to explain things? To me? . . . Captain, I fear you're getting a little above your station."

Another silence. Now the corsair is looking at her thoughtfully. He has probably killed many men, she thinks suddenly, probably looked at them with the same cold-blooded, catlike eyes.

"I won't trouble you any further," he says abruptly. "Forgive me for intruding, Doña Dolores . . . or should I address you as Señora Palma?"

She stands bolt upright, gently tapping her fan against her palm to hide her embarrassment. Embarrassed to find herself embarrassed. At her age. She is the owner of the firm Palma e Hijos.

"You may address me however you wish, as long as you do so with respect."

The man gives a slight nod and turns to leave but then pauses for an instant. He still seems deep in thought. At length, he raises a hand as though suing for peace.

"If all goes to plan we sail next Tuesday," he says, his voice almost a whisper. "Perhaps it might interest you to take a tour of the *Culebra* beforehand. With Don Emilio and Miguel, obviously."

Unruffled, Lolita Palma holds his gaze. She does not blink. "Why might it interest me? I have been aboard a cutter before."

"Because it is your boat too. And it would be interesting for my crew to know that one of their employers—if that is the word—is a woman."

"What purpose would it serve?"

"It's difficult to explain . . . Let's just say you never know when certain things might prove useful."

"I would rather not meet your crew."

The word "your" gives the corsair pause for thought. After a moment, he shrugs. He is smiling vaguely now, as though he were already elsewhere. "They are also your crew. And they might well make you rich."

"You are mistaken, Señor Lobo. I am already rich. Good evening."

Striding away from the corsair, she goes to bid good night to the Sánchez Guineas, Fernández Cuchillero, Curra Vilches and lastly cousin Toño, who offers to escort her home, but she declines. "You stay with your friends," she says. "It is only a short walk."

In the cloakroom, as she is collecting her cape, she encounters Lorenzo Virués. The officer is also leaving because, as he explains, he has to be back on the Isla de Léon by first light. Together, they go down the front steps and out into the street, through the crowd of inquisitive neighbors gathered around the caleches. The officer gallantly walks on her left, wearing his bicorn, his cape over his shoulders and his sword under one arm. They are headed in the same direction, and Captain Virués is surprised to discover she is walking home alone.

"I live only a few streets away," says Lolita, "and this is my city."

The night is still and pleasant. A little chilly. Their footsteps ring out on the narrow cobbled streets. A few votive lamps illuminate the shrine to the Virgin on the corner of Calle Consulado Viejo where a nightwatchman, carrying his pike and lantern, recognizes Lolita and, noticing her companion's uniform, doffs his hat.

"Good evening, Doña Lolita."

"Thank you, Pedro. Good evening to you."

"From the terraces of Cádiz tonight," explains Captain Virués, "you can see the comet everyone has been talking about as it streaks across the skies of Andalucía. Those who claim to know about such things say it portends great turmoil and catastrophe in Spain and Europe. Not that a man would need much knowledge of the dark arts to recognize that. With everything that has been happening."

"What happened in Gibraltar?"

"Excuse me?"

There is a brief silence. Nothing but the sound of footsteps. Lolita Palma's house is close at hand now and she knows she does not have much time.

"Captain Lobo," she explains.

"Ah."

A few more steps without a word. Lolita is walking slowly now and Virués matches his pace to hers.

"You were there together, you told me. You and Captain Lobo. Prisoners."

"That's right," Virués admits. "I was captured during an English raid on a line of trenches we were attempting to open up between the Torre del Diablo and the fortress at Santa Barbara. I was wounded and taken to a military hospital on the Rock."

"Good Lord. Was it serious?"

"Not really." Virués raises his right arm and twists his wrist. "As you can see, they patched me up pretty well. There wasn't much damage, no infection, and no need to amputate. Three weeks later I was allowed to wander the streets of Gibraltar. I was on parole, waiting for an exchange of prisoners to be made."

"And that's where you met Captain Lobo?"

"Yes. That's where I met him."

The officer's tale is brief: bored officers killing time, forced to live off the charity of the English or what little provisions they received from the Spanish side, waiting for the end of the war or for a prisoner exchange that would see them back with their own troops. Even so, they were a privileged category of prisoner, compared to the ordinary soldiers and sailors locked up in jails or brigs, for whom the chances of being sent home were remote. Among the twenty or so officers permitted to move about freely, having given their word of honor not to escape, were officers from the Army and the Armada and also a number of the captains of captured corsairs. This group included only those with a captain's license who had skippered vessels of a certain size and tonnage. There were two or three of them, including Pépé Lobo. He kept himself to himself and did not fraternize with the officers. He seemed more comfortable hanging around with the people on the docks.

"Women of ill repute and so forth?" inquires Lolita Palma lightly.

"More or less. He frequented insalubrious places, certainly."

"But that is not the reason you despise him."

"I never said that I despised the man."

"True. Shall we say you do not like him? That you look down on him?"

"I have my reasons."

They turn into the Calle del Baluarte. As they reach the Palma house, Lolita places her hand on the captain's arm. She has decided to stop beating about the bush. "I cannot let you go without telling me what transpired in Gibraltar between you and Captain Lobo."

"Why are you so interested in this man?"

"He works for an associate of mine . . . and for me, in a manner of speaking."

"I see."

Virués, head bowed, stares thoughtfully at his boots. Then he looks up again.

"Nothing happened between us then," he says. "In fact we barely spoke to one another . . . As I said, he had little time for the company of Spanish officers. Strictly speaking, he was not one of us."

"But he escaped?"

The captain says nothing, makes a vague gesture. He is uncomfortable. Lolita concludes that Lorenzo Virués is not a man to talk about others behind their backs. Or not excessively so.

"Despite the fact that he had given his word," she adds.

There is another brief silence and then Virués nods. "Lobo had indeed given his word. This was why he, like the others, was permitted to move about freely in Gibraltar. And he took advantage of that fact. One dark moonless night, he and two of his men—who had been assigned to a forced work detail down on the docks and whose freedom he bought by bribing the guards, one of whom, a Maltese, deserted and went with them—swam out to a tartane moored offshore, weighed anchor, hoisted the sail and, with a strong easterly wind, made it to the Spanish coast."

"An ugly business," admits Lolita. "After all, he had given his word of honor. I can imagine you were not happy . . ."

"It was not simply that. During the escape, a man was killed and another wounded. One of them, the guard working with the Maltese, was stabbed. And the sailor who was guarding the tartane when Lobo and his men boarded was later found in the sea with his head staved in . . . This meant that the few of us who were free had our parole revoked and we were locked up in the Moorish Castle. I spent seven weeks there before I was sent back in an exchange of prisoners."

Lolita Palma pushes back the hood of her cape. They are standing in the doorway of her house, lit by two lanterns set out by Rosas, the steward, in readiness for the señora's return. Virués doffs his hat, and with a click of his heels, takes his leave. "It has been a pleasure to walk with you," he says. "Might I ask leave to call on you from time to time?" The captain is a genial man, Lolita thinks. He inspires confidence. And trust. If he were a merchant, she would do business with him.

"Have you seen him since then?"

Virués, who was about to put on his hat again, pauses.

"No, but a young comrade, a lieutenant in the artillery, came across him in Algeciras not long ago and wanted to challenge him to a duel . . . Lobo simply laughed in the man's face and sent him packing. He refused to fight."

Lolita can picture the scene perfectly, and despite herself is almost amused. "He does not seem to be a coward to me."

She cannot help but smile to herself. Noticing her smile, the captain frowns, bows deeply and clicks his heels again with excessive formality. Ramrod-straight, contemptuous of the man they are discussing.

"I don't believe he is. In my opinion, his decision not to fight has little to do with bravery. It was more a matter of insolence . . . The word *honor* means nothing to individuals of that kind. But such are the men of today, I fear . . . they are very much of their time. And of times to come."

Two and three-tenth miles away, his cape over his shoulders and one eye pressed to the eyepiece of the Dolland achromatic telescope, Captain Simon Desfosseux observes the lights in the mansion where the English ambassador is holding his reception. Thanks to the carrier pigeons and the information he has gleaned from sailors and bootleggers, the captain knows that tonight Wellesley, the Anglo-Hispanic High Command and the cream of Cádiz society are celebrating the French rout at Chiclana. The powerful lenses of the spyglass make it easy for Desfosseux to locate the building, lit up like an affront against the black lines of the ramparts, ringed by the sea, on which he can make out the vague outline of anchored boats against a sliver of crescent moon.

"Three point five should be enough compensation. Elevation: forty-four . . . Try and set it up for me here, Bertoldi. There's a good lad."

Sitting on a trunk next to him, the firing tables spread out beneath a dim lantern, Lieutenant Bertoldi completes his calculations; he gets to his feet and descends the wooden steps to the redoubt where, in the glow from the torches blazing at the other end of the rampart, he can see the great, black, cylindrical mouth of Fanfan. The 10-inch mortar, trained on its target, is waiting only for Bertoldi to communicate his final corrections to its operators. Taking his eye from the spyglass, Desfosseux looks up and glances at a white blot on the sky's vast expanse of black: the windsock hoisted on a flagstaff next to the observation deck. It flaps gently in the wind, last observed as indicating a fresh breeze from south-southeast. Hence the correction factor of 3.5, to compensate for the crosswind. It could be worse, obviously, but tonight he had hoped for a gentler crosswind or—since he is dreaming of the sort of ideal conditions that would have an artilleryman rubbing his hands with pyrotechnical glee—a strong, steady, following wind from east-southeast, a gift from the god Mars. When it blows, it is possible to create straight lines and almost perfect parabolas, with minimal corrections of zero-point-something. Sheer joy for an artilleryman, an intoxication of powder and cannonfire. Pure glory. It would add a few precious additional *toises* guaranteeing greater range and accuracy across the bay. All these are factors which Desfosseux, a consummate artilleryman, longs for—most especially this evening, since they would favor his plan to put in an appearance at the English ambassador's reception. This is what he and the men are doing here at ten o'clock, having missed their dinner: fine-tuning the mortar.

After a final look through the telescope, Desfosseux clambers down from the observation deck and heads for the redoubt. There, behind the bank of earth designed to protect the gun emplacement, the 10-inch Villantroys-Ruty has pride of place in the middle of its own large rectangular entrenchment; the dark, ominous barrel is raised at an angle to the huge two-wheeled gun carriage capable of supporting 7,371 pounds of bronze. It is trained on Cádiz using the calculations Lieutenant Bertoldi has just given the artillerymen. By the torchlight, he can see the men are sweating, their faces haggard. The company comprises a sergeant, two corporals and eight hollow-eyed, unkempt, unshaven soldiers. The Fanfan boys. All of them, including the NCO—an irritable, mustachioed man from the Auvergne named Labiche—are dressed in garrison caps, their capes unbuttoned and dirty, their gaiters spattered with dry mud. Unlike the officers, who can sleep outside the compound or enjoy the pleasures of Puerto Real and El Puerto de Santa María, they live like moles, constantly moving between ramparts, barbettes and trenches, sleeping under wooden boards piled with earth to protect them from the Spanish firing from their advance post at Puntales.

"Just one moment, Captain," says Bertoldi, "and I'll be with you."

Desfosseux watches the artillerymen work. The operation they are carrying out tonight with Fanfan is one they have performed many times using 12-inch Dedon and 8-inch Villantroys howitzers: to them this is routine—handspike, ladle, linstock, one pace back, mouth open to ensure the blast does not burst the eardrums. To Labiche and his grubby squad, it does not matter a fig whether they are aiming at the English ambassador's reception or at his mother's petticoats. Sooner or later, they either succeed or fail to hit their target; the non-com and the soldiers will go back to their lice-infested blankets and tomorrow morning will be served the same scant rations with foul, watered-down wine. Their one consolation is being based in a garrison where the enemy's strengths have been gauged, where the risks are known and are more or less reasonable, unlike other places in Spain where troop movements expose men to bloody battles and dangerous encounters with gangs of *guerrilleros*. It is true that elsewhere the dangers sometimes have their compensations, opportunities to loot and pillage, to fill your knapsack during raids, marches and overnight billets, whereas in the area around Cádiz, where thousands of French, Italians, Poles and Germans have descended like a plague of locusts—the Germans, as always, are particularly brutal to the local population—there is nothing left to pillage. It would be a different matter if the city, which is as rich as they come, were to finally surrender. But no one has any illusions about that.

"Thirty pounds exactly, Labiche?"

The sergeant, who snapped to attention when Desfosseux appeared, spits a plug of tobacco to the floor, picks his nose and nods. The thirty pounds of powder have been loaded into the breech and the barrel is angled at precisely 44 degrees, based on the corrections provided by Bertoldi. The hollow iron shell, weighing 80 pounds, is filled with lead, sand and only a third of the usual powder charge, with a special fuse fashioned from wood and tinplate in which the oakum burns—or should burn—for 35 seconds. Sufficient time for the internal fuse still to be burning on impact.

"Did you solve the problem with the bush pin?"

Labiche, who is fiddling with his mustache, takes a moment to answer. The copper cylinder which carries the flame to the mortar charge has a tendency to unscrew itself every time it is fired because of the enormous force required to fire the projectile from the barrel. This ends up enlarging the borehole in the breech and reducing the distance obtained.

"I think so, Captain," he says finally, as though still unsure. "We screwed it in cold. I think it'll work fine, but I can't guarantee anything."

Desfosseux looks round the faces of the men and smiles.

"I hope so. Tonight, the *manolos* are having a party in Cádiz. What do you say we liven it up a little?"

The quip barely raises a weak smile. Slides off the greasy skin and sunken eyes. It is obvious that Labiche and his thugs leave enthusiasm to the officer class. They don't care whether the shell reaches its destination or not, whether it kills many, few, or none. All they want is to be done for the night, get something to eat and go back to their bunks to get their heads down.

The captain takes his watch from his waistcoat pocket and checks it.

"Fire in three minutes."

Bertoldi, who is standing near him, consults his own watch. Then he nods, says, "Yes, sir," and turns to the artillerymen.

"Labiche, take the linstock. Everyone to their posts."

Simon Desfosseux snaps shut his watch, slips it into his pocket and carefully goes back up to the observation deck, trying not to trip in the dark and break his leg. That would not be funny. When he gets to the top, he throws his cape round his shoulders, presses his right eye to the telescope and looks at the brightly lit building in the distance. Then he stands up again and waits. How wonderful it would be, he thinks, as he drums his fingernails softly on the copper telescope, if Fanfan sang a perfect note tonight, a deep booming *doh*, crashing through the windows at the English ambassador and his guests with 80 pounds of steel, lead and powder—and with *feeling*. Greetings from the Duc de Belluno, from the Emperor, and from Simon Desfosseux for the role he played.

Ba-boom. The explosion causes the whole observation deck to shudder, temporarily deafening the captain. One eye still open—he closed the other so as not to be blinded by the flash—he sees the fleeting flare light up everything around, sketching out the ramparts, the nearby barracks, the observation deck and the shore by the black expanse of the bay. It lasts barely a second and then everything is dark again, by which time Desfosseux already has his other eye glued to the telescope, focusing it on the point he is trying to observe. Seven, eight, nine, ten, he counts, not moving his lips. In the circular field of the telescope, wavering slightly because of the distance, the lights in the building at which Fanfan is aimed cast a glow against the blurred outlines of the masts of the boats anchored close by. His count has reached seventeen. Eighteen. Nineteen. Twenty. Twenty-one.

A black plume, a jet of spray and foam half the height of the masts rises in the center of the lens, momentarily obscuring the illuminated building on the mainland. Not enough range, the captain thinks gloomily, with the irritation of someone who has bet on one card only for another to appear. Though the calculations were perfect with regard to the aim, the bomb dropped into the sea, having barely reached 2,000 *toises*—a distance that, given the work and the calculations they have put in, is ridiculous. Perhaps the wind over the target was different; or perhaps, as has happened before, the projectile left the barrel too soon, before all the powder had time to ignite. Or the bush pin has come loose again. Desfosseux decides to leave any further thoughts until later, as a series of flashes appear in the embrasures of the fort at Puntales: the Spanish artillery are returning their nocturnal greetings, firing at the Trocadero. He dashes down, then hurries for the nearest casemate—taking rather less care than he did on his way up—just as the first Spanish grenade splits the night above his head and explodes fifty *toises* away, between Cabazuela and the fort at Matagorda. Thirty seconds later, huddled in the shelter with Bertoldi, Labiche and the artillerymen, in the greasy light of an oil lamp, Desfosseux feels the ground, the timber walls and the roof shudder under the hail of Spanish fire. The imperial cannons at Fort Luis respond in a fierce artillery duel fought from opposite shores.

Out of the corner of his eye, the captain sees sergeant Labiche spit a plug of tobacco on the floor, between his crudely darned gaiters.

"It was hardly worth it," grunts the NCO, winking at one of his companions. "Waking them up at this hour."

CHAPTER FIVE

The white queen retreats in disgrace, seeking the protection of a knight whose own position is far from safe—two black pawns are prowling with malicious intent. Stupid game. There are days when Rogelio Tizón loathes chess, and today is one of those days. With his king pinned, castling is an impossibility; already one rook and two pawns down, he plays on only out of respect for his adversary, Hipólito Barrull, who seems totally relaxed, enjoying himself thoroughly. As usual. The bloodbath on Tizón's left flank was triggered by his own foolish error: a pawn moved unthinkingly, a narrow opening and suddenly an enemy bishop piercing his home ranks like a dagger, which within a couple of moves has destroyed a Sicilian defense constructed with great patience and to little effect.

"I'm going to flay you alive, Comisario," Barrull laughs cheerfully, utterly ruthless.

As always, his tactic has been to lie in wait, like a spider at the center of its web, until his opponent makes a mistake, then pounce and tear him to pieces. Tizón, all too aware of what lies in store, hopelessly defends himself. There is little possibility that the professor will lower his guard now. He is always ruthless and precise in the endgame. A born executioner.

"Take that!"

A black pawn closes the circle. The knight's harried steed whinnies, searching for some way to bound from the circle and escape. Barrull's pitiless face, etched by countless hours spent frowning over books, widens beneath his spectacles into a boastful smile. As always when he is at the chessboard, his habitual courtesy gives way to an insolent, almost murderous brutality. Tizón looks up at the paintings that adorn the Café del Correo: nymphs, flowers, birds. There is no help to be found there. Resigned, he captures a pawn, thereby sacrificing his knight, which his opponent immediately takes with a grunt of jubilation.

"Let's stop there," pleads the policeman.

"Another game?" Barrull seems disappointed, his bloodlust not sated. "Don't you want to get your revenge?"

"I've had enough for today."

He gathers up the pieces and stows them in their box. The slaughter complete, Barrull returns to normal. Already, his long, equine face is almost friendly. In another minute, he will be his usual polite, affectionate self again.

"The more observant player always beats the more gifted," he offers his opponent by way of consolation. "It's simply a matter of being alert. Prudence and patience . . . Don't you agree?"

Tizón nods distractedly. He stretches his legs under the table, pushing his chair back against the wall, and looks at the people around them. Conversations, open newspapers, waiters cutting through the curtains of cigar and pipe smoke, carrying chocolate pots, coffee and glasses of cold water. Merchants, members of the Cortes, soldiers, immigrants wealthy and destitute, spongers looking for a free drink or a loan sit around tables or on the patio, coming and going from the billiard room and the reading room. The men of the city bask in late-afternoon indolence, winding down after the day. The café is a bustling hive with its fair share of drones and parasites, which the expert eye of the policeman can detect with a methodical glance.

"How are things going with the footprints in the sand?"

Barrull, who has taken out his snuffbox to take a pinch of snuff, follows Tizón's gaze. The clamor of battle between black and white now forgotten, his expression is kindly, serene.

"It's been quite some time since you mentioned the subject," he adds.

The policeman nods again, keeping his eyes on the crowd. For a moment, he says nothing, then scratches one of his sideburns gloomily.

"The murderer has been quiet for some time now."

"Maybe he's stopped killing," ventures Barrull.

Tizón shifts in his seat, doubtful.

"I honestly don't know," he confesses.

A long silence. The professor looks at Tizón thoughtfully.

"Blazes, Comisario, you almost seem disappointed that nothing has happened."

Tizón turns to look the old man in the eye, and Barrull's mouth forms an O as though he is about to whistle.

"Good God! That's it, isn't it? . . . If he doesn't kill again, you won't find any more clues. You're worried that the man who killed those poor wenches has grown frightened, or weary . . . You're worried that he will remain in the shadows and never be heard of again."

Tizón continues to stare at him blankly, saying nothing. Taking a crumpled kerchief from his pockets, Barrull flicks away the snuff he spilled on himself. Then he extends a forefinger, pointing it at the top button of the comisario's doublet like a pistol.

"It's as though you're afraid he won't kill again . . . afraid that chance will keep him from your clutches."

"There is something meticulous about him," the policeman says gravely. "Something precise. I don't think it has anything to do with chance."

Barrull gives this some thought.

"Interesting," he concludes, leaning back in his chair. "And there is something precise about his crimes. Perhaps he is a maniac?"

Tizón stares at the blank chessboard, at the pieces safely stowed in their box.

"Or perhaps he is playing a game?"

The question sounds naive from the lips of such a man. He immediately realizes this and feels uncomfortable, embarrassed. Barrull, for his part, gives a wary smile. He raises one hand a little, as though absolving himself of responsibility.

"Perhaps. I couldn't say. People are fond of games. Of challenges. But to murder in such a manner goes beyond a game . . . There are people whose instincts are like an animal's, triggered by certain things: by the sound of an explosion, by a feeling . . . Everyone knows that. I would say that this case borders on lunacy, but we know all too well that the limits of madness are not always clear."

He calls over a waiter, who refills their cups with two ounces of java and a fleck of foam. The coffee is excellent, very hot and aromatic—the best in all Cádiz. As he sips, Rogelio Tizón watches a group of men conversing on the far side of the patio. Among them is a suspicious immigrant—his father is in the service of the usurper king in Madrid—and a member of the Cortes whose mail the comisario has opened and read in secret, a precaution which, on the explicit orders of the General Intendant, applies to all members of parliament, civil and ecclesiastical. Tizón has a number of officers to perform this task.

"The murderer could be throwing down a challenge," says the policeman. "To the city. To life. To me."

Another curious look from Barrull. The policeman realizes that the professor is scrutinizing him, as though discovering something unexpected.

"I am unsettled by you taking this so personally. You . . . I mean . . ."

He allows the sentence to hang in the air, shaking his thick gray locks. He goes back to toying with his snuffbox. Eventually he sets it down on one of the black squares on the board, as though it were a chess piece.

"A challenge, you said," Barrull adds after a moment. "From his point of view, perhaps that is what it is. But this is pure speculation. We are building castles in the air . . . These are simply words."

Rogelio Tizón is still studying the patrons in the café. In Cádiz, there is no shortage of spies communicating with the French; one of them was garrotted yesterday at the castle of San Sebastián. As a result, orders have been given for tighter controls on immigrants, even those who claim to be refugees from the occupied territories, and all those without official papers are to be arrested. Though this will entail more work and more worry, it is exactly what Tizón wants: new arrivals, neighbors and the innkeepers who lodge them have seen a rise in official tariffs—and, consequently, in what is charged under the counter. This morning, the owner of a house on the Calle Flamencos Borrachos who was lodging foreigners with no official documents paid him 400 *reales* to avoid a fine of three times as much, and an immigrant, whose passport had been falsified using oxygenated muriatic acid, avoided jail and deportation by crossing his palm with two 100 *real* coins. This means that the comisario's total profit for today already amounts to 30 *pesos*, like thirty shining suns. A well-rounded day.

"Ajax," he says aloud.

Surprised, Hipólito Barrull looks at him over the rim of his coffee cup.

"We talked about similarities between this case and the manuscript you lent me," Tizón goes on. "The other day, reading it again, I found two lines running almost together that unsettled me. *O Woman, silence is the grace of woman*, and further on, *a mute grieving, with no loud wails, but groans, as of a lowing animal*."

Barrull, who has set his cup down on the table, is still staring at him curiously.

"Well?"

"The girls were gagged while they were being tortured—don't you see the connection?"

The professor shakes his head.

"What I see," he answers, "is that you are taking this too far. It has all the makings of an obsession. *Ajax* is merely a play. A coincidence."

"An astonishing coincidence, if it is one."

"You are making too much of this, letting your own ideas take over. I thought you more restrained . . . I'm beginning to regret lending you the manuscript."

There is a pause while Barrull ponders the matter with evident seriousness.

"It has to be coincidence," he concludes. "I don't believe the murderer could have read *Ajax*. It has not yet been published in translation in Spain . . . Or your murderer would have to be a very educated man. And there are not many of them around, even if we include the immigrants and those passing through. We would know the man."

"Perhaps we do know him."

This, the professor admits, cannot be ruled out. But it seems more likely it is mere chance. However, this does not stop Tizón connecting the two, drawing links, real or illusory, in his imagination. There are times when imagination makes it more difficult to analyze a situation dispassionately. As in chess, for example. Imagination may lead one along the right path, but sometimes it makes one go astray. Besides, it is wise to be wary of drawing on one's reserves of knowledge, of piling information onto the facts and obscuring them. More often than not, the simplest route is the most direct.

"The most remarkable thing about the case," he continues, "is not that this monster is murdering girls, or that he whips them to death, or that he does so near bomb sites . . . The most remarkable thing, Comisario, is that all these factors should come together. Do you understand? To go back to the chessboard, it is like a landscape—by studying the position of the various pieces, one can get an overall view of the situation. If we look at the pieces individually, we have no sense of the whole. Getting too close makes it difficult for the observer to evaluate."

Tizón gestures at the clamor and the bustle of the café.

"The city is a complicated place these days."

"It is not simply that. Cádiz is a collection of people, things and positions. And perhaps the murderer *sees* the city as a map on which a story is being played out. A map we cannot see . . . If you could, you might be able to anticipate his next move."

"Like in a game of chess?"

"Perhaps."

Thoughtfully, the professor picks up his snuffbox and slips it into his waistcoat pocket. He trails a nicotine-stained fingernail over the empty chess square.

"Perhaps," he adds, "you should keep a watch on the places where bombs explode."

"I am doing that," Tizón protests, "as much as I can. I have posted officers to every site that seems appropriate—without success. As far as we know, he has not tried again."

"Perhaps your vigilance has deterred him."

"I don't know. Maybe."

"Very well." Barrull adjust his spectacles. "Let us put forward a theory, Comisario. A hypothesis."

Slowly, pausing from time to time to marshal his thoughts, the professor fleshes out his theory. When the French bombs began to fall on the city, the murderer's complex mental world may have taken an unexpected turn. He may have been fascinated by the power of modern technology, the ability to fire bombs at distant targets.

"That would require a certain level of education," insists Tizón.

"Absolutely not. No education would be needed to trigger certain innate impulses or feelings. They exist in everyone. Your murderer could be a man of culture or a complete illiterate . . . Imagine we are dealing with a man who, realizing that some of the bombs do not kill anyone, decides to do their killing for them . . . This is a decision he could have arrived at through complex reasoning or sheer stupidity, but the result would be the same."

Barrull's face seems to light up as he speaks. Tizón watches as he leans forward, laying his hands on either side of the chessboard. This is the expression he always wears when playing chess.

"If the criminal impulse is a primitive one," the professor goes on, "solving the case could depend more on luck than on analysis; on the murderer killing again, making a mistake, on there being witnesses, or some other means of catching him in the act . . . Do you follow, Comisario?"

"I think so. You're suggesting that the more intelligent the murderer, the more vulnerable it makes him?"

"That is one possibility, and certainly one that would make your investigation easier. Such a scenario, however complex and perverse, even if it were the product of a diseased mind, would have a rational motive—a thread you could pull to unravel everything."

"So the more irrational the killer, the fewer the clues?"

"Exactly."

Tizón's gold tooth glitters. He is beginning to understand.

"The logic of horror . . ."

"Precisely. Imagine, for example, that the murderer—either by design or through some irresistible compulsion—wants to leave behind some testimonial linked to the bombs that have fallen. To pay homage to the technology, for example, by killing. Do you follow me? Imagine it's not so far-fetched: precision, technology, bombs and the crimes that connect them."

Barrull leans back, satisfied.

"What do you think?"

"Interesting. But unlikely. You forget you are talking to a dull, unsophisticated policeman. In my world, one plus one always makes two. Without those ones, there can be no total."

"We are simply indulging in fantasy, Comisario. It was your idea. These are words, nothing more—armchair theories. This is merely one possible theory: that the killer murders whenever bombs explode without killing anyone. Let's imagine that he does so with the intention of making good some flaw or deficiency in the technology. It would be fascinating, don't you think? Achieving something that science cannot achieve. This way he can reconcile the point of impact and human life . . . Do you like our hypothesis? We could conjure up half a dozen, some of them coherent, others completely contradictory. And none of them matters a jot."

Tizón, who has been listening carefully, chokes back the words that crowd into his mouth. These poor wretches who were flayed alive were real, he thinks. Their gaping wounds wept blood, their entrails reeked. They have nothing to do with these intellectual abstractions, this coffeehouse philosophizing.

"You think I am wrong to discount the possibility that it could be an educated man? A man of science?"

Barrull makes a vague, uneasy gesture; a wave that indicates he finds the issue too concrete. He did not claim to be so specific. But a moment later, he seems to relent.

"Culture and science do not always go hand in hand," he argues, staring at the blank chessboard. "In fact history has shown that they can move in opposite directions . . . But you're right. It is possible that our murderer has some understanding of technology. And who knows? Perhaps he even plays chess." He throws his arms wide to encompass the whole café. "Perhaps he is here, right now. Close at hand. Paying tribute to his methods."

SWELTERING HEAT. A blaze of light. A riot of people, barefoot or in sandals, people who have known each other all their lives, for whom privacy does not exist. Dark, almost Arabian eyes; skin tanned by sea and sun; youthful, merry voices with the clipped tones particular to the lowliest of classes in Cádiz. Squat tenement houses, women shouting from balcony to balcony, laundry set out to dry, cages with canaries, filthy urchins playing in the dirt of the narrow, unpaved streets. Crucifixes, Christs, Virgins and saints on glazed tiles or in alcoves on every street corner. The smell of the sea, the reek of oil and of every conceivable variety of fish—raw, fried, grilled, dried, salted, putrid—piles of fish heads and bones fought over by cats with greasy whiskers, their fur full of scabs and bald from mange. This is La Viña.

Turning left on the Calle de la Palma, Gregorio Fumagal takes the Calle San Félix and heads into the area of sailors and fishermen. He dodges and weaves, guided by sight, by smell, by hearing, through the empty spaces left in this motley and teeming world. He looks like an alert insect, twitching its antennae. Beyond the houses, looking like an open door or a bottle without a cork, the taxidermist can see part of the Explanada de Capuchinos and a fragment of the city walls near Vendaval, the embrasures with their cannons pointed toward the Atlantic. Fumagal pauses for a minute to remove his hat and mop the sweat from his brow, then walks on past the white, the blue, the ocher houses in search of shade. The fact that he is sweating is particularly unfortunate, since the new English dye he bought yesterday at Frasquito Sanlúcar's shop has begun to run, causing an unpleasant dark staining. His frockcoat is cumbersome, too, and weighs heavily on him; the silk kerchief knotted about his throat pinches more than usual. The sun is high now and the heat oppressive; in this part of the city there is hardly any breeze—the summer is mercilessly announcing its imminent arrival. In a place surrounded by water like Cádiz, where many streets are built perpendicular to each other to create a windbreak, the sweltering, airless heat can be overwhelming.

The Mulatto is at the appointed place, arriving just as Fumagal gets there. He does not seem to walk, but rather to dance, with graceful, measured steps to the rhythm of some primitive melody only he can hear. He is wearing sandals with no socks, no hat, short loose-fitting breeches, and his unbuttoned shirt is tied at the waist with a red band beneath a short, rather shabby waistcoat. His clothing is typical of fishermen and smugglers around here; the Mulatto is more of a smuggler. The grandson of slaves, he was born free and has a little boat that plies the waters, visiting the shores of both enemy and ally. His African blood—more evident in his features than his skin tone, which is a healthy, copper color—is what gives his movements their languid rhythm. Tall, athletic, pug-nosed with thick lips and frizzy hair and sideburns that are beginning to turn gray.

"A monkey," says the Mulatto. "Two feet tall. A fine specimen."

"Alive?"

"For the moment."

"I'm interested," says Fumagal. The two men have stopped in front of a little tavern typical of La Viña: a tiny bar behind a dark, narrow doorway, two large black barrels at the back, sawdust on the floor, a counter and two low tables. It smells strongly of coarse wine and of the olives in an earthenware pot that sits on a nearby cask. They carry on their conversation while the Mulatto orders two glasses of red wine and settles himself by the short counter—a sticky plank with a marble fountain and an engraving of the *guerrillero* known as *Empecinado* ("Bull-headed") hanging on the wall behind. The monkey, explains the Mulatto loud enough for everyone in the bar to hear, arrived on an American ship four days ago. It has a long tail and is as ugly as sin. A rare specimen, said the sailor who sold it to him—a macaque monkey from the East Indies. And fairly depressed, too: perhaps it got used to being in the ship, being at sea. It eats fruit, drinks a little water and spends its days in a cage, legs spread, rubbing its penis.

"I want it to be dead by the time I get it," says Fumagal. "No complications."

"No problem, señor. I'll handle it."

Having discussed the reason for the meeting within earshot of the barkeeper, the two men drain their glasses and leave, heading back to the esplanade overlooking the ramparts and the ocean, far from prying ears. As they walk, the Mulatto picks olives out of a hand callused from hauling oars and cables; every ten or twelve steps, he tilts his head back and, with a loud rasp of his lips, spits the pit as far as he can. As they reach the esplanade, he softly croons a little ditty that has been doing the rounds in Cádiz since March:

Three thousand damned gabachos
We killed in the battle of the Hog
And in revenge they bombed us
But the bomb only killed a dog.

His tone is as scornful as the words. And though he looks toward the ramparts and the ocean as he sings, the Mulatto seems distracted, as though he is thinking about something else. Gregorio Fumagal is irritated.

"Spare me that drivel," he says.

The other man looks at him, eyebrows raised in mock surprise, barely masking his insolence.

"It's not your fault," he says coolly.

"And spare me that, too. My faults are my own business."

"In that case, let's get down to brass tacks, if that suits you."

"If you don't mind. We're already running too many risks to stand around wasting time."

The bootlegger glances around with studied care. There is no one about. The nearest people to them are fifty paces away, a chain gang repairing the rampart, which is being eroded by the sea.

"Your friends asked me to tell you . . ."

"They are your friends too," Fumagal corrects him curtly.

"Fine." The Mulatto makes a vague gesture. "They're paying me, señor, if that's what you mean. Greasing my palm. My real friends are elsewhere."

"Spit it out. Say what you've got to say."

The other man half-turns and gestures toward the street and the city beyond. "They're trying to increase the range of the bombs fired from the Cabezuela. At least as far as the Plaza de San Francisco."

"They haven't managed to reach it yet."

This, the smuggler points out, is not his problem. It is their intention. Then he explains the plan: the cannonades will begin again in a week and the French artillery need a map of the exact locations where the bombs fall, with daily accounts of times and distances, detailing which of the bombs exploded and which did not—although most of them will contain no powder charge. They want Fumagal to calculate distances using the church steeple as a reference.

"I'll need more pigeons."

"I brought some back with me. Belgian, one year old. You'll find the baskets in the usual place."

The two men walk along the Plaza de Capuchinos. Behind the rampart, on the far side of the embrasures and the cannons, they can see the ocean, the coastline and the city walls curving gently toward the Puerta de Tierra and the unfinished dome of the new cathedral; beyond, shimmering in the heat haze, is the white sandy ribbon of the reef.

"When are you going over to the other side again?" asks Fumagal.

"I don't know. Truth is, things are getting pretty tangled. Most weeks, the sea patrols pick up someone crossing the bay without a valid permit. Immigration and espionage have got the authorities on the alert . . . You can't even bribe your way out of things anymore."

They walk a little further in silence, past the work detail of convicts, bare-chested men with kerchiefs tied around their heads, a slick of sweat glazing their scars and tattoos. Bayonets fixed, a group of soldiers in the short jackets and round hats of the Volunteer Corps are idly standing guard.

"A couple of days ago they garroted another spy," the Mulatto says out of the blue. "Fellow called Pizarro."

The taxidermist nods. He is aware of the fact, though not the details.

"Did you know him?"

"No, fortunately." He flashes a cynical smile. "Otherwise we wouldn't be taking this little stroll."

"Did he talk?"

"Now there's a question, señor. Everybody talks in the end."

"I suppose that if it came down to it, you would turn me in."

There is a brief, pregnant silence. Out of the corner of his eye, Fumagal notices a mocking smile on his companion's lips.

"What about you?"

The taxidermist takes off his hat to dab away the perspiration soaking through the sweatband. Confounded dye, he thinks, looking at his fingertips.

"It is less likely that I would be caught," he answers. "My life is unobtrusive. You are taking risks, out there with your boat."

"I'm a notorious smuggler: that's nothing special in Cádiz, everyone's involved in something shady. They don't garrote a man for smuggling round here . . . From that to suspecting me of spying is a big leap. That's why I never carry any papers"—the Mulatto taps his forehead— "it's all in here."

And of course, he continues, there is more to it than that. Their friends on the far shore want information about a floating platform that is being built, from which the Spanish plan to fire on the Trocadero. And about the work being carried out by the English at the redoubts at Sancti Petri, Gallineras Altas and Torregorda.

"That's a little beyond my scope."

"As you say, señor. I'm simply telling you what I was told. They're also very interested in any news about cases of malignant fevers in Cádiz . . . I think they hope the yellow fever will come back and people will start dropping like flies."

"That doesn't seem likely."

The smuggler gives another mocking smile. "Hope is always the last thing to go. Besides, the summer heat might help it along . . . And if there were an epidemic, supply ships would refuse to dock and things would turn ugly."

"I still think it's doubtful. The outbreak last year immunized most people. I don't think that will be the solution."

Seagulls wheel and shriek above the square, drawn ashore by the fishermen. People from the nearby houses lean out through the embrasures and fish, while the bored sentries who patrol the ramparts do nothing to stop them. Sea bream, snapper and sunfish dangle in the air, caught on hooks, or flounder and splash in wicker baskets or wooden crates. Rifles slung over their shoulders, the soldiers come over to see whether anything is biting, sharing a plug of tobacco or maybe a match with the fishermen. In spite of the war, Cádiz continues to live and let live.

"Our friends are asking about the townsfolk," says the Mulatto. "How they are, what they are saying. Whether the people of Cádiz are unhappy about the situation . . . I imagine they still believe the people will rise up, but it seems unlikely. It's not as though people are starving here. And on the Isla de León, where things are much worse and they're closer to the front lines, the Army has everything under control."

Gregorio Fumagal makes no comment. Sometimes he wonders exactly what cloud they are living on across the bay. Anyone who expects a popular uprising to further the imperial cause doesn't know Cádiz. The poor here are fanatically patriotic, passionately in favor of the war, and they support the liberal faction in the Cortes. Everyone in the city, from a captain general to a lowly shopkeeper, fears and flatters the townsfolk. No one lifted a finger when they dragged Governor Solano through the streets to the scaffold. And a few days ago, when a Royalist member of the Cortes expressed opposition to the seizure of assets belonging to the nobility, various mutineers and strumpets wanted to settle the score with him personally—to save his skin, the man had to take shelter aboard a ship belonging to the Royal Armada. One of the reasons it is forbidden to wear cloaks or capes when attending the debates at San Felipe Neri is to make sure the public cannot bring concealed weapons.

"I'm thinking about that poor fellow," remarks the Mulatto, "the one who was executed."

These words hang in the air as they walk another twenty paces in lugubrious silence. The smuggler sways on his long legs in the gentle dance that is his method of walking. Close to him, yet maintaining a certain distance, Gregorio Fumagal takes short, wary steps. His movements never seem automatic; each one is a conscious and deliberate act.

"I don't like to think about it," the Mulatto adds. "The garrotte around his neck, three twists to tighten it round his throat, his tongue sticking out . . . What about you?"

"Stop talking rubbish."

As they reach the Convento de los Descalzos, they encounter a group of women striding gaily across the square carrying pitchers of water. One of them is very young. Embarrassed, Fumagal reaches up and touches his hair to see whether the dye is still running. Looking at his fingertips, he sees that it is. This makes him feel even more filthy. And grotesque.

"I don't think I'll be doing this much longer," the Mulatto says suddenly. "Better to jump out of the net before it's hauled on board with me inside . . . If you play with fire . . ."

He falls silent again, studying Fumagal.

"Are you really taking these risks for the fun of it? For free?"

The taxidermist says nothing and keeps walking. When he removes his hat again to mop the sweat, he notices that his kerchief is wet and dirty. This is going to be a difficult summer, he thinks. In every possible sense.

"Don't forget the monkey."

"What?"

"My macaque monkey from the East Indies."

"Oh, yes . . ." the smuggler peers at him, slightly unsettled, "the monkey."

"I'll send someone to fetch it this afternoon. Dead, as agreed . . . How were you planning to do it?"

The Mulatto shrugs. "Uh, I don't know . . . Poison, I suppose. Or maybe I'll strangle it."

"I'd prefer the latter," the taxidermist says coldly. "Certain substances compromise the preservation of the body. Whatever you do, make sure the skin is unblemished."

"Sure," the Mulatto says, staring at the black bead of sweat trickling down Gregorio Fumagal's forehead.

FRIDAY AFTERNOON. SAILCLOTH suspended from the floor above puts the patio in shade; large planters of ferns and geraniums, rocking chairs and wicker seats are set around the edge of the pond, creating a cool and pleasant ambiance. Lolita Palma takes a sip of maraschino liqueur and sets the glass down on a doily on the table, next to the silver service and the bottles of liqueurs. She bends over her mother to plump the cushions on her armchair. Haughty, garbed in black, with her hair gathered into a lace cap and a rosary lying on the shawl covering her lap, Manuela Ugarte—Tomás Palma's widow—presides over the little family get-together, as she does every afternoon when she feels able to get out of bed. It is visiting time here in the house on the Calle del Baluarte. In attendance is Cari Palma, Lolita's sister, with her husband, Alfonso Solé. Also present are Amparo Pimentel, an elderly widower who is almost one of the family, Curra Vilches and cousin Toño, a regular visitor at this hour and any other.

"You are not going to believe this," he says. "Have you heard the latest?"

"If it's about Cádiz, I'll believe anything," says Curra Vilches.

With his customary easy manner, cousin Toño tells his story. The recent military recruitment drive, expected to swell the Army's numbers with hundreds of men from the first category of recruits—bachelors, and those married men and widowers without children—has been abandoned: barely five out of ten have been called up. They stayed holed up in their houses, searching for documents or exemptions, or enlisted in the local militias in order to evade their responsibilities. The recent battle at La Albuera in Extremadura, where defeating the French came with terrible losses—1,500 Spanish and 3,500 English soldiers dead or wounded—has done little to encourage new recruits. The problem is so great that the Cortes has had to come up with a solution: they have widened conscription to include men in the second and third categories, so that these men, in order to avoid being called up, will turn in the first-category malingerers.

"Does this concern you, Cousin?" teases Cari Palma as she fans herself.

"Absolutely not. Far be it from me to contest anyone for laurels and glory. I am excused by virtue of being the son of a widow, and because I paid the fifteen thousand *reales* required to exempt me from having to gloriously take up arms."

"The fact that you paid is fair enough, but your other excuse . . . Aunt Carmela has been dead for eight years now!"

"That doesn't change the fact she died a widow." Cousin Toño cradles a wineglass in one hand and, with the other, holds a bottle of *manzanilla* to the light and peers at its diminishing contents. "Besides, there's only one war in which I would be prepared to fight: to reconquer Jerez and Sánlucar for the fatherland."

"Now, there's a war in which I'm sure you would fight like a tiger," remarks Lolita, amused.

"Absolutely, *niña*. With a bayonet or any weapon you care to mention. Hand to hand, wine cellar to wine cellar . . . Absolutely. You know the story about King Pepe Botella visiting the area and falling into a vat of wine? The French ran around shouting, 'Throw him a rope! Throw him a rope!' but King Joseph Bonaparte pops his head out and shouts back, 'Noooo! Throw me some ham and cheese!'"

Lolita and the others laugh, though her brother-in-law Alfonso's laugh seems forced. Only her mother remains stiff and aloof. Her expression, distant and disdainful, is evidence of the five drops of laudanum taken three times daily in a glass of orange-flower water to alleviate the pain of the scirrhous tumor slowly eating away at her. Manuela Ugarte is seventy-two years old and does not know her illness is terminal; her eldest daughter is the only person who knows, having sworn the doctor who made the diagnosis to silence. To have done otherwise, she knows, would not have helped matters. The illness seems to be progressing slowly, and the end is unlikely to be quick. Her mother is gradually becoming aware of it, but the pain so far has been tolerable. A hypochondriac by nature, Manuela Ugarte had not left the house for years, even before she developed the cancer that she does not know she has. She spends her days in bed, in her room. Only in the afternoons does she come downstairs for a short while, leaning on her daughter's arm, so that she can sit on the patio in summer—or, in winter, in the drawing room—and receive visitors. Her life is lived within narrow confines, between her domestic whims, which no one questions, her tincture of opium and her obliviousness to her true condition. The ravages of this secret illness are easily attributed to the infirmities of old age, to tiredness, to endless days of dull routine in a life without purpose. Manuela Ugarte ceased to be a wife a long time ago and, as a mother, she did the bare minimum, leaving everything to wet nurses, nannies and governesses. Lolita cannot ever remember her mother giving her a kiss unprompted. Only Lolita's elder brother—Manuela's dead son—could make those expressionless eyes light up. A confident, handsome lad, Francisco de Paula Palma, who traveled the world and learned his trade in Buenos Aires, Havana, Liverpool and Bordeaux, was destined to run the family business and shore it up with a suitable marriage to the daughter of another local merchant named Carlos Power. The French invasion forced him to defer the wedding. Immediately called up to serve in the Cádiz Fusiliers, Francisco de Paula died on July 16, 1808, fighting in the olive groves of Andújar at the Battle of Bailén.

"Remember what happened when they began working on the fortifications for the trench at La Cortadura," says Curra Vilches. "Every man in Cádiz was suddenly a stonemason, working shoulder to shoulder hauling stone. Street parties with music and drinking. Everyone working together: the nobleman, the merchant, the monk and the commoner . . . But within days, some people were paying others to work for them. By the end, hardly a soul was turning up for work."

"Such a terrible shame about the railings," says Cari Palma.

Her mother nods, clearly resentful, but does not say a word. The subject of the railings and the Cortadura is a touchy one in the Palma household. In order to fund defensive works in 1810, with the French at the gates of the city, the Regency not only raised a levy from the citizenry amounting to one million *pesos*, and demolished all the country houses on that part of the reef—including one that belonged to the Palma family, who had already lost their summer house when the French marched into Chiclana—it also demanded that householders donate their wrought-iron gates and window bars. The Palma family did as requested, sending the elaborate wrought-iron gate from their patio: a fruitless offering, since most of the iron went unused when the front line was established on the Isla de Léon, making the Cortadura fortifications superfluous. If anything offends the Palma family's commercial sensibilities, it is not the sacrifices imposed by war—above all, the loss of their late son and brother—but the needless expense, exorbitant taxes and bureaucratic squandering. Especially as it is the merchant class that, as much in time of war as of peace, has kept this city alive.

"They've squeezed us like lemons," says Alfonso, ill-tempered as always.

"Over a paella . . ." adds cousin Toño.

Alfonso Solé remains aloof, sitting bolt upright in his wicker chair, never relaxing for a moment. These visits to the house on the Calle del Baluarte are a social obligation, a fact he makes perfectly clear. For a businessman in his position, visiting his sister- and mother-in-law every Friday is as routine as sending the post. It is a matter of abiding by the unwritten rules laid down by Cádiz gossip-mongers. In this city, family ties entail certain obligations, in keeping with one's class. Moreover, when it comes to the firm of Palma e Hijos, it pays to be prudent. Observing the proprieties is also a means of keeping open lines of credit. If difficulties should arise—war and business are dogged by ill-timed calamities—everyone knows that his sister-in-law will not refuse to help him stay afloat. Not because of him personally. For her sister. As long as the money remains within the family.

The conversation continues on the subject of money. Between sips of tea—he likes to draw attention to the fact he spent time studying in London—Alfonso Solé voices his fear that, with the way things are going, the Cortes might levy a further contribution from the merchants of Cádiz. This, he suggests, would be a terrible decision, given that Customs have already seized more than 50,000 *pesos*, confiscated from individuals in the occupied territories. They could simply give this sum to the treasury.

"It would be the most iniquitous spoliation," protests Lolita.

"Call it what you will. But rather them than us."

Cari Palma nods at every word, flicking her fan open and closed. Visibly pleased by her husband's tenacity, she stares down any possible objections. Her every gesture says, "You're quite right, my love. Well said. Of course, *cariño*." Lolita observes her sister with an experienced, critical eye. Though physically very alike—Cari is more graceful, with her pale eyes and small, perfectly formed nose—they have always had utterly different personalities, even as girls. Frivolous and fickle, more like her mother than her father, the younger of the Palma daughters quickly fulfilled her dreams through a suitable marriage, as yet childless, and a satisfactory social status. Besotted with her husband, or believing that she is, Cari sees life only through Alfonso's eyes and her words come from his mouth. It is something Lolita is accustomed to, but again today she feels the usual vague pang of resentment, not about the present—she is little interested in her sister's domestic arrangements—but about the past: childhood, youth, solitude, melancholy, windows misted with raindrops. Arid afternoons spent in the office poring over business books and ledgers, learning English, arithmetic, accounting, reading about travel and foreign customs while Cari, carefree and superficial, sat before a mirror adjusting her curls or playing with her doll's house. Then, later, when her brother was gone, the responsibility, the sometimes intolerable weight of the family burden, her mother always curt and unreasonable. The disdainful, barely concealed animosity—even during these weekly visits—of her brother-in-law Alfonso and of Cari, the beautiful princess, the queen of the ball, forever scowling and wrinkling her nose because Lolita is the one who, having sacrificed so much, now manages the family firm and works to keep it afloat. It is Lolita who has earned the respect of the city, without giving her brother-in-law a share of the pie.

The bell at the gate rings and Rosas, the steward, crosses the patio and reappears to announce two new visitors. A moment later, Captain

Virués appears, in full uniform, hat trimmed with braid, sword beneath his arm, together with Jorge Fernández Cuchillero, the Creole who has come to Cádiz as a member of the Cortes representing the city of Buenos Aires. He is twenty-seven, blond, elegant and handsome, wearing a charcoal-gray dress coat, a necktie in the American style, striped breeches and high boots. A scar across his face. He is a courteous, friendly young man, and a regular visitor to the Palma house, being descended from an Asturian merchant with whom the Palmas have long had close ties, somewhat strained now by the current upheavals in Argentina. As with other delegates who represent the rebellious American territories, Fernández Cuchillero's political position is a delicate one, a product of the turbulent times faced by the Spanish monarchy, being a member of parliament in a Junta that is in armed conflict with the capital.

"Would you bring some more *manzanilla,*" suggests cousin Toño.

Rosas opens one of the bottles that have been cooling in the well and the new guests settle themselves, commenting about the exorbitant rent—forty *reales* a day—the Creole deputy's landlady is charging him; it has come to a point where he has had to ask the Cortes for help.

"It wouldn't even happen in the Sierra Morena," he says.

The conversation turns to events in Buenos Aires, the offensive launched against the rebels from the military base in Montevideo and the English offer to mediate in peace talks with the rebel territories. According to Fernández Cuchillero, at San Felipe Neri there have even been discussions about offering the English eight months of unrestricted trade with the American ports in return for diplomatic aid. A measure which he, and the other overseas deputies, fully support.

"That is ridiculous," intervenes Alfonso caustically. "If we give the British free access to those ports, they'll never leave . . . They're intelligent people."

"But discussions are already advanced," confirms the Creole phlegmatically. "In fact there is talk that if we reject their proposal, they may withdraw from Portugal, abandoning their base at Badajoz and the plans being drawn up for the battle to defeat Maréchal Soult . . ."

"Sheer blackmail."

"That may be so, señor. But in London they call it diplomacy."

"In that case, the people of Cádiz would have to have their say. What is proposed would mean the end of our trade with the Americas. It would be the ruin of the city."

Lolita toys with the black Chinese fan painted with orange blossoms that lies unopened in her lap. She is irritated to find herself agreeing with her brother-in-law about anything, but on this she does agree. Nor is she ashamed to say so.

"It is bound to happen sooner or later," she says. "Whether or not they act as mediators, the upheaval in the Americas will make trade there much too tempting for England. Having all of that vast market at their disposal. So badly managed by us, and so far away. Subject to so many levies, taxes, restrictions and bureaucracy . . . The English will do what they always do: to us, they will play at being mediators, while at the same time they are stoking the flames, as they have done in Buenos Aires. They have a rare talent for fishing in troubled waters."

"You shouldn't talk about our allies in such a manner, Lolita."

Her mother is silent, head bowed, eyes vacant. It is impossible to tell whether she is following the conversation or in the grip of her laudanum. The rebuke came from Amparo Pimentel. Waving her glass of anisette—this is her third glass, as though she is competing with cousin Toño and his *manzanilla*—she looks utterly scandalized. Lolita Palma is unsure whether the reproach refers to her unflattering views of the English as a nation or to the fact that, as a woman, she expresses herself so freely on matters of politics and commerce. Her favorite priest, the curate at the church of San Francisco, often used his Sunday sermon to gently criticize certain excesses in the exercise of such freedom by ladies of polite Cádiz society. Lolita is not troubled by the criticism—in this city no priest would dare go further, but her neighbor Señora Pimental, though a regular visitor to the Palma house, has always been narrow-minded. Deeply conservative. Doubtless her exemplar of womanhood is Cari Palma: married, prudent, concerned only with her appearance and her husband's domestic bliss. Not some tomboy with ink-stained fingers whose planters are filled with ferns and exotic plants rather than flowers as God ordained.

"Allies?" Lolita looks at her with mild disapproval. "Did you see the sour look on Ambassador Wellesley's face?"

"Not to mention his brother Wellington," interjects Curra Vilches cheerfully.

"They are allies only to themselves," Lolita continues. "Their presence here in the peninsula is simply designed to wear down Napoleon ... They don't care about the Spanish, and they consider the Cortes to be a hotbed of republican sedition. To ask them to mediate in the Americas would be like inviting the fox into the henhouse."

"Jesus, Mary and Joseph," says Señora Pimentel, crossing herself.

Lolita does not fail to notice the discreet, wistful glances Lorenzo Virués directs toward her. This is not the first time the captain has visited the Calle del Baluarte house. Never by himself, and, being the consummate officer that he is, he is never discourteous. Since the ambassador's reception he has visited on three occasions, twice with Fernández Cuchillero and once when, by chance, he encountered cousin Toño on the Plaza de San Francisco.

"Have you been particularly affected by the upheavals in the Americas?" asks Virués.

The question is directed at Lolita, seemingly out of genuine interest rather than courtesy.

"It has affected us enough," she replies. "More than one might wish. The imprisonment of the king and the excesses of the authorities have complicated matters: the Captaincy General of Venezuela and the Viceroyalties of Río de la Plata and Nueva Granada are in open revolt, and the consequent disruption of trade and lack of revenue have left Cádiz with liquidity problems; meanwhile the war with France, the collapse of the market here in Spain and the trade in contraband have unsettled traditional commerce. A number of firms in Cádiz, like Palma e Hijos, have been attempting to recover through local business, warehousing, property and financial speculation, going back to the last resort in times of crisis—more brokers than buyers."

"But this is all just a temporary solution," she concludes. "In the long term, the city is financially doomed."

Alfonso nods, almost grudgingly. From the sour expression on his face, anyone might think Lolita had stolen his thunder. And his money.

"The situation is intolerable. This is why we cannot make any concessions, to the British or to anyone else."

"On the contrary," interjects Fernández Cuchillero, looking out for number one. "We have to negotiate before it's too late."

"Jorge is right," says Lolita. "A businessman accepts his losses when he knows he can compensate with other business . . . If the American colonies become independent, and the ports fall into the hands of the English and the North Americans, we will have no such consolation. The losses would be irretrievable."

"This is why we cannot give an inch," argues Alfonso. "Look at Chile: it is still loyal to the Crown. So is Mexico, despite the revolution led by that lunatic priest—who is a Spaniard, to make matters worse . . . And in Montevideo, General Elío is doing an excellent job. With an iron fist."

These last words are accompanied by an approving clack of Cari Palma's fan. Lolita shakes her head in disagreement.

"That is what worries me. In the Americas, the iron fist will get us nowhere," she says, laying her hand gently on Fernández Cuchillero's arm. "Our friend here is a good example . . . He makes no secret that he supports the radical reforms in his territory, but he is still a member of the Cortes. He understands that it provides an opportunity to deal with the high-handedness and autocracy that have poisoned everything."

"Exactly so," agrees the Creole. "A historic opportunity, one that it would be unforgivable of me not to take part in . . . I tell you this as someone who fought with General Liniers in Buenos Aires under the Spanish flag."

Lolita is familiar with the incident and knows that the Creole is being unduly modest. In 1806 and 1807, during the British invasions of Río de la Plata, Fernández Cuchillero, together with other young aristocrats, battled the English and forced them to surrender; two hard-fought battles in which the British suffered heavy losses with more than three thousand men killed or wounded. The scar across his right cheek is evidence of his courage, the result of a bullet grazing his cheek during the defense of the O'Gorman House on the Calle de la Paz in Buenos Aires.

"When all this is over, we will have come to terms with a new world," says Lolita. "Perhaps a more just world, I do not know. But different . . . Whether or not we lose the Americas, whether or not Cádiz is ruined, whether with the English or without them, our link to the Americas will be through men like Jorge."

"And trade," adds Alfonso sullenly.

Lolita gives a sad, ironic smile. "And trade. Of course."

Captain Virués's eyes are still on her and she cannot help but feel flattered. He is a handsome man, and his blue jacket with its purple collar and lapels gives him a distinguished air. What Lolita Palma feels is a pleasant, intimate sensation, a faint caress of her pride as a woman; it goes no further than that, nor would she permit it to do so. Obviously, it is not the first time that a man has looked at her in this way. Once upon a time she was a rather pretty girl, and even now she might still be considered handsome: her skin is still pale and firm, her eyes dark and sparkling, her figure pleasing. She has slender hands and small feet; and she is of excellent pedigree. Though she dresses soberly, favoring dark colors since her father's death—colors that flatter her when it comes to business dealings—her tastes are those of a sophisticated woman, her dresses and shoes always fashionable. She is still considered to be what people in Cádiz call *a young lady with prospects*, though her reflection in the mirror tells her that those prospects are fading with every passing day. But she is also aware that, to a fortune hunter, she is tempting prey. As cousin Toño is fond of saying, more than one wolf has stalked this little lamb; and in this sense, Lolita has no illusions. She is not one to be dazzled by a man's bearing, by delicate hands, a fashionable frockcoat or a dashing uniform. Her father brought her up to be constantly aware of who she is, something that allows her to meet the attentions of gentlemen with a polite, somewhat reserved attitude. An affected indifference which conceals her distrust. Like the accomplished duelist who, without any fuss, turns his profile to his adversary to reduce the chances of being hit by a bullet.

"I heard that you lost a ship," says Alfonso Solé.

Lolita looks at her brother-in-law, embarrassed. Pompous idiot, she thinks. Clearly annoyed by the drift of the conversation, he is attempting to get his own back with almost childish pique. Heavy-handedly, as is his way. Every day she gives thanks to her father—may he rest in peace—for not making Alfonso a partner.

"Indeed. And the cargo with it."

These few words sum it all up. The tragedy. Four days ago, the *Tlaxcala*, a schooner en route from Veracruz carrying a consignment of 1,200 copper ingots, 300 boxes of shoes and 550 hundredweight of sugar, was seized by the French as it arrived in Cádiz after its sixty-one-day voyage. The capture was made by a corsair felucca that usually operates out of the cove at Rota; some fishermen saw the schooner being boarded some two miles west of Cape Candor.

"You're fortunate that insurance premiums have fallen since the peace with the English," Alfonso points out spitefully. "Besides, you can always recover it with your own corsair."

Lolita, looking at Captain Virués, sees a shadow pass over the officer's face when he hears the word *corsair*. Since their conversation on the night of the English ambassador's reception, neither of them has mentioned Pépé Lobo, but she assumes that Virués is aware of the sailor's adventures. Since being fitted out by the houses of Palma and Sánchez Guinea, the corsair cutter has been mentioned several times in the Cádiz newspapers. Among its first seizures were a polacca carrying a cargo of 3,000 *fanegas* of wheat and the fortunate capture of a brigantine out of Puerto Rico carrying enough cocoa, sugar and dyewood to repay their original investment. The most recent report appeared in *El Vigía de Cádiz* exactly a week ago: "*Arrived into port today a French místico captured by the crew of the corsair* Culebra *en route between Barbate and Cádiz carrying a cargo of* aguardiente, *wheat, leather and mail* . . ." What the newspaper fails to mention is that the *místico* was fitted with six cannons and steadfastly resisted capture; and that, when it finally dropped anchor, there were two gravely injured crewmen aboard the *Culebra* and two more of Pépé Lobo's men at the bottom of the sea.

THE HUGE GAFF-SAIL flaps wildly, causing the cutter to lurch and roll violently while the mast and the black hull of the boat shudder. Astern, next to the two helmsmen struggling to maneuver the leather-encased iron tiller, Pépé Lobo steers the crippled vessel into a headwind that shivers the slack jib and sends the long boom swinging above his head. He can smell the linstocks smoking on the starboard side next to the four 6-pound guns which, on the orders of bo'sun Brasero are pointed at a tartane lurching within pistol range, its triangular sails flapping loose. Lobo knows that, with things as they are, the purpose of aiming the cannons at the prey from such close range is mostly to command respect. Firing would be impossible without endangering his own men; the raucous boarding party, led by Ricardo Maraña and armed with pikes, axes, pistols and cutlasses, have the tartane's crew cornered in the stern, some eighteen men retreating along the deck. On the starboard side, below the mainmast channels, the planking and part of the gunwale have been blown to pieces, indicating the spot where the *Culebra*, having run it down, rammed its prey—the tartane, ignoring the signals, was attempting to escape—just long enough for twenty men armed to the teeth to leap from one ship to the other.

Maraña is a professional. He does this better than anyone. In such situations it is vital not to allow your adversary time to think; Maraña operates with his customary efficiency. Hands on the gunwale of the cutter, keeping a weather eye on the position of the *Culebra*'s sails and sheets with respect to the wind, ensuring they stay abreast of the tartane, Pépé Lobo watches his first mate move across the deck of the captured brig. Pale, hatless, dressed entirely in black, the lieutenant of the *Culebra* brandishes a sword in his right hand, a pistol in his left and another pistol tucked in his belt. Since boarding the vessel, neither he nor his men have had to use their swords or fire a single shot. Overwhelmed by the ferocity of the assault, by the shouting and the appearance of the corsairs, the crew of the tartane seem unsure whether to offer resistance. One or two appear to consider the idea, only to falter and retreat. They are intimidated by the aggressive manner of their assailants, by the shouting and the threats, by the intrepid air of the young leader and the insolent, devil-may-care way he jabs his sword at them and tells them to throw down their weapons. They cower next to the helm, which lurches and jolts since there is no one manning it. The flag of two red and three yellow stripes—flown both by patriots and by those loyal to Joseph Bonaparte—flutters from a short ensign staff on the taffrail. Below it, a man who appears to be the tartane's owner stands waving his arms, as though encouraging his men to resist—or perhaps to discourage them. From the *Culebra* it is possible to see a brawny man grabbing a large knife or a machete and confronting Maraña, but the first mate simply shoves him aside and, with astonishing composure, elbows his way through the crew members to the owner and coolly presses the pistol against the man's chest while, with his other hand, he cuts the halyard of the flag and it plummets into the sea.

Suicidal son of a bitch, mutters Pépé Lobo. He always has to go in with all sails set, heading straight for hell. *El Marquesito*, they call him—The Little Marquis. Lobo is still smiling as he turns to Brasero the bo'sun.

"Clear the decks," he orders. "Make fast the cannons and lower the launch."

The bo'sun blows his whistle and runs the length and breadth of the cutter—seventy-five feet by eighteen—giving the appropriate orders. Meanwhile, aboard the tartane, as the men in the boarding party disarm their adversaries and force them below decks, Maraña goes over to the gunwale and gives the signal—arms raised, wrists crossed—meaning the boat has surrendered and is under their control. Then he disappears into the deckhouse. Lobo takes out his pocket watch and checks the time—9:48 a.m.—then tells the ship's clerk to make a note of it in the log. He looks out to larboard toward the hazy dark shape he can just make out through the gray mists shrouding the coast: they are east of the Aceitera bank, about two miles south of Cape Trafalgar. So ends the pursuit that began at dawn, when from the deck of the *Culebra* a single sail was spotted heading north, having almost crossed the Straits.

Though they approached flying no flag, the crew of the tartane, clearly suspicious, set more sail with the east wind trying to make it to shelter at Barbate. But the swifter *Culebra*, with its copper-sheathed hull, sailing under full canvas including the fore and gaff topsails, gave pursuit for an hour and a half. They hoisted their French corsair flag and in response the tartane hoisted theirs without slowing down; finally Captain Lobo gave the order to haul down the French flag and raise the Spanish corsair flag, and mark the change with a cannon shot. The tartane slackened its sheets, the *Culebra* maneuvered to come alongside so it could get Maraña and his men aboard, and that was the end of the story. For now.

"Bo'sun!"

Brasero rushes over. Dark-skinned, thickset, with gray hair and mustaches, barefoot like most of the crew, Brasero's face, etched with deep lines like knife wounds, is smiling now they have made their capture. The crew of the cutter are in high spirits: while the men busy themselves lowering the launch and deciding who will sail the tartane back to Cádiz or Tarifa, they make guesses about the cargo in her hold and what their share might be once it has been brought ashore and sold.

"Put two men up with a spyglass, I want them looking out for any sail. And keep a weather eye to windward . . . I don't want the Barbate brigantine catching us off guard."

"Yes, señor."

Pépé Lobo is a cautious sailor; he does not want any surprises. The French have a fast, 12-gun brig, moored sometimes near Barbate, sometimes near Sanlúcar, an implacable ship they use to patrol the coast. At sea, the roles in the game of cat and mouse can swiftly be reversed; the hunter can become the hunted. It's a matter of luck, and also of having a good eye and good seafaring instincts. In this occupation, a little healthy doubt and a perpetual mistrust of the weather, the sea, the wind, the sails, the enemy and even your own crew are essential qualities for remaining free and alive. A week ago, the *Culebra* reluctantly abandoned a vessel that had already surrendered—a small schooner, cornered in the cove at Bolonia—when they spotted the sails of the

French brig approaching rapidly from the west; a fact that also forced the corsair to make a tiresome detour into the Straits, where it would be protected by the Spanish gun emplacements at Tarifa.

The launch carrying the ship's clerk, the first officer and the crew who will sail the captured tartane back to port is already pulling away from the *Culebra*, rowing hard against the swell. The tartane is still a pistol shot away, within hailing distance. Ricardo Maraña reappears on deck carrying a brass loud-hailer which he uses to communicate the name, cargo and destination of the captured ship. It is the *Teresa del Palo*, fitted with two 4-pounders, registered in Málaga, en route from Tangier to the mouth of the Barbate River with a cargo of leather, oil and jars of olives, raisins and almonds. Pépé Lobo nods, satisfied. Given the cargo and its destination any Prize Court* would rule it fair game. He glances up at the pennant indicating the wind direction, then out to sea where the clouds scud high in the gray sky. The east wind rose last night and will hold firm, so there should be no problem sailing the tartane back to Cádiz with the *Culebra* as escort. For three weeks now, they have been plying the waters between Gibraltar and the cape Santa María. A few days in port will do everyone good—the plummeting barometer further suggests this is a sensible idea and, who knows, perhaps the Prize Court has reached a decision on one of their previous captures; that way the officers and crew can be paid what is due to them according to the Letter of Marque and their contract with the shipowners. One-third of the proceeds is to be divided among the crew, with seven parts paid to the captain, five to the first officer, three to the bo'sun and the ship's clerk, two parts to each sailor and one to shipboys or cabin boys, not counting the eight parts set aside for the gravely injured, to cover funeral expenses and for orphans and widows.

"Cannons have been secured and tampions fixed, Captain. No sign of a sail on the horizon."

"Thank you, bo'sun. As soon as Señor Maraña and the boarding party get back, trim the sheets."

* A Prize Court is authorized to consider whether or not a ship has been lawfully captured or seized in time of war or under the terms of the seizing ship's Letter of Marque and Reprisal.

"Destination?"

"Cádiz."

The bo'sun gives a broad smile, as does the first helmsman—a strapping blond man nicknamed "the Scotsman," although his name is Machucha and he hails from San Roque. Then, while Brasero heads back toward the bow, checking that everything on deck has been stowed, the sheets and halyards are clear for the maneuver, the linstocks doused, the cartridges stowed in the gunpowder room and the cannonballs in their rack and covered with tarps, the smile spreads to the rest of the crew. They are far from being the worst of men, given what was available, especially since the Army and the Royal Armada are trying to enlist any man capable of carrying a rifle or hauling a rope. Nor were they easy to recruit, given the times. Of the forty-nine men aboard—including a cabin boy age twelve and a deckhand of fourteen—one-third are seamen, fishermen and sailors lured by the prospect of good captures and a guaranteed sum of 130 *reales* a month. Lobo earns 500, and his first officer 350—an advance against future spoils. The rest are made up of harbor rats, ex-convicts with no history of violent offenses who managed to avoid general call-up by bribing recruiting officers, and a handful of foreigners recruited at the last minute in Cádiz, Algeciras and Gibraltar: two Irishmen, two Moroccans, three Neapolitans, an English artilleryman and a Maltese Jew. The *Culebra* has been operating for four months and in that time has made seven captures, which, assuming the Prize Court rules that they were all fair game, is an excellent tally. Enough to satisfy all the men aboard, who are now inured to the sea and battle—fortunately, only two of the captures have resulted in blood being spilled.

Pépé Lobo removes his hat and looks up at the crow's nest above the head of the sail that is snapping and straining at the topping lift in the heavy swell.

"Anything out toward Barbate?"

Nothing, the call comes down, all clear. The launch is already on its way back from the tartane, bearing Ricardo Maraña and his men, as well as the ship's clerk, who is hugging the captured log to his chest. Lobo takes a tinderbox from his pocket and, leaning on the taffrail to shield himself from the wind, lights up a cigar. A corsair ship is a collection of flammable substances, of wood and tar and gunpowder, and only the captain and first officer are allowed to smoke without permission, a privilege Lobo exercises as little as possible. He is not much of a smoker, unlike Ricardo Maraña who, despite his weak lungs and his bloodstained handkerchiefs, smokes cigars by the boxful. Twelve at a time.

Cádiz. Lobo himself is not unhappy at the prospect of dropping anchor there. The cutter needs some refitting and repair and he has to visit the Prize Court, to grease a few palms to speed up the paperwork, though he is confident that the Sánchez Guineas will have taken care of things. But magistrates and bureaucrats aside, the captain of the *Culebra* will be happy to reach terra firma and stretch his legs. This is what he is thinking as he blows smoke between his teeth. It is about time. He feels the need to wander the streets of Santa María and the bars of La Caleta. Yes. Now and then, even he needs a woman. Or several.

Lolita Palma. The memory brings a smile to his lips, one that is brooding and sardonic, since he is smiling to himself. Leaning on the top of the gunwale, with Cape Trafalgar silhouetted in the distance as the mist begins to lift, Pépé Lobo thinks back. There is something about the woman—something that, curiously, has nothing to do with money—that has awakened unfamiliar feelings. He is not a man given to introspection, but a determined hunter looking for an opportunity, for the stroke of luck every sailor dreams of, for the fortune the sea sometimes bestows on those prepared to take risks. Captain Lobo is a corsair of necessity; it is not a vocation, but the result of the way he lives. Of the times he lives in. Since he first shipped out at the age of eleven, he has seen too many pitiful wretches who once stood where he now stands. He does not want to end up in a tavern, telling his life story to young sailors, embellishing it in exchange for a glass of wine. This is why he is patiently, tenaciously chasing after a future somewhere beyond this precarious world, a world he is determined never to return to if he should manage to leave it behind: a small income, a home of his own, a porch where he can sit out in the sun; cold and damp only in rain and winter. With a woman to warm his bed and his belly, not having to listen to the wind howl with a terrible foreboding and an anxious glance at the barometer.

As for Lolita Palma, when he thinks of her his mind is filled with complex ideas. Too complex, given his accustomed thoughts. Though his employer and partner is still a virtual stranger with whom he has barely exchanged a few words, the corsair feels a strange affinity with her; an understanding that includes a certain physical warmth. Pépé Lobo has dropped anchor in too many ports to delude himself. Which is why his reaction to Lolita Palma surprises him. It also worries him, since he is never one to mix business and pleasure. He can have his pick of young, pretty women—now and then he may have to pay in advance, but even this he can find comforting. Or convenient. The heir to the Palma house, on the other hand, is far from being pretty, at least not according to the classical definition of beauty. But she is not unattractive. Not at all. Her features are regular and pleasing, her eyes intelligent, her body shapely, from what one can divine beneath her loose-fitting clothes. Above all, there is something about her manner when she talks, when she is silent, a curious calmness in her poised serenity, a self-assurance that is intriguing, and that—on this crucial point the corsair is not entirely clear—he somehow finds attractive. This is what surprises him. And worries him.

He first noticed it at the end of March during Lolita Palma's visit to the *Culebra*, when the cutter was preparing to put to sea. Pépé Lobo had planted the idea of the visit, and to his astonishment, she came to see the ship—though not immediately—in the company of the Sánchez Guineas. She arrived unexpectedly on a small boat from the port, clutching a parasol, accompanied by Don Emilio and his son Miguel, who had given him just enough notice to make the cutter ready for the visit. Some of the equipment was not yet stowed, one of the 10cwt anchors was on deck, the boom and rigging lay at the foot of the bare mast, and a barge alongside was unloading the iron ballast. But every rope was coiled and in its place, the standing rigging recently tarred, the hull had just had two coats of black paint above the waterline, the gunwales and the railings smelled of teak oil and the deck had recently been scrubbed with holystone. It had been a pleasant, sunny day; the sea was like a mirror. When Lolita Palma came aboard—she refused to be hoisted aboard by windlass, resolutely hiking her skirts and climbing the wooden slats of the starboard gangplank—the cutter looked magnificent, floating at anchor opposite the cape of La Vaca and the battery at Los Corrales, the bows turned into the light breeze blowing along the reef. It was a strange situation. After the initial greetings, Ricardo Maraña, wearing a black jacket and a hastily knotted tie, did the honors with the elegant assurance of a well-bred rake. The men working on deck stepped back, smiling stiffly like simpletons with that mute timidity that seafarers, accustomed to women of easy virtue, demonstrate when faced with a woman who is, or appears to be, a lady. Pépé Lobo, following behind with the Sánchez Guineas, watched his visitor move easily about the boat, thanking the crew with a gentle smile, a nod of the head, asking appropriate questions about this or that. She was dressed in dark gray with a cashmere shawl around her shoulders and an English straw hat, its wide brim turned down slightly, framing her face and emphasizing her intelligent eyes. She was interested in everything: the eight 6-pound cannons, four on either side with two free gunports in the bow, ready to be used if necessary; the sockets into which smaller-caliber blunderbusses and *pedreros** could be slotted, the battens nailed in a fan shape beneath the tiller to provide support for the helmsman in heavy swell, the bilge pump located behind the light-well above the wardroom; the hawse-hole through which the anchor chains would run, and the long, almost horizontal bowsprit slightly to larboard of the central gangway. "All typical," the first officer explained to her, "of this type of light, rapid vessel, fore-and-aft rigged to carry a lot of canvas on a single mast, perfect for corsairs, mailboats and smugglers. The English call it a *cutter,* the French a *côtre;* in Spain we call it a *balandra.*" Contrary to what he expected, Pépé Lobo found the proprietress of the house of Palma knowledgeable on the subject of ships and sailing, so much so that he heard her inquire about the rigging and about how the cutter handled given the lack of shrouds to support the mast in heavy seas, in particular inquiring about the magnificent mast

---

* Short, smooth-bore guns using stone ammunition with barrels of eight to ten calibers that were used in siege and naval warfare.

with its pronounced curve toward the bow. It was made of flexible, re-sistant Riga wood with no knotholes, fashioned from the mainmast of one of the 74-gun French ships from Admiral Rosily's flotilla.

They had a private conversation—the second since she and Pépé Lobo first met—when Lolita Palma declined to visit the between decks. "I would rather remain here," she said. "It is a splendid day, and I find ships' interiors a little uncomfortable; the air tends to be unbreathable. So, if you will excuse me, gentlemen." Ricardo Maraña went below with the Sánchez Guineas, intending to offer them a glass of port in the wardroom while Lolita remained on deck, leaning against the angle of the escutcheon and the gunwale, shading herself with her parasol as she gazed at the imposing fortifications of the nearby Puerta de Tierra, shimmering between the light and the water, at the sails of vessels large and small coming and going from all parts. It was at this point that Pépé Lobo and the heiress to the Palma house spoke for some fifteen minutes, and at the end of their conversation—which touched on no weighty matters, but simply boats, the war, Cádiz and shipping—the captain realized that this uncommonly educated and urbane young woman (he is astonished by her command of English and French nau-tical terminology) was unlike any he had met before. There was some-thing different about her, an inner resolve formed of self-discipline, steadfast convictions and an instinct for judging a man by his deeds and his words. Together with a singular, indefinable charm—"serenity" is the word that keeps coming to Pépé Lobo's mind—related to the pleas-ing appearance of her skin, pale and feminine, the delicate blue veins at her wrists between the lace cuffs and the satin gloves she was wearing that day, to her beautiful lips, always parted when she is listening—even to those, like the corsair, who do not enjoy her wholehearted sym-pathy. This, at least, is what he has concluded from her polite, slightly haughty manner toward him. It is as though, possessed of a lively curiosity—at once considered and impulsive—for everything around her, Lolita Palma has not lost the ability to feel wonder in a world peo-pled by creatures who, when all is said and done, routinely fail to sur-prise her.

Ricardo Maraña reappears. "Everything in order, Captain," he says. "Cargo and destination confirmed, no further news. I've had the hatches sealed and nailed shut."

Maraña never addresses his captain familiarly in front of the crew, a formality Lobo returns. All the boarding party are now back from the tartane. The men stow their weapons in the wicker baskets at the foot of the mast and, riotous and contented, they scatter across the deck recounting details of the capture to their shipmates. With a loud creak of the windlass, six sailors hoist the launch on to the deck, water streaming. Pépé Lobo tosses away the stub of his cigar and comes back from the taffrail.

"So it was a good capture?"

Maraña coughs, fishes a kerchief from his jacket pocket, presses it to his lips and replaces it after an offhand glance at the traces of red spittle.

"I've known worse."

He shares a complicit smile with his shipmates. Following behind the ship's clerk, who is carrying the Letter of Marque, the muster roll and the bill of lading of the captured ship, the captain of the tartane comes on deck. He is a thickset man of a certain age with a ruddy complexion and white sideburns who looks as though the ground has opened up beneath his feet. He is Spanish, as are most of his crew, and there is not a Frenchman among them. Maraña allows him to put his effects in a small trunk retrieved by the boarding party which now lies, pitiful and abandoned, on the deck.

"I regret that I am obliged to distrain your vessel," says Pépé Lobo, touching the brim of his hat. "It will be transported, with its cargo and documentation, since I consider it a fair capture."

As he speaks, he takes his cigar case from his pocket and offers one to the other man, who gruffly pushes it away.

"This is an outrage," the man stammers indignantly. "You have no right."

The captain of the *Culebra* slips the cigar case back into his pocket.

"As my first officer told you, I have an authorized Letter of Marque and Reprisal. You are traveling with cargo destined for an enemy port, which constitutes contraband of war. Furthermore, you did not stop when we hoisted the flag and fired the cannon. You resisted."

"Don't talk rot. I am a Spaniard like yourself. I am simply earning a living."

"We are all earning a living."

"This capture is illegal . . . Besides, you approached flying a French flag."

Pépé Lobo shrugs. "I hoisted the Spanish flag before I fired, so everything was conducted in due form . . . In any case, when we get to port you will be able to lodge a captain's protest. My ship's clerk is at your disposal . . ."

As the tartane's captain is taken below, Lobo turns to his first officer, who has been listening, amused, to the conversation without saying a word.

"Haul aft the sheets. Bearing, southwest by south to avoid the Acitera. Then straight ahead."

"Back to Cádiz, then."

"To Cádiz."

Maraña nods impassively; from his expression, he seems to be thinking about something else. He is the only man on board who does not seem happy at the prospect of putting ashore, but this, too, is part of his character. Pépé Lobo knows that, deep down, the first officer is grateful that he will once again be able to resume his dangerous nocturnal visits to El Puerto de Santa María. The problem would be if either side were to catch him midway. Because, ever true to himself, *El Marquesito* would refuse to be taken alive—*bang, bang* and the sword, probably, accepting the consequences of his actions. Very much his style. And the *Culebra* would be left without a first officer.

"We'll go in convoy with the tartane, escort it. I don't trust that felucca at Rota."

Maraña nods again. He, too, is wary of the French corsair which, since the beginning of the year, has seized many an unwary vessel, Spanish or foreign, that has sailed too close to the coast between Camarón Point and Cape Candor. Even the English and the Spanish navies, being engaged with more important activities, have not been able to curtail its adventures. The French corsair's boldness has grown with its impunity: four weeks ago, on an almost moonless night, right under the cannons of fort San Sebastián, it succeeded in capturing a Turkish schooner carrying a cargo of hazelnuts, wheat and barley. Even the captain of the *Culebra* has had firsthand experience of this dangerous felucca, captained, according to the rumor in Cádiz (the bay is a hive of idle gossip), by a former lieutenant in the Imperial Fleet with a crew of Spaniards and Frenchmen. This is the selfsame corsair—quick to tack to windward with its lateen sails, and heavily armed with six 6-pound guns and two 12-pound carronades—that nearly ruined, or rather further ruined, his last voyage as captain of the merchant polacca *Risueña* between Lisbon and Cádiz, just before he found himself unemployed. This is perhaps why the memory is doubly painful. The fact that he is now armed with eight 6-pound cannons rather changes things. But this is not the only reason. Despite the time that has passed, Lobo has not forgotten his difficulties when the felucca tried to run him down as he sailed into Cádiz. On his list of personal grievances, the felucca and its captain are strongly underlined. Wide as the ocean is, sooner or later one and all are bound to meet. If that moment should happen, Pépé Lobo would be only too happy to settle the score.

CHAPTER SIX

తా

As he does every day after making his round of the cafés, Rogelio Tizón has his shoes shined. The bootblack's name is Pimporro—or at least that is what people call him. Day is gently breaking; the morning sunlight sketches its first lines between the awnings that shade the Calle de la Carne in front of the printseller's shop. The heat is suffocating; one could walk the length of the city and not find a breath of air. Every time a bead of sweat trickles down Pimporro's nose and drops onto the shiny leather, the bootblack—as black as the name of his profession—quickly wipes it away and goes on with his work, sometimes slapping his brush against his palm, not being immune to the showboating common among Caribbeans. *Clack, clack.* As always, the bootblack does his best for Tizón, though he knows the comisario will not pay him. He never pays.

"Other foot, Señor Comisario."

Tizón obediently removes the gleaming boot and places the other on the wooden box before the kneeling figure. Leaning against the wall, his slightly battered summer hat, white straw with a black ribbon, tilted slightly forward; one thumb hooked into the pocket of his waistcoat, his other hand gripping the bronze handle of his cane. Although the battle still continues along the shallow channel separating the Isla de Léon from the mainland, it has been three months since a bomb has landed in Cádiz. This is reflected in the townsfolk's relaxed attitude: women with shopping baskets stand gossiping, maids scrub doorsteps, shopkeepers in their doorways gaze enviously at the idle foreigners strolling up and down and peering into the window of the print shop. On display are engravings of heroes and battles won (or presumed won) against the French and a wide array of pictures of King Fernando—standing, on horseback, full-length and bust—are hung around the door frame; a veritable exhibition of patriotism. Tizón's eyes follow a young woman wearing a mantilla and a skirt with fringing that emphasizes the sway of her hips as she struts past. From a nearby tavern, a boy brings the policeman a cool glass of lemonade, which he sets down blasphemously between two burnt-out candles in an alcove with painted tilework that shows the bleeding image—clearly overwhelmed by the crown of thorns and the stifling heat—of Jesus of Nazareth.

"So there's no news, my friend?" he says.

"Like I said, Señor Comisario"—the black man forms a cross with the thumb and index finger of one hand and kisses it—"nothing at all."

Tizón takes a sip of lemonade. No sugar. The bootblack, who shines shoes in the center of the city, is one of his informants, a small but useful part in the vast network Tizón maintains: pimps, prostitutes, beggars, drudges, barmen, maids, stevedores, sailors, coachmen and sundry petty criminals: pickpockets, highwaymen, watch thieves, fingersmiths and cutpurses. Those well placed to uncover secrets, overhear conversations, witness suspicious events, identify names and faces which the comisario categorizes and files away for later use, for the benefit of his profession or to further his own interests—which are not always the same, but are frequently profitable. Some of these informants, Tizón pays. Others he does not. Most of them cooperate for the same reason that Pimporro the bootblack does. In the city and the times they are living in, where to scratch a living means the right hand cannot know what the left is doing, a little benevolence on the part of the police is the most effective protection. Not to mention that a certain amount of intimidation is brought to bear. Rogelio Tizón is one of those officers who has learned from long experience never to let his guard down or allow the pressure to drop. His is a profession, he knows, that cannot rely on pats on the back and being kind-hearted. It has been this way for as long as there have been policemen in the world. And it is a fact he does his best to reinforce whenever he can, coolly sanctioning even the worst that is said about him in Cádiz, where many people complain as he passes but always—and this is important—under their breath. As it should be. The Roman emperor who would rather be feared than loved was right. Absolutely right, in this world and the next. There are things that can only be achieved through fear.

Every morning, between half-past eight and ten o'clock, the comisario does a round of the cafés to check out any new faces and see whether the familiar ones are still there: the key points on his route are the Café del Correo, the Apolo, the Ángel, Las Cadenas, the Léon de Oro, Burnel's bakery and Cosí's teashop, with a number of other stops along the way. He could delegate the round to a junior officer, but there are things that are for his eyes and his ears alone. These daily rounds give Tizón, a policeman by nature as well as by profession, the opportunity to observe anew the city that is his workplace, to take the pulse where it beats fastest. This is the moment when casual confidences are made, fleeting conversations, meaningful glances; seemingly banal details which, when reconsidered in the calm of his office, with the list of registered foreigners in local inns and boardinghouses, decide his daily routine. Dictate the day's quarry.

"All done, Señor Comisario." The bootblack wipes the sweat from his forehead with the back of his hand. "They're like two jaspers."

"How much do I owe you?"

The question is as much a ritual as the answer.

"For you, it's on the house."

Tizón taps Pimporro's shoulder twice with his cane, finishes his lemonade and carries on down the street, paying special attention, as always, to those who, from their dress and manner, he identifies as foreigners. On the Palillero, he encounters some members of the Cortés heading toward San Felipe Neri. Most of them are young, wearing dress coats open to reveal waistcoats, light hats made of reeds or Filipino hemp, light-colored ties, close-fitting trousers or leather riding breeches with fringed boots in the style of those who call themselves liberals, to distinguish themselves from the dyed-in-the-wool supporters of the absolute power of the king, who dress more formally, tending to favor redingotes and scooped jackets. The latter are referred to as *serviles* by the people of Cádiz, an indication of where popular opinion lies in the increasingly bitter debate over whether sovereignty belongs to the monarchy or to the Spanish people. A debate which leaves the comisario completely cold. Whether liberals or *serviles*, kings, regencies, national juntas, committees of public safety or the Grand Panjandrum of Tamburlaine the Great, whoever rules Spain will always need policemen in order to rule; in order to restore order after they have whipped up the public to adulation or to fury.

Passing the deputies, Tizón instinctively doffs his hat in salute, as punctilious as he would be if—one never knows what may happen—he were ordered to arrest them and put them all in jail. Among their number he recognizes the pale, watery eyes—like raw oysters—of the young Conde de Torenos and the lanky, influential Agustín Argüelles and, among the Americans, Mexía Lequerica and Fernández Cuchillero. Tizón takes his watch from his waistcoat pocket and realizes it is after ten. Although the daily sessions of the Cortés officially begin at 9 a.m. sharp, there is rarely a quorum before half-past ten. Their lordships— and here it makes no difference whether they are liberals or *serviles*— are not early risers.

Turning right onto the Calle de la Verónica, the comisario goes into a small inn run by a man from Cantabria who is also a wine merchant. The owner is behind the bar filling bottles while his wife washes glasses in the sink, surrounded by chorizos hanging from rafters and barrels of salted sardines.

"I have a problem, *camarada*."

The man looks at him charily, a toothpick in the corner of his mouth. He obviously knows Tizón well enough to realize that if the policeman has a problem, it will soon be his.

"Tell me about it."

He comes around the counter and Tizón leads him to the back of the shop near the sacks of chickpeas and crates of dried cod. The woman eyes them suspiciously, her face like vinegar, her ears pricked. She too knows the comisario.

"Last night someone reported people drinking here after hours. And playing cards."

The innkeeper protests. It was a misunderstanding, he says, spitting out the toothpick. A group of foreigners lost their way and came in and he was not about to turn his nose up at a couple of *reales*. That was all. The accusation that there was card-playing is slander. Lies from some bastard of a neighbor.

"My problem," Tizón explains calmly, "is that I have to impose a fine. Eighty-eight *reales*, to be precise."

"But that's unfair, Señor Comisario."

Tizón stares at the Cantabrian until the man bows his head. He is a tall, strapping figure with a thick mustache who hails from Santander in the mountains of Bárcena but has lived in Cádiz all his life. A peaceable fellow, as far as Tizón knows. The kind to live and let live. His only weakness—one he shares with most people—is the desire to pocket just a little more money. The policeman knows that here in the inn, once the street door is closed for the night, card games are played in breach of municipal ordinances.

"The word 'unfair,'" he says coldly, "has just increased your fine by another twenty *reales*."

The innkeeper blanches, stammers his apologies and glances over at his wife. "It's not true there were people playing cards here last night," he protests. "This is a decent establishment. You have no right."

"The fine is now one hundred and twenty-eight *reales*. Watch your tongue."

The man swears indignantly and thumps a sack of chickpeas, scattering some of them across the floor.

"That little profanity I will keep between us," says Tizón, unruffled. "I realize you are agitated, so I will not charge you with public blasphemy. Although, by rights, I should. Nor am I in any hurry. We can stay here all morning if you wish, entertaining your wife and your customers—you objecting, and me increasing your fine. And eventually, I will close the place down. So why don't you just leave things as they are? You've been warned."

"Is there no way we can come to some agreement?"

The policeman makes a deliberately vague gesture. The sort that cannot compromise him. "I was told that the three men who were here last night were foreigners. That seems a little strange . . . Did you know them?"

By sight, admits the innkeeper. One of them is staying at the Paco Peña guesthouse on Amoladores. A man named Taibilla. He wears a patch over his left eye and claims he was in the Army. He insists on being addressed as lieutenant, but the barman does not know if he really is one.

"Does he have money?"

"A little."

"What did they talk about?"

"Taibilla knows some people who bring foreigners in and out. Or maybe he organizes it himself . . . I don't know."

"For example?"

"A young Negro slave. A runaway. They're looking for an English boat for him."

"For free? . . . I doubt it."

"I think he stole his master's silverware."

"That makes more sense. Otherwise it seems a lot of effort for a Negro."

Tizón is making a mental note of everything. He is already aware of the affair—the Marqués de Torre Pacheco filed a report a week ago about a runaway slave who stole the silverware—but the information may prove useful. And profitable. One of his tricks is never to seem unusually interested in what he is being told. That only serves to make the information more expensive, and he likes to buy cheaply.

"Give me something more. Come on."

The man looks at his wife, who is still busy at the sink. "There was something else," he says in a low voice. "They talked about a family over in El Puerto de Santa María who want to come to Cádiz: a civil servant from Madrid with his wife and five children; they are happy to pay for the crossing and for the residency permits if they can get them."

"How much?"

"A thousand *reales* or so, I think they said."

The comisario smiles to himself. He would have arranged things for the man for half that sum. He may well do so, if he can lay hands on him. One of Tizón's many advantages over upstarts like the man with the eyepatch is that, compared with what such scum charge, his prices are a bargain. And they are officially endorsed, respectable, with a genuine seal, no forgeries. After all, it is Tizón's job to certify such documents.

"What else did they talk about?"

"Not much. They mentioned a Mulatto."

"Well, well . . . It seems there was a lot of talk about darkies . . . What about this Mulatto?"

"He's someone else who comes and goes a lot. From what I heard, he regularly goes over to El Puerto."

Tizón notes this detail as he takes off his hat to mop his brow. He has heard of the Mulatto, who apparently owns his own boat running contraband, like many people, but not that he carries people. He decides to investigate the man further. Find out who he talks to and where he goes.

"So what did they say?"

The innkeeper makes a vague gesture.

"Someone wants to visit their family on the far shore . . . I think they said he was a soldier."

"From Cádiz?"

"That's what I heard."

"Soldier or officer?"

"Officer, I think."

"Now that is something . . . Did you get a name?"

"There you've got me."

Tizón strokes his mustache. An officer prepared to cross over to enemy territory is always a danger. He gets there, he talks a bit to ingratiate himself and it's a short step from desertion to high treason. And although deserters fall under military jurisdiction, when it involves the passing of information or espionage, they also come under Tizón's department. Especially these days, when people seem to see spies everywhere. In Cádiz and on the Isla de Léon, severe penalties have been introduced for boat owners who transport deserters and there is an absolute embargo on any immigrant landing without first passing through the Customs ship moored in the bay. On land, anyone who owns a hostel, boardingrooms or guesthouse must give details of any new guests; and everyone in the city is required to have an officially stamped residency card. Tizón knows that Governor Villavicencio has already prepared a more draconian law which calls for the death penalty in the case of grave infractions, though so far he has not enacted it. In the current circumstances, rigorously enforcing the law would mean executing half the population and jailing the other half.

"Very well, my friend. If they should come back, listen carefully and tell me everything. Understood? In the meantime, close up when you are supposed to close. Mind your own business, and no card-playing."

"What about the fine?"

"Today is your lucky day. We'll say forty-eight *reales.*"

THE SUFFOCATING HEAT of the city feels no better in the sunshine, Tizón realizes, as he steps out into the street and crosses the Plaza San Juan de Dios on the way to his office at the Comisaría de Barrios, an old building with iron railings next to the convent of Santa María near the Royal Jail. Though the morning is already well advanced, crowds of people are milling around the fruit and vegetable stalls and the fishmongers beneath the awnings that stretch from the Town Hall to El Boquete and down to the docks. Swarms of flies buzz, drawn by all this exposed food. Tizón loosens the tie that is pinching his throat and fans himself with his hat. With some relief, he takes off his jacket, so he is in waistcoat and shirtsleeves—though made of fine linen, the shirt is already soaked with sweat—but there are some things that a gentleman and a comisario cannot permit himself. A gentleman he is not (nor does he claim to be), but being a comisario entails a certain level of decorum. Not everything about his position is an advantage.

As he turns the corner by the stone gate of Santa María, Rogelio Tizón spots his deputy, Cadalso, in the distance, accompanied by his secretary. They have clearly been waiting for some time, because they hurry to meet him looking as though they have important news. The news must be grave, the comisario thinks, for his secretary—an office rat and self-professed enemy of sunlight—to come outside on such a hot day.

"What's happened?" he asks, as they reach him.

They quickly bring him up to speed. The body of a dead girl has been found. Tizón feels all the heat drain from him. When he can eventually bring himself to speak, his lips feel frozen.

"How did she die?"

"She was gagged, Señor Comisario, and her back was flayed open with a whip."

He looks at them, bewildered, attempting to digest this information. It is impossible. He tries to think quickly but he cannot; his mind is deluged with ideas.

"Where was she found?"

"Not far from here. In the patio of a ruined house at the end of the Calle del Viento, next to the corner . . . She was discovered by some children who were playing nearby."

"Impossible."

The secretary and the deputy stare at their boss curiously. One of them adjusts his spectacles while the other knits his obtuse brow.

"There's no doubt about it," says Cadalso. "She was eighteen, and lived in the area . . . Her family had been looking for her since last night."

Tizón shakes his head, though he does not quite know why. The murmur of the sea lapping at the nearby ramparts suddenly seems deafening, as though the waves were directly beneath the boots so recently shined by Pimporro. It makes him all the more confused. A strange chill creeps into every part of his body, into the very marrow of his bones.

"I'm telling you it's impossible."

He is shivering, and realizes that his subordinates have noticed. Suddenly he feels the need to sit down somewhere. To think things through slowly. Alone.

"You are sure she was killed in the same manner as the others?"

"Exactly the same," Cadalso confirms. "I've seen the body. I've been looking for you for some time . . . I posted a guard and told him not to let anyone near and to allow no one to touch the body."

Tizón is no longer listening. Impossible, he mutters under his breath. Absolutely impossible. Cadalso is staring at him, puzzled.

"Why do you keep saying that, Comisario?"

"Because no bomb has fallen there."

He blurts out the words as though in protest. And, of course, they sound ridiculous, even to his ears. So he is not surprised to see Cadalso and the secretary exchange a worried glance.

"In fact," he adds, "no bombs have fallen in the city for weeks now."

THE LITTLE CONVOY, four gray carts drawn by donkeys, clatters across the second pontoon bridge and moves along the left bank of the San Pedro River heading for the Trocadero. Sitting in the back of the last cart—the only one with a canopy to protect travelers from the sun— legs hanging over the side, his sword between them and a kerchief pressed to his face to avoid having to breathe the dust kicked up by the mules, Captain Desfosseux watches as the white houses of El Puerto de Santa María vanish into the distance. The trail curves round, following the line of the coast between the wasteland that adjoins the river and the shore at low tide, a wide expanse of mud and moss with the sandbar of San Pedro in the foreground and, in the background, retrenched behind its ramparts and the still blue of the sea, Cádiz.

Simon Desfosseux is reasonably satisfied. The carts are carrying the cargo he had hoped for; moreover, he has just spent two peaceful days in El Puerto enjoying some of the comforts of the rearguard—a cozy bed and decent food instead of his usual daily ration of black bread, half a pound of stringy meat and half a liter of sour wine—while waiting for the convoy to make its slow way from Seville, escorted by a detachment of dragoons and infantry. The latter did nothing to prevent it being attacked twice by guerrillas: once at the inn run by the Biscayan in the foothills of the Sierra de Gibalbín and the second time in Jerez, as they forded the Valadejo River. Eventually, the carts arrived yesterday having suffered minor losses, one dead and two wounded, though the death was all the sadder since the victim was a young bugle boy who disappeared on his way to fill canteens from a nearby brook and turned up naked and lashed to a tree, looking as though he had taken rather too long to die.

Lieutenant Bertoldi, traveling in the first cart, appears by the side of the road, buttoning his fly, having just relieved himself in a clump of bushes. Wearing neither hat nor sword, jacket and waistcoat open to reveal his belly, he is panting from the heat. His skin is as tanned as a redskin on the American prairies.

"Climb up and keep me company," says Desfosseux.

He reaches down and helps Bertoldi into the shade in the back of the cart. Having thanked him, the lieutenant covers his nose and mouth with the filthy kerchief he has been wearing around his neck.

"We look like highwaymen," says the captain, his voice muffled by his own kerchief.

Bertoldi laughs. "In Spain," he says, "they all look like highwaymen."

Longingly, he looks back toward the rearguard camp where he enjoyed two wanton days of enforced idleness. His presence had been unnecessary, but Desfosseux had insisted on bringing him along, knowing that the lieutenant would benefit from a break away from Spanish cannonfire in a place where his only worry would be having to walk in a straight line with several bottles inside him. And from what he has heard, this is exactly how it was. Of the two nights, Bertoldi spent one drinking in a wine cellar and the other in a brothel recently opened for officers on the Plaza del Embarcadero.

"Those Spanish women," he says wistfully. "'You French son of a bitch,' they say while they're taking their clothes off, like they want to gouge your eyes out. So exotic, don't you think? So primitive, with their fans and their rosary beads. They look like gypsies, but they charge you like they're princesses. Bloody whores . . ."

Desfosseux is looking dispassionately at the scenery. Thinking about his own problems. From time to time, in the kind of affectionate gesture a mother hen might give her favorite chicks, he half-turns to contemplate the cargo in the back of the cart, covered with tarpaulins, and carefully packed in straw inside wooden crates. His adjutant peers inside, smiling beneath his kerchief.

"All things come to he who waits," he says.

Desfosseux nods. The wait has been worthwhile—at least, he believes it will have been worthwhile. The convoy is transporting fifty-two special bombs from the Seville Foundry made specifically for Fanfan: spherical projectiles for a 10-inch Villantroys-Ruty howitzer with no handles or eyebolts, perfectly calibrated and polished to create two different models, named Alpha and Beta. Each cart is carrying eighteen of the first type and thirty-four of the second. The Alpha is a conventional bomb like a grenade weighing 72 pounds, with a hole for a fuse and filled with a carefully balanced mixture of lead and gunpowder. The Beta, which is totally spherical and has no fuse or powder charge, simply contains inert lead packed with sand—which causes it to fragment on impact—bringing its weight to 80 pounds. These new bombs are the result of the trials and experiments Desfosseux has been carrying out for several months in the gun battery at Cabezuela, the fruit of lengthy observations, sleepless nights, failures and partial successes; this is the cargo being carried by the convoy, together with five new 10-inch howitzers which were cast in Seville, like Fanfan, though with a number of technical improvements.

"We should use powder that is slightly damp," says the captain, out of the blue.

Bertoldi looks at him, surprised. "Do you never stop thinking?"

Desfosseux points to the dusty road. This is how he came up with the idea. He pulls down his kerchief, and is smiling from ear to ear.

"It was foolish of me not to think of it sooner."

His assistant knits his brow, considering the idea. "It makes sense," he concludes.

"Of course it does," says the captain. "It entails increasing the initial thrust of the explosion within the eight feet of the cannon's bore. If the barrel were shorter, it would not make much difference; in fact dry powder might work better. But with long-bore, high-caliber howitzers cast in bronze, like Fanfan and his new brothers, the less violent combustion of slightly damp powder might increase the thrust of the projectile."

"It's just a matter of proving it, surely? Since they won't give us mortars, we will use damp powder."

They laugh like schoolboys behind a master's back. No one will ever succeed in convincing Simon Desfosseux that they would not get better results with mortars rather than howitzers, extending their range to cover the whole of Cádiz. But the word *mortar* may not be uttered among Marshal Victor's general staff. And yet the captain knows that in order to achieve what is asked of him, he requires a larger caliber than any howitzer. He is tired of reiterating that a dozen 14-inch mortars with cylindrical breeches and an equal number of 40-pound cannons would allow him to raze Cádiz to the ground, terrify the populace and force the insurgent government to seek refuge elsewhere. With such means at his disposal, he would be prepared to sign any harebrained guarantee that within a month he would plow the city and sow it with bombs. And with grenades as God ordained them, fitted with fuses that explode when they reach their target. But no one will listen to him. Marshal Victor, on the direct orders of the Emperor and the drones at Imperial High Command, cannot bring himself to argue with Napoleon over the least whim or idea, and insists on using howitzers against Cádiz. Which, as the marshal repeats every time the subject is raised, means projectiles must reach the city by whatever means, regardless of whether or not they explode. All this in order to generate a convenient story for the newspapers in Madrid or Paris—*Our cannons have the center of Cádiz under constant bombardment,* or something like that; the Duc de Belluno continues to prefer a lot of noise to little effect. Simon Desfosseux, whose only concern in life is to trace parabolas with projectiles, suspects that even the noise is not guaranteed. Nor is he convinced that Fanfan and his brothers, even if they were loaded with the Greek alphabet from Alpha to Omega, would be enough to satisfy his superiors. Even with this new equipment from Seville, it will be difficult to attain a range of 3,000 *toises*. The captain calculates that, with a strong east wind, the right temperature and all other conditions being favorable, he might make four-fifths that distance. Reaching the center of Cádiz would be a miracle. Fanfan's location relative to that of the church steeple on the Plaza de San Antonio is precisely 2,870 *toises*, a distance that Desfosseux calculated on the map and is now etched onto his brain.

Rogelio Tizón looks like a man possessed. He has been pacing up and down for some time, stopping now and then only to retrace his steps. He examines every doorway, every corner, every inch of this street he has been searching now for hours. His apparent indecisiveness is like that of a man who, having lost something, searches everywhere, checking and rechecking pockets and drawers, constantly returning to the same place convinced he will find some trace of what was lost, or remember how he came to lose it. The sun has almost set and the Calle del Viento has begun to fill with shadows. Half a dozen cats are lying on a pile of rubble in front of a house on which an armorial shield, eroded by the weather, can be seen behind the laundry hanging from the upper windows. This is a poor fishermen's neighborhood, situated on the highest point, in the oldest part of the city near the Puerta de Tierra. There is barely a trace of its former magnificence: a few merchants and a number of ancestral houses which have been converted into tenements inhabited by poor families with too many children, and, since the French siege began, by soldiers and immigrants of slender means.

The building where the dead girl was found is slightly beyond the bend in the street, almost on the corner of a little square which opens out at the far end, near the Calle de Santa María and the walls of the convent that bears the same name. Tizón slowly retraces his steps, glancing left and right. All his certainties have fallen apart, and he is finding it impossible to reorganize his thoughts. He spent half the afternoon verifying the terrible truth: no bomb has ever fallen here. The most recent bomb sites are at least three hundred yards away on the Calle del Torno and next to the Iglesia de Nuestra Señora de la Merced. This time, even twisting the facts, it is impossible to find a connection between the girl's death and the point of impact of the French bombs. Which is hardly surprising, he thinks bitterly. When all is said and done, there was never any solid evidence that such a connection existed. Nothing but footprints in the sand. The flights of an imagination playing tricks on him. Drivel. Tizón thinks about Hipólito Barrull and this serves only to irritate him further. His chess partner at the Café del Correo will laugh when he tells him.

The policeman goes into the house, which smells of neglect and filth. The late afternoon sun is waning rapidly and the hallway is already in darkness. There is a rectangle of sunlight on the patio beneath two floors of windows with no glass and balconies from which the wrought-iron railings have long since been ripped down. On the broken tiles of the patio, two brownish stains—dried blood—indicate the spot where the girl was found. She was taken away at midday after Tizón had checked the body and performed the necessary investigations. She was just like the other three: hands tied behind her back, a gag stuffed into her mouth, her back stripped bare, flogged and flayed to reveal each vertebra from neck to waist, her shoulder blades and the beginnings of the ribs. On this occasion, the murderer was even more cruel; the body looked as though a wild animal had ripped at it with its teeth and devoured the flesh. The girl must have suffered horribly. When Tizón removed the gag, he noticed that she had broken several teeth clenching them in her agony. It is a piteous sight. Next to the dried crust of blood is a yellow stain that still reeks. One of Tizón's men—men inured to such atrocities—vomited his guts up when he saw the body.

Tía Perejil has confirmed she was a virgin. Like the other victims. And once again this was not what had interested the offender. From what Tizón has established, the girl disappeared early last night as she was heading back to her house on the Calle de la Higuera, having visited a sick relative on the Calle Sopranis and bought a pitcher of wine for her father. The crime does not appear to have been impulsive: the girl made a habit of leaving her relative's house at the same time every day. The murderer must have been watching her for some time; yesterday he followed her for a short while, approached her just as she reached the derelict house and dragged her into the patio—the pitcher was found smashed in the doorway. He probably knew the place and had looked it over to see if it would suit his purpose. Although this part of the Calle del Viento is not very busy, there are people coming and going. The murderer's feat shows considerable daring, given that he might have been surprised by a passerby or a prying neighbor. And he must have been very self-possessed. To bind and gag the victim and flay her in this way, lash after lash, would have taken at least ten or fifteen minutes.

Something in the air intrigues the policeman, though it takes some time before he becomes conscious of this. It has to do with the atmosphere—or rather the lack of it, the change in it. It is as if this is a point in space where temperature, sound and even smell have been suspended to create a vacuum. Something like moving unexpectedly from one point to another, through a point where the air is absolutely still. It is a curious sensation, especially on the Calle del Viento—a street named after the wind and not by chance, since it is close to the sea wall and the gales that blow in from the ocean. The cats, who have followed Tizón into the house, distract him from these thoughts. Silently, they creep closer, with the watchful eyes of hunters. Although this is their territory, and the area is overrun with rats, there were bite marks on the dead girl's body. One of the cats tries to rub itself against Tizón's boot, and he lashes out with his cane, sending it scurrying back to join the others licking at the pool of dried blood. Tizón sits down on the cracked steps of a ruined marble staircase and lights a cigar. When his thoughts return to the victim, the strange feeling has dissipated.

Four deaths and not a single worthwhile clue. And now, the situation is becoming even more complicated. Although it might be possible to get the girl's family to stay quiet this time—in the other cases, Tizón paid people off—several neighbors saw the body. The news will already be all over the area. And to complicate matters further, an unwelcome figure has entered the picture: Mariano Zafra, owner, editor and sole reporter on one of the newspapers that have proliferated in Cádiz since the freedom of the press was proclaimed—an unfortunate event, in the comisario's opinion. Zafra is a champion of radical ideas, and his activities make sense only in the current climate of political intrigue. His paper *El Jacobino Ilustrado* is published once a week, running to four pages that cover the debates at the Cortes, some news and a variety of completely unsubstantiated rumors in a section entitled "Calle Ancha," a column as meddling, petty-minded and scandalmongering as its author. Once a supporter of Godoy* and, after the Prime Minister's disgrace, a fervent supporter of King Fernando, more recently a vigorous defender of the Throne and the Church, becoming gradually more liberal as those members of the Cortes have found favor with the citizens of Cádiz, Zafra is an opportunist who can jump sides without so much as a blush. His pamphlets have little influence on public opinion beyond a handful of taverns in the insalubrious area where he lives near El Boquete, in cafés where people will read anything, and among the constituent delegates who read everything written about them, ready to applaud or excoriate depending on whether they are considered coreligionists or adversaries. But though it is a far cry from the *Diario Mercantil*, *El Conciso* or *El Semenario Patriótico*, at the end of the day *El Jacobino Ilustrado* is nonetheless a newspaper. Journalism has become the glorious god of this new century. And the authorities—Governor Villavicencio and General Intendant García Pico, for example—are wary of challenging it, even when it entails the sort of gross libel Zafra publishes. In fact Zafra, given his zealous extremism—not a week goes by without him calling for nobles to be guillotined, generals to be executed and a people's assembly established—has been nicknamed by wags the Robespierre of El Boquete.

The fact remains that early this afternoon, when the body of the murdered girl was still here in the patio and Tizón was searching for some clue, his assistant Cadalso came to tell him that Mariano Zafra was at the door, asking for permission to come in. The comisario went out and had the busybodies move back so he could take the journalist aside and tell him in no uncertain terms to mind his own business.

"A girl has been murdered," the man protested. "And she's not the only one. I can think of at least one or two more who were killed recently."

---

* Manuel de Godoy, "Príncipe de la Paz," prime minister of Spain from 1801 to 1808.

"That has nothing to do with this case."

Tizón had taken Zafra's arm in an almost friendly gesture and walked him down the street to get him away from the crowd around the doorway. The polite gesture did not deceive anyone and Zafra was certainly not taken in. After a couple of attempts, he managed to pull free and confronted the comisario.

"Well, I'm afraid I don't agree. I think they are related."

Tizón glared down at this little man wearing badly darned stockings and filthy shoes with brass buckles, his necktie pinned in place with a topaz—doubtless fake. His crumpled hat was lopsided, his fingernails stained with ink, and the pockets of his bottle-green frockcoat spilled over with scraps of paper. His eyes were pale. Perhaps intelligent.

"And on what do you base such a foolish idea?"

"A little bird told me."

Unruffled as always, Tizón coolly considered the problem. The possible moves on the chessboard. Clearly someone had let the cat out of the bag. It was bound to happen sooner or later. On the other hand, although Mariano Zafra was not particularly dangerous—his reputation as a journalist was negligible—the consequences of him printing anything could be profound. The last thing Cádiz needed was to find out that a murderer had been stalking the streets for some time, killing young girls—to say nothing of *how* he killed them. There would be widespread panic, and the first poor bastard suspected of anything would be strung up by a furious mob. And, predictably, they would demand to know who was responsible: who had kept the matter secret? Who was so incompetent that they failed to catch the killer? Et cetera. The serious newspapers would be quick to jump on the story.

"Let's try to be responsible, Zafra my friend. And discreet."

This was the wrong tone, thought Tizón as he said the words and saw the expression on the man's face. A tactical error on his part. The Robespierre of El Boquete was a man who grew taller as his enemy grew weaker.

"Don't try to pull a fast one, Comisario. The people of Cádiz have the right to know the truth."

"Forget about rights and such rubbish. Let's be practical."

"What authority do you have to dictate to me?"

Tizón glanced left and right, as though expecting someone to appear with a certificate confirming his authority. Or perhaps to check that there were no witnesses to the conversation.

"The authority of someone who can smash your head in. Or make your life a living hell."

Zafra flinched. Took a step back. It was now his turn to glance around, worriedly.

"That sounds like a threat, Comisario?"

"You don't say."

"I'll inform on you."

Tizón allowed himself a little laugh. Short, derisive. As friendly as the gold tooth glinting in his smile.

"To whom? The police . . . ? I *am* the police, *hombre*."

"I mean to the Law."

"Sometimes I am the Law. Don't make me angry."

The silence between them was longer this time. The comisario was expectant, the journalist brooding. Fifteen seconds ticked by.

"Let's be reasonable, *camarada*. You know a lot about me. As I do about you."

Tizón's tone was conciliatory. A donkey driver offering a carrot to the mule he has just beaten with a stick. Or is about to beat—this, at least, is how Zafra interpreted it.

"We have freedom of the press," he said. "I assume you have heard of that?"

Zafra's tone was defiant. The little rat is not a coward, thought Tizón. After all, not all rats are. Some of them are capable of eating a man alive.

"Don't talk such rubbish. This is Cádiz. Your newspaper, like every newspaper, is protected by the government and the Cortes . . . I can't stop you publishing whatever you like, but I can ensure you suffer the consequences."

Zafra raised an ink-stained finger. "You don't frighten me. Others have tried to silence the voice of the people, and look what happened to them. The day will come when—"

Zafra drew himself up until he was standing on the tiptoes of his badly shined shoes. With a curt gesture, Tizón interrupted him. "Don't make me waste my breath," he said. "And don't waste yours. I want to offer you a deal." At this last word, the journalist looked at him in disbelief. Then he brought his hand to his chest.

"I do not make deals with blind instruments of power."

"Listen, don't try my patience. What I am offering you is reasonable."

In a few brief words the comisario explained what he had in mind. As and when necessary he would provide information to the editor of *El Jacobino Ilustrado*. And to him alone. He would keep him up to date, withholding only information that might compromise the investigation if it were made public.

"In return, you will look after me. A little."

The other man looked at him suspiciously. "And what exactly do you mean by that?"

"Praise me to the skies: our Comisario de Barrios is wise, essential to the maintenance of civil peace, et cetera. The investigation is going well and we expect new developments at any moment . . . I don't know. You're the writer. The police are working day and night, Cádiz is in good hands, things like that. The usual."

"You are making fun of me."

"Absolutely not. I'm telling you what we are going to do."

"I prefer the freedom of the press. My freedom as a citizen."

"I have no intention of interfering with your freedom to print whatever you like. But if we do not come to some arrangement, your own freedom may be jeopardized."

"Explain yourself."

Thoughtfully, Tizón gazed at the bronze head of his cane: a round ball in the shape of a large walnut. Capable of splitting a man's head with a single blow. Calmly, the journalist followed the direction of his gaze. A tough customer, thought Tizón. He had to acknowledge that although the man's principles could change according to the whims of popular opinion, he was prepared to defend them tooth and nail for as long as he held them. To anyone who did not know the man, he seemed almost respectable. But Tizón had the advantage of knowing him.

"Would you like me to beat around the bush, or shall I tell you straight?"

"Tell me straight, if you would be so kind."

A brief pause. Just long enough. And then Tizón moved his bishop into play.

"The fourteen-year-old Moorish boy who works in your house, the one you bugger from time to time, he could cause you a problem. Or two."

It was as though an embolism had suddenly drained all the blood from Zafra's body. White as a sheet of paper before it is put into the printing press. The pupils in his pale eyes shrank until they all but disappeared.

"The Inquisition has been suspended," Zafra finally whispered with some effort, "and it is about to be abolished."

But his tone was not so defiant. Rogelio Tizón knew too much. Zafra's bearing was that of a man who had not had breakfast or lunch and was about to go without dinner. A man whose belly was empty and whose head was suddenly full. About to faint. At that moment, Lobo's gold teeth glittered again. "I don't give a shit about the Inquisition," said Tizón. "But as you can imagine, there are various options. One would be to deport the boy, since he has no more papers than a wild rabbit. Another would be to arrest him and make sure the old lags in the Royal Jail broaden his horizons. A third possibility has just occurred to me: demand a medical examination before a trustworthy judge and then force him to prosecute you for sodomy. The unspeakable crime, as you know. That is how we used to refer to it in front of the fools at the Cortes and the Constitution. In the good old days."

Zafra was stammering now. "How long? No one knows . . . How long have you known this?"

"About the boy? For a while. But each to his own, and I don't like to interfere in other people's private lives. But having to wipe my ass with that rag you publish is a different matter."

Sitting on the staircase of the derelict house, Tizón tosses away his cigar without finishing it. Perhaps it is the smell of this place, but the smoke tastes bitter. The last light drains from the cloudless sky and the rectangle of light vanishes from the patio tiles, where the cats are still licking at the dried blood. There is nothing further to be done here. Nothing to clear up. All his predictions have come to nothing, leaving a gaping void as empty as this house. The comisario remembers the piece of twisted lead in his desk drawer and shakes his head. For months now he has been waiting for some strange event, some crucial insight that would allow him to see the chess game as a whole. The possible and the impossible. Now he knows this idea has cost him too much time; he has been waiting meekly, and this girl's death is the result of his indolence. Rogelio Tizón has no regrets, but the thought of this sixteen-year-old girl, her back slashed to shreds, her eyes wide with horror, her teeth broken from clenching them as she died, makes him feel physically sick. This picture is overlaid with those of the other murdered girls. Forcing him to face the ghosts that stalk the darkness of his own home. The silent woman who moves about the house like a shadow; the piano that no one plays anymore.

BARELY A GLIMMER of daylight remains. The comisario gets to his feet, takes a last look at the cats licking the tiles and walks down the dark corridor toward the street. Governor Villavicencio was right after all. It is time to put together a list of undesirables, ready for the moment when Cádiz begins to demand that someone put a face to the killer. For the moment, a couple of calculatedly ambiguous confessions should be enough to keep things under control while they wait for the results of his meticulous work or some stroke of luck related to politics or the war: upheavals that make this chaos seem orderly. But such thoughts do little to dispel the sense of failure, the helplessness he feels before this closed door; now dark, uncertain, affording barely a chink of light but which, until today, had fueled the hope that he might glimpse some spark within, might grasp the gambit that allows the patient chess player to move deep into his opponent's territory.

As he steps out into the dark street, a sudden sound like ripping sailcloth makes the comisario start. He turns to see where it is coming from and as he does, the dark hallway belches out a tongue of yellow flame that briefly lights up the porch and the street, bringing with it a rain of dust and gravel. Then comes the boom of the explosion, causing everything to tremble. Shaken by the blast—his eardrums ache like they have burst—Tizón staggers, throwing up his arms to protect himself from the shards of glass and plaster falling all around. He takes a few steps then falls to his knees in the thick, suffocating cloud of dust. When he finally comes to his senses, he feels something hot and sticky against his neck. He brushes it off, and as he does so briefly panics that it might be part of his own body. But what he discovers is a length of intestine attached to the tail of a cat.

All around, the ground is scattered with red dots: twisted, glowing fragments that rapidly cool and darken. Corkscrews of lead. Still dazed, Tizón instinctively bends down and picks one up, only to drop it instantly as the metal burns his fingers. When finally his ears stop ringing and he looks around in the darkness, the first thing that strikes him is the silence.

THE FOLLOWING DAY, in shirtsleeves, wearing a rubber apron and carrying a homing pigeon, Gregorio Fumagal walks over to the eastern edge of the terrace and carefully surveys the area. With the fine weather and the glut of foreigners, the roofs of many houses have become camping grounds, with whole families living like nomads in makeshift tents of canvas and sailcloth. It has begun to happen on the Calle de las Escuelas, where Fumagal owns the top floor of his building. For simple reasons of discretion, the taxidermist does not rent out his own terrace, but there are immigrants living on some of the neighboring terraces and it is not unusual to see people nosing about at all hours. This has forced him to tread warily, just as, when he first began his clandestine contact with the far shore, he dismissed the housemaid who had been working for him. He now does his own housework, his breakfast is a bowl of milk with bread crumbs, and he eats his other meals in the Perdiz inn on the Calle Descalzos, or at La Terazza between the Calle Pelota and the Arco de la Rosa.

The coast is clear. Standing between the laundry to shield himself from prying eyes, and having already checked that the tube carrying the message is tied with silk thread to the bird's tail, Fumagal releases the pigeon, which flutters for a moment, gaining height, then flies off between the towers of the city heading for the bay. In a few short minutes, the message detailing the points of impact of the last five bombs will be in French hands. The very same points are marked on his map of Cádiz, the fretwork of penciled lines growing every day into a fan that spreads out across the city from the eastern walls. On the map, the maximum range of the bombs has extended a whole inch westwards— there is one on the edge of the Murga and another on the corner of the Calle San Francisco and Calle Aduana Vieja—all this without following winds, which increase the trajectories. Things may improve further when the east winds pick up. Perhaps.

Gregorio Fumagal feeds the pigeons, pours water into their drinking trough and closes the dovecote. Then he goes back inside, leaving the glass door to the terrace open, and descends the short staircase to his workshop. There on the marble slab, among the glassy stores of the stuffed animals on perches and in display cases, his newest creation is beginning to take shape: the macaque monkey from the East Indies looks splendid. The taxidermist is pleased. Having skinned the animal, removed and cleaned the bones, he left the hide to soak for several days in a solution of alum, sea salt and cream of tartar bought at Frasquito Sanlúcar's shop—where he also acquired some new hair dye which does not run when he sweats—before creating the internal framework using thick wire, cork and stuffing made from oakum inside the reconstructed skeleton, then slowly fitting it inside the carefully prepared pelt.

It is a hot morning. The light streaming through the terrace door and spilling down the steps grows brighter as the sun reaches its height, illuminating the workshop and making the glass eyes of the stuffed animals glitter. The steeple bell at the nearby Iglesia de Santiago rings out—the midday Angelus—and is answered by the clock on the dresser chiming twelve. Then once again there is silence, broken only by the sound of Fumagal's instruments. He works skillfully using needles, awls and string, filling and securing the cavities, checking against the drawings lying next to the table. Preliminary sketches of the pose he has decided on for the monkey: standing upright on a dried, varnished branch, the tail loose and carefully curled, the face looking slightly over the left shoulder, staring at the future viewer. In choosing the right pose for the macaque, the taxidermist consulted natural history books, engravings from his collection and drawings he himself has made. Not a single detail is overlooked. This is the most delicate part of the process: finding a lifelike posture that will complement the body, taking great care over the eyelids, the ears, the mouth, the texture of the fur. To a large extent this determines the final preparations, the finishing touches that will make—or fail to make—the piece lifelike, accentuating or marring its perfection. Gregorio Fumagal is aware that to overlook any imperfection—the slightest graze on the skin, a careless stitch, a tiny insect left inside the stuffing—will disfigure the piece and, over the years, may ruin it. After almost thirty years in this profession, he knows that every stuffed animal is still, in some sense, alive, and each ages differently under the effects of light, dust, the passage of time and the subtle physical and chemical processes taking place inside. Dangers the taxidermist must guard against using all his skill and every technique of his art.

A tremor in the air that makes the glass panes in the terrace door quiver is followed, a moment later, by a muffled explosion, the sound dampened by the distance and by the houses in between. Interrupted just as he begins sewing the base of the macaque's tail using overcast stitches, Fumagal stops and listens intently; the hand holding the threaded needle hovers in midair. *This one did explode,* he thinks as he goes back to his work. *And not far away: somewhere near the Iglesia del Pópulo, probably. No more than five hundred paces.* The possibility that a bomb might one day strike his house or even him has occurred to him from time to time. Any one of his pigeons might provoke a reply that could be dangerous or even fatal. The taxidermist has many plans for his old age—some likely, some unlikely—but the idea of sacrificing himself like Samson in the Temple of the Philistines is not among them. But every game has its rules, and this one is no exception. In fact he would not care if a bomb were to fall nearby, ideally on the Santiago church, silencing the bells which ring out every day—with particular insistence on Sundays and holy days—accompanying the hours he spends here. If there is an excess of anything in Cádiz—a microcosm of all that is bad about Spain—it is convents and churches.

In spite of his affinity for those laying siege to the city—or rather for the Enlightenment tradition of the previous century, to which the Revolution and the Empire are heirs—there are some things Gregorio Fumagal finds difficult to tolerate, and the Napoleonic restoration of the cult of religion is one of these. The taxidermist is merely a humble merchant and artisan who has read books and studied creatures both living and dead. But he believes that mankind, ignorant of Nature and failing to abide by its laws, has rejected knowledge in favor of imaginary systems; inventing gods and the priests and kings anointed by them, meekly submitting to men who are their equals and who exploit this fact to enslave them; spurning reason and unaware of the key fact: everything that exists does so within the natural order, in which chaos is as common as its opposite. Having read the philosophers on these matters, and studied death at close hand, Fumagal is of the opinion that Nature cannot act otherwise. It is Nature and not some impossible God that dispenses order and disorder, pleasure and pain. It is Nature that propagates both good and evil, in a world in which neither screams nor prayers can alter the immutable laws of creation and destruction, their fearful inevitability. It is within the order of things that fire should burn; that is its nature. It is also within the order of things that man should kill and devour other animals whose flesh he needs. And that man should do evil, since it is in his condition to hurt. There is no more edifying example of his theory than death accompanied by terrible suffering beneath a heaven incapable of sparing one whit of that pain. Nothing could be more instructive about the nature of the world;

nor more comforting when confronted with the notion of a superior intelligence whose intentions, should they exist, are criminally unjust. This is why the taxidermist believes that there is a consolatory, almost Jacobin moral certainty to be found in terrible disasters and atrocities: earthquakes, epidemics, wars, massacres. Even in the most terrible crimes which clarify the mind, and force mankind to face the cold reality of the Universe.

"You should be thinking about this in terms of physics, of concrete experiments," says Hipólito Barrull. "Looking for some supernatural explanation is ridiculous in this day and age."

Rogelio Tizón listens attentively as he walks, head bowed, staring at the cobbles of the Plaza de San Antonio. He clasps his hat and his cane behind his back. The walk has cleared his head after the three games of chess at the Café del Correo: two won by the professor, the third a stalemate.

"Question reason," Barrull continues.

"Reason laughs in my face when I question it."

"Analyze the visible world, then. Anything at all rather than resorting to this hocus-pocus."

The comisario looks around. The sun has already set and the temperature dips as the sky grows dark above the lookout towers and terraces. A number of caleches and sedans are stationed outside Burnel's teashop and the Café de Apolo, and in the fading light crowds of people are strolling along the plaza and the nearby Calle Ancha; well-heeled families from the neighboring houses, children running and bowling hoops, priests, soldiers, penniless refugees slyly looking for cigar stubs in the gutters. Serene and confident, the city is taking its ease among the demi-columns, the orange trees and the marble benches, enjoying the leisurely summer sunset. As ever, the war seems very remote. Almost unreal.

"The visible world," Tizón protests, "implies that what I've just told you is true."

"And therefore it is. Unless the visible world has tricked you, which is possible. You have to remember that sometimes unforeseen coincidences do occur. Effects whose apparent causes are utterly unrelated."

"There have already been four separate instances, Professor. Or perhaps three plus one. The similarities are obvious, and they are clearly connected. I simply cannot work out the key."

"And yet there must be one. In the order of things there are no unprompted actions. Bodies act upon one another. Each alteration is the result of factors both visible and unseen . . . Nothing can exist without them."

They leave the square, and still at a leisurely pace, head toward the Mentidero. Behind the window shutters and in some of the shops that are still open, lights are beginning to flicker. Barrull, who lives alone and usually has a frugal dinner, has a hankering for an aubergine tortilla from the inn on the Calle del Veedor. They go inside and lean for a while on the counter next to the lamp which emits an oily black smoke, among crates of overseas produce and wineskins. The professor drinks a small glass of *pajarete** and the comisario a glass of cold water.

"In general terms, your murderer is not an isolated case," Barrull continues while he waits for his food to arrive. "Every human being acts by virtue of his own energy, and that passed on by the bodies with which he interacts. For every effect there is always a cause. A link."

The tortilla arrives, steaming and succulent. The professor offers some to Tizón, who shakes his head.

"Think about men in ancient times," Barrull continues. "They saw planets and stars moving across the heavens, but they did not understand why until Newton explained the forces that heavenly bodies exert on each other."

"Gravity . . ."

"Exactly. Some forces or causes can remain beyond our understanding for centuries. Like the connection between these bombs and this murder. Their criminal gravity."

The professor pensively eats a piece of tortilla, reflecting on what he has just said. After a moment, he nods vehemently.

* *Pajarete*, sometimes called "blended sherry," is a vinous liqueur to which boiled must is added.

"If a body has mass, it falls," he goes on. "If it falls, it will collide with other bodies and communicate that motion to them. It acts upon them. Everything is governed by the laws of physics. Including men and bombs."

He takes a sip of wine. With satisfaction, he contemplates the contents of his glass in the lamplight, then takes another sip. When he sets it down again, a smile plays across his equine face.

"Give me matter and motion, Descartes said, and I will create a world . . . or destroy it."

"But this time the crime was committed before the bomb fell," Tizón points out.

"That has happened only once. And we do not know why."

"Listen, the murderer has killed four times. Each time the manner was identical. And the fact is that shortly beforehand, a bomb fell in precisely the same spot. Do you really think coincidence has anything to do with it? . . . Reason tells me that this connection exists."

"You will have to wait for further proof."

At this, both men fall silent. Tizón turns and looks out of the door to the street. When he turns back to Barrull, he can see the man is deep in thought. Through the reflection of the lamp on his spectacles, his half-closed eyes glitter with curiosity.

"Tell me something, Comisario . . . If you had the choice at this moment to catch the murderer or give him another opportunity to prove your theory, what would you choose?"

Tizón does not answer. Holding Barrull's gaze, he slips a hand into the pocket of his frockcoat, takes a Havana cigar from the Russian leather case and puts it between his teeth. He offers one to the professor, who shakes his head.

"At heart you are a man of science," Barrull says, clearly amused.

Setting a few coins on the counter, they go out into the street where the last of the daylight is fading. Other shadows stroll unhurriedly along the street. Neither man speaks until they reach the Mentidero.

"The problem," says Tizón finally, "is that this reduces the possibility of catching him . . . Until now, we thought we might catch him by keeping an eye on the sites where bombs had exploded. Now, there is no way of anticipating his movements."

"Let us be logical," argues Barrull after a moment's thought. "The man has killed four times, and on three of these occasions, the bomb fell before the murder was committed. In the most recent case, however, it fell afterward. It is impossible to establish whether the connection was unfounded from the start, the result of an error or random chance, which would invalidate everything. A second possibility is that the connection is genuine, that the sequence has been interrupted or changed by chance or circumstances. There is a third possibility, that the modus operandi has changed—whatever that may mean—that this represents a new phase in the series, the reason for which we do not yet know but which must have a logical explanation. Or, at the very least, it must not conflict with the natural laws of the world in which both murderer and policeman exist."

"Careful with the word *chance*, professor," warns Tizón. "You yourself told me it is a common excuse."

"That's very true. It is the explanation that requires the least effort. All too often, we use the idea of chance to conceal our limited understanding of natural causes. Of the immutable law whose mysterious strategy moves the pawns on the chessboard . . . We use chance to explain observable incidents in which we are incapable of discerning order or method. Man, in fact, attributes to chance all those effects for which the connection to cause remains hidden."

Tizón has stopped to strike a match against the wall. He brings the flame to the tip of his cigar.

"*All is possible, when 'tis a god contrives,*" he murmurs, blowing smoke to extinguish the match.

In the darkness, he cannot see Barrull's face, but he hears the laugh.

"Well, well, Comisario. Still puzzling over Sophocles, I see."

They stroll across the Plaza Mentidero toward the ramparts and the sea, weaving through dark groups of people huddled on benches, on chairs, on blankets spread out on the ground, their silhouettes flickering in the light of oil lamps, lanterns and candles set in pots or glasses.

Since the fine weather arrived, many families from neighborhoods threatened by the bombing have taken to spending their nights here on the Plaza Mentidero and the neighboring Campo de Balón, drinking wine and playing guitars into the early hours.

"So, let us examine the facts," says Barrull. "Since it defies reason that someone could deliberately and precisely predict the sites where the bombs will fall and use those locations to commit murder, there remains only one possibility: the murderer *intuits* the point of impact . . . or to put it in scientific terms, his actions are driven by forces of attraction, by probabilities we cannot formulate."

"You mean he is simply one element in something more complex?"

"Perhaps," says Barrull. "The world is full of elements which have no apparent relation to each other. But when some are mixed with others, the resulting force can produce surprising—or horrifying—results. Combinations to which we have not found the key. It seems likely that primitive man would have been astonished to see fire suddenly appear, whereas today we know we simply mix iron filings with sulfur and water. Complex actions are simply a combination of simple actions.

"In which case," Barrull concludes, "your murderer might be a physical, geometrical or mathematical factor . . . I don't know. One element in relation to others: victims, topographic localization, the trajectories of the bombs, perhaps their contents. Gunpowder, lead. Some explode while others do not, and he murders only when they explode—or when they are going to."

"But only when the bombs kill no one."

"This further complicates matters. Why in some cases and not others? Does he make a conscious choice? What prompts him to act in those cases? Obviously, it would be useful to interrogate him. I am sure even he would not be able to answer these questions. Some, perhaps, but not all. I doubt that anyone could."

"Some time ago, you said we could not rule out the idea that he is a man of science."

"I said that . . . ? Very well. Now that we are dealing with a murder that took place in advance, I am not so sure. It could be anyone. Even a brainless, illiterate monster is capable of reacting to complex stimuli: though he must have something in his head that functions scientifically."

A slightly brighter area marks out the space between the artillery park and the Candelaria barracks at the far end of the plaza. In the distance, it is possible to make out the glow of the lighthouse at San Sebastián, which has just been lit. The comisario and the professor reach the small arbor of the Paseo del Perejil, near the waterwheel, and turn right. By the ramparts, people stand staring at the far shore of the bay, silhouetted by the last waning ribbon of sunset.

"It would be interesting to know what is inside his head," says Barrull.

The glow of the comisario's cigar lights up his face.

"Sooner or later I will find out. That I promise you."

"I hope you do not apprehend the wrong man. For if you do, I foresee a terrible future for some poor wretch."

They carry on walking in silence, past the ramparts, wandering beneath trees on the Alameda. The Iglesia del Carmen is shrouded in shadow, the church doors closed, its twin spires soaring above the imposing facade.

"Whatever else you do, remember this," adds the professor. "Torture has just been abolished by the Cortes."

That's what they say, Tizón is about to reply, but he says nothing. He spent this very afternoon interrogating, in his usual manner—the only effective manner—a foreigner who was found yesterday furtively watching the young seamstresses coming out of the dressmakers' workshops on the Calle Juan de Andas. It took several hours of rigorous interrogation, much sweat from Cadalso, and much screaming from the suspect, muffled by the thick dungeon walls, to establish that he was not responsible for the murders. Tizón, however, is planning to keep him locked up for a while, in case things become complicated and it is necessary to appease the mob. When you have a suspect in hand, it matters little whether he is guilty, or only seems to be. And a confession made in front of a clerk who is deaf to anything but the jingling of the money he is paid is a confession nonetheless. It has not yet come to

this with Tizón's prisoner—an unmarried, middle-aged worker from
Seville, a refugee in Cádiz—but you never know. Tizón does not care
that the deputies at San Felipe Neri have spent months debating
whether or not to adopt a law similar to the English habeas corpus
or to reinstate the Aragonese law, both of which forbid arresting someone without prior inquiries proving they may have committed a crime.
His opinion, unlikely to be changed by debates in the Cortes or fatu-
ous liberal nonsense, is that good intentions are one thing, but reality
is a very different matter. With or without such new laws, experience
has proved that there is only one method of getting the truth from
people—it is a method as old as the world, or at least as the policeman's
profession. And the margin of error, inevitable in such methods, is off-
set by a high rate of success. You cannot make a tortilla without breaking eggs, not in the inn on the Calle Veedor or in a police cell. Tizón
has broken a few eggs in his time. And fully intends to go on breaking
them.

"With or without the Cortes, I will get inside his head, Professor. I
guarantee it."

"First you have to catch him."

"I will do." Tizón looks around, bitter and suspicious. "Cádiz is a
small town."

"But full of people. I fear your claim is uncertain. A voluntarism
that is understandable, given your profession and the circumstances,
but it is hardly rigorous . . . You have no concrete reason to assume you
will catch him. It's not simply a matter of following your nose. The
solution, if one exists, will be arrived at by more complex, scientific
means."

"The manuscript of *Ajax* . . ."

"Listen to me, my dear friend, don't fall back into your old ways. I
know the play; I translated it. It is poetry, not science. You cannot solve
this case based on a text written in the fifth century BC . . . It is all very
well for firing the imagination, for conjuring the images and meta-
phors that permeate the sort of overheated novels read by ladies now-
adays. But it leads nowhere."

They have stopped in front of Tizón's house and are leaning against

a buttress in the ramparts between two watchtowers. The figure of a
sentry can be seen moving near the closer of the two, his bayonet glittering above his head. On the far side of the wall are dark shapes, the
hulls and masts of Spanish and English ships anchored nearby. The
night is so peaceful, even the sea is calm. All is boundless and silent, the
dark mass of water, the rocks at low tide, the sand and seaweed.

"Sometimes," Barrull continues, "when our senses cannot grasp
certain causes and their effects, we fall back on our imagination, which
is the least trustworthy of guides. Nothing in this world is exempt from
the natural order. Every action—and I insist on this—can be explained
by invariable, necessary laws . . . Therefore, let us draw the rational
conclusion: there are universal codes we do not understand."

Tizón tosses the stub of his cigar into the sea.

"Many things, I tell you, can be known by mortal eyes," he murmurs,
"but before he sees it happening, no man can foretell the future . . ."

Barrull gives a snort of disapproval, or perhaps exasperation.

"You and Sophocles are beginning to bore me. Even in the improbable, though not impossible, event that the murderer is familiar with
the text and has been inspired by it, the fact that the fourth girl was
murdered *before* the bomb dropped makes it a rather secondary detail.
Small change in this tragedy . . . If I were you, and were as sure of what
I was saying, I would devote my time to establishing where and when
future bombs will fall."

"Yes, but how?"

"That, I don't know." Barrull's laugh rings out in the darkness.
"Perhaps you could ask the French?"

CHAPTER SEVEN

ℭ

Ite, missa est. The eight o'clock mass at San Francisco ends. At this hour, the faithful are few: some men standing or sitting in the side pews and about twenty women in the nave, kneeling on cushions or on mantillas laid on the ground. With these last words and the priest's blessing, Lolita Palma closes her missal, makes the sign of the cross and walks toward the door, dipping her hand in the font of holy water set against a wall covered with votive offerings in wax and brass. She does not come to mass every day, but today would have been the birthday of her father—a devout man, though not excessively so, he always attended mass before beginning his day's work. Lolita knows that Tomás Palma would be pleased to see her here, commemorating his birthday this way. At other times, she is reasonably faithful to the precepts of her Catholic education, goes to mass on Sundays and sometimes takes communion after confessing to an elderly priest, an old friend of the family who does not ask impertinent questions and dispenses light penances. Nothing more. She read widely even as a girl; the product of a modern education, like many middle-class women in Cádiz, the heiress to the Palma fortune has a liberal view of the world, of business and of life. This is consistent with the formal practice of Catholicism, which in her case is sincere, but tempers its extremes, freeing her of the sanctimonious attitude customary to her sex and her times.

The square is bustling with people. The sun is not yet high and the temperature is pleasant.

A number of foreigners from a nearby boardinghouse—the Posada de París, now renamed the Posada de la Patria—are sitting around tables set out in the street, having breakfast, watching the passersby. The local shopkeepers open their doors and take down the wooden shutters from their windows to show off their merchandise. Women kneel to scrub the doorsteps in front of their houses. Others are sprinkling water on the pavement to keep down the dust or are watering plants on their balconies. Lolita lifts her mantilla and allows it to fall back onto her shoulders—she is wearing her hair in a braided coil, pinned with a mother-of-pearl comb at the nape of her neck. She slips the missal into a black satin bag, lets her fan dangle from the cord on her right wrist and walks toward the shops between the corner of the Calle de San Francisco and the Calle del Consulado Viejo, where there are second-hand bookshops and shops selling prints and engravings. Before going home, she plans to walk down to the Plaza de San Agustín to collect some books and order some foreign newspapers. Then, as every day, she will go back to her office.

She does not see Pépé Lobo until he is right in front of her, coming out of the bookshop with a package under one arm. The corsair is wearing a frockcoat with gilt buttons, long nankeen breeches that reach his ankles, and buckled shoes. When he sees her, he stops dead and doffs his bicorn hat.

"*Señora*," he says.

Somewhat flustered, Lolita Palma returns the greeting. "Good day, Captain."

She was not expecting this encounter. Nor, it seems, was he. He looks uncertain, hat in hand, as though trying to decide whether to put it on again and carry on walking, or stay put and exchange pleasantries. She too is hesitant, ill at ease.

"Taking a stroll?"

"I have just come from mass."

"Oh."

He looks at her curiously, as though he was expecting a different response. *I hope he doesn't take me for some Holy Mary*, Lolita thinks fleetingly, and is immediately irritated by the thought. *What do I care what such an individual thinks of me?*

"Are you a regular patron of bookshops?" she asks pointedly.

The corsair does not seem to notice the insolence. He turns and looks back at the shop he has just left, then gestures to the package under his arm. He smiles to defuse the situation—an ivory-white slash across his tanned face.

"Not really, excepting for my work," he says simply. "This is the *Naval Gazetteer*, in two volumes. An English captain died of a fever and they auctioned off his belongings. I knew some of the books would end up here."

Lolita nods. Such auctions are frequent in the little market down by the Puerta de Mar when ships arrive after long, insanitary voyages. The stark stories of a life spread out on canvas groundsheets, like flotsam from a shipwreck: a carved whalebone, some rope, a pocket watch, a knife with a grimy handle, a pewter mug engraved with initials, a miniature portrait of a woman and sometimes a book or two. A sailor's trunk holds very little.

"How sad," she says.

"For the Englishman, of course." Lobo pats his package. "But fortunate for me. It is a fine book to have aboard . . ."

The corsair trails off, the last word dying on his lips. He seems to hesitate over whether to conclude matters or talk a little more, trying to find a happy medium between politeness and expediency. Lolita also hesitates, and begins to be amused by the situation.

"Cover yourself, Captain, please . . ."

Pépé Lobo is still bareheaded; finally he puts his hat on. He is wearing the coat he always wears, frayed at the sleeves, but the fine cambric shirt is new and freshly laundered and his white tie is knotted at two points. Now it is her turn to smile to herself. The nervousness she senses in him moves her a little—this vague, acutely masculine clumsiness, combined with that calm expression which now and then intrigues her—*and I cannot think why*, she says to herself. *Or perhaps I can. An individual in his profession is accustomed to women of a very different class. I suppose he is not accustomed to dealing with women as employers or business partners. To women having the power to give him work or take it away.*

"Do you speak English?"

"I can get by, señora."

"Did you learn it in Gibraltar?"

She said this without thinking. Or almost without thinking. He looks at her thoughtfully. Curious, perhaps. Those green eyes, so feline, now hold her own. Wary. A cautious cat.

"I spoke a little English before that. But yes, in Gibraltar, I improved it."

"Of course."

They stare at each other a moment longer, silent once more. Studying one another. In Lolita's case, she is also studying herself. She feels a singular combination of curiosity and suspicion that is both irksome and pleasant. The last time she saw the corsair, the tenor of their conversation was very different—professional, in front of others. It occurred a week ago at a meeting in her office. The Sánchez Guineas were in attendance to finalize the sale of the French místico *Madonna Diolet*, which, after two months before the Prize Court—and after greasing the palms of sundry court officers—had finally been declared a fair capture, with its cargo of leather, wheat and *aguardiente*. The king's share having been paid to the Treasury, Pépé Lobo took the third due to the crew—of which, in addition to the 25 *pesos* per month he is paid as an advance against captures, he will take seven parts. He also takes charge of the monies owed to the families of crew members who died or were injured during the captures: two parts each, in addition to a share of the general kitty set aside for invalids, widows and orphans. In her office, the corsair's manner was brisk and efficient and particularly scrupulous about the state of the accounts; he meticulously checked every digit of the monies owed to his men before appending his signature on each page. His attitude, Lolita noticed, was not that of a suspicious man worried about being cheated by the shipowners; he was simply confirming the figures, calculating the amount for which he and his men had risked their lives, within the cramped confines of the cutter. Outside, the wind, the waves, the enemy; inside, the smell and the damp and the overcrowding. One tiny cabin in the stern for the captain, another with bunks separated by curtains for the first officer, the bo'sun and the ship's clerk; the rest of the crew took turns sleeping in the shared hammocks on the open deck, with no protection from wind or sea, while the cutter pitched and rolled at the whim of the ocean and the war, constantly on the alert, in keeping with the old sailor's maxim: "One hand for you, the other for the king." As she watched him read and sign the papers in her office, Lolita realized that a man is not only a good captain at sea, he must also be one on land. She also realized why the Sánchez Guineas held Pépé Lobo in such high esteem and why, in times like these with sailors in short supply, there was no shortage of men willing to sign up aboard the *Culebra*. As Miguel Sánchez Guinea once said to her, "Pépé Lobo is the sort of man the girls in port go crazy about, and men would give their shirt for."

They are still standing in the street outside the secondhand bookshop. Staring at each other. The corsair tips his hat to indicate that he must be on his way. Suddenly, Lolita Palma finds herself wishing he would not go. At least not yet. She wants to prolong this curious sensation, the unfamiliar tingle of fear or wariness that so kindles her curiosity.

"Would you walk with me, Captain? I have some packages to collect. Books, in fact."

She says the words with a self-assurance that surprises even her. She is calm, or at least that is the impression she wishes to convey. But the pulse at her wrists quickens. Pépé Lobo looks at her, unsettled for a moment, then smiles again. A sudden, candid smile. Or so it seems. Lolita looks at his firm jawline, the shadow of stubble already visible, although he doubtless shaved this morning. His bushy dark-brown sideburns are long, as is the fashion, half covering his cheeks. Pépé Lobo is not a sophisticated man, a gentleman like Captain Virués, nor is he a man of good family accustomed to frequenting the cafés of Cádiz and strolling along the Alameda. Not by a long chalk. There is something crude about him, accentuated by the strange paleness of his feline eyes. Something primitive, perhaps dangerous. A broad back, strong hands, a solid presence. In short, a man. And yes, dangerous is the word. It is not difficult to imagine him in shirtsleeves, hair wild, covered in sweat and salt spray, shouting orders and curses amid the smoke of cannonfire, with the wind whistling in the rigging on the cutter where he earns his living. Nor is it hard to imagine him on rumpled sheets beneath the body of a woman.

This last thought unsettles Lolita Palma. She tries to think of something to say to hide her confusion. She and the corsair are walking down the Calle San Francisco—not looking at each other, not speaking, a hand's breadth apart.

"When do you put out again?"

"Eleven days from now. If the Armada gives us the necessary permissions."

She clasps her bag in front of her. They come to the corner of the Calle del Baluarte and walk on. Slowly.

"Your men will be happy. The French *místico* turned a generous profit. And we have another capture still to be adjudicated."

"Indeed. The problem is that many of them have already sold their share of the capture to various merchants in the city. They would rather have money now, even if it is less, than wait for the decision of the Prize Court . . . And, of course, many have already spent it . . ."

Lolita can easily imagine the sailors of the *Culebra* squandering their money in the backstreets of El Boquete and the sordid dives of La Caleta. Nor is it difficult to picture Pépé Lobo squandering his.

"I suppose that is good for business," she ventures. "They will be eager to put out to sea again to earn more."

"Some, yes; others less so. It is not an easy life."

Above their heads, on every balcony, plants spill through ornate railings of wrought iron, like a hanging garden along the length of the street. In front of a toy shop, a group of filthy urchins wearing tattered caps peer enviously at the pasteboard figurines and horses, at drums and spinning tops and toy wagons hanging from the doorjamb.

"I fear I am distracting you from your business," she says.

"Don't worry. I was heading back to the port. To the ship."

"You have no home here in the city?"

The corsair shakes his head. When he was on land he needed a place to live, he tells her, but not now. Especially given the prices in Cádiz. Keeping a home or a room here costs a lot of money, and everything he possesses will easily fit in his little cabin.

"That's true. But you have money now."

Once more the white slash of a smile opens in his tanned face.

"A little, yes. As you say . . . but one never knows. Life, like the sea, can be a bitch." He touches his hat. "Please forgive my language."

"Don Emilio tells me you deposited all of your money with him."

"Yes. He and his son are decent men. They give a fair rate of interest."

"Might I ask a personal question?"

"Of course."

"What drew you to the sea?"

Pépé Lobo pauses for a moment before answering, as though weighing the matter.

"Necessity, señora. Like almost all the sailors I know . . . Only a fool would go to sea by choice."

"Perhaps I would have been such a fool, had I been born a man."

She says it as she walks, looking straight ahead. And she can feel Pépé Lobo staring at her. When she turns toward him, she can still see a hint of astonishment in the sailor's eyes.

"You are a curious woman, señora, if you will permit me to be so bold."

"Why would I not permit it?"

On the corner of the Calle de la Carne, by the Iglesia del Rosario, a group of locals and passersby are discussing a poster on the convent wall. It is a message from the Regency concerning the recent military operations, including the failure of General Blake's foray into the Condado de Niebla and the fall of Tarragona to the French. Next to the official poster is another; this one is anonymous, commenting in caustic terms that responsibility lies with the English General Graham and his lack of interest in saving the Spanish garrison. With the exception of Cádiz, which, thanks to its ramparts and its cannons, is still free, the news from elsewhere in the Peninsula is frequently bad: incompetent generals, undisciplined troops, the British acting according to their own whims, and a blurring of the boundaries between guerrillas and gangs of murderous highwaymen. From one defeat to another, as cousin Toño quips, and so on to the final victory. Which is surely out there somewhere.

"You know you do not have a good reputation, Captain? I am not, of course, referring to your abilities as a sailor."

A long silence. Long enough for them to walk some twenty paces, side by side, as far as the little Plaza de San Agustín. *What possessed me to say such a thing?* Lolita Palma wonders, bemused. *What right do I have? I barely recognize the silly fool talking in my stead, irritable and insolent with this man who has done me no wrong—a man I have met barely half a dozen times.* A moment later, when they come to the Librería Salcedo, she stops suddenly and looks the corsair in the eye, confident and determined.

"Some say you are not a gentleman."

She is intrigued to see he is neither embarrassed nor angered by her remark. Pépé Lobo stands stock-still, the package containing the *Naval Gazetteer* under one arm. His face is calm, but he is not smiling.

"Whoever told you such a thing is quite right: I am not a gentleman, nor do I claim to be."

It is neither an apology nor a boast, but said with complete sincerity. He does not look away. Lolita tilts her head a little to one side, appraising.

"What a curious thing to say. All men aspire to be gentlemen."

"Not all, as you can see . . ."

"I am shocked by your cynicism . . . Is that what I should call it?"

A quick blink. He seems surprised by this term. Cynicism. *Perhaps he is not aware of it,* she thinks; *perhaps for him everything is straightforward. His life is so different from mine.* A faint smile plays on the corsair's lips.

"Call it what you will, it has its advantages," says Pépé Lobo. "These are not times for civilities such as 'You fire first' . . . Not if a man wants to eat . . . even if it is only the worm-eaten hardtack, rancid bacon and watered-down wine we get aboard ship."

He falls silent and looks around: the church doorway beneath the statue of Saint Augustine, the pigeons pecking at the bare soil of the square, the windows of shops open for business, the bookcases on display outside the Salcedo bookshop, just like those nearby on Calle

Hortal, Calle Murguía and Calle Navarro. He gazes at everything as though he were simply passing through, as though seeing them from a distance, as an outsider.

"It is very pleasant talking with you, señora."

There is no sarcasm in his remark, something that surprises Lolita.

"Why . . . ? It can hardly be because of what I say, I fear . . ."

"It is not what you say."

Lolita Palma stifles the urge to flick open her fan and cool herself vigorously.

"Would you care . . . ?" The corsair begins, but stops himself. Once again there is a silence—brief, this time.

"I think perhaps it is time you went on your way, Captain."

Pépé Lobo nods, he seems distracted. Or preoccupied.

"Of course."

He touches the brim of his hat, murmurs "By your leave . . ." and makes to depart. Lolita unfolds her fan and spends a moment or two fanning herself. Just as he is about to leave, Pépé Lobo glances at a picture of a landscape. She follows his gaze.

"It is called a dragon tree," she says. "Have you ever seen one?"

The corsair stops, his head tilted slightly as if unsure he has heard her correctly.

"There are two extraordinary specimens in Cádiz," she adds. "In Latin it is *Dracaena draco*."

It is clear from his face he thinks she is mocking him. Seeing his expression—confusion, curiosity—Lolita feels the secret pleasure of drawing a man into a world of improbabilities.

"One is on the Plaza de San Francisco, quite near my house . . . From time to time I visit it, as one might an old friend."

"What do you do when you get there?"

"I sit on the bench opposite and look at it. And think."

Without taking his eyes off her, Pépé Lobo shifts the package to his other arm. For some minutes now, he has been studying her as though she were an enigma, and she notices how pleasurable it is to be looked at in this way. She is more in control of her actions, her words. It calms her. She feels the urge to smile, but restrains herself. Everything unfolds more easily this way.

"Do you know much about trees?" he asks finally.

"A little. I am interested in botany."

"Botany . . ." the corsair echoes in a barely audible whisper.

"Exactly."

His inquisitive feline eyes are still gazing into hers.

"Once . . ." Pépé Lobo ventures, "I took part in a botanical expedition."

"Really?"

He nods, satisfied by the look of surprise on her face.

"Back in 'eighty-eight, I was first mate on the ship that brought home a group of botanists, together with their pots and plants and seeds and so forth." He pauses deliberately. "And do you know the strangest thing? Can you guess what the ship was called?"

Lolita's excitement is genuine. She almost claps her hands.

"In 'eighty-eight? Of course I know; it was called the *Dragon*—like the tree."

"You see?" The corsair's smile broadens. "It's a small world."

She can hardly get over her surprise. The world is filled with strange twists of fate.

"I can't believe it . . . twenty-three years ago, you brought Don Hipólito Ruiz to Spain from El Callao!"

"I'm afraid I don't remember the names of the gentlemen aboard. But clearly you know all about it."

"Of course I do . . . That expedition to Chile and Peru was extremely important: those plants are now in the Botanical Gardens in Madrid. And I have several books at home by Don Hipólito and his partner Pavón . . . They even mention the name of the ship . . ."

Once again, they consider each other in silence.

"How interesting." Her voice is calmer now. "You must tell me all about it, Captain. I would very much enjoy that."

Another pause. Short-lived this time. The fleeting glimmer in the corsair's eyes. "Now?"

"No, not now," she says, shaking her head gently. "Some other day, perhaps . . . when you come back to port again."

SERIOUS, GRUFF, MASCULINE, three men are sitting on wicker chairs in the shade of the vine, passing a tobacco pouch from hand to hand, striking a flint to spark the tinder and light their cigarettes. The glass pitcher, half-full of wine, has already circulated several times.

"That makes two thousand *duros* to be divided up," says Curro Panizo.

Panizo is a salter, a friend and neighbor of Felipe Mojarra, who is now looking at him thoughtfully. Tempted by the idea. They have been discussing the ins and outs of the matter for a while.

"The nights are short, but there is time enough," Panizo insists. "To get there, we simply need to swim along the channel quietly, like my son and I did the other night."

"How far did you get?"

"As far as La Matilla, near the dock. We saw two other launches there, but further off. More difficult to steal."

Mojarra grabs the pitcher, throws his head back to take a long draft of red wine, then gives it to his brother-in-law Bartolo Cárdenas—a thin, wiry man with hands as gnarled as vines—who takes a drink and passes it on to Panizo. The sun shimmers on the still water of the nearby salt flats, and casts a haze over the distant pinewoods and the gentle slope that rises to Chiclana. Mojarra's little cabin—a modest dwelling with two rooms and a patio with grapevines, geraniums and a small kitchen garden—lies outside the village in the Isla de Léon, near the tidal creek of Saporito, at the end of the long road that runs from the Plaza de las Tres Cruzes.

"Explain it to me again," says Mojarra. "In detail . . ."

Panizo patiently recaps. A gunboat, about forty feet long. Moored in the Alcornocal channel near the mill at Santa Cruz. Guarded by a corporal and five soldiers who spend most of their time sleeping, because it's a safe area for the *gabachos*. He and his son spotted the boat while on a reconnaissance mission to see if people were still taking sand to build fortifications. They spent all day hiding in the scrubland, staking out the area, planning the job. And it should be easy. Past the Camarón channel, through the swampland and the shallow tidal creeks to the main channel, taking care not to be spotted by the English gun batteries at San Pedro. From there, swim slowly to Alcornocal. Coming back should be easier, with an ebb tide and a pair of oars. If there's a favorable wind, all the better.

"Our officers won't be happy," protests Mojarra.

"They haven't got the guts to do it themselves. And even if they did, they'd keep the reward and not give us a *real*. It's a lot of money, Felipe."

Mojarra knows that Curro Panizo is absolutely right. The Spanish authorities will pay a reward of 2,000 silver *reales* for the capture of a boat equipped with cannons or howitzers. They pay 10,000 *reales* for a boat with minor artillery, and 200 for every captured enemy sailor or soldier. And most important, in order to encourage such captures they pay promptly, in hard cash. At least that is what they say. In these straitened times—when most sailors and soldiers are owed twenty months' back pay, and all claims are met with a blunt "we do not have the authority to help you"—to make two thousand *duros* in cash overnight would be a fortune. Especially for people as poor as this: Mojarra and Panizo are poachers and salters, and Mojarra's brother-in-law Bartolo Cárdenas works as a ropemaker at a rigging plant in La Carraca.

"If the Frenchies catch us, we're done for."

Panizo smiles avariciously. He is thickset, his bald head tanned by the sun, his beard streaked with gray. He wears a butcher's knife tucked into a broad belt—once black, now a faded gray—and a shirt that has been patched and darned, with calf-length breeches made of sailcloth. His bare feet are as callused as Mojarra's.

"For that amount of cash, let them try," he says.

"I'm in too," chimes Cárdenas.

"If you want to steal figs, you have to climb trees . . ."

The three men smile gleefully, picturing it. They have never seen so much money all together—they have never seen so much money at all.

"When will we do it?" asks Mojarra.

An explosion rings out in the distance and all three look to the east, beyond the Saporito creek, toward Chiclana. It is unusual for the French to be shelling at this time of day, but you never know. In general, they shell the Isla de Léon, where there is heavy fighting along the front, and frequently at night. Many people live holed up in the basements of houses that have them. Mojarra's house has no cellar, so when there is shelling his family has no choice but to seek refuge in the Carmelite convent, in San Francisco or in the local parish church, which has thick stone walls. But only when there is time. If the shelling comes out of the blue, all he and his wife can do is press themselves against the walls of the hut, hug their children and pray.

Mojarra's wife—hair in a bedraggled topknot, skin lined with wrinkles, breasts sagging beneath a coarse cotton blouse—also heard the distant boom. She appears in the doorway, drying her hands on her apron, and looks out toward Chiclana. Her expression is not one of fear, but of weariness and resignation. Her husband sends her back indoors with a glance.

"We could do it five days from now," whispers Curro Panizo. "There will be no moon, so it will be pitch dark."

"But they might have moved the gunboat by then."

"It's permanently moored there, by a small jetty. It's the gunboat they sail up the narrow waterways to fire on the English gun battery at San Pedro . . . I was told that by a deserter we captured; we found him hiding in the salt lake at La Pelona, waiting for darkness so he could swim across to the other side."

"And this boat has a cannon?"

"A big one—we saw it with our own eyes. Six or eight pounds, the *gabacho* told us."

Smoke swirls from the hand-rolled cigarettes; the wine pitcher makes another round. The men look at each other gravely. They can all see the problem.

"Three men won't be enough."

"I'll bring my lad along," says Panizo.

The boy is fourteen—named Francisco, like his father (they are known as Curro and Currito)—and is quick and agile as a squirrel. Though he is too young to enlist in the fusiliers, he sometimes goes on reconnaissance missions with his father. Just now, he is sitting on the bank of the Saporito thirty paces away, fishing line in hand, hoping to catch something. Panizo told him to stay put and not bother them until he was called. Tough and old enough to risk his life, he is not old enough for adult conversation. Or for cigarettes and wine.

"Any more and we're likely to be spotted," interjects Mojarra's brother-in-law. "We could get shelled by the English battery at San Pedro, or by our own troops as Maseda . . . or be caught by the *gabachos* on our way back."

"Four sounds about right," agrees Mojarra. "The three of us and the stripling."

"That makes . . ." Panizo counts on his fingers, ". . . five hundred *duros* each."

Cárdenas looks sidelong at Mojarra, but his brother-in-law says nothing. It is only fair: the kid will be risking as much as any of them. Between him and Curro Panizo, *compadre* is more than just a word.

"We should get away with it," he says.

They drained the carafe on the last round. Mojarra gets to his feet, grabs it by the neck and goes into the house for a refill. The wine is cheap, bitter, but it is all they have. It fires their bellies and stiffens their resolve. Next to the spent embers in the chimney breast his wife, Manuela Cárdenas, helped by a girl of eleven, is preparing food: a frugal *gazpacho* with a single clove of garlic, strips of dried pepper pounded with oil, vinegar and a little bread and water. Two other girls—one, eight, the other, five—are sitting on the floor playing with some blocks of wood and a ball of twine next to Mojarra's elderly, crippled mother-in-law, who is dozing in a chair beside the rain barrel. Their eldest daughter, Mari Paz, is in Cádiz, working as a housemaid for the Palmas. With what she earns and the rations her father receives as a fusilier, the family have enough to eat and drink.

"We're talking about five thousand *reales*," Mojarra whispers, standing next to his wife.

He knows she has overheard. She turns her weary eyes to him and stares at him in silence. Her wizened skin and the wrinkles around her eyes and mouth attest to the ravages of time, the daily grind of chores, the unremitting poverty; to seven pregnancies in a few short years, three of which ended in miscarriages. As Mojarra refills the wine pitcher from a wicker-covered demijohn, he can read the words left unspoken in his wife's eyes: *It is a long way to go, husband; with the ga-bachos there, it might as well be the ends of the earth, and who will pay us if they kill you? There will be no one to provide food if you are lying dead in the canals. You already risk too much every day, why tempt fate?*

"Five thousand *reales*," he insists.

She turns away, expressionless. Fatalistic as the times, as her situation, as her downtrodden sex. Her brother Cárdenas, who was taught to read and to count, has already worked out the sums: 3,000 two-pound loaves of bread; 250 pairs of shoes; 300 pounds of meat; 800 pounds of ground coffee; 2,500 *cuartillos* of wine . . . These are just some of the things they could buy if Felipe Mojarra were somehow—by hauling, rowing, or by God's help—able to transport the French gunboat from Santa Cruz through half a league of shallow tidal creeks, salt marshes and no man's land. Food; lamp oil; firewood to cook with and to heat the hut in winter; clothes for the girls who run around half-naked; a new roof for the house; new blankets for the straw mattress in the bedroom with its smoke-grimed walls where they all sleep together, parents and children. A respite from this abject poverty relieved only by a fish caught in the creek, or a bird shot over the salt flats—something that has become more difficult because even poaching, the only thing that helped them get by, has gone to hell since the war, with a whole army entrenched on the Isla de León.

Mojarra goes back outside, squinting into the glare of sunlight reflected on the still waters of the creeks and salt marshes. He hands the pitcher to his friend and his brother-in-law, who throw their heads back and let the stream of wine pour down their throats. They click their tongues contentedly. With long blades they cut tobacco into their calloused palms and roll more cigars. The long line of prisoners returning from work on the Gallineras fortifications is framed against the sunlight, escorted by marines, shuffling slowly along the path by Saporito Creek that leads back to the arsenal at La Caracca.

"We leave here in five days," says Mojarra, "as soon as it's dark."

FROM THE DOCK of the Jarcia de Puerto Real, Simon Desfosseux observes the nearby enemy coastline. His expert eye, accustomed to gauging distances, whether actual or on a map, functions with the meticulous precision of a rangefinder: three miles exactly to Punta Cantera, one and six-tenths to the headland at Clica, one and a half to Carraca and the formidable gun battery located in the former prison barracks in the northeast corner of the Santa Lucía arsenal, heavily defended by the Spanish with twenty field guns, including 24-pound cannons and 9-inch howitzers. This extensive deployment, with angles of fire crossing those of other gun emplacements, makes this section of the enemy front line unassailable, protecting as it does the channels by which French vessels might launch an attack and providing cover for the gunboats that periodically harass the imperial forces. This happened some three days ago when a flotilla anchored close to the dock at Puerto Real was attacked by gunboats that had sailed under cover of darkness from the enemy coast. By daybreak there were ten gunboats, four more with howitzers and three bombers which, while the seas remained favorable, fired more than twenty grenades and two hundred round shots, causing considerable damages to ships, equipment and buildings near the port. Indeed, there were eleven separate hits on the building next to the quay known as the Casa Grenada or the Casa de las Rosas, a provisions store and guardhouse. All in all, a minor disaster, with many dead and wounded. As a result, Marshal Victor, fuming from every curl of his sideburns, bawled at General Menier, *de facto* commander of the division responsible for Puerto Real, dismissing him as a complete imbecile. Simon Desfosseux was sent posthaste from the Trocadero, with full authority and orders to analyze the situation and ensure—to quote the Marshal's words verbatim—*that such a bloody stupid cock-up would never happen again.*

Sergeant Labiche, whom Desfosseux brought with him to lend a hand, is approaching. The NCO is no genius, nor does he have a head for battle, but he is the only man the captain can spare just now. And at least Labiche gives the right impression. Perhaps the change of scenery has given him a burst of energy—or perhaps he is simply taking out all the accumulated boredom and frustration of life at the Trocadero on his subordinates here—but for the past two days this man from the Auvergne has been barking orders like a foreman, swearing at the local troops and impugning the mothers who bore them.

"The cannons have arrived, sir."

"I want them unloaded immediately, please. And prepare the gun carriages."

The air is thick with the smell of low tide. Next to ships grounded in the mud—many of them no more than charred frames—the white blots of seagulls spatter the stretch of greenish shore alongside the docks, where Desfosseux is pacing amid a bustle of soldiers coming and going with carriages and carts. The captain made a study of the situation as soon as he arrived yesterday morning; by the afternoon he set everyone to work and kept them working, without a break, through the night into today. It is now just after 4 p.m. and a detachment of sappers, aided—reluctantly, given the sweltering heat—by marines and artillerymen, have just finished placing the last gabions filled with mud and sand to protect the new bulwark: a semicircular rampart from which six 8-pound guns, three on either side, will cover the entire stretch of coast around the village. In principle.

Desfosseux wanders over to the square to look at the iron tubes stacked on mule carts. These are old artillery pieces, six feet long, each weighing more than half a ton, brought from El Puerto de Santa María to be fitted to the Gribeauval gun carriages that are currently being lashed into position. The Duc de Belluno's haste means that the cannons will have to be fired from the parapet with no embrasures and no protection for the artillerymen, beyond a three- to five-foot-high rampart formed by the mud and gabions, supported with planks and stakes driven into the ground. This, Desfosseux reckons, should be enough to keep the Spanish gunboats at a distance, at least during daylight hours, although he is a little worried about certain changes in the enemy's artillery deployment—a fact he has made clear to his superiors. His information was brought up to date by an English officer who defected to the French side after a duel: longer-range cannons at the Lazareto battery, the reinforcement of the English redoubts at Sancti Petri and Fallineras Altas, the deployment of additional Portuguese troops and artillery to Torregorda, including 24-pounder field guns and 36-pounder English carronades. All of this lies beyond Desfosseux's area and does not worry him unduly. There is, however, a new threat to the Trocadero: plans are afoot to throw a pontoon from the battleship *Terrible* to be used as a floating battery, firing at elevated angles on Fort Luis and the Cabezuela to silence Fanfan's shelling of Cádiz. Or to try. In this siege—which is a combination of blind man's buff, a house of cards and a game of dominoes—every new development, every move, however slight, can have complex repercussions. And the Imperial Artillery, with Simon Desfosseux at the center of its web, is forced to play the part of a firefighter tackling a blaze with a single bucket of water, constantly running here and there without ever putting it out.

Slipping off his uniform jacket, with little concern for his rank, Desfosseux goes over to Sergeant Labiche's men, who are unloading the cannons amid the shriek of ropes and pulleys, setting them on the wooden gun carriages painted olive green. Their bases are shaped like an inclined plane on a limber set of rails to dampen the recoil. The sheer weight of the iron tubes makes installation a slow and painful process, further aggravated by the men's lack of experience. *So cackhanded,* Desfosseux thinks; *they should be made to run the gauntlet.* But he doesn't blame them. There is a genuine scarcity of artillerymen in the six regiments that cover the coastline between the Trocadero and Sancti Petri, weakened by poverty and the inevitable casualties of war. In such a situation, even the halfhearted Labiche is a boon, since at least he understands his position. In the gun batteries trained on Cádiz itself, Desfosseux has been forced to make up the numbers using ordinary infantrymen. Even here, in Puerto Real, with the exception of two artillery corporals, five soldiers and three Navy artillerymen who arrived with the cannons from El Puerto de Santa María—their blue frockcoats with red piping distinguishing them from the white breast-plates of the infantrymen—those dealing with the field guns are drawn from the Line regiments.

The gun carriage creaks. The captain jumps back with a start, narrowly avoiding a wheel that would have crushed his foot to a pulp. The devil take it, he thinks. Take him and the Spanish gunboats and Marshal Victor and his infuriating whims. Any officer could have seen to the artillery at Puerto Real, but in recent months not a shell can be fired in either direction without the Duc de Belluno and his general staff considering it the exclusive territory of Simon Desfosseux. "I'm giving you everything you asked for, Captain," the Marshal said at their last encounter. "Or everything I can. So just sort things out and don't trouble me unless it's with good news."

The upshot of all this is that now every last high-ranking artillery officer in the Premier Corps—including General of Brigade d'Aboville, who has taken over from Lesueur—harbors a deep-seated loathing of Desfosseux; a barely concealed contempt, evident in their manner and their ordinances. The Marshal's right eye, they call him. The Ballistics Genius, the Marvel from Metz, etc. . . . the usual. The captain knows that any one of his superior officers would gladly give a month's pay to have a Villantroys-Ruty howitzer explode in his face, or a providential Spanish bomb finish him off. Let the rifle change his tune, in the neat euphemism common in the Imperial Army.

Taking out his pocket watch, Desfosseux checks the time: it is 4:55 p.m. He is eager to be finished here and to return to the Cabezuela, back to Fanfan and his brothers. Though he knows they are in the capable hands of Lieutenant Bertoldi, he is worried that he has heard no shelling since he has been here. They had agreed that, if the wind were not unfavorable, eight shots would be fired on Cádiz: four inert shells filled with lead and sand, and four containing a powder charge.

The captain has been more than satisfied recently. The curve on the map indicating the range of the shelling has gradually been moving toward the west of the city and now covers a third of the urban area. From the reports he has had, three lead-filled shells recently fell near the Tavira Tower; its height makes it a perfect reference point when aiming. This means that the impact sites are now only 190 *toises* from the main square, the Plaza de San Antonio, and only 140 *toises* from the Oratory of San Felipe Neri where the rebel Cortes meets. With this information, Desfosseux feels optimistic about the future: he feels certain that very soon, given favorable weather conditions, his shells will exceed a range of 2,700 *toises*. Even now, with an adjustment of fire toward the stretch of bay where the English and Spanish warships are moored, he has managed a direct hit. True, the shot was not very precise and little damage was done, but it forced the warships to weigh anchor and move further off, next to the bastions of Candelaria and Santa Catalina.

Almost all of the 8-pound cannons are now on their limbers. Filthy and sweaty, the soldiers continue hauling on the ropes, pushing from behind. The burly sappers conscientiously toil away, in silence as always. The artillerymen leave most of the work to them, doing only the bare minimum. As for the infantry, they shirk whenever they can. Labiche viciously clouts one soldier around the ear, then gives him a kick in the backside.

"I'll rip your liver out, you blackguard!"

Desfosseux takes the NCO aside. "Do not hit the men in my presence." He says this in a low voice, so as not to undermine him in front of the men. Labiche shrugs his shoulders, spits on the ground, goes back to work and five minutes later deals out two more blows.

"I'll have your hide . . . feckless wastrels! Come on, you bastards!"

The sweltering heat is made worse by the fact there is no breeze. Desfosseux mops the sweat from his brow, then picks up his jacket and wanders away from the dock toward the water butt set in the shade on the corner of the Calle de la Cruz Verde, next to the watchtower. Almost all the Spanish residents have deserted their homes in Puerto Real, willingly or by force. The village is now one vast military camp. Through wrought-iron railings as high as the houses, broken windows can be seen; empty rooms, doors and furniture smashed to smithereens, mattresses and blankets lying on the ground. Everywhere there are piles of ash from the campfires. The patios of the houses, now used as stables, stink of horse dung and are buzzing with flies.

The captain drinks a ladle of water and, sitting in the shade, slips a hand into his pocket and takes out a letter from his wife—the first in six months—which he received yesterday morning just before leaving the Cabezuela battery. This is the fifth time he has read it, and once again it stirs no real feeling in him. *My dearest husband,* it begins, *I send up my prayers to God that He will keep you safe and in good health.* The letter, written four months ago, is an exhaustive, droning catalog of family news—births, marriages and funerals, minor domestic incidents, the echoes of a city, of a life so distant that Simon Desfosseux reads through it unmoved. His interest is not even piqued by the news that 20,000 Russian troops are massing along the Polish border and that the Emperor is intending to wage war on the Czar. Poland, Russia, France, Metz: they are all so far away. There was a time when this feeling of indifference worried him. A time when he felt guilty about it. That was in the early days, as the army marched south through unfamiliar terrain, leaving a seemingly well-ordered world further and further behind. But things are different now. In this circumscribed world, with its routine and its fixed certainties, his lack of interest in anything that may be happening more than 3,000 *toises* from here is constructive, almost comforting. It frees him from melancholy and homesickness.

Desfosseux folds the letter and slips it back into his pocket. He spends a moment watching the men working on the semicircular redoubt, then looks out toward the Trocadero. He is still worried that he has heard no shots from Fanfan and his brothers. He allows his mind to wander, calculating trajectories and parabolas, letting himself be swept along as though in an opium haze. At last the Tavira Tower is almost within range, he thinks with satisfaction. This is wonderful news. The center of Cádiz is almost in his grasp. The last carrier pigeon to cross the bay brought with it a miniature map of that sector of the city, precisely indicating the points of impact: two on the Calle de Recaño, one on the Calle del Vestuario. Lieutenant Bertoldi was literally jumping for joy. As he often does, Desfosseux wonders about the agent who is sending them this information, the man whose dangerous work helps him place these triumphant points on the map. The man, he assumes, is a Spaniard, or perhaps a Frenchman who has long since been naturalized. He does not know his name, or what he looks like; whether he is a soldier or a civilian, a selfless ally or a simple mercenary, a traitor to his country or a hero in a noble cause. He does not even pay this man: the general staff deals with such details. His only links to the man are the carrier pigeons and the secret trips across the bay made by the Spanish smuggler they call the Mulatto. But the Mulatto gives him only essential information. Whatever the truth, whoever is sending the messages must have powerful reasons for doing so. A brave and cool-headed man, judging by what he does. Living in the shadow of the gallows would unnerve an ordinary man. Desfosseux knows that he would find it impossible to live like that, an exile in hostile territory, unable to trust anyone, fearing the heavy tread of soldiers or police on the stairs, in constant danger of being suspected, exposed, of suffering the torture and ignoble death reserved for spies.

The cannons have now been installed on their gun carriages and are pointing over the parapet at the bay. The captain gets to his feet, leaves the shelter of the shade and goes back to the dock to supervise the final adjustments. As he walks, he hears an explosion from the west, a powerful *buh-boom* that is all too familiar. His trained ear can tell it comes from precisely two and a half miles away. He turns and gazes out past the Trocadero; half a minute later he hears a second blast, then a third. Standing on the wharf, shading his eyes with his hand, Desfosseux gives a satisfied smile. The shots from the 10-inch Villantroys-Ruty are unmistakable: perfect, compact, the clean blast of the powder charge, the emphatic echo that follows *buh-boom*. A fourth shot. Nice work, Maurizio Bertoldi. He knows how to do his duty.

Buh-boom. The fifth explosion fills the captain with a sense of pride, gives him a warm feeling inside. This is the first time he has heard the howitzers on the Cabezuela from a distance, the first time he has not been there to oversee every last detail. But everything sounds as it should: magnificent. The last shot was Fanfan: he can hear the slight difference in tone; the blast is deeper and more abrupt than the others. Recognizing it even at this distance fills Simon Desfosseux with a curious tenderness. Like a father watching his son take his first faltering steps.

"The prisoner has disappeared . . . ? Is this some kind of joke?"

"Absolutely not, señor. Heaven forfend."

There follows a long, tense silence. Rogelio Tizón coolly holds the furious gaze of Eusebio García Pico, General Intendant and Chief of Police.

"The man was your prisoner, Tizón, he was your responsibility."

"As I said, he escaped. These things happen."

They are in the office of García Pico, who is installed behind his immaculate desk—not a scrap of paper on it—by a window overlooking the courtyard of the Royal Jail. Tizón is standing, clutching a folder of documents. Wishing he was somewhere else.

"The circumstances of the escape are curious indeed," García Pico mutters, almost to himself.

"That is true, señor. We are investigating the matter thoroughly."

"What exactly do you mean, thoroughly?"

"As I said. Thoroughly."

It is as good a word as any. In fact for more than a week now the prisoner in question—the man caught spying on the young seamstresses on the Calle Juan de Andas—has been lying at the bottom of the bay, wrapped in a canvas tarpaulin weighed down by cannonballs and a grapnel. Eager to secure a preemptive confession, Tizón made the mistake of entrusting the task to his assistant Cadalso and a pair of henchmen who were somewhat heavy-handed. The suspect was not in good health, and the interrogation clearly proved too much.

"It is not really a problem, señor. No one knows about it . . . well, very few people."

García Pico motions gruffly for Tizón to sit.

"You brought this on yourself," he says as Tizón takes a seat and lays his folder on the desk. "The murder of the last girl did not pass unnoticed."

"Nothing but an unsubstantiated rumor . . ." corrects the comisario.

"But people were demanding explanations. I even had two members of the Cortes asking me about the case."

"Only for two days," protests Tizón, "and they assumed it was an isolated incident. After that the matter was completely forgotten. There is so much upheaval in the city. So many tragedies, to say nothing of the bombs. With so many foreigners and soldiers about, there is no shortage of criminals. Just yesterday an English sailor stabbed a soldier who was strangling a prostitute in El Boquete. There have been seven violent deaths so far this month, three of them women. Fortunately, there is almost nothing to connect that last girl's death with the previous murders and we managed to persuade everyone to remain silent."

García Pico stares at the file on his desk as though it is full of someone else's problems.

"Damn it all! You said you had a suspect. The perfect scapegoat—those were your very words."

"And so I did," admits Tizón. "But as I said, he escaped. We were planning to release him, keep him under observation and arrest him again, in order not to break the new laws . . ."

García Pico raises his hand in a vague gesture. He shifts his gaze from the comisario and stares into space, focusing on some point between the closed door and the inevitable painting of His Majesty Fernando VII—beloved martyr of his country, now languishing in some French dungeon—who gazes down with bulging eyes that hardly inspire confidence.

"Spare me the details."

Tizón shrugs. "As part of our investigation, two of my men took him to the scene of the most recent crime, and he escaped. Unfortunately."

"It was an oversight, was it not?" The Intendant is still staring into the middle distance. "He escaped due to an oversight. Just like that."

"Precisely, señor. The relevant officers have been punished."

"Harshly, I imagine."

Tizón decides to ignore the sarcasm.

"We are still looking for him," he says calmly. "It is our number one priority."

"Number one?"

"Or thereabouts."

"I've no doubt it is."

García Pico's gaze slowly returns to focus on the comisario. Now his expression is weary, as if he is overwhelmed by everything: by Tizón, this situation, the sweltering heat, Cádiz, Spain. And by the explosion that rings out just at that moment near the Puerta de Tierra, making both men turn toward the open window.

"Let me read you something."

He opens a desk drawer, takes out a printed sheet of paper and reads the first lines aloud: *"Torture is hereby abolished forever in all the territories and dominions loyal to the Spanish Crown, and with it the associated practice of threatening and intimidating defendants using means which are abusively and illegally referred to as coercion; it is further decreed that no judge, tribunal or court of law may order or sanction torture."*

At this point he stops and looks up at Tizón. "What do you think?"

The comisario does not so much as blink. *Do you really think it's worthwhile reading me these bedtime stories?* he thinks to himself; *I am heading up the police in a city where the poor man can have himself acquitted for eighty* reales, *a craftsman for two hundred and a rich man for two thousand.*

"I'm aware of the statute, señor. It was published five months ago."

García Pico sets down the document on his desk and studies it, trying to think of something to add. Finally, he thinks better of it and files it in the drawer. Then he points his right index finger at Tizón.

"Listen to me. You slip up once more and we'll have everyone down on top of us. Including the newspapers with their habeas corpus and all the rest of it . . . It is a very sensitive subject. Even the most respectable conservative deputies have been taken in by these newfangled ideas. Or they pretend to be. No one dares challenge them."

García Pico clearly misses the good old days, when things were straightforward and blunt. Tizón nods guardedly. In his own way, he misses them himself.

"I don't think that will really affect us, señor. Look at *El Jacobino Ilustrado* . . . It is defending the actions of the Comisariado. 'Impeccable humanist rigor,' it said last week. 'A modern police force,' and so on. 'An example to other nations.'"

"Are you joking?"

"No."

García Pico glances around him as though something stinks. At length he turns an icy stare on Tizón. "I don't know how you fixed things with that worm Zafra, but the *Jacobino* is a rag . . . I am more worried about the serious newspapers: the *Diario Mercantil* and the others . . . The governor is watching our every move with a magnifying glass."

"I'm taking care of it, señor."

"You are? Really? Well, listen to me very carefully. If the newspapers come looking for a suspect, I'll throw you to the wolves."

The newspapers have got other things to worry about, the comisario reassures him phlegmatically. The recent cases of malignant fever have the townsfolk worried; they fear there may be another outbreak of yellow fever. At the Cortes, the deputies have even discussed moving out of the city, because the overcrowding and sweltering heat make it unpleasant. News of the war also keeps the populace distracted, and what with General Blake's fiasco at Niebla, the surrender of Tarragona, the fear of losing the whole of the Levant and the rising cost of tobacco from Havana, there is more than enough to keep idle tongues wagging in the cafés on the Calle Ancha. And in addition, there is the forthcoming foray against the French under the command of General Ballesteros.

"How do you know about that?" García Pico starts in his chair. "That is a military secret."

The comisario looks at his superior in genuine surprise.

"You know about it, señor. I know about it. That is normal. But everyone else knows about it too. That is Cádiz."

They stare at each other in silence. García Pico is not a bad man, the comisario thinks coolly—or no worse than any other, himself included. The General Intendant is simply trying to hold on to his job and adapt to the new regime, to survive the young blades and the visionary philosophers of San Felipe Neri who, without one whit of common sense, have turned the world upside down. The problem with this war is not the war itself, it is the mayhem it brings.

"Leaving the matter of those poor murdered wretches aside," says García Pico, "there is something else that worries me. There are too many people coming and going between Cádiz and the enemy coast . . . too much smuggling and so on."

"So on?"

"You know very well what I mean. Espionage."

The comisario shrugs his shoulders. "That is surely normal in times of war? More so in Cádiz."

García Pico opens another drawer in his desk but this time he does not take out anything. He closes it again slowly, thoughtfully.

"I have had a report from General Valdés . . . His surveillance fleet have captured two spies in the past three weeks."

"As have we, señor. It is not just the Navy and the Army who deal with such matters."

García Pico gives a dismissive wave.

"I know that. But there was an unusual detail in his report. On two occasions there was mention of a Negro or a Mulatto who has been operating between the shores of the bay."

Rogelio Tizón has no need to rack his brains: he knows the Mulatto. He has been intending to deal with this matter ever since his conversation with the innkeeper on the Calle de la Verónica. So far, he has not discovered anything concrete: all his men have been able to establish is that someone is trafficking people between the shores. This is the first time the word *espionage* has come into the story, though Tizón is not about to admit this to his superior.

"The report may well be referring to a boatman we have had under surveillance for some time now," he says cautiously. "He has been mentioned by a number of our informants as someone not to be trusted . . . We know he is involved in smuggling; we have been investigating his involvement in spying."

"Well, don't let this suspect get away. And keep me informed on the matter . . . Oh, and on the matter of the murdered girls."

"Of course, señor. We are deploying all our art."

The other man looks at him as if trying to detect a note of sarcasm in this last statement; Tizón braves the scrutiny with impassive innocence. After a moment, García Pico seems to relax a little. He knows the comisario very well, or thinks he knows him. It was he who appointed him to the post when he became General Intendant two years ago, a decision he has never regretted. At least not until today. The comisario's methods are a barrier to shield his superior officers from any awkward situations. Efficient, discreet and with no political ambitions, Rogelio Tizón is a useful man in difficult times. And in Spain, these are difficult times.

"Regarding these young women, I have to admit that you have done a fine job. Kept everything under control . . . As you say, no one has made the connection between the four murders."

Tizón allows himself a faint, deferential smile, with just the right note of complicity. "And anyone who has made the connection has kept their mouth shut. Or I've shut it for them."

García Pico flinches again and sits up in his chair. "I don't need to know about that."

There is a brief hesitation. He glances up at the wall clock next to the window. Interpreting this action, Tizón picks up his file and gets to his feet. García Pico stares at his hands.

"Remember what the governor said," he says pointedly. "If there's any scandal about these murders, we'll need a culprit."

Tizón bows slightly—a faint nod of the head, not an inch more than absolutely necessary.

"We are working on it, señor. Trying to lay our hands on him . . . I have every neighborhood police captain sifting through their files, and every officer that can be spared is pounding the streets."

"I'm not sure I made myself clear; I mean someone who is actually guilty."

Tizón does not even blink. He looks as smug as a cat sitting beside an empty cage, brushing feathers from its whiskers.

"Of course, señor. A genuine culprit. Understood."

"And this time I don't want him to escape, understood? Remember what I just read to you, for Christ's sake. Do whatever it takes so he does not *have* to escape."

FLAMING TORCHES DRIVEN into the sand beneath the ramparts cast their flickering light on La Caleta, leaving in silhouette the boats and light vessels bobbing in the high tide next to the silent shore. The night is clear. The waning moon will soon arch across the starry vault of the heavens. There is not a breath of wind, not a single ripple on the calm black waters. The vertical flames of the torches cast a reddish glow on the dingy bars and flamenco cabarets that run along the sandstone walls where, at this time of year, there are seafood restaurants by day and dance halls by night. A lenient attitude is taken to law and order along this half moon of hard, flat sand between the reef at San Sebastián and the Castillo de Santa Catalina, on the western tip of the city overlooking the Atlantic. Since La Caleta is outside the city walls, the curfew is not enforced here and through the city gate leading down to the beach comes a steady crowd of people with safe-conduct passes or enough money to bribe the guards. From the ramshackle bars comes the sound of glasses, of fandangos and boleros, the click of castanets, the voices of flamenco singers, of sailors, soldiers, immigrants with fat wallets and those looking for someone to buy them a bottle, young gentlemen slumming it, Englishmen and boatmen plying their trade. With warships moored nearby to protect the area from French shelling, the place is thronged with officers and crewmen. Everywhere there is the clamor of conversation, loose women laughing, guitars playing, voices singing, drunkards roaring and brawlers fighting. The nighthawks and the scapegraces of Cádiz come to La Caleta to find pleasure in the second summer of the French siege.

"Good evening . . . Could I have a moment of your time?"

Seated at a table made of bare boards nailed together, Pépé Lobo exchanges a quick glance with Ricardo Maraña; then looks up at the stranger who has just stopped in front of him, a curious man with a hook nose and a round straw hat, carrying a walking stick, sporadically outlined against the distant flashes from the San Sebastián lighthouse.

Wearing a gray redingote, open to reveal a waistcoat, and a pair of rumpled breeches, he looks disheveled. His long, thick sideburns are of a piece with his bedraggled mustaches and the dim light makes his eyes look even darker. Perhaps dangerous. Like the handle of his cane, which Lobo cannot help but notice: a large brass knob fashioned like a walnut, ideal for splitting a man's skull.

"What do you want?" the sailor says, without getting up.

The other man gives a little smile, a fleeting, deferential smile that does not reach his eyes—a vestige, perhaps, of jaded courtesy. In the light of the torches planted in the sand, there is the flash of a gold tooth.

"I am the Comisario of Police. My name is Tizón."

The corsairs glance at each other again—the captain of the *Culebra* is intrigued; Maraña, as always, indifferent. Pale, thin, elegant, dressed all in black from his necktie to his boots, the young man leans back in his chair, stretching out one leg that shows signs of a limp. With a glass of *aguardiente* on the table—the half bottle already in his belly does not affect his manner—and a cigar smoldering in the corner of his mouth, he turns slowly, halfheartedly, to look at the interloper. Pépé Lobo knows that, like himself, his first mate does not like policemen. Or Customs officers. Or naval officers. Or anyone who interrupts other people's conversations in La Caleta at eleven o'clock at night when alcohol has begun to make tongues and thoughts slow.

"We didn't ask who you were, we asked what you wanted," says Maraña curtly.

The intruder calmly ignores this insult, notes Pépé Lobo, the word *policeman* immediately dissipating the alcoholic fog in his brain. The man is clearly thick-skinned. Another brief smile, another flash of the gold tooth. The grimace is a reflex, the corsair decides, a part of his job. As potentially lethal as the sturdy pommel of his cane or the dark, expressionless eyes which are as disconnected from his smile as if they were twenty paces apart.

"It concerns my work . . . I thought perhaps you might be able to help me."

"You know who we are?"

"Indeed, Captain, you and your lieutenant. That is to be expected in my job."

"And what do you want from us?"

The other man seems to hesitate for a moment, perhaps wondering how best to broach the subject. Finally, he decides.

"It is the lieutenant I need to speak with . . . This is probably not the right moment, but I am aware that you are putting out to sea shortly. When I saw him here, I thought perhaps this way I could avoid disturbing him tomorrow . . ."

I hope the first mate has not got himself mixed up in something, thinks Pépé Lobo. They can ill afford trouble, being two days from weighing anchor. But he decides that it is not his business. In principle. He overcomes his curiosity and makes to get to his feet.

"I will leave you alone, then."

Maraña immediately puts a hand on his arm to stop him.

"The captain has my complete confidence," he says to the policeman. "You may speak in front of him."

The other man, still standing, wavers. Or maybe pretends to waver.

"I don't know whether I should . . ."

He is watching them closely, as if deliberating. Waiting for some word, some gesture, perhaps, but the corsairs say nothing, do nothing. Pépé Lobo is still seated, waiting, watching his first officer out of the corner of his eye. Maraña stares impassively at the policeman, as cool as a gambler waiting for a card to set either side of his knave. Lobo knows the kind of existence his first mate leads: a dangerous game in which every day the young man rashly risks his life.

"It is a delicate matter, gentlemen," says the policeman. "I would not wish to—"

"Skip the prologue," cuts in Maraña.

The man gestures to a chair. "May I sit?"

Receiving no response, he grabs the back of the chair and sits down some distance from the table, setting his hat and his cane on his lap.

"Very well, I shall be brief. I have had reports that when in Cádiz, you have been making trips to the other side . . ."

Maraña goes on looking at him without blinking. His eyes, which can burn with a fire when roused, are calm. "I don't know what trips you are referring to," he says languidly. The policeman is silent for a moment, then tilts his head and looks out to sea as though indicating the direction. "Your excursions to the Puerto de Santa María," he says finally, "at night, aboard boats owned by smugglers. You made just such a trip last night. There and back."

A slight cough, quickly stifled. The young man laughs insolently in the policeman's face.

"I don't know what you're talking about. Besides, it's no business of yours."

Pépé Lobo sees the gold tooth gleam again in the red torchlight.

"That's true, of course. It's not really my business . . . but that's not the issue . . . I have reason to believe that the boat you took is owned by a man I am interested in. A smuggler, a Mulatto . . ."

Deadpan, Maraña crosses his legs, takes a long draw on his cigar then slowly, deliberately exhales. He shrugs his shoulders wearily.

"All right. That's enough. Good evening."

The hand holding the cigar gestures toward the beach, and the gate back to the city, but Tizón remains seated. He is clearly a patient man, thinks Pépé Lobo; patience is obviously a virtue in his godforsaken job. Those hard, dark eyes leave no room for doubt: it is obvious that the policeman dispenses with niceties when it comes to settling a score. These days no one can be certain that they will not end up on the wrong side of the law. Pépé Lobo is confident that, despite his youth, his insolence and the *aguardiente* fueling his contempt, Maraña is as aware of this fact as he is, and is accustomed to judging a man by his looks and his words in the way that a bird may be recognized by its droppings.

"I fear you have got the wrong impression, señor . . . I have not come to talk to you about smuggling."

A gust of laughter causes Pépé Lobo to turn toward the nearest bar, where a barefoot dancer, accompanied by a guitarist, is engaged in a spirited flamenco, pounding the wooden boards and hiking her skirt up to show off her bare legs. A group of English and Spanish officers have just arrived to cheer her on. The corsair pulls a face as he sees them settle in. Among the Spanish officers is a face he recognizes: Captain of Engineers Lorenzo Virués. A reminder of past unpleasantness and present antipathy. For an instant, the image of Lolita Palma's face flickers before his eyes, sharpening his bitter hostility toward the officer. This merely adds to the disagreeable turn the evening has taken.

"What concerns me is more serious," the policeman is telling Maraña. "We have reason to believe that a number of boatmen and smugglers are passing information to the French."

On hearing this, Pépé Lobo suddenly forgets about Lolita Palma and Lorenzo Virués. *I hope not*, he thinks with a start. *Curse the lot of them: Ricardo Maraña, this woman he's been visiting in El Puerto, and this dog poking his nose into things.* The captain of the corsair fervently hopes his lieutenant's nocturnal excursions will not end up complicating his life. Two days from now, if the wind is set fair to leave the bay of Cádiz, the *Culebra* should be out on the open sea with a full crew, cannons ready, all sails set, ready for the hunt.

"I don't know anything about that," says Maraña brusquely.

Maraña's pulse has not quickened, Pépé Lobo notices; it is as regular as that of a snake sleeping in the sun. He has just taken a deep swig of *aguardiente* and replaced the empty glass precisely on the ring of moisture he had lifted it from a moment before. He is as serene as a man prepared to gamble his booty on a hand of *rentoy*, to challenge a man to a fistfight, to leap from the deck of one ship to another amid the creaking of timber and the smoke of musket fire. Looking upon life—and upon himself—with a permanent sneer of disdain.

"Sometimes a man may know things without realizing he knows them," says the policeman.

"I can't help you."

There follows an awkward silence. Eventually Rogelio Tizón gets to his feet.

"This is Cádiz," he says with emphasis. "Smuggling is a way of life here. But *espionage*, now that is a different story . . . Help to fight it, and you are serving your country."

Maraña laughs under his breath. The glow of the torches and the flashes from the distant lighthouse accentuate the dark circles around his eyes and the pallor of his face. The laugh ends with a hacking cough which he does his best to mask, quickly taking a kerchief from the sleeve of his jacket and bringing it to his mouth, and dropping his cigar on the ground. He returns the kerchief to its place without bothering to look at it.

"I shall bear that in mind. Especially the part about serving my country."

The policeman watches him intently and Pépé Lobo has the disagreeable impression that he is filing the lieutenant's face away in his memory. *Insolent little shit*—he can read the words in Tizón's tight-lipped expression—*I hope one day I have the opportunity to settle the score with you.* Tizón certainly seems to be a heartless man, a cold fish. *I only hope*, thinks Pépé Lobo, *that I never have to play cards with these two. It would be impossible to tell their hands by looking at their faces.*

"Should you decide that you have something to tell me, I am at your disposal," concludes the comisario. "The same applies to you, Captain . . . My office is on the Calle del Mirador, opposite the new jail."

He puts on his hat and swings his cane, about to leave. He pauses a moment longer.

"One more thing," he says, turning back to Maraña. "If I were you I would be careful about making trips at night. They might lead to nasty encounters. And consequences."

Maraña looks at him with undisguised indifference. In the end he nods twice, very slightly, and leaning back in his chair pushes aside his coattail to reveal the varnished wooden butt of his snub-nosed pistol.

"Ever since they invented *this*, consequences can go both ways."

The comisario bows his head a little, as though thinking about pistols, directions and consequences; he rakes the sand with the tip of his cane. After a little sigh, he gestures as if writing on the air.

"I shall make a note of that," he says with deceptive suaveness. "And in passing, I should remind you that the use of handguns by individuals is forbidden in Cádiz."

Maraña holds his gaze, smiling thoughtfully. In the flickering light from the torches and with the strumming of the guitar the shadows seem to dance across his face.

"I am not an individual, señor. I am an officer with a Letter of Marque from the king . . . We are outside the city walls, and therefore your authority does not extend here."

Tizón nods with exaggerated formality.

"I shall make a note of that, too."

"Well, when you have finished making notes, might I suggest you go to hell."

The gold tooth glitters one last time. A promise of trouble to come, thinks Pépé Lobo, if ever the lieutenant's path should cross that of the forces of law and order. The sailors say nothing and watch as the comisario heads back along the beach toward the reef and the city gate. Maraña considers his empty glass gloomily.

"I think I'll order another bottle."

"Don't bother. I am leaving . . ." Lobo is still watching the policeman. "So did you go to El Puerto with the Mulatto?"

"I may have."

"Did you know he was a suspected criminal?"

"Nonsense." The young man pulls a scornful face. "Besides, it's no concern of mine."

"Well that bastard seemed to know what he was talking about. I expect it's his job. To be informed."

The two corsairs sit in silence for a moment. They can still hear the cheering and the music from the flamenco bars. The comisario has melted into the shadows under the arch of the Puerto de la Caleta.

"If there is espionage involved," says Pépé Lobo, "it could cause problems for us."

"Don't you start, Captain. I've had enough for one day."

"Are you planning to go over tonight?"

Maraña does not answer. He has picked up his empty glass and is toying with it.

"This changes things," Lobo persists. "I cannot risk you being picked up two days before we put out to sea."

"Don't worry . . . I'm not planning to leave Cádiz."

"Give me your word on it."

"Absolutely not. My private life is my own affair."

"This is not about your private life, it's about your duty to the ship. I can't afford to lose my first officer two days before we sail."

Maraña stares out at the lighthouse. His word of honor, as Pépé Lobo knows, is one of the few things he values. Maraña sets great store by something which most people—and the captain cheerfully includes himself among their number—consider a tactic or a ploy which does not commit you to anything. Keeping his word at all costs is simply one more aspect of his dark, rebellious character. Just one more form of despair.

"You have my word."

Pépé Lobo drains his glass and gets to his feet.

"I'll go and get more *aguardiente*. And have a piss while I'm about it."

He crosses the sand to the bare-board floor of the nearest bar and asks them to bring another bottle to his table. As he does so, he passes the group of men Captain Virués is sitting with and realizes the officer has recognized him. The corsair carries on walking to a dark corner near the city walls that smells of filth and urine, beneath the San Pedro walkway. He unbuttons his breeches and relieves himself, one hand leaning against the wall; then he buttons himself up again and retraces his steps. As he crosses the floor of the bar, a number of Virués's fellow officers stare at him, curious. Clearly the captain has said something about him and, seeing two Redcoats among their number, Pépé Lobo suspects he has mentioned Gibraltar. It would not be the first time; Virués evidently spoke of the matter to Lolita Palma. The memory of it makes him furious. It is difficult to forget her comment when last they spoke: "Some say you are not a gentleman." He has never pretended to be one, but he does not care for the idea that Virués might be announcing the fact at society soirées.

As the corsair walks on, flashes of memory return from that night in Gibraltar—the darkness over the port, the stress of waiting, the danger and the whispers, the stabbed sentry lying on the ground, the freezing water before they clambered aboard the tartane, the muffled struggle with the Navy guard, the splash as the body fell into the black water, the hiss of sail being hoisted as the anchor was raised and the boat gliding across the bay, heading westward towards freedom. All this while Virués and his kind lay sleeping, dreaming of the exchange of prisoners that would send them back to Spain, honor intact, uniforms pressed, with their habitual look of superiority. They are all cut from the same cloth, like the young fop who had challenged him to a duel in Algeciras after the prisoner exchange only to have Pépé Lobo laugh in his face and send him packing. Things are different now. At least they seem to be. Maybe it is the *aguardiente*, the guitars. Maybe things would have been very different had it not been some beardless stripling who had challenged him to a duel in Algeciras, but Virués himself. That stupid, stuck-up son of a bitch.

Without thinking about what he is doing, or about the consequences of his actions, the corsair turns and heads back to the officers' table. *What the hell are you doing?* he thinks. But it's too late to change tack now. There are three Spaniards and two Englishmen with Virués. The latter, a captain and a lieutenant, are wearing British naval uniforms. The three Spaniards are captains: one wears the uniform of an artilleryman while the other two are dressed in the light-blue jackets with yellow lapels of the Irish Regiment. They all look up, startled by his presence.

"Do we know each other, señor?" he asks Virués, who looks at him, flustered. The group is silent; on tenterhooks. The only sound is the music of the flamenco show. Clearly the Captain of Engineers was not expecting this. Nor was Pépé Lobo. *To the devil with it*, he thinks again, *what am I doing here, picking fights like some drunken tosspot?*

"I believe we do," answers Virués.

Pépé Lobo coolly appraises the captain's face, impeccably shaven despite the lateness of the hour, his dark mustache and fashionable whiskers neatly trimmed. A fine-looking man, he thinks, not for the first time. Captain of Engineers, no less. A man with an education and a bright future, with or without the war, the sort of man whose path has already been carved out for him. A gentleman, as Lolita Palma would say—as she *did* say. Just the sort to offer a scented kerchief to a lady, or holy water as she leaves a church.

"I thought as much. You were one of the men in Gibraltar, sitting around on their asses waiting for a convenient prisoner exchange . . ."

The words hang in the air. Virués blinks, sitting up slightly in his chair. Unsurprisingly, none of the officers is smiling now. The Spaniards are open-mouthed; the English have not understood what was said.

"I was on parole, bound by my word of honor, señor. As were you."

Virués stresses the last two words haughtily. The corsair gives him an insolent smile.

"Yes, on parole, and in the company of these upstanding English gentlemen . . . I see that you still count them as friends."

The officer frowns, his initial puzzlement fast becoming irritation. Pépé Lobo spots him glancing down at the sword that leans against his chair. The corsair, for his part, is unarmed. He never carries a weapon when on land, and certainly not when drinking. Not even his sailor's knife. It is a lesson he learned as a young man traveling from port to port, watching other men hang.

"Are you picking a quarrel with me, señor?"

The corsair thinks about this for a moment. It is certainly an interesting question. Eventually, having mulled it over, he shrugs his shoulders.

"I don't know," he answers honestly. "What I do know is that I don't care for the way you look at me. Nor for what you have been saying about me behind my back."

"I have said nothing I would not say to your face."

"For example?"

"That in Gibraltar you did not behave like a gentleman . . . That your escape, in direct breach of the rules, put everyone in an embarrassing position."

"By 'everyone,' I assume you mean cretins such as yourself."

Murmurs of indignation around the table. There is a rush of blood to Virués's face. He gets to his feet like the well-bred man he is: slowly, serenely. Pépé Lobo sees the man's fists clench and this gives him a thrill. The other officers remain seated, looking at each other, especially the English officers—clearly they do not understand a word of Spanish, but that is hardly necessary. The scene being played out is international and needs no translation.

Virués brings a hand up to his immaculate shirt collar as if to adjust his necktie. His struggle to maintain his self-control is obvious. He pushes aside the tail of his frockcoat, puts one hand on his hip and stares down at the corsair, over whom he towers by some six inches.

"That is a filthy slur."

Pépé Lobo says nothing. Sometimes words offend, but he is an old seadog. He simply looks Virués up and down—as though carrying the knife he does not have—sizing him up like he is calculating where best to stab if the man should lift a finger. As though he has divined his intentions, the captain remains stock-still, staring at him curiously, politely menacing. Or barely menacing at all.

"I demand an honorable resolution, señor."

At the word "honorable," Pépé Lobo sneers. He all but laughs. *Let's leave military honor out of this*, he thinks. *Why don't you kiss my ass?*

"Spare me the propriety and the posturing. We're not at Court, or even in a guardroom."

The officers around the table are hanging on every word. Pépé Lobo's jacket is unbuttoned; he holds his arms away from his body like a wrestler, which is exactly what he looks like just now, with his broad shoulders and powerful hands. His instincts as an old salt, together with a long experience of seedy harbor bars and what goes on there, make him alert, anticipating every movement, both probable and improbable. Calculating risks. That same experience now warns him of Ricardo Maraña's silent presence behind him. Smelling trouble, the Little Marquis has come over and is hanging back, ready to wade in if there is a brawl. Dangerous as always. *Pray God he does not decide to go for the gun tucked into the belt under his jacket*, thinks Lobo. *Because too much* aguardiente *can play tricks on a man, as it has done to me tonight. Here I am standing in front of this imbecile, with no way forward unless he makes the first move, and no way back without admitting defeat, for flouting a simple rule: never stir up trouble at the wrong time or in the wrong place.*

"I demand satisfaction," says Virués.

The corsair stares toward the reef as it sweeps out past the Castillo de Santa Catalina. It is the only place nearby that offers a modicum of privacy, but luckily it will not be uncovered by low tide for another two hours. Lobo feels a violent urge to punch the captain, but he has no desire to fight a duel, with seconds and the whole ridiculous protocol that would entail. The idea is absurd. Dueling is forbidden by law. He would probably lose his Letter of Marque and the command of the *Culebra*, something the Sánchez Guineas would take very badly. Not to mention Lolita Palma.

"I put out to sea two days from now," he says neutrally.

He said it in precisely the right tone, staring straight ahead, as if thinking aloud. No one can accuse him of backing down. Virués looks at his companions. One of them, a Captain of Artillery with a gray mustache and a respectable air, shakes his head slightly. The captain is wavering, and Lobo can see it. *This is my chance*, he thinks. *Better to leave this for another day, when it can be handled more discreetly.*

"Don Lorenzo is on duty early tomorrow," says Gray Mustache. "We are heading back to the Isla de Léon before dawn, Captain Virués, myself and these gentlemen."

Imperturbably, Pépé Lobo continues to stare at Virués.

"That makes things difficult, then."

"So it would seem."

Both sides are hesitating now. The corsair hides his relief. The time will come, he thinks, and then we shall see. He wonders if his adversary is as relieved as he is—his intuition assures him that he is.

"In that case, let us leave this conversation to another time."

"I trust we will meet again soon, señor," says Virués.

"You can dispense with the *señor.* It clearly sticks in your craw. But, yes, we shall meet again soon, my friend. And then I will wipe the smile off your face."

The captain's face flushes again. For an instant, Lobo thinks Virués is about to hurl himself at him. *If he tries to punch me*, Lobo thinks, *I'll smash that bottle and slash his face, and damn the consequences.*

"I am no friend of yours," growls Virués indignantly. "And if tonight I did not—"

"That's right. You did not . . ."

The corsair lets out a crude, insolent laugh. As he does so, he slips a hand into the pocket of his jacket, takes out two silver coins, tosses them to the innkeeper, turns his back on Virués and stalks off. Behind him he can hear Ricardo Maraña's erratic footsteps on the wooden planks, then on the sand.

"I don't believe it . . . You dare lecture me about being careful and five minutes later you're spoiling for a duel."

Pépé Lobo laughs again, this time at himself.

"It must be the *aguardiente.*"

They walk along the stretch of red-tinted sand toward the boats beached by the walkway at San Sebastían. Maraña has caught up with the captain and now limps along next to him, watching him in the faint glow from the torches set into the sand. He looks at him curiously, as though seeing him for the first time.

"I'm sure that's what it was," says Lobo after a while. "The *aguardiente.*"

CHAPTER EIGHT

೮೦೦

It is shortly before dawn. The east wind, blowing hard across the barren landscape of the salt marshes, whips up swirls of dust that blot out the stars. The dust, like a thousand invisible needles, stabs the eyes of the four men—three adults and a boy—who have been wading through mud and darkness for several hours. Armed with swords, hatchets and knives, they advance slowly; their faces are covered with cloths or kerchiefs to shield them from the blustering wind, which is blowing so hard that every time they have to leave the channels and the tidal creeks to walk for a stretch on dry land, it instantly dries the salt and mud on their clothes.

"There's the main channel over there," whispers Felipe Mojarra.

He stops and hunkers down, cocking his ear, between the branches of saltwort that scratch his face. All he can hear is the whistle of the wind in the undergrowth and the rush of water in the channel: a black streak, visible only by the faint reflections in the darkness.

"We'll have to get wet again."

Thirty *varas*, the salter reminds himself—that is how wide the channel is along this stretch. Fortunately, since they have lived all their lives in the salt marshes, he and his comrades know how to keep afloat. One by one they line up along the bank: Curro Panizo; his son Currito; Mojarra's brother-in-law Cárdenas. Silent, single-minded shadows. They left the Isla de Léon at nightfall and, barely visible through the dust clouds, managed to cross the Spanish lines to the south of the Isla de Vicario, crawling on their bellies under the cannons of the San Pedro battery. From there, shortly before midnight, they swam across the Camarón channel and trekked through half a league of no-man's-land, negotiating the maze of gullies and tidal creeks in the darkness.

"Where are we?" asks Cárdenas in a low voice.

Felipe Mojarra is not sure. The dust whipped up by the east wind has disoriented him. He is afraid of having miscounted the creeks they crossed, of going too far and stumbling right into the French trenches. So he stands up, pushes aside the dark bushes and peers into the darkness, doing his best to protect himself from the stinging sand and wind. When his poacher's eyes have adjusted to the gloom, he sees a dark shape that looks like the rib cage of a huge skeleton: the rotting hull of a ship, half sunken in the mud.

"This is the place," he says.

"And there are no *gabachos* on the other side?" asks his brother-in-law.

"The nearest French are at the mouth of the creek that leads to the mill. We'll be safe here."

He crawls down the short slope to the water's edge, followed by the others. When he reaches the muddy shore, he stops to check the short sword slung over his shoulder is still secure and that the six-inch pocket-knife tucked into his belt will not hamper his swimming. Then, slowly, he wades into the dark water—so cold it takes his breath away. When he can no longer feel the bottom, he begins to move his arms and legs, keeping his head high, kicking out toward the far shore. The distance to be swum presents no difficulty, but the high wind swelling the water, and the tide which has just begun to turn, sweep him off course. He must not get out of breath. Behind him, he hears Cárdenas splashing. His brother-in-law is the least able of the four—Panizo and his son both swim like fish—but he has taken the precaution of tying two hollow gourds to himself so that he will not go under. In other circumstances, they would have had to make sure his energetic splashing did not alert the French; fortunately tonight, everything is drowned out by the gale.

It has proved to be a good day for Felipe Mojarra and his companions. When the east wind blows hard across the salt flats, it shrouds everything in a pall of sand and dust. Some time ago, on one of his first reconnaissance missions with Virués, Mojarra overheard the captain attempting to persuade an English officer that it would not be a good idea to use traditional fascines to surround the San Pedro gun battery. It would be better to use sisal, Virués insisted—something farmers in Andalucía used to fence in their gardens. The Redcoat refused to budge and, following orders, built defenses round the camp using fascines. By the time the east wind had been blowing for five days, the trench was filled with sand and the parapet buried under it. The English officer having finally been persuaded of the effectiveness of sisal—an old salter knows more tricks than the devil himself, Virués remarked, giving Mojarra a wink—the fence around the San Pedro battery now looks like more of a garden than a fortress.

Mojarra crawls out of the channel, shivering as he slithers like a snake across the muddy bank, where he is joined by the others. Some six hundred *varas* away, framed against a faint blue light, a hill, dark with pine groves, rises up to Chiclana. Following the bank of the channel, the village, now heavily defended by the French, is a little more than half a league away.

"Single file," whispers the salter. "And keep it slow."

He goes first, clambering over the low ridge of earth, then crawling on all fours through the freezing water of the salt marsh. A little further on, when they are sure they will not be seen in the dawn light, the four men wade, up to their waists in water. The muddy terrain makes progress difficult. From time to time, there is a sudden splash or a muttered curse, and they have to free each other from the treacherous mire. Fortunately they are facing into the gale, so any sound is carried downwind, away from prying ears. The tide ebbs; water drains into the channel and out into the bay, exposing the salt marsh, from which no one has harvested salt since the French arrived. Mojarra knows they are running late. Between the clouds of sand and dust whipped up by squalls of wind, he can see that the narrow band of sky is already veering from murky blue to ocher, the dawn emerging behind the pine groves of Chiclana. We'll get there only by the skin of our teeth, he thinks. But with a bit of luck we'll make it.

"They're over there," hisses Curro Panizo. "By the mouth of the little creek, next to the wooden jetty."

Mojarra crawls up the bank and carefully pushes aside fronds of saltwort and wild asparagus. A faint silvery light reflects on the maze of tidal creeks, like rivulets of molten lead, marking out the mouth of the Alcornocal channel where it widens near the mill at Santa Cruz—which, though still in shadow, he knows is nearby. To his left, where it joins the channel that runs down from Chiclana, beside the little jetty and the boathouse Mojarra knows well (they were here before the war), he sees the long, flat outline of the gunboat.

"Where is the guard?" Panizo asks.

"At the far end of the jetty . . . We can creep closer to the boat, following the salt banks. The rest of them will be asleep in the boathouse."

"Let's go then. It's getting late."

The shape of the nearby pine grove is beginning to emerge as the four men cross the last salt bank and wade into the thick mud. In the grayish-yellow light the wooden boathouse is now visible, as well as the little jetty and the gunboat moored alongside. Mojarra breathes a sigh of relief when he sees it is not grounded in the mud but floating, its mast tilted slightly toward the bow and the sail furled around the lateen yard. This will make things easier; they can ride the stiff easterly wind and sail out into the main channel, instead of having to row like hell with the *gabachos* on their tail.

"I can't see the sentry."

Panizo pops his head over the ridge and looks round, then scuttles back.

"On the right, next to the jetty. Sheltering from the wind."

Mojarra finally picks out the dark, stationary figure—*with a bit of luck, the man's asleep*, he thinks. He has untied the sword slung over his shoulder and listens as the others do likewise. Panizo has a boarding ax, while Cárdenas and young Currito have cutlasses. He feels a shudder run through him, up from his groin—a feeling he always gets when carrying a knife.

"Ready?" Three whispers of assent.

Mojarra takes three deep breaths. "It's all in God's hands now."

The four men scrabble to their feet, make the sign of the cross and advance cautiously, stooping slightly so as not to be seen, listening to the crunch of dry salt beneath their bare feet. *Twenty thousand* reales *if we can get the gunboat across the Spanish lines*, Mojarra thinks again. *That's five thousand for each one of us, if we make it back alive. Or for our families.* The faces of his wife and daughters flash through his mind, only to be swept away by the pounding of his heartbeat, a rush of blood hammering in his ears, drowning out the howling wind that chills his damp clothes.

Thock . . . The sentry does not even have time to cry out. He was asleep. Not stopping to think about the dark figure he has just run through with his sword, Mojarra walks on to the boathouse, finds the door and kicks it open. The four men are silent. Jostling each other, they rush inside; all that can be seen in the faint light that filters in from outside are five or six figures lying on the floor. The room smells of mildew, sweat, stale tobacco, wet clothes and grime. *Thock, chsss, thock, chsss.* Methodically, as though lopping branches off a tree, the four men slash and hack. The last of the figures, awake now, does have time to scream. He lunges brutally at them, scrabbling for the door, letting out a desperate howl of terror. *Thock, thock, thock. Chsss, chsss, chsss.* Mojarra and his companions get it over with quickly. Who knows if there are others nearby, others who might have heard the screams? Then they pile out of the boathouse, greedily sucking in lungfuls of air, all but collapsing on the sand, brushing from their clothes the blood that stains their hands and faces.

They run down to the jetty without looking back. The French gunboat, still afloat, bobs in the wind. The tide is ebbing more quickly now, laying bare the muddy banks of channels and creeks in the harsh dawn light. Unless something goes wrong, they still have time. Only just, Mojarra thinks, but they have time.

"Go and take any weapons you can find, kid."

Currito Panizo sets off for the boathouse like a cannonball while his father, Cárdenas and Mojarra leap aboard the gunboat. They untie the lateen yard and pull on the halyard to raise the yard, having taken in the reefs of the sail which unfurls in the wind with a crack; the boat lists toward the side of the channel just as young Currito is running back, carrying four rifles and two gun belts complete with cartridges, bayonets and swords.

"Hurry up, lad! We're leaving!"

A slash of the saber to prow and another to stern as the boy jumps aboard, and his cargo clatters noisily on to the deck of the boat. It is a long, narrow, shallow-draft vessel, ideally suited for a war waged by gunboats in the maze of tidal creeks around the Isla de Léon. It must be about forty feet in length, Mojarra calculates. It is a fine boat. There is a cannon in the bow—a 6-pounder by the look of it, a handsome piece—mounted on a sliding gun carriage, and there are two small brass *pedreros* in the stern, one on either side. This guarantees that they will get a reward of at least 20,000 *reales*. Possibly more. Assuming, of course, they make it home.

With the mooring lines cut, and urged on by the wind, the sail swelling on the right side, the gunboat pulls away from the jetty; it glides slowly at first, and then with unsettling speed it sails down the middle of the Alcornocal channel. In the stern, manning the tiller, careful to keep the vessel in the deepest part of the narrow channel—all would be lost if they were to run aground—Mojarra tries to calculate the ebb of the tide and how best to take the bend where the Alcornocal joins the main channel. Currito and Cárdenas are hauling the sheet and adjusting the sail while Panizo steers in the prow. It is light enough now for the men to see each other's faces: unshaven, dark circles under their eyes, their skin streaked with mud and *gabacho* blood. They are all on edge, knowing what they have done, but they have no time to think about that.

"We did it!" Cárdenas yells, jubilant, as if he has only just realized.

"We're going to be rich!" Panizo echoes from the bow.

Mojarra is just about to tell them not to count their chickens, when the enemy does it for him. A shout in French comes from the shadows that still shroud the bank of the channel, followed immediately by two dazzling flashes. *Bang. Bang.* The shots do not reach the gunboat, which is at the mouth of the Chiclana channel. More shots ring out from the opposite bank—a few bullets, fired blind, sending up jets of spray—while Mojarra leans all his weight on the tiller to tack westward into the current of the big channel. The weight of the cannon in the bow makes it easier to hold a straight course, but difficult to maneuver. Wind and tide finally converge; the boat speeds into the current with the wind behind and the lateen yard almost horizontal. Anxiously, Mojarra surveys the flat landscape and the low banks. He knows that there is a French advance post by the next confluence, and that the ashen light filtering through the clouds of dust will make it easier for the enemy to aim as they pass. But they have no choice but to carry on and hope that the poor visibility will thwart the *gabachos*.

"Get the oars ready. We might have to use them when we get to the San Pedro channel."

"We won't need them," protests Panizo.

"Best to be prepared. There's going to be a lot of mud around the islets. I don't want to take any risks, what with the current and this wind . . . We might have to row through that section . . . Where's the flag?"

While Panizo senior and Cárdenas set the oars into the rowlocks, Currito Panizo takes a folded scrap of cloth from his belt. He shows it to Mojarra with a wink, setting it down between the breeching ropes that secure the cannon. His mother sewed the flag two nights ago by the light of a tallow candle. Since they had no yellow fabric, the middle band is white, cut from an old bedsheet, while the red bands came from the scarlet lining of an old cape that belonged to Cárdenas. The finished flag, which measures about three feet by two, looks very like those flown by the gunboats of the Royal Armada; when they run it up the mast, it will ensure the Spaniards and the English do not fire on them when they see the boat appear out of the Chiclana channel. For the moment, it is better to leave it where it is, since the only people likely to fire are the French—and they will fire for all they're worth, thinks Mojarra anxiously, watching as they speed toward the mouth of the creek. Once they have passed the enemy's advance post, there are still 1,500 *varas* of no-man's-land to cross before they emerge into the main channel near the Spanish front lines, the gun batteries of San Pedro and the Isla de Vacario. But that will all come later. First they will have to run the gauntlet. Alerted by the shots, the French gunners up ahead will be ready and waiting to fire—at almost point-blank range.

"Hit the deck! . . . We're nearly there!"

The French post is barely visible from this part of the creek, but in the gray light filtering through the eddies of dust that swirl along the bank, Mojarra can see ominous figures peering through the undergrowth. He leans on the tiller, trying to steer the gunboat toward the other side of the channel, as far as possible from the shore, keeping an eye on the bank of thick mud now uncovered by the fast-receding tide.

The French are already firing. The bullets whistle through the air above the gunboat, or fall short, sending up plumes of spray. *Plop. Plop.* A harmless splashing that sounds like stones being skimmed across a river. Clinging to the tiller, Mojarra keeps his head as low as possible, careful not to lose sight of the black mudbank. For all he knows, there could be twenty soldiers in the *gabacho* post. That would mean that in the sixty long seconds the gunboat is within firing range—assuming they don't run aground and end up riddled with bullets—the French will have enough time to fire off fifty rounds. It sounds like they've made a good start. There's too much firing, Mojarra thinks gloomily; this is how a wild duck must feel as it flaps desperately, trying to outdistance the shooting party. Too terrified even to quack.

"Watch out!" Curro Panizo yells.

This is it, thinks Mojarra. The gunboat is now directly opposite the advance post; the French are adjusting their aim. The bullets hammer all around like hailstones while the wind whips away the smoke from the rifle shots. The chorus of *ziaang* and *plop* grows louder, but now there is another, more menacing, sound: the dull crack of bullets hitting the boat's wooden hull. One shot splinters the gunwale barely inches from Mojarra. Others rip through the sail or bury themselves in the mast above the crouching figures of Panizo, Cárdenas and Currito.

Gripping the tiller, doing his utmost to prevent the wind from taking the boat off course, all Mojarra can do is grit his teeth, keep as low as possible—his every muscle aches as he waits for a bullet to strike home—and pray that none of these lead slugs has his name on it.

Crack, crack, crack. The hail of bullets is coming thick and fast. Mojarra pops his head over the gunwale, checks how far they are from the right bank, how deep the water is; he adjusts the tiller and, turning back, sees Cárdenas, his brother-in-law, on the deck of the gunboat, clutching his head in his hands while blood gushes through his fingers and trickles down his arms. Cárdenas has let go of the sheet—the sail is whipped around by a sudden gust of wind, the boat sheers and almost crashes into the bank.

"The sheet! F'Christ's sake, haul aft the sheet!"

Gunfire crackles all around. Leaping over the injured man, Currito tries to grab the rope, which flails in the air as the sail flaps wildly. Mojarra leans his full weight on the tiller, turning it first one way, then the other, desperately trying to keep it from running aground on the mudbanks. Eventually, Curro Panizo manages to grab the rope; he hauls the sheet astern and the sail—by now riddled with a dozen bulletholes—catches the wind again.

The last shots go wide and are left behind as the gunboat speeds away from the French post and into the gentle double-curve that leads to the San Pedro channel. One last bullet hits the sternpost and buries itself in the rudder, sending up a shower of splinters that hit Mojarra in the neck—without causing any damage, but giving him a terrible shock. Damn those fucking Frenchies, mutters the salter, still gripping the tiller; damn Napoleon and all his dead. Suddenly, he remembers the boathouse, the whistle of sword and ax, the stench of butchery, the blood that has since dried on his hands and under his fingernails. He tries to think about something else. About the twenty thousand *reales* to be divided between the four of them. Because, if nothing else goes wrong, all four will make it home: Curro and Currito Panizo are tending to Cárdenas, who is sprawled on his back on the gun carriage, his face pale and covered in blood. "Just a flesh wound," Curro informs him. "It doesn't look too serious." Picking up speed now, the gunboat glides down the middle of the channel; already Mojarra can see the little islands of mud left by the ebb tide at the mouth of the creek. In another hundred yards or so, the gunboat will come into view of the English battery on the far bank. Mojarra yells to Currito to get the flag ready. "We don't want the Redcoats firing on us from San Pedro."

From this distance, he can see that there is still enough space to sail between the muddy islands. They won't need the oars just yet. He shifts the tiller, pointing the bow toward the stretch of open water rippled by the wind and the current, between the two flat banks of black mud emerging inch by inch as the tide drops. Mojarra glances back one last time at the flat landscape, the channels and the tidal creeks on both sides. A flock of avocets—they seem reluctant to fly north this year, as if they too are scared of the *gabachos*—wade along the muddy shore on spindly legs, flapping black-striped wings, sheltered from the wind by a high ridge covered with shrubs.

"Raise that flag now, lad . . . We need the Redcoats to see it."

By now the sail will be visible from the gun battery, he thinks, and the English must have heard the shots. But better to be safe. In a flash, Currito Panizo, who has already attached the flag to a halyard, hoists it above the lateen yard to the top of the mast. A moment later, with a firm tug on the tiller, Mojarra steers the gunboat between the islands, then changes tack, heading north into the mouth of the main channel.

"Haul down the sails! . . . Get to your oars!"

Slumped against the gun carriage, clutching his injured head, Cárdenas moans from time to time. *Ay, mamá*, he whimpers. *Ay, ay, ay* . . . Curro and Currito Panizo scrabble to slacken the sheet, lower the lateen yard and make fast the sail. Then each grabs an oar and, facing the bow, feet wedged against the thwarts in front, they begin to row frantically. Between their heads, in the distance, Mojarra can already see the sisal parapets, the low walls and the cannon embrasures of the English stronghold. Just at that moment, there is a gust of wind from the east, the haze of dust lifts and the first ray of sunlight illuminates the red and white flag fluttering fiercely on the mast of the captured gunboat.

THE MALE ORGAN or spermatic fluid must be located within the female uterus, and in contact with the embryonic seed such that they are fertilized clandestinely, since otherwise it is impossible to explain the fecundity of the seed, which presumes the interaction of both sexes . . .

Lolita Palma stands, rereading these lines. Then she closes Cavanilles' *Description of Plants*, gazing at the dark leather covers of the book in her botanical workshop. She is quiet, thoughtful. Then she returns the volume to its shelf, crosses to the window that overlooks the street, and rolls down the venetian blind. She is wearing only a light dressing gown of Chinese silk that falls to her flat sandals, and her hair is pinned up. It is impossible to concentrate in such heat, and the streaming sunlight she needs to work or read brings with it the hot muggy air from outside. It is *siesta* time, but unlike most people in Cádiz, Lolita Palma does not sleep, preferring to spend these few hours on her plants or her reading, enjoying the tranquility of the hushed house. Her mother is reclining amid her pillows and her laudanum vapors. Even the maids are resting. This is the only time, except at night, that Lolita reserves for herself; ever since she took charge of the house of Palma e Hijos, her days have been dictated by the customs of her trade. She is in her office from eight o'clock until two-thirty; she has lunch, brushes her teeth with powdered coral and myrrh water, her hair is brushed and combed by her maid Mari Paz, then it's back to her office from six o'clock until eight; a stroll before dinner along the Calle Ancha, the Plaza de San Antonio and the Alameda, some shopping and a little light refreshment at Cosí's café, or perhaps Burnel's. Sometimes—rarely—she has a meeting at an acquaintance's house, or in her own salon or patio. The war and the French occupation have long since put an end to summers spent in the family house in Chiclana. Lolita still feels an aching wistfulness for the place: the pine groves and the nearby beach, the orchards beneath whose trees she would stroll at dusk, tea taken at the hermitage of Santa Ana and trips by caleche to Medina Sidonia. The quiet walks through the country-side, collecting and identifying plants with old Professor Cabrera, who taught her about botany. And when night fell the moonlight spilled through the open windows, so bright and silvery that you could almost read or write by it, lulled by the constant chirrup of crickets and the croak of frogs in the nearby irrigation ditches. But that cherished world where she spent the endless summers of her childhood and her youth has long since vanished. Those who have been to Chiclana tell her that these days the house and its grounds have been laid waste, converted into barracks and forts or falling to rack and ruin, the French having diligently looted everything. God knows what will be left of that happy world, already so remote, when these uncertain times are finally over.

The soft glow of the gold-leaf tracery that adorns the books and the herbaria penetrates the gloom. On the far side of the room, opposite the street window, dewdrops from ferns mist the panes of the glassed-in balcony, like a hothouse, which overlooks the patio. Outside, the city is silent. Not even the rumble of a French bomb, distant or close—for the shelling from the Trocadero has been coming ever nearer—breaks the warm silence of the afternoon. It has been four days since the French shelled the city, and with no bombs, the war once again seems impos-sibly remote. Almost alien to the regular, everyday pulse of Cádiz, as it has always been. The most recent glimpse of war took place yesterday morning, when the citizenry went up to their terraces and watchtowers with telescopes and spyglasses to watch as a French brigantine and a corsair felucca flying the same flag emerged from the inlet at Rota to do battle with a small convoy of tartanes coming from Algeciras, es-corted by two Spanish gunboats and an English schooner. The blue of the ocean was filled with smoke and cannonfire for almost two hours. The westerly breeze gently stirred the distant sails as the people of Cádiz enjoyed the spectacle, sometimes applauding, sometimes jeering when things looked grim for the allies. From her lookout tower, even Lolita Palma, accompanied by the wise eyes of old Santos ("That tar-tane to windward is in dire straits, Doña Lolita; they'll hunt it down like a sheep that's strayed from the flock"), followed the fate of the ships, the distant roar, the smoke from the cannonfire. Eventually the

French—who had the advantage of the west wind, which becalmed the English schooner and made it impossible for the Spanish corvette that quit its moorings to get close—managed to get away, having captured two boats right under the cannons of the Castillo de San Sebastián.

Three weeks earlier, with her spyglass resting in the embrasure of the same tower, alone this time, Lolita Palma had watched the *Culebra* sail out of the bay. Now, in the half light of her library, she well remembers the east-northeasterly wind rippling the full tide as the corsair cutter—steering close to the rocks by Las Puercas and the shallows at Fraile to keep away from the French gun batteries—first sailed straight out toward the open sea, then, with the wind on the beam, rounded the city walls toward the reef of San Sebastían. Then, letting out more sail—it looked as though they had hoisted the gaff topsail and the third jib on the long bowsprit—she watched as it tacked due south, off into the vast blue immensity, the white speck of the sails growing smaller until they disappeared from the lens of her spyglass.

Much later, the waning day and the streaks of purple in the eastern sky found Lolita Palma still in the tower, gazing at the empty horizon. Standing motionless, just as she is now in her study. Still focused on the last glimpse of the cutter as it disappeared; surprised to find herself still there. Only once before could she remember staring out at the empty sea: it was on the afternoon of October 20, 1805 as the French and Spanish fleets commanded by Admirals Villeneuve and Gravina left port—a long and painful departure with much tacking and little wind, while a multitude of fathers, sons and brothers, wives and relatives watched in silence from their terraces and watchtowers, or from the city walls, staring out to sea even after the last sail had long since disappeared: those men heading to meet their grim fate at Trafalgar.

Leaning against the wall of her study, Lolita Palma remembers. The watchtower, the sea. The feel of leather and brass from the spyglass in her hands. The wrenching sensation of some vague absence, and a sadness filled with strange foreboding. *What did any of that have to do with the* Culebra? she thinks now, angry at herself. And suddenly, the cautious, thoughtful smile of Pépé Lobo flashes into her mind like a gunshot, sending a shudder through her. His wary, catlike eyes gazing serenely at her, accustomed to looking at the sea and at women. "Some say you are not a gentleman." This was what she had said to him, and she will never forget his response; simple, confident, never taking his eyes from her: "I am not a gentleman, nor do I claim to be."

Lolita opens her mouth like a fish gasping, and takes a deep breath of warm air. Once, twice, three times. She slips a hand into the opening of her damp peignoir and runs it over her bare breast, feeling the same quickening pulse she felt in her wrists that day, during their encounter on the Plaza de San Francisco—their conversation about the dragon tree painted on her fan. She hears her own words as though spoken by someone else, by some strange woman. "You must tell me all about it, Captain. I would very much enjoy that . . . Some other day, perhaps . . . when you come back to port again." Lolita cannot forget his firm, tanned hands; his chin, though freshly shaved that morning, already showing signs of dark stubble. His thick hair and long whiskers, bushy but impeccably trimmed. Masculine. That smile like a white streak across his suntanned face. She pictures him as he is right now, standing on the deck of the cutter, hair ruffled by the wind, eyes half-closed against the sun's glare. Scouring the horizon for his next prey.

Lolita Palma stands by the window, listening to the silent city. Even with the blinds closed, the warm air seeps through the slats. The days of strong easterly winds are over and Cádiz once again feels like a ship drifting on warm, still waters, becalmed on its own Sargasso Sea. A ghost ship, aboard which Lolita Palma is the only crew—or the only survivor. This is how she feels now in the silence and the sweltering heat, leaning back against the wall, thinking of Pépé Lobo. Her body feels damp, the back of her neck wet. Beneath the silk, small beads of sweat trickle down her thighs.

•

THE TALL, IMPOSING mass of the Puerta de Tierra stands out against a dark sky strewn with stars. Following the whitewashed walls of Santo Domingo convent, Rogelio Tizón turns left. A street lantern illuminates one corner of the Calle de la Goleta; the other side is shrouded in shadow. As the policeman's footsteps resound, a figure emerges from the darkness.

"Good evening, Señor Comisario," says Tía Perejil.

Tizón does not return the greeting. The midwife has just opened the door, revealing the flickering light of an oil lamp within. She steps inside, closely followed by Tizón, picking up the lamp to light their way down the narrow corridor, with its peeling walls that smell of mildew and cats. Though it is hot outside, in here it feels cold. As though the hallway leads to a different season of the year.

"My friend says she will do what she can."

"I hope so."

The old woman pulls aside a curtain. On the other side is a miserable little room, its walls covered with blankets from Jerez on which hang religious icons, engravings of saints, ex-votos made of wax and tinplate. On a carved wooden dresser, incongruously elegant, is a small shrine with a crystal urn depicting the Christ of Humility and Patience, lit by votive candles floating in a bowl of oil. The center of the room is taken up by a *mesa camilla*—a table with a heater underneath—on which stands a brass candlestick; the flickering candle casts shadows and light on the features of the woman sitting opposite, her hands on the table.

"Here she is, Señor Comisario, La Caracola."

Tizón does not remove his hat. Without ceremony, he sits in the empty chair, his cane between his knees. Unmoving, eyes vacant, she returns his gaze. She is a woman of indeterminate age, between forty and sixty: her hair is dyed copper, her face has something of the gypsy about it, her skin is smooth. One of the fat, bare arms lying on the table is adorned with gold bangles—at least a dozen of them, the policeman calculates. Around her neck she wears a huge crucifix, a reliquary and an embroidered scapulary bearing a picture of the Virgin that he cannot identify.

"I've already explained to my friend what it is that's worrying you," says Tía Perejil, "so I'll leave the two of you alone."

Tizón nods but says nothing, busy lighting a cigar as the midwife's footsteps disappear down the hallway. Then he looks at the other woman through a smoke ring that melts into the candle's flame.

"What can you tell me?"

Silence. Tizón has heard tell of La Caracola—it is his job to hear about everyone—but he has not set eyes on her until now. He knows she moved to the city six or seven years ago and worked selling fritters in Huelva. In Cádiz she is celebrated as a pious woman and a clairvoyant. Poor people constantly pester her for advice and cures. It is her stock-in-trade.

The woman has closed her eyes and is mumbling something inaudible. A prayer, perhaps. Not a promising start, thinks Tizón—the gypsy mystic routine.

"He will kill again," the clairvoyant whispers after a moment. "This man will kill again . . ."

She has a curious voice, Tizón realizes. Tormented and shrill, it sets his teeth on edge and reminds him of the wail of an animal in pain.

"How do you know it's a man?"

"I know."

Tizón sucks on his cigar thoughtfully. "I didn't need to visit you to find out that," he says. "I worked it out for myself."

"My friend told me that . . ."

"Listen, Caracola," the comisario says, his hand raised in warning. "Don't give me any mumbo jumbo. I'm here because I'm clutching at every straw I can . . . And you never know. It can't hurt to try."

This much is true. The case has been going round and round in his head for so long he decided to consult the clairvoyant—although he wasn't getting his hopes up, obviously. He is an old dog, and a mangy cur at that, and this is not the first charlatan he has met in his life. But as he has just said: it can't hurt to try. It is no more illogical than the fact that the last time the murderer killed it was *before* the bomb fell. At that point, Tizón decided not to discount any possibility, any idea, however absurd. His visit to the clairvoyant is simply a shot in the dark, one of the many strange things he has tried—and, he fears, will go on trying—since the last murder.

"Do you believe in the grace bestowed on me by God?"

"Do I believe in what?"

The woman stares at him suspiciously, saying nothing. The tip of Tizón's cigar blazes as he takes a long draw.

"I don't believe in your grace, or anyone else's for that matter."

"Then why did you come here?"

A good question, the comisario has to admit. "It's my job," he says. "It is a difficult investigation . . . But be careful: as I'm sure your friend has told you, I'm not a man you should cross."

A black cat appears out of the shadows, weaves through the legs of the table and comes to rub itself against Tizón's boots. Filthy beast.

"Just tell me the truth. Do you see anything that might help me? If you don't, it doesn't matter. I'll go . . . All I ask is that you don't waste my time."

La Caracola sits, frozen, unblinking, staring at some uncertain point behind the comisario. Finally she closes her eyes—Tizón takes the opportunity to kick the cat away—and, a moment later, she opens them again. She looks blankly at the cat whimpering next to her, then at the policeman.

"I see a man."

The comisario leans his elbows on the table irritably, smoldering cigar clamped in the corner of his mouth.

"You've said that already. What I'm interested in is the link between the murders and the places the French have shelled."

"I don't understand what you mean."

"Is there a connection between the two . . . between the murdered girls and the bombs?"

"What bombs?"

"The bombs falling on Cádiz, you stupid bitch."

The woman looks him up and down, at first disconcerted, then with disdain.

"Your soul is hardened," she says after a moment. "You do not believe. This makes it difficult for God's grace to shine on me."

"Make an effort. I must believe in something; after all, I'm here."

Her eyes glaze over again and she stares at something over Tizón's shoulder. Her hands clutch the scapulary she wears round her neck for the time it takes to say two Hail Marys. Eventually La Caracola blinks and shakes her head.

"It's impossible. I can't concentrate."

Tizón takes off his hat and scratches his head, discouraged, resisting the urge to stalk out. He puts his hat back on. Cautiously, the cat circles him, taking a path that stays out of reach of his boots.

"Try again, Caracola."

The woman sighs and turns to the picture of Christ on the dresser, as though calling Him as witness to her good faith. Then she stares into the void again. Three Hail Marys this time, Tizón calculates.

"Wait. I see something."

There is a brief pause. Her eyes half-closed, she raises one hand in a tinkle of golden bracelets.

"A cave . . ." she says, "a dark place."

The comisario leans forward across the table. He has taken the cigar from his mouth and is staring at La Caracola.

"Where? Here, in the city?"

The woman's eyes are still closed, her hand still raised. Now she moves her hand as though pointing.

"Yes. A grotto. A sacred place."

Tizón frowns. *Let's get this over with*, he thinks.

"Are you talking about the Sacred Grotto?"

The Oratory of La Santa Cueva is an underground church next to the church of Nuestra Señora del Rosario. He knows it well, as does everyone: it is a chapel, a place of worship. As respectable a place as one could think of. *If this is the place she means, I'll lop her head from her shoulders with my cane then burn her damned hovel to the ground.*

"Is this some kind of joke?"

The woman sighs. She leans back in her chair and looks at the policeman reproachfully.

"I cannot do it. You have no faith. I cannot help you."

"You pathetic charlatan . . . What has one thing got to do with the other?"

He slams his cane on the table, sending the candlestick tumbling to the floor, where the flame goes out.

"I'll have you put in jail, you old baggage."

The woman scrambles to her feet and scuttles backward, her hands raised, fearing that the next blow will be aimed at her. The faint light from the floating candles dimly illuminates her face, a mask of fear.

"If you speak of this to anyone, I swear I will kill you myself."

Resisting the impulse to beat her to a bloody pulp, the comisario turns on his heel and blindly gropes his way down the hallway, tripping over the cat—which he sends yowling with a savage kick—and out into the Calle de la Goleta in a miasma of fury. He takes a few steps, swearing viciously under his breath, embarrassed and more angry with himself than with the clairvoyant. *Superstitious, gullible fool*, he mutters over and over as he walks hurriedly through the dark, narrow streets of Santa María, as though in his haste he might leave all this behind. *How could you have thought it would work, even for a moment? How could you? What a stupid, absurd, grotesque, pathetic way to make a fool of yourself.*

He does not calm down until he reaches the corner of the Calle de la Higuera, where he pauses in the darkness. The hazy sound of guitars drifts down from the tenements. Shadows move around him, hovering in doorways or loitering on street corners; there is a murmur of male voices, women laughing, whispered conversations. The place smells of vomit and cheap wine. Tizón has tossed away the cigar he was smoking, or dropped it along the way—he cannot remember. He takes another from the Russian leather case, strikes a match on the wall and lights it, shielding the flame with his hand. *"Many things, I tell you, can be known through mortal eyes; but before he sees it happening, no man can foretell the future . . ."* This fragment of *Ajax*—he can almost recite Barrull's translation by heart—rings in his head as he walks through the dark alleys of the fishermen's quarter, sucking deeply on his cigar. Never before has he felt so lost, unable to find a single clue to guide him. Never before has he felt this bitter helplessness that paralyzes all thought and makes him want to bellow like an agitated bull, searching for some invisible—perhaps nonexistent—enemy on whom he can vent his frustration and rage. It is as if he is pounding his head against a wall: a wall of mystery and silence, against which all his experience, his logic, his skills as a policeman are useless. Since this case began,

Rogelio Tizón no longer sees Cádiz as familiar territory, the personal fiefdom he was wont to wander with impunity. The city has become a chessboard, an inhospitable wasteland of unfamiliar squares, unexpected angles of attack. A tangle of geometric lines he does not understand, with a multitude of unidentifiable pieces which move about before his eyes, like a challenge or an affront. Four pawns captured so far, and not a single clue. Every day is a slap in the face, as time passes and he remains at a loss, rooted to the spot. Waiting for some glimmer of logic, some sign, some glimpse of the chessboard that never comes.

He walks a little way, swinging his cane. On a small square next to the tower of La Merced, he comes upon a lantern made of card and green paper and in its faint glow he spies a woman pacing up and down; she wears no hat, only a shawl thrown over her shoulders. As the policeman passes, she stops and tantalizingly adjusts her shawl to offer a peek of her low-cut bodice. The green light illuminates her face. She is young; very young. Sixteen, perhaps seventeen. Tizón does not recognize her; the girl must be one of the flood of refugees recently arrived in the city, driven here by war and starvation. The good thing about being a woman in times such as these, he thinks cynically, is you can always make enough money to eat.

"You want a good time, señor?"

"Can I see your papers?"

The girl's expression changes; she can tell from his tone and his manner he is a policeman. With a weary gesture, she slips a hand into her bodice and takes out her papers bearing an official stamp. Tizón does not bother to look at them. He is looking at her: she has a pale complexion, blond hair, pleasing curves. There are dark circles under her eyes. He or one of his subordinates probably stamped the documents in exchange for the usual fee, or as payment for some service from her madame or pimp. Live, take your cut, and let live, that is the way. The girl puts away her papers and looks across the street, waiting for the policeman to be on his way. The comisario looks at her coolly. Close up, she looks even younger, and more fragile. She may be only fifteen years old.

"Where do you do it?"

A weary shrug. Resigned. Still looking toward the far end of the street, the girl reluctantly points to a nearby doorway.

"In there."

"Let's go."

Rogelio Tizón does not pay whores. He sleeps with them whenever he chooses. For free. This is one of the privileges of his position in the city: he has official impunity. Sometimes he calls in at old widow Madrazo's bawdy house—an elegant establishment on the Calle Cobos—or Doña Rosa's place, or the whorehouse run by an elderly Englishwoman behind the Mentidero. When the mood takes him, he also pays infrequent visits to the most sordid places in the city, to Santa María and the dark alleys opposite the Puerta de la Caleta. When it comes to such women, the comisario is anything but gracious. Or when it comes to women in general. It is common knowledge among those who sell their bodies in Cádiz that an encounter with Rogelio Tizón is never pleasant. Every woman who knows him, regardless of whether or not she is a whore, eyes him warily when he crosses her path. Not that he gives a tinker's curse. Whores are meant to be whores, as far as he is concerned—something he is prepared to teach them if they don't already know it. There are many ways to impose respect. Fear is traditionally one of these, and often a staunch ally of efficiency.

A seedy ground-floor room. A woman in widow's weeds standing by the door who disappears as soon as she recognizes the policeman. A straw mattress, a pillow and some sheets, a jug and washbasin, a crooked candlestick with a single candle lit. The overpowering dank, stale smell of all the naked bodies who have been here before him.

"What do you want me to do, señor?"

Tizón is standing, motionless, studying her. He is still wearing his hat, clutching his cane, smoking the meager cigar stub that is burning away between his fingers. He tries again to understand, and fails. Like a musician listening for an unfamiliar, jarring note. A hunter when he hears a beating of wings nearby or a rustle in the undergrowth. The comisario does not take his eyes off the young girl, trying to divine in her some key to those horrors of which even he is incapable, pressing helplessly against a wall of mystery and silence.

Automatically, unself-consciously, she undresses. It is obvious that, in spite of her youth, she is accustomed to her work. The bodice laces, the petticoat, the stockings, the long blouse that covers her modesty since she has no underskirt. Eventually she stands naked, motionless, the candle casting a glow on her slim, shapely body, the heft of her small, pale breasts, the curve of her hip, her slender legs. She looks even more fragile. She stares at the policeman, as though waiting for instructions, as though she finds his passivity and his silence unsettling. Tizón sees a flicker of panic in her eyes that seems to say, *Oh dear God, he's mad . . . He's one of those.*

"Lie on the bed, facedown."

Her sigh is barely audible, as she imagines—or knows—what lies ahead. Obediently, she crosses over to the straw mattress and lies down, legs together, arms outstretched. She buries her face in the pillow. This will not be the first time someone has made her scream, Tizón thinks, and not out of pleasure. When he tosses away the stub of his cigar and moves toward her, he sees the purple marks, the bruises on her thighs, her hips. The work of a particularly passionate customer, perhaps. Or her pimp letting her know who's boss.

"The other he lashes upright to a pillar, and seizing a thick strap from a heavy horse-harness, flogs with a whistling double lash, mouthing such insults as no mortal man but some demon had taught him . . ." The lines from *Ajax* run through the policeman's mind with menacing precision. So this is how it happened, he thinks, looking at the girl's naked body. This is how he has them lie when he flays their body to the bone, when he murders them. He raises his cane and traces a line from the nape of the whore's neck down her back. He does it slowly, conscious of every inch of flesh. Trying to understand, even as he teeters over the abyss, the motives of the murderer he is hunting down.

"Spread your legs."

With a quiver, the girl obeys. The tip of his walking stick continues its slow descent to her buttocks, the violent shudders racking the young girl's body, sending tremors up the wooden cane to the brass pommel. Her face is still buried in the pillow. Her knuckles are white, her fingers clutching the sheets. She is trembling with fear.

"No, please . . ." she whimpers, her voice muffled. "Please!"

A shudder of horror runs through Tizón, making his skin crawl, shaking him from head to foot, as if he truly were on the edge of an abyss. He feels dazed, like someone has just hit him; all he can see is a boundless, terrifying darkness that makes him stumble backward, bumping into the washstand, sending the jug crashing to the floor, splashing water everywhere. The crash brings him to himself again. For a moment he stands stock-still, cane in hand, staring insensibly at the naked body in the candlelight. Finally, from the pocket of his jacket he takes a doubloon worth two escudos—his fingers are colder than the gold—and tosses it onto the sheets next to the girl. Then, moving almost soundlessly, he turns on his heel and disappears into the night.

THE SKY IS filled with plumes of black smoke from the Trocadero all the way to Puntales, following the curve of the bay. It has been thirty-two hours since Simon Desfosseux dared raise his head above the parapet, since there is fighting all along the line. This is not targeted shelling of Cádiz or the advance positions at Puntales, La Carraca and the Zuazo Bridge, but a duel between the massed artillery of every French and Spanish gun battery and bastion, a furious exchange with both sides returning shot for shot. It began early yesterday morning when, after a slew of bad news including the Spanish landing at Algeciras and forays by irregular forces along the coast near Ronda, the guerrillas crossed the main channel of the Isla de Léon at various points, attacking the French advance posts near Chiclana. The fighting, centered chiefly on the Olivar tavern and the Casa de la Soledad, was supported by gunboats from Zurraque, Gallineras and Sancti Petri which sailed up the narrow channels while maintaining their fire. The shelling spread along the line, tit-for-tat fire degenerating into wholesale bombardment, even after the Spanish retreat. Having slaughtered or laid waste to everything in sight, they pulled back, taking armaments and prisoners, spiking cannons and blowing up munitions dumps. According to the outriders delivering messages along the front line, the guerrillas crossed back over the main canal in the early hours of this morning, attacking the advance posts on the salt flats at Polvera and the mills at Almansa and Montecorto; they were still fighting there when the eastern section of the bay erupted in cannonfire. The situation is so desperate that Captain Desfosseux, under orders from his superiors, has been dispatched to supervise the conventional shelling from the Cabezuela and Fort Luis against the Spanish fort at Puntales, less than a thousand *toises* away, on the outcrop of the reef at the narrowest point of the bay, directly opposite the Trocadero.

The blasts shake the ground and send shudders through the gabions, the fascines and the wooden parapets. Huddled in one of these bastions, Desfosseux points his spyglass through an embrasure, but prudently keeps the lens some distance from his right eye, since the shock of a previous explosion almost embedded it in the socket. He has not slept for a day and a half, and has eaten nothing but dry bread and drunk nothing but muddy water—given that the shelling has left a number of soldiers disemboweled, none of the sutlers is prepared to leave their shelter. The captain is filthy and sweaty. The explosions have left a layer of dust over his hair, face and clothes—not that he can see himself, but a look at any of the men around him informs him that he too must appear haggard, starving, miserable; red-rimmed eyes spilling dusty tears down mud-spattered faces.

The captain trains the spyglass on Puntales, small and squat behind its defensive walls set among the reef's black rocks, now exposed at low tide. Seen from this side of the water—flanked to the right by the immense fortification of the Puerta de Tierra a mile and a half away, and to the left by the no less solid and imposing Cortadura—the Spanish fortress looks like the prow of a stubborn ship, the six field guns set in their embrasures aimed exactly at Desfosseux's vantage point. At intervals of methodical regularity, one of the embrasures is lit up by a flash, and some moments after the howitzer's boom comes the sound of an enemy projectile, grenade or solid iron cannonball exploding near the French battery. Nor are the French artillerymen sitting around idly; the shells from the 18-pound and 24-pound cannons and the 8-inch howitzers crash upon the Spanish fortress, raising clouds of dust that sometimes blot out the defiant flag fluttering above it—every four or five days the defenders hoist a new flag, the previous one having been ripped to shreds by shrapnel. For some time now, the captain has admired—as one professional to another—the solid expertise of the artillerymen on the other side. Over the past eighteen months of shelling, they have developed unfailing skill and tenacity. To Desfosseux, this is entirely in keeping with the Spanish character: though lazy, ill-disciplined and faltering on the battlefield, they can be very daring when swept along by pride or the urge to kill, and their proud, long-suffering nature makes them formidable in defense. They veer constantly between military incompetence, political farce and religious fanaticism on the one hand, and on the other fierce, senseless patriotism, almost suicidal loyalty and a bitter hatred of the enemy. The Puntales fortress is an obvious example. The troops garrisoned there live under the constant shelling of the French, but constantly, implacably, they return fire, shell for shell.

One of those shells has just landed in the adjacent bastion, near the 18-pound cannons. A black grenade—almost visible as it whizzed through the air—hit the upper parapet, bounced, then rolled down next to a barricade of earth and gabions, smoke trailing from the fuse, about to explode. The captain, kneeling up to see where it fell, hears the screams of the gun crew as they throw themselves on to the deck supporting the gun carriage, or take shelter as best they can. Then, as Desfosseux huddles inside his embrasure, an explosion shakes the bastion; dirt, shards of wood and rubble rain down all around. It is still raining earth when he hears a long, blood-curdling howl. When the captain puts his head above the parapet again, he sees several soldiers carrying the screaming artilleryman, the stump of his thigh—the rest of his leg has been blown away—gushing blood.

"Kill those bastard *dagos*!" yells Lieutenant Bertoldi, who is already on his feet, goading his men, urging them on. "An eye for an eye! Avenge your fallen comrade!"

They're good lads, thinks Desfosseux, as he watches the men rush back to their field guns, then load, aim and fire. After everything that has happened, and everything that awaits them, they are still capable of urging each other on—proud of the gallant resignation in the face of the inevitable that characterizes the French soldier. Even after a year and a half buried in the cesspit that is Cádiz, the arse end of Europe and canker of the Empire, with the rump of rebel Spain reduced to one impregnable island.

The roar of cannonfire resumes, with mounting intensity—the men have to keep their mouths open so their eardrums do not burst. It is almost impossible to see Puntales for the clouds of dust raised by the shells exploding, one after another, temporarily silencing the Spanish guns.

"We're doing the best we can, Captain."

Brushing the dust from his jacket, his head uncovered, his skeptical smile framed by his grubby blond whiskers, Lieutenant Bertoldi comes and stands next to the embrasure where Desfosseux is perched with his spyglass. He tilts his head slightly to peer at the enemy positions, then leans back against the parapet, facing the opposite direction.

"This is stupid . . . all this noise and dust for nothing."

"Our orders are to shell the *dagos* all along the lines," says Desfosseux resignedly.

"And that's what we're doing, Captain. But it's a waste of time."

"One day you're going to get yourself court-martialled, Bertoldi . . ."

The two officers exchange a look of hopeless complicity. Then Desfosseux asks how things are going and the lieutenant, just back from an inspection, playing the dashing hero amid the shelling—the captain did the last inspection at daybreak—gives his report: one dead and three injured in La Cabezuela. Five wounded, two of them gravely at Fort Luis, and a 16-pound cannon destroyed. As for the enemy positions, he has no idea.

"They're probably giving us the finger," he says.

Desfosseux has gone back to his telescope. Along the reef, between Puntales and Cádiz, he notices a convoy of carts and people on foot—almost certainly delivering provisions to the Isla de Léon under heavy escort. Or perhaps reinforcements. He passes the spyglass to Bertoldi and indicates where he should look. The lieutenant winks and puts the lens to his other eye.

"I want you to fire on them," says the captain, "if you would be so kind."

"Yes, sir."

Bertoldi hands back the spyglass and walks over to the 24-pound cannons. Simon Desfosseux does not permit his precious Villantroys-Rutys to play a part in this thunderous maelstrom—like his adjutant, he believes it to be utterly absurd. Like an attentive parent keeping his children safe from the perils of the world, the captain keeps Fanfan and the other 10-inch howitzers he fires on Cádiz out of this duel. These magnificent, delicate guns are reserved for the specific task of extending his range, *toise* by *toise*, into the heart of the city. He is not prepared to squander their carefully cast bronze, their condition or their operational lifespan—which in field guns of this caliber is limited, and constantly at risk from some tiny chink, some minor defect in the alloy—on a military exercise utterly unrelated to the reason for their creation. Therefore, as soon as the general shelling began, Sergeant Labiche and his men immediately implemented Captain Desfosseux's orders for such situations: pile up more earth, gabions and fascines around the howitzers and cover them with thick tarpaulins to protect them from dust, stones and ricochets. Every time a shell falls nearby, or looks as though it might score a direct hit on the redoubt, Desfosseux feels his heart tighten, terrified at the idea of even one gun being put out of operation. He wants this absurd, chaotic bombing to end, for the lives of besiegers and besieged to return to their customary routine, leaving him to deal with the only thing that matters: gaining the two hundred *toises* which, according to the map in his hut, still separates the shells that have attained the greatest range in Cádiz—exploding near the Tavira Tower and on the Calle de San Francisco—from the steeple of the church on the Plaza de San Antonio.

CHAPTER NINE

A gray, leaden sky. The temperature is mild. Above the watchtowers of the city, the autumn breeze trails ragged, murky clouds from the west.

"I've got a problem," says the Mulatto.

"As have I," says Gregorio Fumagal.

The two men stare at each other, weighing up the gravity of what they have just heard, its consequences for their personal safety. That, at least, is how Fumagal sees things. He doesn't like the way the smuggler smiles as he glances from left to right at the people bustling around the market stalls in the Plaza San Juan de Dios—a faintly sardonic smirk. If you think you've got problems, it seems to say, wait until you hear mine.

"You go first," says the Mulatto at length, in a weary tone.

"Why?"

"Mine is complicated."

Another silence.

"Pigeons," ventures the taxidermist warily.

"What about them?" The Mulatto seems surprised. "I brought you three baskets of twelve last time." He gestures discreetly toward the Puerta de Mar and the far side of the bay. "Belgian pigeons, as always. Raised right here . . . I'm guessing that should be enough to be going on with."

"You guess wrong. A cat got into the pigeon loft. I don't know how, but it did. And it decimated the flock."

The smuggler looks at Fumagal, incredulous.

"A cat?"

"Yes. Only three of the pigeons survived."

"Three cheers for the cat . . . clearly a patriot."

"I don't find that amusing."

"I'm guessing it's been stuffed and mounted by now."

"I didn't manage to catch it in time."

The two men walk a short distance in silence; Fumagal notices the Mulatto looking sideways at him, as though wondering if he is being serious—something he wonders himself. It is mid-morning and the hum of conversations on the square between the port and the City Hall is a cacophony of accents from every part of Spain, from her colonies and foreign lands: refugees of every sort, ladies of Cádiz with baskets on their arms nibbling on prawns from paper cones, porters lugging sacks and packages, stewards making the daily purchases, people in all sorts of hats, *monteras, catites,** broad-brimmed *tamboras,* the blue and tan clothes of sailors.

"I don't understand why we are meeting here," says the taxidermist cantankerously. "This place is hardly what one would call discreet."

"Would you rather I visited you at home?"

"Of course not. But this place . . ."

The Mulatto shrugs. He is dressed, as always, in rope sandals and an open shirt; the top button of his breeches is open and he wears no stockings. He is carrying a large hessian sack. His apparel is in stark contrast to Fumagal's hat and purple frockcoat.

"It's for the best, with the way things are."

"Things?" The taxidermist half-turns, anxiously. "What do you mean?"

"Just that. Things."

They walk a little and the Mulatto says no more, but simply strolls along with his indolent, rhythmic gait. Fumagal, ill at ease—he has always abhorred physical contact with others—manages to weave through the crowds that mill around the stands. The air is heavy with

---

* *Montera*—a hat traditionally worn as part of Iberian folk costume, covered in astrakhan fur with an inner lining of velvet. The image of a saint is sometimes printed on the lining as a talisman of good luck; *catite*—a traditional Andalusian hat with a high conical crown and a wide brim with upturned edges.

the smell of burnt oil from the fried-fish stand, next to awnings made
of old sailcloth where stallholders offer succulent shellfish. Further
away are the stalls selling vegetables and meat: mostly pork, bacon,
lard, live chickens and slabs of beef from Morocco. Everything arrives
by boat, and is unloaded on the docks or the Atlantic beaches—in
Cádiz, no one cultivates even the smallest plot of land, let alone rears
livestock. There is no room.

"You mentioned that you had a problem," says the taxidermist finally.

The Mulatto's thick lips contract in an unpleasant smile. "The net
is tightening."

"Pardon?"

The Mulatto gestures back toward the Puerta de Mar, as if someone were following him. "I mean they're watching me as closely as a
three-legged crab."

Gregorio Fumagal lowers his voice. "They're watching you? . . .
What do you mean?"

"They've been prowling around, asking questions."

"Who has?"

There is no response. The Mulatto has stopped at a stall where the
fish roll their white eyes and the sardines have scarlet heads. He wrinkles up his nose as though sniffing them.

"That's why I wanted to meet you here," he says eventually. "To
prove I've got nothing to hide."

"Are you mad? They could be following you right now."

The smuggler tilts his head, considering this possibility, and nods
calmly. "I can't say they're not. But this way, it's just an innocent meeting. Like you having ordered another specimen for your collection . . .
Have a look, I brought you this rather pretty American parrot."

He opens his sack to show Gregorio Fumagal its contents, even
takes the bird out for the benefit of prying eyes: it is about fifteen inches
high with a yellow beak; the plumage is bright green, the lateral feathers scarlet. Fumagal recognizes it as a chrysotis, from the Amazon or
possibly the Gulf of Mexico. A fine specimen.

"Dead, just how you like them. And no poison to spoil things. This morning I stabbed a needle through its heart, or thereabouts."

He places the bird back in the sack and gives it to Fumagal. "This one is a gift," he says. "I won't charge you for it."

The taxidermist glances around furtively. No one in the crowd is watching—or seems to be.

"You could have written to me," he protests.

The Mulatto makes a wry face. "You forget, I can barely write my own name . . . Besides, I wouldn't think of leaving a paper trail. You never know."

Now Fumagal glances behind him toward the Puerta de Mar and the narrow area of El Boquete, to the section of market that sells secondhand clothes and items from ships, chipped porcelain from the East Indies, earthenware and tin, sailors' tools and other junk. On the far side of the square, on the corner of the Calle Nueva, outside an inn frequented by shipping agents and merchant captains, a number of well-dressed men sit reading newspapers or watching the bustle of people.

"You are putting me in danger."

The Mulatto clicks his tongue. He clearly does not agree. "You've been in danger for a long time, señor. Just like me . . . It comes with the territory."

"So what exactly is the purpose of this meeting?"

"To tell you I'm shipping out."

"What did you say?"

"I'm leaving Cádiz . . . You've lost your link with the other side."

It takes the taxidermist several paces to digest this information. He realizes that something terrible is looming over him. One more unexpected, dangerous desertion. He feels a sudden chill, though his frock-coat is buttoned to the throat.

"Are our friends aware of this?"

"Yes. And they agree. They said to tell you they'll be in touch . . . asked you to keep them informed, if you can."

"And how do they know I'm not being watched too?"

"They don't. But if I were you, I'd burn any compromising papers. Just in case."

Fumagal's mind is racing, but it is difficult to calculate the risks and the probabilities, to weigh up the future. Until now, the Mulatto has been his only link to the outside world. Without him, he will be left almost deaf, dumb and blind. With no instructions; abandoned to his fate.

"Have they considered the idea that perhaps I too would like to leave Cádiz?"

"They're leaving that up to you. Though obviously they would prefer you to keep a steady course. To carry on as long as possible."

The taxidermist considers the matter, gazing up at the City Hall—like almost every other building in the city, it is flying the red and yellow flag of the Royal Armada. He could do nothing, of course; hibernate like a bear and not lift a finger until they send him a new contact. Bury himself while everything goes back to normal. The question is, how long will that take, and what might happen in Cádiz in the meantime? He is surely not the only spy here, but this knowledge is not useful to him. He has always acted as though he were.

"And do you think I should stay?"

The Mulatto clicks his tongue apathetically. He is standing in front of a stall selling shaving soap, lucifer matches, pocket mirrors and other cheap knickknacks.

"What you do is no business of mine, señor. Every man wants what he wants. I want to get out of here before I end up with a garrote round my throat."

"But without pigeons, I can't communicate. The alternatives are slow and dangerous."

"You'll have to sort it out. I don't think you'll have too much difficulty."

"When were you planning to leave?"

"As soon as possible."

Leaving the square behind them, the two men stop on the corner of the Calle Sopranis, beneath the Torre de la Misericordia. In the doorway of the City Hall, a sentry from the urban militia in his round hat and white gaiters, bayonet fixed to his rifle, is leaning against one of the arches; he is chatting with two young women and looks rather less than soldierly.

"Well," says the Mulatto. "This is goodbye, then."

With curious intensity, he studies the taxidermist, who has no difficulty working out what he is thinking. It's a question of principle, he thinks; a matter of loyalties, though God knows to what. From the viewpoint of the pragmatic, mercenary Mulatto, there is not enough money to pay him for what he is doing.

"If I were you, I'd get out of here, no doubt about it," the smuggler says suddenly. "Cádiz is becoming dangerous. And you know the old saying: if you play with fire, eventually you're bound to get burnt . . . Even being caught by the army or the police is not the worst thing that could happen. Remember the poor bastard the mob caught the other day? Beaten to a pulp and then strung up by his feet . . ."

Remembering the incident, the taxidermist feels his mouth go dry. The luckless foreigner found himself in the street accused of being a French spy. Hounded by the mob, with no place to hide, he was clubbed to death and his body strung up outside Los Capuchinos. No one even knew his name.

The Mulatto falls silent now. Unusually, his half smile is not mocking but thoughtful—or curious.

"You decide what you need to do. But if you want my opinion, don't spend too much time making your mind up."

"Tell them that I'll stay here for the time being."

For the first time since they've known each other, the Mulatto looks at Fumagal with something akin to respect.

"All right," he says. "It's your neck, señor."

THE ATMOSPHERE IS solemn. At one end of the presidential table, flanked by two impassive guards, above a vacant chair, the young king Fernando VII presides over the assembly (with worrying indifference, in Lolita Palma's opinion) in the form of a portrait that hangs below the baldachin of the Oratory of San Felipe Neri, between a pair of Ionic columns made of stucco and gilded card. The principal altar and the side chapels have been curtained off. In the main section, a succession of speakers troop up to the two speakers' platforms, surrounded by benches and sofas set in two semicircles. Despite the array of silk and linen, of soutanes and secular garb, fashionable clothes and attire that belongs to an earlier age, the predominant colors are the sober black and gray of the respectable gentlemen who, at the Extraordinary and General Cortes of the Spanish Nation, represent the peoples of peninsular Spain and her Overseas Territories.

This is the first time that Lolita Palma has attended a parliamentary session. She is dressed in deep purple, with a fine cashmere shawl and an English cloth hat, its broad brim turned down to frame her face and tied with ribbon beneath her chin. Her fan is Chinese, black, painted with a floral scene. Ordinarily, women are not permitted to attend sessions of the Cortes, but today is an exception; moreover, she has come at the invitation of two deputies: the American, Fernández Cuchillero, and Pepín Quipo de Llano, Count of Toreno. She finds herself moved by the passionate solemnity of the proceedings, the fervent tone of the speeches and the seriousness with which the president oversees the debates. These do not merely concern the Constitution they have been tasked with drawing up, but also the war and other affairs of government, since the Cortes is—or claims to be—the representative of the king in exile and the head of the nation. The matter under discussion today is the British Crown's demand for free trade with the American ports. Because this subject concerns her directly—and because she is curious—Lolita decided to accept the invitation. With her, alongside a number of business acquaintances from Cádiz, are Emilio Sánchez Guinea and his son. They are seated on the benches reserved for guests, facing the diplomatic corps, including Ambassador Wellesley, the Minister Plenipotentiary of the Two Sicilies, the Portuguese ambassador and the Archbishop of Nicaea, who is also the Papal Nuncio. There are few people in the upper galleries of the oratory reserved for the general public: the uppermost is empty and there are about thirty in the lower gallery, most of whom look poor and unemployed, together with a handful of foreigners and a few journalists busily noting down every word that is said.

And what is being said is this: it is one thing to be loyal to one's allies, but to kowtow to the commercial interests of a foreign power is a very different matter. The speaker is Lorenzo Villanueva, deputy for Valencia—Miguel Sánchez Guinea tells Lolita the names of those she does not recognize—a short-sighted, courteous cleric with moderately reformist views. The cleric says he shares the concerns voiced by his fellow speaker, Señor Argüelles, about the trade in contraband with the American ports the British have been engaged in for some time, in exchange for their support of Spain in the war against Napoleon. Villanueva fears that the commercial treaty demanded by London will irreparably damage Spanish interests overseas. Et cetera.

Lolita, who has been listening attentively, realizes that there are a large number of clerics in the assembly and that many of them, in spite of their ecclesiastical role, support national sovereignty over an absolute monarchy. But everyone in Cádiz knows that, with the exception of radical reformers and die-hard royalists, the position of the majority of the deputies is flexible: they change their position depending on the subject under debate, they shift and are contradictory, and sometimes ideologically paradoxical. In general terms, the majority of members are in favor of reform, despite their catholic or royalist origins. On the other hand, in the liberal atmosphere of Cádiz, those in favor of national sovereignty enjoy greater support than those who defend the absolute powers of the monarch. This means that the former—who are, moreover, better orators—find it easier to impose their point of view, placing their opponents under considerable pressure from public opinion in a city radicalized by the war, where the lower classes, were they to slip out of control, could prove dangerous.

This is another reason why certain delicate matters are debated in private. Lolita is aware that the issue of British trade and the American ports is one that is generally discussed *in camera*—something which has encouraged the gossip and scandalmongering that today's open session is intended to allay. But the debates have proved more polemical than expected. The Count of Toreno has just taken the floor to denounce a poster that has appeared on walls around the city, entitled *The Americas Bankrupted by Free Trade with Foreigners.* The poster criticizes the concessions made to English businesses and ships and attacks the American members of the Cortes, who are asking that all the ports be opened to free trade. But, he insists, the Spanish cities whose trade would be damaged by such a measure deserve to be heard, as their interests are very different.

"They have this right," concludes the young man, holding up the poster, "because it is our trade that will pay, indeed is already paying, a terrible price for these capitulations in the Americas."

His words are greeted with applause from the gallery and a number of the guests. Even Lolita feels the urge to clap, but she restrains herself, and congratulates herself on her prudence when the president of the assembly, ringing his bell, calls the session to order and threatens to clear the public galleries.

"Look at Sir Henry's face," whispers Miguel Sánchez Guinea.

Lolita glances at the British ambassador. Wellesley is sitting stock-still in his seat, his whiskers disappearing into the collar of his green velvet jacket as he leans toward the interpreter, who quietly translates any phrases he does not understand. As ever, his expression is gloomy—though this time, Lolita thinks, with good reason. It can hardly be pleasant to be criticized by an ally, especially one whose conservative wing—opposed to political reform and the idea of patriotic renewal—you have spent considerable influence and money supporting. London's boycott of any initiative by the Cortes that would reinforce national sovereignty in Spain, its influence overseas and its control over the revolutions in the Americas, frequently verges on contempt.

"He couldn't buy everyone."

It is now the turn of the American deputies, among them Jorge Fernández Cuchillero. Lolita, who has never seen her friend speak in public, listens to him with interest. He argues eloquently in favor of reforming the rules of trade with the Americas, for three pressing reasons: to placate the British allies, to satisfy those overseas demanding urgent reform, and to shore up the position of those loyalists in the

Americas who have vigorously opposed the independence movement. It is vitally important, he adds, to rescind some of the trade rules with the Indies, which are incompatible with the freedoms required in these modern times.

"If the Cortes proclaims that all Spaniards—whether in Europe or the Americas—are equal, a conclusion logically follows," the Argentinian adds. "Those in Europe are allowed free trade with England, so by the same token their compatriots in the Americas should be permitted the same freedom . . . It is simply a matter, *señorías*, of enshrining in law what is already practiced daily but clandestinely."

Another American deputy takes the floor in support of his compatriot, the representative of the viceroyalty of Nueva Granada, José Mexía Lequerica—handsome, educated, perceptive and a freemason. He paints a grim picture, blaming inflexibility to American interests for the wars currently raging here, and in Río de la Plata, Venezuela and in Mexico, where the capture of the rebel priest Hidalgo—news of his execution is expected any day—does not, in his opinion, guarantee an end to the upheaval. Far from it.

"The way to ensure that ties do not break," he concludes, "is to make sure there is enough slack in the rope—not tighten it until it snaps."

"Leaving us to rot . . ." mutters Miguel Sánchez Guinea irritably.

Lolita Palma fans herself, spellbound, eager not to miss a word of the debates. She finds it normal that Fernández Cuchillero, Mexía Lequerica and the other American deputies should argue in favor of their home countries—and that the reactionary deputies or those who are lukewarm about national sovereignty should be staunchly supporting the English, as they consider the latter to be the best defenders of monarchy and religion against the revolutionary rabble. But she also knows that, in the opinion of most people in Cádiz, Miguel Sánchez Guinea is right: equal rights to free trade would bankrupt the continental ports in Spain. She reflects on this as she listens to the Aragonese deputy, Mañas, who has interrupted to ask whether the proposed free trade would also allow the British free access to ports in America and the

Philippines, reminding members of the competition between the Chinese silk trade and that of Valencia, though the latter is of superior quality. Fernández Cuchillero takes the floor again, insisting that the North Americans and the British have long been trading in that region clandestinely.

"What we are proposing," he says in summation, "is to legalize the existing contraband trade. To regulate the inevitable."

A number of other American deputies speak in support of the member from Río de la Plata, as does Capmany, the conservative Catalan deputy widely considered to be the voice of the English ambassador at the Cortes. Another deputy intervenes to suggest that it might be possible to authorize free trade between Britain and the Americas for a limited period, only for Mañas to respond—looking deliberately toward the diplomatic benches—that the phrase "limited period" is not part of the English vocabulary. One only has to think of Gibraltar. Or to remember Menorca.

"Our trade," he says categorically, "our industry, our Navy, will never recover if we permit foreigners to trade freely with our territories in the Americas and Asia. Any such concession would be a nail in the coffin for the ports of Spain . . . Mark my words, gentlemen, cities such as Cádiz would be wiped off the map."

Amid the applause—this time, Lolita Palma cannot help but join in—Mañas adds that he is in possession of letters from Montevideo proving that England has been supporting the rebels in Buenos Aires (at this, Ambassador Wellesley squirms in his seat); and that in Veracruz, the English are demanding a shipment of five million *pesos* in Mexican silver; and that, with or without the war with Napoleon, the British government will not rest until it has dismantled Spain's overseas territories, a market it is determined to control. Amid murmurs of "Aye, aye!" and "No, no!" the deputy from Aragon concludes his speech by dismissing the proposals as "intolerable blackmail," words that provoke uproar on the diplomatic benches and in the public gallery—almost resulting in a scandal when the English ambassador gets to his feet and storms out. The president of the Cortes rings his bell to restore order and announces a break in the proceedings, warning that the session will resume *in camera*. Talking animatedly, the public and the deputies file out and the guards close the doors.

Out on the street, as a chorus of heated voices discuss what has just happened, Lolita and the Sánchez Guineas go over to Fernández Cuchillero, who is standing with Mexía Lequerica and a number of other deputies from the Americas. All are arguing in favor of the proposal.

"Your new system would ruin us, señor," Miguel Sánchez Guinea splutters angrily to the member from Río de la Plata. "If our American compatriots are able to trade freely with foreign ports, Spanish merchants will not be able to compete with their prices. Don't you realize? This would force us to take ruinous measures at greater risk and expense . . . What you and your friends are proposing would be the *coup de grâce* for our business, it would mean the end for what remains of our Navy, and it would bankrupt Spain while she is fighting a war, without industry or agriculture."

Fernández Cuchillero roundly denies this. Lolita Palma barely recognizes in him the gentle, shy young man who visits her family. The subject confers on him a self-assured dignity, an old-fashioned gravitas. Authority.

"The proposal is not mine," he responds. "You are speaking to someone who, despite his place of birth, is loyal to the Spanish Crown. As you know, I do not approve of the treachery of the Junta in Buenos Aires . . . but history and the times we live in have decided matters. The Spanish Americas have needs, but they are helpless to satisfy them. The Creoles demand the profits legally due to them so the poor can escape their misery. But we are bound to a system decided here in Spain, which solves nothing."

The Calle de Santa Inés is filled with people arguing over what happened during the session, moving from one group to another, popping in to the little inn nearby where some of the deputies grab a bite to eat. The group that has gathered around the American deputies is still standing on the steps of the oratory. It is by far the largest group, mostly made up of local merchants. Their faces betray their fear and, in some cases, naked hostility. And though it directly concerns her, even Lolita Palma feels little sympathy for what she has heard this morning about free trade and the English. After all, the future of Palma e Hijos is at stake.

"You people are simply trying to avoid paying taxes," someone says. "Trying to steal our business."

One hand in the pocket of his frockcoat, Fernández Cuchillero turns calmly to the speaker.

"Such a course of action would be entirely legitimate," he says. "After all, that is what happened in the thirteen English colonies in North America. Everyone wishes to improve his lot in life, and being stubborn is not the answer . . . But make no mistake, the future will come. It is significant that a number of the loyal American administrations that previously claimed to be Spanish and complained that they were under-represented at the Cortes now call themselves 'colonies.' It is a short step from there to declaring independence. But you people do not seem to realize that fact . . . My country is a fine example. There, the talk is not of the reasons for the uprising, but of *reconquering* Buenos Aires."

"But there are those who have remained loyal, señor. Cuba, for example, the viceroyalty of Peru, and many others."

Now it is José Mexía Lequerica's turn to speak. Lolita Palma knows him because of their shared passion for botany. She has met him on a number of occasions at Master Cabrera's house, in the gardens of the College of Surgeons and the bookshops on the Plaza de San Agustín. A noted philosopher of the French school, a stalwart supporter of equality between the Americas and peninsular Spain, José Mexía Lequerica lives on the Calle Ahumada with Gertrudis Salanova, a striking young lady from Cádiz who is not his wife—as everyone in the city is aware. Lolita has seen them strolling brazenly, arm in arm, along the Plaza de San Antonio and the Alameda. Given his status as an eminent politician, the relationship is the subject of much salacious gossip.

"Make no mistake," says Mexía in the soft accent of his native

Quito, "there are many in the American territories who have remained loyal to Spain because they fear an uprising by the Indians or the Negro slaves. They see the Spanish monarchy as a force upholding law and order . . . But if they felt confident enough to deal with such a situation themselves, that might change matters—"

"What we need is a firm hand," someone interrupts. "We must force the rebels to yield to legitimate authority . . . Have they no shame? Taking advantage of the war with France and the abduction of the king to sue for independence is not simply disloyal—it is a disgrace!"

"No, I'm afraid I disagree," says the American. "It is simply an opportunity. The chaos in Spain has brought things to a head . . . Even here, what with the generals, the Regency and the Juntas tripping over each other, no one seems able to decide how best to fight this war."

There is a sudden, awkward silence. Lolita sees people glance at each other. Even Mexía seems to realize that he has gone too far: he waves his hand as if to erase the words he has just spoken.

"That a man like you should say such a thing . . . you, a deputy at the Cortes," splutters Miguel Sánchez Guinea angrily.

Mexía turns to face the young man, as Miguel's father pats him on the arm, urging him to let the matter rest. "That is precisely why I must say it, señor," Mexía replies, a little haughtily. "Because one day history will judge us."

There is an angry roar from the crowd—Lolita recognizes the voice: it is Ignacio Vizcaíno, a leather merchant who has been bankrupted by the revolution in Buenos Aires. "This whole thing is a conspiracy engineered by the English to force us out of the Americas."

Mexía smiles scornfully, turning his back, as if this comment does not deserve a response. It is left to Jorge Fernández Cuchillero to answer.

"It is nothing of the kind," he says calmly. "In fact, very few people in the Americas would go so far. That is why we are here, working to draw up a constitution which will benefit the peoples on both sides of the Atlantic. One that will put an end to the privileges of an indolent aristocracy, a feckless administration, and a fanatical and all too often ignorant clergy. That is why I am standing here talking to all of you . . . trying to get you to understand that if the ties between our countries are broken, they cannot be repaired."

The doors of San Felipe Neri reopen; the session is about to begin again, this time with no one in the public galleries. Miguel Sánchez Guinea raises his finger, determined to have the last word before the American deputies take their leave, when all conversation is suddenly interrupted by an explosion nearby that causes the ground and the surrounding buildings to shake. Lolita Palma turns and looks toward the Tavira Tower. Just beyond it, a cloud of yellowish smoke rises above the houses.

"That was close," says the leather merchant.

The crowd quickly disperse. People scamper away, avoiding the middle of the street, seeking shelter in the houses nearby. News comes that the bomb exploded on the Calle del Vestuario, demolishing a house. Quickening her step, Lolita heads in the opposite direction, with Don Emilio taking her arm, and Miguel Sánchez Guinea leading the way. Glancing back she sees the deputies, dignified and unperturbed, walk deliberately toward the steps of the oratory.

"I THINK YOU might like to come downstairs, Comisario."

Rogelio Tizón lays down the papers he has been reading on his desk and looks over at his assistant: six feet of deferential brute force standing in the doorway.

"Why? What's happened?"

"Number eight. I think you might be interested in what he has to say."

The Commissioner for Districts, Vagrants and Transients gets up and leaves his office. Cadalso steps to one side to allow him to go first and they head down the corridor, footsteps making the rickety wooden floor creak, toward the stairwell next to a dusty skylight that overlooks the Calle del Mirador. The gloomy spiral staircase leads down to the cellar and the dungeons. When they reach the bottom, Tizón buttons his frockcoat self-consciously. The air is cold and dank and the light filtering through the narrow, barred loopholes high up on the walls does little to relieve the sense of confinement.

"What did he say?"

"He's confessed to making trips to the far shore, Comisario, but there is something else."

"Something important?"

"It might be."

Tizón shakes his head skeptically. Like the big old dog he is, Cadalso has little imagination, but is utterly dependable. This is useful when blindly following orders, but it has its limitations. Tizón's deputy is hardly a genius when it comes to knowing what is important. But you never know.

"Is the interrogation still going on?"

"For more than two hours now."

"The devil . . . A hard case, then . . ."

"He's starting to soften."

"Make sure things don't go too far, like they did with the suspect from the Calle Juan de Andas . . . If that happens again, you and your pals will end up breaking rocks in the penal colony in Ceuta."

"Don't worry, sir." Cadalso bows his head apologetically. "It's slower using the *tabla*. But we'll get there."

"I hope so."

They walk along the narrow passage—the cell doors, with the exception of number eight, are secured with hefty padlocks—and into a large, bare room. The sentry sitting on his stool leaps to his feet when he sees the comisario. They walk on, their footsteps ringing out in another narrow passageway, its walls grimy and cracked. At the far end is a door. Cadalso opens it with obsequious attentiveness and Rogelio Tizón steps inside. It is a windowless room with a table and two chairs, lit by a tallow lantern hanging from the ceiling. In one corner there is a bucket of dirty water and a flannel.

"Leave the door open—get some air in here."

A man in underdrawers is lying face up, his kidneys aligned with the edge of the table, his bare torso arched backward into empty space, his head dangling inches from the floor. The prisoner's arms are shackled behind his back, and he is flanked by two burly henchmen. One is perched on the table, gripping his thighs and his legs; the other is supervising. *If only the fine gentlemen at the Cortes could see this*, thinks Tizón, smiling to himself. The good thing about the table is that it leaves no marks. In this position, the prisoner slowly asphyxiates. It is simply a matter of time, as the lungs strain, the kidneys ache and the blood rushes to the head. When it's over, you simply stand the prisoner up and he looks bright as a new pin. Not a single inconvenient bruise.

"Has he said anything else?"

"He's confessed to contact with the French," says Cadalso. "Making trips to El Puerto de Santa María, to Rota and Sanlúcar. Once, he went all the way to Jerez to see a ranking officer."

"What was the purpose of these visits?"

"To find out about the situation there. He also carried messages and packages."

"From whom? To whom?"

A pause. The henchmen and Tizón's assistant exchange worried glances.

"That is something we have not yet ascertained, señor," says Cadalso warily. "But we're working on it."

Tizón studies the prisoner. The man's negroid features are racked with pain, his eyes, half-open, have rolled back in his head. The Mulatto was arrested last night just as he was about to set off for the far shore—and judging by all the equipment he was carrying, he had no intention of coming back.

"Does he have accomplices here in Cádiz?"

"Absolutely." Cadalso nods vehemently. "But we have not been able to get any names out of him."

Tizón approaches the prisoner, hunkering close to the man's face. From here, he can see the curly hair, the pug nose, the sparse beard beginning to grow in. His skin is dirty and greasy. The Mulatto gapes, like a fish out of water, and Tizón can hear his labored breaths, a choking death rattle brought on by his position. There is a damp stain on the floor from which the sour smell of fresh vomit wafts. Cadalso, he realizes, had the grace to mop it up before coming to fetch him.

"What has he said that might be of interest to me?" he asks his assistant.

Cadalso moves closer, after another furtive glance at the henchmen, who are still pinning the prisoner's legs to the table.

"We managed to get a couple of things out of him . . . Something about pigeons."

"Pigeons?"

"That's what it sounded like."

"The kind that fly?"

"I don't know of any other kind, sir."

"What about these pigeons?"

"Pigeons and bombs. I think he meant carrier pigeons."

Tizón slowly gets to his feet again. He has a vague, unsettling sensation in his mind. A fleeting, half-formed idea.

"What else?"

"At some point he said, 'Ask the man who knows where the bombs are falling.'"

"And who exactly would that be?"

"That's what we're trying to find out."

An idea now appears to him like a long, dark corridor behind a half-open door. Tizón steps away from the table. He does so carefully, feeling that any sudden movement might cause that door to slam shut.

"Put him in a chair."

With Cadalso's help, the henchmen lift the prisoner, who howls in pain as they move him. Tizón watches him blink rapidly, confused, as though waking from a trance, as he is carried across the room, feet dragging along the floor. Once he is seated, hands still shackled behind his back, with a guard on either side, Tizón brings over the other chair, spins it around and sits, arms folded on the back.

"I'm going to make this easy for you, Mulatto. People who collaborate with the enemy go to the garrote . . . and the case against you is open and shut."

He pauses, giving the prisoner a moment to adjust to his new position, to allow the blood to flow back—and giving him a chance to take in what he has said.

"You can cooperate," he says finally, "maybe save your own neck."

The Mulatto gives a loud, ragged cough. He is still choking. A spray of spittle lands on Tizón's knees, but he does not flinch.

"Maybe?"

He has the deep voice of men of his race, but he has a curious complexion, thinks Tizón. A white Negro. As if someone scrubbed the color from his skin with soap.

"That's what I said."

The prisoner's eyes flicker with contempt.

The bull hasn't been thrashed hard enough, thinks Tizón. But it would be better to leave him as he is for now—Tizón does not want the Intendant and the governor on his back. One body at the bottom of the bay is enough.

"Tell your mother," spits the Mulatto.

Tizón hits him. A quick, vicious slap: palm open, fingers together. He waits three seconds, then gives him another. The sound rings out like a whip crack.

"Shut your filthy mouth . . ."

A thread of snot hangs from one of the Mulatto's nostrils, but he still musters the strength to smirk. A proud, insolent sneer that almost succeeds in becoming a smile.

"I'm not much longer for this world, Comisario. Don't tax yourself, and don't tax me."

"My point exactly," says Tizón. "There's no need for either of us to tax ourselves. The deal is, you answer my questions and then we'll leave you in peace until a judge decides what to do with you."

"A judge, no less. What a luxury."

Another slap, loud as a gunshot. Cadalso takes a step forward, about to intervene, but Tizón raises a hand to stop him. He can deal with this himself. He is in his element.

"We *will* get it out of you, Mulatto. As you can see, we're in no hurry. I can make you an offer. But as far as I'm concerned, we can make it brief . . . Bombs and pigeons: do you follow me?"

The man says nothing, but looks at him uncertainly. The swagger has gone. Tizón knows his job; he knows that this sudden change has nothing to do with the blows. They are simply a flourish, like a matador brandishing his cape. The beast is elsewhere. In situations like this, showing some of your cards can have a miraculous effect, depending on who you are dealing with. With someone of even moderate intelligence, the most obvious thing is to look him in the eye.

"Who is this person you mentioned who knows where the bombs fall? And how does he know?"

Another pause, longer this time, but Tizón is patient by profession. The Mulatto looks at the table thoughtfully, then back at the comisario. Obviously he is weighing up what little future lies ahead of him, making calculations.

"Because he is responsible . . ." he says finally, "for checking the bomb sites and sending back information . . . He's the one who is keeping score."

Tizón does not want to mess things up, to overlook any possibility, any probability. Nor does he want to raise his hopes. His tone is careful, as though his words were made of fine crystal.

"Does he also know where the bombs will fall? Could he guess?"

"I don't know. Maybe."

This is too good to be true, thinks the comisario—a shot in the dark with someone else's gun. Nothing but smoke. If Professor Barrull were here, he would burst out laughing and stalk out of the room. *A chess player's guesses, Comisario. You're building castles in the air, as usual. This is nothing but smoke and mirrors.*

"Give me his name, my friend."

He makes the suggestion quietly, carelessly, as though it is not remotely important. The prisoner's dark eyes bore into his. Then he turns away, uncertain once more.

"Listen, Mulatto . . . you've told us he uses carrier pigeons. I can check to see who in Cádiz keeps pigeons—it would only take me two days to find out for myself. But if I have to get by without your help, I don't owe you anything . . . Do you understand?"

The Mulatto swallows hard, twice. Or he tries to. His mouth is actually too dry to swallow. Tizón orders one of the henchmen to bring some water.

"What difference does that make?" asks the Mulatto finally.

"Not much. But it means either I owe you a favor, or I don't."

The man takes his time to think this over. He tears his eyes from the comisario for a moment and watches the henchman return with a jug of water. Then he tilts his head to one side and Tizón sees a smile play on his lips, the same smile he could not quite manage earlier. It is as if the Mulatto is privately savoring some desperate, secret, particularly funny joke.

"His name is Fumagal . . . He lives on the Calle de las Escuelas."

A POUND OF white soap, two pounds of green, two more of mineral soap and sixteen ounces of rosemary oil. While Frasquito Sanlúcar wraps the order, and pours the scented oil into a small flask, Gregorio Fumagal inhales the scents of the shop with pleasure. It smells of soaps, essential oils and pomades, and among the crates of cheaper merchandise are the pleasing colors of the more sophisticated goods, carefully protected in glass jars. On the wall, the long, narrow barometer forecasts changeable weather.

"The green soap contains no copper sulphate, does it?"

Beneath his thinning red hair, the shop owner's freckled face takes on an offended look.

"Not a drop, Don Gregorio, have no fear. This is a serious establishment . . . The soap is made with extract of acacia, which is what gives it such a lovely color. It is very popular, the ladies love it."

"With so many people in Cádiz, I'm sure trade is thriving."

Sanlúcar admits that he cannot complain. The truth is that, as long as the *gabachos* maintain their siege, he will have no shortage of customers. People seem to be attending more to their personal appearance. Even salves and pomades for gentlemen—carnation, violet, heliotrope—are selling well. "Smell this. Exquisite, is it not? To say nothing of the soaps and toilet waters for ladies. Business is booming."

"I can tell. You certainly have no shortage of stock."

"Why would there be any shortage? With the English as our allies, we have goods arriving from all over the world. See this alkanet root I

use to dye the soaps? I used to have it shipped in from Montpellier—
now I get it from Turkey, and it's cheaper."

"And you still have as many female customers?"

"You have no idea! Ladies of every class. From local women to
high-class ladies. And lots of rich immigrants."

"It's strange, given the current state of affairs."

"Well, I've given it a lot of thought: I think that's precisely why they
come. It's as though the war is giving people a thirst for life, they want
to go out and meet people, they want to look their best . . . Like I said,
I can't complain. It's true that I'm a careful businessman. It is not
enough for the products to smell good and be pleasing to the touch,
they have to be displayed to their best advantage. I make sure they look
good."

Frasquito Sanlúcar finishes packing the order, hands it across the
counter to Fumagal and wipes his hands on his gray smock. "That will
be nineteen *reales*," he says. While the taxidermist rummages in his
pocket and takes out two silver *duros*, Sanlúcar taps out a jolly rhythm
on the counter with his knuckles. *Tum-te-te-tum Tum Tum*. The tapping stops suddenly as they hear a muffled explosion in the distance. It
is barely audible. Both men look towards the door. Outside, the passersby barely seem to react. The bomb obviously fell on the far side of
the city, thinks Fumagal as Sanlúcar gives him his change and goes back
to rapping out a rhythm on the counter. It is not surprising that people
in this area are not troubled by the French artillery. The area around
the Mentidero is outside the range of the shelling from the Cabezuela.
And, according to the taxidermist's calculations, it will remain that way
for a long time. Too long, unfortunately.

"Be careful, Don Gregorio. Even if the French are firing at random, you never know what they might hit . . . How are things near
you?"

"We get some shells falling but, as you say, it's random."

Tum-te-te-tum Tum Tum. Gregorio Fumagal steps out into the
street with his package under his arm. It is early, and the street is still in
shade. Hoarfrost covers the cobblestones, the balustrades, the railings

and the plant pots. In spite of the explosion he has just heard, the war seems as remote as ever. An olive seller, driving a donkey weighed down with jars toward El Carmen and the Alameda, is hawking his wares—*green olives, black olives, queen olives*, he calls. Fumagal encounters a water-seller with a barrel on his back. On one of the first-floor balconies, a young servant, her arms bare, is shaking out a mat, watched from the street corner by a man who is leaning against the wall and smoking.

The taxidermist heads down the Calle del Óleo toward the city center, engrossed in his own thoughts. In recent days, his thoughts have been less than serene. As he passes a coal yard, he steps off the pavement to avoid the people queuing to buy *picón*—cheap charcoal. Winter is just around the corner, the rains are getting heavier and already people are having to light the little braziers under the tables known as *mesas camillas*. Turning off the street, Fumagal glances over his shoulder and sees that the man who was smoking on the corner is behind him. It could be a coincidence—indeed, it probably is—but the mounting sense of danger makes him uneasy. Ever since war came to the city and he made contact with the French camp, uncertainty has been his constant companion; but recently, particularly since his conversation with the Mulatto on the Plaza San Juan de Dios, he has been continually fretful. Gregorio Fumagal is no longer receiving any news, any instructions. Now he is working blind, not knowing whether his messages have arrived. He no longer has any guidance, and no means of contact other than the pigeons he sends toward the Trocadero. Their numbers are steadily dwindling, and he has no idea how to replace them. When he sends the final messenger fluttering off, the tenuous link that binds him to the far shore will be broken. At that point, his solitude will be complete.

In the little square at the end of the Calle del Jardinillo, Fumagal stops in front of a haberdasher's window and casually glances behind him again. As the tall man passes and keeps walking, the taxidermist watches him out of the corner of his eye: his dress is slovenly, an ill-fitting frockcoat and a battered round hat. He could be a policeman, but he could equally be one of the hundreds of unemployed immigrants who wander around with a safe-conduct in their pocket that exempts them from being conscripted to fight in the war.

Imagination is the worst thing, Fumagal thinks as he walks on, and the fear that spreads through his body like a malignant tumor. Now is the time to draw a distinction between reality and experience: reality tells Fumagal that he does not know whether he is actually being followed, while experience tells him that, given the circumstances, it is all too likely. Thinking about it logically, it seems more than probable. But this conclusion is not a tragedy; in fact, it might even be a relief. To die would not be so bad, after all. The taxidermist believes that the fate of every man depends on imperceptible forces within the framework of universal laws. All things eventually come to an end, including life. Like animals, like plants, like minerals, one day he too will have to give back his borrowed particles to the universal store. It happens every day; indeed, he contributes to it. It is a consequence of the laws of nature.

On the Plaza del Palillero, between the stalls selling engravings and newspapers from Monge and from Vindel, locals and passersby crowd around recently posted notices and discuss their contents. One of them gives notification that the Cortes, at the request of the Regency, has recently approved a tax requiring the inhabitants of the city to contribute twelve million *pesos* to the upkeep of the naval forces and fortifications. They're bleeding us dry, someone shouts. King or no king, nothing changes. The other poster offers news that the City of Havana, against the express orders of the Cortes, has repealed the decree emancipating black slaves, calling it detrimental to the island's interests, and positing that it might have the same effect on Cuba as a similar French law did on Santo Domingo: revolution and anarchy.

Fools, thinks Fumagal as he passes the crowd, barely pausing to give them a contemptuous glance. At least it should give them something to talk about for a couple of days. Ancient traditions have left these people with an affinity for their chains: kings, gods, parliaments, decrees and proclamations that change nothing. The taxidermist believes that humanity moves from one master to another, and is made up of miserable wretches who believe themselves free while acting against their natural inclinations, incapable of realizing that the only true freedom is that of the individual and consists in allowing oneself to be swept along by the forces that control us. The actions of mankind will always be governed by fate; or the amoral Natural Order and the relationship between cause and effect. Something that makes the word *evil* moot. Paradoxically, society condemns the very inclinations that characterize it; but that condemnation is merely a flimsy barrier against the dark impulses of the heart. The human animal, stupid to the point of insanity, prefers illusions to a reality that in itself disproves the notion of a Supreme Being who is merciful, intelligent and just. Surely it is an aberration for a father to place a weapon in the hands of a fractious child and then condemn that child for using it to kill.

"Where did the last bomb fall?" Fumagal asks a blacksmith who is making a fishing lure in the doorway of his forge.

"Nearby, opposite the Candelaria . . . It didn't do much damage."

"No victims?"

"No, thanks be to God."

Residents and soldiers are working among the rubble on the little square. The bomb, Fumagal notices when he gets there, fell right in front of the church without damaging the houses on either side and, although it exploded, the size of the site—with the buildings set far apart—has meant that damage was limited to a few broken windows, some chipped plasterwork, and a few broken roof tiles. The wind is blowing from the west, he notes, something which probably contributed to the bomb falling in this part of the city, further east and not as far as the last four bombs. Pretending to be curious and blending in with the other onlookers—some boys are picking up twisted shards of lead from the ground—Fumagal walks slowly, concentrating, counting his steps, calculating the distance, using as his reference the corner post on the Calle del Torno, the remains of an old Moorish column. With or without the Mulatto, whether he has pigeons or the pigeon loft is empty, he is determined to carry on what he is doing, fulfilling the ritual according to his personal standards—inevitable and deliberate.

Gregorio Fumagal has counted seventeen steps when he notices that someone in the crowd seems to be watching him. It is not the same man he saw earlier, but another, of average height, wearing a gray cape and a bicorn hat. Maybe they have several people watching him, he thinks. Or perhaps it is just his mind playing tricks again, something that is beginning to seem like an incurable disease. The taxidermist believes that all men are diseased, infected at birth by the contagion that is life and by its madness, the imagination. And when fear arises, the imagination runs out of control, giving birth to fanaticism, to religious terrors and madness, and—he smiles savagely at this thought—to great crimes. Simple people despise great crimes, ignorant of the fact that they require the same passion and tenacity as great virtues; oblivious to the fact that the most virtuous of men could, by an imperceptible confluence of correctly aligned forces, become the most criminal of men.

On an arrogant impulse that he does not trouble to analyze, but which is merely the logical outcome of his earlier reasoning, Fumagal puts his head down and walks briskly, feigning preoccupation, and deliberately collides with the man in the bicorn.

"Excuse me," he says, barely glancing up.

The man mumbles something unintelligible and moves aside; Fumagal smugly goes on his way. Come what may, he has no intention of fleeing the city. Socrates, obedient to the unjust laws of his own country, also refused to flee his jail cell when the door was left open for him. He accepted the rules, confident—as Gregorio Fumagal is—that by his very nature Man can act only as he acts. Everything is necessary—such is the dogma of fatalism.

AT THE FOURTH attempt, the lock opens soundlessly. Rogelio Tizón warily pushes the door, slipping his picklocks into his pocket. The procedure took less than three minutes. In his long experience of dealing with pickpockets and other thieves of the kind known in their profession as *gentlemen of industry*, the comisario has acquired a number of skills, one of which is the ability to use picklocks—he is a *rum dubber*, in thieves' cant—which has proved extremely useful. Ever since padlocks and door locks were invented, there are few secrets that cannot be discovered by the skillful use of picklocks, skeleton keys, hacksaws, files and diamond-point tools.

The policeman moves slowly down the hallway, checking every room: bedroom, water closet, dining room, and then the kitchen, which has a stove burning wood and coal, a sink, a meat safe and a rat trap baited with a piece of cheese next to the pantry door. Everything is spotless and orderly, even though it is the home of a bachelor—by now, Tizón has found out everything he can about the suspect. The workshop is at the end of the corridor and when the comisario gets there, the light streaming from the door onto the terrace bathes the room in a golden glow. It reflects off the glass eyes, the beaks, the varnished claws of stuffed animals on perches and in display cabinets; it shimmers on glass jars filled with embalmed birds and reptiles.

Rogelio Tizón opens the glass door and goes up to the terrace. At a glance, he takes in the whole city: the watch towers, the chimneys, the laundry hung out to dry. Then he checks the pigeon loft, finds three birds there, after which he goes back down to the workshop. There is a brass clock on a dresser and a bookcase containing some twenty volumes, almost all illustrated tomes on natural history. Among them, he finds an old, well-thumbed edition entitled *Historiae natrualis de avibus* by someone named Johannes Jonstonus, as well as two volumes of the *Encyclopédie* and a number of other banned French books, all hidden between apparently innocent covers: *Émile, La Nouvelle Hélloïse, Candide, De l'esprit, Lettres philosophiques* and *Système de la nature*. A strange smell permeates the room, of alcohol mingled with unfamiliar substances. In the center is a large marble table on which something is covered with a white sheet. Pulling it aside, the comisario discovers the body of a large black cat, disemboweled and already half-stuffed, its eye sockets filled with cotton wool and the body cavity with wadding, through which protrude pieces of wire and string. Rogelio Tizón is not a superstitious man, yet he cannot help but feel a certain foreboding at the sight of the animal, the color of its fur. Ill at ease, he covers the body again, doing his best to leave the sheet exactly as it was before. The sight of the cat's carcass and the stuffy atmosphere of the room suddenly make him feel nauseous. Tizón yearns to light a cigar, but the lingering smell of tobacco smoke would let the owner of the house know an intruder had been here. *The whoreson*, he thinks as he looks around, brooding. *Accursed, damnable whoreson.*

Next to the marble table is a lectern with a sheaf of notes: details about the animals he has stuffed and the various stages of the process. The comisario moves over to another table, between the terrace door and a display case inhabited by the frozen figures of a lynx, a barn owl and a monkey. On this table are flasks of glass and porcelain containing chemicals, and instruments similar to those a surgeon might use: saws, scalpels, pincers, saddler's needles. Having inspected everything, Tizón moves over to a third table, large and fitted with drawers, set against the wall beneath various branches on which a pheasant, a falcon and a bearded vulture perch. Their poses are extremely lifelike—this man is clearly a master of his art. On the table is an oil lamp and a number of papers, which Tizón quickly leafs through, trying to replace each one exactly as he found it—more notes concerning natural history, sketches of animals and suchlike. The first drawer in the table is locked and the key is nowhere in sight, so Tizón again takes out his picklocks, selects one of the smallest, slips it into the lock and with a little effort—*click, click*—he manages to open the drawer. Inside he finds a neatly folded map of Cádiz, measuring about three palm-lengths by two, similar to those that can be purchased anywhere in the city and which many families have hung on their walls to mark the places where French shells have fallen. This one, however, is hand-drawn in black ink; the detail is thorough and precise, and the legend in the bottom right-hand corner gives scales in both Spanish *varas* and French *toises*. In the margins are marked lines of latitude and longitude, but the numbering does not relate to the historic meridian of Cádiz, nor the meridian of the Naval Observatory on the Isla de Léon. Paris, perhaps, thinks Tizón. A French map. It is professionally drafted, similar to those used by the military, which is undoubtedly where it came from. But what is most striking is that the owner has not simply marked the places where bombs have fallen, as others in the city might do. Instead, they are carefully identified using numbers and letters, and are connected by penciled lines to a gradated semicircular reference point located on the east of the map—the direction of the French artillery fire from the Trocadero. Together, the marks form a network of lines and circles carefully traced using various instruments in the drawer: slide rules, measuring rods, compasses, set squares, a large magnifying glass and a good-quality English compass in a wooden case.

The comisario is spellbound by this strange web etched over the original paper—like a cone with its vertex pointing eastward; the codes, the circles drawn with a compass around each point of impact. For a long time he stands in front of the table, staring down at the map, swearing under his breath. It is as if, when looked at as a whole, what at first seems to be a jumble of crisscrossed lines is a second map superimposed upon the first: one that charts a strange, sinister labyrinth Tizón has been unable to see, or even sense, before today. A parallel city governed by dark forces that defy ordinary logic.

I've got you now, he thinks coldly, only to add a moment later: *at least, I've got the spy. He won't get away now.* He rummages in the drawer and finds a little book in an oilcloth slipcase listing the code of numbers and letters attributed to each point of impact, the street names, the precise latitude and longitude, the distance in *toises,* so it is possible to calculate the point of impact with reference to buildings and easily identifiable landmarks. All of this is crucially important, and yet the comisario's eyes keep drifting back to the circles traced around the places where the bombs fell. He has a sudden flash of inspiration and, picking up the magnifying glass, he looks for four specific places: the alleyway between Santo Domingo and La Merced, Lame Paco's Tavern, the corner of the Calle de Amoladores and Rosario, and the Calle del Viento. All are carefully marked, but there is nothing to distinguish them from the others—only the codes that relate to the data in the oilskin notebook, making it possible to determine which bombs exploded and which did not. All four exploded, as did about fifty others.

Tizón puts everything back in its place, closes the drawer, locks it again with his picklock and stands for a moment, deep in thought. Then he walks over to the bookcase, takes down each volume and leafs through them to check whether there are any documents hidden between the pages. In the copy of *Système de la nature, ou des Lois du monde physique et du monde moral,* by a certain M. Mirabaud, published in London, he finds a number of passages underlined in pencil. One of these stands out:

> There is no cause, however minute, however remote, that does not sometimes produce the greatest and most immediate effects on man. It may, perhaps, be in the parched plains of Lybia, that are amassed the first elements of a storm or tempest, which, borne by the winds, approach our climate, render our atmosphere dense, and thus operating on the temperament, may influence the passions of a man . . .

Contemplating what he has just read, the comisario is about to close the book when, as he flicks quickly through the pages, his eye falls on another passage, also underlined:

> It is in the natural order that fire burns, because it is of its essence to burn. It is in the natural order that the wicked man should do evil, because he is of his essence evil.

Tizón takes his notebook from his pocket and jots down the two paragraphs before replacing the book on its shelf. He glances at the clock on the dresser and realizes that he has already been here too long. The owner might come back at any moment, although he has taken precautions against such an eventuality: he has two men trailing the suspect and a boy, a fast runner, who will dash back the moment the suspect starts to head home; he also has Cadalso and another officer posted at either end of the street, ready to give the alert. In principle, such precautions are unnecessary since the map, together with the Mulatto's confession, are more than evidence enough for them to arrest the taxidermist and hand him over to the military tribunal, where, with no right of appeal, they would snap his neck with a few quick twists of the garrote. Nothing could be easier, especially in these days when Cádiz is particularly sensitive to acts of war and espionage. But the comisario is in no hurry. There are some murky points he would like to clarify first, theories to be tested and suspicions to be confirmed. Arresting a man who stuffs animals, underlines disturbing passages in books and sends messages to the French informing them where their bombs have fallen seems of little importance just now. What he wants is to work out whether there is some different, parallel way of reading the map he has just locked in the desk drawer—a direct connection between the man who lives in this house, four French bomb sites and four murdered girls, three after and one before those same bombs fell. A meaning that is perhaps pulsing underneath the spider's web of penciled lines that pinions the map from east to west. A premature arrest could change the scenario, leaving the mystery forever unresolved and Tizón with only a captured spy and a host of suspicions that might never be confirmed. This is not what he is looking for today, searching among the bodies of dead animals, through drawers and cupboards for the key to the secrets which, for some time now, have forced him to live among brooding ghosts. The comisario is searching for a solution to the riddle which once seemed simple but which, since the preemptive murder on the Calle del Viento—the bomb falling *after,* not *before*—seems unfathomable. In order to be proven or refuted, his theory requires that all the pieces on the chessboard remain in play, each moving freely according to its rules. As his friend Hipólito Barrull would say, he needs empirical evidence. Preventing the potential murderer of four girls from killing again would be a public service, a heroic and a patriotic act. But from another point of view, it would obviate any possibility of testing his powers of reasoning and their limits. This is why Tizón has decided to be patient, to be as still as the animals who even now are staring at him with their glass eyes from perches and display cases. He will keep watch over his prey, do nothing to alert him, and wait for more bombs to fall. After all, Cádiz is not short of targets. And any game of chess requires a piece to be sacrificed sometimes.

CHAPTER TEN

ᘓᘔ

The day is cool and cloudy, a light northerly breeze rippling the waters of the canals. Felipe Mojarra leaves his house early—broad-brimmed hat pushed down over his eyes, his gamebag and cape thrown over his shoulders, horn-handled knife tucked into his belt—to walk the quarter of a league of tree-lined road that leads from the village on the Isla de Léon to the military zone and San Carlos hospital. Today he is wearing a pair of rope sandals. He is going to visit Cárdenas, his brother-in-law, who is slowly convalescing from the bullet that grazed his skull as they were bringing the French gunboat back from the mill at Santa Cruz. The bullet merely splintered the bone, but there were complications when the wound became infected, and Cárdenas is still very weak. Mojarra visits him as often as possible, whenever he is not on duty with the guerrillas or accompanying Captain Virués on reconnaissance missions. The salter always brings some food prepared by his wife and chats for a while with Cárdenas over a cigar. But the visits are always grueling, not so much because of his brother-in-law, who is more or less holding up, but because of the atmosphere in the hospital. It is no one's idea of a good day out.

Mojarra walks along the straight roads of the military district, between the serried ranks of naval barracks, past the church square and enters the building on the left, after showing his papers to the guard. He walks up the stairs and has hardly crossed the vast hall connecting the two wards before he feels a familiar shiver of unease at being inside this disagreeable place, its constant low, monotonous murmuring, the groans of hundreds of men lying on bare boards on mattresses of straw and corn husks, lined up such that, from the door, they seem to stretch forever. Then comes the smell, also familiar—which, though expected, is no less sickening. The open windows do little to dissipate the fetid odor of rotting, ulcerous flesh and the sickly stench of gangrene beneath the bandages. Mojarra removes his hat and the checked kerchief he wears beneath it.

"How have you been?"

"As you can see. Not too good, but still alive and kicking."

His eyes are shining and red-rimmed from the fever. He looks terrible. His unshaven face is gaunt, his cheeks hollow. His head has been shaved and the wound—exposed, to make it easier to drain—looks trivial when one looks around this ward filled with the injured, the crippled and the maimed. There are soldiers, sailors and civilians wounded not only during the recent fighting along the front line and the incursions into occupied territory, but also from battles fought last year at El Puerto, Trocadero and Sanlúcar, the disaster suffered by Zayas' Division at Huelva, General Blake's forays into the Condando de Niebla and the battle of Chiclana; suppurating sores, gaping cuts that have still not healed, amputated stumps with purple suture scars, heads and limbs with wounds from bullets or sabers, patches over blinded eyes or empty sockets. And always the constant, muted moaning that seems like a distillation of all the pain and sorrow in the world.

"What did the surgeons say?"

Cárdenas heaves a sigh. "That I'll have to take it slowly . . . that I'll be here for a while yet."

"I think you're looking a lot better."

"Come on, don't treat me like a fool. And give me a smoke."

Mojarra takes out two small cigars, handing one to his brother-in-law and putting the other in his mouth, then lights both with his tinderbox. With some difficulty, Cárdenas sits up on the edge of the mattress—the sheets are grubby, the blanket old and threadbare—and takes a deep, satisfied draw on the cigar. The first in two weeks, he claims. Damn tobacco. From his gamebag, Mojarra takes out a package tied with string: cured meat, salted tuna, a small earthenware jar of stewed cod with chickpeas, a flask of wine and a bundle of six cigars.

"Your sister sent this. Make sure your *compañeros* here don't steal it all."

Glancing around warily, Cárdenas stows the package under the pallet of his mattress. He sets the earthenware jar on the floor beside his feet.

"How are your girls?"

"Good."

"And the one in Cádiz?"

"Even better."

The brothers-in-law smoke while Mojarra tells Cárdenas the latest news. There have been more forays into the tidal creeks, and the French are on the defensive—shelling over the Isla de Léon and the city, but causing little damage. There are rumors that General Ballesteros and his men have retreated to Gibraltar and the safety of the English cannons, as the *gabachos* have been threatening to take Algeciras and Tarifa. A military expedition has set sail for Veracruz to fight the Mexican insurgents. Mojarra himself narrowly missed being forcibly enlisted with some of the other villagers, but Don Lorenzo Virués rescued him, insisting he was needed here.

"So how is your captain?"

"Same as always, you know . . . Still sketching, still getting me up before dawn . . ."

"Have we lost any battles lately?"

"Every one, except Cádiz and the Isla."

Cárdenas gives a bitter scowl, baring his gray, fleshless gums. "They should line up twenty generals and shoot them all for treason."

"It's not just the generals, Bartolo. The problem is no one can agree what to do—it's every man for himself. The soldiers do their best, only to get themselves killed; they decide to pull together, and still they are slaughtered . . . It's hardly surprising so many are deserting, running off into the mountains. The way things are we have more and more *guerrilleros* and fewer soldiers."

"And the Redcoats?"

"Still here, still doing what they always do."

"At least the English know exactly what they want."

"That they do. They do their job and they don't give a shit about us."

A pause. The two men smoke in silence. Mojarra cannot help but stare at the cross-shaped wound on his brother-in-law's head, which looks like an open mouth whose lips have been slashed. Inside the wound is a dirty, oozing scab.

"I heard they shot Father Ronquillo," says Cárdenas.

Mojarra nods. Ronquillo, the parish priest in El Puerto, hung up his cassock the day the French burned down his church and led a group of men who started out as patriots and ended up as cutthroats, ruthlessly robbing and murdering travelers and peasants. Eventually, the ex-priest and his men defected to the French.

"About a month ago, our guerrillas laid an ambush for him near Conil," Mojarra explains. "They gave him a good hiding, then shot him."

"He's better off dead. He was a bad lot."

A sudden howl makes Mojarra turn his head. Lying on his back, writhing naked on the bed, is a young man whose arms and legs have been strapped down. He arches his body violently, grinding his teeth, clenching his fists, every muscle tensed, eyes bulging, letting out short, staccato cries of rage. No one else seems to pay him any mind. A soldier from the Cantabria battalion, Cárdenas explains, wounded seven months ago during the battle of Chiclana. He has a French bullet in his brain that cannot be removed, and now and then it triggers these terrible convulsions. There he is, not healing, not dying, one foot on either side of the abyss. He is moved from bed to bed so his screams and howls are distributed equally around the ward. Some talk of suffocating him with a pillow in the night, so the poor bastard might rest in peace, but no one has dared do it because the surgeons seem particularly interested in his case; they come to see him regularly, take copious notes, and show him off to visitors. When they moved him here, his fits and convulsions kept Cárdenas awake for three nights, but eventually he grew accustomed to it.

"You can get used to anything," he tells Mojarra.

At the mention of the battle of Chiclana, Mojarra pulls a face. Quite recently it was discovered that men injured in the battle were dying of neglect and starvation here in San Carlos hospital, and that the money raised to buy bacon and chickpeas for the stewpot had been embezzled by officials. The minister at the Royal Treasury responsible for the hospital reacted immediately, condemning the Cádiz newspaper that had published the story. Thereafter, everything was settled through bribes, visits by members of the Cortes, and there was a slight improvement. Thinking about the scandal, Mojarra looks around at the bedridden men, and at those who stand by the windows or move about the ward like ghosts, propped up by walking sticks and crutches—giving the lie to words like "heroism," "glory" and other such terms used and abused by the young and the credulous, by those who are in no danger of ending up in a place like this. Those Mojarra sees are men like himself who have fought for their captive king and their subjugated country, brave men and cowards, brought low by cold steel or a bullet. The ill-fated defenders of the Isla de Léon, of Cádiz, of Spain itself. He could easily have been one of them, he thinks. It might have been him lying here in place of his brother-in-law, his head split open with a wound that refuses to heal, or the poor wretch strapped to the bed, writhing, an ounce of lead buried in his brain.

Suddenly, Mojarra feels afraid—not the ordinary fear he feels when bullets whistle by, when every muscle and tendon tenses, waiting for the one that will knock him over. Nor is it the slow dread of waiting for a battle to begin—the most terrible fear of all—when the landscape, even in brilliant sunlight, seems gray and you feel a strange ache creep up through your chest to your mouth and your eyes, forcing you to take slow, deep breaths. The fear he feels now is different: it is sordid, petty. Selfish. He feels ashamed of this inchoate fear that turns the cigar smoke bitter in his mouth, that urges him to leap to his feet, rush out of here, run home and hug his wife and daughters so that he might feel whole. Alive.

"What happened about the gunboat?" asks Cárdenas. "When are they going to pay us?"

Mojarra shrugs. The gunboat. Two days ago he returned to Naval Headquarters to claim the promised reward. He has lost count of how many times he has been there. Three hours standing in line, cap in hand as usual, only for some surly bureaucrat to say—in a matter of thirty seconds, and without deigning to look at him—all in good time, be patient. There are too many leaders, officers and soldiers who have gone for months without being paid.

"It's going to take a little time. That's what they said."

Cárdenas looks at him anxiously. "But tell me honestly . . . you did go, didn't you?"

"Of course I went. And Curro has been there several times too. Each time they send us packing. You have to remember it's a lot of money, and times are hard."

"What about Captain Virués? Couldn't he talk to someone for you?"

"He says that with matters such as this, there's nothing to be done. It's beyond his influence."

"They were happy enough to see us when we showed up with the boat. The Navy Commander himself came down to shake hands with us, remember? He even bandaged my head with his kerchief."

"You know how it is; things are always different in those first moments."

Cárdenas brings a hand to his forehead as if to touch the open wound, but stops an inch from the edge.

"I'm lying here for the sake of five thousand *reales.*"

Mojarra says nothing; he does not know what to say. He takes a last drag on his cigar, lets it fall to the floor and grinds it with the heel of his sandal. Then he gets to his feet. Cárdenas's red-rimmed eyes stare up at him miserably. Indignantly.

"We pulled it off," he says. "You, me, Curro and the lad. And what about those French bastards we slaughtered, lying there asleep in the dark . . . ? Did you tell them all that?"

"Of course I did . . . Don't worry, everything will be fine."

"We earned that money," Cárdenas insists. "That and more . . ."

"We have to be patient." Mojarra lays a hand on his brother-in-law's shoulder. "I'm sure it will come through in a day or two. When they get the money from America."

Cárdenas shakes his head wearily and lies back on the mattress, curling up as though he were cold. His feverish eyes stare into space.

"They promised . . . twenty thousand *reales* for a gunboat with its cannon . . . That's why we did the job, isn't it?"

Mojarra picks up his cloak, his gamebag and his hat, walks past the rows of straw mattresses and leaves the hospital, fleeing the horrors hidden in the folds of the flag.

TWENTY MILES WEST of the Espartel cape. The last cannon shot brought down their quarry's main topsail, which falls to the deck, a tangle of spars, rigging and canvas. At almost the same instant, the crew heave to and hoist the French ensign.

"Lower the launch," orders Pépé Lobo.

Leaning on the starboard gunwale, in the stern of the *Culebra*, the corsair looks at the captured vessel, bobbing on the waves, its sails aback, held there by the fresh easterly breeze. It is a medium-tonnage, square-rigged *chambequín*, with three 4-pounders on each side which surrendered after the briefest of battles—two carronades on either side, resulting in little damage—following a five-hour pursuit which began at daybreak when the lookout spotted it heading out into the Atlantic. It had to be one of the enemy vessels—part corsair, part merchant ship—that frequent the Moroccan ports, bringing supplies to the French-occupied coastline. Given the course it was steering before it realized it was being pursued, the *chambequín* must have put out from Larache last night intending to gain the open sea, sailing west to evade the English patrols, before tacking northward toward Rota or Barbate under cover of darkness. Once its topsail is repaired, and manned by a crew from the *Culebra*, it will be bound for Cádiz. The ship's bell rings the quarters with two double-peals. Ricardo Maraña, who has exchanged a few words with the crew of the *chambequín* using the loudhailer, comes back from the bow, passing the four 6-pound cannons on the starboard side, still aimed at the captured vessel to avoid any last-minute surprises.

"The crew is French and Spanish, the skipper is French," he informs Pépé Lobo, satisfied. "Out from Larache, as we suspected.

They're carrying a cargo of cured meat, almonds, barley and oil . . . It's a good capture."

Pépé Lobo nods while his first officer, with his usual nonchalance, slips two pistols in the wide belt of his black jacket, straps on his sword and goes to join the boarding party, equipped with cutlasses, blunderbusses and pistols. Given the flag the *chambequín* is flying and the cargo it is carrying, no Prize Court would dispute its lawful seizure. Word has already spread across the deck: elated at the prospect of such a large booty with no bloodshed, the crewmen heartily clap Maraña and his men on the back.

Picking up the spyglass lying next to the binnacle, Pépé Lobo extends it, puts his eye to the lens and looks toward the raised poop deck of the other ship, whose crew are busy gathering up the fallen sail and securing the rigging. Three men stand at the foot of the mast, looking desolately toward the *Culebra*. One of them, sporting a thick beard and wearing a black pea jacket and narrow-brim hat, seems to be the captain. Behind him, on the far side, the apprentice pilot—or maybe a deckhand—throws something overboard. A book of secret codes, perhaps; or official correspondence; or a French Letter of Marque; or all of the above. When he sees this, Lobo calls to Brasero the bo'sun, who is still manning the cannons.

"Nostromo!"

"Aye, Captain!"

"Get the loudhailer and tell the crew of the *chambequín* to move toward the bow! And if they throw anything else overboard—if they so much as spit over the side—we'll fire another cannon shot."

As Brasero delivers the order, the captain of the *Culebra* looks over the side to see if the launch is in the water. The boarding party are now all aboard and the men are setting the oars into the rowlocks as Maraña lowers himself over the side. Pépé Lobo looks toward the Moroccan coast, which is not visible, although the weather is fair and the horizon clear. Once the *chambequín* is manned, Pépé Lobo intends to tack a little landward and keep an eye out for any other prey—these are good waters for hunting—before escorting the captured vessel home.

"All hands! Ship ahoy to starboard!"

Pépé Lobo looks up irritably toward the crow's nest; the lookout is pointing northward.

"What ship?"

"Looks like a two-master. Square-rigged, all sails set!"

Hooking the spyglass over his shoulder, Lobo crosses the deck beneath the boom that is swaying with the half-furled mainsail. Heaving himself on to the gunwale, he climbs a little way up the ratlines, opens out the telescope and peers through it, trying to compensate for the lurch and roll of the swell.

"It's a brigantine!" the lookout calls down from above his head.

The yell comes a moment before Pépé Lobo identifies the rig of the ship, which is now gaining on them rapidly thanks to a fresh easterly wind swelling its sails. It is indeed a brigantine. Packing all sails—jibs, topsails, topgallants and royals—it is five miles out and making good speed with the wind on its port quarter. It is not yet possible to see which flag she is flying, if she is flying any, but there is no need. Lobo closes his eyes, cursing his fate, then opens them and peers through the spyglass again. He thinks he recognizes the intruder. He can hardly believe his misfortune, but the sea likes to play these little games. Some you win, some you lose. The *Culebra* has just lost.

"Get the boarding party back here now! All hands on deck!"

He barks the orders while he slides down a shroud line, and as soon as his feet hit the deck he heads back to the stern, ignoring the crew, who stare at him bewildered or scan the horizon. On his way he bumps into Maraña, scrabbling aboard and giving him a searching look. Lobo has only to jerk his chin northward and the first officer understands.

"The Barbate brigantine?"

"It could be."

Maraña stands gazing at him expressionlessly. Then he leans over the side, looking down at the launch; its crew, at their oars, are hanging on to the chain of plate with a boathook and look up quizzically, not sure what is happening.

"All aboard! Get that launch out of the water!"

It could be an English ship, thinks Pépé Lobo, though he's had no news of one in this area of the Straits. But he is not about to take any risks. The cutter is fast, but the French brigantine—if that is what it is—is much faster, especially with the wind on the beam and all sails set, which will be the case if they decide to give chase. It also has greater firepower—twelve 6-pound cannons to the *Culebra*'s four. And a larger crew.

"It's the French brigantine!" comes a call from the crow's nest.

Lobo does not need to be told twice. "Set the mainsail, set the foresails, port tack!"

The launch is back on deck, water streaming from it. The boarding party have put down their weapons and are lashing the boat to the skid beam beneath the boom in front of the mast, while Maraña barks orders and Brasero the bo'sun pushes the laggards toward their stations. There are disappointed mutterings on deck. Bewildered at first, they have come to realize the danger bearing down on them; the men rush to brail the mainsail up; it unfurls with a crack of canvas while, in the bow, the standing jib and the foresail are hoisted, clacking on the staysail sheets.

"Trim the mainsail! Trim the foresails!"

The men haul aft the starboard sheets, and the cutter heels three points to starboard as the wind fills the sails. Still standing in the stern, Pépé Lobo operates the wheel himself until the bearing on the compass mounted on the companion hatch reads west by south; he repeats the bearing to the Scotsman, the chief helmsman, and hands him the tiller. A quick glance tells him that the sails are catching the wind and the cutter responds—whipped on like a thoroughbred racehorse by the unfurled canvas on its lone mast—cleaving the waves and gathering speed as the crew finish trimming the sheets.

"That's a small fortune we're leaving back there," mutters the steersman. Like his captain and most of the crew, he glares back in frustration at their abandoned prey. Their course takes them within pistol range of the other ship, close enough for the corsairs to witness its crew's confused looks turning to joy, to hear their mocking catcalls, to see their obscene gestures. As they leave the *chambequín* behind, Pépé Lobo feels a twinge of bitterness as he watches the enemy captain wave his hat in the air while his men run the French flag back up the mast.

"Can't win 'em all," says Ricardo Maraña, who has come back to the bow and is leaning against the leerail with his habitual languor, thumbs hooked into the belt in which he stows his sword and his pistols.

Pépé Lobo does not answer. He shields his eyes against the sunlight and stares at the water, then up at the pennant indicating the wind direction. The corsair is busy calculating bearings, wind and velocity. As effortlessly as if he were tracing them on a chart, he maps out in his mind the zigzag of lines, angles and the distance he intends to cover in the next few hours, in order to put as much water between the cutter and the brigantine which, as soon as it identifies the *chambequín* and has been assured of its reward, will certainly give chase. If this is the French brigantine that plies the waters between Barbate and Guadalquivir, it is a fast ship, 800 feet in length and weighing in at 250 tons. With a fresh wind on the beam or on the quarter, this would give it a maximum speed of ten, perhaps eleven knots—considerably greater than the cutter's seven or eight. The *Culebra*'s one advantage is its superior ability to sail close-hauled; its large fore-and-aft sail allows it to hug the wind more closely than the square-rigged brigantine, and consequently outrun it by at least a couple of knots.

"The easterly should hold," sighs Ricardo Maraña, staring at the sky. "Until tomorrow at any rate . . . That's one blessing, at least."

"Well, thank God for that, because I was beginning to think he had us cursed!"

Having vented his spleen—Maraña smiles a little at the captain's comment, but says nothing—Pépé Lobo takes out his pocket watch. He knows that he and his first officer are thinking the same thing: there are only five hours' daylight left. The plan is to keep a southwest course until dusk, heading out into the Atlantic, and then tack northeast, working to windward to lose the brigantine under cover of dark. That is the theory. The main thing is to keep a safe distance between them until that time comes.

"One mile an hour," says Lobo. "That's as much as we can let the brig gain on us . . . Best set the flying jib and the foretopsail."

The first officer looks up at the mainsail—the vast expanse of canvas, swelled by the wind, braced to leeward and held in place by the gaff and the boom, urges the cutter on, aided by the foresail and jib set on the long bowsprit.

"I don't trust the topmast," Maraña almost whispers, so the helmsman does not overhear. "One of the French cannonballs grazed the mast just above the cap . . . Carrying that much canvas, it might well split if the wind freshens any more."

Pépé Lobo knows his first mate is right. Given their bearing, in a high wind and carrying a press of sail, the cutter's lone mast might break if they set any more canvas. It is the one drawback of this class of swift, easily manageable ship: its speed comes at a price. It can be as delicate as a *señorita*.

"That's why we're not going to set the topgallant," he tells Maraña. "As for the rest, we have no choice . . . Go to it, pilot."

Maraña nods wearily. He sets down his sword and his pistols and calls the bo'sun—Brasero is making sure the cannons are secured and hatches battened—then goes over to the mast to supervise the maneuver. In the meantime, Pépé Lobo corrects the Scotsman's course by two points then directs his spyglass over the cutter's wake. The *chambequín* has set its sails again and is heading toward its savior, while the brigantine is still gaining fast. When he sets down the telescope and looks back toward the bow, the lone mast is carrying more sail, which flutters briefly before swelling in the wind, as the men trim the topsail sheets: the flying jib above, straining at the grommets of the standing jib and the foresail, the foretopsail braced on its yard above the crow's nest. As it catches more wind, the *Culebra* surges forward, slicing through the water, leaning more to leeward, the gunwale so close to the water that spray crashes over the cannons, water coursing down the deck to the scuppers such that everything is soaked. Leaning in the angle formed by the stern taffrail and the leerail, feet spaced wide apart to compensate for the steep inclination, the corsair once again bemoans the prey they have had to leave behind. Leaving aside his share of the plunder, he knows the capture would have impressed Don Emilio Sánchez Guinea and his son Miguel. And even Lolita Palma.

For a moment, Pépé Lobo thinks about Lolita ("When you come back to port again . . ." she had said when last they spoke), as the *Culebra* keeps a straight course, surefooted, riding the Atlantic, slicing through the heavy swell. A blast of icy water leaps from shroud lines to stern, drenching the captain and the helmsmen, who duck in an attempt to avoid it. Shaking out his frockcoat, soaked to the skin, his hair disheveled, the corsair wipes his face on his sleeve to get rid of the salt stinging his eyes. Then he turns back to look out across the wake of the cutter toward the distant sails of the brigantine. As Maraña said earlier, at least that's one blessing. Chasing down a ship takes hours, and the *Culebra* is running like a hare.

"Come on, then," Pépé Lobo mutters savagely. "Catch me if you can, you bastard!"

THE CLICKING OF bobbins, the swish of silk and the rustle of dresses on the chairs and the sofa, its arms adorned with lace covers. Glasses of sweet wine, chocolates and sweetmeats on the side table. The skirts of the table have been lifted and beneath it burns a copper brazier, warming the room and filling it with the sweet scent of lavender. The walls, papered in vermilion, are hung with a large mirror, engravings, painted ceramic plates and a couple of fine oil paintings. A lacquered Chinese sideboard stands out among the pieces of furniture, and a cage with a cockatoo. Through tall windows opening on to balconies, the trees of San Francisco convent can be seen, gilded in the late afternoon light.

"They say Sagunto has fallen," remarks Curra Vilches. "And that Valencia might well be next."

Doña Concha Solís, the mistress of the house, gives a start and sets down her work for a moment.

"God would not permit such a thing."

She is a heavy woman in her sixties, with gray hair pinned up into a bun. She wears earrings and bracelets of polished jet, and a black woolen shawl draped around her shoulders. Her rosary and her fan lie on the table beside her.

"He simply would not allow it," she says again.

Next to her Lolita Palma, in a dark brown dress, its collar trimmed with white lace, takes a sip of her wine. She sets the glass down on the tray and returns to the embroidery in the frame on her lap. Her character and social standing make her ill-suited to needle, thread and thimble, but she is in the habit of visiting her godmother's house on the Calle del Tinte twice a month, for a gathering of women who sew, embroider and make bobbin lace. This afternoon, they are joined by Doña Concha's daughter, Rosita Solís; her daughter-in-law, Julia Algueró, who is five months pregnant; and Luisa Moragas, a tall, blond woman from Madrid—she and her family are refugees here in Cádiz—who rents the top floor of the building. Completing the group is Doña Pepa de Alba, widow of General Alba, whose three sons are all in the military.

"Things are not going well," Curra Vilches continues assertively between stitches. "General Blake was defeated by the French at Suchet and his army disbanded. People are afraid that the whole of the Levant will fall to the French . . . And if that is not bad enough, Ambassador Wellesley, who is enraged with the Cortes, has threatened to withdraw not only the English troops in Cádiz, but also those of his younger brother, the General Wellington."

Lolita Palma smiles and remains tactfully silent. Her friend speaks with a military assurance that certain generals might envy. Anyone would think she spends her time surrounded by mortar fire and drumrolls, like some brazen serving wench.

"I've heard that the French are also threatening to march on Algeciras and Tarifa," adds Rosita Solís.

"That's true," says Curra authoritatively. "They plan to take them by Christmas."

"But this is terrible. I can't understand why our army is capitulating so easily . . . I cannot believe that a Spaniard is any less brave than a Frenchman or an Englishman."

"It is not a question of bravery, but of experience . . . Our soldiers are peasants, farmers with no military training, recruited indiscriminately. They have no experience on an open battlefield. That is why so many of them desert, cry 'treason!' and take to their heels . . . With the guerrillas, it is a very different matter. They choose the time and place to fight. They are in their element."

Lolita Palma laughs. "You speak just like a general, Curra," she says, without looking up from her needlepoint. "Very forthright, and extremely well informed."

Her friend laughs too, looking down at the work in her lap. This afternoon she is wearing her hair in a graceful coiffure tied up with ribbons that bring out the color of her cheeks, which are charmingly flushed from the heat of the brazier.

"It is hardly surprising," she says. "We women have more common sense than many a respected strategist—the sort who assemble armies of ignorant peasants and leave them to fall apart with the first puff of wind, with thousands of poor wretches running through the fields only to be ruthlessly cut down by the enemy cavalry."

"Poor things . . ." chimes in Rosita Solís.

"Poor indeed . . ."

They sew in silence, brooding about sieges, battles, defeats—the world of men that reaches them only as a distant echo. And the consequences. A small, plump, lazy dog rubs up against Lolita Palma's feet then disappears into the hallway just as a nearby clock tolls five. For some time, the only sound is the clack of Doña Concha's bobbins.

"These are sad times," Julia Algueró says eventually, turning to General Alba's widow. "Have you any news of your sons?"

"The two elder boys are doing well. One is in Ballesteros's army, and the other is stationed here in Puntales . . ."

There is a painful silence. All the ladies around the table understand. Julia Algueró bends solicitously toward her host, her swollen belly filling out her ample tunic. She speaks as one mother to another.

"And the youngest boy? Is there any news?"

Doña Alba shakes her head, staring down at her needlework. Her youngest son, captured during the battle of Ocaña, is being held prisoner in France. She has had no news of him for some time.

"Everything will be fine, you'll see."

Doña Alba gives a stoic smile. It cannot be easy to smile at such a time, thinks Lolita Palma. It is a thankless role: a hero's widow, and mother to three soldiers, constantly having to live up to expectations.

"Of course."

The bobbins click and the needles jingle. The seven women carry on with their work—they are making Rosita Solís's trousseau—as the light wanes. The conversation shifts easily between domestic events and local gossip: Mrs. So-and-so who recently gave birth; some woman who has just been married or widowed; the financial problems of such-and-such a family or the scandal of Doña So-and-so and the lieutenant from Ciudad Real; the vulgarity of Doña What's-her-name, who leaves her house without a maid, her hair uncombed and barely washed; the French bombings; and the essence of musk the perfumer at the Mentidero has just got in from Russia. The fading light that streams through the windows and reflects in the large mahogany-framed mirror is just enough to light the room. Swathed in this golden glow, Lolita Palma finishes embroidering the initials *R.S.* on a fine cambric handkerchief, cuts the thread and allows her mind to wander far from Cádiz: the sea, islands, the distant coastline, a seascape of white sails and sunlight shimmering on rippling water. A man with green eyes gazes out, and she gazes at him. With a shudder that is almost painful, she comes down to earth.

"Two days ago, I ran into Paco Martínez de la Rosa in Cosí's teashop," Curra Vilches says. "Every time I see him he looks more handsome, with that gypsy air of his—so dark-skinned, and those coal-black eyes . . ."

"A little too handsome, perhaps, and a little too black . . ." says Rosita Solís maliciously.

"What about him?" asks Luisa Moragas, confused. "I have seen him once or twice and he seems a personable young man. Sensitive."

"Sensitive. That is precisely the word."

"I would never have thought . . . !" says Doña Maragas, shocked, realizing what is being said.

". . . and yet it's true."

"So anyway," Curra Vilches continues. "I ran into this young liberal at Cosí's, in the company of Atoñete Alcalá Galiano, Pepín Queipo de Llano and some others of the same political persuasion—"

"Simpletons, the lot of them," interrupts Doña Concha. "A fine crowd!"

"At any rate, they told me that the theater is definitely being re-opened. In a matter of days."

Rosita Solís and Julia Algueró clap their hands. The mistress of the house and the widow Alba scowl.

"Another victory for those preening boys who call themselves philosophers," Doña Alba protests.

"It is not just them. Some deputies from the anti-reformist movement have declared their support."

"The world is upside down," complains Doña Concha. "We don't know which way to turn."

"Well, I for one think it is a fine idea," insists Curra Vilches. "Keeping the theater closed deprives the city of pleasurable, wholesome entertainment. After all, many plays are put on in private houses that charge admission . . . Last week Lolita and I were at the home of Carmen Ruiz de Mella, where they put on a short comedy by Juan González del Castillo, and *The Maidens' Consent*."

At the mention of this scandalous play, the lady of the house gets the bobbins of her lace in a tangle.

"The play by Moratín? That Frenchified fop? It's disgraceful!"

"Don't exaggerate, godmother," Lolita Palma interjects. "It is a fine play: modern, respectful and clever."

"Fiddlesticks!" Doña Concha takes a sip of water to calm her indignation. "What about Lope de Vega, what about Calderón . . . ?!"

The general's widow clearly concurs. "Reopening the theater seems a frivolous idea," she says as she completes a stitch. "People seem to forget we are at war, even if it is not always apparent here in Cádiz. People are dying on battlefields and in cities all over Spain . . . It is disrespectful."

"Well, I view it as good, honest entertainment," protests Curra Vilches. "Theater is the product of good society and the fruit of the wisdom of a people."

Doña Concha gives her a withering, scornful look. "Well, well, Curra, you sound just like a liberal. I'm sure that's something you read in *El Conciso.*"

"No," Curra says, laughing gaily. "I read it in the *Diario Mercantil.*"

"That makes little difference to me, *hija.*"

Luisa Moragas intervenes. Married to an official with the Regency, and having fled Madrid with her family when the French invaded, she confesses that she is surprised by the casual way that Cádiz women talk about military and political issues—the way they seem to talk about everything.

"Such independence would be unthinkable in Madrid or Seville . . . even among the upper classes."

Doña Concha tells her that it is only to be expected. In other cities, she adds, all that is asked of women is that they dress elegantly, move gracefully, utter inane pleasantries and be skilled in the use of a fan. Whereas everyone in Cádiz, man or woman, is eager to understand how things work. The port and the sea have much to do with it. Having been exposed to foreign trade for centuries, the city enjoys an almost liberal tradition, one in which many young women of wealthy families are educated. Unlike what happens in the rest of Spain—and, indeed, in other civilized countries—in Cádiz it is not unusual for women to speak foreign languages, read newspapers, discuss politics and, should it be necessary, take over the running of the family business, as her goddaughter Lolita did following the deaths of her father and her brother. Such things are considered acceptable, even praiseworthy, as long as they do not overstep the boundaries of decorum and good breeding.

"But it is true," she concludes, "that in the confusion of war, many of our young people have lost some perspective. There are too many soirées, too many balls and gaming tables and uniforms . . . There is too much talk of freedom, too many charlatans speechifying, within the Cortes and without."

"People are too concerned with their own amusement," asserts the widow Alba, without looking up from her sewing.

"Not everything is about amusement," protests Curra Vilches. "The world no longer belongs to absolute monarchs, it belongs to everyone. The theater is a good example. Paco de la Rosa and a number of others firmly believe that theater can be a means of educating the people . . . It offers a platform to proclaim the new ideas about patriotism and nationhood."

"The people? You've hit the nail on the head, *niña*," says Doña Concha. "What these men want is a republic of guillotiners and atheists who will hold the monarchy to ransom. And one of the ways of achieving that is by competing with religion. By replacing the pulpit with the theater. By preaching their message from the stage. A lot of rot about national sovereignty, as they call it, and not much about religion."

"The liberals have nothing against religion. Almost all of the ones I know go to mass."

"Of course they do"—Doña Concha looks around her triumphantly—"to the Iglesia del Rosario, because the parish priest there is one of them."

Curra Vilches is not about to be contradicted. "Just as the conservatives go to the old cathedral," she says sagely, "because they preach against the liberals."

"You can hardly compare the two, my dear."

"Well, I think that patriotic theater is a good thing," says Julia Algueró. "It is important that the people be educated regarding civic virtues."

Doña Concha turns her fire on her daughter-in-law.

"That's just how things started in France," she snaps, "and we've all seen what happened there: kings guillotined, churches looted and a populace with no respect for anything. And if all that were not enough, Napoleon. Cádiz," she adds, "has already seen what the people are capable of when they become an unruly mob. You only have to remember what happened to poor General Solano, and similar incidents. Freedom of the press has only served to make matters worse, with all these pamphlets littering the streets, the liberals and the anti-reformists constantly squabbling and the newspapers setting one against the other."

"The people need education," Lolita Palma interjects. "Without it, there can be no patriotism."

As is her way, Doña Concha gives Lolita a long hard look that mingles affection with disapproval at hearing her say such things. Lolita knows that, despite the time that has passed, in spite of everyday reality, her godmother still cannot accept the idea that she is still a spinster. "Such a pity," she constantly tells her friends. "A spinster at her age. And it is not as though she's a plain girl. She has a wonderful head on her shoulders and is so sensible in the way she runs the household, the business, everything. But there it is. She will end up being left on the shelf, poor thing."

"There are times, my dear, when you talk like those feckless idlers at the Café de Apolo . . . What the people need is food, and to have the fear of God and respect for their rightful king drummed into their heads."

Lolita smiles gently. "There are other things in life, Godmother."

Doña Concha has set down her cushion and her bobbins and is fanning herself vigorously, as though suffocated by the conversation and the heat from the brazier.

"Perhaps," she concedes. "But none of them decent."

THE PINE SHAVINGS burning next to the cockpit give off an oily, dirty smoke. The flames feebly illuminate the enclosure, casting a reddish glow on the sweaty faces of the men crowded around the ring in which two cocks are fighting: their feathers clipped back to the vanes and cut into bevels, their spurs fitted with steel spikes, their beaks stained with blood. The men cheer in delight or disappointment at every peck and lunge, betting money according to the vagaries of the fight.

"Bet on the black, Captain," advises Lieutenant Bertoldi. "We can't lose."

His sword leaning against the palisade surrounding the cockpit, Simon Desfosseux observes the scene, fascinated by the brutality of the fighting cocks—one scarlet, the other black with a collar of white feathers, its hackles raised for the fight. Some twenty French soldiers are cheering them on, and a number of Spaniards from Joseph Bonaparte's militias. Above the roofless timber enclosure looms the starstrewn sky and the dark, fortified cupola of the former hermitage of Santa Ana.

"The black, the black," Bertoldi insists.

Desfosseux is not sure this would be such a good bet. Something in the poker-faced expression of the red cockerel's owner advises caution. The lean, gray-haired Spaniard, swarthy as a gypsy, his eyes impassive, is hunkered next to the cockpit. He looks rather too indifferent for Desfosseux's liking. Either he cares little for his bird and the money at stake, or he has a trick up his sleeve. The French captain is no expert on cockfighting, but he has seen a number of them in Spain and he knows that a weakened, wounded animal can suddenly recover and, with a well-aimed slash of its beak, crush its adversary. Some birds, in fact, are specifically trained to seem exhausted, about to breathe their last, until the odds turn in their favor: only then do they attack and kill.

The spectators howl excitedly as the scarlet cock draws back in the face of a fierce onslaught by its opponent. Maurizio Bertoldi is about to force his way through the crowd to add a few more francs to his bet, but Desfosseux places a hand on his arm.

"Bet on the red," he says.

The Italian stares bemusedly at the gold napoleon his superior officer has just placed in his hand. Desfosseux insists, serious and assured.

"Trust me."

Bertoldi nods. After a brief hesitation, he adds a *media onza* of his own money to the napoleon before giving it to the man in charge of the cockfight.

"I hope I don't regret it," he groans as he returns.

Desfosseux says nothing. Nor is he following the progress of the fight. His attention has been drawn to three men in the crowd. They noticed the flash of coins and the leather purse the captain slipped back into his cloak pocket and are staring at him with an intensity that is far from reassuring. All three are Spanish: one wears peasant garb— rope sandals and a striped blanket thrown around his shoulders—

the other two are wearing the dark woolen frockcoats trimmed with red, the breeches and the gaiters of the rural militia that operate as support to the French army. The militia are usually made up of dubious individuals, mercenaries not to be trusted: *guerrilleros*, criminals and smugglers—it is difficult to distinguish in Spain—who have sworn allegiance to King Joseph and now hunt down their former comrades, receiving a third of everything they confiscate from enemies and criminals, real or imaginary. Cruel, fickle, benefiting from total impunity and apt to inflict all manner of abuse and humiliation on their compatriots, the militiamen can prove more dangerous than the rebels themselves; they rival them in atrocities committed on roads, in fields and farmhouses, robbing and pillaging the very people they are sworn to protect.

Staring at these three somber faces, Captain Desfosseux once again considers the twin traits he considers particular to the Spanish: chaos and cruelty. Unlike the English soldiers and their ruthless, intelligent, unfailing courage, or the French, resolute in battle though far from home and fighting chiefly for the honor of their flag, the Spanish still seem to him to be a mess of contradictions: incongruous bravery, gallant cowardice, inconstant steadfastness. During the Revolution and the military campaigns in Italy, the French—ill-equipped, ill-dressed and with no military training, quickly became veterans obsessed with their country's glory. Meanwhile the Spanish, as though atavistically predisposed to accept defeat and distrust their leaders, gave up at the first shot, and the whole army descended into chaos before the battle had even begun. And yet, despite this, they are capable of dying with dignity, uncomplaining, seeking no quarter; they defend themselves with astonishing ferocity, whether in skirmishes, hand-to-hand combat or great sieges. After each new defeat, they display an extraordinary single-mindedness, an ability to regroup and return to the fray, as resigned and vengeful as ever, yet never for a moment humiliated or disheartened, as though to fight, suffer defeat, flee and regroup were the most natural things in the world. It is something the Spanish themselves call *General Never Mind*. And it means they are to be feared. This is the one thing that never fails them.

As for the cruelty of the Spanish, it is something Simon Desfosseux has witnessed on numerous occasions—the cockfight is a fitting symbol. The resignation with which these laconic people accept their fate rules out all compassion for those who fall into French hands. Even in Egypt the French did not suffer such agonies, horrors and privations as here in Spain, and this has led the French to commit all manner of abuse. Surrounded by an invisible enemy, their fingers are forever on the trigger; they are continually looking over their shoulders, knowing their lives are in constant danger. In this barren, rugged country with its rutted highways, the soldiers of the Imperial Army, weighed down like pack animals come sun, hail, wind or rain, are forced on marches that would traumatize men with no burden to carry. And at every turn, whether at the outset, on the march, or when they finally reach the place where they might rest, there are constant skirmishes with the enemy—not pitched battles where, once fought, survivors might rest awhile around a campfire, but insidious ambushes, throat-slitting, torture and murder. Desfosseux is aware of two recent events that serve to confirm the disturbing nature of the war in Spain. A sergeant and a soldier of the 95th Line Infantry, captured at the Marotera inn, reappeared a week ago, pressed between two boards, their bodies sawn in half. And four days ago, in Rota, a local man and his son returned a horse and equipment belonging to a guard from the 2nd Dragoons who was billeted with them, insisting that he had deserted. Eventually the soldier was found, his throat slit, hidden at the bottom of a well. The man insisted the dragoon had tried to rape his daughter. Father and son were hanged, but only after their hands and feet had been hacked off and their house looted.

"Look at the red cock, Captain—he's holding his own."

Bertoldi is excited. The cock, apparently cornered by its opponent on one side of the ring, suddenly displays hitherto unsuspected reserves of energy; with a furious slash of its beak, it gouges a gaping wound in the breast of the other cock, which totters backward, flapping its clipped wings. Desfosseux glances quickly at the owner's face, seeking some explanation for this turn of events, but the Spaniard is still staring at the bird, seeming utterly unsurprised by both its earlier weakness and its sudden improvement. The cocks launch themselves into the air in a frenzied battle, lashing out with beaks and spurs. Once again the black cock is forced to retreat, flailing, eyes gouged and bleeding, before finally collapsing at the feet of the red cock—which ruthlessly pecks it to death, throws back its blood-spattered head and crows triumphantly. Only now does Desfosseux perceive a slight change in the bird's owner. A fleeting smile, at once jubilant and contemptuous, that vanishes as he gets to his feet, picks up his bird and looks around with cruel, expressionless eyes.

"It just shows you can never trust a cock," says Bertoldi approvingly.

Desfosseux stares at the quivering red bird, drenched in blood—its own, and that of its adversary—and feels a shudder like a premonition run through him.

"Or its owner," he says.

The two artillerymen collect their winnings, divide them up and, swaddled in their gray capes, step out of the cockpit and into the dark night. A dog lying in the shadows starts and struggles to its feet as they appear. In the faint light from the cockpit, the captain can see that one of its hind paws is missing.

"A fine night," says Bertoldi.

Desfosseux assumes his assistant is referring to the money that is weighing down his purse, since a night such as this, with cloudless skies and stars, is something they have both seen many times as soldiers. They approach the old hermitage of Santa Ana, on the brow of the hill that overlooks Chiclana—they are spending two days resting here, on the pretext of collecting supplies for the Cabezuela. By day, this fortified peak with its gun battery affords a panoramic view: sweeping on one side from the salt flats of Isla de Léon and Puerto Real to the Atlantic Ocean and the English stronghold of Sancti Petri Castle at the mouth of the channel; on the other, the snowcapped mountains of the Sierra de Grazelma and Ronda. Now, in the darkness, all that is visible is the outline of the hermitage amid the mastic and carob trees and the pale ribbon of pathway snaking down the hill; a few lights in the distance—probably military campfires—on the Isla de Léon and near the Carraca arsenal; the low, half-moon infinitely reflected in the canals; and the tidal creeks stretching out toward the curve of the horizon. Nestling at the foot of the hill is the village of Chiclana, drab and doleful from all the pillaging, occupation and war, ringed by the vast black nothingness of the pine forests with their perimeter of whitewashed houses, and bisected by a tributary of the Iro River.

"That dog is after us," says Bertoldi.

So it is. The animal, a shadow moving among shadows, is hobbling after them. Turning to look, Simon Desfosseux can make out another three shadows following behind.

"Watch out, the *dagos* are after us too," he warns.

He has hardly finished the sentence when the Spaniards fall on them, steel glittering in the darkness like lightning flashes. Before he has time to draw his sword, Desfosseux feels a wrench on his arm and hears the blade slice through his cape. Simon Desfosseux is no intrepid warrior, but neither is he about to stand there and let them cut his throat. He ducks to avoid the next thrust, launches himself against his attacker, attempting unsuccessfully to knock him down and draw his sword. Close by he hears furious shouts, ragged breathing, the sounds of a tussle. For an instant he wonders how Bertoldi is faring, but he is too busy trying to save his own skin for this to be more than a fleeting thought.

"Help!" he screams.

A blow to the face leaves him seeing stars. The blade slashes at his cloak again and he feels a trembling in his groin. *They're going to butcher me like a pig*, he thinks. The men struggle with him as they try to pin down his arms—so they can stab him, he thinks in a burst of panic. They smell of sweat and oily smoke. Now he thinks he can hear Bertoldi scream. With a desperate effort the captain manages to break free, throws himself down the hill and rolls a short distance between the rocks and brambles. This gives him just enough time to slip his right hand into the pocket of his cape and take out the gun he is carrying. It is a short, small-caliber pistol that would look more at home in the hands of a perfumed dandy than a military officer, but it is lightweight, easy to carry and at short range can put a bullet in a man's gut as easily a cavalry pistol *modèle An XIII.** Cocking it with the palm of his left hand, Desfosseux just has time to raise the gun and aim it at the nearest shadow bearing down on him. The powder flash lights up a pair of startled eyes in a whiskered, dark-skinned face, then there is a groan and the sound of the figure stumbling backward.

"Help!" Desfosseux yells again.

In answer he hears something in Spanish that sounds like a curse. The dark shapes that had been wrestling with Desfosseux now rush past him down the hill. The Frenchman, who has knelt and managed to unsheath his sword, swings at them as they pass, but slices the air without making contact. A shadowy figure leaps at Desfosseux, who is about to stab again when he recognizes Bertoldi's distraught voice.

"Captain? Are you all right, Captain?"

The guards are running down the path from the hermitage, carrying a lantern, light glittering on their bayonets. Bertoldi helps the captain to his feet. In the light of the lantern, Desfosseux can see the lieutenant's face is covered in blood.

"It is a miracle we got out alive," Bertoldi says, his voice quavering.

They are now surrounded by half a dozen soldiers, asking what happened. While his adjutant explains, Simon Desfosseux slots his sword back into its scabbard and returns his pistol to his pocket. Then he looks down the hill for his attackers, who have vanished into the darkness. An image flashes into his mind of the red cock, cunning and cruel, strutting around the cockpit, hackles raised, drenched in blood.

"She was some whore from Santa María," says Cadalso.

Rogelio Tizón looks down at the form covered with a blanket; only the feet are visible. The corpse is lying on the ground, next to the wall of an old abandoned warehouse on the corner of the Calle del Laurel: a dark, narrow, crumbling building with no roof. The stumps of three thick beams frame the sky above the remains of a staircase which leads nowhere.

Crouching down, the comisario pulls back the blanket. This time,

---

* A French flintlock cavalry pistol first used circa 1806. Year 13 refers to years post the French Revolution.

though accustomed to such horrors, he feels overwhelmed. From Santa María, according to Cadalso. In his mind, memories interweave with ominous forebodings. The memory of a naked girl, lying facedown in the half-light. Her entreaties. Please, no. Please. *Please don't let it be her,* he thinks, overcome. Too obvious a twist of fate. Too much of a coincidence. As he reveals the flayed back, between the tatters of clothing torn to the waist, the stench rips at his nostrils and his throat like a claw. This is not the stench of decomposition—the girl can only have been dead since last night—it is the strange smell that has become all too familiar: the smell of flesh whipped so viciously, so deeply, that the bones and the entrails are revealed. It smells like a slaughterhouse in summer.

"Holy Mother of God," exclaims Cadalso behind him. "I'll never get used to what he does to them."

Holding his breath, Tizón takes a handful of the girl's hair—filthy, matted, plastered to her forehead with dried blood—and pulls gently, lifting the head so that he can see her face. Rigor mortis has already set in, so the movement also lifts the stiff neck a little. The comisario stares at what looks like a grubby waxen mask, marked with purple bruises. Dead meat. Almost a thing. Or perhaps there is no "almost"—there is nothing human about the yellowish complexion, the milky eyes staring sightlessly beneath half-closed lids, the mouth still gagged with a kerchief intended to stifle her screams. At least it's not *her,* he thinks as he lets go of the dead girl's hair. It is not, as he feared, the girl he met after his conversation with La Caracola. The naked body in which, to his horror, he glimpsed his own abyss.

He covers the corpse with the blanket, and gets to his feet. A number of people have appeared on their balconies and he knows that this time it will be impossible to keep the death secret. *This is what we have come to,* he thinks. He quickly weighs up the pros and cons, the immediate consequences of the event. Even in the exceptional circumstances that currently prevail in the city, five identical murders is too many. There is no room for maneuver. At best, he might manage to avoid a public scandal, to keep the gossipmongers and journalists at bay, but he will still have a great deal of explaining to do to the Intendant and the governor. They haven't got time for hunches, theories and experiments. To them, only the facts are important; they will want a culprit. And if one is not forthcoming, they will need someone to blame. The murderer's head on a plate, or his own.

Swinging his cane thoughtfully, his other hand in the pocket of his frockcoat, hat tilted over his eyes, Tizón contemplates the narrow street, divided in two by a right angle: on one side, it leads toward the Santiago district, on the other toward Villalobos. No shells have fallen here. This was the first thing he checked when he learned that a body had been discovered. The closest—a shell that did not explode—fell two weeks ago next to the building site of the new cathedral. This means one of two things: either his hypothesis is unfounded, or it will be confirmed in the coming minutes or hours by a French bomb. Looking up, he coldly observes the surrounding buildings, the facades and the terraces that, given their orientation, are more likely to be hit by a bomb fired from the far side of the bay. His attention is drawn to a dozen or so neighbors peering down from their balconies. He should warn them, he thinks. Should inform them that any moment now a shell is likely to fall right here, maiming or killing them. He would be curious to see their faces. Get the hell out of this place as fast as you can, because a bomb is about to drop. A little bird told me. Or, in official terminology: evacuate the Calle de Laurel and the surrounding area immediately for—hours? days?—on the basis that the Commissioner for Districts, Vagrants and Transients suspects that a murderer is operating according to strange magnetic attractions and mysterious coordinates. The peals of laughter would be heard as far as the Trocadero. And it is unlikely that the Intendant and the governor would find it amusing.

In the coming minutes or hours, he thinks again . . . He steps into the street and looks around. This very moment—the thought sends a shudder of fear through him—it is possible nothing will happen, or that a bomb will fall from the sky and explode right where he is standing. As it did last time on the Calle del Viento. That cat, blown to pieces. The thought of it makes him move with exaggerated care, as though a few steps this way or that will determine whether he becomes the point of impact of a French shell. Then, for a brief instant, as if he has found a point where the very air itself has disappeared, leaving only a strange vacuum, Tizón is overcome by a disturbing feeling of unreality. As though he is walking along a clifftop, he thinks, and feels the powerful lure of the abyss, a vertigo he has never noticed. Or barely. Excitement might also describe the sensation. Curiosity, fascination or uncertainty. There is something darkly pleasurable about it. Unsettled by this train of thought, the policeman suddenly feels exposed, physically vulnerable. This is how it must feel for a soldier to clamber out of his trench within range of an invisible enemy. He tosses his head, glancing around as though trying to shake off some baleful dream. The neighbors continue to watch from their balconies; Cadalso stands over the body of the girl; the nightwatchmen on the corner keep busybodies away. As he comes to his senses again, Tizón glances around quickly, looking for the most sheltered spot on the street; as he makes rapid calculations, he tries to take into account the fact that the French are firing at the city from the east.

Next comes the murderer, of course. Standing in a doorway, he considers the word *next*. Not without a sense of irony. In fact, he is surprised by his own uncertainty about the order of his priorities. Bombs and murderers. Places that have a *before* and an *after*. The fact is, he realizes, he finds it extraordinarily vexing to have to deal with one aspect of the problem without resolving that which is most unclear. But now there has been a fifth victim, he has no choice. The prime suspect has been located and his superiors are clamoring for a name. Indeed, as soon as news of this fresh horror spreads through the city, they will be pounding on their desks and demanding that Tizón produce a suspect. This time the news will spread, however many mouths he manages to silence. All these stupid people on their balconies, the newspapers piecing together the facts. Thinking back. With this degree of pressure, all the other elements will have to wait, or be cast aside. The comisario is infuriated by this possibility—or, more likely, this certainty. It would be disappointing to find himself obliged to neutralize the killer without first understanding the curious rules of physics that determine his game. To know whether he is the absolute author or a mere agent in this complex web. The key to the puzzle, or merely a piece.

"What do we make of this man Fumagal?"

He has walked back to where Cadalso is standing, staring down at the blanket-covered corpse as he methodically picks his nose. His assistant makes a noncommittal gesture. His job is not to interpret the facts, but to note them down meticulously and inform his boss. Cadalso is one of those whose sleep is never troubled. Like a baby.

"He's still being watched, señor. Two teams worked in shifts outside his house last night."

"And?"

There is an awkward silence while Cadalso tries to work out whether this monosyllable requires a detailed answer. "And nothing, señor."

Tizón taps the ground with the ferrule at the end of his cane.

"He didn't go out last night?"

"Not that we know of. The officers swear he was at home all afternoon. Then he went out to dinner at a little tavern, La Perdiz, stopped off briefly at the Café del Ángel and came home early. The lights in his windows went out at about a quarter past nine."

"A little too early . . . Are you sure he didn't go out again?"

"That's what the lookouts said. Those who were on duty swear they didn't move from the spot during their shifts and the suspect did not even appear in his doorway."

"The streets are dark. He could have got out some other way . . . out the back . . ."

Cadalso knits his brow, and considers this possibility for a moment.

"It would be difficult," he says. "The house doesn't have a back door. The only way would be for him to lower himself from a window onto the patio of the house next door. But if I may say so, señor, it doesn't seem likely."

Tizón brings his face close to his assistant's.

"What if he went out on to the terrace, and from there crossed over to the house next door?"

A pregnant silence. Guilty, this time.

"Cadalso . . . I am going to rip your head off."

Tizón's assistant hangs his head in shame.

"*Imbeciles!*" spits Tizón. "You bunch of cretinous imbeciles."

Cadalso babbles some ridiculous excuse which the comisario brushes aside with a wave of the hand gripping the cane. He would rather deal with the practicalities. Time is short and they need to focus. First and foremost they must make sure the bird does not fly the coop.

"What is he doing now?"

Cadalso looks at Tizón meekly, a whipped dog trying to win back its master's favor. "He's still in the house, Señor Comisario. Everything seems normal . . . I doubled the surveillance, just in case."

"How many guards are there now?"

"Six."

"That means you tripled it, cretin."

Mental arithmetic. Cádiz is a chessboard. There are clever moves and perfect moves. What marks out an intelligent player is foresight and patience. Tizón would like to be intelligent, but he knows he is merely cunning. And experienced. That will have to do, he concludes wearily.

"Get the body out of here. To the morgue."

"Aren't we going to wait for Tía Perejil?"

"No. We don't need to check whether this girl was a virgin like the others."

"Why not, señor?"

"You told me yourself she was a whore . . . idiot!"

He walks out into the middle of the street and looks around, trying to recapture what he felt a moment ago when he was considering the possibility—one that still worries him a little—that a bomb might fall on him. It is not something concrete, only a faint, almost imperceptible, impression. Something to do with sound and silence, with wind and the absence of wind, with the density—or the texture, if that is the right word—of the air at this precise spot in the street. And this is not the first time he has felt it. Looking around, moving very slowly, Rogelio Tizón racks his brains. He is now convinced that he has experienced precisely the same sensation before, or its effects—a strange sense of déjà vu, when the mind seems to recognize something that happened in the past, in other circumstances or another life.

The Calle del Viento, he suddenly remembers. He experienced the same sensation of emptiness in the derelict house where the last dead girl was found. That same peculiar certainty that, in a specific place at a particular moment, the very air seemed to change, as though this particular spot were somehow different from the rest. A void, a point of absolute nothingness, isolated from its surroundings by an invisible bell jar, draining it of air. Still staggered by this discovery, he takes a few random steps, trying to find the spot where he was standing earlier. Eventually, not far from the body, at the right angle formed by the street, he once again has the impression of penetrating the same singular, constricted space where the air is still, sounds seem muffled and distant, and even the temperature feels different. An almost perfect sensory vacuum. The feeling lasts only for a moment, then fades. But it is enough to make the comisario's hair stand on end.

CHAPTER ELEVEN

ᗝᗢ

In recent days the winter westerlies have brought hazy sunsets to the city. The sky has long since veered from red to bluish gray, thence to black. On the bay, flags have been hauled down, and the still shapes of the anchored ships have melted into the darkness. These early hours of night bring an impatient dew, leaving railings damp, cobblestones slippery and the ground glistening under the lone, ghostly light—a lantern on the corner of the Calle del Baluarte and the Calle San Francisco. It does little to dispel the shadows, but is surprising, like an altar lamp in a dark, abandoned church.

"Nonsense, I won't hear of you walking home alone! Santos!"

"Yes, Doña Lolita?"

"Fetch a lantern and escort the señora."

At her doorway, a woolen shawl about her shoulders, her hair plaited into a coil at the base of her neck, Lolita Palma bids goodnight to Curra Vilches. Her friend protests that she is perfectly capable of walking on her own for the short distance to her house in Pedro Conde, opposite the Customs House. This is Cádiz, and at her age she has no need of an escort. Really, a fan to swat flies is all she needs!

"Don't annoy me, my dear," she objects, raising the wide lapels of her cape. "And don't trouble poor Santos: he is having his dinner!"

"Not another word," Lolita says. "With things as they are, I won't have you walking around on your own."

"What twaddle! I'm telling you, I'm off."

"Absolutely not . . . Santos!"

Curra Vilches insists, but Lolita refuses to let her leave. It is late, and the rumors about women being murdered in the city have everyone on edge. With a killer on the loose, this is no time to stand on ceremony. The authorities maintain that the rumors are merely fabrications, and there have been no reports in the newspapers; but Cádiz is a parish pump, and the word on the street is that the murders are real, the police are unable to catch the killer and the military have gagged the newspapers, trampling over the freedom of the press under the pretext that there is a war on and it would create widespread panic. Everyone knows that.

The manservant returns carrying a tinplate oil lamp, and Curra Vilches finally sees reason. She has spent the evening at Lolita's house helping her out. The last day of every month in Cádiz is traditionally reserved for stock-taking and balancing the books, meaning that offices and businesses are open until midnight; so, too, are currency exchanges, banks, importers and shipping agents. In a routine she inherited from her father, Lolita Palma spent the afternoon supervising the Palma e Hijos employees in the ground floor office while they did the accounts; Curra kept her company, oversaw the domestic chores and tended to her mother.

"She seemed in good form. Given her condition."

"Go on, go. Your husband will be wanting to have dinner."

"Him?" Curra Vilches adopts an insolent pose, hands on her hips beneath her cape. "With things as they are in Cádiz, he is up to his neck in correspondence and account books just like you . . . He barely notices I'm there. This would be the perfect day to commit adultery. For married women in Cádiz, the last day of every month is an extenuating circumstance . . . any confessor would make allowances."

"Don't be so ridiculous, Curra," Lolita says, laughing.

"Mock if you must. But what doctors prescribe for days such as these is a lieutenant in the grenadiers, a naval officer or something . . . a man who knows nothing about currency exchanges or double-entry bookkeeping, but brings a flush to your cheeks and has you fanning yourself whenever he is within shooting range. With elegant whiskers and tight-fitting breeches."

"Don't be so vulgar."

"I am nothing of the kind, my dear. It is you who is being dull. I tell you, if I were single and in your position, it would be a very different story. I wouldn't spend my life with half a dozen penpushers shut up in some gloomy office, or pressing lettuce leaves into albums."

"Go on, get out of here . . . Santos, light the way for Doña Curra."

The lamp lights the pavement in front of Curra Vilches, who wraps herself up in her cape and walks behind the old manservant.

"You're wasting away, my dear," she says, turning back one last time. "Take my word for it . . . you're throwing your life away."

Leaning against the gate, Lolita Palma laughs into the darkness. "Go . . . and be careful, you brazen hussy."

"Goodnight, Mother Superior!"

Lolita walks back down the path, closing the gate behind her, and crosses between the ferns planted in large tubs in the tiled courtyard. Next to the well, a large candelabrum illuminates the arches and columns of the marble staircase leading to the upper floors and their glassed galleries. A few steps to the right, a door leads off the patio to the ground-floor offices, with another door, used for deliveries and tradesmen, opening on to the Calle de los Doblones. Here are the fine goods store, the small parlor, the main commercial office and a second office where the manager and two clerks—a junior and a bookkeeper—work by lamplight, leaning over desks strewn with copies of letters, account books, bills and invoices. When Lolita comes in, stepping around the charcoal brazier that heats the room, they nod in greeting—she has forbidden them from standing up when she enters the office. Only Molina, the head clerk, who has been with the firm for thirty-four years, gets to his feet, coming to greet her from behind the frosted-glass panel that demarcates his workspace. He is wearing black oversleeves with ink stains, and has a goose quill tucked behind his ear.

"I have calculated the unpaid invoices from Havana, Doña Lolita . . . at one and a half percent, it comes to 3,700 *reales* in protest charges."

"What are the chances we might recoup any of it?"

"Very slight, I fear."

She listens to her chief clerk, careful not to let her anxiety show—just a brief frown that might be taken for concentration. Carry it forward. One more loss. Equivalent to a year's salary for one of her employees. The weariness she feels is not simply due to the day's work, which is not yet finished. The French blockade, the general lack of liquidity, the problems in the Americas, all these things are slowly strangling the merchants of Cádiz, despite the apparent boom in business some are experiencing due to the war. Palma e Hijos is no exception.

"Log it in the accounts ledger. And when you have the Manchester and Liverpool invoices ready, bring them to my office." Lolita glances around at the clerks. "Have you all eaten?"

"Not yet."

"Tell Rosas to prepare something. Some cold meats and wine. You have twenty minutes."

She pushes the door to the little parlor which leads to the Calle de los Doblones, with its engravings of seascapes and its dark wooden frieze, crosses the hall and goes into the main office. Unlike the private office upstairs, which she usually uses outside business hours, this one is large and imposing, its decor unchanged since her father's or grandfather's time: a large desk and a bookcase, two worn leather armchairs, three model ships under glass, a framed map of the bay of Cádiz on the wall, an almanac of the Royal Company of the Philippines, an English grandfather clock, a metal map cabinet in one corner, and a thin barometer that constantly reads *Stormy*. On the desk—mahogany, like the rest of the furniture in the house—are a blue-glass oil lamp, a hand bell, a brass ashtray that belonged to her father, a Chinese porcelain inkstand, a portfolio and two books with marked pages: *Promptuario Aritmético* by Rendón and Fuentes, and *The Art of Double-Entry Bookkeeping* by Luque and Leyva. Lifting her skirts—she is wearing a simple brown cashmere skirt with a short jacket, allowing her to work in comfort—Lolita sits down at her desk. She rearranges her shawl about her shoulders, turns up the oil lamp and stares at the empty chair opposite. Don Emilio Sánchez Guinea was sitting there some hours ago, mid-afternoon, as they discussed the current state of affairs—which, in the opinion of the heiress to Palma e Hijos (or, indeed, any clear-sighted person in Cádiz), looks uncertain. The precise term Sánchez Guinea used was *harrowing*.

"People don't seem to realize what's happening, *hija*. When this war and this liberal pox is over, when we have lost the Americas for good, that will be the end of us . . . Political hysteria does not create business; nor does it put food on the table."

It was a frank and honest professional discussion. Neither of them labored under any illusions about the hard times that were to come. The complications of converting treasury bonds into cash; the sluggish flow of funds into the city; problems with investments in marine insurance; and, most of all, the difficulties for many businesses of keeping their credit, which was dependent as much on one's reputation as it was on discretion about other people's predicaments.

"I'm tired of fighting, Lolita. For twenty years this city has had to deal with all the misfortunes of the world. The wars with France and with England, the upheaval in the Americas, the epidemics . . . Add to that a government in disarray, exorbitant taxes, the loans to the Crown and to the Cortes, the capital losses in territories occupied by the French. And now we're being told that there are corsairs in Río de la Plata working for the rebels . . . Too much fighting, *hija*, too much disappointment. I feel old just thinking about it. I wish this madness would end, so I could retire to my *finca* in El Puerto—if I ever get it back . . . Well, I suppose it's just a matter of patience. I only hope I will live to see it . . . Luckily I have my son, who is gradually taking over the helm."

"Miguel is a good boy, Don Emilio. Clever and hardworking."

The old merchant smiled sadly. "Such a shame that your father and I never managed to get the two of you . . ."

The words hung in the air. Lolita smiled too, a gentle, reproachful smile. This had long been a delicate subject.

"He is a good boy," she said again. "Too good for me."

"I wish you had married him."

"Don't say that. You have a wonderful daughter-in-law; you have two beautiful grandchildren and another on the way."

Don Emilio shook his head forlornly. "Being clever and hardwork-

ing may not be enough for us to get through this. I don't envy him the
days to come . . . What lies ahead for all you young people when this
war is over? The world will never be the same again."

A silence. Sánchez Guinea smiled affectionately. "You should . . ."

"Don't start, Don Emilio."

"Your sister has no children, nor does it look like she will have any.
If you . . . I don't know." He looked around sorrowfully. "It would be
such a pity if all this . . . you know."

"If the House of Palma should end with me?"

"You're still a young woman."

Lolita raised a warning hand. She never allowed anyone, not even
Don Emilio Sánchez Guinea, to venture any further on this subject.
Not even her dear friend Curra Vilches.

"Please, let's talk about business."

The old merchant shifted in his seat uncomfortably. "I apologize,
hija . . . I have no wish to interfere."

"You are forgiven."

They talked about business matters: freight, Customs duties, ships,
the difficulty of opening up new markets to compensate for those lost
in the Americas. Sánchez Guinea, aware that Palma e Hijos had recently begun trading with Russia, tried to sound out Lolita. Conscious
of this—affection and business interests do not mix—she confined herself to the superficial details: two trips made by the frigate *José Vicuña*
to St. Petersburg with cargoes of wine, cinchona bark and cork with a
ballast of salt on the voyage out; castor oil and Siberian musk—much
cheaper than that from Tonkin—on the return. Nothing that Sánchez
Guinea and his son did not already know.

"You also seem to be doing well with flour."

Lolita said that she had no reason to complain. Importing flour
from North America—there are fifteen hundred barrels of it in warehouses at the dock—has proved a lifeline for Palma e Hijos in recent
times.

"For Russia too?"

"Perhaps. If I can manage to ship it before it is spoiled by the
damp."

"I wish you every success. Times are hard . . . just look at poor Ale-jandro Schmidt. He lost the *Bella Mercedes* and all its cargo in the shallows off Rota."

Lolita nodded. Obviously she had already heard. A month ago, strong headwinds and treacherous seas had forced the boat aground on the occupied French coast, where it was looted as soon as the storm passed: two hundred boxes of Chinese cinnamon, three hundred sacks of pepper from the Maluku Islands, and a thousand yards of Canton linen. It would take some time for the house of Schmidt to recover from such a loss, if indeed it ever did. In these times, when too much was sometimes risked on a single voyage, the loss of a ship could be fatal.

"I have a business proposition that might interest you."

Lolita looked at Don Emilio warily. She recognized the tone. "This business—would it be done by the right hand or the left?"

A pause. Sánchez Guinea lit a fat cigar from the oil lamp.

"Don't get ahead of yourself," he said eventually, narrowing his eyes with sly charm. "What I am proposing is a good venture."

Lolita leaned back in the leather armchair and shook her head mistrustfully. "The left hand, then," she concluded. "As you know, I do not like to stray far from the everyday."

"That is what you said about the *Culebra*. And you see, that turned out to be an excellent business proposition . . . That reminds me— I don't know whether you know, but the Tavira Tower has just hoisted a black ball. They have spotted a frigate away to windward and a cutter making its way up the coast with the west wind. Did you know?"

"No. I have been dealing with paperwork all day."

"The cutter might well be ours. I assume it will round the lighthouse tonight and, if the wind doesn't change, it should be back in the bay tomorrow morning."

With some effort, Lolita dismissed Pépé Lobo from her thoughts. This was neither the place nor the time, she thought.

"Let us talk about something else, Don Emilio. The *Culebra* is a corsair ship with a Letter of Marque and Reprisal. Smuggling is a very different matter."

"And yet half our rivals engage in it without any compunction."

"That does not matter. There was a time when you yourself . . ."

She fell silent, out of respect. Sánchez Guinea stared at the gray ash forming at the end of his cigar.

"You're right, *hija*. There was a time when I would have had no truck with such business. Neither smuggling nor slave trading, although your grandfather Enrique was happy to trade in Negro slaves . . . But none of that matters. Times have changed . . . we have to adapt. What with the French and the greed of our own authorities, I am not about to allow myself to be fleeced." He leaned forward slightly, ash falling on to the mahogany desk. "What I am talking about . . ."

Lolita Palma gently pushed the ashtray toward him. "I don't wish to know."

Sánchez Guinea, cigar clenched between his teeth, looked at her intently. Persuasively.

"It is *more or less* honest: seven hundred hundredweight of cocoa, two hundred boxes of cigars and a hundred and fifty bales of leaf tobacco. All of it left in Santa María cove at night . . . An English xebec will bring it from Gibraltar."

"What about the City Hall, what about Customs?"

"That is by the way. Almost."

She shook her head again, affectionately. Gave a short, disbelieving laugh. "This is contraband, pure and simple. Barefaced smuggling. And it cannot be done in secret, Don Emilio."

"Who says it will be? This is Cádiz, remember. Officially, we will have nothing to do with it. Everything has already been organized. All the hinges are oiled, so nothing will squeak. There is no problem."

"Then why do you need me?"

"To share the financial risk. And the profits, of course."

"I'm not interested. And it is not because of the risks, Don Emilio. I know that as far as you are concerned . . ."

Sánchez Guinea leaned back, finally resigned to her decision. He gazed sadly at the pristine ashtray, gleaming against the dark wood, burnished by the touch of three generations.

"I know. Don't worry, *hija* . . . I know."

Through the closed window, a fleeting sound of voices comes from the Calle de los Doblones—young men from La Viña or La Caleta talking and laughing on their way to a fandango in some tavern in El Boquete, a few notes played on a guitar. Then the night and the street fall silent again. Alone in her office, Lolita Palma stares at the empty chair on the far side of the desk. She can still remember her old family friend's crestfallen air as he got up and walked to the door; she can still remember every word of their conversation. She cannot stop picturing Schmidt's *Bella Mercedes*, grounded in the shallows near Rota, its cargo looted by the French. Palma e Hijos would find it difficult to recover from such a blow. These days, they take a risk with every ship and every crossing, at the mercy of corsairs and the fickle moods of the sea.

Molina, the chief clerk, knocks then pops his head round the door.

"Excuse me, Doña Lolita. I have brought the invoices for Manchester and Liverpool."

"Leave them with me. I'll talk to you about them later."

A single peal rings out from the nearby tower of San Francisco; its watchman signals when he sees a flash from the French gun batteries at the Trocadero, one peal for every bomb. Moments later, a blast causes the windows to rattle a little—a grenade exploding not far away. Lolita Palma and the chief clerk look at each other in silence. When Molina takes his leave, she barely leafs through the papers he has brought, but sits motionless, shawl around her shoulders, her hands in a circle of lamplight. The word *corsairs* runs through her mind. Just before sunset, she left the office and called in to see her mother, where she found Curra Vilches sitting next to the bed, as patient as only a friend can be, playing cards with her. Then she and Santos went up to the lookout tower on the terrace and, resting the English telescope against the window, spent a long time watching the cutter making its way northward, slowly working to windward against the hazy red of sunset, a couple of miles west of the city walls.

THE NARROW, ORDERLY streets that run between the lofty houses of well-to-do Cádiz seem to blend into a gray and sullen sky which thickens to the west of the city. It is a sky that promises wind and rain, determines Pépé Lobo with a glance. For days now, the barometers have been continuously falling, and the corsair is glad that the *Culebra* is safely anchored on the bay by half a ton of iron rather than out on the open sea, furling sails and battening down everything against the storm. Yesterday the cutter dropped anchor in three fathoms of water among the other merchant ships, opposite the jetty by the Puerta de Mar, aligned with the breakwater at San Felipe and the tidal shallows at Los Corrales. It had been a calm night, with a wet, still mild westerly breeze. There were several flashes from the gun battery at the Cabezuela, but the shells that whistled through the darkness above the masts of the ships did not disturb anyone's sleep.

Having set foot on terra firma at first light, just three hours ago, Pépé Lobo walks along the Calle de San Francisco toward the square and the church, feeling as if the ground is still lurching and rolling— the inevitable effect of forty-seven days at sea. He is dressed formally, in a manner befitting a captain on shore: dark breeches of coarse serge, shoes with silver buckles, a blue jacket with brass buttons and a black sailor's bicorn hat, with no trim but sporting the red cockade that marks him out as corsair to the king. This attire is invaluable when arriving in port and attempting to deal with the inevitable bureaucratic, judicial and Customs procedures; given the way things are in the city, it is al- most impossible to get anything done without wearing some kind of uniform. There are half a dozen different kinds at Cosí's teashop, both inside and at the tables on the corner of the Calle del Baluarte: mem- bers of the Cádiz Volunteers, an officer from the Royal Armada and two British soldiers wearing red coats, legs bare beneath their kilts. The place is also thronged with civilians, both men and women; among them it is easy to identify the journalists from *El Conciso* because of their ink-stained fingers and the papers spilling out of their pockets, and the immigrants from French-occupied territories because of their indolent air and old-fashioned, patched and threadbare clothes. Sev- eral of them are sitting idly around tables on which there is nothing more expensive than a glass of water.

A beggar is seated on the ground, leaning against the wall and blocking a clockmaker's doorway. The owner tells him to move on, but the man pays him no heed. In fact, he makes an obscene gesture. As Pépé Lobo passes, the beggar looks up at him.

"Spare a little change, Brigadier, for the love of God . . ."

Pépé Lobo is surprised by the barely concealed impertinence of the man's tone, the almost mocking way he embellishes the corsair's rank. Without stopping, Lobo gives the beggar a quick glance: his gray hair and beard are dirty and unkempt. It is impossible to guess his age: he could be thirty, he could be fifty. He is wrapped in a long, brown coat that has been patched and darned and, in an attempt to elicit pity, the right leg of his breeches is pinned up to reveal the stump where his limb was amputated below the knee. Just one of the hordes of men and women scratching a living on the streets of Cádiz; they are constantly moved on by the police toward the area by the docks, but return to the fray every day, scrabbling for what crumbs they can find in this part of the city. The corsair carries on walking, then suddenly stops, his attention drawn to a bluish tattoo, faded by time, on the beggar's forearm. It looks like an anchor flanked by a cannon and a flag.

"What was your ship?"

The beggar looks into his eyes, unsettled at first. Eventually, he looks down as though he understands. He stares at his own tattoo, then looks up again at Pépé Lobo.

"The *San Agustín* . . . Eighty guns. Commanded by Don Felipe Cajigal."

"She was lost at Trafalgar."

The beggar gives a toothless grimace that once upon a time might have been a smile. He gestures to the exposed stump. "She's not the only thing that was lost there."

Lobo stands motionless for a moment. "You've had no help, I suppose," he says finally.

"Oh, I've had help, señor . . . My wife, she went out to work as a whore."

Now it is the corsair who nods slowly, thoughtfully. Then he slips a hand into his pocket and takes out a *duro* on which the head of old King Carlos looks off somewhere to the right as though all this has nothing to do with him. As he takes the silver coin, the beggar looks up curi-

ously at Pépé Lobo. Then he lurches forward a little, draws himself up
in a surge of unexpected dignity, and brings two fingers to his temple
in salute.

"Gunner Cipriano Ortega, sir. Second battery."

Captain Lobo goes on his way. And with him goes the grim sadness
of any sailor who has braved the seas and the fortunes of war when he
sees another sailor crippled and destitute. It is not so much pity as
a concern for his own fate—for the future that lies in wait after the
insidious hazards of his profession, the ravages of battle, injuries from
bullets, cannonballs and shell fragments. An acute awareness of one's
own vulnerability, constantly at the mercy of time and fortune—or
misfortune—which might well cast a broken, miserable wretch up onto
the shore, just as the sea throws up the shattered hulk of a shipwreck.
Perhaps one day, he too will end up like this, thinks Pépé Lobo as he
walks away from the beggar. But as he does so, he brushes the thought
aside.

He spots Lolita Palma, wearing black taffeta and her shawl, emerging from a bookshop, her umbrella under one arm, slipping on her
gloves. She is accompanied by her maid, Mari Paz, who is carrying
some packages. This is not a chance encounter. The corsair has been
looking for her since he left the Sánchez Guineas's office in El Palillero
half an hour ago. He called at her house on the Calle del Baluarte,
where the steward, who claimed not to know when his mistress would
return home, suggested he look here. The manservant said she was
headed for the Botanic Gardens and then to the bookshops on the
Plaza San Agustín, or perhaps on San Francisco. And when books are
involved, he said, she is usually gone for some time.

"What a surprise, Captain."

She looks handsome, the corsair notes, just as he remembered. Her
skin is still firm and soft, her face pleasing, her eyes serene. She wears
no hat or any other adornment, aside from a pearl necklace and pair of
simple silver earrings. Her hair, pinned in a chignon by a tortoiseshell
comb, and the delicate Turkish shawl—black, embroidered with red
flowers—draped casually about her shoulders give a touch of individu-
ality to the simple dress that elegantly accentuates her waist. The very

picture of a lady of Cádiz, the corsair smiles to himself. It is obvious in her breeding, in her manner. Two thousand five hundred years of history, or thereabouts—Lobo is not so well versed in things that do not relate to his profession—cannot but leave a mark upon a city and its women. Even upon Lolita Palma.

"Welcome back to terra firma."

Pépé Lobo finds himself attempting to justify his presence here. He has a number of pressing matters he needs to resolve this morning, and Don Emilio Sánchez Guinea suggested he speak to her before dealing with them. He can accompany her back to her office, if she would like. Or he could call on her to discuss the matter at a more convenient time. As he says all this, the corsair watches her look up and study the gray sky.

"Let us talk now, if you like. Before it begins to rain . . . I usually take a walk at this time of day."

Lolita Palma dismisses her maid, who walks off with the packages toward the Calle del Baluarte and stands, staring at the corsair as though it is now his turn to make the decisions. Lobo hesitates and then, with a gesture, proposes two alternatives: the nearby café, or a stroll along Calle del Camino past the Alameda, toward the city walls and the sea.

"I would prefer the Alameda," she says.

The corsair nods as he puts on his hat again. He is irritated with himself, and amused—surprised and amused, in fact—by his irritation. By the strange shyness that prickles at his eyes, his hands; that makes his voice hoarse. And at his age . . . Never before has he felt intimidated by a beautiful woman. It is almost funny. But the serene gaze, the composure of this woman facing him—his superior and his partner, he twice reminds himself—kindles in him a pleasurable feeling of tranquility. A shared peace. A close, strangely accessible warmth, as though he might simply reach out and place his hand on Lolita Palma's graceful neck and feel the beat of her pulse, the delicate heat of her flesh. He laughs to himself—she looks at him quizzically for a moment and he fears that something in his face has betrayed his thought, or his silent laugh—then dismisses this absurd idea, and returns to his senses.

"Are you sure you don't mind walking, Captain?"

"Not at all."

They stroll down the middle of the cobbled street, he on her left, as he informs her of the latest news. The *Culebra*'s recent campaign was not unsuccessful, he explains, struggling to concentrate. Five captures, including an important ship, a French schooner flying under a Portuguese flag sailing from Tarragona to Sanlúcar with a cargo of fine fabric, shoe leather, saddles, bales of wool and letters. Lobo took the letters to the naval authorities, but everything seems to indicate that the ship and its cargo will be declared a fair capture. The other four vessels are of lesser value: two tartanes, a pink and a felucca carrying herring, raisins, iron staves and salt tuna. Not much more. Aboard the felucca, a Portuguese smuggling ship out of Faro, was a sack containing two hundred and fifty gold pieces bearing the head of King Pepe.

"Since the felucca may prove to be a problem when it comes before the Prize Court," he says, "I took the precaution of depositing the gold under seal in Gibraltar so that no one can touch it."

"Were there any problems with the other ships?"

"No. They all surrendered at the first shot. The felucca tried to mislead us at first, hoping its flag would offer it protection, but then it tried its luck, forcing us to chase it from Tarifa to Carnero point. But it didn't fire the two four-pounders it had aboard."

"And our men, are they all well?"

It pleases him that she said *our men* rather than *your men*.

"All well, thank you."

"So what is this matter you wished to discuss with me?"

The French have tightened their grip on Tarifa, he explains, just as they did on Algeciras. It seems likely they will soon control that whole stretch of coastline. There is talk that General Laval has laid siege—or is about to do so—with ten or twelve thousand soldiers, cavalry and artillery. Every possible aid is being sent from Cádiz, but it does not amount to much. There are not enough ships and the English, though they have a colonel and a number of men in the city, are not prepared to divert any of their vessels. The most serious problem is communication, the ability to send and receive dispatches. Don Cayetano Valdés, the commander of the bay, claims he cannot spare a single gunboat.

"In short," he concludes, "the *Culebra* is being commandeered by the Royal Armada for a month."

"You mean they have requisitioned it?"

"They have not gone quite so far."

"What do they plan to do with it?"

"Run official dispatches to and from Tarifa. The *Culebra* is swift and she handles well . . . It makes sense."

Lolita Palma does not seem overly concerned. She has obviously already had some word of this, the corsair thinks. Some prior warning.

"You would continue to command the ship, I assume?"

Lobo smiles confidently. "I have not been told otherwise."

"It is too much . . . We could not possibly agree without adequate compensation . . . And with things the way they are, the Armada is in no position to pay anyone. Like everything else, it is completely bankrupt . . . or worse."

The Sánchez Guineas offered the same opinion, the corsair tells her evenly. However, it is unlikely the Armada would replace him as captain of the cutter. Officers are also in short supply, with every man available working for the fleet patrolling the bay and the canals.

"Whatever the case may be," he adds, "the Crown will take care of the cost of equipment and the crew's salaries, and will defer our Letter of Marque for as long as the ship is in service . . . I have little faith that they will pay the crew, to be honest. They don't even pay their own men. But they cannot refuse us the equipment. We can make the most of it to stock up on gunpowder and other supplies and to mend the rigging. I can also try to get gunlocks for the cannons."

Lolita Palma nods unthinkingly. Pépé Lobo could not fail to notice the difference in her voice when she discusses official matters. Her tone is harder, colder. Almost metallic. The corsair gives her a quick sidelong glance. Lolita stares straight ahead, walking toward the ramparts at the end of the street. A beautiful face, he thinks. Although *beautiful*, the word traditionally used to describe women, is somehow not quite appropriate in this case. Her nose is perhaps a little too straight, too willful. The mouth can seem a little harsh. Though it can probably be gentle, depending on her mood—on the person who is kissing her. For several steps he is lost in thought, wondering whether anyone has actually kissed her.

"When do you put out, Captain?"

The corsair gives a sudden start. *Don't be ridiculous,* he chides himself.

"I don't know. Soon, I expect . . . as soon as I receive the order . . ."

The street has led them to the Plaza de los Pozos de la Nieve. To their left is the Alameda, where the tall palms and the trees stripped bare by winter are ranked in three parallel lines along the city walls, all the way to the spires of the Iglesia del Carmen; the ocher bastion of Candelaria juts out into the ashen sea like the prow of a ship.

"Very well," Lolita Palma says with a shrug. "I don't think we can stop them . . . I shall take charge of insurance and the warranties. With the Royal Armada, one never knows. Don Cayetano Valdés can be a difficult man, but he is reasonable. He is an old acquaintance . . . and very likely to become Governor and Captain General of Cádiz, if the rumors are confirmed that Villavicencio is joining the new Regency after Christmas."

They have stopped by the city walls, next to the first trees and the stone benches on the Alameda. From here, the bay seems like a gray, cold, gently rolling extension of the square. Not a breath of wind ripples its surface, which melts into the mist along the coast and the low clouds that shroud the headland of Rota and the Puerto de Santa María on the far side of the bay. Lolita Palma leans her gloved hands on the carved ebony and ivory pommel of her black umbrella.

"I gather you were in Algeciras during the evacuation."

"Yes, I was."

"Tell me what you saw. All anyone here knows is what the newspapers published this week said: the usual tales of boundless heroism by our compatriots and the heavy losses suffered by the enemy . . . you know."

"There is not much to tell," says the corsair. "We were moored in Gibraltar, having brought in the Portuguese felucca when the shelling started and the people fled to Isla Verde and to the ships. I was asked to help, so I sailed in as close as possible—carefully, because it is a treacherous stretch of coastline. We spent several days ferrying refugees and soldiers along the line, and kept working until the French captured the city and began firing at us from the hills of Matagorda and the Villavieja Tower."

He gives a brief, almost reluctant account, glossing over the rest: the terrified women and children without food or shelter, shivering with cold in the wind and rain, sleeping on the hard, rocky ground of the island or on the decks of the ships. The last soldiers and guerrillas from the volunteer forces, having demolished the little bridge across the river Miel and defended the avenues during the mass evacuation, escaped along the beach, where the French infantrymen hunted them like rabbits. Through his spyglass Lobo saw a solitary sapper go back and try to carry his injured mate to safety, but he was captured by the enemy before he could reach the last boat.

A bell tolls some streets away in the San Francisco bell tower. A single peal. A number of caleche drivers, fishermen and passersby run to the nearest houses for shelter.

"Artillery fire," says Lolita Palma with eerie composure.

Pépé Lobo looks toward the Trocadero, though buildings block his view of that part of the coastline.

"It will hit in fifteen seconds," she adds.

She stands, motionless, staring at the gray sea. The corsair notices that her hands are gripping the handle of her umbrella, clenched with unfamiliar, almost imperceptible tension. Instinctively, he moves closer to her, placing himself in the imagined trajectory of the shell. An absurd gesture. The French bomb might land anywhere. It might even hit them.

Lolita Palma turns and looks at him curiously. Or so it seems to him. On her lips, he can see a faint smile—of gratitude, perhaps. Certainly spontaneous. They stand there for a moment, their bodies close, studying each other in silence. Perhaps too close, thinks Lobo, suppressing the urge to take a step back. That would only make matters worse.

A muffled explosion behind the line of buildings; far off. Somewhere near the Customs House.

"It did not have our name on it," she says.

She is smiling openly now, almost gently, as she did that day when they talked about the tree painted on her fan. Once again he finds himself admiring her composure.

"Do you know who rings the bell at San Francisco when the bombs are coming?"

The corsair says that he doesn't, so she tells him: a novice from the convent, a volunteer, performs the task. The English ambassador, seeing her from his balcony making obscene gestures toward the French lines between the peals, asked to meet her and gave her a gold piece. Lobo has surely heard the ballads about it, sung to the strains of guitars in the taverns and bars of the city. Nothing, not even war, can silence the local wits.

"But not all the ballads are so charming," Lolita says. "People say women are being killed."

"Killed?"

"Yes. Murdered. In horrible ways."

The corsair has heard nothing about this, so she tells him what she knows. Which is not much. The newspapers have not published a word about it, perhaps so as not to panic the public. But rumors abound that young girls have been snatched off the streets and beaten to death—at least two of them. And God knows what other atrocities have been committed. With so many strangers and soldiers in the city, there is no way of knowing. Few women dare go out at night anymore.

Pépé Lobo frowns, ill at ease. "There are times when I am ashamed to be a man."

He says it spontaneously, without thinking. Something to fill the silence after what she had said. But he sees Lolita Palma observing him curiously.

"I don't think you have anything to be ashamed of."

They look into each other's eyes for a long moment, which the corsair wishes would last even longer.

"I might surprise you, señora."

Another silence. A fine drizzle is falling; tiny raindrops settle on the woman's upturned face, heralding the coming storm. But she does not move, does not open her umbrella—she simply stands next to the edge of the rampart, framed by the gray expanse of fog and sea behind her. He should offer to shelter her, thinks the corsair. But he does not move. In fact, he should say or do something to defuse the moment, to break the silence. But none of the possibilities tallies with what he wants to do at this moment.

"Did you buy anything interesting?" he says eventually. For something to say.

She looks at him, puzzled, not knowing what he is talking about. Lobo gives a faint, forced smile.

"The bookshop. On the square."

The raindrops glitter on Lolita Palma's face. Behind her, the gray vastness of the sea is now dotted with tiny splashes shifting in flurries on the breeze that blows from the mouth of the bay.

"We should—" the corsair begins.

"Oh, I see," she says abruptly, turning away. "Yes, something very interesting. The complete six volumes of *La Flora española* by Joseph Quer . . . A beautiful copy in excellent condition."

"Ah."

"Printed by Ibarra."

"Really."

It has begun to rain in earnest. A sudden swell brings waves crashing over the rocks at Las Puercas, out on the bay.

"We should go back," murmurs Lolita Palma.

Lobo nods while she opens her umbrella. It is large enough to cover them both, but she does not invite him to shelter under it. They walk back slowly past the leafless saplings as the rain grows stronger. The corsair is accustomed to braving the elements aboard ship, but is surprised that she does not seem concerned. Glancing sideways, he sees her lift her skirt a little with her free hand to avoid the puddles beginning to form.

"We have another matter pending," he hears her say suddenly.

He turns to her, bemused. He feels water drip from the corners of his hat, soaking his jacket. He should take it off and wrap it around her shoulders to protect her shawl, but is unsure how such a gesture would be seen. Too intimate, probably. Too forward. With or without the rain, Cádiz is a small city. Here, reputations can be made or lost through idle gossip.

"The dragon tree," explains Lolita Palma. "Remember?"

Pépé Lobo smiles, somewhat taken aback. "Of course."

"And your botanical expedition. You promised to tell me all about it."

Were she any other woman, the corsair thinks, he would have long since wiped the raindrops from her face, her hair, brushed them away with his fingertips. Slowly; careful not to alarm her. But she is not any other woman—she is herself. And that is precisely the problem.

"Shall we say tomorrow?"

Pépé Lobo takes five steps before he responds to this question.

"It will still be raining tomorrow," he says gently.

"Of course. How foolish of me . . . Let us say the first fine day, then. Before you put out again, or when you return."

The silence is broken only by the patter of raindrops. They walk along the glistening pavement of the Calle de los Doblones, in the shelter of the houses. On the corner, some twenty paces away, is the Palma house. When Lolita speaks again, her manner has changed.

"I envy you your freedom, Señor Lobo."

The tone is colder, more neutral. The word *señor* restores order.

"That is not what I would call it," says the corsair.

"You don't understand, Captain."

They have reached the front door of the house, in the shelter of the wide, dark passageway which leads to the railings and the inner courtyard planted with ferns. Pépé Lobo removes his hat and shakes it while Lolita closes her umbrella. He can feel the weight of his wet jacket on his shoulders. His waterlogged silver-buckled shoes create a puddle on the tiles.

"A man is free when his life is how he wishes it to be," she says. "When he is held back by no one but himself."

At this moment, in the dim light that streams from both courtyard and doorway, framed by the shadows behind her, raindrops still glittering on her face, she is truly beautiful, thinks Lobo. She stares up at him, seeming to look right through him to somewhere distant, remote. To distant seas and boundless horizons.

"Had I been born a man . . ."

She breaks off, and fills the silence left by her words with a wistful, barely perceptible smile.

"Fortunately, you were not," says the corsair.

"Fortunately?" She looks at him surprised, almost shocked, though he cannot understand the reason. "Oh no, oh heavens. You . . ."

She has raised her hand, as though to stop her mouth, to prevent it uttering another word. But the hand hovers in midair.

"It is getting late, Captain."

She turns, opens the gate and vanishes into the house. Pépé Lobo is left standing in the passageway, contemplating the empty courtyard. Then he puts on his hat and goes out into the street, into the rain.

WEARING AN OILSKIN carrick coat and hat, huddled close to the wall to shelter from the rain, Comisario Tizón stares down at the body lying a few feet away, alongside the pile of rubble it was found under some three hours ago. The bomb fell last night, bringing down part of a house on the alleyway behind the Divina Pastora chapel. Four of the residents were injured, one of whom is in critical condition—an elderly man already in bed, crushed when the building collapsed. But the shock came this morning, when the rubble was being cleared and the building shored up by residents attempting to salvage their possessions. The woman whose body was discovered among the ruins of the ground floor—formerly a carpenter's workshop—was not killed by the explosion, nor by falling debris: she was gagged and bound and her back had been flayed raw with a whip. The driving rain that sluices the body sprawled amid the wreckage and soaks its blood-matted hair gradually washes away the brick and plaster dust to reveal a back so viciously mutilated that bones and entrails are visible, glistening under the rain, from the base of the skull to the hips.

"Her head was partly crushed by falling debris, so it won't be easy to identify her," comments Cadalso, who comes over dripping wet and shaking himself. "She looks young, like the others."

"Maybe someone will be looking for her. Take down anything you can and have someone investigate."

"Yes, señor, right away."

Rogelio Tizón steps away from the wall, around the rubble, and walks down the alleyway to the Calle del Pasquín. The rain continues to fall, more gently in this part of the city whose streets, laid out at right angles to each other, create an effective windbreak. Swinging his cane, the comisario looks at the neighboring houses, the damage caused by the bomb, the narrow doorway at the end of the alley that leads into a church whose facade overlooks the Calle de Capuchinos. Obviously the woman died before the bomb fell. The murder again *preceded* the impact, just as it did on one of the two previous occasions: the Calle del Viento. But on the Calle del Laurel no bomb fell, either beforehand or afterward—something which leaves the comisario even more puzzled. All this will further complicate matters when he meets with the governor and the Intendant, he thinks uneasily; he will have to decide what he can and cannot tell them. But that will have to wait. Right now, he is looking for something the precise nature of which he does not understand, but he is convinced he will find it nearby, in the air, in the streets. A sensation similar to the one he experienced at the other crime scenes: that fleeting, almost perfect vacuum, as though in that precise spot a bell jar had extracted all the air, or conferred on it a sinister stillness. An empty space, devoid of movement, of sound; he believes he will recognize it.

But this time, he feels nothing. Tizón paces the street from end to end, step by step, sniffing around stubbornly like a bloodhound. He studies every detail of his surroundings. But the rain and the damp obscure everything. Suddenly he realizes that yesterday afternoon and last night, when the girl was probably murdered, it had not yet begun to rain. Perhaps this is what it is, he thinks: some peculiarity of the air, or the temperature. Or God knows what. It may be that his imagination is making absurd connections; maybe he is going mad. Ready to be locked up in Caleta asylum.

Beset by these disturbing thoughts, the comisario has made his way around the block to the whitewashed stone portico of the Divina Pastora, where there is a shrine with a seated figure of the Virgin stroking the neck of a lamb. The chapel door is open and, without taking his hat off, the policeman peers inside and looks around. At the far end, beneath the barely visible gildings of the high altar, burns a lone sanctuary lamp. A kneeling figure in mourning dress gets to her feet, blesses herself with holy water from the font and walks out past the comisario. It is an old woman wearing a black shawl and carrying a rosary. When Tizón goes back into the street, the woman is walking away toward the Capuchin monastery. The comisario watches her until she disappears from view. Then, in the shelter of the doorway, he lights a cigar and smokes, watching the whorls as they dissolve slowly in the damp air. He wishes he could feel no regret, no disquiet at the scene he has just left behind in the rubble of the narrow alley. One dead woman, or six, or fifty, changes nothing: the world still turns, wheeling toward the abyss. Besides, he thinks, all things have their allotted time in the suicidal order of things—in life, and in its inexorable outcome, death. Every event when observed moves at its own pace, with its own particular rhythm. Every question must give ample opportunity for its answer. He is not the guilty party here, thinks Tizón, exhaling another plume of smoke. He is merely a witness to these events. It is a thought he hopes he can cling to with equal conviction tonight, at home, in his bare living room, as his wife stares at him silently, reproachfully, next to the closed piano. And all these fine words do not change the fact that yesterday the dead girl in the alley was still alive.

"Fuck!" he says aloud, grim and glowering.

He takes his pocket watch from his jacket and studies the hands.

Then he drops the stub of his cigar and crushes it beneath the wet heel of his boot.

The time has come, he thinks coldly, to pay someone a little visit.

RAIN PATTERS OVERHEAD, on the terrace and the bare boards of the empty pigeon loft. Next to the door, whose panes of colored glasses do nothing to enliven the hazy gray light from outside, Gregorio Fumagal, wearing a dressing gown and a woolen nightcap, is burning the last of his papers in the stove. There is little left: a handful of notebooks which record the places where bombs landed, their geographic coordinates, estimated distances, dates and sundry other details. Page by page, everything is burned as the taxidermist opens the iron grille and, after a quick glance, tosses loose sheets and ripped pages into the flames. Earlier, having stripped them of their innocuous covers and torn them to shreds, he burned a number of prohibited books by French philosophers. They were longtime companions of his thoughts, of his life, yet today he watched them burn with little regret. None of this must be found here.

He is not some naïve fool, nor is he blind. The unfamiliar people who discreetly dog his steps every time he goes out have not escaped his notice. Every night before he retires, he has observed from his bedroom window—the only one that directly overlooks the street—the same figure, standing motionless in the shadows on the corner where the Calle de las Escuelas meets the Calle de San Juan. And as he wanders through the city, stopping nonchalantly in front of some shop or tavern, a sideways glance is enough to confirm the presence of ominous companions: silent men with plain clothes and fearsome faces. All these things mean that he no longer harbors any illusions about the future. In fact, when he considers the situation objectively—what he has done and what they could do to him—he is surprised that he is still a free man.

Everything in the stove has been turned to embers and ashes. All that remains is the map of the city, his masterwork. The key to everything. Fumagal looks sorrowfully at the folded sheet of paper, worn now with use, on which penciled lines and curves, spreading out from the east, form a complex conical web overlaying the urban tracery of Cádiz. This is the fruit of a year of meticulous and dangerous work. Day upon day of endless walks, of calculations and covert observations that give the map extraordinary scientific value. Every detail is set down here, or is effectively referenced: the geographic disposition, angle of incidence, the speed and direction of the prevailing wind for almost every impact, blast radius, areas of uncertainty. The military importance of this map for those laying siege to Cádiz is incalculable. This is why, in spite of the dangers he has faced recently, Fumagal has held on to it until today in the hope that eventually his contact with the far side of the bay—interrupted when the Mulatto left—will be reestablished. But nothing happened, and the danger has escalated. The last pigeons he sent to the Trocadero, carrying messages in which he outlined the critical nature of the situation, were met with silence. Every day that passes serves merely to reinforce the taxidermist's belief that he has been abandoned to his fate. A fate that, in this perilous period of his life (the days pass like a strange dream, through which he wanders uncertainly like a sleepwalker), he has deliberately forced. But there are some aspects that are inevitable. Circumstances that no one can choose or spurn. Or not entirely.

He rips the map of Cádiz into four pieces, crumples each into a ball and tosses them into the stove. That, he thinks, is everything. A whole life, a whole worldview reduced to ashes. The cold, implacable geometry of a universally ordered system taken to its logical, necessary conclusion, but whose savage finale remains incomplete. The word *finale* reminds him of the small black vial, its glass stopper sealed with wax, that he keeps in one of his desk drawers: a concentrated opium solution that represents his gentle, peaceful route to freedom and equanimity, should the worst come to the worst. The flames blaze more intensely now, illuminating Gregorio Fumagal's haggard face and, behind him, the display cases and perches from which the glassy eyes of stuffed animals stare vacantly into space—witnesses to the tragedy that has befallen the man who rescued them from putrefaction, dust and oblivion.

There is nothing on the marble table now. It has been some time since the taxidermist has felt able to work. He lacks the necessary concentration to wield the scalpel, the wire and the oakum wadding. He lacks the peace of mind. And for the first time that he can remember, he lacks the determination. Perhaps *courage* is the word he cannot bring himself to say. In recent weeks, the empty pigeon loft has chipped away at too many foundations, too many convictions. When he contemplates what he has become, his urgent need to face the immediate future and the rest of his life—if either of these extend beyond a few short hours— Fumagal cannot find the strength to overcome his own apathy. Even burning the compromising documents and books does not seem imperative. It is simply a logical act, the consequence of previous actions. An almost instinctive reflex born of loyalty or allegiance to those on the far side of the bay, or perhaps—and this seems more likely—to himself.

The doorbell rings. A single, brief peal. Fumagal closes the stove door, gets to his feet and goes out into the hallway. He slides back the grille of the peephole. Standing on the landing is a man he does not recognize, wearing an oilskin hat and a carrick coat that drips water on the floor. He has a strong, aquiline nose, like the beak of some bird of prey; his face is framed by bushy whiskers connected by a mustache. He carries a heavy cane, topped by a fearsome brass pommel.

"Gregorio Fumagal? This is the Comisario of Police. Can you open the door, please?"

Of course he can, the taxidermist silently decides. Not to do so at this stage would be futile and grotesque. What is happening is simply what was bound to happen, eventually. Surprised by his own calm, he draws back the bolt. As he opens the door, he thinks again about the small glass vial in the desk drawer of his workshop. Perhaps it will soon be too late to avail himself of it; but an insatiable curiosity overshadows all other thoughts. Curiosity, he concludes—perhaps he is using the word simply as a justification, as a cowardly excuse to go on breathing, to go on observing for a little longer.

"May I?" says the comisario.

Without waiting for an answer, he steps indoors. As the taxidermist moves to close the door, Tizón blocks him with his cane, forcing him to leave it open. Before following him, Fumagal glances down the stairs to the next landing, where he sees two men with round hats and dark capes.

"What do you want from me?"

The policeman, who has not removed his hat, nor unbuttoned his carrick coat, stands beside the marble table in the middle of the workshop, swinging his cane as he glances around. He does not look as though he is inspecting an unfamiliar place, but rather as though he is checking everything is as it was. For a moment, Fumagal wonders when he might have been here before—and how he managed to leave no trace of his visit.

"*He sits transfixed among those slaughtered by his sword. Clearly plotting some baleful deed . . .*"

Fumagal blinks, puzzled. The comisario spoke these words as he looked around before turning back toward him. His tone is dramatic, as though declaiming something. And it is certainly a quote, but the taxidermist does not recognize it.

"Excuse me?"

The comisario glares at him. There is something unsettling in those eyes, something beyond his policeman's swagger. A steely glint of hatred both vast and contained.

"You don't know what I'm talking about? Good Lord."

He takes a few steps, running the brass pommel of his cane over the marble dissecting table. A slow, ominous shriek of metal.

"Let's try our luck again," he says after a brief silence.

He has stopped in front of the taxidermist, staring at him—a look more personal than official.

"*A man who, having plotted the murder of the entire army, then marched by night against us in order to take us with his sword . . .*"

He says it in the same declamatory tone, his eyes blazing.

"Does that sound more familiar?"

Fumagal is taken aback. This is not what he has been waiting for these past days. "I don't know what you're talking about."

"I see. Tell me something, have you ever read *Ajax*?"

Still puzzled, Fumagal holds the comisario's gaze, trying to get his bearings. "Ajax?"

"Yes. You know, Sophocles."

"Not that I can remember."

Now it is the policeman's turn to blink. Only for a fleeting instant. And in this brief instant, Fumagal allows himself to hope that all this is simply a misunderstanding. That the target is not him, but someone else. An error of policing, the result of malicious gossip. Anything. But the next words he hears put an end to any such hopes.

"Let me tell you something, *camarada*." The comisario leans over the stove, opens the door, glances inside and then closes it again. "Last Thursday at six a.m., in accordance with the sentence passed by a drum-head court-martial, the Mulatto was garroted in the dungeons of the Castillo de San Sebastián . . . You read nothing about it in the papers, of course. Being a delicate matter, it was conducted *in camera*, as is usual in such cases."

As he speaks, he glances at the terrace door, opens it and peers out at the stairs, then carefully closes it. He takes a few steps and stops in front of the stuffed monkey in a display case.

"I was there, that morning," he goes on. "There were three or four of us. The Mulatto went to his death with some dignity, by the way. Smugglers are usually such crude men; as, indeed, was he. But every man has his limits."

As the policeman talks, Fumagal casually moves around the desk, one step closer to the drawer containing the vial of opium. Inadvertently or intentionally, the comisario moves between him and the desk.

"We had a number of interesting conversations, the Mulatto and I," he continues. "You might say that, toward the end, a point of agreement was reached . . ."

Tizón pauses for a moment and gives a faint, wolfish smile, flashing his gold tooth. Then he goes on: "A point of agreement is always reached, señor, I assure you. Always."

This last word sounds like a threat. There is a fresh pause, during which the comisario studies the other stuffed animals before continuing. The Mulatto, he says, talked about Fumagal. At some length: carrier pigeons, messages, trips across the bay, the French, et cetera. Later the comisario visited this house to have a look around. Leafed through some papers, pored over the map of the city with all those curious marks and tracings. Extremely interesting.

"Do you still have it?"

Fumagal does not answer. The comisario looks resignedly at the blazing stove.

"A pity. I had rather hoped . . . A mistake on my part. But there were other aspects . . . I had to be sure, you understand, I had to give you . . . well, you know, *camarada*. I had to give you another opportunity."

He pauses, as if in thought. At length, he lifts his cane, bringing the brass pommel close to Fumagal's chest without making contact.

"Are you sure you've never read Sophocles, señor?"

Sophocles again, thinks the taxidermist. It is like some absurd joke he doesn't understand. Despite his precarious situation, he is becoming irritated.

"Why do you keep asking me that?"

The comisario laughs grimly under his breath. There is no humor in the sinister, ill-omened laughter, Fumagal realizes. Again he glances surreptitiously toward the locked desk drawer, now and forever beyond reach.

"Because a friend of mine will take great delight in mocking me when I tell him."

"Am I under arrest?"

Tizón stops for a moment and studies the man. A look of surprise on his face. "Of course. Obviously you are under arrest . . . What else were you expecting, señor?"

Then, without warning, he lifts his cane and slams it hard three times against the marble table. The sound brings the two men in the stairwell running. Out of the corner of his eye, Fumagal sees them standing in the door of the workshop, waiting. The policeman has moved closer now, so close Fumagal can smell his fetid breath, thick with tobacco. The steely, baleful eyes bore into his and Fumagal once again sees the flicker of revulsion he noticed earlier. The taxidermist takes a step back: for the first time he feels fear—nothing less than abject physical terror. He is afraid this man will beat him with the heavy pommel of his cane.

"Gregorio Fumagal, I am arresting you for spying on behalf of the French, and for the murder of six women."

What most shocks Fumagal is the comisario deliberately failing to address him as *señor*.

CHAPTER TWELVE

Rumor has it—the war abounds with rumor and gossip—that Marshal Suchet is about to march into Valencia, and that Tarifa will fall in a matter of days; but Simon Desfosseux is unconcerned. All that concerns him at this moment is ensuring that the wind and the flurries of rain coming through the cracks in his hut do not put out his fire, on which he is boiling up a pot of water with a mixture of toasted barley and a few grains of dreadful coffee. Above the captain's head, the storm produces ominous groans from a roof made of planks and branches held together with rope and nails. The rain, in violent gusts, seeps through every little gap, soaking the shelter. Sitting on a makeshift bench that does little to protect him from the mud and the damp, Desfosseux draws his cloak around his shoulders and pulls on an old woolen cap. His filthy black fingernails poke through his threadbare gloves. In foul weather, life in the trenches becomes unbearable; all the more so on the Trocadero, a low, almost level spit of land jutting into the bay, exposed to the wind and the sea. The lower gun batteries are all but flooded by the swollen waters of the canal and the San Pedro River, creeping up over the sandbar and the high-water line.

In this filthy weather, it is pointless to think about Fanfan and its brothers. For four days now they have been unable to shell the city. The howitzers are silent, covered with heavy tarpaulins. Meanwhile Sergeant Labiche and his men, buried in their shelter, up to their gaiters in mud, are cursing everything and everyone. The weather means supplies have been cut off and the Cabezuela is not receiving rations—not even the quarter rations of salted meat, bitter watered-down wine and four days' worth of black bread (which is mostly bran) that the artillerymen have been getting in recent weeks. The starvation that, in the last months of 1811, is cutting a swath through whole populations and looks set to devastate the Peninsula is now beginning to hit the French troops; the supply chain is finding it increasingly difficult to get a grain of wheat or a pound of meat in this hostile terrain of ghost villages left derelict by war. And of all the Imperial Army, those in the Premier Corps, at the southernmost tip of Andalucía, are furthest from the supply centers; communications, always prey to guerrilla raids, are now cut off by the foul weather that is lashing the coastline, causing rivers to burst their banks, flooding roads and sweeping away bridges.

"Tie up that damned tarpaulin!"

Lieutenant Bertoldi, who has just come in shaking the water from his patched and threadbare cloak, apologizes and secures the oilcloth over the doorway. Seeing his assistant's filthy, gaunt face still smiling despite being forced to squelch through this world of mud and water, Desfosseux feels he should apologize for his brusqueness, but he is too despondent even for that. If people were to make amends for every ill-tempered outburst of the past few days, everyone would be constantly apologizing to everyone else. Desfosseux simply nods, and gestures to the stewpot on the fire.

"It will brew in a minute, but I can't vouch for what it will taste like."

"As long as it's hot, that's fine by me, Captain."

The concoction begins to boil. Carefully, Desfosseux takes the pot off the heat, and pours some steaming liquid into a tin cup, which he passes to Bertoldi. Desfosseux uses a chipped, blue-china bowl—a piece of crockery from a wealthy house in Puerto Real, looted at the start of the war—and sips, almost taking pleasure in burning his lips and tongue. There is no sugar, no honey, nothing to sweeten the brew. It doesn't really taste much like coffee but, as Bertoldi said, at least it is hot. And quite bitter. All it takes is a little imagination while it warms the belly.

Maurizio Bertoldi moves about, trying to get his sore leg comfortable. Three weeks ago, he was hit by a shard from a Spanish shell while supervising the gun battery at Fort Luis. His leg was bruised—nothing serious, but he is still hobbling. And the weather doesn't help.

"They're dealing with the deserters in half an hour . . . next to the large barracks, at the changing of the guard."

Desfosseux looks at him over the rim of his china bowl. Bertoldi scratches his red whiskers and shrugs.

"All officers and men must be present," the captain adds. "Orders. No excuses."

The two artillerymen drink in silence as flurries of rain lash the hut, trickling through every crack in the roof. A week ago, taking advantage of low tide, four men from the 9th Light Infantry, sick to death of the hunger and deprivation, abandoned their sentry posts, leaving their rifles and ammunition, intending to defect to the enemy. One of them managed to swim as far as the Spanish gunboats anchored by Punta Cantera, but the others were captured by a patrol boat and brought back to the Trocadero. The execution, after a summary court-martial, was to have taken place in Chiclana two days ago, but the weather made it impossible for the prisoners to be transported. Tired of waiting, Marshal Victor has now ordered that the three men be executed here. In such terrible times as these, as morale is sapped and treacherous thoughts stir in the men, it will serve as a warning to make an example of these deserters. That, at least, is what is hoped.

"Let's go, then," says Desfosseux.

They finish their coffee, wrap themselves up in their cloaks; the captain straps on his sword and trades his wool cap for his old bicorn covered with oilcloth. They push the tarpaulin aside and step out into the mud. Beyond the churning banks of the peninsula, the bay is seething with gray spume and spindrift. The ghostly smudge of Cádiz is barely visible in the background. There is a rumble of thunder as lightning streaks across the leaden sky, silhouetting the dark spit of land and the masts of ships at anchor on the heavy swell, bows facing southeast.

"Be careful here, Captain. The bridge is shaking like it's alive."

The rising waters threaten to sweep away the wooden footbridge that spans the drainage ditch between the second and third gun batteries. Simon Desfosseux crosses it carefully, afraid that he might well be dragged out to sea. The path runs along a partially flooded trench, protected from Spanish shells by gabions, fascines and a wall of earth. With every step, Desfosseux's boots sink into the mud, and water seeps through the cracked soles up to his ankles, saturating the rags wrapped around his feet. A few paces ahead, Bertoldi hobbles and squelches, his body hunched against the wind that howls between the gabions, creating waves in the thick, brown mire through which the skirts of his cape trail carelessly.

Beyond the main block, where the gun carriages, limbers and other artillery equipment are stowed, and which sometimes serves as a temporary jail for prisoners, there is a gully that leads down to the Trocadero canal, some seventy *toises* wide, which now roils thunderously with a deluge of muddy water. Muffled up in capes or cloaks, some gray, some brown, their hats and shakos dripping water, 150 officers and soldiers stand silently, expectantly, forming a crude semicircle around the gully. Desfosseux notices that Sergeant Labiche and his men are also here, watching this scene with grim, mutinous fury. In theory, the men should be in perfect formation, but what with the weather and the torrential rain, no one is minded to follow regulations.

In the doorway of the barracks, Simon Desfosseux sees two Spanish officers: sheltering under a canvas awning, they are observing the scene from a distance, watched over by a sentry, his bayonet fixed. Both are wearing the blue uniform of the enemy Armada. One has his arm in a sling, while the other has a lieutenant's stripes on his frockcoat. Desfosseux knows that yesterday the storm dragged their felucca off its anchor, and sent it careering toward Trocadero. With considerable skill, the lieutenant hoisted the sails so that he could control the boat and managed to bring it ashore on the beach at the Cabezuela rather than dashing it on the cruel rocks nearby. Then he tried to burn the ship—the rains made it impossible—before he was captured together with his first mate and twenty crewmen. Now, the Spaniards are waiting to be transported to Jerez, the first stage of their journey to captivity in France.

At the bottom of the gully, near the canal bank, the three deserters stand waiting for the sentence to be carried out, each guarded by two *gendarmes* wearing their distinctive bicorn hats—immaculate as ever, despite the rain—with rifles pointed downward beneath their blue capes. Standing next to Bertoldi among a group of officers, Captain Desfosseux peers curiously at the prisoners. They are standing in the driving rain, without capes or hats, hands tied behind their backs; one in a waistcoat and shirtsleeves, the other two in sodden blue combat jackets, their breeches—made from brown twill requisitioned from a local convent—spattered with mud. Someone mentions that the man in shirtsleeves is a corporal, someone named Wurtz from the 2nd Company. The other two look very young. One, a skinny redheaded boy, glances around in terror, shivering so hard—from cold or fear— that he has to be supported by the *gendarmes.* A colonel dispatched from the Duc de Belluno's headquarters—cursing silently at having to travel from Chiclana in this weather—moves toward the prisoners, brandishing a piece of paper. His progress is hindered by the muddy ground, boggy in some places and slippery in others. Twice he almost falls.

"Let's get this farce over with," someone behind Desfosseux mutters under his breath.

The colonel attempts to read the sentence aloud, but is drowned out by the wind and the rain. After the first few words he gives up, folds the sodden piece of paper and gestures to the *gendarmes'* warrant officer, who exchanges a few words with his men; the infantrymen who make up the firing squad reluctantly congregate next to the barracks. The prisoners have been turned to face the canal while they are being blindfolded. The officer in shirtsleeves struggles. One of his companions—a short, dark-haired boy—acquiesces meekly, but the moment the *gendarmes* step back, the red-haired boy's legs give way and he falls on his backside in the mud. His wails can be heard all through the ravine.

"They should have lashed them to posts," says Bertoldi, shocked.

"A couple of sappers drove stakes in," explains the captain, "but the ground was too soft and the rain washed them away."

The firing squad lines up behind the prisoners: twelve men with rifles and a lieutenant from the 9th Regiment, his sword drawn, wearing a blue cape, rain coursing from his hat. By order of Marshal Victor, the executioners belong to the same regiment as the prisoners. The infantrymen look sullen and it is clear they have no desire to be here: rain glistens on their black oilskin shakos and their cloaks, protecting the rifles' gunlocks from the rain. The redheaded youth is still sitting in the mud, hands tied behind his back, howling. The man in shirtsleeves tilts his blindfolded face back slightly as though he does not want to miss the moment when they shoot him. The leader of the firing squad is now saying something, resting his sword on his shoulder; then he lifts his arm and the rifles are raised—some of them very slowly—so they are more or less horizontal. In principle, four men are to aim at each of the prisoners, who are standing with their backs to the firing squad, silhouetted against the raging torrent of the channel.

Simon Desfosseux does not hear the order being given. He sees only the flash of the rifles—rather than the regulation fusillade, the shots ring out randomly, halfheartedly, and several rifles fail to fire—and the white cloud of powder smoke dissolving in the rain.

"Fuck, fuck," mutters Bertoldi. "Fuck."

An utter shambles, thinks Desfosseux, almost vomiting up the brew he drank half an hour earlier—but a shambles somehow befitting the day and the situation they are in. The prisoner in the waistcoat falls facedown in the mud, the rain quickly spreading a scarlet stain down the sleeves of his sodden shirt. But the short, dark-haired boy, who fell on his side, thrashes about in the mire as if trying to crawl away, although his hands are still tied behind his back; he leaves a trail of blood as he lifts up his face like a sightless man trying to work out what is happening around him. As for the redhead, he is still sitting on the ground without a scratch on him, wailing in terror as the rain pounds down.

Simon Desfosseux has no difficulty hearing every word of the tirade that the colonel from Chiclana unleashes on the lieutenant, or the one he in turn lets loose on the sheepish firing squad. The soldiers gathered around the ravine look at each other or blatantly curse their senior officers. No one knows what to do. After a brief hesitation, the lieutenant draws his pistol from under his cloak, stumbles past the prisoner kneeling in the mud and pulls the trigger on the man crawling away, but the spark merely scorches the damp gunpowder and the gun fails to fire. Flustered, the lieutenant fumbles with his weapon, then turns to the firing squad and orders them to reload their rifles. However, everyone, including Desfosseux, knows that with the rain and the wind this is pointless.

"You'll see, they'll end up butchering them with bayonets . . ." mutters an officer.

Bitter laughter ripples through the group. Down below, in the gully, the situation is settled by a sergeant in the *gendarmes*, a heavyset officer with a thick mustache. With great composure—and without waiting for orders—he takes a rifle from one of his men, strides over to the wounded man crawling through the mud and shoots him at point-blank range; he exchanges the rifle with another, then marches over to the redhead sitting on the ground and puts a bullet through his head. The boy slumps forward, his body hunched like a rabbit. The sergeant hands back the rifle and tramps through the mud, without so much as a glance at the bewildered lieutenant, then salutes the colonel from general staff, who—equally confused—returns the salute.

Slowly the men drift back to their posts, some muttering darkly, or glancing back at the three corpses on the bank.

Lieutenant Bertoldi stands watching as the two Spanish naval officers are led back into the barracks. "I don't like the fact that the *manolos* got to see that," he says.

Pulling up the wet collar of his cloak and ducking his head down against the driving rain, Simon Desfosseux reassures his adjutant.

"Don't worry . . . they do the same on their side. No one can outdo the Spanish when it comes to cruelty."

The captain tramps through the muddy trench, heading toward the waterlogged footbridge, hoping that the fire in his hut is still burning so he can dry his clothes a little and warm his numbed hands. Perhaps they'll be lucky, he thinks with a smile: perhaps the coffee will still be warm. It seems incredible to him that in such desperate circumstances, a sip of coffee, a hunk of stale bread or—the height of luxury these days—a pipe or a cigar can seem so important. He sometimes wonders if he will ever be able to adapt to ordinary life, if he should survive: seeing the faces of his wife and his children every day; gazing at a landscape without instinctively calculating trajectories and points of impact; lying in a meadow and closing his eyes without a nagging dread that a *guerrillero* might creep up on him and cut his throat.

As he trudges on through the muddy water, he hears behind him the squelching and muttering of Maurizio Bertoldi.

"You know what I think, Captain?"

"No. And I don't want to know."

More squelching. After a long pause, as though he has taken the time to consider his commanding officer's words, the lieutenant speaks again. "Well . . . If you don't mind, I'm going to tell you anyway."

Another brutal gust of rain. Simon Desfosseux presses his hat down firmly and bows his head. "I do mind. Just shut up."

"This war is a piece of shit, Captain."

The naked man, huddled in a corner of the cell, raises a hand to shield his face as Rogelio Tizón bends down and peers at him. Lips split and swollen, face bruised from the beatings, eyes ringed with dark circles from pain and lack of sleep, the man cowering in front of him is barely recognizable as the one he arrested five days ago in the house on the Calle de las Escuelas. With a practiced eye, the comisario evaluates the injuries and considers the possibilities of the situation, which are reasonably elastic. Some time ago he summoned a relatively trustworthy doctor—a drunken quack who spends most of his time doing medical examinations for the whores in Santa María and La Merced—whose professional diagnosis was that the suspect could withstand further interrogation. "His pulse is strong, his breathing normal, given the circumstances. In moderate doses and with a little caution you can keep up the good work, I think." Then, with another half ounce weighing down the pocket of his smock, the doctor—Casimiro Escudillo, better known in the brothels of Cádiz as "Dr. Wormer"*—went straight to

---

* Wormer—a tool used to clean a cannon.

the nearest wine merchant to convert his remuneration into liquid form. And so Tizón is still here, aided by the ubiquitous Cadalso and another agent, "keeping up the good work"—interrogating Gregorio Fumagal, or what is left of him.

"Let's start again from the beginning, *camarada*," says Tizón, "if you don't mind."

The taxidermist whimpers as he is lifted and carried across the windowless dungeon, feet dragging on the floor, to the table, where he is laid face up. His grimy, almost hairless skin, slick with sweat, shimmers in the dim glow of the tallow candle. While one of the henchmen sits on the suspect's legs, holding him in place, Rogelio Tizón sits with his arms resting on the back of a chair he has placed close to Gregorio Fumagal's head which, like his upper body, is dangling over the table edge into the void. The prisoner's mouth gapes as he struggles to breathe, his face flushed purple as the blood rushes to his head. Over the past five days, he has confessed to so many crimes that he could be garroted as a spy ten times over, but none of them truly interests the comisario. Tizón leans closer and in a hushed, almost intimate tone, he recites the list:

"María Luisa Rodríguez, sixteen, Puerta de Tierra . . . Bernarda Garre, fourteen, Lame Paco's Tavern . . . Jacinta Herrero, seventeen, Calle de Amoladores . . ."

He carries on: six names, six ages (none older than nineteen), six places in Cádiz. He leaves long pauses between the victims, giving Fumagal a chance to fill in the gaps. Tizón finishes his list and sits, motionless, his mouth still inches from the taxidermist's ear.

"And the fucking bombs," he adds finally.

Suspended upside-down, his features racked with pain, Fumagal's gaze is blank. "Bombs," he whispers feebly.

"That's right. The marks on your map, remember? The places where they landed. Special places. Cádiz."

"I've already told you everything . . . about the bombs . . ."

"I'm afraid you haven't. Take my word for it. Come on, try to remember. I'm worn out and so are you . . . All of this is just a waste of time."

Fumagal flinches as though expecting a blow. Another one. "I've told you everything I know," he whines. "The Mulatto . . ."

"The Mulatto is dead and buried. He was garroted, remember?"

"I . . . The bombs . . ."

"Exactly. The bombs that exploded, the murdered girls. Tell me about it."

"I don't know . . . anything . . . about the girls."

"Too bad." Tizón's lips curl into a smile, though his face is grim. "With me, it's always better to know than not to know."

The taxidermist shakes his head wildly, desperately. After a moment he shudders and lets out a long, guttural howl. With professional curiosity, the comisario watches a thread of spittle trickle from the corner of Fumagal's mouth.

"Where have you hidden the whip?"

Fumagal moves his lips ineffectually, as though unable to form the words. "The . . . the whip?" he says eventually.

"Exactly. The whip made of braided wire. The tool you used to flay them."

Fumagal shakes his head again. Tizón quickly glances up at his assistant, who stands beside the table holding a bull's pizzle. Cadalso administers a single lash, hard and fast, between Fumagal's thighs. The suspect's wail becomes an agonized howl.

"It's not worth it," Tizón says with savage gentleness. "Take my word for it."

He pauses momentarily, studying the prisoner's face. Then he glances up at Cadalso; the whip cracks again and Fumagal's howl rises to a shriek of terror and despair. The comisario's trained ear analyzes it, straining to hear the precise note he is expecting—and which, he realizes angrily, is not there.

"María Luisa Rodríguez, sixteen, Puerta de Tierra . . ." he patiently begins again.

More groans. More lashes and screams. More carefully calculated pauses. The liberal gentlemen of the Cortes would do well to see this, thinks Tizón during one such pause, with their prattle about Utopia, national sovereignty, habeas corpus and all that drivel.

"I'm not interested in why you killed them," he says after a pause. "At least, not yet . . . I just want you to confirm the place where each girl died . . . And also the point about the bombs falling before or after . . . Do you follow me?"

The taxidermist's eyes, bulging from their sockets, stare at him. In them, Tizón thinks he can see a flicker of understanding. Or of madness.

"Tell me, and you'll finally be able to get some rest too. Our friends here will get some rest too. Everyone will be able to rest."

"The bombs . . ." Fumagal whispers hoarsely.

"That's it, *camarada*, the bombs . . ."

The lips continue to move, but no sounds come. Tizón leans closer, listening carefully.

"Come on. Just tell me . . . Six bombs, six murdered girls. Let's get this over with."

Up close, the prisoner reeks of sweat and putrefaction, of clammy, bloated flesh. As they all do after a few days of treatment, or "keeping up the good work," in the words of Dr. Wormer.

"I don't know . . . anything . . . about any girls."

The whisper bursts forth like a death rattle. It is followed by a jet of vomit. The comisario, who had his ear almost pressed to Fumagal's lips, jumps back in disgust.

"It's a pity you don't know."

Brutish, devoid of any imagination or initiative, Tizón's assistant stands gripping the whip, waiting for the order to flog the prisoner again. The comisario dissuades him with a glance.

"Take it easy, Cadalso. It looks as though this may take some time."

A RAY OF sunlight pierces the blanket of low cloud that still hangs above the hills of Chiclana on the far side of the Saporito channel, the Sancti Petri canal and the maze of tidal creeks and salt flats. As Felipe Mojarra steps out of his house, the dawn light breaks through the mist and glitters on the gray waters, swollen by the rains and the high tide. Walking past the low vine—its gnarled branches now leafless for the winter—Mojarra stares at the tangle of sludge, brushwood and reeds that the storms have washed up against the nearby embankment and the walls of his shack, laying waste to the vegetable garden.

The damp, bitter cold gnaws at his bones. With a broad-brimmed hat over the kerchief tied about his head, a blanket worn like a poncho and his rope sandals strung around his neck, Mojarra leans down, strikes the flint of his tinderbox and lights a hand-rolled cigar. Then he takes the long French rifle from his shoulder and leans on it, smoking, while he waits for his daughter. Too many women in the house, he thinks. Though if he had had a son—he sometimes envies his friend Curro Panizo for having a son—the war would probably have killed him by now, as it has so many. No one can predict when fortune or misfortune will strike, all the more so with the *gabachos* around. The truth of the matter is that Mojarra cannot bear goodbyes; this morning he wanted to spare himself the sight of his daughter Mari Paz weeping and hugging her mother, her grandmother, her little sisters. She is heading back to Cádiz, after spending Christmas on the Isla de Léon. "You should all be thankful that her mistress gave her time off," he'd said angrily, suddenly abandoning his breakfast—a hunk of stale bread dipped in wine—and going outside to wait for her. It is not as if the girl is going to the ends of the earth. War or no war, whether here on the island or anywhere else in Spain, now is not the time for mawkishness and tearful goodbyes. Tears are for funerals, and life has to be lived wherever you find yourself: in a fine house in Cádiz or in hell itself.

"Whenever you're ready, Father."

Mojarra looks at his daughter as she walks down the path; her bundle in one hand, wearing a dark skirt and a shawl that covers her head, accentuating her big, dark, soulful eyes. She is as delicate as her mother was at that age, before the cares of work and childbirth ground her down. She is almost seventeen. An age when he should be thinking of marrying her off as God intended, if he can find a suitable man, someone serious and decent, someone able to take care of her. The sooner the better, were it not for their current circumstances. But Mari Paz working as Señora Palma's maidservant is what keeps the family going at present; Mojarra cannot afford to support everyone on the little he gets as a volunteer with the local fusiliers: a little meat for the stewpot and a few coins when there is money to pay him. There is still no news of the reward for the gunboat they brought back from Santa Cruz. The various appeals he and Curro Panizo have made have proved fruitless; Cárdenas, his brother-in-law, died in hospital two weeks ago without seeing a penny of it, only to be tossed out of his bed like a dog while his fellow patients stole his tobacco. Mojarra takes comfort in the fact that at least Cárdenas had no family to take care of. He left no widow, no orphans. Sometimes Mojarra thinks ideally a man should leave nothing behind him. Freed of such worries, he would act more decisively. Less cautiously, less fearfully.

"Be careful when you get to Chato's tavern," the salter says sternly between puffs on his cigar. "Don't talk to anyone, and keep yourself covered with your shawl, do you hear me?"

"Yes, Father."

"When you arrive in Cádiz, go straight to your mistress's house before it gets dark. I don't want you stopping off anywhere . . . I don't like the rumors that have been going around."

"Don't worry."

Mojarra belches smoke, making his face appear sterner than he feels.

"That's exactly what I want. Not to worry . . . The coach driver is trustworthy, but he has enough to worry about already, what with his horses and so forth."

The girl protests, a little mockingly. "Perico the cooper is coming too, Father—remember? I'm not a fool, and I won't be traveling alone."

How grown up she is, thinks Mojarra. *All this time working in Cádiz, and here she is almost defying me.* "Even so," he grunts.

Father and daughter walk through the village toward the main square. The streets are lined with houses whose windows are protected by bars embedded in the narrow pavements. Women kneel on their doorsteps with buckets and cloths, or wash the dirt path outside their houses with dishwater.

"You do what I tell you. And don't trust anyone."

On the main street, between the Carmelite convent and the parish church, merchants and innkeepers are opening up and queues are beginning to form for bread, wine and oil. Opposite the Imprenta Real de Marina, a blind man with a loud voice is hawking copies of the *Regency Gazette* hot off the press. Carters and mule drivers come and go, making deliveries, and here and there amid the somber colors of civilian clothes is a garish flash of uniform: local militiamen in round hats and short jackets, ordinary soldiers in tight breeches, elaborately trimmed frockcoats with cuffs and lapels in various colors, pointed hats, leather helmets or shakos with red cockades. Since the French arrived, the island has seemed more like a barracks. As they walk, Mojarra greets the occasional neighbor or acquaintance, but he does not stop. Next to the Zimbrelo house is a fritter stand with a pan of smoking oil.

"Did you have any breakfast?"

"No. What with my sisters crying, I didn't have time."

After a brief hesitation, Mojarra shifts his rifle to his other shoulder, slips a hand into his meager purse, takes out a copper coin and buys two penny fritters wrapped in greasy paper. He gives them to his daughter; one for now, one for the journey, he says as she protests. He tells her to fasten her shawl tighter, then taking her arm, he leads her away from the stall, directing a furious glare at two Engineering Cadets in purple frockcoats and bearskin helmets who are staring shamelessly at the girl while they queue to buy fritters.

"My mistress says I should learn to read and write, and count too . . . . She says I'm bright enough."

"That costs money, *hija*."

"She says if I want to and I study hard, she'll pay. There's an old widow who lives above the apothecary on the Calle del Sacramento, a decent woman—she teaches reading and writing and sums for five *duros* a month."

"Five *duros*?" Mojarra splutters, outraged. "That's a small fortune."

"I told you, she said she would pay. And she will give me an hour off every afternoon to study, if you agree. Even cousin Toño says I should make the most of the opportunity."

"Tell your mistress to mind her own business. And tell this cousin of hers to watch his step . . . Tell him a knife in the belly and a quick flick of the wrist will dispatch a poor man as quickly as a gentleman with a gold watch in his pocket."

"My God, Father. You know that Don Toño is a perfect gentleman, even if he is always joking around. And he's very charming."

The salter glowers angrily at the ground. "I know what I'm talking about."

Leaving the town hall square behind, father and daughter come to the avenue that leads down from the Convento de San Francisco. It is here, next to the watering trough outside the blacksmith's forge, between the Naval Observatory and the municipal slaughterhouse, that the carriages bound for Cádiz stop. The journey takes less than three hours by landau or caleche, but that is expensive. It will take six to eight hours for Mari Paz to get there on the slow cart, which is scheduled to stop at Torregorda, at Chato's tavern and at the Cortadura barricade—two and a half leagues along the reef from the sea to the far end of the bay, with stretches of it lying within cannon shot of the enemy. The very thought that the French might fire at his daughter fills Felipe Mojarra with murderous rage, an urge to make his way through the tidal creeks and slit the throat of the first *gabacho* he finds.

"A respectable woman has no need of arithmetic or the ability to read," he says, having considered his response for several paces. "All you need to know is how to sew, how to iron and how to make a stew."

"There are other things in life, Father. Education . . ."

"With everything you've learned, from your mother, in that fine house where you work, and from watching the ladies and gentlemen, you have more than enough education for when you marry and have your own house."

Mari Paz's laugh is soft, silvery. A laugh that brings a childlike freshness to the air. The freshness of the little girl that Felipe Mojarra has almost forgotten.

"Me, marry? Come now, Father. Don't even think of such a thing." Her tone is at once artless, affronted and vain. "Who would want me? . . . Besides, a woman does not have to marry. Look at Señorita Palma—she is still single. And she is so elegant and serious, she is . . . I don't know . . . such a lady."

In spite of himself, the salter finds that the girl's warm tone and her laughter move him deeply. We should leave nothing behind, he thinks again, suddenly gripped by a nameless panic. He looks at his daughter, unsure whether to kiss or scold her; in the end, he does neither. Instead, he simply tosses away the stub of his cigar and shifts his rifle to his other shoulder.

"Come on, finish your fritter."

LEANING OVER THE parapet of the city wall next to the Royal Jail, Rogelio Tizón gazes out at the sea. To his left, beyond the Puerta de Tierra, misty and yellow, is the long, low line of the reef leading to the mainland, to Chiclana and the Isla de Léon. To his right, the sky is cloudless. The air seems fresher, though even now a dark band of cloud is once again looming over the horizon. In this direction, the sweeping panorama of the city moves from the uncompleted new cathedral, taking in the watchtowers of the houses, the Capuchin convent, the low squat dwellings of the Viña district and the distant ocher point of the San Sebastián castle, with its lighthouse protruding into the mouth of the bay.

"Fancy a little sea bass, Señor Comisario?"

Along the wall overlooking the sea are a dozen regulars who make their living using rod, bait and line, selling their catch from door to door at the inns and the lodging houses. One of them, a gypsy named Caramillo from El Boquete—a regular informer and a member of the mob who dragged General Solano through the streets during the uprising in 1808—has come over and is politely offering Tizón one of the three large fish floundering at the bottom of his bucket.

"It would be my pleasure to give it to you, Don Rogelio. I can bring it to your house later, if you like."

"Get out of my sight, Caramillo. Off with you!"

The man meekly retreats, limping slightly. He seems to bear Tizón no grudge for the beating seven or eight years ago that left him with one leg half an inch shorter than the other. But the comisario has no appetite for fish or meat, nor for dealing with riffraff. Not this morning, anyway—not after the little chat he had an hour ago, at the Harbor Master's Office, with Governor Villavicencio and the General Intendant García Pico. The day had started out well enough. After a cup of coffee in the Café del Correo, leafing through *El Censor General* and *El Conciso* (one *servile*, the other liberal) to see how the Tyrians and Trojans are getting along, and then a shave at the barbershop on the Calle Comedias—gratis, as usual—the comisario made a lucrative tour of his usual stomping grounds. He visited his best shark-like smile on a couple of bars where the owners' uneasy conscience and the need to appease the relevant authorities made it possible for him to line his pockets without much resistance. Thirty *pesos* is a tidy profit for a single morning's work: a hundred *reales* from an ironmonger on the Calle de la Pelota for having an immigrant widow with no official papers residing and working—in every sense, malicious neighbors insisted—on the premises; another five hundred from a silversmith on the Calle de la Novena for receiving stolen goods, to whom Tizón bluntly offered a choice between lining his pocket and the unpleasant alternative of a 9,000-*real* fine or six years in Ceuta prison.

But after that, things had turned black. Twenty minutes in the office of the military and political Governor of Cádiz were enough to ruin Rogelio Tizón's mood. He had gone to the governor's office to speak to García Pico concerning a matter which, for reasons of discretion, neither the governor nor the Intendant were prepared to discuss in writing. There is no room in the current climate for pointless risks or blunders.

"We still can't prove anything for certain," Tizón explained uneasily as he sat at the governor's imposing desk. "Obviously, we can prove that he is a spy . . . but for the other matter we need more time."

Listening, General Don Juan María de Villavicencio brought the tips of his fingers together in an almost pious gesture. He bowed his venerable, gray-haired head over his black necktie, his gold-rimmed spectacles dangling from the buttonhole of his frockcoat. Finally he spoke.

"If he has confessed to being a spy," he said curtly, "you should turn him over to the military authorities."

Cautiously, respectfully, Tizón explained that this was not the issue. In Cádiz there was no shortage of spies—or people suspected of spying—so one more or less would make no difference. There was, however, serious evidence linking the prisoner to the murdered girls. Something that put matters in a very different light.

"Is this certain?"

The comisario's hesitation was barely noticeable. "It is very probable," he said coolly.

"Then what are you waiting for? Get me a confession."

"We are working on it," Tizón said, allowing himself a wolfish smile of thinly veiled self-satisfaction. "But the new policing regulations impose certain limitations . . ."

But when he turned toward García Pico, expecting to get his support, Tizón's smile drained away. Solemn, the Intendant was determined to stay out of the fray, not to get involved. Not here, at least. Not in front of the governor. The one thing clear from his expression was that he seriously doubted that Rogelio Tizón would feel constrained in any way by policing regulations, or any other damn thing.

"What are the chances that the suspect is indeed our murderer?" asked Villavicencio.

"Reasonable," said Tizón. "But some aspects are unclear."

The governor eyed him suspiciously. An old dog. A sea dog, thought Tizón, smiling at his own joke.

"Has he admitted anything?"

Another wolfish smile, more ambiguous this time.

"Some things, yes . . . but not much."

"Enough to take the matter before a judge?"

A careful pause. Feeling the heat of García Pico's anxious gaze, Rogelio Tizón made a vague gesture and said, not yet, señor. It might take a couple of days. Or a little longer. Then, having spent the whole interview on the edge of his seat, he leaned back in his chair. He was beginning to feel hot; he was glad he had taken off his coat before coming in.

"For your sake, I hope you know what you're doing."

Silence. The governor's coldness was in stark contrast to the temperature of his office. As though a lifetime at sea had permanently chilled Villavicencio to the bone. The fire burning in the hearth, beneath a huge painting of a naval battle of uncertain outcome, gave off a scorching heat, yet Villavicencio seemed cool and comfortable in his thick frockcoat. His pale, delicate hands protruded from the striped cuffs—a watchmaker's hands, thought Tizón—and on the left one he still wore the emerald given to him by Napoleon at Brest, a point of pride or perhaps a reminder of his social standing. After a moment's hesitation, the comisario dismissed the idea of taking out his kerchief and mopping his brow. The gesture might be misinterpreted.

"In any case," he said, "the public needs a culprit. And we have him: a self-confessed spy, suspected of . . . Well, it can all be arranged. I know a number of journalists."

The governor waved his hand contemptuously.

"I know them too. Rather better than I might like . . . But what if he is not our man? What if we announce our news and then tomorrow the real murderer kills again?"

"This is why I did not make the arrest public, señor. Everything has been handled discreetly. Even the spying has not been mentioned yet . . . For the moment, this man has simply disappeared off the face of the earth."

Villavicencio nodded distractedly. All of Cádiz is aware he will not be in this post much longer: he is one of the most eligible candidates for the new Regency, to be elected in the coming weeks. He will almost certainly be replaced as governor by Cayetano Valdés, who is currently commanding the fleet that is defending the bay: a tough, experienced sailor, a veteran of the battles of Trafalgar and San Vicente, with a reputation for being brusque and plainspoken. That is why this matter needs to be settled now, thought Tizón. With Valdés as governor, a man with considerably less political sophistication than Villavicencio, there would be no question of insinuations, equivocations or half measures.

"I expect everything to be done according to form," said the governor suddenly. "I mean your investigation."

"My investigation?"

"The interrogation. I assume it will be conducted without any intemperance and . . . um . . . unnecessary violence."

García Pico finally opened his mouth. He was shocked, or attempted to appear so. "Of course, señor. That would be unthinkable . . ."

Villavicencio paid him no heed. He looked Tizón directly in the eye. "In some respects, it is a good thing that you are responsible for these proceedings . . . Military jurisdiction is less flexible. Less . . ."

"Pragmatic?"

I couldn't help myself, Tizón thought. *A pox on that filthy tongue of mine.* The two men glowered at him. His sarcasm had not passed unnoticed.

"The new laws," said the governor after a pause, "stipulate that the period of detention be limited and the interrogation methods restrained. All this will be set down in black and white in the new Constitution . . . But anything concerning this particular prisoner will not be official until the two of you make it public."

García Pico was not best pleased by this use of the plural. Out of the corner of his eye, Tizón saw the Intendant squirming uncomfortably in his chair. And moreover, the governor went on, as yet no one had informed him of the matter. Officially, of course. There was no need to shout it from the rooftops. Making this affair public would put everyone in a difficult position. There would be no way back.

"On that point, you need have no worries," García Pico said quickly. "Technically, this arrest has not yet taken place."

A patrician, approbatory silence. Villavicencio moved his fingertips apart, nodded slowly, then brought them together again with the precision he might bring to regulating the micrometer of a sextant.

"This is not the time to lock horns with the Cortes. Those liberal gentlemen . . ."

He fell silent, as though there were nothing more to add; Tizón realized that this was neither a confidence nor an omission. Villavicencio was not one to make such a slip, nor to share political confidences with his subordinates. He was simply reminding them of his position with regards to the debates conducted at San Felipe Neri. Although the Governor of Cádiz was scrupulously impartial, it was no secret that he sympathized with the royalist diehards and, like them, trusted that King Fernando would return to restore order and wisdom to the nation.

"Of course," said García Pico hurriedly. "You have nothing to fear."

"I shall hold you responsible, Intendant." The stern look was not directed at García Pico, but at Tizón. "And you, of course, Comisario . . . There must be no public statement before the matter is resolved. And not a word in the newspapers before we have a duly signed confession."

At this, without stirring from his seat, Villavicencio gave a wave with the hand bearing the imperial emerald—a cursory dismissal, immediately understood as such by García Pico and the comisario, who got to their feet. The gesture of a man accustomed to giving orders without words.

"It goes without saying," said the governor as they were getting up, "that this conversation never took place."

They were halfway to the door when he unexpectedly spoke again.

"Are you a religious man, Comisario?"

Tizón turned, bewildered. There could be nothing casual about such a question coming from the mouth of Don Juan María de Villavicencio, a seaman with an illustrious career, a man who attended mass and took communion every day.

"Well . . . um . . . like most people, señor . . . More or less."

The governor gazed at him almost curiously from behind the vast, imposing desk. "In your shoes, I would pray that the spy you have under arrest does turn out to be the killer of those girls." He pressed his fingertips together again. "That no one kills another girl . . . Do you understand what I'm saying?"

Cunning old bastard, thought Tizón, though his face remained impassive. "Perfectly," he answered. "But as your Lordship said, it would be wise for us to have someone in reserve. Just in case . . ."

Villavicencio raised his eyebrows with studied grace. As though racking his brains to remember.

"I said that? Really?" He glanced at the Intendant as though appealing to his memory of events, but García Pico made an ambiguous gesture. "I certainly do not remember expressing myself in such terms."

Now, standing by the sea wall, the memory of his conversation with Villavicencio unsettles Rogelio Tizón. The certainties of the past days have given way to the qualms of the past hours. Together with the governor's words and the deferential, logical attitude of García Pico, this has left him feeling vulnerable; like a king on a chessboard watching pieces disappear that might have allowed him to castle safely. And yet these things take time. If his position is to remain secure, he must proceed with caution. This is his strategy. Haste is the most terrible of all enemies. Objectively, one dram more or less on either side will tilt the scale—the limit between the possible and the impossible, between certainty and delusion—as surely as a hundredweight.

There is a distant explosion somewhere in the center of the city. The second one today. With the cloudless sky and the change of wind, the French have begun shelling from the Cabezuela again. The blast, muffled by the buildings in between, has Tizón worried. It is not the bombs or the damage they might cause—he has long since grown accustomed to those. But they are a constant reminder of how weak his position could be—perhaps how weak it is, he thinks anxiously—in this game he is playing: this house of cards that might be brought down by the news he most fears, a piece of news that, in some strange sense, he awaits with a mixture of curiosity and anxiety. The confirmation that he has made a mistake would relieve him of the agony of uncertainty.

The comisario steps away from the parapet and the city walls, taking a route that in recent days he has taken so often it has become a routine: slowly retracing the path between the six sites where the girls were murdered, attentive at every step to the slightest change in air or light, in the temperature, the smells, the sensations he experiences. Calculating and recalculating the subtle chess moves of an unseen adversary whose complex mind, as unknowable as the idea of God, merges with the map of Cádiz, a singular city ringed by the sea, buffeted by the winds. It is a city whose physical form—the streets, the squares and the buildings—Rogelio Tizón can no longer see; he sees only a mysterious terrain, menacing and abstract as a fretwork of whip marks: that same disturbing tracery he glimpsed on the skin of the murdered girls, and which he recognized—or thought he recognized—in the map Gregorio Fumagal says he burned in the stove of his workshop. The secret plan of an urban space which seems to correspond—in every line and curve—with the mind of a murderer.

WHILE COMISARIO TIZÓN is brooding about the trajectories and parabolas of bombs in Cádiz, Pépé Lobo—moored off Los Lances beach at Tarifa, forty-five miles southeast of the city—watches the plume of spray that a 12-pound French bomb has just thrown up, less than a cable's length away from the bowsprit of the *Culebra*.

"Don't panic," he reassures the crew. "It's just a stray shot."

On the deck of the cutter, anchored at four fathoms with all sails furled and flying the ensign of the Spanish Navy, the crew watch the pall of smoke drifting along the ravine on the far side of the town walls. Since nine o'clock, under a leaden sky, the French infantry have been making an assault on the breach to the north of Tarifa. The continual rumble of rifles and cannonfire can be clearly heard a mile out, borne on the offshore wind that holds the *Culebra* with the beach off its starboard bow, the town on the beam and Tarifa island to stern. Near the cutter, anchored broadside on—the better to aim their gun batteries— two English frigates, a Spanish corvette and several gunboats carrying cannons and howitzers are firing at intervals on the French positions; the white smoke from their gunpowder drifts toward the corsairs as they watch the battle. There are a dozen other smaller vessels moored nearby: feluccas and tartanes, waiting to see how things play out. If the enemy breaks through the powerful defenses of the town walls, these vessels will have to rush to help evacuate the local population and any survivors among the 3,000 Spanish and English soldiers who have been defending the town tooth and nail.

"The French are still piling into the breach," says Ricardo Maraña.

The first officer, who has been peering through the telescope, now passes it to Pépé Lobo. The two men are standing in the stern of the cutter, next to the tiller. Maraña, hatless and dressed, as always, in black, wipes the corners of his mouth with a kerchief which he stuffs into the sleeve of his jacket without so much as a glance. With one eye closed and the other pressed to the lens, Pépé Lobo scans the coastline from Santa Catalina Fort, almost in line with the Guzmans' castle, all the way to the smoke-shrouded ramparts and the suburbs razed by the shelling. On the far side are the hills from which the enemy attack was launched, dotted with agave and prickly pear and sudden flashes of red from the artillery fire.

"Our lads are giving them hell," says Lobo.

His lieutenant shrugs his shoulders coldly. "I just hope they hold out. I'm sick to death of these hurried, last-minute evacuations . . . old hags with bundles of dirty laundry, screaming kids and women asking where they can have a piss."

There is a silence, broken only by the distant thunder of battle. Ricardo Maraña looks up critically at the flag fluttering from the mast—two red stripes, one yellow, bearing the Royal Arms: castle and lions rampant. Meanwhile Pépé Lobo notes that the offshore wind seems to be shifting to a fresh north-northwesterly. This will be a god-send if, as they have been expecting for some time, the order comes from Tarifa to weigh anchor.

"And I'm sick of this too," adds Maraña disdainfully. "If I had wanted to serve my country, I'd have joined the Armada, darned my uniforms and ended up with a salary in arrears like everyone else."

"You can't win 'em all," says Pépé Lobo, smiling.

A short ragged cough. The kerchief appears again.

"True."

Lobo points the telescope toward the town walls; between the eddies of dust, he can make out the diminutive figures of men engaged in fierce fighting, fending off the French for as long as possible. Half an hour ago, a naval lieutenant—arriving on a boat from the city with a package of official dispatches to be shipped to Cádiz—reported that the French had noticed the breach last night and, considering it auspicious, mounted a 9 a.m. assault from the trenches they had excavated along the ravine in the preceding days. According to the naval lieutenant, four enemy battalions of grenadiers and chasseurs marched in serried ranks, but finding themselves up to their knees in mud, as a result of the recent rains, and under constant fire from the defenders, the assault was quickly thrown into confusion and by the time they reached the town walls it had lost much of its momentum. An hour and a half later, little has changed: the French are still attempting to scale the walls and the defenders are holding them back without artillery—the anchored ships cannot shell the area around the breach—only rifles and bayonets.

The crew of the *Culebra* discuss the morning's events, pointing out the plumes of smoke that indicate heavy fighting. Perched on the gunwale, leaning against a shroud line, wielding a second telescope, Brasero the bo'sun tells them what he can see. Pépé Lobo leaves them in peace. He knows that every man aboard shares the opinion of the first officer. For the most part these men are smugglers and the sort of port rabble who sign a roster or a police confession with a cross. Lobo recruited them in the sleazy taverns along the Calle de los Negros, the Calle de Sopranis and El Boquete; most of them on the run, trying to evade enforced conscription. Not one of these forty-eight men—including the first officer and the ship's clerk—signed up with the *Culebra* with the intention of spending their time under military command, giving up the free life of a corsair, the thrill and the spoils of the chase in exchange for a meager wage from the Royal Armada, of which they know they might never see a peso. Their most recent campaign had put at least 250 *pesos* in every man's pocket—three times as much in Pépé Lobo's—with seven vessels already declared fair captures, and six more still before the Prize Court, to say nothing of the 150 *reales* a month every sailor got from the moment he signed up. This is why, though he has not said so, the captain completely understands why his men are, like himself, heartily sickened by the twenty-two days they have wasted as a mailboat under naval command—ferrying soldiers and dispatches from place to place, far from their hunting waters; forced to serve as auxiliaries to a Navy which, like the Royal Customs, they would ordinarily avoid like the plague—since there is hardly a man aboard whose conscience is clear, or whose neck is safe from the rope.

"Signal on the tower," calls Ricardo Maraña.

Pépé Lobo shifts the telescope toward the lighthouse on the island where the flags have just been hoisted. "That's us," he says. "Tell the men to get ready."

Maraña steps away from the taffrail and heads back toward the crew.

"Silence on deck! Prepare for action!"

More flags. Lobo can read them without the need for his telescope: one white and red, followed by a blue pennant. He has no need to consult the secret signal book he keeps in a drawer of the binnacle above the companionway. This one is easy: *Set sail immediately*.

"Let's go, Lieutenant."

Maraña nods and strides across the deck, giving orders while the sudden thunder of bare feet makes the boards shake. Brasero the bo'sun, having clambered from the shrouds, blows his whistle and dispatches men to work the halyards and the capstan whose bar is already in place.

"Heave around and up!" roars the lieutenant. "Break out the jib!"

Pépé Lobo steps aside so the Scotsman and the other steersman can take the helm; he glances warily over the taffrail toward the rocks, half hidden by the sea, half a cable length from the stern and the foot of the island. When he looks to prow again, the anchor is at short stay.

"Port tack," he orders the helmsmen.

The cutter's long bowsprit turns away from the coast and the wind, while the men straddling it loosen the sail ties securing the jib and the foresail. A moment later the first triangular sail is made fast to the forward end of the bowsprit, the slack sheets quickly hauled in and secured. Like a thoroughbred racehorse impatiently champing at the bit, the *Culebra* bridles a little as the rigging grows taut, ready for the off.

"Slacken the mainsail sheet! Set the sail!"

The sailors loosen the main brails and the sail opens out with a creak of wood and canvas, flapping in the fresh north-northwesterly. Lobo quickly glances again at the sunken rocks, which are a little closer now. Then he checks the compass and visually traces the course; he needs to keep the cutter well to starboard of the dangerous shallows at Los Cabezos, four miles west-northwest of here opposite the Peña Tower. The mainsail is almost set and the vast expanse of canvas is beginning to take the wind. The anchor is now being secured to the cat-head; the ship lists elegantly to port and cleanly glides away from its mooring.

"Set the foresail! Trim the sheets!"

Another stray French cannonball—or perhaps it was fired deliber-ately, the enemy seeing the cutter getting under way—raises a column of water and spray far off to starboard. Meanwhile, the ships still at anchor continue shelling the enemy on land. With all necessary canvas set around its sole mast, the *Culebra* now gathers speed, close-hauled, powerfully cleaving the water, which is almost glassy, being in the lee of shore. Hands behind his back, feet well apart to compensate for the heeling of the ship, Pépé Lobo looks back one last time at Tarifa, its north wall still wreathed in a pall of smoke and sparks. He is not sorry to be getting out of here. Not sorry at all.

"Back to Cádiz," says Maraña.

Having finished his work on deck for the moment, the first officer ambles back casually, hands in pockets, to stand next to the captain. Lobo however cannot help but notice the contented note in his first officer's voice, or the smiles on the faces of a number of crewmen, in-cluding Brasero. Perhaps they will be able to spend a day in port, and go ashore. It would be a welcome break after three weeks at sea, with the ground shifting and everybody muttering under their breath. Per-haps the ship's owners will have managed to persuade the authorities to give the *Culebra* back its Letter of Marque, and they can finally stop bucketing about like a messenger boy for the Royal Armada.

"Yes," Pépé Lobo says, thinking about Lolita Palma. "Back to Cádiz."

"The Silent Street"—the very name of the Calle del Silencio seems like a taunt. It is as though the city itself, crouching within its labyrin-thine web of streets and alleys, is mocking Rogelio Tizón. This is what the comisario is thinking as, by lantern light, he holds on to his hat and ducks through the gaping hole in the wall of the Castillo de Guardia-marinas, a dark, decrepit stone building that has stood empty for fif-teen years. Tizón knows that this is no ordinary place; this is where the old Cádiz meridian once ran. In earlier times, the square tower that still stands in the south corner housed the Naval Observatory, while the northern part was reserved for the Royal Armada naval academy until both observatory and academy were moved to the Isla de Léon. It was subsequently used as a barracks, then, after a failed attempt to locate the new prison here, it was bought by a private individual only to be later abandoned. Even the homeless refugees looking for somewhere to live avoid these ruins, because of the falling masonry, the crumbling roofs and the poor condition of the beams.

"Some kids from the Calle del Mesón Nuevo found her," Cadalso informs him. "Two brothers."

Until now, Tizón had hoped it might be a mistake, a random coincidence that would not alter the equilibrium of things. But as he steps into the old parade ground, with Cadalso lighting his way through the mounds of rubble, that hope vanishes. At the far end of the courtyard, next to the portcullis at the foot of the keep, walled up with stones and planks, the flickering flame of a lantern casts an arc of light on the ground. And lying facedown in that semicircle is the body of a young woman, her back flayed to shreds with a whip.

"A pox on God and his whore of a mother!"

The brutal blasphemy shocks Cadalso, who is far from being a pious man. The deputy clearly does not like what he sees on the comisario's face. When Tizón turns to look at him, Cadalso has gone pale.

"Who knows about this?"

"The kids . . . and their parents, of course."

"Anyone else?"

Cadalso nods toward a pair of dark, cloaked figures standing guard over the body, just beyond the circle of light.

"The corporal and a nightwatchman. The boys reported it to them."

"Make it clear that if anyone breathes a word about this, I'll rip their eyes out and stuff them up their ass—understood?"

"Yes, señor."

A brief pause. Ominous. The cane swings gently. "That includes you, Cadalso."

"Don't worry."

"On the contrary, I do worry . . . and you should worry too, if you know what's good for you."

Tizón struggles to compose himself, to remain calm, not to surrender to the panic convulsing his insides. He is five paces from the body. The corporal and the nightwatchman step forward and salute him. They have checked everything, the corporal tells Tizón, leaning on his pike. As far as they know, there is no one hiding in the building. And none of the neighbors—aside from the two boys—noticed anything suspicious. The girl is very young, no older than fifteen. They believe they have identified her as a maid working in the Posada de la Academia, a local boardinghouse, but given the extent of her injuries and the lack of light they cannot be sure. They estimate she must have been murdered shortly after sunset, because the boys were playing in the courtyard during the afternoon and saw nothing.

"What were they doing back here after dark?"

"They live nearby—only fifty paces away. After dinner, their dog escaped from the house and they went looking for it. Since they often play here, they thought the dog might have come here . . . When they stumbled on the body, they told their father and he alerted us."

"Do you know the father?"

"A cobbler. A decent man, by all accounts."

Tizón dismissed them with a nod. "Go and stand guard by the main entrance," he tells them. "Don't let anyone in: no neighbors, no busybodies, not even King Fernando himself. Is that clear? Go on, then." He takes a deep breath, thinks for a moment; he slips his fingers into his jacket pocket then hands Cadalso a gold half *onza*, telling him to go to the cobbler's house and give it to him, after making the situation clear. For his cooperation, and for any inconvenience.

"Tell him if he keeps his mouth shut and doesn't obstruct the investigation, he'll get the other half in a couple of days."

Cadalso and the nightwatchman melt into the darkness. Once he is alone, the comisario circles the body of the girl, remaining outside the ring of light cast by the lantern. He is careful to consider every possibility, every clue before he moves closer. All the while he is grappling with two, parallel feelings: bitter indignation at the difficult position in which this new murder—to call it "unexpected" would be excessive, he admits with perverse honesty—puts him with his superiors, and a profound fury that shakes him to the core, faced with this evidence of his miscalculation and failure. The certainty of his own defeat at the hands of the malign, the cruel, the obscene forces of this city, which he is beginning to despise with his very soul.

There can be no doubt, he realizes as he approaches the body. He picks up the lantern by its wire handle and holds it high, illuminating the scene. No one could imitate these wounds, even if he tried. The hands tied behind the back, the mouth gagged, the back bare, crisscrossed with deep gashes that reveal a labyrinth of clotted blood and exposed bone. And the distinctive smell of butchered flesh, the stench of the slaughterhouse Tizón knows so well and which he realizes he will never be able to blot out from his memory. The girl is not wearing shoes and the comisario looks around for them, to no avail. He finds only a flannel mantilla, tossed next to the hole in the wall. The shoes are probably still out on the street where the killer grabbed her before dragging her in here. She could have been knocked out by a blow, or she may have been conscious and struggling to the end. The gag and the fact that her hands are tied points to the latter, although they may simply have been additional precautions on the part of the murderer, in case the whiplashes brought her round. He hopes that this is how it was, that the girl was unconscious the whole time. Fifteen years old, he confirms, kneeling down and bringing the lantern closer so he can study her face, the glassy half-open eyes gazing into the nothingness of death. Whipped without mercy, like an animal, until she died.

Getting to his feet, the comisario looks up into the inky sky above the castle. Dark stretches of cloud hide the moon and much of the sky, but a handful of stars burn with an icy glimmer that seems to register the coldness of the night air. Rogelio Tizón brings a cigar to his lips but does not light it; instead he stands for a moment, staring at the heavens. Then he walks back to the gap in the wall, lighting his way with the lantern, which he hands back to the corporal and the nightwatchman.

"I want someone to find that poor wretch's shoes. They won't be far away."

The corporal blinks, confused. "Shoes, Señor Comisario?"

"Yes, God damn you. Shoes. I'm not speaking Chinese! Now get moving . . ."

He steps out into the Calle del Silencio and looks both ways before heading right. In the yellow glow of the municipal streetlight burning opposite the Mesón Nuevo, at the far end of the Calle de los Blancos, he can just make out the ruined archway in the north wall of the Castillo de Guardiamarinas, leading to the Calle San Juan de Dios. Tizón walks under the arch and peers into the shadows. In the distance, to the left, are the streetlights of the Plaza del Ayuntamiento. He presses his hat down and pulls up his collar against the damp sea air—the Atlantic is only a few steps away at the other end of the street.

The comisario stands motionless for a moment, then retreats into the shelter of the archway; he strikes a match and prepares to light the cigar still dangling from his lips. Suddenly, as he cups his hand around the flame, he thinks better of it and snuffs out the match. Because what he is looking for, if it truly exists, will require a keen sense of smell and every other sense on the alert. So he slips the cigar back into the case and walks slowly along the Calle del Silencio, watchful as a hunter, stalking out sensations and sounds that crouch in the dark hollows of the city. He does not know exactly what he is looking for. An emptiness, perhaps. Or a smell. Perhaps a breath of wind, or the sudden absence of it.

He is trying to calculate where and when the next bomb will fall.

CHAPTER THIRTEEN

ⱷ

Past the open door and the white marble step with the sign engraved in black reading *Café del Correo*, to one side of the twin arches leading into the columned courtyard, Comisario Tizón and Professor Barrull have just finished their second game of chess. The rumor of war hanging over the squares of the chessboard gradually fades: a king still stands in the back row—the policeman was playing white—mercilessly pinned by a knight and a queen. A few squares forward, two pawns stare each other down, each blocking the other's path. Tizón is licking his wounds, but the subject of the conversation shifts to a different chessboard.

"Five hours later the bomb fell, Professor, right on the corner of the Calle del Silencio, by the Guardiamarinas archway . . . thirty feet, as the crow flies, from the courtyard where the girl's body was found."

Hipólito Barrull is listening attentively, cleaning his spectacles with a kerchief. They are sitting at their usual table, Tizón leaning his chair back against the wall, legs stretched out under the table. Two bowls of coffee and two glasses of water sit among the captured chess pieces.

"This bomb did fall," says the comisario, "as did the one at Divina Pastora. But not the time before. On the Calle del Laurel, a girl was murdered but no bomb fell, either before or after. That changes things. It changes the rules."

"I don't see why," the professor says. "Perhaps it just means that even the murderer is fallible . . . That his method, or whatever you want to call it, is not perfect."

"But the places . . ." Tizón breaks off, unsure. Barrull looks at him attentively. "There's something about the places . . ." the comisario says after a brief hesitation. "I've noticed it. There's something different about the atmosphere."

Barrull nods thoughtfully. After the massacre he has just enacted on the chessboard, his equine face has regained its normal courteous expression. He no longer looks like the ruthless opponent who, barely five minutes ago, was mocking and insulting Tizón—damn your eyes, Comisario, I'll rip out your liver, and so forth—as he marshaled his pieces with homicidal fury.

"I see," he says. "You mentioned something of this before . . . How long have you been mulling over this idea? Weeks?"

"Months. And the more I think about it, the more convinced I am."

Barrull nods, shaking his mane of gray hair. Then he carefully adjusts his spectacles. "This may simply be like your obsession concerning *Ajax*," he suggests. "Or that spy you arrested . . . You became obsessed and that clouded your judgment. False clues lead to false conclusions. This is not scientific—it is more akin to fiction. Perhaps you have rather too much imagination for a police officer."

"It's too late to change my vocation now."

Barrull greets this remark with an oblique, complicit smile. Then the professor nods to the chessboard.

"There is a part of you I know well," he says. "The part played out here. And I'm not sure that the word *imagination* truly applies. Rather, it is the contrary. You have a keen intuition when playing chess. You know how to look at things. When you're sitting here as my opponent there is nothing fictional about your play. You are not one of those players who get swept up in fantastical but foolish strategies, which simply make things easier for the opponents. That is why I enjoy playing you. You allow yourself to be trounced methodically."

Tizón lights a cigar; the smoke rises to join the thick pall trapped beneath the courtyard's glass roof, through which streams of late afternoon sunlight illuminate the upper balustrade. Then he glances around warily, on the lookout for anyone who might be listening in. As usual, a goodly number of customers occupy the wicker chairs and wooden benches set out on the patio. Paco Celis, the owner, watches from the kitchen doorway, while waiters in white aprons bustle about with pots of coffee and hot chocolate and pitchers of water. Sitting together at an adjacent table, a cleric and three gentlemen are reading newspapers in silence. Their presence does not trouble Tizón; they are members of the Royal Academy, come from Madrid to Cádiz to seek refuge. They are regular patrons of the Correo and he knows them by sight. The clergyman, Don Joaquín Lorenzo Villanueva, is also the member for Valencia at the Cortes, an active constitutionalist and—despite his tonsure—an exponent of liberal ideas. One of the other men is Don Diego Clemencín, a scholar of about fifty, who now earns his living editing the *Regency Gazette*.

"There are places," Tizón insists, "strange places."

Hipólito Barrull studies the comisario carefully, narrowing his eyes, which seem smaller still through the thick lenses of his spectacles.

"Places, you say?"

"Yes."

"Very well. In reality it is not so far-fetched."

There is a scientific basis for the phenomenon, the professor explains. Eminent researchers have noted something similar. The problem is that, compared to dioptrics and astronomy, the science of meteorology is still in its infancy. Nonetheless, it is indisputable that particular places can have particular atmospheres. The heat of the sun, for example, acts upon the earth and the air, and variations in temperature can be indicative of many things, including storms gathering in specific places.

"The example of a gathering storm seems a good analogy to me," Barrull adds. "A series of circumstances—temperature, wind, atmospheric pressure—come together to create a precise condition at a precise moment. This gives rise to rainstorms, lightning . . ."

As he lists these phenomena, Barrull places a nicotine-stained finger on different squares of the chessboard. Rogelio Tizón leans forward, listening carefully. He glances around at the other customers again, then says in a low voice: "Are you telling me it could also prompt someone to kill, or a bomb to fall . . . ? Or both of these things simultaneously?"

"I am not saying anything. But it is possible. Anything that has not been comprehensively disproved remains possible. Modern science surprises us daily with new discoveries. We have no idea of its limits."

He raises his eyebrows, absolving himself of any personal responsibility. Then he reaches out toward the thin line of smoke rising from the burning tip of Tizón's cigar, waves his hand and waits until the whorls and spirals of smoke settle once again into a straight line. The wind, for example, he explains. Air in motion. The comisario mentioned wind, or subtle variations in it at certain points in the city. Recent studies of winds and breezes have led us to believe that, during the day, wind direction shifts to form a clockwise circle in the northern hemisphere and an anti-clockwise one in the southern hemisphere. This would make it possible to establish a stable relationship between specific locations, atmospheric pressure and the intensity of the wind. It is an interaction of constant, cyclical causes and transitory, local forces, of undetermined frequency—a given set of circumstances should give a specific set of results. Does Tizón understand what he is saying?

"I am trying to understand," says the comisario.

Barrull takes his snuffbox from the pocket of his old-fashioned jacket; he toys with it, but does not open it.

"By your hypothesis, nothing would be impossible in a city like this. Cádiz is a ship at the mercy of wind and sea. The streets and the houses have been built to withstand them, to channel or to temper them. You talk of winds, sounds . . . even smells . . . All of these things are in the air, in the atmosphere."

The policeman looks again at the captured chess pieces on each side of the board. At length, he picks up the white king thoughtfully and sets it down among them. "It would be funny if, in the end, the murders of seven young girls were the result of atmospheric conditions . . ."

"And why not? It has been proven that certain winds, based on their moisture levels and temperature, act directly on the humors, triggering changes in temperament. Madness and crime are more common in areas subject to constant or frequent pressure . . . We know very little about the dark chasms of the human mind."

The professor finally opens the snuffbox, takes a pinch, snorts it and discreetly sneezes with pleasure. "Obviously, all this is very vague," he adds, shaking snuff from his jacket. "I am no scientist. But every general law of Nature also applies in the most specific circumstances . . . What holds true for a continent, equally holds true for a street in Cádiz."

It is now Tizón's turn to place a finger on the chessboard, on the empty square where the vanquished king stood.

"Let's imagine," he says, "that there are specific locations, geographical points where the phases of physical phenomena are related, or where they combine to behave differently than in other places . . ."

He allows these last words to hang in the air, inviting Barrull to complete the thought. The professor, once again toying with his snuffbox, turns to look at the people on the patio. Pensive. A waiter hurries over, thinking that they must want something, but Tizón dismisses him with a glance.

"Well," Barrull begins, after reflecting on the matter a little longer, "we would not be the first to think this is true. Almost two centuries ago, Descartes considered the world to be a *plenum:* a stable construct composed of or filled with 'subtle matter,' inside which are tiny cavities or eddies. Like the cells of a honeycomb, with matter swirling around them."

"Say that again, Don Hipólito. Slowly."

The professor slips the snuffbox back into his pocket and looks at the comisario. Then he looks down again at the chessboard.

"There's not much more I can tell you. What you are talking about are specific points where the physical conditions are distinct from the area surrounding them. Such points are known as vortices."

"Vortices?"

"Exactly. Compared to the vast immensity of the universe, a vortex is a minuscule point in which things happen . . . or do not happen. Or happen in a different way."

A pause. Barrull seems to be considering his words, discovering unexpected perspectives in what he has just said. Eventually, his lips curl into a smile.

"Distinct places that act upon the world," he says. "Upon individuals, things, upon the movement of the planets . . ." He stops, as if he dare not say more.

Tizón, who has been sucking on his cigar, takes it out of his mouth. "On life and death . . . ? On the trajectory of a bomb?"

The professor looks troubled, as if he has gone too far—or fears he has. "Listen, Comisario. Don't set too much store by me. What you need is a man of science . . . I am merely a reader. A curious man who knows a thing or two. I am speaking from memory, and no doubt making some mistakes. Here in Cádiz, there is no shortage of—"

"Answer my question, please."

The word *please* seems to surprise Barrull. This may be the first time he has heard it from Rogelio Tizón's lips. The comisario himself cannot remember uttering the word in years. If ever.

"The idea is not aberrant," says the professor. "Descartes maintained that the universe as a whole consists of vortices whose movements determine the movement of the objects within it . . . Newton later dismissed this concept in favor of forces that act at a distance, through a void; but he could not prove his theory conclusively, perhaps because he was too good a scientist to blindly believe in it . . . Eventually, the mathematician Euler, while attempting to explain the movement of the planets according to Newtonian physics, partially revived Descartes' hypothesis, arguing in favor of Cartesian vortices . . . Are you following me?"

"Yes, though with difficulty."

"You read French, don't you?"

"I can get by."

"There is a book I could lend you: *Lettres à une princesse d'Allemagne, sur divers sujets de Physique et de Philosophie*. These are letters written by Euler to the niece of Frederick the Great of Prussia, who was very interested in such matters. In them, he explains the idea of these eddies or vortices in a way that is accessible to mere mortals such as ourselves . . . Would you care for another game, Comisario?"

It takes a moment for Tizón to work out what sort of game, until Barrull nods toward the chessboard.

"No, thank you. You've annihilated me enough for one day."

"As you wish."

The policeman stares at the straight line of smoke rising from his cigar. Then he waves his fingers and watches as it becomes whorls and spirals. Lines, curves and parabolas, he thinks. Corkscrews of air, of smoke, of lead, with Cádiz as the chessboard.

"Distinct places where things happen, or do not happen," he repeats aloud.

"Exactly." Barrull, putting away the chess pieces, pauses and looks at him. "And which act upon their surroundings."

A hiatus. The sound of ebony on boxwood as the pieces are placed in the coffer. The murmur of conversations, the clack of ivory balls from the billiard room.

"That said, Comisario, I would not take all this too literally . . . Theories are one thing; the exact reality of things is something else. As I said, even men of science sometimes doubt their own conclusions."

Tizón stretches his legs under the table again, pushing his chair back against the wall. "Even if it were true," he says, thinking aloud, "it only solves one half of the problem. We would still need to discover how the murderer can pinpoint these points or vortices in the earth's atmosphere and identify what will happen there . . . filling the vortex with his own matter."

"Are you asking me whether a murder or a falling bomb can be considered a physical phenomenon, as natural as rain or a thunderstorm?"

"Or the hideous human condition."

"Good Lord."

"You told me yourself that nature abhors a vacuum."

The professor, who has finished stowing the pieces and closed the case, looks at Tizón with something akin to surprise. Then he fans himself with his hat.

"Pfff. It is not wise for fools such as us to venture onto this terrain, my friend . . . I fear we are straying too far into the realm of imagination, into fiction. This is beginning to sound absurd."

"There is a basis in fact."

"It is far from clear that there is a basis in fact. Imagination, triggered by necessity, anxiety or some other cause, can play terrible tricks on us. You should know that."

"I have stood in these vortices, Professor. I have felt them . . . There are points where . . . I don't know . . . places in the city where everything shifts imperceptibly: the quality of the air, sound, smell . . ."

"What about temperature?"

"I couldn't say."

"In that case, you need to conduct a proper scientific experiment, using the necessary tools. Barometers, thermometers . . . You know. Just the way you would measure the meridian."

He smiles as he says this, it is a joke. Or seems to be. Tizón looks at him gravely without saying anything. Questioningly. The two men stare at each other for a moment then, eventually, the professor adjusts his spectacles and his smile broadens.

"Preposterous vortex hunters . . . Why not?"

The light is waning in the house on the Calle del Baluarte. At this time of day, the bay is bathed in a melancholy, golden light the color of caramel, as the sparrows fly back to roost in the city's watchtowers and the seagulls fly off toward the beaches of Chiclana. As Lolita Palma steps out of her office, climbs the staircase and crosses the covered gallery, that last glow is already fading in the patch of sky above the courtyard and the shadows are gathering along the arcade, around the pool, among the large planters filled with ferns and flowers. Lolita has worked all afternoon with the chief clerk, Molina, and a secretary, attempting to salvage what they can from a business deal that has gone awry: 1,000 *fanegas* of pure wheat flour shipped from Baltimore which has turned out to be adulterated with corn flour. They spent the morning checking the samples—contamination can be confirmed by the appearance of yellow flakes when nitric acid and potassium carbonate are added to the flour—and the rest of the day writing letters to suppliers, banks and the North American shipping agent involved in the matter. All very disagreeable. This entails a substantial financial loss, to say nothing of the damage to Palma e Hijos' reputation with the consignees, who will now have to wait for a new shipment of flour or make do with what they have.

As she passes the living room, she notices the burning embers of a cigar and a shadowy figure sitting on the divan, silhouetted against the last rays of light from the twin balconies that overlook the street.

"Are you still here?"

"I wanted to smoke a cigar in peace. You know your mother cannot bear the smell."

Cousin Toño does not move. In the gathering dusk, his dark dress coat is barely visible; only the pale gleam of his waistcoat and cravat. Nearby, the glowing charcoal of a small brazier that smells of lavender warms the room.

"You should have had them light a fire in the hearth."

"It's hardly worth it. I shall be going in a moment . . . Mari Paz brought me the brazier."

"Are you staying to dinner?"

"No, thank you. I can't, honestly. As I said, I'll just finish this cigar and be on my way."

He shifts a little as he speaks. The glow of the brazier is reflected in the lenses of his spectacles, and in the glass he is holding. Cousin Toño has spent much of the afternoon with Lolita's mother in her room, as he does whenever Doña Manuela Ugarte does not have the energy to get out of bed. On such occasions, he spends a short while on the patio with Lolita, and the remainder of the afternoon with his aunt, chatting, playing cards and sometimes reading to her.

"Your mother seemed in good form. I almost had her laughing at one or two of my jokes . . . I read her twenty-five pages of *Juanita or The Kind-Hearted Foundling*. A romantic novel, Cousin. It almost had me in tears."

Lolita Palma picks up her skirt and sits on the divan. Her cousin shifts a little to make room for her. She can smell the cognac and tobacco on him.

"I'm sorry I missed that. My mother laughing and you crying . . . that's a news story worthy of *El Diario Mercantil*."

"Don't mock, I'm being serious. I swear on the wine cask at Pedro Ximénez's tavern. If this is a lie, may I never see her again!"

"Who? My mother?"

"The wine cask."

Lolita laughs. Then she taps his arm. "You're nothing but a foolish winebibber."

"And you are a pretty little witch . . . You always were, even as a child."

"Pretty? Don't talk such nonsense."

"No, I said witch. A bewitching witch."

Cousin Toño shakes with laughter and the glowing tip of his cigar quivers. The Palmas are his only family. His daily visits are a ritual he has kept up ever since his mother brought him here as a boy. She died some time ago, but her son carried on the tradition. He treats the place as if it were his own home, which is in fact a three-story house on the Calle de la Verónica where he lives with his manservant. A private income from his properties in Havana allows him to live a life of idleness. He rises at noon, visits the barber at twelve-thirty, lunches in an upstairs dining room at the Café de Apolo where he reads the newspapers before taking a siesta in an armchair downstairs; he visits the Palma house mid-afternoon, followed by a light dinner and an evening spent in conversation with friends at the Café de las Cadenas, and sometimes a game of cards or billiards. The thirteen hours a day he spends sleeping considerably dilute the effects of the two bottles of *manzanilla* and the various spirits he consumes every day: there is not a fleck of gray in his thinning hair, the paunch that strains the buttons of his double-breasted jackets is noticeable but not excessive, and his unfailing good humor does much to stave off the ravages to his liver which, Lolita suspects, is by now the size and texture of two pounds of *foie gras*. But cousin Toño doesn't care. As he says when she affectionately scolds him, better to die on your feet, a glass in your hand, laughing and surrounded by friends, than to grow old on your knees, withered and boring. Now pour me another glass, *niña*. If it's not too much trouble.

"What were you thinking about, Cousin?"

There is a sudden serious silence. The tip of his cigar flares twice in the gloom. "I was remembering."

"Remembering what . . . ?"

There is another pause before he answers. "Us, here," he says finally. "When we were little. Scampering around this room. Or you playing upstairs on the terrace . . . Going up into the tower with the spyglass. You would never let me play with it, even though I was older than you. Or maybe that was why. You with your hair in plaits and always behaving like a wise little mouse."

Lolita Palma nods slowly, though she knows her cousin cannot see. How far off they seem to her, those children, herself and Toño and the others. They are still there in the past, strolling through some impossible paradise, spared from rationality and the passing of the years, like that little girl who used to watch the white sails of the ships pass by from the watchtower on the terrace.

"Will you come to the theater with me, the day after tomorrow?" she asks, lightening the mood. "With Curra Vilches and her husband. They are playing *Finding Truth through Doubt* by Lope de Vega and a short farce called *The Soldier Swaggering*."

"I read about that in *El Conciso*. I'll pick you up here dressed to the nines."

"Try not to be too scruffy."

"Are you ashamed of me?"

"No. But if you brushed your hair and ironed your clothes, you would be much more presentable."

"You wound me deeply, Cousin! You don't like my exquisite jackets? They are the latest fashion, made to measure by the Bordador de Madrid."

"I should like them more if you did not spill cigar ash all over them."

"Ouch. You harpy."

"You overgrown buffoon."

The living room is almost dark now, but for the light at the tip of cousin Toño's cigar and the glow from the brazier. The windowpanes of the balconies stand out against the blackness with an almost violet phosphorescence. Lolita hears her cousin pour himself more brandy from a bottle close at hand. For a moment, neither of them speaks, waiting for the shadows to engulf everything. Eventually, Lolita gets to her feet, fumbles for the box of matches and the oil lamp on the dresser, lifts the tulip shade and lights the wick. The flickering flame illuminates the paintings on the walls, the dark mahogany furniture, the vases of artificial flowers.

"Don't turn it up too bright," says cousin Toño. "We are fine just as we are."

Lolita adjusts the wick until the flame is as small as it can be, casting only a faint reddish glow that gilds the outlines of furniture and objects. Her cousin sits on the divan, smoking, his glass in one hand, his face in shadow.

"Just before you came in," he says, "I was thinking about those afternoon visits with my mother and your mother and the whole family—those elderly aunts and second cousins—all dressed in black, drinking hot chocolate in this very room, or down on the patio . . . Do you remember?"

Moving back to the sofa, Lolita nods again. "Of course. There are few of us left these days."

"And the summers we spent in Chiclana? Climbing trees to pick fruit and playing in the garden in the moonlight. With Cari and Francisco de Paula . . . I used to envy the wonderful toys your father always gave you. Once, I tried to steal a toy soldier, but I was caught."

"I remember that. The beating you got."

"I nearly died of shame, and it was a long time before I could look you in the eye again." A long, thoughtful pause. "That was the end of my career as a criminal."

He falls silent. A strange, unexpectedly gloomy silence, utterly at odds with his cheerful disposition. Lolita Palma takes his hand; it lies limply in her own. He does not respond to her affectionate squeeze. To her surprise, she notices his hand is cold. After a moment, he takes it away.

"You were never one for dolls and dollhouses . . . You always wanted to play with your brother's tin swords, his lead soldiers and wooden ships . . ."

The silence seems very long this time. Too long. Lolita can guess what her cousin will say next; and he can probably sense that she knows.

"I think a lot about Paquito," he murmurs at length.

"So do I."

"I suppose his death changed your life. I sometimes wonder what you would be doing now if . . ."

The glow from the cigar vanishes as Cousin Toño carefully stubs it out in the ashtray.

"I mean . . ." he says, his tone different now, "to be honest, I can't imagine you married, like Cari."

Lolita smiles to herself in the darkness. "Cari and I are very different creatures," she says gently.

Cousin Toño agrees. He gives a snort rather than his usual brazen laugh. "You and I will both end up alone," he says. "Just like Cádiz." Then he falls silent again. "What was the name of that boy? Manfredi?"

"Yes. Miguel Manfredi."

"That is something else that changed your life."

"You never know, Cousin."

This time he lets out a belly laugh, and becomes his old self again. "The fact remains that here we are, you and I: the last of the Cardenals and the last of the Palmas . . . a confirmed bachelor and a woman who has been left on the shelf. As I said, just like Cádiz."

"How can you be so boorish and so rude?"

"It takes practice, *niña*. Copious quantities of the nectar of the vine and years of practice."

Lolita knows that her cousin has not always been a confirmed bachelor. For many years, as a young man, he was in love with a woman named Consuelo Carvajal, a beautiful woman who was courted by many and was proud to the point of arrogance. Cousin Toño was desperately in love with her; he acceded to her every whim. But she was cruel; she liked to play *la belle dame sans merci* at the expense of Toño

Cardenal. For a long time, without ever spurning his advances, she allowed herself to be wooed. Just as one might exploit a faithful servant, she presumed upon the devotion of this tall, witty young man, she ruled over him like an empress, subjecting him to all manner of humiliations, which he bore with unfailing good humor and his big-hearted canine loyalty. He went on loving her even when she married someone else.

"Why did you not go to America? You were considering it after Consuelo married."

Cousin Toño sits, silent and unmoving, in the lamplight. Lolita is the only person with whom he ever mentions the name of the woman who ruined his life. He always speaks of her without spite or bitterness, only with the melancholy of someone who has lost and is resigned to his fate.

"I was lazy," he murmurs. "It's one of my many qualities."

His tone is different now, lighter, more carefree; and there is the sound of cognac splashing into his glass. "Besides," he adds, "I need this city. Even with the French just across the bay, here in Cádiz we live in a haven of calm. Neat, orderly streets that run at right angles to each other, or obliquely, as though trying to hide themselves in their own dead ends. And that sense of seclusion bordering on sadness that, as you turn a corner, can erupt into the heaving bustle of life. Do you know what I love most about Cádiz?"

"Of course I do. The liquor in the taverns and the wine from the merchants."

"That too. But what I really love is the smell of the streets, like the cargo hold of a ship: salted meat and cinnamon and coffee . . . the scent of our childhood, Lolita, the smell of the past. And above all, I love those street corners where you see a painted board with a boat on a blue-green sea, and a sign above bearing the most beautiful words in all the world: *Goods from overseas and from the colonies.*"

"You are a poet, Cousin," Lolita laughs, "I've always said so."

THE EXPERIMENT HAS been a disaster. Rogelio Tizón and Hipólito Barrull have scoured the streets of Cádiz all day in the hope of glimpsing a trace of this other map of the city, the secret, disquieting map the comisario has sensed. They set out early, accompanied by Cadalso, who carried the equipment recommended by the professor: a good-sized Spencer barometer, a Megnié thermometer, a detailed city map and a small pocket compass. They started off near the Puerta de Tierra, where the first murdered girl was found more than a year ago now. Then they took a caleche out to Lame Paco's Tavern, and walked back to the city, map in hand, looking for the slightest clue, meticulously retracing the route: Calle de Amoladores, Calle del Viento, Calle del Laurel, Calle del Pasquín, Calle del Silencio. At every place, the process was the same: locating the spot on the map, calculating its position with respect to the cardinal points and the position of the French gun batteries at the Cabezuela, studying the surrounding buildings, their angle of incidence with the wind and any other useful details. Tizón even brought the meteorological records of the Royal Armada for the days on which the girls were murdered. And while the comisario moved around, obsessive as a bloodhound sniffing out a difficult prey, the trusty Cadalso watched from a distance, patiently awaiting his orders. In the meantime Barrull compared the data, the actual temperature and barometric pressure, assessing possible variations between one spot and the next. The results are disappointing: except for the fact that there was a light easterly breeze in all the locations and the atmospheric pressure was relatively low, there is no common pattern, or if there is it is impossible to determine; nor did they register an anomaly in any of the sites they visited. At only two spots did the pocket compass display any significant deviation: but in one of these, on the Calle de Amoladores, this may have been due to the presence of a scrap-metal merchant nearby. Otherwise, the experiment produced no new information of relevance. If places did exist where the conditions were different, there was no measurable evidence of them. They were impossible to find.

"I fear your perceptions are too subjective, Comisario."

"Are you suggesting I imagined it?"

"No. I'm saying that, with the humble tools at our disposal, it is impossible to find any physical confirmation of your suspicions."

Cadalso has already been sent off, laden with equipment, and the two men are discussing the scant findings of the day as they walk past the Convento de los Descalzos, heading for the Plaza de San Antonio and a tortilla in the Café Veedor. They encounter few people along this stretch of road: a street vendor selling contraband cigars—who quickly ducks out of sight when he recognizes Tizón—and a mahogany cabinetmaker working in the doorway of his shop. The afternoon is dry and sunny, and the temperature is pleasant. Hipólito Barrull is wearing a bicorn hat, tilted slightly and pushed back off his forehead; the black cloak over his shoulders is open to reveal his old-fashioned jacket and his thumbs are hooked into his waistcoat pockets. Walking alongside him, his mood as black as thunder, Tizón swings his cane and stares at the ground in front of his feet.

"What we would need," Barrull continues, "is to be able to compare the atmospheric conditions of each location at the precise moment the murders were committed and the moment the bombs fell . . . to verify whether there are any constants aside from the light easterly breeze and the low pressure. Then we could draw lines connecting the sites according to pressure, temperature, wind speed and direction, time and any additional factors that occur to us . . . To create the map you are seeking is impossible with the science we have today—all the more so with the humble means at our disposal."

Rogelio Tizón is not prepared to surrender just yet. Though the evidence is overwhelming, he clings to his conviction. He insists that he experienced these sensations himself: the subtle shift in the quality of the air or temperature; even the smell seemed different. It was like being in a vacuum under a bell jar.

"Well, you felt no such thing today, Comisario. I watched you scurry around in vain all day, cursing under your breath."

"Perhaps it was not the right time," Tizón admits sullenly. "Perhaps it has something to do with the weather, specific conditions . . . Perhaps it happens only at favorable moments relating to each crime, each bomb."

"I'm prepared to allow for any possibility. But you have to admit that, from a serious, scientific viewpoint, it seems highly unlikely."

Barrull moves to one side to allow a woman leading a small boy by the hand to pass.

"Have you read the book I lent you—Euler's letters?"

"Yes, but I didn't get very far. I can't say I'm sorry. It would probably have led me down another blind alley, like your translation of *Ajax*."

"Perhaps that is precisely the problem . . . too much theory leading to an overactive imagination. And vice versa. The most we could possibly establish is that there are places in the city that share similar conditions—temperature, wind speed and so forth. Or an absence of the same . . . And that these places may exert a sort of pull, or magnetism, which has two effects: it attracts bombs that explode, and the actions of a murderer."

"Even so, it's something," protests Tizón.

"Perhaps, but it's something for which we do not have a single scrap of evidence. Nor have we any proven link between the bombs and the murders."

The policeman shakes his head, implacable. "This is not coincidence, Hipólito."

"Very well, then: prove it."

They have stopped near the convent on the little square that leads to the Calle de la Compañía. The shops and the flower stalls are still open. People are strolling between the Calle del Vestuario and the Calle de la Carne, or have gathered around the four barrels that serve as tables outside the Andalucía tavern. Half a dozen boys with grimy knees, armed with swords made of wood and cane, are scuffling on the ground outside the workshop of Serafin the cutler, playing Frenchmen and Spaniards. No quarter is given to prisoners.

"There's no need for books or theories or imagination," says Rogelio Tizón. "Call them vortices or curious places or whatever you like. The fact remains that they exist. I have detected them myself. The way a chess player might . . . In the same way that sometimes, when you touch a chess piece—before you've moved it and I know what you're going to do—I feel a sense of impending disaster."

Barrull shrugs, hesitant rather than skeptical. "But your senses failed you today. Your *sentiment de fer*, as they say in fencing."

"That's true. But I know that I am right."

Barrull stops for a moment, then continues walking. After a few paces, he stops again, waiting for Tizón to catch up. The comisario is walking slowly, head down, his brows knitted, staring at the ground. He has known moments in his life that were more hopeful, less troubled. The professor waits for him to draw level before he speaks again.

"Nevertheless, since we are hypothesizing . . . Has it occurred to you that the reason you experience these sensations is that you share a certain receptive affinity with the murderer?"

Tizón looks at him suspiciously. Three seconds.

"Don't goad me, Professor," he mutters. "Not this late in the day."

But Barrull is not prepared to give up. A particular level of understanding may exist, he says, an ability to sense these sporadic shifts that the comisario has been seeking. After all, there are people who experience premonition dreams, visions of the future. To say nothing of animals, which can sense earthquakes or catastrophes before they occur. Human beings may have a similar sense, the professor suggests. Partial, perhaps. Atrophied after centuries of disuse. But there will always be exceptional individuals. Therefore the murderer may have the gift of precognition. At first he would be drawn to these places by the same forces or conditions that cause the bombs to fall there. Later, with practice, he might refine this ability such that he can anticipate them.

"As I said, an exceptional individual," says Barrull.

Tizón sighs, exasperated. "An exceptional scoundrel, you mean."

"Maybe so. Perhaps, to paraphrase D'Alembert, he might be classified as one of those *'obscure and metaphysical entities, which only serve to cast shadows on a science that is in itself clear* . . .' But let me tell you something, Comisario: there is nothing to prevent you being one also, since you share a certain instinct with the killer. This would place you, paradoxically, on the same level as this monster . . . and better able to understand his impulses than the rest of his fellow citizens."

They have turned the corner and are now slowly making their way up the Cuesta de la Murga, beneath the green railings and shutters of the balconies. Barrull turns and looks at the comisario, eager to see the effect of his words.

"Disturbing, don't you think?"

Tizón does not answer. He is thinking about the young prostitute in Santa María lying facedown, naked, defenseless. Remembering himself standing over her, sliding the tip of his cane over her pale skin. Remembering the bottomless pit of horror he sensed for an instant inside himself.

"This might explain why your obsession with this case goes beyond the professional," continues the professor. "You know what you are looking for. You instinctively recognize it . . . Maybe in this case, science is merely a hindrance. Maybe it is simply a matter of time and chance. Who knows? You may simply happen upon the murderer and immediately know it is him."

"Recognize him as a brother whose instincts I share?" The comisario's voice is harsh, menacing. Tizón can hear it himself, can see the expression on Barrull's face.

"Devil take it, that is not what I meant at all," says the professor. "I am deeply sorry if I have offended you. But the truth is that none of us knows the dark recesses we carry within us, nor how fragile our boundaries can be."

Once again he falls silent for a moment, then adds: "Let us just say that, in my opinion, this is a game that can only be played on its own chessboard. A place where even science cannot help . . . Perhaps you and the killer see the city differently from how others see it."

The comisario's laugh is anything but cheery. In fact, he quickly notices, he is laughing at his own shadow. At the portrait which, by chance or by design, Barrull is painting of him.

"Dark corners, you say."

"Yes, exactly. Yours, mine . . . anyone's."

Suddenly, Tizón feels a need—a burning need—to explain himself. "I had a daughter once, Professor."

He stops dead, tapping the ground impatiently with his cane. He feels a mute rage shake him to the roots of his hair, a surge of loathing and incomprehension.

Barrull's face has changed; he now looks at Tizón in surprise. "I know," the professor says softly, suddenly embarrassed. "I heard about it. A terrible tragedy . . ."

"She died when she was a little girl. And when I see those girls—"

At this, Barrull almost leaps out of his skin. "I don't want to hear anymore," he interrupts, raising his hand. "I forbid it."

Now it is Tizón's turn to be surprised, but he says nothing. He stands facing Barrull, waiting for an explanation.

"I value our friendship too much," the professor finally says, reluctantly. "Though I know that where you are concerned the word is relative . . . Let us say that I appreciate your company. Can we leave it at that?"

"As you wish."

"You are a man who never forgives weakness in others, Comisario . . . I think that if the pressure of these events led you to confide too much in me now, you might later regret it. I mean about your life. Or at least your family."

Having said this, Barrull pauses, as if considering what he has just said. "I would not wish to lose my best chess opponent."

"You're right," Tizón says.

"Of course I'm right. I am almost always right. I am also hungry . . . So why don't you buy me that tortilla and something to wash it down with? I think I've earned it today."

Barrull sets off again, but Tizón does not follow. He is still standing next to a building on the corner of the Calle de San Miguel. High up, in a niche, the Archangel Michael, sword in hand, is trampling a demon underfoot.

"Come here, Professor . . . Do you notice anything?"

Barrull looks at him in astonishment. Then, following his gaze, he looks up at the statue. "No," he says cautiously. The comisario goes on staring.

"Are you sure?"

"Absolutely."

Suddenly clearheaded, Rogelio Tizón wonders whether what he is experiencing right now preceded the moment when he looked and saw the archangel, or whether seeing it triggered this sinister, familiar feeling—the one he has been searching for all morning. The feeling of stepping for an instant into the rarefied space in which everything, the quality of air, of sound, of smell—the comisario notices there is no smell—is subtly, briefly altered, diluted by the vacuum until they disappear completely.

"What's happening, Comisario?"

For an instant, even Barrull's voice seems to come from afar, distorted by some vast distance. *What is happening is that I have just stepped into one of your accursed vortices, Professor,* Tizón is tempted to answer. Instead, he jerks his chin toward the statue of St. Michael and then looks around him, at the street corner, the buildings nearby, trying to engrave this space on his memory as much as in his senses.

"Stop pulling my leg," Barrull says, suddenly realizing what is going on, but his cheery expression turns grave when he sees the comisario's frozen gaze.

"Here?"

Without waiting for a reply, he walks over to Tizón and, like him, looks up, and then around. Eventually he shakes his head, discouraged.

"It's useless, Comisario. I fear you are the only one . . ." He pauses and looks at Tizón again. "A pity we gave the instruments to your assistant to take back," he says. "It would have been useful . . ."

Tizón motions for him to keep quiet. He is still standing, staring upward. The sensation was fleeting; now he feels nothing. Now all he sees is a statue of St. Michael in a niche on the Cuesta de la Murga at six o'clock in the evening, on a day like any other. And yet it was here, there can be no doubt. For an instant, he stood on the threshold of that strange, familiar void.

"Perhaps I'm going mad," he says eventually.

He feels the professor's worried gaze. "Come now, don't talk nonsense."

"In a way, you suggested it yourself earlier . . . I'm like the killer."

Tizón has begun walking in circles, very slowly, carefully observing every detail of his surroundings. Tapping the ground with his cane like a blind man.

"You said something once . . ."

He stops, remembering what the professor said. He would not like to see himself in a mirror right now, Tizón thinks as he notices the way Barrull is looking at him. And yet, some things are not perfectly clear in his head. Somber affinities: the ripped flesh of a woman, emptiness and silence. And today the wind is blowing from the east.

"You should ask the French, that's what you said—remember?"

"No. But I'm sure I probably did."

Tizón nods, although he is not really paying attention. He is having a conversation with himself. From his niche, sword held aloft, the arch-angel seems to be watching defiantly. Scornful, with the desolate, grim rictus that suddenly flashes like a whiplash across Tizón's face.

"You may well be right, Professor. Perhaps now is the moment to ask."

It is Saturday night. The excited theater crowd pouring out of the Calle de la Novena on to the Calle Ancha are chatting about the evening's entertainment. From the doorway of the café on the corner of the Calle de la Amargura, a haunt of foreigners and sailors, Pépé Lobo and his first officer Ricardo Maraña silently contemplate the throng. The two corsairs—their titles official since the *Culebra*'s Letter of Marque was restored five days ago—came ashore this morning and are now sitting at a table in front of an earthenware bottle (already half-empty) of Dutch gin. The glow of the street lamps that line the main street of Cádiz illuminates the parade of elegant apparel: frockcoats; redingotes; dress coats; nankeen gaiters; cloaks and *surtús* in the fashions of London and Paris; watch chains and expensive jewels; ladies in fur wraps and embroidered shawls, though there are also bonnets that come down to their eyebrows or broad-brimmed hats; short jackets embroidered with shells and silver *peseta* buttons; suede breeches; skirts with frills or flounces; the humble brown coats and capes of the ordinary folk heading home to their houses in Viña or the Mentidero. Un-surprisingly, there are attractive women of every caste and class. There are also deputies from San Felipe Neri, immigrants—some solvent, others less so—members of the local militias, Spanish and English mil-

itary officers sporting stripes, epaulettes and cockades. Each night the
theater, the only public entertainment in the city since the Cortes approved its reopening some months ago, finds the great and the good
filling the stalls and the loges, although the common people are to be
found higher up in the gods. Given that performances start early, the
night is still young and the temperature mild for this time of year, most
of the crowd are not yet ready to call it a night: gaming tables, salons
and fine conversation await those with wealth and position; taverns,
guitar music, billiards, flamenco and cheap wine will entertain the
lower classes and those with a proclivity for such things. And they are
many.

"Look who we have here," says Maraña.

Pépé Lobo follows his first officer's gaze. Lolita Palma, accompanied by various friends of both sexes, is walking among the throng.
Lobo recognizes cousin Toño and Jorge Fernández Cuchillero, the
deputy for Buenos Aires. Lorenzo Virués is also present in full regalia:
his dress sword, shoulder flashes indicating his rank as Captain of Engineers on his blue frockcoat with purple revers, his hat adorned with a
red hackle and a silver cockade.

"Our boss," says the lieutenant with his habitual indifference.

Lobo notices that Lolita Palma has seen him. She briefly slows her
pace and graces him with a polite smile and a slight nod of the head.
She looks beautiful, in a dark-red dress cut in the English style, a black
Turkish shawl around her shoulders and a small emerald brooch pinned
at her breast. She wears leather gloves and is carrying a long satin purse
of the sort used to carry a fan and opera glasses. She wears no other
jewelry except for a pair of simple emerald earrings. Her delicate velvet
hat is held in place with a silver hatpin. As she draws level, Lobo gets to
his feet and bows slightly. Without interrupting her conversation with
her friends, or taking her eyes off the corsair, she casually places a hand
on cousin Toño's arm, who stops, takes out his pocket watch, and says
something that makes the whole company erupt in peals of laughter.

"She is waiting for you to go over and say hello," says Maraña.

"That's how it seems . . . Will you come with me?"

"No. I am only a first officer and I'm perfectly happy to sit here with my gin."

After a brief hesitation, Lobo takes his hat from the back of his chair and walks toward the group. As he does so, he spies Lorenzo Virués giving him a disdainful look.

"What a pleasant surprise, Captain. Welcome back to Cádiz."

"We dropped anchor this morning, señora."

"I know."

"Tarifa was saved in the end. And we have been relieved of duty . . . Our Letter of Marque has been reinstated."

"That, too, I know."

She offers her hand and Lobo bows and takes it briefly, barely brushing it. Lolita Palma's tone is warm, calm and courteous. Ever the mistress.

"I don't know whether you know everyone . . . Don José Lobo, captain of the *Culebra*. You have certainly had dealings with many of my friends: my cousin Toño, Curra Vilches and her husband, Carlos Pastor . . . Don Jorge Fernández Cuchillero, Captain Virués—"

"I know the man," the officer says curtly.

The two men exchange a brief, hostile glance. Pépé Lobo wonders whether Virués's hostility relates to the unfinished business at La Caleta, or whether Lolita Palma's presence tonight is like a Knave of Swords in a game of tarot. We were planning to have a drink in Burnel's café, she says with impeccable poise. Perhaps you would care to join us.

The sailor gives her a discreet smile. A little awkward.

"Thank you for your kind offer, but I am with my first officer."

Lolita glances toward the café table. She recognizes Ricardo Maraña, having met him when she visited the *Culebra*, and gives him a gracious smile. Lobo has his back to his first mate, so cannot see him, but he can imagine his response: a graceful nod of the head as he raises his gin in salute. Never introduce me to someone I don't know, he once said.

"He is welcome to join us."

"He is not exactly sociable . . . Another time, perhaps."

"As you please."

As they say their goodbyes with the usual pleasantries, Deputy Fernández Cuchillero—in an elegant gray cape with saffron revers, carrying a cane and a top hat—remarks that he would welcome the opportunity to converse with Señor Lobo awhile, to hear his account of what happened at Tarifa. A valiant defense, from what has been said, and a bitter blow for the French. In fact, the Cortes war commission will be discussing the matter on Monday.

"Perhaps I might invite you to lunch tomorrow, Captain, if you have no other plans?"

The corsair looks quickly toward Lolita Palma. The glance slips into the void. "I am at your service, señor."

"Excellent. Twelve-thirty at the posada Cuatro Naciones—how does that suit? They serve a fine oyster *empanada* and a *menudo con garbanzos.** They also have decent wines from Portugal and the Canary Islands."

Pépé Lobo thinks quickly. He does not care a fig about the Cortes war commission, but the deputy, aside from being a friend of the Palmas, would make a powerful political ally. The association could prove useful. In these uncertain times, and given the parlous nature of his profession, one never knew.

"I shall be there."

Captain Virués scowls, clearly not best pleased by this turn of events.

"I doubt the man has much to tell you," he says cuttingly. "I don't believe he ever set foot in Tarifa . . . From what I've heard, his mission was merely to ferry official dispatches."

There is an awkward silence. Pépé Lobo's eyes briefly meet Lolita Palma's, then he stares at the officer.

"That is true," he says calmly. "From my ship, we were only able to watch the bullfight from the ringside . . . It is a little like your own situation, señor. I constantly see you here in Cádiz when you are posted to the front lines on the Isla de Léon . . . I can imagine how painful it

---

* A stew of meat (usually tripe) and chickpeas.

must be for a soldier here, so far from the gunfire and the glory, dragging his sword from one café to the next." The corsair stares coolly at
Virués. "You must feel sorely aggrieved."

Even in the faint yellow glow of the street lamps, it is clear that the
captain has gone pale. Pépé Lobo's keen eyes, accustomed to brawls
and difficult situations, are quick to notice the captain's reaction: his
left hand instinctively reaches for his sword, but he stops himself. This,
they both know, is neither the time nor the place. Certainly not in the
presence of Lolita Palma and her friends. Still less so given that Captain Virués is an officer and a gentleman. Armed with this knowledge
and the impunity it affords him, the corsair turns his back on the officer, nods politely to Lolita Palma and her companions, and—feeling
her worried gaze upon him—returns to the table where Ricardo
Maraña is sitting.

"Are you not crossing the bay tonight?" he asks his lieutenant.

Maraña looks at him with vague curiosity.

"I had not planned to."

Pépé Lobo nods gravely. "In that case, let us find ourselves some
women."

Maraña is still staring at him inquiringly. He turns to look at the
group as it makes its way toward the Plaza de San Antonio. He watches
them in silence for a moment, then ceremoniously empties the rest of
the gin into the two glasses.

"What class of women, Captain?"

"The sort of women befitting this hour."

A dignified smile—world-weary and a little lewd—creases the pale
lips of the *Culebra*'s first officer.

"Would you prefer a preamble of wine and dancing at La Caleta or
the Mentidero, or the more basic pleasures of the whores at Santa
María and La Merced?"

Pépé Lobo shrugs. He has just swallowed a large, acrid mouthful of
gin that burns his stomach and puts him in a foul temper, although
perhaps he was already in bad humor—from the moment he clapped
eyes on Lorenzo Virués.

"I don't care, as long as they're quick and they won't want to chat."

Maraña finishes his drink, considering the matter. He takes a silver coin from his pocket and leaves it on the table.

"Let's go to Scabies Street," he suggests.

THERE IS SOMEONE crossing the bay at this very moment. But the boat is not heading toward El Puerto de Santa María; instead the prow is pointed slightly farther east, toward the sandbar exposed by low tide at the mouth of the San Pedro River near the Trocadero. The silence is broken only by the soft lapping of water against the boat. The lateen sail, swelled by a fresh westerly breeze, is a black triangle framed against a star-strewn sky. It lists as the boat moves on, leaving behind the dark shapes of the Spanish and English ships that lie at anchor, the solid black line of the city walls, and the scattered lights of Cádiz.

Rogelio Tizón boarded the boat at Puerto Piojo almost an hour ago, after its owner—one of the few smugglers still prepared to brave the waters of the bay—managed, for a price, to persuade the guards on the pier at San Felipe to close their tired eyes. Now, sitting under the sail, with the collar of his coat turned up so it reaches his eyebrows, the comisario keeps his arms folded and his head down, waiting for them to arrive at their destination. The cold and damp seep through his clothes and make him wish he had worn another coat beneath his redingote. It is surely the only precaution that he failed to take tonight. The only loose end. He has spent several days planning this trip, down to the last detail; and he has not been tight-fisted, disbursing as much gold as necessary to guarantee an initial contact, a discreet route and a suitable welcome in complete privacy, quiet and secure.

The comisario is becoming impatient. He has already spent too long here; he feels out of place on the water in the darkness, far from his milieu, from the city. He feels *vulnerable*. He is not accustomed to the sea and the bay, still less to this strange sense of gliding through the darkness toward the unknown, chasing an obsession, or the truth. Stifling the urge to smoke—the boat owner warned him that the glowing tip of a cigar would be visible for miles around—he leans back against the mast, which drips with evening dew. Everything aboard is sodden: the wooden bench on which Tizón sits, the gunwale of the boat with oars set into the rowlocks, the coarse fabric of his coat and the soft felt of his hat. Even his whiskers and his mustache are dripping; he feels as though his very bones are damp. Irritably, he looks around. The owner is a dark, silent shape sitting in the stern beside the rudder, and his mate is huddled half asleep in the bow. For them, this is routine; it is how they earn their daily crust. Above their heads, the starry expanse of the heavens spans the bay's sweeping curves, tracing the almost invisible arc of the horizon. Beneath the sail foot, far beyond the port bow, the comisario can just make out the lights of El Puerto de Santa María and off the starboard beam, less than a mile away, the long, low form of the Trocadero peninsula.

The comisario thinks about the man he is to meet there—someone whose identity it has cost him time and money to discover. He wonders what the man is like, and whether he will be able to understand what it is he is looking for. Whether the man will be prepared to help him capture the murderer who, for more than a year, has been playing a sinister game of chess, using the city and the bay as his board. He also wonders, somewhat worriedly, whether he will make it there and back again without some stray bullet or cannonball catching him unawares in the darkness. Rogelio Tizón has never risked his job and his life as he is doing tonight. But he is prepared to descend into hell itself, if necessary, to find what he is seeking.

CHAPTER FOURTEEN

༄

"What you describe is a very curious problem."

By the light of a candle inserted in the neck of a bottle, Simon Desfosseux studies the man sitting before him. The face is sharp-featured, melancholy, typically Spanish. The thick curly mutton-chop whiskers blend into the mustache, framing a pair of eyes that are dark, impassive—and probably dangerous. From his appearance, he could be a soldier or a *guerrillero*, one of those who would flee the battlefield but prove fearsome and cold-blooded in an ambush or a surprise attack. From what Desfosseux knows, the visitor is a policeman, but not just any policeman. He clearly had sufficient money and influence to get here—with both Spanish and French safe-conducts in his pocket—without being arrested or killed.

"It is a problem I will not be able to solve without your help, Commandant."

"I am only a captain."

"Ah. My apologies."

He speaks French passably well, Desfosseux notes. His *R*'s are a little harsh, and he sometimes hesitates, looking away and frowning as he gropes for words, or simply uses the Spanish equivalent. But he can make himself understood. Much better, Desfosseux has to admit, than his own command of Spanish, which barely extends beyond *buenos días señorita, cuánto cuesta?* and *malditos canallas*.

"Are you sure about everything you have told me?"

"I am sure of the facts . . . seven girls murdered, three of them in places where bombs fell shortly afterward: your bombs."

The Spaniard is sitting on a rickety chair with a map of Cádiz—

which he took from the pocket of the long brown redingote that comes down to his bootlaces—spread out on the table in front of him. Lieutenant Bertoldi, who is standing guard outside to ensure the interview is not interrupted, checked the coat as he arrived, to make sure the man was unarmed. Simon Desfosseux is sitting on an empty crate, leaning back against the peeling walls of the converted munitions depot; it is an old house, just off the road that runs between the Trocadero and El Puerto de Santa María, near the sandbar where the visitor disembarked a little more than an hour ago. Their experience of the Spanish has left the French mistrustful, and the captain is no exception. His hat lies on the table, he wears his military cape around his shoulders, and he has his sword between his legs and a loaded pistol on his hip.

"In each case, the wind was blowing from the east, as I told you," the policeman continues. "A light breeze. And the shells in question exploded."

"Would you be so good as to point out the exact locations again?"

They pore over the map once more. In the candlelight, the Spaniard points to the places in the city marked in pencil. Despite his scepticism—this still sounds like nonsense—Desfosseux's curiosity is piqued. They are, after all, discussing trajectories and impacts. Ballistics. Though what the policeman is showing him seems far-fetched, it clearly relates to the work he does every day. With his calculations, his hopes and frustrations.

"It is absurd," he says, leaning back again. "There cannot be any connection between—"

"There is. I don't know what it is, or how it happens, but there is."

There is something genuine in his expression, Desfosseux notes. If there were some flicker of obsession or fanaticism, it would be easy; he could end the interview right now. Good night, thank you for coming and telling me your bizarre story, señor. *Hasta la vista.* But that is not the case. What Simon Desfosseux sees in front of him is calm, assured conviction. This does not seem like the fantasy of an unbalanced mind. And there was nothing in the way he recounted his story to suggest there is anything fanciful about this man—something that would, in any case, be uncommon in a policeman. All the more so, to judge by his appearance, in a hard-bitten veteran like this one. In fact, thinks Desfosseux, it is difficult to believe the man has any imagination at all.

"This is why you thought that the man was spying for us . . ."

"Exactly," the Spaniard says with a strange half smile. "There was a connection—and I mistakenly thought that Gregorio Fumagal was that connection."

"What happened to him?"

"He is awaiting trial. Awaiting the fate reserved for spies . . . You know as well as I do that we are at war . . ."

"The firing squad?"

"I assume so. It is no longer my concern."

Desfosseux thinks about the man with the pigeons, a man he has never met—someone he knew only through the messages he sent, until one day they ceased to arrive. He never knew the man's motives, whether he was spying for France for money or for patriotic reasons. Until today, he did not even know his name, or his nationality. Military intelligence and such matters would be dealt with by General Macquery, the new chief of staff of the Premier Corps since the departure of General Semellé. It is a murky, complicated world and one about which Simon Desfosseux would prefer to know as little as possible. But he misses the pigeons. The dispatches he now receives—the Imperial Army obviously has other informants in the city—lack the rigorous precision of those written by the man who was arrested.

"You took a considerable risk coming here like this."

"Oh, well . . ." The policeman gestures vaguely around him. "This is Cádiz, you understand? People cross the bay all the time. I suppose for a French soldier it might be difficult to understand."

He says this offhandedly. With typical Spanish gall, thinks Desfosseux. The man is watching him carefully.

"Why did you agree to meet me?" he asks finally.

It is the captain's turn to smile.

"Your letter piqued my curiosity."

"Thank you."

"Don't thank me yet." Desfosseux shakes his head. "There's still time to turn you over to the *gendarmes* . . . I don't much like the idea of finding myself before a court-martial accused of conspiring with the enemy."

A short, dry laugh.

"Don't worry about that. My safe conduct has been stamped by imperial headquarters in Chiclana . . . Besides, I'm only a policeman."

"I never much cared for policemen."

"I have never much cared for bastards who kill fifteen-year-old girls."

The two men stare at each other in silence: the Spaniard calm, un-ruffled; the Frenchman pensive. Then Desfosseux leans over the map of Cádiz again and stares at the penciled marks, moving from one to the next. Until now, he has thought of them only as points of impact. Successful targets since, in six of the seven cases, the bombs landed and exploded as intended. For the man sitting before him, however, the marks mean something else: they are the concrete reminders of seven girls who were murdered after having been horribly tortured. What-ever his reservations about the way in which the case has been inter-preted, at no point does Desfosseux doubt the veracity of the facts. And although he would not give his life or his fortune—if he had one—for this man, still he knows the man is not lying. At least, not consciously.

"It goes without saying that this conversation never took place," he says finally.

Never, the Spaniard echoes in the tone of one intimately familiar with nonexistent conversations. He has taken out a fine leather cigar case and offers one to the captain, who takes it and slips it into his pocket—he'll make it last by cutting it up. The wind has a major influ-ence, Desfosseux explains, moving his hand over the map, on both the trajectory and the point of impact. Truth be told, many factors contrib-ute: the temperature, the humidity, the condition of the gunpowder. Even the ambient temperature can cause the bore of the cannon to expand or contract, thereby affecting the shot.

"In fact, one of my problems is that I can't manage to get bombs to land where I want them to . . . at least not always."

The policeman, who has put away his case and is now holding an unlit cigar, points one end of it toward the marks on the map.

"What can you tell me about these?"

"A quick glance says it all. Look: five of the bombs fell within a sector to the south of the city, the area closest to us . . . Only this one here traveled further, to the outer limit of our range."

"These days, they go further."

"Indeed." Simon Desfosseux has a satisfied expression. "We are gradually getting there. Eventually, we will be able to shell the whole city, take my word for it. But at the time, this shot here . . ."

"An alley off the Calle del Pasquín, behind the chapel of the Divina Pastora."

"Precisely. That one was a lucky shot. It was a long time before I was able to achieve such a range again."

"Are you saying that at the time you were not aiming for that particular spot?"

Desfosseux sits back, slightly irritated.

"I was aiming to hit whatever I could, monsieur. In fact, sometimes I still fire like that. At random . . . Accuracy is less important than distance."

The Spaniard seems disappointed. The unlit cigar now clenched between his teeth, he looks again at the map as if he no longer recognizes it.

"So you're saying you never know where your bombs are going to fall?"

"Sometimes I do, sometimes I don't. It would be possible to predict if, when the shot was fired, I had all relevant data: the expanding force of the powder charge, temperature, relative air humidity, wind speed and direction, atmospheric pressure . . . But that is impossible. And even if it were possible, we do not have the capacity to do the calculations."

The comisario has placed a hand on the table. It is rough and callused, the fingers stubby, nails bitten to the quick. One finger traces the streets as though following a precise route.

"And yet someone does have the capacity: the murderer. He achieves the precision your men cannot."

"I doubt that he does so consciously." Desfosseux is irritated by the policeman's tone. "No one could perform these calculations with such accuracy . . . no one human."

This has been one of the fundamental problems of artillery since it was devised, adds the captain, ascertaining the geometric figure traced by a projectile under specific conditions. Galileo himself tackled the problem. And this has been his principal challenge in Cádiz: dealing with those elements of a cannon that alter the trajectory of the bombs. The temperature of the barrel, air resistance and friction. Because still air is one thing, wind is a very different matter. And here it is the wind that matters. Cádiz is a city in which winds weave a veritable labyrinth.

"No doubt about that."

"I don't doubt it: I have been shelling the city for months."

The Spaniard bends down and lights his cigar from the candle in the bottle. Through the closed shutters—there is no glass in the windows—comes the sound of carts rolling along the road outside, the voices of soldiers giving the watchword, and Lieutenant Bertoldi's reply. Then silence descends again.

"Even if what you have told me is true," Desfosseux continues, "it can only be a matter of probabilities. I don't know whether your murderer is a man of science, but his mind is clearly capable of calculations that scientists have been attempting for centuries . . . He sees the landscape through different eyes. Perhaps he can detect things: constants, curves and points of impact. He may even have intuited a theorem first proposed a century ago by the mathematician Bernoulli: the effects of Nature approach a constant when such effects are studied in large numbers."

"I'm not sure I follow." The policeman has taken the cigar from his mouth and is listening intently. "Are you talking about chance?"

Quite the reverse, explains Desfosseux. He is talking about probability. Of mathematical certainty. There is nothing, for example, in what he does—from the direction of the howitzers to the moment they are fired—that does not depend on factors such as night and day, wind, weather conditions and other such things. Consciously or unconsciously, even he and his men act according to these probabilities.

The Spaniard's face lights up. He understands, and for some reason this seems to reassure him. To confirm what he has been thinking.

"What you are telling me is that, although even you cannot control where your bombs land, they do not fall at random, but in accordance with certain laws of physics?"

"Exactly. According to some code which we are as yet unable to decipher—though modern science is making considerable progress—the curve described by each of my shells is as precisely determined as the orbits of planets. The only difference between the two stems from our ignorance. And, in that case, your murderer—"

"*Our* murderer," the Spaniard corrects him. "He is as closely linked to you as to me."

His tone is not sarcastic—at least, it does not seem so. There's no way out of this now, thinks Desfosseux. And yet, as he goes deeper into this theory, he experiences a singular pleasure. A new way of looking at things that is appealing, attractive. Not unlike discovering the hidden keys to some cryptogram or some scientific mystery.

"Very well, as you wish . . . What I was trying to say is that this man is somehow capable of calculating the range of probabilities with considerable accuracy. Imagine you could feed all the data we discussed earlier into a machine that would give you an exact location and an approximate time . . ."

"Our murderer would be that machine?"

"Yes."

A cloud of smoke briefly veils the policeman's face. He leans his elbows on the table, fascinated.

"Probabilities, you say . . . And this can be calculated?"

"Up to a point. As a young man, I spent some time studying in Paris. I had not yet joined the army, but I was already intrigued by physics and chemistry. In 1795 I attended a number of classes given by Pierre-Simon Laplace at the Arsenal . . . Have you heard of him?"

"I don't believe so."

"It doesn't matter," Desfosseux explains. "Monsieur Laplace is still alive; he is one of the most eminent mathematicians and astronomers in France. At the time, his chief interest was chemistry, including the gunpowder and metallurgy used in the casting of cannons. In one of his classes, he asserted that we know that, of several possible events, a single one ought to occur; but nothing induces us to believe that one of them will occur rather than the others. However, comparing the situation to similar, earlier situations, it becomes clear that some of the possible events will probably not occur."

Desfosseux pauses for a moment. "I don't know whether this is too . . . abstruse for you?"

The policeman gives a twisted smile, his profile lit by the glow of the candle.

"Too complicated for a policeman, you mean? Don't worry, I can get by. You were saying that the experiment allows one to eliminate possibilities that are less probable than others."

Desfosseux nods. "That's correct. The process involves reducing all the events of the same kind to a certain number of equally possible cases, and determining the number of cases favorable to the event whose probability is sought. Do you follow?"

"Yes . . . more or less."

"To recapitulate: the murderer must have this mathematical understanding—whether it functions consciously or instinctively. Given predetermined physical conditions, he would rule out all those trajectories and points of impact that are impossible, and reduce the probability to absolute certainty."

"*Ah, coño. Era eso.*"

The policeman spoke in Spanish and Desfosseux looks at him, puzzled.

"Excuse me?"

Silence. The comisario pores over the map of Cádiz. "Obviously, this is just a theory," he murmurs, as though thinking about something else.

"Of course. But it is the only one that, in my view, offers a rational explanation for what you have told me."

The policeman remains bowed over the map, spellbound. The smoke from his cigar weaves spirals around the candle flame.

"Would it be possible for you to fire at a precise area of the city at a specific time?"

His expression is different now, Desfosseux notes; the eyes seem harder. For a fleeting instant, the captain imagines he sees the glitter of a gold tooth. Like a wolf's fang.

"I don't think you are aware of the seriousness of what you are suggesting."

"You're wrong," the policeman replies. "I am all too aware. So, what do you say?"

"I could try to do it, obviously. But as I already told you, as far as accuracy is concerned . . ."

Another puff on his cigar followed by another cloud of smoke. There are moments when the policeman seems to become animated.

"The bombs are your problem," he says coolly. "Mine is to track down a murderer. I will give you coordinates of specific locations. Places that are within your range." He gestures to the map. "Which areas of the city are most accessible?"

Desfosseux is flabbergasted. "I don't know . . . This is highly irregular. I . . ."

"What the devil do you mean, irregular? It's your job."

Desfosseux ignores the insolent tone. After all, without realizing it, the policeman has hit the mark. Desfosseux now leans over the map, moving the candle closer so he can see more clearly. Lines and curves, weight and fuses. Distances. In his mind, he traces perfect parabolas, precise points of impact. It is like relapsing into a chronic fever, and he allows himself to be swept up by it.

"Given the right conditions, and the range we can currently attain, these would be the most accessible zones." With his index finger he traces a line along the eastern part of the city. "Almost all this sector, two hundred *toises* to the west of the city walls."

"From the cape of San Felipe to the Puerta de Tierra?"

"More or less."

The Spaniard seems satisfied. He nods, not looking up, then indicates one of the penciled marks.

"This point here is within the zone, the corner of the Calle de San Miguel and the Cuesta de la Murga. Could you target this spot at pre-arranged days and times?"

"I could. But as I already told you, not accurately . . ."

Desfosseux does some rapid mental calculations, estimating weight and the necessary powder charge to provide thrust. It could be done, he concludes, given favorable conditions and no strong headwind or crosswind to deflect the shell or reduce its range.

"Do they need to explode?" he asks.

"It would be helpful."

The captain is already thinking about detonating devices, about the new fuses he designed which burn more steadily. At this distance, they are infallible—almost. He is convinced he can do this. Or at least he can try.

"I can't guarantee the accuracy . . . I can tell you in strict confidence that I have spent months trying to hit the Customs House where the Regency meet. But nothing."

"It is the area that interests me. Anywhere around this spot." It is now the policeman who leans over the map.

"For a while I wondered if you weren't some sort of a madman," Desfosseux says. "But I made some inquiries after I received your letter . . . I know who you are and what you do."

The policeman says nothing but simply stares at him, the smoldering cigar between his teeth.

"In any case," says Desfosseux, "why should I help you?"

"Because no man, be he French or Spanish, likes to see young girls murdered."

It is a fair answer, the captain has to admit. Even Lieutenant Bertoldi would agree with such a statement. But he does not want to go further on to this terrain. The wolfish fang he glimpsed a moment before dispelled any illusions he might have. The man in front of him is not a humanitarian, merely a policeman.

"We are at war, monsieur," he says, distancing himself. "People die every day in their hundreds, in their thousands. In fact, it is my job as an artilleryman in the Imperial Army to kill as many inhabitants of the city as I can . . . and that includes you, and these girls."

The policeman smiles. Fine, the expression says; no more tugging at the heartstrings.

"Very well, I get the point," he says abruptly. "You know you should help me. I can see it in your face."

Now it is Desfosseux's turn to laugh. "I've changed my mind. You really are a madman."

"No. I am simply fighting my own war."

He says this with a shrug of his shoulders and a gruff, unexpected candor that makes Desfosseux think. He can understand what the policeman said perfectly. Everyone has his own parabolas and trajectories to deal with.

"What about my man?"

The policeman looks at him, confused. "Which man?"

"The one you arrested."

The Spaniard's expression softens. He has understood, but he does not seem surprised by this turn of the conversation. It is almost as though he has been expecting it.

"Do you really care?"

"Yes. I want him to live."

"Then he shall live"—a cryptic smile—"I promise you."

"I want you to send him back to us."

The policeman tilts his head as if considering the matter.

"I can try, but that is all," he says finally. "But that, too, I promise you: I shall try."

"Give me your word."

The comisario looks at him with surprise.

"My word is not worth a damn, *monsieur le capitaine*. But if it is within my power, I will send him to you."

"So, what is your plan?"

"I plan to set a trap." The wolfish canine tooth glitters again. "And bait it, if I can."

THE SUN SHIMMERS on the water, its dazzle illuminating the white city within the dark girdle of its walls, as though all the light held captive by the blanket of low cloud is spilling from the heavens. Dazzled by the sudden glare, Pépé Lobo squints, bringing his hat forward and pressing it down so it is not swept away by the wind. He is standing beneath the shroud lines on the starboard bow, and he has a letter in his hands.

"What the hell are you planning to do?" asks Ricardo Maraña.

They are speaking privately, in low voices. Hence Maraña's rather familiar tone. The first mate of the *Culebra* is leaning on the gunwale next to the captain. The cutter is anchored a short distance from the jetty, prow facing into the strong south-southeasterly wind, with the boom pointed toward Puntales and the far end of the bay.

"I haven't decided yet."

Maraña skeptically tilts his head to one side. He clearly does not approve. "It is lunacy," he says. "We sail tomorrow morning."

Pépé Lobo looks at the letter again: neatly folded in four, sealed with wax, the handwriting elegant and clear. Three lines and a signature: Lorenzo Virués de Tresaco. It was brought out to him half an hour ago by two army officers who arrived in a boat rented from the jetty—they sat tensely, stiffly formal in their white gloves and frockcoats (somewhat damp from the spray), swords between their legs, while the boatman rowed against the wind and asked permission to hitch on to the chainplate. The officers—a lieutenant in the Engineers and a captain in the Irish Regiment—elected not to come aboard, merely passing up the dispatch and leaving without waiting for a response.

"How soon do you have to reply?" Maraña asks.

"Before noon. The meeting is set for tonight."

He gives the letter to the first officer, who reads it in silence then hands it back.

"Was the insult really so serious? It didn't look so from where I was sitting."

Lobo shrugs fatalistically. "I called him a coward in front of all those people."

Maraña gives the thinnest of frozen smiles. "Well," he says, "it's your problem. You don't have to go."

The two sailors stand in silence, listening to the wind howl in the shroud lines overhead, as they stare at the jetty and the city beyond. Around the cutter pass sails of every kind: square sails, lateen sails, lug sails. Boats and small crafts move across the rippling water, weaving between the tall merchant ships, while the English and Spanish frigates and corvettes ride at anchor farther away, safely out of range of the French artillery, grouped around two 74-gun British warships, their sails furled and topsails lowered.

"The timing is bad," Maraña says suddenly. "We are about to put out again, after all those wasted weeks . . . These men all depend on you."

He turns and gestures to the deck. Brasero the bo'sun and the rest of the crew are tarring the rigging and caulking the spaces between the boards, after which the deck will be scrubbed and polished with holystone. Pépé Lobo looks at their sweaty, weather-beaten faces, little different from the faces one might see through the bars of the Royal Jail—indeed, some of their number came straight from there. The tattooed bodies and unmistakable features of seafaring lowlife. In the past forty-eight hours, the crew has lost two men: one was stabbed yesterday during a brawl on the Calle Sopranis, and the other is in the hospital with the French pox.

"You'll have me in tears, with your talk of all our brave men . . . You'll break my heart."

Maraña laughs heartily now, only to stop suddenly, seized by a wet, hacking cough. He leans over the side and spits into the sea.

"If anything should go wrong," says Lobo, "you can easily take my place aboard."

Still catching his breath, the lieutenant takes a kerchief from his sleeve and wipes his mouth.

"Don't make me angry," he says, his voice still hoarse. "I like things the way they are."

There is a blast, some two miles off the port bow. Almost immediately, a cannonball fired from the Cabezuela ten seconds earlier splits the air above the *Culebra*'s mast, heading for the city. The men on deck look up, following the path of the shell, which lands on the far side of the wall with no noise and causing no apparent damage. Disappointed, the crew go back to their chores.

"I think I shall go," says Lobo. "You will be my second."

Maraña nods as though this were part of his job. "We need a third man," he says.

"Hogwash. You'll be more than enough."

Another blast from the Cabezuela; another shell rips through the air, causing everyone to look up. This one, too, seems to cause little damage.

"The place they are proposing is not bad," says Maraña evenly. "The reef by Santa Catalina will be deserted at low water. That will give you enough time and space to settle the matter."

"And since it lies outside the walls, we need not feel constrained by the ordinances of the city . . . We can claim to be acting within the law."

Maraña tilts his head, vaguely admiring. "Well then. I've studied our little soldier from Aragon. He clearly bears you ill will"—he looks at Lobo coolly—"since Gibraltar, I suppose."

"I am the one who bears him ill will."

Still looking out toward the sea and the city, Lobo notices that his first officer is staring at him intently. When he turns to face him, Maraña looks away.

"Personally, I would use a pistol," suggests Maraña. "It is cleaner and quicker."

His words are interrupted by another coughing fit. This time his kerchief is stained with spots of blood. He folds it carefully and stuffs it back into his sleeve.

"Listen, Captain, you still have a few things to do aboard this ship. Responsibilities and so forth. Whereas . . ." He pauses for a moment, lost in thought. As though he has forgotten what he was about to say. "Whereas I'm running out of cards. I've nothing to lose."

He leans over the gunwale, gaunt and ashen, as if straining for the fresh air his damaged lungs so clearly lack. His elegant, close-fitting black frockcoat, with its fine cloth and long tails, accentuates the distinguished image he projects of the prodigal son of a good family who has washed up here by chance. As he looks at the Little Marquis, it occurs to Lobo that Maraña turned twenty-one two months ago and will not live to see twenty-two—that he is doing everything in his power to prevent it.

"I am a crack shot with a pistol, sir. Better than you."

"Go to hell, Maraña."

"At this point, I don't care if I'm playing with fives or aces," the first mate says with habitual hauteur. "It would be better than dying in some tavern, spitting blood."

Pépé Lobo raises his hand. He does not like the turn the conversation has taken. "Forget about it. This individual is my concern."

"I have a taste for certain things, as you know." The lieutenant's lips curl into an ambiguous, slightly cruel smile. "I like to live life on the edge."

"Not at my expense. If you're in such a hurry to die, throw yourself overboard with cannonballs stuffed in your pockets."

Maraña does not answer, as though he is seriously weighing the advantages of this suggestion. "It's the señora," he says finally. "That's what this is about, isn't it."

It is a statement rather than a question. The two men stand for a moment in silence, gazing out at the city, spread before them like a vast ship; depending on the light and the water, it sometimes seems to float, and sometimes seems stranded on the black outcrop of rocks. Eventually, Maraña takes out a cigar and puts it in his mouth.

"Very well. I hope you kill the bastard. For the nuisance he has caused."

THE ADMINISTRATIVE OFFICE of the Royal Armada is in a two-story building on the main street of the Isla de Léon. For half an hour now Felipe Mojarra—wearing a dark jacket, a kerchief on his head, a knife in his belt and a pair of rope sandals—has been waiting in the narrow corridor on the ground floor with some twenty other people: sailors in uniform, peasants, elderly men, and women dressed in black carrying children in their arms. There is a fog of tobacco smoke, and a murmur of conversation, all of which revolves around the same thing: unpaid pensions and overdue salaries. A marine in a short blue jacket with yellow belting across the chest stands guard in front of the Office of Payments and Arbitration, leaning against a wall filthy with damp and handprints. After some time, a clerk pops his head around the door.

"Next."

Everyone turns to Mojarra, who makes his way through the crowd and steps into the office with a polite *"buenos días,"* which goes unanswered. He knows the building well from his previous visits: the corridor, the office and those who work here. Behind a small desk strewn with paperwork and surrounded by filing cabinets—on one of which there is half a loaf of bread and an empty wine bottle—a sub-lieutenant is working, aided by a clerk. The salter stands in front of the desk. He knows both men—the sub-lieutenant is always the same one, the clerks work in shifts—but he also recognizes that, to them, he is merely one more face among the dozens they see every day.

"Mojarra, Felipe . . . I've come to find out where things stand with the reward for the capture of the gunboat."

"Date?"

Mojarra gives the relevant details. He remains standing, since no one offers him the chair that languishes in a corner: it has been put there deliberately, to make sure that those who enter do not sit on it. While the clerk looks through the filing cabinets, the sub-lieutenant returns to the papers on his desk. After a moment, the clerk sets down a large ledger and a wallet of handwritten documents.

"Mojarra, you said?"

"That's right. It should also be recorded under the names Francisco Panizo and Bartolomé Cárdenas, now deceased."

"I don't see anything."

The clerk, standing next to the officer, points to a line in the ledger. Having read it, the sub-lieutenant opens the wallet and searches through the documents until he finds the right one.

"Ah, here it is. Request for a reward payment for the capture of a French gunboat at Santa Cruz mill . . . Case pending."

"What did you say?"

The sub-lieutenant shrugs his shoulders without looking up. He has protruding eyes, his hair is thinning, and he needs a shave. He looks exhausted. The carelessly unbuttoned collar of his blue jacket reveals a shirt that looks less than clean.

"I said the matter is pending," he says listlessly. "It has not yet been dealt with by the relevant authorities."

"But the piece of paper here . . ."

A brief, disdainful glance—that of a busy civil servant.

"Do you know how to read?"

"Not very well . . . No."

The officer taps the document with a paperknife.

"This is a copy of the original report: the request filed by you and your companions, which has not yet been approved. It requires a signature from the captain general, then one from the administrator, and finally one from the Treasurer of the Navy."

"But they should already be there, I think."

"Your claim hasn't been rejected: you should count yourself lucky."

"It has been a long time."

"There's no point telling me." The officer lifts the knife and, with a gruff, weary gesture, indicates the door. "It's not as if it's my money."

Considering the matter closed, he looks down at his papers. Then, noticing that Mojarra has not moved, he looks up again.

"As I told you—"

He breaks off when he sees the expression on Mojarra's face, the hard features of a man weathered by the sun and winds of the salt marshes. His eyes move to the man's hands, the thumbs hooked into his belt, either side of the knife.

"Listen to me, señor." The salter's tone has not changed. "My brother-in-law died because of that French gunboat . . . I have been fighting on the Isla de Léon since the war started."

He says no more, but stands, staring at the officer. His calm is merely a front. *One more insolent remark*, he is thinking, *and as God is my witness I might well do for you, and sign my own death warrant.* The sub-lieutenant, who seems to read his mind, glances quickly toward the door and the Navy guard on the other side. He changes tack.

"This is just how these things happen; they take time . . . The Armada is short of funds, and this award is a lot of money . . ."

His tone is different—strained and conciliatory, softer, more wary. These are uncertain times, what with the Constitution being decided; you never know who you might run into some dark night in the street. Standing next to him holding the documents, the clerk watches the scene play out wordlessly. Mojarra thinks he can see a secret satisfaction in the way the man is eyeing his superior.

"We are poor people," the salter protests.

The sub-lieutenant shrugs helplessly. Now, at least, he is sincere—or attempting to appear so. "Do you get paid, my friend?"

Mojarra nods uncertainly. "Sometimes. And we get a little food for the pot."

"Then you're lucky. Especially about the food. Because those people out in the hallway are poor, too. They cannot fight, they cannot work, so they do not even have what you have . . . Take a good look at them as you leave: old sailors left destitute because they cannot get their pensions, invalids, widows and orphans who receive no help whatsoever, salaries that have not been paid for twenty-nine months now. Every day I see people come through that door who are worse off than you . . . What do you expect me to do?"

Without answering, Mojarra turns to leave. Then he stops for a moment in the doorway.

"To treat us with a little humanity," he says hoarsely. "To show us a little respect."

ON THE REEF left exposed by low tide, 500 *varas* beyond Santa Catalina Castle near La Caleta, a lantern set on the uneven, shelled limestone illuminates two men, who stand, fifteen paces from one another, at opposite extremes of the circle of light. Neither wears a hat or coat. Traditionally, they should be in shirtsleeves or bare-chested—too much fabric increases the risk from shrapnel and infections if a bullet should hit home—but it is two o'clock in the morning and bitterly cold. Too little clothing might cause a man's hand to shake as he aims, to say nothing of the fact that the slightest shiver might be misinterpreted by the witnesses: off to one side, silent and grave, stand four men muffled up in topcoats and capes, intermittently picked out in the glare from the lighthouse at San Sebastián. Of the two men facing each other, one wears a blue uniform waistcoat, close-fitting breeches in the same color and military boots, the other is dressed in black. Even the scarf masking the collar of his shirt is black. Pépé Lobo has decided to follow the expert advice of Ricardo Maraña: bright colors merely make it easier for an opponent. As you well know, Captain. In profile, and in black, you offer a more difficult target for a bullet.

Standing perfectly still, the corsair tries to calm his nerves as he waits for the signal. He breathes slowly, clearing his mind—forcing himself to focus only on the man facing him. His right hand hanging by his side, he presses a long-barreled flintlock pistol—ideally suited to the task at hand—against his thigh. Its twin is in the hand of his opponent; Pépé Lobo cannot make him out clearly, since, like the corsair himself, he is standing on the edge of the circle, ghostly in the lamplight, halfway between light and shadow. The duelists will be able to see more clearly when the signal is given and they walk toward each other, toward the lantern. The rules agreed by the seconds are simple: a single shot, with each man free to choose the moment to open fire as they advance toward each other. From afar, he who fires first has the advantage, but risks missing his target at such a distance. At close range it is easier to aim, but he who hesitates too long before squeezing the trigger may find himself with a bullet in the chest. It is like playing blackjack: if you go bust you lose, but you also lose if you fail to make the points.

"Prepare yourselves, gentlemen," one of the seconds announces gravely.

Without turning, Pépé Lobo glances at the group: two officer friends of his opponent, a surgeon and Ricardo Maraña. Ample witnesses to attest afterward that no one was murdered and that the duel was conducted outside the city walls in a spirit of honor and decency.

"Ready, Señor Virués?"

Although there is not a breath of wind, and the only sound is the murmur of the sea lapping against the rocks, Pépé Lobo does not hear the reply, but sees his opponent nod without ever taking his eyes off the corsair. Having drawn lots, Virués has his back to the sea, while Lobo stands on the part of the reef that leads to La Caleta and the star-shaped fortifications of the Castillo de Santa Catalina. In fifteen minutes the rising tide will likely come up to his bootlaces. But by then this matter will have been settled and one or other, if not both of them, will be sprawled on the wet rock, where the lantern light now shimmers on small pools left by the ebb tide.

"Ready, Señor Lobo?"

With some difficulty—his mouth is dry—the corsair utters the terse "yes" required. He has never fought a duel before, but he has shot many men or faced them with swords in the heat of battle, on decks slick with blood, the air thick with splinters and shrapnel from enemy cannonfire. In a job such as his, where survival is the only birthright one can risk to earn a crust, life and death are mere cards dealt by Fortune. His trump card tonight is the professional sangfroid of a man accustomed to danger—something, Lobo knows, that is equally true of his opponent. Grudges and quarrels aside, he knows that it is not fear of public opinion that brings Virués here tonight, but an old score, which he too has long postponed since the business in Gibraltar.

"Prepare to advance, gentlemen . . . On my signal."

In the moment before he clears his mind and focuses on raising the pistol and advancing on his opponent, a last thought flickers through Pépé Lobo's brain: today, he wants very much to live. Or, more exactly, to kill his adversary. To wipe him from the face of the earth forever. The corsair is not motivated by some idea of honor; at this point in his life and his profession, it matters little to him. He leaves honor, its posturing and the hellish burden of its grisly consequences to those who can afford such luxuries. He has come here to the reef at Santa Catalina with the intention of shooting Lorenzo Virués: putting a bullet in his chest and wiping the stupid, supercilious expression from his face. Virués is a man who sees the world in the simplistic terms of a bygone age; a man who, by birth or by chance, knows nothing of how hard it is to be forced to live in his shadow, nor how cold it is outside. Whatever happens—Lobo thinks one last time before focusing on his own life-or-death struggle—Lolita Palma will think it was because of her.

"Advance!"

All around him now is shadow and gloom; the darkness is like a black curtain beyond the circle of light, which grows brighter as Lobo slowly advances, careful to remain in profile. He stares fixedly at his adversary, also moving, closer now, more visible. One pace. Two. It is a matter of keeping a sure footing and a constant aim—this is what it comes down to now. It is not reason but instinct that gauges the distance, decides when to open fire, checks the finger tensed on the trigger, struggling against the urge to fire before the other man does. To fire and be done with it. The corsair advances carefully, teeth clenched, his every muscle tensed for the dull impact of half an ounce of lead. Three paces now. Or perhaps four. It seems like—perhaps it is—the longest walk in the world. The ground is uneven, making it difficult for the hand that grips the pistol—his arm extended and flexed slightly at the elbow—to keep a steady aim.

Five paces. Six.

The flash startles Pépé Lobo. So focused is he on edging closer and keeping the pistol steady, he does not even hear the shot. He simply notices the sudden flare from his opponent's gun and has to struggle not to pull his trigger. A bullet passes less than an inch from his right ear with the ominous buzz of a lead blowfly.

Seven paces. Eight. Nine.

Pépé Lobo feels no satisfaction or relief, only a sense that he might now live a little longer than seemed likely five seconds ago. He has managed to hold fire, though this is not how duels usually play out. His pistol aimed, he continues to advance. In the glow of the lantern, now only a few paces away, he sees the contorted face of Lorenzo Virués. The officer stands stock-still, the smoking pistol still half-raised as though he is caught in the moment between realizing he has fired and the certain knowledge of disaster. The corsair knows what is expected of a man in such circumstances. He also knows that it is not what he plans to do. The course of action much favored by polite society would be to fire without advancing any further, or to deliberately shoot into the air now that the heat of the moment has cooled. After the first exchange—usually simultaneous—no gentleman would shoot his opponent in cold blood at point-blank range.

"For the love of God, señor!" cries one of the seconds.

It may be a reproach, thinks Lobo. A call to honor or a plea for mercy. Virués, for his part, does not say a word. His eyes are fixed, as though hypnotized, by the barrel of the pistol coming toward him. Not for a moment does he look away, not even when Pépé Lobo draws level with him, lowers his gun, pressing the nose against Virués's right thigh, and fires, shattering his leg.

THE NIGHT IS almost pitch black; the faint glow of the waning moon outlines the whitewashed terraces and the watchtowers of the tall houses. A municipal street lamp burns in the distance near the convent, but the glow is too far off to reach the low, narrow portico where Rogelio Tizón is crouching. Further up the Cuesta de la Murga, the shrine of the Archangel Michael trampling Satan is barely visible in the gloom.

But in the distant glow of the street lamp, a pale figure is moving slowly. Tizón watches as the figure draws closer, passes beneath the archangel's shrine and carries on up the hill. The comisario takes a moment to study the crossroads, then leans back against the wall again. As he expected, it is going to be a long night. One of many, he fears. But patience is the cardinal virtue of the hunter. And tonight he is hunting. Using live bait.

The pale figure turns and, retracing its steps, walks back toward the corner. In the hushed silence of the street, where no lights flicker in the shuttered windows, comes the sound of hesitant footsteps. Unless Cadalso has fallen asleep, thinks Tizón, he should see the bait as it moves along the section of the street he is watching from an apothecary's window on the Plaza de la Carnicería. At the far end of the route, another agent has been posted on the Calle del Vestuario, next to the street lamp by the convent. Between the three of them, they have the whole block and its adjoining streets under surveillance, with the shrine as the main axis. The original plan was to cover a larger area, with additional officers posted in the surrounding streets, but at the last moment Tizón changed his mind, fearing that too many men might create suspicion.

The bait stops next to a doorway, framed against the distant lantern. From his hiding place, the comisario can clearly see the pale smudge of the white shawl intended to act both as a lure for the killer and a visual reference for him and his officers. It goes without saying that the girl has no idea of the danger she is in or the true nature of the role she has been called upon to play—a fact that surprises no one, given that Rogelio Tizón is involved. She is a young prostitute from La Merced; the same girl that some months ago Tizón saw naked, sprawled facedown on a filthy bed as he traced the tip of his cane along her back and peered into the abyss of his own dark desires. Her name is Simona. She is sixteen now and, in the light, she looks less fresh and innocent than she did then—the time she has spent plying her trade in Cádiz has left its mark—but at first glance, with her blond hair and pale skin, she is young, delicate. Tizón had little trouble convincing her: fifteen *duros* to her pimp—a man named Carreño—on the pretext of luring local married men to later blackmail them. Or something of the sort. Whether Carreño swallowed this cock-and-bull story does not matter: he pocketed the money, and the future leniency of the comisario, asking no questions—and certainly not whether this had anything to do with the rumors he had heard about young girls being murdered around the city. That was none of his business, still less so if Rogelio Tizón was involved. Besides, as he said when he agreed to the deal, that is what whores are for, señor. To be whores and do the bidding of magnanimous police commissioners. As for Simona, she accepted the situation with the resignation of a woman meekly doing the bidding of her man—whoever that might be. After all, it made no difference to her whether the clients were married men or bachelors, soldiers of rank or otherwise, or whether she walked this street or that. She'd still have to scratch the same itch.

The pale smudge of the shawl has begun to move off down the

street again. Rogelio Tizón watches as the girl walks to the corner of the Calle del Vestuario then stops, a still shadow framed in the lamplight. A little while ago, the comisario's interest was piqued when a man strolled past her, but he turned out to be just another passerby and the girl, having been duly forewarned, paid him no heed. Her instructions were precise: do not approach anyone, simply be on the alert. So far, three men have passed; only one of them stopped, to hurl abuse at her, before going on his way.

Time is passing and Tizón is exhausted. He would like to sit on the steps in the shelter of the doorway, lean against the wall and take a nap. But he knows this is unthinkable. He clings to the hope that Cadalso and the other officer have likewise resisted the urge to close their eyes. Half asleep, images of the street randomly flicker through his mind: the shadows, the pale smudge of the white shawl pacing up and down, memories of the murdered girls. There are pictures of the city too, a vast chessboard, its squares all black in the darkness. Struggling to keep his eyes open, Tizón pushes his hat back off his forehead and unbuttons his coat, hoping the chill night air will shock him awake. Damn it all. Right now, he would give his soul to be able to smoke a cigar.

He shuts his eyes for a moment, and when he opens them again the girl is close by. As she paces up and down, she has casually contrived to position herself near him. She stops next to the doorway, facing the street, a shawl around her shoulders and her head bare, doing nothing that might reveal the policeman's presence. She is wily and discreet, Tizón thinks; he stares at the curve of her shoulders, lit by the soft glow of the moon above the houses.

"I've had no luck tonight," the girl whispers, her back to the comisario.

"You're doing a good job," he says in the same low voice.

"Thought that last gent was going to stop, but he didn't. Just stared at me and walked past."

"Did you get a look at his face?"

"Not really. The lantern was too far away . . . He looked strong, though, with a face like an ox."

The description piques the comisario's interest for a moment. One of the things he has recently been wondering is how a man's features might relate to his character and his proclivities. Among the many false leads he has blindly followed up in this investigation is a theory he discovered in a book lent to him by Hipólito Barrull some months ago: *De humana physiognomonia*. The treatise was written two hundred years ago, but its hypothesis is of considerable interest to the policeman: to what extent is it possible to deduce the virtues and vices of an individual from his physical traits? It is a speculative art (to call it a science would be excessive, as the professor qualified when he lent him the book) according to which dangerous people, those predisposed to crime and delinquency, have a tendency to reveal such propensities in their face and body. At the time, Tizón devoured the book and then spent days wandering the streets of Cádiz, constantly on the alert, hawk-eyed and suspicious, attempting to find the face of the murderer from among the thousands he encountered every day—seeking out the pointed heads that foretell evil, the low brows suggestive of stupidity and slow-wittedness, the thin or conjoined eyebrows indicating a proclivity for vice, the horse-like teeth suggestive of wickedness, the misshapen ears of the lecherous goat, the flared nostrils of shamelessness and cruelty— as Tizón remembers, an ox-like face was linked to cowardice and sloth. The experiment ended one sunny morning when, stopping in front of the window of a fan shop to light a cigar, the comisario saw his own reflection and realized that, according to the theories of physiognomy, his aquiline nose was an unambiguous sign of nobility and magnanimity. That very afternoon he gave the book back to Barrull and wiped the matter from his mind.

"If you want, Comisario, I can entertain you a little."

Simona says this in a whisper, her back to him, looking out into the street as though she is alone.

"A quick frig, won't hardly take a minute."

Tizón does not doubt the girl's willingness, but it takes him less than three seconds to dismiss the idea. This is not the time or place.

"Maybe some other time," he says.

"As you like."

Indifferent, Simona sets off again toward the Calle de San Miguel, melting into the darkness until all that is visible is her white shawl. Rogelio Tizón moves away from the walls and shifts his position, stretching his numbed limbs. Then he looks up at the night sky, beyond the house with the shrine to the archangel. A singular fellow, that Frenchman, he thinks to himself, with his field guns and trajectories and his initial reluctance; in the end, unquenchable curiosity got the better of his misgivings. The policeman smiles, remembering the way the artillery captain requested recent data, exact details of the ideal points of impact and how best to communicate them across the bay. Let us hope he keeps his word tonight.

Again comes the urge to close his eyes, images from this night mingling in his befuddled state with remembered nightmares. The mutilated flesh, the exposed bones, the fixed, staring eyes covered with a film of dust. And a distant voice whose accent and sex it is impossible to determine, whispering words like *here*, or *to me*. The comisario nods off for a second, waking with a start, and looks up toward the Calle de San Miguel expecting to see the faint gleam of the white shawl. For a moment he thinks he sees a dark shape moving, a shadow gliding along the wall opposite. Sleep fashions its own ghosts, he thinks.

He cannot see the shawl. Perhaps Simona has stopped at the end of the street. First worried, then panicked, he scans the darkness. He cannot hear the girl's footsteps. Stifling the urge to rush from his hiding place, Tizón carefully pokes his head out, trying to make sure he is not too visible. Nothing. Nothing but darkness on the corner of the street and the faint glow of the lantern in the distance. In any case, she should be heading back by now. Too much time has passed. Too much silence. The image of the chessboard again appears before him. The ruthless smile of Professor Barrull. You didn't see that move coming, Comisario. He's got away from you again. You've made a mistake and lost another piece.

The surge of panic hits him as he rushes from the doorway, running blindly toward the dark corner. Finally he sees the shawl, a white stain discarded on the ground. Tizón races past it, comes to the corner and anxiously looks around, trying to see through the shadows. Only the faint glow of the waning moon, now hidden behind the flat roofs, reveals the bluish outlines of the balcony railings, the dark frames of windows and doorways, magnifying the blackness of every corner, every hidden recess in the soundless street.

"Cadalso!" he yells frantically. "Cadalso!"

At the sound of his voice, one of the shadowy corners, a niche that extends like some frightening crack into the dark heart of the little square, seems to stir, as though a shadow has come to life. At the same moment, a door is flung open behind the comisario; the rectangle of light cuts the street like a knife blade, and he hears Cadalso's footsteps pounding toward him. But by now Tizón is already running, plunging into the murky square. As he comes closer, he can just make out a crouching shape which suddenly splits into two figures: one sprawled on the ground, the other running quickly, hugging the walls of the houses. Without stopping at the first, the comisario attempts to catch up with the second figure as it crosses the street, heading for the corner of the Cuna Vieja; it is framed for an instant in the light, a black figure running quickly and soundlessly.

"Stop, police! Stop!"

Lights and candles appear in some of the windows along the street, but Tizón and the shadow he is chasing have already left them far behind, cutting rapidly through the square on the Calle de Recaño toward the Women's Hospital. The comisario can feel his lungs burning from the strain, and he is further hampered by his cane—he lost his hat along the way—and the long redingote flapping around his legs. The shadow is moving with incredible speed, and he finds it increasingly difficult to keep pace.

"Halt! Halt! Murder!"

The distance between them now is insurmountable, and the hope that some neighbor or passerby might join the pursuit is fading—they are moving too quickly through the streets, it is a winter's night and almost two o'clock in the morning. Tizón can feel his strength failing. If only he had brought his pistol, he thinks.

"Son of a bitch!" he howls impotently as he comes to a halt.

Already he is gasping for breath, and this last yell finishes him off completely. Hunched over, wheezing with the hoarse rattle of a pair of bellows, gasping for air to soothe his red-raw lungs, Tizón attempts to lean against the wall of the hospital and gradually slumps until he is sitting on the ground, dazed, at the corner where the shadow disappeared. He sits there for some time, catching his breath. Eventually, with great effort, he gets to his feet and limps back on aching legs to the Plaza de la Carnicería, where lamps now burn in the windows and locals in nightshirts and nightcaps are leaning out or standing in their doorways. The girl is being cared for by the apothecary, Cadalso says, as he comes over holding a dark lantern. Simona was brought round with smelling salts and vinegar compresses. The killer only succeeded in dealing a single blow, knocking her unconscious.

"Did she see his face? Anything at all?"

"She is still too dazed to think clearly, but it does not seem so. The attack was sudden and from behind. She barely noticed he was there before he had a hand over her mouth . . . She thinks he was a short man, but strong and agile. She didn't see anything else."

We will have to start all over again, thinks Tizón gloomily in a haze of frustration and exhaustion.

"Where was he planning to take her?"

"She doesn't know. Like I said, she passed out at the first blow . . . but I think he intended to drag her to the gallery behind the rope warehouse when we came down on him."

This use of the plural infuriates the comisario.

"*We* came down? Where the devil were you, idiot? He must have passed right under your nose."

Cadalso says nothing, shamefaced. Tizón, who knows him only too well, correctly interprets his reaction, though he cannot bring himself to believe it.

"Don't tell me you fell asleep . . ."

The lieutenant's continued silence confesses to his guilt. Once again, he looks like a lumbering, dull-witted dog, waiting, ears down and tail between his legs, for his master to beat him.

"Listen, Cadalso . . ."

"Yes, señor."

Tizón stares at him, repressing the urge to split the lieutenant's head open with his cane.

"You are a half-wit."

"Yes, sir."

"I would gladly shit on you from a great height, you and your mother and the Blessed Virgin herself."

"Whatever you think fit, Don Rogelio."

"Numbskull. Asshole."

Tizón is incensed. He still cannot believe that they have failed. They had him almost in their grasp. At least, he consoles himself, the killer has no reason to suspect that this was a trap. It might simply have been an unfortunate encounter with a nightwatchman. A coincidence. Nothing, in short, that would prevent him from trying again. Or that, at least, is what the comisario is depending on. Resigned, and smothering his contempt, he looks around: the locals are still leaning out of doors and windows.

"Let's go and see the girl. And tell these people to get back inside. There is a real danger that—"

He is interrupted by a long whine that splits the air. A ripping sound heading for the Calle de San Miguel. As though someone were viciously tearing a piece of cloth over their head.

Then, forty paces away, the bomb explodes.

CHAPTER FIFTEEN

࿇

In Cádiz, many royal and municipal ordinances are enacted only to be ignored. The ordinance regulating excessive public displays during Carnaval is a case in point. Though officially no ball, music or spectacle is authorized, in practice everyone celebrates the "farewell to the flesh" preceding Lent. And though the French shelling has intensified in recent weeks—although, even now, many bombs fail to explode or fall into the sea—the streets are teeming with people: the common masses celebrating in their local area while polite society, as ever, moves between soirées in private houses and boisterous revelry in the cafés. After midnight, the city teems with costumes, masks, water squirters, and every conceivable type of powder and confetti. Families and groups of friends and relatives wander from house to house, past groups of Negroes—slaves and freedmen—who roam the streets playing drums and reed flutes. In the long and bitter argument among the public and in the Cortes about ignoring Carnaval and being abstemious because of the war, those who favored showing the French that life goes on as normal have clearly prevailed. On the terraces hang paper lanterns with candles, which can be seen from the far shore of the bay, and many of the ships at anchor have lit their beacons, throwing down the gauntlet to the enemy artillery.

Lolita Palma, Curra Vilches and cousin Toño are walking arm in arm through the Plaza San Antonio, laughing as they weave through groups of wild revelers wearing masks. All three are in costume. Lolita is wearing a full mask of black taffeta that leaves only her mouth visible, and is dressed as a harlequin with a black and white domino by way of a cowl. Curra, true to herself, is elegantly dressed in a military frockcoat and a shirt with three layers of frills and flounces, a sutler's cap and a mask painted with thick mustaches. Cousin Toño is wearing a Venetian mask and is dressed as a handsome bullfighter: a short, richly embroidered jacket, close-fitting tights, his hair secured in a short ponytail and, tucked into his belt in place of a rapier, three Havana cigars and a flask of *aguardiente*. They are coming from the ball at the Consulado Comercial, having spent a pleasant evening of music and drinking with friends: Miguel Sánchez Guinea and his wife, Toñete Alcalá Galiano, Paco Martínez de la Rosa, Jorge Fernández Cuchillero, the member for Buenos Aires, and other young liberal members of the Cortes. Now, having excused themselves to get a breath of air, chaperoned by cousin Toño, the two women have decided to take a stroll and sample the street festivities, to see how the other half lives.

"Let's go to the Café de Apolo," suggests Curra Vilches.

This is the one day of the year when women are admitted to cafés in Cádiz; habitually, they frequent the less masculine world of the teashops with their sorbets and cold drinks, pastries, sweetmeats and mahogany finger bowls.

Cousin Toño protests. "Are you mad? You want me to step into the lion's den with two beautiful women? Good Lord, they will eat you alive."

"Why so?" asks Lolita Palma. "After all, we are escorted by an elegant gentleman."

"By a brave and valiant bullfighter," corrects Curra Vilches.

"Besides," Lolita adds, "behind these masks, no one will be able to tell whether we are beautiful or ugly."

Resigned to his fate, her cousin heaves a doubtful sigh and heads for the café on the corner of the Calle Murguía.

"Ugly? You are a pair of turtle doves, *niñas*. Besides, in Cádiz during Carnaval, no woman could possibly be ugly."

"This is the chance of a lifetime for me!" Curra Vilches gaily claps her hands.

Lolita Palma laughs, her arm through her cousin's. "And for me!"

The three stroll past the caleches and private carriages lined up on one side of the square, the coachmen passing around a wineskin, and cross the threshold beneath the wrought-iron lyre that gives the establishment its name. The Café de Apolo is cousin Toño's regular haunt and, as they enter, the head waiter recognizes him despite his disguise, greeting him politely with a deep bow and accepting a silver *duro* as a tip.

"A table with a view, Julito. Somewhere these ladies will be comfortable."

"I don't know whether we have any tables free, Don Antonio."

"I'll wager another *duro* that you do . . . and see, I lose."

The second coin glitters briefly in the waiter's hand before he slips it—now you see it, now you don't—into the pocket of his apron.

"Let me see what I can do."

Five minutes later, surrounded by the merry throng in the colonnaded courtyard, the three are seated around a folding table which a waiter has brought down from upstairs—the women with glasses of cinnamon liqueur, and cousin Toño with a bottle of sweet sherry. The building has four storys: the two upper floors, accessed from the Calle Murguía, are a lodging house for travelers; below these are the spacious courtyard and the first floor with its dining hall and various rooms where impassioned liberals usually hold court. Today, the lower floors are bubbling with excitement. Chandeliers and candelabras are everywhere, candlelight glittering on jewelry, satins, embroidery work and sequins. From up above comes a rain of colored confetti and the sound of mirlitons and bladder pipes while a string orchestra plays softly beneath the arcades. There is no dancing, but waiters weave between the tables amid singing and lively chatter. The conversations, the laughter and the cigar smoke create a merry atmosphere. Lolita Palma eagerly takes in the spectacle while cousin Toño—who has pushed back his mask to put on his spectacles—is smoking and clinking glasses; Curra Vilches, with her usual candor, is making pointed comments about the dresses, costumes and people all around.

"See the woman in the green bodice and the white wig? I'm sure that's Pancho Zangasti's sister-in-law."

"Do you think so?"

"I told you, she is . . . And that man nibbling her ear is not her husband!"

"Currita, you can be so uncouth."

As usual, the café is thronged with men—society gentlemen, officers in civilian clothes, foreigners. But there are many women too, sharing tables on the patio and in the side rooms, or leaning over the balustrade. Some are respectable ladies accompanied by their husbands, relatives or friends. Others—Curra Vilches elegantly, mercilessly dissects them—are less sophisticated. Carnaval breaks down barriers, sweeps aside the social conventions that are rigorously enforced in Cádiz during the rest of the year. In these unsettled times, which have made the city a microcosm of Spain itself, Cádiz remains open to all, but everyone knows their place. If they do not, or if they should forget, there is always someone to remind them of it. Regardless of the war and the Cortes, this is still the case; even the costumes and the carnival atmosphere cannot equate the unequal. Perhaps, thinks Lolita Palma, one of the young liberal philosophers with their café debates, their homilies and their meetings advocating enlightenment, nationhood and justice will change things. Or perhaps not. At the end of the day, those who sit in the Cortes at San Felipe Neri are priests, noblemen, scholars, lawyers and military officers. There are no merchants, shopkeepers or commoners, though they claim to speak for and represent them. The king is still a prisoner in France, and the much debated national sovereignty is nothing more than a sheaf of paper known as the future Constitution. This much is clear even in the communal celebrations of the Café de Apolo. The people of Spain, of Cádiz, together in one place, but not mingling—or only to a certain degree.

"Another drink?"

"Why not?" Lolita accepts another glass of liqueur. "Though I fear you are intent on ruining my reputation, Cousin."

"Look at Curra . . . I don't hear her complaining."

"Ah, but she is utterly shameless."

Confetti still rains from the floor above, like multicolored snow.

Taking off a glove, Lolita Palma fishes some pieces of confetti out of her drink and sips it slowly. From where she is sitting she can see a sea of masks: elegant, graceful, ingenious and vulgar; but there are also people here wearing no mask and everyday clothing. And as she glances around the room, scanning the faces and the fashions, she spots Pépé Lobo.

"Is that not your corsair?" asks Curra Vilches, unconsciously following her gaze.

"Yes, that's him."

"Where are you going?"

Lolita Palma will never know—though she will spend the rest of her life wondering—what possessed her to get up that Carnaval night in the Café de Apolo, to the surprise of cousin Toño and Curra Vilches, and walk over to Pépé Lobo's table disguised by her mask and cowl. Perhaps her daring was brought on by the liqueur, or perhaps by the heady feeling of intoxication in which she seems to glide, weightless and serene, her senses heightened rather than dulled; it is an exhilaration brought on by the music and the dreamlike rain of confetti that fills the space that separates them, amid the clamor of happy voices and coils of smoke. The captain of the *Culebra* is alone, though Lolita notices that there are two glasses set out with the bottle on the marble table. As always, he is wearing his blue frockcoat with gilt buttons, open to reveal a white waistcoat and a shirt with a wide black necktie knotted at the throat. He is studying the people in the café, amused, though a little aloof; not really taking part in the festivities. Sensing her presence, Lobo looks up at Lolita just as she stops. The sailor's green eyes, glittering in the candlelight, look her up and down, at the mask and the black silk cowl she drew up as she walked over. Then he looks her up and down again. He clearly does not recognize her.

"Good evening, harlequin," he says with a smile.

The smile opens a white cleft in his weather-beaten skin between the thick, brown whiskers. Without getting to his feet or taking his eyes off her for a moment, Lobo leans over the table, pours some *aguardiente* into a glass and offers it to Lolita; thrilled at her own daring—she can feel the horrified gazes of Curra Vilches and cousin

Toño watching her from afar—she takes it and brings it to her lips, though she takes only a small sip: the strong liqueur burns her mouth and tastes slightly of aniseed. Then she hands the glass back to the sailor, who is still smiling.

"Have you lost your tongue, harlequin?"

His tone is curious now—or interested. Lolita Palma, wondering who the second glass might be for, says nothing for fear that her voice will give her away, reveling in the pleasurable freedom the disguise affords her, something akin to fearlessness, although she knows that it cannot last. It is beginning to be uncomfortable. And dangerous. And yet, to her surprise, she realizes she is at ease here, standing next to Pépé Lobo's table, brazenly staring at his face from behind her mask. Enjoying being close to those glittering green eyes, the rough handsome face of the corsair; that smile, at once so serious and serene; those lips, so masculine—she longs to touch them. *What a pity there is no dancing here,* she thinks impetuously. *Not that I care for dancing, but it is something one can do without speaking, without those tiresome words that bind and compromise.*

"Wouldn't you like to sit down?"

She shakes her head, about to turn on her heel. In that moment she sees the first mate of the *Culebra,* the young man named Maraña, weaving between the tables toward them. The other glass is intended for him. *It is time to go,* she thinks—*back to Curra Vilches and cousin Toño, to the rational world.* And yet, as she makes to leave, Lolita Palma does something spontaneous, something that shocks even her. Carried away by the same impulse that first carried her across the room, she walks around the table where Pépé Lobo is sitting and as she passes behind him, she brushes a gloved hand across his shoulders, stroking the coarse fabric of his frockcoat. As she leaves, she sees the baffled way he is looking at her.

The walk back to her table is never-ending. Halfway there, she feels a presence next to her. A hand seizes her wrist.

"Wait."

Now she truly has a problem, she thinks as she stops and turns toward him, suddenly calm. The green eyes gaze intently into hers. In them Lolita can see a mixture of curiosity and surprise.

"Don't go."

She remains unruffled by his presence. The alcohol coursing gently through her veins gives her a courage and composure she has never known. The man's hand, still grasping her wrist, is firm, but his grip is light. He does not squeeze, holding her by his will rather than brute force. This is the hand that shot Lorenzo Virués, she thinks, leaving him a cripple for the rest of his days.

"Let me go, Captain."

And in that moment, Pépé Lobo recognizes her. Lolita can see the dawning realization on his face: surprise, disbelief, amazement, embarrassment. Her wrist is free now.

"Well, well . . ." he murmurs. "I . . ."

For some obscure reason she basks in this moment of triumph, in the confusion of this man whose laugh has suddenly faded, snuffed out like a candle flame. He glances around him curiously, as though wondering how many people were in on the joke. Then he looks at her gravely.

"I apologize," he says.

He is like a boy who has been scolded, she thinks, vaguely moved by the flicker of innocence she believes she glimpses in the corsair's face—a fleeting glance, perhaps. The almost childlike way he spreads his hands, bewildered. Maybe, she thinks suddenly, this is how he looked as a child, before he first put out to sea.

"Are you enjoying your evening, Captain?"

Now it is his turn to be silent, and Lolita feels a private exhilaration at the nebulous power she holds over this man. Something in her atavistic womanhood, born of flesh and of the ages. She studies his beard—though he shaved some hours ago, it is already darkening his firm, strong chin between the sideburns that almost reach the corners of his mouth. For a second, she wonders what his skin smells like.

"I was surprised to see you here."

"Imagine how I feel."

The green eyes have recovered their composure, twinkling again in the candlelight. Curra Vilches, presuming something is amiss, has got up from the table and is coming toward them. Lolita calmly raises a hand.

"Everything is fine, 'Officer.'"

Through the mask, Curra looks from one to the other inquiringly.

"Are you sure?"

"Absolutely. Tell our tipsy toreador that I am going to take some air . . . It's too smoky in here."

A silence. Then Curra's puzzled voice: "Alone?"

Lolita can imagine her friend's jaw dropping behind the cardboard mask with its painted mustaches, and almost bursts out laughing. It is not often she swaps roles with Curra Vilches.

"Don't worry. This gentleman will escort me."

Rogelio Tizón steps aside to avoid the bucket of water thrown from a window above. Then, resigned to the inevitable, he elbows his way through a group of women dressed up as witches, who prod him good-humoredly with their brooms on the corner of the Calle de los Tres Hornos. This is a popular area—families of craftsmen and laborers. The houses are close together, life is lived on the streets, and everyone knows everyone else. On many of the terraces there are makeshift tents rented out to refugees and foreigners. Some of the streets are lit by torches that give off coils of dark, oily smoke. Despite the ban on dancing out of doors—a fine of ten *pesos* for men and five for women, according to the latest municipal edict—people are out on their balconies throwing water and bags of powder on passersby or out in the street in animated groups, playing guitars, bandurrias, trumpets, whistles and rattles. There is much laughter and joking, and the conversations are marked by the accent and merry disposition of Cádiz's common people. Twice the comisario encounters a group of Negro freedmen roaming the streets to the rhythm of pipes, singing in thick Caribbean patois.

Ma mama doan' wan'
Me a-go to the beach

'cuz de soldiers there
doan' treat a girl right

A boy in a purple burnoose and slippers armed with a bladder on a stick makes a rush at Tizón, ready to hit him, but the comisario blocks him with his cane.

"Get out of here," he says, "or I'll rip off your head."

The boy scurries away, terrified by the glare and the harsh tone of the policeman, who continues to make his way through the crowd, studying the masked faces all around. Now and then, when he spots a girl he trails her a little way, watching for anyone who attempts to approach or follow her. Sometimes he keeps up the surveillance through several streets, staring at every masked face, waiting for the slightest suspicious movement to hurl himself at some stranger, rip off the mask and reveal the face—the face he has seen so often in his nightmares—of the man he is seeking. Other times, it is not a young girl but a strange costume, a curious look that catches his eye, and he follows the man, watching his every move, his every step.

On the Calle del Sol, next to the chapel, Tizón spots a man in a long hooded black robe and a white mask who stands, motionless, watching the crowd. Something about the man's demeanor arouses the comisario's suspicions. Perhaps, thinks Tizón, taking cover behind a group of revelers, it is the way he seems to set himself apart: solitary, aloof from the festivities. The man's eyes seem cold, distant—too distant for someone who has taken the trouble to put on a Carnaval costume and come out into the street to have fun. This man is not having fun, he is not interacting with anyone. The cowled head moves slowly from side to side, watching people as they pass. He does not seem to bat an eyelid when three giggling girls, dressed in colored ponchos and straw hats, their faces painted black, rush up to him, spray him with water and then scamper down the street. He merely watches them go.

Cautiously stepping from behind the revelers, Rogelio Tizón moves toward the stranger. For an instant, he seems to stare at the comisario, then he turns and quickly walks away. It might be mere coincidence, thinks Tizón. But it might not be. Quickening his step so as not to lose sight of the man, the comisario follows him as far as the Calle del Sacramento; just as he is about to rush over and grab him, eager to rip off the mask, the stranger goes over to join a group of men and women in costumes who greet him by name, clearly delighted to see him. There is a burst of laughter, someone produces a wineskin and the latecomer pushes back his hood, takes off his mask and, holding the wineskin high, aims a long draft squarely at his gullet, just as Rogelio Tizón walks past him, feeling utterly foolish.

THE SMELL OF fried fish, of fritters and burnt sugar. Small paper lanterns flicker in the meager hovels of the fishermen's district in La Viña. On the long, straight Calle de la Palma, these points of light look like fireflies lined up in the darkness. The faint glow reveals groups of locals; there is a hum of conversation, clinking glasses, laughter and singing. On the corner of the Calle de la Consolación, next to a lantern on the ground that barely illuminates their legs, two men and a woman dressed up in sheets that look like shrouds are drunkenly singing about *Good old King Pepino** who, they rhyme, *was very fond of vino.*

"I don't usually frequent this neighborhood," says Lolita Palma, fascinated by everything.

Pépé Lobo steps between her and a group of boys running past with lighted torches, bladders and syringes of water. He turns to look at her. "We can head back, if you prefer."

"No."

The black taffeta mask she is wearing completely hides her face beneath the domino hood. When she says nothing for long periods, Lobo feels as though he is walking beside a shadow.

"It's pleasant . . . Besides, the night is glorious for the time of year."

From time to time, as it has done just now, the conversation drifts back to the weather, to the trivial details of their surroundings. It happens when the silences drag on too long and they find themselves in a blind alley of words that neither of them cares—*dares* is perhaps the

---

* A reference to Joseph Bonaparte—so named for having the fountains of Madrid run with wine to celebrate his investiture.

right word—to utter. Lobo knows Lolita Palma feels the same way. And yet, how pleasurable it is to be lulled by these silences, by the languid indolence of this aimless stroll—by the unspoken amnesty of Carnaval which abolishes all responsibilities. And so, for more than half an hour the corsair and the lady have idly roamed the streets of Cádiz. From time to time, a slight stumble, the sudden appearance of a group of revelers, or the shock of a masked figure blowing a whistle or a trumpet nearby, causes them accidentally to brush against each other in the darkness.

"Did you know, Captain, that dancers from Cádiz were all the rage in ancient Rome?"

They are standing on the corner of the Calle de las Carretas, in the light of an oil lamp. Outside the half-open door of a tavern, a group of costumed women are dancing—ready to vanish should a nightwatchman appear—surrounded by a circle of dandies, sailors and gypsies, whose rhythmic clapping makes any music unnecessary.

"I didn't know," Pépé Lobo admits.

"Well, it's true: the Romans used to fight over them." Lolita's tone is easy and self-confident, the voice of a hostess showing off her city to a foreigner. *And yet it is I who am escorting her*, thinks Lobo. *I wonder how she comes by such poise.*

"In another age," she adds after a moment, "that is something else I would have had to do, I fear . . . Palma e Hijos, shipper of fine dancers."

She breaks off and laughs quietly; the captain is unsure whether she is joking.

"Dancers," Lobo says.

"Just so: dancers and tuna in escabeche: these are the things that have brought Cádiz her fame and fortune . . . Though the dancers were less fortunate than the tuna: the Emperor Theodosius banned their dancing for being too lascivious. According to Saint John Chrysostom, they were dancing with Satan himself."

They continue on their way, leaving the dancers behind. Above the broad street, the ample expanse of the heavens is thronged with stars.

At every turnoff to their left, Pépé Lobo notes the soft, slightly damp westerly breeze coming from the city walls and the Atlantic, which lies a mere three hundred paces beyond the Capuchinos esplanade.

"Do you like the people of Cádiz, Captain?"

"Some."

They walk a few paces in silence. Sometimes Lobo can hear the soft rustle of the domino silk. Close up, he can smell Lolita's distinctive perfume, unlike that usually worn by women of her age. But it is delicate and pleasant. Fresh, not too intense. Bergamot, he thinks absurdly, though he has never smelled bergamot.

"There are some I like and some I do not care for," he adds. "As in any city."

"I know so little about you."

The words sound like a lament. Almost a reproach. He takes her hand to help her step around an unhitched carriage, its shafts resting on the ground. The sailor shakes his head.

"Mine is a commonplace story: the sea as a means of escape."

"You were very young when you arrived from Havana, were you not?"

"To say I *arrived* is to overstate the matter. Rather I left . . . To arrive would be to return with thousands of *reales*, a Negro manservant, a parrot and several crates of cigars."

"And a shawl of Chinese silk for a woman?"

"Sometimes."

Lolita Palma walks a few steps in silence.

"Have you ever bought a shawl?"

"Sometimes."

They pass the Calle de la Palma, with its twin rows of fireflies. There are fewer people now; before them is the shadowy esplanade of San Pedro and, on the right, the dark hulking mass of El Hospicio. Lobo stops, ready to retrace his steps, but Lolita Palma walks on toward the rampart a short distance away, and the blue-black expanse of the sea beyond. The water shimmers yellow at regular intervals, in the beam of the San Sebastián lighthouse.

"I seem to remember"—Lolita is thoughtful—"that I once heard you say only a fool would go to sea by choice. Can it be true that you do not love the sea?"

"Is this some jest? It is the most terrible place in the world."

"Why then do you still ship out?"

"Because I have nowhere else to go."

They come to the bastion above La Caleta. Close by, they can distinguish a watchtower and the dark figure of a guard. Lanterns at regular intervals illuminate the sweeping curve of white sand below; from the ramshackle bars and taverns built of timber and sailcloth that cluster against the city wall comes the sound of music, laughter and merriment. In the half light, against the black background of the sea, it is possible to make out the pale outlines of boats grounded on the muddy bank and, closer in, the gunboats at anchor. In Cádiz, thinks Pépé Lobo, all roads lead to the sea.

"I would love to go down there," Lolita Palma says.

The corsair almost flinches. Even during Carnaval and wearing a mask, the dive bars of La Caleta with their sailors, whores and music are no place for a lady.

"That would not be a good idea," he says, embarrassed. "Perhaps we should—"

"Calm yourself," she cuts in, laughing. "I was expressing a desire, not an intention."

They fall silent again, leaning against the stone parapet. Standing within a hand's-breadth of each other, breathing the damp air with its tang of sand and salt, Lobo is keenly aware of the woman's physical presence. He can almost smell the warmth of her body next to his shoulder—or imagines he can.

"Are you waiting for some stroke of fortune?" asks Lolita Palma, returning to their earlier conversation.

That is one way of putting it, thinks Lobo. A stroke of fortune.

At length, he nods. "That is what I'm looking for, and if I should find it, I would turn my back on the sea forever."

"I thought . . . I don't know," she says, seeming genuinely surprised, "I thought you liked this life. The adventure."

"You thought wrong."

Another silence. Suddenly, Lobo feels a pressing need to speak; to explain something he has never cared to tell anyone before now.

"I live as I do because I cannot live by any other means. As for what you call 'adventure' . . . well, I would trade all the adventure in the world for a few sacks of gold coins . . . If one day I should retire, I will buy a plot of land as far as possible from the ocean, in some place with no view of the sea . . . I will have a house and a trained vine that I can sit under of an evening, watching the sun set without having to worry about whether the ship is dragging its anchor, or whether I need to reef the sails before I can get a good night's sleep."

"And a wife?"

"Yes . . . I don't know. Maybe. Maybe even a wife."

He breaks off, disconcerted. She asked the question dispassionately, coldly. As though it were merely one more item on the list Lobo had begun. And it is precisely this detachment—artless or deliberate?—that unsettles the corsair.

"It seems to me you are close to achieving all that," Lolita Palma says. "I mean, amassing enough money. So you can retire inland."

"It's possible. But it is impossible to know until it happens."

At intervals a beam sweeps across them from the castle lighthouse, at the far end of San Sebastián reef. The dark figure of the guard paces slowly along the sea wall. Lolita Palma still wears her checkered hood, but she has taken off her mask. Lobo gazes at her profile, sporadically illuminated by the distant flare.

"Do you know what I like about seafaring men, Captain? I like the fact that they have traveled much and say little. What they know they have seen with their own eyes; they have learned without reading it in books. Sailors feel no real need for company, since they have always been alone. And there is something naive, something innocent about them—they set foot on land as though stepping into some dangerous, unfamiliar place."

Lobo listens in astonishment. So this is how others see him. This is how she sees him.

"You have a pretty notion of my job, but an inaccurate one," he says. "Some of the vilest scum I've ever encountered, I met aboard ship, and not just on the fo'c'sle. And forgive me for saying so, but I would never for a minute leave you alone with my crew . . ."

Lolita almost flinches, then reverts to her former tone: "I know how to take care of myself, señor."

The pride of the Palmas. The corsair smiles in the darkness. "It is not a question of what you know."

"I have been handling sailors ever since I was a child. My house . . ."

Stubborn. Self-assured. She stares out to sea, her profile silhouetted against the distant light.

"You know us by sight, señora. And from what you have read in books."

"I have eyes, Captain."

"Do you? And what do you see when you look at me?"

She says nothing, her lips parted slightly. The delicate balance of their conversation has been shattered. She seems at a loss; Lobo is seized by a strange feeling, something like remorse. Besides, the question was rhetorical.

"Listen . . ." says the corsair, "I am forty-three years old and incapable of sleeping for two hours straight without waking up to wonder where I am, whether the wind has turned. My stomach is ruined from the swill I eat on board ship, and I get headaches that last for days . . . When I spend too long in the same position, my joints creak like those of an old man. When the weather changes, every bone I've broken—or had broken for me—aches. And all it would take is one storm, one mistake by the pilot or the helmsman and I could suddenly lose everything I possess. To say nothing of the possibility that . . ."

He leaves the sentence unfinished. He is thinking of disfigurement and death, but he does not want to go there. He does not want to talk about that, about his true fears. In fact, he is wondering why he told her what he did; what he is trying to prove to this woman—or what he is trying to ruin, or sabotage, at any cost. Perhaps it is the urge to turn to her, to throw caution to the devil and take her in his arms.

The sentry is now back in his watchtower; there is a brief flicker of flame as he lights up a cigar. The star fort of Santa Catalina appears and disappears in the beam from the distant lighthouse, which also picks out the rocky headland and the patrol boat guarding the gunboats. Lo-lita Palma stares out to sea.

"Why did you do what you did to Lorenzo Virués?" The mention of broken bones seems to have reminded her of the incident.

Pépé Lobo looks at her harshly. "I did nothing to him he did not bring upon himself."

"I was told you did not conduct yourself . . ."

". . . like a gentleman?" The corsair laughs as he says the words.

Lolita Palma stands for a moment in silence.

"You knew he was a friend of mine," she says eventually. "A friend of the family."

"And he knew that I am captain of one of your ships. The two cancel each other out."

"What happened in Gibraltar?"

"To hell with Gibraltar! You know nothing about that. You have no right . . ."

A brief pause. When Lolita speaks again her voice is low, almost a whisper. "You are right. God knows you are right."

The remark surprises Pépé Lobo. The woman is standing motionless, obdurately staring out at the sea, at the darkness. The guard, who can surely see them from his watchtower, begins to sing. His voice is low, neither happy nor sad—a dark, guttural moan that seems to come from far away, from down the years. Lobo can barely make out the words.

"I think perhaps we should go," says the corsair.

She shakes her head. Her mood seems almost gentle again.

"Carnaval comes but once a year, Captain Lobo."

She suddenly seems young, fragile—were it not for her eyes, which never waver, never stray for a moment from the corsair's as he leans down and kisses her mouth, slowly, gently, as though giving her the opportunity to pull away. But she does not pull away. Pépé Lobo feels the sweet softness of her half-open lips, feels her body tremble, at once powerless and unyielding as his arms enfold her, draw her to him. They stand frozen for a moment, Lolita swathed in her domino cape whose hood has fallen back, wrapped in this man's embrace, silent and utterly calm. Her eyes never close, never leave his. Then she draws back and gently brings a hand up to his face, neither drawing him closer nor pushing him away. She holds him there, palm open, fingers splayed, stroking his face like a blind woman trying to imprint the image on her warm hand. When she finally withdraws it, she does so slowly, as though every inch that separates her hand from the corsair's face causes her pain.

"It is time to go back," she says calmly.

SIMON DESFOSSEUX IS having trouble sleeping. Before going to bed, he spent a long time making calculations for a new slow-burning fuse he has successfully been working on for several weeks, and also reading the most recent dispatch from the far shore: a message from the Spanish police comisario suggesting a new area to the east of the city which he is requested to shell at specific dates and times. Now lying in his hut, staring into the darkness, Desfosseux has the uncomfortable feeling that something is amiss. In his short, restless sleep, he thought he heard strange noises, hence the uncomfortable feeling when he woke.

"*Guerrilleros! Guerrilleros!*"

A scream comes from nearby and he sits bolt upright on his cot. He realizes with mounting panic that the noise he heard while he was asleep was the crackle of gunfire. Now he can clearly hear the rifle shots as he fumbles for his breeches and his boots; he adjusts his nightshirt as best he can, grabs his sword and his pistol and stumbles for the door. He is barely outside before an explosion rings out, lighting up everything around: the gabions, the trenches, the timber blockhouse and the soldiers' quarters. The barracks from which the blast came are now burning fiercely—someone clearly tossed in a bomb made of tar and gunpowder. Silhouetted against the conflagration, half-dressed soldiers run in all directions.

"They're inside the camp!" someone yells. "The *guerrilleros* are here and they're inside!"

Desfosseux thinks he recognizes the voice as that of Sergeant Labiche, and feels his skin tremble. The artillery base is a pandemonium of stampeding men, screams and the blaze of gunfire; of shadows, lights, shapes and figures moving, crowding together or facing off against each other. It is impossible to distinguish between friend and foe. Attempting to retain his composure, the captain retreats, keeping his back against the hut wall. He checks that there is no enemy near, then looks over at the fortified position housing Fanfan and his brothers: in the trench protected by thick planks and fascines that leads to the gun emplacement, he can see flashes of gunfire and the glint of swords and bayonets. Men are fighting in hand-to-hand combat. Only now does he finally realize what is happening. This has nothing to do with *guerrilleros:* this is an all-out assault from the beach. The Spanish have landed, intent on destroying the field guns.

"Over here!" he screams. "Follow me! We have to save the guns!"

This is all because of Soult, he thinks suddenly. Of course. Marshal Soult, commander-in-chief of the French army in Andalucía, personally relieved Marshal Victor as head of the Premier Corps and is currently doing a tour of inspection: Jerez, El Puerto de Santa María, Puerto Real and Chiclana. Tonight he is billeted less than a mile from here, and tomorrow he is scheduled to visit the Trocadero. So the enemy decided to get up early and arrange a warm welcome for him. Knowing the Spaniards—and he believes he knows them by now—that is likely to be the reason for this raid. Something similar happened last year during the visit of King Joseph. Damn them all, damn the *manolos* and the marshal. In Simon Desfosseux's opinion, none of this has anything to do with him or his men.

"To the gun battery! Defend the gun battery!"

In answer to this rallying cry, one of the shadows nearby fires a bullet that misses him by inches, raising a shower of splinters from the hut behind. Desfosseux carefully steps out of the light. He hesitates, reluctant to use his sword, for he knows the Spanish are fearsome in hand-to-hand combat; he has had enough of the clash and clang of heavy blades in his worst nightmares. Nor does he want to discharge his only pistol, since the outcome is uncertain. The decision is taken out of his hands by a group of soldiers who set upon the enemy with rifles and bayonets, clearing a path. Good lads, the captain thinks, relieved as he rushes to join them. They may be feckless and complaining when things are slack, but when the time comes they are raring to fight.

"Come on! We have to protect the field guns!"

Simon Desfosseux is the antithesis of an imperial hero. His idea of a warrior's glory is relative—he does not even think of himself as a warrior, but there is a time and a place for everything. And he is beside himself at the thought of the *manolos* laying hands on his precious Villantroys-Ruty howitzers, recently joined by new field guns—christened Lulu and Henriette by the troops—cast in Seville, for which he has high hopes. And so, leading a party of half a dozen men, his sword drawn, the captain dashes toward the embattled position, a chaos of guns, screams and steel. Soldiers are fighting in utter confusion, illuminated by a sudden burst of flame that shoots above the barrack roofs. Desfosseux spots Lieutenant Bertoldi, in shirtsleeves, lashing out with the butt of a rifle.

Close by—too close, thinks the petrified captain—he hears voices in Spanish. *Vámonos*, they seem to be saying. *Vámonos*. A small group of shadows who have been crouching in the darkness suddenly emerge and rush toward Simon Desfosseux. He does not know whether the enemy are attacking or retreating, he knows only that they are headed straight for him; when they are four or five paces away, there is a brief flash of gunfire and several bullets whistle past him. He can also see the glint of naked steel glimmering red in the glow from the distant blaze. His panic mounting as he sees them marching toward him, Desfosseux raises his pistol—a bulky *An IX* cavalry pistol—and fires blindly into the crowd, then flails about with his sword, hoping to keep the enemy at bay. The blade narrowly misses one of the men, who dashes past the captain, head down, stabbing at him with a short knife that barely brushes Desfosseux's nightshirt, then disappears into the darkness.

It is not easy to retreat with a knife in one hand and a spent rifle in the other. The long, French Charleville musket slows Felipe Mojarra as he runs from the gun battery, but his honor as a salter forbids him from leaving it behind. No man worthy of the name would come back without his gun, and Mojarra has never abandoned his, even in the most dire circumstances. These days, rifles are in short supply. But the assault on La Cabezuela has been a disaster. Some of the comrades running with him through the darkness, desperate to reach the beach and the boats that should be waiting for them—pray God they have not left!—are muttering about betrayal, as they always do when things go wrong; the incompetence of their leaders, the lack of organization, the utter contempt with which ordinary soldiers are treated . . . it was doomed from the start. The assault, scheduled for 4 a.m., was supposed to be made by a team of fourteen British sappers, led by a lieutenant, and a detachment of twenty-five men from the Salt Marsh Fusiliers, supported by four gunboats from the docks at Punta Cantera, with half a light infantry company from the Guardias Españoles on the beach to support the offensive and the re-embarkation of the troops. But at the appointed hour, the infantry still had not shown up and the boats waiting on the dark bay off the Cabezuela, their oars wrapped in rags to muffle the splash, were at risk of being spotted. Faced with the dilemma of either waiting or retreating, the English lieutenant decided to press on immediately. *Goh a-hed*, Mojarra heard him say, or something of the sort. Someone muttered that he was clearly determined to have his slice of glory. At first the landing—in pitch darkness since there was no moon—went well. The Salt Marsh Fusiliers moved silently across the beach and the first French guards had their throats cut before they realized; but then, without anyone knowing why, things began to go wrong—an isolated gunshot, then another, degenerating into a free-for-all of burning buildings and indiscriminate gunfire— and soon the English and Spanish troops were not fighting for control of the gun battery, they were fighting to save their own skins.

This is what Felipe Mojarra is doing right now: running for his life, running toward the beach, panicked at the thought of tripping in the darkness and smashing his skull. With one hand he holds his knife; the other is still clutching his rifle. And all the while, with the fatalism so characteristic of his race, he is thinking: *sometimes you win, most times you lose*. But tonight he is desperate not to lose—not to lose everything. Mojarra knows that if he is captured, his life will not be worth a brass farthing. To be caught by the *gabachos* while armed and wearing civilian

clothes is an automatic death sentence for a Spaniard. The Frenchies
are particularly brutal to prisoners with no uniform, whom they refer
to as *guerrilleros*—even if they have been fighting with regular soldiers,
and have the red cockade sewn on to their caps or their clothing next
to the pictures of saints, the medals and the scapulars. This was how
Felipe Mojarra lost both his cousins three years ago, after the battle of
Medellín, when Marshal Victor—the same man who until recently led
the siege against Cádiz—ordered four hundred Spanish soldiers, most
of them wounded, to be shot simply because they were wearing peasant
clothes.

Mojarra feels sand beneath his feet, though he is wearing sandals—
in the darkness, you never know when you might step on something
that could hurt you. The ground is soft and pale. The beach and the
shoreline are no more than five hundred feet away; the tide is high. Out
in the bay, the Spanish gunboats are firing at intervals on Fort Luis and
the eastern part of the beach, protecting the flank of the retreating
troops. Mojarra knows the risks of spending too much time in the
open, which would expose him to a bullet from friend or enemy; he
veers slightly left toward the shelter of the ruined Matagorda fort. His
eardrums are throbbing from the effort of running, and he cannot seem
to catch his breath. All around him on the beach, shadows are running
pell-mell: a confusion of Englishmen and Spaniards, all desperate, like
him, to make it to the water's edge. Beyond the fort, he can see the
flashes of the French guns like a string of firecrackers. A few stray bullets whistle past; meanwhile, a shot from a Spanish gunboat falls short
of its target, exploding with a deafening blast in a narrow tidal creek,
and the fleeting blaze lights up the crumbling black walls. Mojarra runs
on, and is about to overtake someone ahead of him, but before he can
catch up there comes another gunshot and the figure crumples to the
ground. Mojarra rushes past without stopping, without even looking,
other than to make sure he does not trip over the body. He reaches the
shelter of the Matagorda wall, where he pauses to catch his breath,
glancing anxiously across the beach as he snaps the blade of his knife
back into the horn handle and tucks it into his belt. There is a launch
not far off: he can just make out the long shadow near the shoreline. A

moment later, it is clearly visible in a flash of cannonfire from the gunboats; the launch bobs on the black water, oars raised, with men already
aboard or splashing through the shallows to reach it. Without thinking, Mojarra slings his rifle over his shoulder and dashes for the boat.
The soft sand makes the going difficult, but he manages to run fast
enough. He plunges into the water up to his waist, grabs the side of the
boat and clambers aboard as hands grab his shirt, his arms, and hoist
him in.

There are still shouts of "Treason!" as more dark shapes come running, framed against the distant fire, and scrabble to get aboard. As he
falls between the benches, Mojarra lands on someone, who lets out a
howl of pain and something unintelligible in English. He tries to move
away and, struggling to get up, instinctively puts out his hand and leans
his weight on the man's bare torso. The howls of the Englishman are
louder still. As he pulls his hand away, Mojarra discovers a large piece
of the man's charred skin stuck to his palm.

It is raining as though water were flowing from an open tap, gushing
down from the low, black clouds. The violent thunderstorm that punished Cádiz this morning has given way to a steady torrential downpour. Everything is saturated; the rain drums on the roofs and the
houses, pooling in puddles, forming rivulets in the sand sprinkled over
the cobbles to prevent horses' hooves slipping. Sodden flags and garlands of flowers, battered by the rain, hang from the balconies. Sheltering in the doorway of the church of San Antonio, amid a throng of
people wearing oilskins or carrying umbrellas—hundreds more of
them crowd beneath the awnings and balconies—Rogelio Tizón
watches the ceremony that, despite the weather, is taking place beneath
the marquee erected in the center of the square. Spain, or that part of
it symbolized by Cádiz, now has a Constitution. The solemn procla-
mation was made this morning, and the foul weather has done little to
mar the festivities. Given the risk of French bombs—which in recent
weeks have become more frequent and more accurate—a pageant of
deputies and other dignitaries followed by a *Te Deum* in the cathedral
was considered ill-advised. It was feared that the enemy might try to

commemorate the event after their own fashion. And so the proceedings were moved to the Iglesia del Carmen, opposite the Alameda, beyond the range of enemy artillery. Excited crowds—the whole of Cádiz has turned out, irrespective of class or profession—have staunchly braved squalls and showers, and even a large tree that suddenly came crashing to the ground without any damage: in fact this incident seemed to add to the elation as bells rang out in every church, the cannons on the square and in the warships at anchor thundered, to be answered by every French gun battery on the far shore of the bay. Celebrating, in their own way, since today, March 19, 1812, is also Joseph Bonaparte's saint's day.

Now, well into the afternoon, the formalities are continuing and Rogelio Tizón is surprised by the resilience of the crowd. Having spent the morning being lashed by the storm, the townsfolk are braving heavy showers to listen eagerly to a reading of the Constitution, something which has been performed twice already: once before the Customs House, where the Regency erected a portrait of Fernando VII, and again at the Plaza del Mentidero. When the third ceremony here in San Antonio concludes, the official procession, followed by the public, will move through the crowded streets to its final scheduled stop: the port of San Felipe Neri, where they are awaited by the deputies who this morning received a freshly printed copy of the Constitution— already nicknamed *La Pepa*, in honor of the feast of St. Joseph. And it is curious, thinks Tizón, gazing around him, to see how—for a few hours at least—the proceedings have been greeted with unanimous acclaim and general enthusiasm. Even those most critical of the constitutional enterprise seem to have succumbed to the collective outpouring of joy and hope, and joined in the pomp and ceremony. The policeman has been surprised to see the most reactionary monarchists, those virulently opposed to any whiff of national sovereignty, taking part in the events, applauding with the crowds—or at least putting on a brave face and biting their tongue. Even the two rebel deputies, a man named Llamas and the delegate from Vizcaya, Eguía, who had refused to ratify the text approved by the Cortes—the former declaring himself opposed to national sovereignty, the latter hiding behind the privileges of his province—duly signed and pledged with the others this morning, when they were faced with the choice of doing so or finding themselves stripped of their Spanish nationality and forced to leave the country within twenty-four hours. When it comes down to it, the comisario thinks cynically, such miracles are brought about as much by prudence and fear as by patriotic fervor.

The reading has concluded now and the solemn pageant moves off. The troops lining the route present arms, their uniforms sodden from the rain; escorted by a cavalry unit, the cortège heads toward the Calle de la Torre, to the rhythm of a marching band that is utterly drowned out by the torrential rain, but applauded nonetheless by those lining the streets. As the procession passes the church, Rogelio Tizón sees the newly appointed Governor of Cádiz and Commander-in-Chief of the Navy, Don Cayetano Valdés: somber, wiry, ramrod-straight with side-burns that come down to the collar of his frockcoat. Wearing the uniform of a lieutenant general, the man who captained the *Pelayo* at the battle of San Vicente and the *Neptuno* at Trafalgar walks slowly and impassively through the deluge, holding a red morocco-bound copy of the Constitution, which he shields as best he can. Since Villavicencio was appointed to the Regency and Valdés took over the position of military and political governor of Cádiz, Tizón has met with him only once, accompanied by Intendant García Pico; the results were unsatisfactory. Unlike his predecessor, Valdés is a man of liberal ideas. He also turns out to be a blunt, tactless individual with the gruff manners of a sailor who has spent most of his life under arms. With him there can be no subterfuge, no implicit understandings. From the moment they first explained the case of the murdered girls, he made himself absolutely clear to the comisario and the Intendant: if results were not forthcoming, he would seek out those responsible. As to the means used in conducting this or any other investigation, he assured Tizón—about whose background he seemed to be extremely well informed—that he would not tolerate prisoners being tortured, arbitrary arrests, nor any abuses that would contravene the new rights laid down by the Cortes. "Spain has changed," he said, before dismissing them from his office. "There is no way back, either for you or for me. Perhaps it is best that we all know where we stand."

Watching the procession with a critical eye, the comisario remembers the words of this man, now walking solemnly through the pouring rain. He cannot help but wonder what will happen if the king now held prisoner in France should return. Beloved by his subjects—who know nothing of his character and intentions (private reports Tizón has read of his conduct during the Escorial conspiracy, the mutiny of Aranjuez* and the imprisonment in Bayonne** do not show him in a flattering light)—when young Fernando VII returns to Spain he will discover that in his absence, and in his name, a group of visionaries inspired by the ideas of the French Revolution have turned the traditional order upside down on the pretext that, deprived of their monarch—or abandoned by him—and delivered into the hands of the enemy, the Spanish people have had to fight for themselves and enact their own laws. And so, even as he watches the new Constitution being proclaimed, Rogelio Tizón, who knows little about politics, but has considerable experience plumbing the depths of the human heart, cannot help but wonder whether the mob now cheering and applauding in the rain—the same brutal, illiterate mob that dragged General Solano through the streets, and would as likely do the same to General Valdés—would not cheer and applaud just as enthusiastically if the situation were reversed. He also wonders whether, when he returns, Fernando VII will meekly accept this new state of affairs or whether he will side with those who insist the Spanish people are not fighting for some chimerical national sovereignty, they are fighting for God and King. So Spain might return to how it was; and these claims of sovereignty might become nothing more than usurpation and presumption. A nonsense that time will reverse.

Rain is still hammering down on the Plaza de San Antonio. In a thunder of hooves and festive music, the procession slowly moves along

---

* Popular uprising against Carlos IV, forcing him to abdicate in favor of his son Fernando VII.
** Bonaparte invited Carlos IV and Fernando VII to Bayonne to "resolve the problem" then forced both to renounce the throne of Spain.

beneath the sodden flags and the bunting hanging from the balconies. Leaning back against the door of the church, the comisario takes a cigar from his case and lights it. Then he calmly surveys the joyful throng around him, people of every class and creed enthusiastically applauding. He carefully studies every face, as though committing each one to memory. It is a professional reflex, a precaution. At the end of the day, whether liberal and royalist, the struggle in Cádiz is simply a new variant on the never-ending struggle for power. Rogelio Tizón has not forgotten that until recently—on the orders of his superiors, in the name of King Carlos IV—he was throwing people in jail for distributing books or pamphlets promulgating the very ideas now being carried through the streets by the governor, handsomely bound in red leather. And he knows that with or without the French, whether absolute monarch, national sovereignty or Pepa the flamenco singer sitting enthroned at San Felipe Neri, whoever governs Spain, as anywhere, will always have need of prisons and policemen.

AT NIGHTFALL, THE French shelling intensifies. Sitting at the desk in the botanical study, warmed by a small brazier, Lolita Palma listens as the explosions merge with the thunder of rain and wind. The rain is still hammering down; the wind howls as it lashes against the ramparts and the houses, trying to clear a path through the labyrinthine streets around San Francisco. The whole city is like a ship, lurching and rolling, straining at the reef that anchors it to the mainland, about to be dismasted of its towers by the gale and the curtain of black water, merging in the darkness with the breakers that roll off the Atlantic into the bay.

Asplenium scolopendrium. The leaf of the Hart's-tongue fern is almost a foot long and two inches wide. By the light of an oil lamp, Lolita Palma studies it through a powerful, ivory-handled magnifying glass, observing the sporangia which form parallel ridges diagonal to the midrib. It is a beautiful plant, first described in Linnaeus and common in the woodlands of Spain. In the house on the Calle del Baluarte, there are two magnificent specimens in pots on the glassed-in balcony Lolita uses as a hothouse.

Another explosion, closer than the last, not far from the end of the Calle de los Doblones. The sound of the blast is muffled by the buildings in between, and partly drowned out by the roar of the rain and the wind. Tonight the rainstorm and the shelling are both so fierce that the bell tower of the Iglesia de San Francisco, which usually marks the flashes seen at La Cabezuela, is silent. Impassive, Lolita Palma presses the cutting in a cardboard herbarium between two large sheets of thin paper, sets down the magnifying glass and rubs her tired eyes—she fears that soon she will need to wear spectacles. She gets to her feet and, stepping past the glass case in which she keeps dried specimens, rings the small silver bell on the dresser next to the bookcase. Mari Paz, her maid, appears almost at once.

"I am going to bed."

"Very good, señorita. I will get everything ready right away."

Another explosion in the distance—this time somewhere toward the center of the city. "God preserve us"—the maid blesses herself as she leaves the study. Later, she will go downstairs to sleep on the ground floor, where the servants take shelter when there is shelling. Lolita stands, motionless, caught up in the howl of the wind and rain. Tonight, she thinks, there will be many candles lit to saints in the homes of sailors.

Through the open door, she catches her reflection in the hallway mirror: hair fashioned into a braid, a simple gray house dress adorned only by a fringe of lace at the collar and cuffs. The hallway is dim and, with the lamplight behind her, this figure of a woman gazing at her reflection looks like an old-fashioned painting. She brings her hands to her throat; the gesture begins as coquettish, then becomes lingering and reflective until finally she freezes in this pose, staring at herself and thinking how much she looks like the portraits, darkened by time, that hang on the walls of this house amid the chiaroscuro of furniture, knickknacks and family memorabilia. The portrait of a bygone age—never to be regained—fading like a ghost among the shadows of the slumbering house.

Suddenly, Lolita Palma looks away from the mirror, lets her hands fall to her sides. Seized by an overpowering urge, she goes to the window overlooking the street, flings it wide open and stands, letting the storm soak her dress, the flurries of rain drench her face.

THUNDERBOLTS ILLUMINATE THE city. Slashes of lightning rip across the black sky, the crash of thunder merging with the rumble of the French artillery and the steady, remorseless response of the Spanish guns at Puntales, matching them shot for shot.

Wearing his waterproof carrick coat and oilskin hat, Rogelio Tizón is prowling the old districts, dodging the streams of water that spill from the roofs. In the taverns and the bars, those who have not yet gone home are still celebrating the momentous day; the comisario can hear the clink of glasses, songs, music and cries of *"Viva la constitución!"* through doors and windows as he passes.

A blast rings out nearby, on the Plaza de San Juan de Dios. This time the shell exploded as it landed, sending shockwaves through the dank air, causing the windowpanes to rattle. Tizón pictures the artillery captain, whom he has now met, training his field guns on the city in a futile attempt to put an end to the festivities. A queer fish, that Frenchman. For his part, Tizón has kept his side of their curious bargain. Three weeks ago, having pulled a few strings and greased the necessary palms, the comisario managed, purportedly as part of a prisoner exchange, to have Gregorio Fumagal repatriated to the far shore. Or more precisely, he repatriated the gaunt, shambling specter that is all that remains of the taxidermist after a long spell in the windowless dungeons of the Calle del Mirador. The Frenchman has been keeping his side of the bargain too. Like a gentleman. Three times, on prearranged days and hours, shells from his howitzers have fallen more or less where Tizón hoped they might; so far, the experiment has produced no results, except for destroying two houses, killing one person and injuring four others. Each time he had the locations surrounded by officers, each time he used a different bait—war and poverty have left no shortage of desperate girls in Cádiz—but on no occasion did anyone who might have been the killer appear. It should be said the weather in recent days—what with the rain, and no easterly wind—has not been auspicious. Tizón—who is not so obsessed that he doesn't realize his net is full of holes—does not hold out much hope of success, but he is not ready to give up. After all, he thinks, a man is more likely to catch a fish by casting a net, however threadbare, than by casting no net at all. Meanwhile, by combing the city, comparing previous crime scenes with locations that have similar characteristics, the comisario—or the strange force currently guiding his actions—has been drawing up a list of places he believes are conducive to what he is expecting and hoping for. The method he uses to identify these places is convoluted, at times almost illogical—even Tizón is not convinced it works. It is partly based on experience, partly on intuition: places with derelict houses, courtyards and abandoned warehouses; patches of waste ground far from prying eyes; streets where a man can easily hide or escape; recesses and alcoves where the wind behaves in a certain way; nooks where Tizón has felt that disturbing sensation—whether real or imagined, on this he and Hipólito Barrull have yet to agree—that sudden absence of air, of sound and smell as though he has stepped into a vacuum. Those damned vortices, whatever they're called, whatever they are: those eddies of horror, at once alien and intimate. Given the means at his disposal, the comisario knows he cannot cover all these places simultaneously. Nor can he be sure that there are not a host of other, similar places that he has missed. But he can—and has—set up a system of random controls. To return to the fishing metaphor, it is like casting his net into waters where he cannot be sure there are fish, but where he knows, or thinks he knows, that fish might congregate. And every day, with or without bait, Tizón visits each of these sites, studies them on the map until he knows every corner by heart, organizes covert patrols by nightwatchmen and calls on the eyes and ears of the network of informants he has always had, but now keeps on the alert by means of a clever and efficient combination of bribery and threats.

The Arco del Pópulo is one of those places that worry him. Deep in thought, the comisario stares at the vaulted passageway. Situated just behind the City Hall, the place is central, busy, and there are several houses and businesses in the area, though tonight, with the storm, all that is visible in the darkness is closed shutters and water cascading everywhere. And yet Rogelio Tizón *knows* this is one of the marks on the map-chessboard that disturbs his sleep by night and his peace of mind by day: his opponent has seven captured pieces, and he only an inkling of the game. He has spent two nights keeping watch here with an attractive piece of bait—a young girl he found on the Calle de Hercules—to no avail. But even if the killer did not keep his appointment, the bomb did, falling in the early hours two nights ago, a few feet from where Tizón is now standing, on the little square on the Calle de la Virreina. This is why, despite the rain and his exhausting day, the policeman is circling the area, reluctant to go home. Though the conditions are wrong—what with the storm, the wind and the lightning—he is still wandering around, inspecting every corner, every shadow, trying to understand. Trying to see the world through the eyes of the man he seeks.

For an instant, in the faint glow from the lamp beneath a sacred image on the wall, the policeman sees a shadow at the mouth of the tunnel—a dark shape that was not there a moment earlier. Suddenly the comisario is on the alert, like a dog scenting prey. Furtively, trying to make sure he is not seen, Tizón creeps toward the safety of the nearest wall, trusting that the driving rain will drown out the sound of his boots splashing through the puddles. He stands, clutching his brass-handled cane, feeling the water stream off his hat and his waterproof coat. The shadow—a scrawny masculine figure standing near the lantern—does not move. Eventually the policeman decides to creep closer, cane at the ready. He is midway through the passageway when the figure clearly hears his footsteps echoing under the vaulted roof.

"Damned wine," a voice says. "Can't stop pissing it out."

The voice sounds young and blasé. Tizón stops when he draws level with the figure, thin and dressed in black, now more clearly visible against the darkness. He finds he does not know what to say. He tries to think of some reason for standing here rather than going on his way.

"This is no place to be relieving yourself," he says curtly.

The other man seems to weigh up the relevance of this remark.

"Saw your timber!" he says finally, his voice trailing off into a fit of coughing. Tizón peers at the man's face, but can only see his profile against the lamplight. After a moment, he hears a rustle of fabric—the man is presumably doing up his fly—and now the flickering glow lights up the gaunt face, the dark sunken eyes of a handsome man of about twenty, looking contemptuously at Tizón.

"Mind your own business," he says.

"I'm a police commissioner."

"I don't give a curse what you are."

He is closer now and reeks of wine. Tizón does not care for the man's insolence, still less for his disparaging tone. For a moment, his natural instinct is to dance the head of his cane over the man's head then go on his way. Stupid young whelp. Just then Tizón realizes he has met him. Something to do with ships. He remembers a seaman. Clearly an officer—that would explain the wine and the arrogant swagger, very different from the insolence of the jack tars, the braggarts, and the dandified young men of Cádiz. There is a haughty tone to this man's voice—a lad from a good family.

"Is there some problem?"

A second voice from behind him almost makes the comisario start. The other man comes toward him. Turning, Tizón sees a swarthy figure with thick sideburns wearing a blue jacket with gilt buttons. The lamplight glitters in his pale, calm eyes.

"Are you together?" asks Tizón

The silence implies an affirmative. Tizón swings his cane in his right hand. There is no problem, he explains, other than the one posed by his friend. The other man looks at him evenly. He wears no hat and his hair is wet from the rain. Lamplight shimmers on his wet shoulders. He also stinks like a cheap tavern.

"I heard the word *police*," the man says finally.

"I am a police commissioner."

"And your job is to make sure no one pisses in the street, when the heavens themselves are pissing on us?"

He says this in a calm, ironic tone. A bad start. For his part, Rogelio Tizón has finally recognized the two men: a couple of corsairs, a captain and his lieutenant, who he talked to down at La Caleta one night last summer. A conversation as disagreeable as this one (though not quite as damp), it happened during the investigation into smugglers and trips across the bay that led him to the Mulatto.

"My job, my friend, is to do whatever I see fit."

"We are no friends of yours," snaps the younger man.

Tizón thinks quickly. The urge to split the lad's head open with his cane is even stronger—he suddenly remembers he felt the same way last time—but these are coarse men and the matter would not be so easily resolved. This is the sort of situation where, if a man is not careful, being hotheaded can leave him cold and dead. Especially in a dark alleyway with two men who are drunk, but not sufficiently drunk that they have passed the dangerous, aggressive phase. And there is no nightwatchman close by to come to his aid. They have probably all taken refuge in the nearest tavern, what with the rain, Tizón thinks. So when he speaks again, he decides on a moderate, more conciliatory tone.

"I was tailing someone," he admits with calculated candor. "In the darkness, I made a mistake."

A flash of lightning illuminates the tunnel like a flare of cannonfire, framing the three men in silhouette. The one with the sideburns— Captain Lobo of the *Culebra*, Tizón suddenly remembers—stares at the comisario without saying anything, as though mulling over what he has just said. Then he gives a brief nod.

"We've met before."

"We had a conversation," Tizón confirms. "Some time ago."

Another brief silence. This is not the kind of man to prattle or threaten, thinks Tizón. Nor is his friend. The corsair nods again.

"We were in a tavern nearby with some revelers . . . My friend came out to get some air and relieve himself. We put out to sea tomorrow."

Now it is Tizón's turn to nod. "I mistook your man for someone else," he says.

"Then everything is settled?"

"So it would seem."

"Very well, then. I wish you good luck on your rounds."

"And I you with your tavern."

From inside the tunnel, Tizón watches as the two men, reduced once more to dark shapes, step out into the downpour and plunge into the darkness, only to reappear now and then in a lightning flash like the crack of gunfire. Only now does the policeman remember the whole story: this Captain Lobo is the same man who, the story goes—nobody has been able to prove anything and the witnesses are saying nothing—shot a Captain of Engineers two months ago in a duel on the reef near Santa Catalina. A tough bastard.

CHAPTER SIXTEEN

୨୦୨

The shimmer of light and salt. Tall white houses tower above the treetops along the Alameda; window boxes burgeon with flowers on wrought-iron balconies and watchtowers painted green, red and blue. Cádiz looks just as it does in a painting, thinks Lolita Palma as she steps out of the church and adjusts the cream lace mantilla carefully pinned to her decorative tortoiseshell comb. Shielding her eyes against the dazzling sunlight with her fan, she goes down to join the guests standing at the foot of the Mexican-style spires of the Iglesia del Carmen. It is a magnificent day, perfect for the christening of Miguel Sánchez Guinea's son. The ceremony now over, the baby dozes in the arms of his godparents, swaddled in linen and lace, being lavished with kisses, compliments and fond hopes for a long and prosperous life, one that is rewarding for his family and the city. "You gave me a Moor; I give you back a Christian," the godmother says to the child's father, in keeping with tradition. Even the French artillery seems to be celebrating the happy event: firing began from the Trocadero just as the ceremony ended. In fact, shelling is now an everyday occurrence, but being out of range of the French bombs, the assembled company pay little heed to the rumbling drone, one to which the city is long since inured.

"At least there's some music!" quips cousin Toño, cutting the tip off a Havana cigar.

Lolita Palma looks around. The guests—men in pale top hats, women wearing combs with mantillas of white, cream or black lace, according to their age and social standing—are milling around between the church and the Candelaria fort, chatting pleasantly. Gradually, people begin to drift away and, ignoring the coaches and caleches lined up around the square, they stroll along the Alameda toward the place where the banquet is being held. The ladies walk arm in arm with husbands or relatives, children run and play, everyone delighting in this stroll, this view—as though it belonged to them, which in a sense it does—the pristine panorama of sea and sky stretching out beyond the city walls toward Rota and El Puerto de Santa María.

"Tell us about last night, Lolita," says Miguel Sánchez Guinea. "They say it was a huge success."

"It certainly was a success, though I was frightened half to death."

The conversations—at least those of the men—chiefly revolve around business matters and recent military developments, which have been ill-starred as ever for the Spanish: Alicante falling into French hands, and General Ballesteros being routed at Bornos. There are rumors the French are about to launch an attack on La Carraca, weakening the defenses of the Isla de Léon and threatening the city, but no one believes them. Behind the city walls, Cádiz feels impregnable. But the real topic of interest to both sexes this morning is the play that some of those present saw last night at the theater on the Calle de la Novena. It was the premiere of *What a Job Can Achieve*, a minor but rather ingenious comedy recently penned by Francisco de Paula Martínez de la Rosa, much anticipated because it contained a withering indictment of the anti-liberals who, in exchange for stipends and a comfortable, well-paid position, have suddenly demonstrated a suspicious enthusiasm for constitutional ideas. Lolita saw the play from her private box, where she was joined by Curra Vilches, her husband, cousin Toño and Jorge Fernández Cuchillero. The theater was far from full, but the stalls were buzzing with a large coterie of friends and supporters of the author: Argüelles, Pepín, Queipo de Llano, Quintana, Mexía Lequerica, Toñete Alcalá Galiano and others. There were many ladies present. Several of the comical scenes in the play met with loud applause, but the real climax came when, midway though the farce, a French bomb grazed the roof of the theater and fell nearby. Pandemonium ensued and some of the audience fled, but others stood and demanded that the show carry on—which it did, to thunderous applause, thanks to the great sangfroid of the actors. Lolita Palma was among those who stayed until the end.

"Weren't you afraid?" asks Miguel Sánchez Guinea.

Curra confesses that she and her husband shot out of the theater "like a cannonball."

Lolita laughs. "I was intending to leave with them," she says. "I rushed out of my box, but seeing that Fernández Cuchillero and Toño and the others were not moving, I just stood there like a fool. And all the time I was thinking, 'Another bomb and that will be the end of all of us.' Luckily there was no other bomb."

"And what did you think of the play?"

"A little contrived, but it's amusing and well worth seeing. The character of Don Melitón is very droll . . . You know Paco de la Rosa. He wrote it with his usual wit."

"And his usual pomposity," quips Curra Vilches.

"Don't be so unkind . . . Those who stayed to the end gave him an ovation."

"Of course they did; they were part of his clique."

The banquet is being held in the Posada Inglesa, on the Plaza de los Pozos de la Nieve next to the Café de las Cadenas. Owned by an Englishman who has settled in Cádiz, and staffed by English waiters, it is one of the most elegant restaurants in the city. As they arrive, the guests are shown to the large, spacious first-floor dining room, its windows overlooking the bay and the house of the late, hapless General Solano, which is still in ruins after all the pillaging and the fire three years ago. For the ladies and the children, set out on large Mexican silver salvers belonging to the Sánchez Guineas, there is a cornucopia of almond and cinnamon biscuits, marzipan sweetmeats, Savoy cakes and cream tarts accompanied by orangeade and lemonade, French hot chocolate, English tea and Spanish cinnamon milk. In addition, for the gentlemen, there is coffee, liqueurs, and boxes of Havana cigars. In no time at all, the first floor of the *posada* is thronged with joyous friends and relatives drinking the health of the newly christened child and his family. The tables are piled with purses of satin and silver mesh, fans inlaid with mother-of-pearl, cigar cases of fine leather. The greatest merchant families are all here to pay tribute to the next generation of one of their own. They have known each other for centuries, and down the years they have gathered for baptisms, communions, weddings and funerals. They believe themselves to be the lifeblood of the city, the powerful muscle that drives work and wealth. The dozen families gathered on the top floor of the Posada Inglesa represent the real Cádiz: money and business, the risks, the failures and the successes that keep this city and its memory alive—Atlantic and Mediterranean, ancient and modern, reasonably cultivated, reasonably liberal, reasonably heroic. But reasonably worried too, not so much about the war—that, too, is merely business—but about the future. The ladies chatter about children and aunts and servants, about dresses they have had made for them by a seamstress on the Calle Juan de Andas, about the new fashions recently arrived from England and the stylish shops on the Plaza de San Antonio, the Calle Cobos and the Calle Ancha, about bed drapes and counterpanes in white muslin—the latest in bedroom fashion—and about the flag being sewn by the Society of Patriotic Ladies to present to the artillerymen of Puntales. Meanwhile, their husbands talk about this or that ship arriving, the dire financial situation and the upheavals, uncertainties and hopes brought about by the French siege and by the escalating insurrection in the American colonies, which has been cynically encouraged by the English—while in Cádiz, through their ambassador, they have spent months sabotaging constitutional progress and supporting the servile Absolutists.

"They should send more troops overseas to suppress this perfidy," says someone.

"This barbarous obscenity," adds another.

"The problem, as always, is that we would be the ones to pay. It would be our money," a third man says sardonically.

"What else can they do? There's no one else in Spain they can sink their fangs into."

"They have absolutely no shame. Between the Regency, the Junta and the Cortes, they've bled us like stuck pigs."

Don Emilio Sánchez Guinea—wearing a sober dark gray tailcoat, breeches and black silk stockings—has taken Lolita aside at the far end of the table, near the window that overlooks the bay. They too are discussing the grave financial situation. Having contributed one million *pesos* to the war effort last year, Cádiz once again finds itself forced to provide more loan capital, like the seven and a half million *reales* that recently financed the disastrous military campaigns in Cartagena and Alicante. Now there are rumors—and when it comes to taxes, rumors invariably prove to be true—that there is to be another direct levy based on a published list of company fortunes. Emilio Sánchez Guinea is outraged. In his opinion, to air such matters in public is just as detrimental to those who run their businesses well as it is to those who run them badly; the former because they will find themselves even more harried, the latter because business depends on the good name of a company, so making public the finances of certain houses will do little to help them obtain credit. In any case, calculating risk is a delicate matter at the moment, with colonial revenues stagnant and little capital about.

"It is madness," the elderly merchant says, "attempting to impose direct taxation in a merchant city such as Cádiz where the only reliable measure of a business is its reputation . . . It would be impossible to calculate without allowing other people to poke their noses into our ledgers. And that would be disgraceful."

"Well, they shall not get to see my books," Lolita says decisively. Her face is grave, pensive; her expression tight-lipped and severe. "I shall make sure of that."

Her mantilla is now draped around her shoulders, her hair swept up and pinned with a tortoiseshell comb. Next to her hands, which are crumbling an almond tart over the tablecloth, lies a fan, a velvet purse and a glass of cinnamon milk.

"People say you have been having problems," says Sánchez Guinea in a low voice.

"That I have been having problems *too*, you mean."

"Of course. Like myself, and my son . . . like everyone."

Lolita nods, but says no more. Like many merchants in Cádiz, she is owed almost five million *reales* by the public treasury—of which, to date, she has not recovered more than a tenth: 25,000 *pesos*. If the debt remains unpaid, it could bankrupt her. It would certainly force her to suspend payments.

"I have it on good authority that the government has received payments from London and has neatly arranged its finances without paying a penny to its creditors . . . It did precisely the same with the recent revenues from Lima and Havana."

"I can't say it surprises me," Lolita says. "But this is precisely why I am worried. Any serious blow and I would find myself without the funds to continue."

Sánchez Guinea shakes his head despairingly. Lolita thinks he looks exhausted; not even his grandson's christening seems to cheer him. Too much grief and worry have sapped the peace of mind of this man, once her father's partner and dearest friend. "It is the end of an era," she has often heard him say. "Cádiz as I knew it is dying, and I am dying with it. I do not envy the younger generation, those who will be here in fifteen or twenty years." More than once he has talked about retiring and leaving the business to Miguel.

"What news of our corsair?"

The old man's face lights up as he asks the question, as though a sea breeze has cleared away his melancholy thoughts. He even smiles a little. Lolita moves her hand toward her glass, but does not touch it.

"He is faring well," she says, glancing out of the window toward the bay. "But the Prize Court has been moving slowly. What with Gibraltar, Tarifa and Cádiz, everything is moving at a snail's pace . . . You know as well as I that the *Culebra* may be a boon, but it is no solution. Besides, there are fewer and fewer French and foreign ships prepared to brave these waters. They should sail out beyond the Cabo de Gata. They might find easier pickings."

Don Emilio smiles, amused, remembering Lolita's initial resistance to becoming involved in anything to do with corsairs.

"You have clearly decided to take this business seriously, *niña*."

"What choice do I have?" She smiles too, a little at her own expense. "Times are hard."

"Well, we may have another capture to add to the list. A cutter was sighted this morning just past Torregorda, escorting another ship . . . It might well be our Captain Lobo with more prey."

Lolita does not so much as blink. She has already had this information from the watchtower.

"If it is the corsair," she says finally, "we must make sure she puts out again immediately."

"Further east, you propose?"

"Exactly. Now that Alicante has fallen, there should be more French sea traffic in the area. They could use Cartagena as a base."

"Not a bad idea . . . not bad at all."

They both fall silent. Now it is Sánchez Guinea's turn to gaze pensively out the window, then to survey the room. All around is the hum of conversation, the chatter of ladies, the laughing and shrieking of children. The celebrations carry on, oblivious to the harsh realities of a world that is crumbling outside—the only inkling of which is the occasional explosion of a French shell. Miguel Sánchez Guinea, who has been mingling with his guests, notices that his father and Lolita Palma are engaged in a private conversation; he makes a move to join them, smiling, a cigar in one hand and a drink in the other. But his father stops him with a warning gesture. Dutifully, Miguel raises his glass and turns on his heel.

"What news of the *Marco Bruto*?" Once again, Don Emilio speaks in a concerned whisper.

At this question, a shadow crosses the face of the heir to the house of Palma. For some time now, the mere mention of the ship has been keeping her awake at night.

"Nothing as yet. She is late arriving . . . She was scheduled to put out from Havana on the fifteenth of last month."

"And you do not know where she is?"

Lolita makes an ambiguous gesture. "Not yet. But we are expecting her any day now."

There is a long and pregnant silence. As experienced merchants, they both know that the ship may well be lost: some accident at sea; the French corsairs; misfortune. There are ships that can make or break a business with a single voyage. The *Marco Bruto*, by far Palma's largest brigantine—280 tons, a copper-sheathed hull, carrying four 6-pound guns—is heading for Cádiz with a cargo of singular importance: a valuable consignment of grain, sugar, indigo and 1,200 copper ingots from Veracruz; indeed, a small part of the shipment is destined for Sánchez Guinea's own business. What he does not know—friendship is one thing and business another—is that, hidden beneath the ingots, the brigantine is carrying 20,000 silver *pesos* belonging to Lolita, intended to restore her liquidity and maintain her local credit. Should it be lost, the blow would be almost insuperable—made all the worse by the fact that, given the delicate nature of the venture, the marine insurance has been covered by Palma e Hijos.

"I realize you have risked a great deal on this shipment, *hija*," Sánchez Guinea says at length.

Lolita says nothing. She gazes into the middle distance as though she did not hear the last words uttered by this old friend of her father. After a moment, she shudders almost imperceptibly, then smiles a sad, worried smile.

"I don't think you realize, Don Emilio . . . With things as they are, I have risked everything."

She turns away again and gazes out at the ocean from which Cádiz's fortunes and disasters arise. In the distance, side by side, the sails of two ships swell in the nor'easter as they move into the bay, careful to give a wide berth to the French gun batteries as they pass Las Puercas and the Diamante.

Pray God the brigantine arrives soon, she thinks anxiously, Pray God she comes home safely.

LEANING ON THE port bow of the *Culebra*, spyglass to one eye, Pépé Lobo watches the sails of the ship rapidly approaching from Rota headland; two masts tilted slightly to stern, a spike bowsprit, triangular lateen sails taut from the wind on the beam.

"She's a místico," he says. "One gun each to port and starboard, and another in the bow. She's flying no flag."

"A corsair?" Standing next to the captain, Ricardo Maraña stares at the approaching vessel, shielding his eyes with his hand.

"Probably."

"When I first saw her, I assumed she was the felucca anchored near Rota."

"As did I. But there's no sign of a sail in the inlet . . . The felucca has clearly found a new hunting ground."

Lobo passes the telescope to his first officer, who carefully studies the boat, its sails shimmering in the late afternoon sun.

"We've not seen her in these waters before . . . Could she be the one from Sanlúcar?"

"Maybe."

"What is she doing so far east?"

"If the felucca is off hunting elsewhere, she might have taken over. Just to see if there's anything around."

Maraña is still peering through the spyglass. At a glance, he can see what the místico is up to.

"She's trying her luck . . . testing the water."

Pépé Lobo looks to windward. Sailing in convoy with the *Culebra*, crewed by a boarding party, is the cutter's most recent prize: a 90-ton Neapolitan schooner, the *Cristina Ricotta*, captured without resistance four days ago off Cires point, heading to Málaga from Tangier with a cargo of wool, leather and salt meat. Coming into the bay of Cádiz, and anticipating the presence of corsairs and the threat from the French fort at Santa Catalina, which fires on any ship that comes too close to land, Pépé Lobo has taken care to keep the schooner on the starboard side of the *Culebra*, two cables distant, the better to be able to protect her should there be any threat. The *Culebra* herself is sailing cautiously, flying no flag, her long bowsprit pointed toward Rota inlet, hugging the nor'easter; all sails are set, including the foretopsail, with half the crew manning braces and sheets and Brasero the bo'sun leaning on the windlass two paces behind the captain and the first mate. He has one eye on the maneuvers, the other on the eight 6-pound guns, which are primed and loaded. Meanwhile, the rest of the crew have been armed and ready ever since the sail first appeared from behind the headland at Rota.

"Do we come about, or keep a steady course?" Maraña asks, folding the telescope.

"Let's keep things as they are for the moment. The místico shouldn't cause us any trouble."

The lieutenant nods, hands back the telescope and turns to look at the schooner sailing aweather, maintaining the agreed distance and dutifully obeying all signals from the cutter. Like his captain, Maraña knows that the enemy corsair does not have sufficient firepower to tackle them head-on; with only three guns compared to the *Culebra*'s eight, any attempt would be suicidal. But at sea, it is wise to take nothing for granted, and the French corsair, fearless by virtue of her profession, is doing precisely what they would do in her position: coming as close as she can, circling like a wary predator, waiting to see whether some stroke of luck—a change of wind, a false maneuver, a shot from Santa Catalina dismasting the cutter—might give her the opportunity to pounce.

"We can pass Los Cochinos and Fraile with a single tack," says Maraña, "but we'd have to steer pretty close to Rota."

He says this with his usual aloofness, as though observing the maneuver from land. It is simply an objective comment, not intended to influence his captain's decision. Pépé Lobo looks out toward the enemy headland and the town beyond it, then turns back toward Cádiz, white and sprawling behind the imposing city walls. With a glance at the swell and at the weathervane fluttering at the top of the cutter's lone mast, Lobo quickly calculates the strength and direction of the wind, speed, course and distance. In order to avoid the rocks at the mouth of the bay they will have to tack toward Cádiz, then Rota, then back toward the city again. This means steering dangerously close to the French gun batteries, with little margin for error. It might first be wise to teach the místico a little respect. Just in case.

"Stand by, Lieutenant."

Maraña turns to Brasero, still leaning on the windlass.

"Nostromo! Ready to go about!"

As Brasero turns and makes his way across the listing deck, getting the crewmen into position, Pépé Lobo tell his first mate the plan.

"We'll launch a broadside at the místico, just to keep her at a safe distance . . . We'll wait until the last minute and fire just before we come about."

"One shot from each gun?"

"Yes. I don't think we'll dismast her with a broadside, but I want to give her the fright of her life . . . Can you handle the first shot?"

The lieutenant gives a faint smile. True to his character, Ricardo Maraña is staring out to sea as though thinking about something else, but Lobo knows that he is mentally calculating the conditions of fire and the range of the cannons. Reveling in the prospect.

"You can count on me, sir."

"Come on then, we come about in five minutes."

Opening the telescope and attempting to compensate for the list of the deck, Pépé Lobo studies the enemy corsair. She has tacked slightly to windward. Her lateen sails mean that she can luff a little more, to come closer to the course that the cutter and the schooner will take when they come about. Through the spyglass, Lobo can clearly make out the two guns, one on each side, and the long bow chaser peeping through a gunport just to port of the horn bowsprit. A 6-pounder, maybe an 8-pounder. Nothing that should pose a serious threat, but you never know. To quote a saying he himself coined, at sea no precaution is needless: one reef more means one hitch less.

"Ready to come about!"

While the crew ready the braces and sheets, Lobo heads for the stern, passing the gunners bending over their cannons under the supervision of the lieutenant.

"Don't show me up, lads," he says. "We're in full view of Cádiz!"

A chorus of laughter and cheers goes up. The men are keyed up because of the captured ship and the prospect of going ashore. Besides, they have enough training and experience to know that the enemy corsair is no match for an adversary of their size. Next to the launch stowed beneath the trysail boom, those crewmen who are not busy with the maneuver or manning the cannons are laying out weapons for fighting at close quarters, if it should come to that: rifles, pistols and brass pedreros that slot into the sockets on the gunwales, ready to be charged with small bags of grapeshot. Lobo surveys his crew, satisfied with himself. In the six months they have been plying the Straits together, the harbor scum he recruited in the sleaziest bars of Santa María, La Merced and El Boquete have proved themselves to be an able crew, both when a capture has called for skillful maneuvering, and *in extremis*— two boardings and four serious skirmishes to date—when it has required close combat and casualties. Aboard the *Culebra*, true to the contracts they signed, every man jack is prepared to do what is necessary—they always have one eye on the possible spoils, but not one of them balks at difficulty or danger. For as Pépé Lobo well knows, there are no heroes aboard the *Culebra*—nor cowards—only men doing their jobs: professionals resigned to the hard life aboard ship, scraping by on the meager salary of a corsair.

"Signal the schooner! Prepare to come about!"

A red pennant is quickly raised and lowered to the tip of the lower foretopsail yard on the starboard bow. In the stern, the Scotsman and the other helmsman hold the tiller firm on the appointed course. The captain is standing next to them on the lee, gripping the hatchway hood, looking along the gunwale at the line of cannons, muzzles peeping through the gunports. Brasero the bo'sun is standing at the foot of the mast among the crewmen, facing the stern, waiting for the order. Ricardo Maraña is standing next to the first port cannon, right hand clutching the lanyard that activates the gunlock, left hand raised to indicate he is ready. The other three gunners on the port bow do likewise.

"Bring the schooner about!"

A blue signal flag is hoisted to the yardarm and as it is, the *Cristina Ricotti* hauls the wind, its sails ashiver. Lobo takes one last glance at the enemy místico. It is less than three cable lengths away, almost within range, given that the broadside will be fired from the leeside, which is listing heavily.

"Ready about!" Lobo calls to the helmsmen.

They heave the tiller to port and the *Culebra*'s bowsprit veers from the cove at Rota until it is pointed toward the enemy fort at Santa Catalina. Braces and sheets quickly calm the slight fluttering of the canvas, now close-hauled. The místico is no longer directly off the port bow but more abeam, within the arc of fire of the guns.

"Hoist the colors!"

The merchant ensign is raised—two red and three yellow stripes with the central escutcheon affirming its condition as a corsair for the king of Spain—and flutters in the breeze. As soon as the flag reaches the peak of the mainsail, Lobo turns to his first officer.

"Over to you, pilot!" he yells.

Unhurried, peering through the cannon's sights, calculating the angle of fire and the roll as he whispers orders to the gunners to adjust the piece using the chocks and handspikes, Maraña waits for a moment, holding the lanyard, then finally jerks it. With a boom and a cloud of cordite smoke, the cannon recoils, checked by the breeching ropes. Five seconds later the other three guns resound and the smoke is still clearing on the port quarter when Pépé Lobo gives the order to back the wind.

"Hard alee! Pay out the sheets!"

"God preserve us!" says the Scotsman, making the sign of the cross, and downs the helm.

The bowsprit sail flutters as the bow turns through the wind. Beneath the mast, Brasero's men brace the topsail hard to haul to the wind on the new course.

"Trim sheets! Rudder amidships!"

Tacking to port now, the *Culebra* cleaves the water sailing parallel to the schooner, which has forged ahead a little, trysails and jib taut, making good speed. Ricardo Maraña is already back in the stern, hands in the pockets of his tight black jacket, sporting his usual blasé expression, as though he is just back from a leisurely stroll along the beach. Pépé Lobo opens the telescope and points it at the enemy místico, wind on her beam as she comes about. There is a tear in her foresail which the fresh nor'easter extends, ripping the canvas from top to bottom.

"Fuck them," says Maraña apathetically.

THE GAME CONCLUDED fifteen minutes ago, but the pieces on the chessboard are still in place, indicating the final position: a white king pinned by a black rook and knight, and a lone white pawn at the far end of the battlefield, just one square away from being crowned a queen.

"Maybe sometime in the future, science will make it possible to determine such things," says Hipólito Barrull, "but for the moment, it is difficult, almost impossible."

Alongside the captured pieces lie a dirty ashtray, an empty coffee pot and two small cups with dregs at the bottom. It is late; aside from the two players, the Café del Correo is deserted. The silence is remarkable. Most of the lights on the terrace have been extinguished and for some time now the waiters have been stacking the chairs on top of the tables, emptying the brass spittoons, sweeping and mopping the floor. Only the corner where Barrull and the comisario are sitting has been left untouched, lit by a single lantern whose flame has all but guttered out. From time to time the manager, in shirtsleeves, pops his head out to see whether they are still here, but does not disturb them and discreetly retires. If the man breaking the municipal ordinance regarding café closing times is the Commissioner for Districts, Vagrants and Transients—who is famously hot-tempered besides—there is nothing to be said. After all, he makes the rules.

"Three traps, Professor, with a different bait each time . . . and so far, nothing."

Barrull wipes his spectacles using a kerchief that is stained with snuff.

"But nor has he killed again, from what you've told me. Perhaps it was the shock of almost being caught . . . Perhaps he won't kill again."

"I doubt that. Someone who has gone so far is not likely to stop because of a minor shock. I am convinced he is simply waiting for the right moment."

Barrull replaces his glasses. His chin, freshly shaved this morning, is already beginning to show signs of a gray beard.

"I am still flabbergasted about the little matter of the French artilleryman. Getting him to cooperate . . . It is truly astonishing. And I am grateful to you for telling me about it. It shows you trust me."

"I need you, Professor, just as I need the French artilleryman." Tizón picks up one of the black knights and twirls it between his fingers. "Each of you makes good something that I lack; helps me go further than I could alone. You with your knowledge and your intelligence, he with his bombs."

"It's incredible. If news of this were to get out . . ."

The policeman laughs quietly, confidently—scornful of what others might know. "It will not get out."

"And the French officer is still cooperating?"

"For the moment."

"How the devil did you manage to persuade him?"

The policeman looks at him with jaded cynicism. "Thanks to my natural charisma."

He sets the ebony chess piece back on the table with the others. Barrull is staring at Tizón curiously.

"What he told you about Laplace and probability theory is absolutely correct," he says. "Another mathematician, a man named Condorcet, also studied this problem."

"I've not heard of him."

"It doesn't matter. He published a book—one I'm afraid I cannot lend you, because I do not own a copy—entitled *Thoughts on the method of determining the probability of future events* . . . in French, obviously. In it, he poses questions such as, if an event has occurred a specific number of times in the past, and at other times has not occurred, what is the probability that it will occur again?"

The comisario takes a cigar from his leather case and leans across the table.

"'The effects of Nature approach a constant when such effects are studied in large numbers . . .'" he says, or rather recites. "Would that be what you are getting at, Professor?"

"Well, well . . ." Barrull's yellowish smile betrays admiration. "You truly are a rough diamond, Comisario."

Tizón leans back in his chair and smiles too. "With work, even a fool can learn. Even a fool like me . . . Do you think I might be able to find this book in Cádiz?"

"You could look, but I suspect it would be difficult. I read it some years ago in Madrid. However, to talk about probabilities is one thing; certainties are a different matter. The gap between them is wide. And it can be dangerous to bridge that gap with imagination rather than reason."

Barrull waves away the cigar case Tizón proffers, instead taking his snuffbox from his jacket pocket.

"Although I understand your enthusiasm," he continues, "I am not entirely convinced that all this theorizing . . . I don't know . . . It can be counterproductive. An excess of erudition can stifle ideas."

He takes a pinch of snuff, brings it to his nostril, snorts deeply. He sneezes, blows his nose, then looks back at Tizón.

"It was a pity he escaped from you that time . . . Do you think he suspected it was a trap?"

The policeman shakes his head vigorously.

"I don't think so. It could easily have been an accident. If a murderer kills in the street, it would hardly be surprising if, sooner or later, he is interrupted in his crime . . . It is simply a matter of time."

"But since then, several bombs have fallen in other parts of the city. There have been victims."

"That is none of my business. They are beyond my jurisdiction, so to speak."

The professor looks at him again thoughtfully. Analytically, perhaps.

"Be that as it may, you are not completely innocent in this. Not anymore."

"I trust you are not referring to the crimes."

"Of course not. I am talking about this sense that you share with the murderer, this awareness. Your curious intimacy."

"A criminal affinity?"

"Good Lord, Comisario. What a horrid thought."

"But that is what you are thinking."

Barrull considers this for a moment then shakes his head. No, he says—at least not in the sense Tizón intends. Barrull believes, because it has been scientifically proven, that there are links between living creatures, or between them and Nature, which cannot be explained by the rational mind. Notable experiments have been conducted using animals, and also human subjects. This may explain how the murderer's crimes anticipate the bombs, and the comisario's intuition about the murderer's intentions and crime scenes.

"Do you mean thought transference? Mesmerism and such things?"

Barrull nods vigorously, shaking his mane of gray hair. "Something of that nature, yes."

The café owner reappears on the terrace to see if they are still there.

"We should go," says the professor, "before Celis takes his courage in both hands and throws us out. As commissioner of police, you should set an example . . ."

Reluctantly, Tizón gets to his feet, picks up his straw hat and his cane, and they head for the door as Barrull continues to expound his theory. He once knew two brothers, he explains, whose mutual sympathy was so intense that if one of them suffered an ache, the other displayed the same symptoms. He also recalls the case of a woman whose body developed open wounds identical to those suffered by one of her friends, on the same day at the same time, in an accident several leagues away. And he is sure that Tizón must have dreamed things which later came to pass, or experienced situations which he was convinced had happened before.

"There are dark corners of the mind," he concludes, "upon which reason and science have yet to shed any light. Now, I am not saying that you have created a mental bridge with the mind of the murderer or that you know his intentions . . . All I am saying is that it is possible, for reasons I do not understand, that you have entered his territory. His sphere of consciousness. This might make it possible for you to perceive things we cannot see."

They have walked slowly, as far as the Calle del Santo Cristo. Only the light of the moon illuminates the terraces and the towers soaring above their heads.

"If that were the case, Professor, if my senses had created such a bridge, then perhaps . . . I don't know. Perhaps my nature is inclined toward such things."

"Toward crime? I cannot believe it."

Barrull walks a few paces in silence, seeming to brood on these words. At length he growls, dismissing the possibility—or eager to do so.

"Truthfully, I do not know. Perhaps it would be more exact to talk of a capacity for sensing horror, the dark chasms that reside within all human beings . . . Even me, for example. You yourself pointed out— and I entirely agree with you—that when playing chess I become a disagreeable soul, even cruel."

"Inhuman, if you will forgive the word."

Laughter in the darkness.

"I forgive you."

They walk a little further, each caught up in his own thoughts.

"But all this is a long way from the issue of those girls being beaten to death," Tizón says finally.

"Of course. Neither of us could do such a thing. But you have been obsessed with this case for more than a year. For professional reasons, of course. And personal reasons, too, I imagine, though they do not concern me."

Unsettled, almost irritated, the policeman swings his cane.

"Perhaps someday I will tell you—"

"I don't wish you to tell me anything," Barrull interrupts him. "I know already. Every man is a slave to what he says, and master of what he leaves unsaid . . . For the rest, after so many years spent facing each other across the chessboard, I have come to know you just a little. What I wanted to say to you is that this lingering obsession might have produced certain . . ."

"Delusions?"

"Repercussions is the word. To my mind, a hunter is always marked by the hunt."

They have walked down the Calle Comedias and arrived outside an inn called La Manzanilla. There is a chink of light beneath the closed door. Barrull gestures to the place.

"I know you are an abstemious man, Comisario, but I would gladly rinse my gums. All this hypothesizing has made me thirsty. Might you be persuaded to abuse your authority a little more, for my benefit?"

Tizón nods and knocks on the door with his cane until the innkeeper appears, drying his hands on his gray smock. He is a young man, and looks tired.

"I'm closing up, Señor Comisario."

"That can wait another ten minutes, my friend. Give us two glasses of *manzanilla*."

They prop themselves at the dark wood bar, staring at the huge barrels of old wines from Sanlúcar. In the rear, next to some hams and barrels of herring, the innkeeper's father is eating potato stew with cuttlefish and reading a newspaper by lamplight. Barrull raises his glass in a toast.

"To hunting."

Tizón raises his glass in turn, though he barely wets his lips. The professor drinks in short sips while picking at the little plate of four olives the innkeeper has set out. Thinking about it, he continues, a hunter is not a bad analogy: someone who, having stalked an animal for a long time, will be familiar with its territory, its watering holes, the places where it sleeps and eats, its hiding places and its habits. After a while, the hunter will come to imitate the animal's behavior, will come to see this space as something personal. He will adapt to the terrain, making it his own until finally he becomes one with the prey he is stalking.

"It's not a bad example," Tizón admits.

Barrull looks at the innkeeper washing glasses in the sink, then at the man's father, still reading in his corner. When he speaks again, he lowers his voice.

"Previously, when we have spoken about this case, you used chess as an analogy. And perhaps you are right . . . the city is the battlefield. The chessboard. A field of play which, whether you like it or not, you share with the murderer. It is for this reason you see Cádiz in a way the rest of us cannot."

He looks thoughtfully at the plate before him, then eats Tizón's two olives.

"And even if it should end someday," he continues, "your view of the city will never be the same again."

He takes out his purse to pay for the *manzanillas*, but Tizón waves it aside and calls the innkeeper over. Put it on my slate, he says. The two men leave the bar and walk slowly toward the Plaza del Ayuntamiento, their footsteps echoing in the empty streets. The lantern on the corner of the Calle Juan de Andas lengthens their shadows across the cobbles in front of the closed dressmakers' shops.

"What do you intend to do now, Comisario?"

"I intend to keep to my plan for as long as possible."

"Vortices? Calculating probabilities?"

Barrull's tone is gently mocking, but Tizón is not offended.

"If only I could make such calculations," he says candidly. "There are locations that fascinate me. I have explored them, I have spent days—weeks—studying every detail."

"Are there many?"

"Three. One is beyond the range of the French shelling; as such, I have dismissed it in principle . . . The other two are more viable."

"For the murderer?"

"Of course."

Tizón says nothing for a moment, but lifts the tail of his frockcoat. In the dim light, Barrull can see the stock of the double-barrel Ketland revolver tucked into his belt.

"This time he will not get away," Tizón says grimly. "I plan to be prepared."

He notices that Barrull is staring at him with evident consternation. Tizón is aware that this is the first occasion, in all the time they have known each other, that the professor has seen him with a firearm.

"Has it occurred to you that, by intervening, you are altering the murderer's play? Disturbing his thoughts or his intentions?"

It is Tizón's turn to be surprised. Arriving at the Plaza San Juan de Dios, they feel a fresh, salt breeze coming in off the sea. A caleche is parked nearby, the driver sleeping on his coachbox. To their left, beneath the twin peaks of the Puerta de Mar, the guards are changing shift. They are lit from the landward side by a lantern that gives the stone a yellowish hue and glitters on the white belting of their uniforms, the cold steel of their bayonets.

"I hadn't thought about it," says the policeman.

He is silent for a moment, considering this new perspective. Eventually he nods in agreement. "You mean that this may be why he has not killed for some time?"

"It's possible," says Barrull. "Perhaps, because you have meddled with the bombs, modified—if I can put it this way—the artless random element of the French artilleryman's shelling, you have also altered the murderer's game plan. Unsettled him . . . Perhaps he will not kill again."

Tizón tilts his head sullenly, one hand patting the hard shape of the pistol beneath his frockcoat.

"Or perhaps he will take up the challenge," he says, "and play me at my own game."

CHAPTER SEVENTEEN

꩜

The last light of day is fading, melting slowly before the encroaching purple of night as it slips between the terraces, the towers and the spires. As Lolita Palma arrives by carriage at the Mentidero—accompanied by her maid, Mari Paz, and the first officer of the *Culebra*, Ricardo Maraña—the west-facing windows of the houses shimmer with the last red beams guttering into the sea. So begins the hour—so much a part of Cádiz and so beloved by her—when the sea gleams faintly; when hushed sounds travel great distances like the hammer-blows of a shipwright working on the docks; when men fishing from the city walls head home, their rods over their shoulders, beneath the unlit street lamps; when idlers return from watching the sunset out beyond San Sebastián lighthouse; when lamps and candles are lit in shop windows and in doorways, piercing the tentative, tranquil darkness the city settles into every evening.

At dusk, the Plaza de la Cruz de Verdad, known as the Mentidero, resembles a village fair. Telling her maid and the coachman to wait for her on the corner of the Calle del Veedor, Lolita Palma accepts Maraña's hand and steps down from the carriage, drapes a black lace mantilla around her head and shoulders and, accompanied by the young sailor, walks among the tents. Children are running and playing while entire families sit on the ground, cooking on open fires and preparing to sleep under the stars. In recent weeks the French shelling has intensified, and its range has extended. Now bombs fall with unsettling regularity and, though the number of victims is not excessive—many shells still do not explode, therefore causing little damage—those living in the most exposed neighborhoods make the most of these balmy nights to shelter in this part of the city, safe from the artillery fire. Improvising bivouacs using blankets, straw mattresses and sailcloths, they occupy the square and a part of the esplanade which runs between the twin bastions of Candelaria and Bonete. Every evening at sunset the area around the Mentidero is transformed into a nomadic camp—citizens and immigrants, cheerfully resigned, gather until the early hours in local inns and restaurants or at the makeshift bars set up in the street, where wine, conversation, music and song go some way toward allaying their discomfort.

Pépé Lobo is having dinner on the corner of Calle de Hércules opposite the Café del Petit Versailles, at a dubious establishment known as the Negro's bodega, which specializes in grilled sardines, roast octopus and red wine. In fine weather, the owner sets up a deck outside with three or four tables, mostly frequented by sailors and foreigners, who in turn attract those women who, after dark, prowl the streets and the neighboring alleys. Lolita Palma, spotting the corsair—who seems unaware of her presence—stops, leaving Ricardo Maraña to walk on alone. She has spent more than an hour searching the city for Lobo: first at the Sánchez Guineas' office, where she was told he had dropped by earlier this afternoon; then down at the docks, where she found the *Culebra* ready to weigh anchor as soon as there is a lull in the strong nor'easter that has been blowing across the bay for the past two days. The *Culebra*'s first officer, hearing of her arrival from a boatman, immediately came ashore—it is a matter of life and death, she told him, offering no further explanation—and with his usual cold, polite formality, offered to accompany her to the Mentidero, where he believed the captain was having dinner. Now Lolita watches as the lieutenant approaches Pépé Lobo's table, bending to exchange a few brief words, then turning toward her. The captain looks at her in astonishment, then says something to Maraña, who shrugs. Lobo sets down his napkin, gets to his feet and, not bothering to don his hat, weaves through the crowd toward her. She does not give him time to say the words clearly forming on his lips: "What brings you here?"

"I have a problem," she says brusquely.

The sailor seems taken aback. "Serious?"

"Extremely so."

Lobo glances around him, awkwardly. His first officer is now sitting at the table, watching them as he pours himself a glass of wine.

"I'm not sure that this is the place," says the corsair.

"It hardly matters." Lolita speaks with a calmness that surprises herself. "The French have captured the *Marco Bruto*."

"My God . . . When did it happen?"

"Yesterday, off Punta Candor. A Royal Armada gunboat brought the news this morning. She spotted our ship on a reconnaissance mission to the cove at Rota. Both ships are anchored there, the *Marco Bruto* and the corsair felucca that captured her . . . She must have sailed too close to land."

Lolita feels the man's eyes watching her anxiously. Having carefully considered her position, she has come here determined, having rehearsed every word, every gesture. But her calm exterior is an act of will. There is a powerful inner fury. It is not easy to meet those pale, questioning eyes. The corsair struggles to speak.

"I'm sorry," says Lobo. "This is a terrible misfortune."

"There is nothing to be gained by being sorry. This is not a misfortune, it is a catastrophe."

What comes next is not merely a sudden burst of honesty. Lolita Palma tells him everything, because she knows that it is her only hope. The inescapable conclusion. And so she tells him about the valuable cargo of copper ingots, sugar, grain and indigo dye the brigantine is carrying, but she also tells him about the 20,000 *pesos* crucial to the survival of the family business—to say nothing of the value of the ship itself and the goods and chattels aboard.

"From what I have been able to ascertain," she concludes, "the French are intending to move the ship to Sanlúcar and unload her there; given the storm, they have been forced to take shelter at Rota . . . I assume that as soon as the wind changes, they will weigh anchor. The jetty at Rota is too small to berth her there."

Having stooped slightly to listen to Lolita, Lobo now straightens up and glances around him once more. Eventually, he looks at her again.

"This nor'easter could hold out for another two days . . . Why aren't they unloading her on the beach?"

Lolita Palma does not know. Perhaps, with the Spanish and English gunboats nearby, they do not dare. Moreover, the felucca is based out of Sanlúcar, so perhaps they simply want to get her there. They may also be wary of the fact that *guerrilleros* operate on the Río Salado, so the French would be disinclined to transport the cargo by land.

"Are you genuinely interested in what I am saying, Captain?"

She poses this question with a hint of irritation that borders on disdain. She has noticed that once again he has turned away, as if heedless of what she is saying, and is looking at the lamps and lanterns being lit in nearby shops and buildings. After a moment she sees him screw up his eyes.

"You were looking for me in order to tell me this?"

Finally, he looks at her again, mistrustful. Just as he might look at the sea, she thinks. Or at life. Now is the moment to tell him.

"I want you to retrieve the *Marco Bruto*."

She has said it—has managed to say the words—her voice low and measured. She lifts her chin and stares at him, unblinking, intent, as she strives to hide the fierce beating of her heart. *How ridiculous it would be*, she thinks suddenly, fearfully, *to faint here in the street. Without my smelling salts.*

"Is this some jest?" says Pépé Lobo.

"You know it is not."

She cannot be sure now that her voice did not quaver. Those green eyes seem to be scrutinizing every inch of her.

"That is why you came here?"

It is not really a question, nor is there any surprise in his tone. Lolita Palma does not answer. She cannot. Sometimes these days she feels a terrible weariness, a frailty almost like a sickness. The erratic pounding of her heart has slowed now; the space between each beat is longer. She has gone as far as she can go, and she knows this. The corsair surely knows it too, for, after a brief hesitation, he reaches out his hand, just enough to brush her elbow, as though inviting her to walk a little way with him. She follows the man's slight gesture, meekly allowing herself to be led. After a moment, she hears his voice again.

"It would be impossible to get to the ships at Rota . . . They will have anchored them over three and a half fathoms as always, between the headland and the rocks. Protected by the gun batteries at Gallina and Puntilla."

At least he did not laugh, she thinks, relieved. Nor did he say anything untoward, which is what she feared. Though skeptical, he simply sounds solemn, correct. He seems genuinely intent on explaining to her why he cannot do as she asked.

"You could try at night," says Lolita, coldly. "If the nor'easter holds, all you would need to do is cut the mooring rope and hoist a sail and for the brigantine to drift away from land . . ."

She says no more, hoping her words will be enough. Enough for him to see things as she sees them; as she has spent all day imagining them, poring over the map of the bay in her study until it is imprinted on her brain. She notices him give her a sidelong glance—admiration, perhaps; a little hopeful, or maybe a little amused. But the surprise in his voice seems genuine.

"Well now, you seem to have studied the matter thoroughly."

"My life depends on it."

The Plaza del Mentidero stretches out toward the esplanade, the ramparts and the sea, between the artillery park and the military barracks at Cadelaria. Between the makeshift tents where families have huddled are open fires on which stewpots simmer. From somewhere nearby comes the sound of children shrieking, a few melancholy notes of a guitar. In the last row of houses there is a coal yard; in the doorway a woman in a black shawl sits dozing in a chair, surrounded by brooms tied together with cane. Behind her, the ghostly glow of an oil lamp illuminates sacks and baskets of coal.

"When the wind shifts, the *Marco Bruto* will leave the cove," ventures Pépé Lobo. "It would only be possible to attempt what you're suggesting when she is on the open sea, far from the gun batteries."

"By then it might be too late. They will travel armed, perhaps even with an escort. We would lose the element of surprise."

Lolita Palma detects a skeptical smile playing across the corsair's lips. Since that night at Carnaval, nothing about those lips goes unnoticed by her.

"This is a job for the Royal Armada, not for us."

Drawing on her last reserves of calm, Lolita looks once more into those green eyes. Lobo is gazing at her in such a manner that, for a moment, she does not know what to say. *Oh, God*, she thinks. *Perhaps it is because of the way I see him now. Because of what I am doing or what I want him to do. Because of what I am proposing to do to him, to his ship and his crew.*

"The Armada will not deal with matters relating to an individual," she says finally, with perfect equanimity. "At best, if we manage to get the *Marco Bruto* out of the inlet at Rota, some gunboats from La Caleta might escort her back home . . . but no one will guarantee anything."

"Have you been to the Harbor Master's Office?"

"I spoke to Valdés in person. And that is how things stand."

"But the *Culebra* is a corsair not a warship . . . Neither the ship nor my crew are up to what you are asking of us."

They are now on the windy esplanade near the arbor and the small, half-withered garden next to the munitions dump. The city walls are just ahead, the watchtowers and cannons swathed in a fading haze of indigo. In the damp, salty breeze, the lace of Lolita's mantilla flutters against her face.

"Listen to me, Captain. I told you about the twenty thousand *pesos* aboard the *Marco Bruto*, but there is something I have not said . . . In addition to the usual reward for recapturing her, I will add ten percent of that sum."

"Forty thousand *reales*? Are you in earnest?"

"Absolutely. Two thousand silver *pesos*. An amount which, for each of your men, is equal to a fifth of everything he has earned to date at a single stroke. To say nothing of the official reward for her recapture."

There is a sustained, appraising silence. She notices his lips purse.

"This is clearly important to you," says the corsair.

"It is critical. I do not think Palma e Hijos can survive her loss."

"The situation is truly that bad?"

"It is agonizing."

Unexpected, candid, almost brutal, her answer surprises even her. She holds her breath for a moment, bewildered, unable to bring herself to turn away from this man who is staring at her so solemnly. Perhaps it was a mistake to speak so freely, to go so far, she thinks anxiously. Certainly she would never have made such a frank confession to Don Emilio, or to his son Miguel. Not in these words—not to them, nor to anyone. Lolita Palma is too wary and too proud. And she knows this city. In an instant, she realizes that Pépé Lobo understands all these things too, as though he can read her mind. The thought is strangely comforting.

"To attempt it would be suicide," says the corsair after a moment.

They are standing by the parapet of the city walls—just as they did on the night of Carnaval, thinks Lolita—and she, like Lobo, is staring out to sea, past the swell that breaks against the rocks at Los Cochinos, all the way to the few distant lights on the headland at Rota, across six miles of choppy water and white salt spray.

"With a stiff wind like this," the corsair continues, "the only way to do it would be to sail close, approach the cove from the French fort at Santa Catalina and then come in as close as possible to shore . . . That would mean coming within firing range three times."

"There is no moon. That affords a certain advantage."

"But it brings disadvantages, too. Risks. Like running aground in the darkness on the rocks at Gallinas . . . It's a dangerous stretch of coastline."

Lobo places both hands on the parapet, as though on the gunwale of his ship. Lolita notices his manner as he stares out at the bay; surely it must be the same as when he is aboard the *Culebra*. His is the wary, preoccupied expression of a man who takes nothing for granted, at sea or on land. As though he can never trust anything or anyone.

"Besides," Lobo continues, "even if we could get there, we would have to split the crew and put a boarding party on the brigantine, something that could not be done without attracting attention . . . to say nothing of the fact that the felucca is anchored nearby and heavily armed: two 12-pound carronades and six 6-pound guns . . . What you are asking would mean the cutter and her crew braving the field guns of the French batteries, boarding the brigantine and perhaps doing battle with the feluccas . . ."

"Exactly."

For the love of God, thinks Lolita as she hears her own words. *I do not know how I came by this cold logic, but I give thanks for it—for this desperate need that allows me to speak in this way, this calm that restrains me from throwing myself at him, forcing him to take me in his arms again.*

The corsair nods slowly, tilting his head to one side. He seems to have reached some conclusion, one she cannot intuit.

"I don't know what you think of me, but I can assure you . . ."

He breaks off—or rather, he allows the words to die away in a vague, strangely masculine sigh. His voice and the silence that follows make the hairs on the back of Lolita Palma's neck prickle. She shudders, both with physical desire and selfish hope. In a flash, hope prevails over desire and all that is left is the urge to pose the inevitable question.

"Can it be done?"

Pépé Lobo laughs, softly, quietly, but making no attempt to hide it. As if some invisible figure has just said something funny, in a whisper Lolita did not hear. This laugh gives her hope, yet it shocks her. Only a man who has heard the devil himself laugh, she thinks, could laugh as he does.

"We can try," murmurs the corsair. "The sea is capricious . . . We may succeed and we may fail."

"All I ask is that we try."

Lobo looks down at the dark waves lapping at the foot of the ramparts, at the foam carried on the wind that gives the rocks a curious phosphorescence.

"Admit it is too much to ask."

"I admit it."

The corsair is staring at the wisps of luminous sea spray. *Of all the men in the world,* Lolita thinks suddenly, *of all those I have met or will ever meet, he is the one I know best. And he has only held me once.*

"Why should I do it?"

She hesitates before answering, still stunned by the realization. By the unspoken power she has glimpsed for the first time. Everything suddenly seems so simple, so obvious, that she is astounded by her own naïveté: by how she could have surrendered that night—so long ago already, impossible now—have pressed herself against his chest, breathed in his scent, feeling beneath her awkward, tremulous hands his brawny muscular back. More firm, more solid than she could ever have imagined. Not until this moment did she realize the fearful consequences that fleeting moment imposed upon this man now standing, head bowed, staring at the sea.

"Because I am asking you."

She says this firmly, but is careful in her words and her tone, keenly aware that the slightest false move might cause Lobo to look up, to see her in a different light, to awaken from this dream of phosphorescent spray. Then everything would be lost in the darkness gathering in the shadows at the foot of the sea wall.

"They might kill me," he says with touching simplicity. "Me and all my men."

"I know."

"I don't know whether the crew will agree to it . . . No one can force them. Not even me."

"I know that, too."

"You . . ."

He has lifted his head and is looking at her in the last glimmer of light; but for him it is too late. When she hears this last word, Lolita falters for an instant in her purpose, but she immediately feels her determination return and holds her tongue. There is nothing but the sound of the wind, the lapping of water on the rocks.

"Damnation," whispers Pépé Lobo.

Lolita is surprised by the terseness and precision of the word. And so she remains silent. Not all victories are sweet, she is thinking. Not victories such as this.

"You have never known anything about me," says the corsair.

It is not a regret, she realizes; simply a matter-of-fact observation. Sad, perhaps. Or resigned.

"You are wrong. I know everything about you."

She spoke more warmly than she intended; realizing this, she pauses for a moment, uncertain. Once again she feels that fleeting weakness of surrender, a moment of tenderness. They are too far apart tonight for her to breathe his scent.

"Everything," she says again, her tone more brusque.

Now she finds herself thinking about what she has said and realizes it is the truth.

"That is why I came to you," she adds quickly. "Because I know everything I need to know."

She sees him turn away. He cannot bring himself to look at her face—or perhaps he needs to hide his own.

"I will need to think . . . to talk to my crew. I cannot promise anything."

"Of course. I understand. But we do not have much time."

A smack. He slams his hands hard against the parapet. The slap echoes against the bare stone.

"Listen. I cannot promise anything, and you cannot expect me to do it."

Lolita is staring at him intently, almost in surprise. Men are fools, she thinks. Even this one.

"You are wrong. As I already told you, I can."

Seeing him move toward her, she takes a step back.

"You kissed me once, Captain."

She says this as though the memory will be enough to keep him at bay. The sailor laughs again. This time his laugh is louder, more bitter—and one Lolita finds unpleasant.

"And that," he says, "gives you the right to do as you please with my life?"

"No. It gives me the right to look at you as I am doing now."

"Curse the way you look at me, señora. And curse this city."

He takes another step toward her, and defiantly she backs away. And so they stand, frozen, facing one another. Watching each other in the gathering darkness.

"If this were any other place in the world, I would—"

Pépé Lobo suddenly breaks off, as if the dying light robs him of words, confounding any argument he might make. *And he is probably right*, she thinks. *For that I am indebted to him.*

"As would I," she says gently.

There is nothing calculated in what she says. Her voice is quiet, the words a fond regret passing between them. She cannot see his eyes, but she sees him shake his head forlornly.

"Cádiz," she hears him murmur.

"Yes. Cádiz."

Only now does she dare to touch him, hesitantly, like a little girl approaching some furious animal. She lets her hand rest gently, weightlessly, on his shoulder. And beneath her fingers, through the fabric of his frockcoat, she feels the corsair's tense muscles tremble.

A Map of the Port of Cádiz as drawn up by Brigadier Don Vicente Tofiño de San Miguel of the Royal Armada. Pépé Lobo stands, poring over the printed chart of the bay, calculating distances with a pair of compasses set to precisely one nautical mile, according to the scale in the top right corner. Lit by the gimbal lamp mounted on the bulkhead, the map is spread out on the desk of the narrow cabin underneath a skylight, whose glass is covered by a thin layer of salt. This blurs the cloudless, star-strewn sky that is wheeling slowly about the Pole Star, high above the long boom, the furled sail and the lone mast of the cutter. The bulkheads and the cross-timbers creak with every strong gust from the nor'easter that whistles through the rigging; it hauls on the mooring chain, sending violent shivers through the *Culebra*, which cants slowly to port, to starboard, anchored over three fathoms in sand and mud between the breakwater at San Felipe and the rocks at Las Corrales.

"The men are on deck," says Ricardo Maraña, clambering down the companion ladder.

"How many are we short?"

"The bo'sun has just arrived with eight more men . . . There are only six still ashore."

"Could be worse."

"Could be."

Coming over to the desk, Maraña peers at the map. Moving across the coarse paper, Pépé Lobo spins the compasses, measuring out the exact distance—three miles—separating the cutter from the gun battery in the French fort of Santa Catalina, on the easternmost point of the cove at Rota. From this point, heading westward, the coast describes the five-mile sweeping double curve of the inlet, from the fort to the small headland on Puntilla, and from here to the cape at Rota. The captain of the *Culebra* has penciled a circle around each of the six French gun batteries defending this stretch of coast: aside from Santa Catalina, with its long-range field guns, they are the Ciudad Vieja, Arenilla, Puntilla, Gallina and the 16-pound cannons the Imperial Army has positioned within villages around the little wharf at Rota.

"Right now, the darkness and the tide are in our favor," explains Pépé Lobo. "We can take a port tack, hauling the wind as far as the sandbank at Galera . . . From there we tack as far as Puntilla, then we run down the coast, careful to take soundings, working to windward as much as possible. The advantage is that no one will expect the enemy to come from that side . . . If anyone does spot us, it will be some time before they realize we're not a French ship."

The first officer is still bent, impassive, over the map. Pépé Lobo sees that he is carefully studying the three penciled circles on the far left of the inlet. The young man says nothing, but Lobo knows what he is thinking: there are too many cannons, and they are too close. To reach its target, the *Culebra* will have to glide through the darkness past a long line of guns. All it would take is one suspicious sentry, one rocket flare, one patrol boat, and they would have the full might of all these batteries firing at them at point-blank range. And the oak sides of the cutter, which is as lithe and nimble as a girl, are not those of a ship of the line. There is a limit to the beating they can take before she sinks.

"What do you think, pilot?"

Maraña gives an apathetic shrug. Pépé Lobo knows his first officer would have the same reaction if he were suggesting they make straight for Santa Catalina fort and shoot it out with the heavy field guns.

"If the wind shifts even a little, we'll not be able to get close to where the *Marco Bruto* is moored."

He says this coolly, as always, with his usual professional detachment. And not a word about the gun batteries. Yet, like his captain, Maraña knows that if they cannot do this before daybreak, and the French cannons come upon them at dawn, then neither the *Culebra* nor the ship she is to recapture will ever leave the cove.

"In that case, too bad," says Lobo. "We simply sail on, and that's an end to it."

The two men stand up and Pépé Lobo stows the map. Then he looks at Ricardo Maraña. The first mate has not offered a single opinion since the captain confided his intention to rescue the *Marco Bruto*. His only questions have been technical ones, related to the maneuver and how the crew of the *Culebra* should be deployed to execute the plan. Now, with his elegant, long-tailed frockcoat buttoned to the throat, the lieutenant wears his usual expression of ennui, as though in the coming hours they were intending to conduct some commonplace operation—a tiresome, routine maneuver.

"What do the men think?"

Maraña shrugs his shoulders. "Opinions vary. But the promise of an extra forty thousand *reales* and the prospect of a bounty for recapturing the ship have cheered them."

"Have many requested leave to go ashore?"

"Not that I am aware of. Brasero has them on a short leash."

"Make sure you wear your pistol, Lieutenant. Just in case."

Opening a locker in the bulkhead, the captain takes out a loaded weapon and tucks it into his belt, beneath his frockcoat. He is no more apprehensive than usual, but realizes that this is a delicate moment—

with the safety of land nearby, there is still time for crewmen to ask awkward questions, to plot among themselves, before they get under way. Though it may sail under a flag that bears a three-towered castle and a lion rampant crowned, a corsair ship lacks the rigorous discipline of the Royal Armada; the line is more easily crossed between restlessness and mutiny. Once at sea and in the heat of action, every man will do what is expected, will fight for his ship and for his life. He will defend his own interests. These men have spent many months at sea, suffering hardship and danger. They are owed money, money that they could lose were they to fail to fulfill the contracts they signed. Once at sea, it will be too late for second thoughts.

Ricardo Maraña is standing at the foot of the companion ladder, stifling a coughing fit. Not for the first time, Pépé Lobo admires his first mate's unruffled calm. In the glow of the paraffin lamp, the pallid lips Maraña has just wiped with a kerchief—spotted with blood, as usual—seem paler than usual. They flicker into the briefest of smiles as Lobo comes toward him, adopting the more formal tone they use on deck.

"Ready for action, pilot?"

"Ready, Captain."

Before they climb the ladder, Pépé Lobo pauses for an instant.

"Have you something to say?"

Maraña's smile broadens. It is cold and aloof as always. It is the same smile he flashes when in some sleazy bar, shuffling cards over a table piled high with money; he wins or loses with the same equanimity, without blinking, as indifferent to chance as he is to the life in which his ravaged lungs are pitted in a suicidal struggle. To achieve such perfect disregard requires a long lineage, Lobo thinks; it requires countless generations of gamblers or good breeding—possibly both.

"Why would I have something to say, Captain?"

"You're right. Let's go up."

As they step on to the wet, slippery deck beneath the star-strewn sky, the crew gather into dark groups in the bow, between the mast and the bowsprit. The wind, which has not shifted, blows hard through the rigging, the taut ropes vibrating like the strings of a harp. Scattered city lights glow off the port bow, beyond the silhouettes of the 6-pounders lashed to their gunports.

"Nostromo!"

The sturdy figure of Brasero the bo'sun steps forward.

"Yes, Captain."

"Crew?"

"Forty-one, not counting yourselves, señor."

Pépé Lobo walks over to the bilge pump behind the anchor winch. The men move aside to let him pass, their conversations petering out. Lobo cannot see their faces, nor they his. Even the stiff wind is not enough to eliminate the smell of bodies and tattered clothes: sweat, vomit, rotgut wine from taverns left hardly an hour beforehand, the dankness of loose women. The unmistakable reek that, since the dawn of time, has followed every sailor when he comes aboard.

"We are going to steal ourselves a ship," Lobo says, raising his voice.

He speaks for less than a minute. He is not a man of words, and his crew have no fondness for speeches. Besides, they are corsairs, not hapless conscripts aboard a warship who are forced to read the Royal Armada ordinance every week to instill in them the fear of God and of their superiors: threats of corporal punishment, including death, and if that were not enough, the fires of hell itself. With corsairs, it is enough to talk of bounty, and if possible, to offer precise figures. So this is what he does. Briefly, in short, clear sentences, he reminds them of their earnings to date, the monies being held by the Prize Court and the 40,000 *reales* that will be shared among them, in addition to the reward for recapturing this ship, increasing their total earnings, since signing on, by a fifth. On the far shore of the bay, he says, there are French corsairs; maybe the *Culebra* will have a fight on her hands while they hug the shoreline, but the darkness and the wind are in their favor. And on the way back—he speaks of this as though it is a certainty, though he cannot help but notice the mute, skeptical expression on Ricardo Maraña's face—the allied guns will provide cover.

"And while we're at it," he adds, "we'll launch a broadside at the bastard felucca the *gabachos* have anchored there."

Laughter. Lobo walks back along the deck, his men patting his arm and slapping his back. Everything now is instinctive, a result of the bonds that have forged between the crewmen during their long campaigns. It owes less to camaraderie and discipline than to blind obedience and straightforward efficiency. It is the knowledge that they are skippered by a sensible, successful captain who does not take unnecessary risks, who protects his captures, his ship and his crew and, when ashore, manages the spoils of their campaigns wisely. Everyone here knows that hard work and risk come at a price. This is the loyalty Pépé Lobo expects of his men tonight, the commitment he will need to sail through the darkness to the far end of the bay, tacking skillfully, fighting if necessary, to return with the *Marco Bruto* in tow.

When he reaches the starboard ladder between the third cannon and the launch stowed on deck, Lobo leans over the gunwale and looks down at the shadowy figure waiting in the rowboat alongside: a servant with the Palma house, an old sailor who usually carries messages when they are in port.

"Santos!"

The man stirs—he was clearly dozing.

"Yes, Commander!"

"We're about to set sail. Inform your mistress."

"Like a bullet!"

There is the sound of oars slapping the water as the dark form of the boat sheers off from the cutter, rowing with the wind abeam, heading back to the jetty. Pépé Lobo walks past the helm, back to the stern; he leans on the taffrail on which the boom rests, next to the ship's chest containing instruments and charts. The wood is wet, but despite the breeze that is coming off the bay, the temperature is mild. His frock-coat unbuttoned over his shirt, Lobo takes the pistol from his belt and stows it in the chest. Then he stares out at the sleeping city behind the line of walls, the twin peaks of the Puerta de Mar beyond the pier, the shadows of the anchored ships; a few lights reflect on the black water amid flecks of spray whipped up by the wind.

Perhaps right now she is awake, he thinks. Perhaps she is sitting, reading a book, looking up now and again to check the time, imagining what he and his men might be doing at this moment. Perhaps she is anxiously counting the minutes. Or perhaps—and this seems more likely, from what Lobo knows of her—she is asleep, oblivious to everything, dreaming about whatever it is that haunts the dreams of women. For a moment, the corsair imagines the warmth of her body, her eyes as they open in the morning, her languid movements as she wakes, the sun streaming through the window and lighting up her face. It is a sunrise that some of the men aboard the *Culebra* may not live to see.

I know everything about you. Those were her words as she stood by the sea wall at dusk, as she asked him to sail his ship and his crew beneath the enemy guns at Rota. *I know everything I need to know,* she said, *and that gives me the right to ask what I am asking; to look at you as I am doing now.* Leaning on the damp taffrail, the corsair remembers how, behind the billowing folds of her mantilla, her gaze seemed fixed on the purple darkness while cold, calculating words precise as the scale on a sextant, spilled from her lips. And all the while—with that awkwardness that men have always felt when faced with the enigma of the flesh, of life and death—he watched, not daring to kiss her again, as her face melted into the darkness. On this journey into oblivion—the journey that began as soon as he pored over the map in his cabin—he will take with him nothing but the voice, the physical reality of this woman, her warm, unattainable shape melting into the shadows that are encroaching on their fate. *If this were any other place in the world, I would . . .* That was all he managed to say before he broke off; he did not need to say more, for in making this singular confession, everything was sealed between them—the corsair was resigned to the inevitable. Resigned to making this journey without protest, without looking back. Simply one more man setting out on a road of no return, on a sea with no winds to guide him home; with no fears, no regrets—since nothing would be left behind, and he could take nothing with him. But finally, at the last moment, she found the will to speak. And this changed everything. *As would I.* Her words, as melancholy as the violet light fading on the bay, quavered with an age-old tremor from down the centuries; the keening of a woman in an ancient city looking out over the sea wall. The impossibility of return makes death itself seem even more deadly. And her hand on his arm, as weightless as a sigh, merely sealed his hopeless fate.

"The crew are ready, Captain."

The smell of tobacco smoke is whipped away by the wind. The dark, slender form of Ricardo Maraña appears at the taffrail, the glow of his cigar lighting his face. The deck is alive with the sound of bare feet, men's voices, the creak and screech of block and tackle.

"Then give the order. Let's sail."

"Yes, sir."

The cigar glows briefly as the first mate turns.

"Ricardo . . . er, Lieutenant?"

A brief silence. Confused, perhaps, Maraña stops where he is.

"Sir?"

There is surprise in his voice. Just as they never speak in familiar terms in front of the crew, not even when ashore, so never before has Pépé Lobo called him by his first name.

"It looks to be a short, tough trip."

Another silence. Then the lieutenant's laugh booms out in the darkness until eventually it is strangled by a coughing fit. The cigar traces a red arc across the bow and drops into the sea.

"Just get us to Rota, Captain. Then let the devil take care of his own."

IN HIS HUT, by the weak flame of a candle end, Simon Desfosseux dips his pen into the inkwell and sets down calculations and results in a thick notebook, a technical diary of the campaign which he keeps methodically. He does this at the close of every day, with his usual meticulousness, dispassionately noting every success, every failure. In recent days, the artilleryman has been satisfied: certain improvements in the specific gravity of the bombs, implemented after difficult negotiations with General d'Aboville, have increased their range. For two weeks now, using perfectly spherical grenades with no fuse and thirty pounds of sand in place of a powder charge, the Villantroys-Ruty howitzers have been managing to hit the Plaza de San Antonio, in the heart of the city. This implies an effective range of 2,820 *toises*, made possible by the extremely delicate balance of sand and lead which, carefully introduced into the projectile in successive layers, compensates for the 95-pound weight of the shells fired at a 45-degree angle. Admittedly, having no charge and no fuse, they never explode, but at least they land where they are supposed to land—more or less. There are occasional deviations—which worry Desfosseux—of up to 50 *toises*, calculated using the two spires of the church as reference. With things as they are, it is an admirable achievement, one that has allowed *Le Moniteur* to report—to Marshal Soult's great satisfaction—that the Imperial Army are shelling the whole of Cádiz. As for the bombs that are intended to explode, an ingenious combination of fuses, primers and newly devised detonators—the fruit of endless calculations and laborious work by Maurizio Bertoldi—now means that, when the wind, temperature and humidity are favorable, one in ten will reach its target, and the fuse will burn long enough for it to explode. Reports received from Cádiz are enough to save face and to appease the marshal—though they stress the fear and damage caused, rather than fatalities. Desfosseux, however, feels deeply humiliated; he is still convinced that if his superiors would only allow him to use mortars rather than howitzers, and large-diameter shells with longer fuses rather than grenades, his success in extending range would be matched by increased destructive power, and his shells would raze the city to the ground. But, just like the absent Marshal Victor, Soult and his general staff, careful to pander to the Emperor, refuse to hear mention of the word *mortar*; all the more so now that Fanfan and his brothers are finally hitting their targets—or almost. In fact the Duc de Dalmatie himself—this is Jean Soult's imperial title— congratulated Desfosseux some days ago during a routine inspection of the Trocadero. The duke was in unusually good spirits. A messenger, one of the few to cross the Despeñaperros gorge without being strung up from a tree and disemboweled by the *guerrilleros*, brought newspapers from Madrid and Paris containing articles about the bombing of Cádiz, as well as news that the convoy transporting the last consignment of paintings, tapestries and jewels looted by Soult in Andalucía had arrived safely on the far side of the Pyrenees.

"Are you sure you don't want that promotion, Captain?"

"No, sir." Desfosseux clicked his heels impeccably. "Though I am grateful for the offer. As my superior officers are aware, I would prefer to remain at my current rank."

"Really? You said that to Marshal Victor in person?"

"Yes, sir."

"Do you hear that, gentlemen? A queer fish."

Desfosseux closes his notebook and sits brooding. After a moment, he checks his pocket watch, then opens the empty munitions crate he uses as a desk and takes out the most recent message, received this morning from the Spanish policeman. After a silence lasting two weeks, this curious individual has now asked him to fire on a specific point in the city five days from now at 0400 hours precisely. The letter includes a penciled sketch of the area where the bombs are to fall; the captain, who knows the streets of Cádiz like the back of his hand, does not need a map to work out where it is: the little Plaza de San Francisco, situated next to the convent and the church that bear the same name. It is well within range of the exploding shells, as long as there is not a stiff westerly breeze. A relatively easy target to hit with a conventional exploding charge, providing the bombs do not decide to veer right or left—the cursed things sometimes seem to have minds of their own—or fall short and land in the sea.

A colorful character, this commissioner, thinks Desfosseux, putting a match to one corner of the letter and watching it burn. Not exactly likable, it has to be said, with that hawk-like face and those eyes that blaze with suppressed fury, fierce determination and a thirst for vengeance. Ever since their clandestine meeting on the beach, Simon Desfosseux has not replied to the Spaniard's communications. Such a measure would be reckless and dangerous. Not for himself, since he can claim the man is an informant helping him to select targets, but for the policeman himself. This is not a time for misunderstandings or fine distinctions. Desfosseux doubts whether the Spanish authorities would accept the idea of one of their policemen colluding with the enemy, setting targets for some of the bombs that fall on the city, destroying property and lives. This man Tizón seems to blithely accept such risks, but Desfosseux has no intention of making them worse by some indiscretion. Not even the loyal Bertoldi, who helped with their meeting, is aware of what was discussed; he still believes that Tizón is a spy or an informant. As far as the captain is concerned, he has kept his part of their agreement, arranging matters so that at the appointed day and time, Sergeant Labiche and his men fire several shots at prearranged locations, always using grenades containing a powder charge and fuse. After all, they are simply shelling—they do not care where the bombs land. As for the story of the murdered girls, Desfosseux imagines that if Tizón is successful, he will send a message to this effect. In the meantime, Desfosseux is prepared to keep his promise. Not indefinitely, of course. He has to draw the line somewhere.

Getting to his feet, the artilleryman checks his watch again. He picks up his coat and hat, snuffs out the candle and, pushing aside the blanket that serves as a door, steps out into the darkness. The sky is filled with stars and the northeasterly breeze fans the flames of a nearby campfire, on which soldiers are warming a pot of the usual brew of toasted barley and "coffee grounds" that do not smell like, taste like or contain a single grain of coffee. The leaping flames cast a red glow on the barrels of the rifles, and shadows dance across their spectral faces.

"Fancy a beaker, Captain?"

"Maybe later."

"There probably won't be any left later."

Desfosseux stops, takes the tin beaker offered to him and, careful about where he steps, carries it to the watchtower a short distance away. It is a mild night, despite the wind. Summer is coming, bringing with it scorching heat—as much as a hundred degrees in the shade—and swarms of mosquitoes from stagnant pools that torment the army day and night. At least, thinks Desfosseux, sipping the warm brew, the northeasterly breeze makes a change from the muggy heat of the wind the Spanish call *solano*, a sirocco that blows in from Africa, bringing terrible fevers and sweltering nights, drying up the riverbeds, killing the plants and driving people insane. People say that most of the murders in this country—which is criminal by nature—are committed when the *solano* is blowing. A shocking case took place in Jerez only three weeks ago. A lieutenant colonel in the dragoon guards who was living with a Spanish woman—many officers allow themselves this luxury, while the troops are left to vent their lust in brothels or rape women at their own risk—was stabbed to death by the woman's husband, a normally peaceable local bureaucrat who had sworn allegiance to King Joseph. No motive could be determined for this crime beyond the personal, under the influence of this hot wind that boils the blood and unhinges the mind.

Simon Desfosseux finishes his drink, sets the empty beaker on the ground and climbs the creaking ladder that leads to the observation deck, converted into a blockhouse using thick planks of pine from the forests of Chiclana. Five minutes from now, over at Fanfan's battery, Lieutenant Bertoldi will fire the last shots of the day at a range of targets including the Plaza de San Antonio, San Felipe Neri and the Customs House; in doing this he is observing what in recent months has become a ritual, by which several bombs are fired at the limit of the range at daybreak, lunch, dinner and shortly after midnight. It is a basic routine: the bombs now cause more damage than before, but no one expects that they will change anything. Not even the Duc de Dalmatie.

Peering through an embrasure, Desfosseux stares out at the landscape, the vast expanse of the bay, the scattered lights of the sleeping city, the distant flare of San Sebastián lighthouse. There are lights in some of the windows near the Isla de Léon, and the campfires of both armies create a sweeping arc in the distance along the canals of Sancti Petri, marking out a front line that has not moved an inch in the fourteen months since the battle of Chiclana. Nor is it likely to move now, unless in retreat. With the bad news coming in from all over the Peninsula, the defeat of Marshal Marmont by Wellington at Arapiles as the English march into Salamanca, rumors of a general retreat northward are rife in Andalucía.

Nonetheless, Cádiz is still here. Removing the lens cap from the powerful Thomas Jones night glass mounted on a tripod, a wide-barrelled instrument almost a meter in length—six months and mountains of frustrating paperwork were necessary to get one for La Cabezuela—Desfosseux scans the dark city, pausing over the Customs

House where the Regency meet. Together with the Oratory of San Felipe Neri, where the rebel parliament meet—farther off and more difficult to aim at—the Customs House is one of his favorite targets. After several failed attempts, Desfosseux has successfully managed to hit the building with a number of well-aimed shells. It is something he plans to do again tonight, if Bertoldi's hand remains steady and the northeast wind does not play havoc with the trajectories.

Just as Simon Desfosseux is about to turn away from the telescope, he sees a dark shape pass slowly across the lens. Moving the glass to the right, the captain follows it curiously. Finally he realizes that the shadow, magnified and flattened against the vast black expanse of the bay by the powerful lens, is a ship, all sails set, hugging the wind, slipping silently through the darkness like a ghost.

IN THE TERRACE watchtower, cooled by the breeze from the north window, Lolita Palma is also peering through a spyglass. The line of the coast, where the constellations of stars piercing the blue vault of the firmament pass away, is barely visible against the black vastness of the bay. Below the horizon, darker still in this last hour of night, there are no lights save for the intermittent flare of the San Sebastián lighthouse to the left, and a few dim specks—the campfires at Rota—which look like low stars, faint and tremulous in the distance.

"Day is about to break," says Santos.

Lolita looks right, toward the east. Beyond the darks hills of Chiclana and the peak of Medina Sidonia, a faint blue line is appearing on the horizon. It will be more than an hour before the light chases the shadows from the point on the bay on which her telescope has been trained for over an hour, attempting to penetrate the inky blackness. Her heart is in her mouth as she looks for any sign that the *Culebra* is close to its objective—but there is nothing but darkness; everything seems eerily calm. The wind may have delayed them, she thinks, forcing them to tack more often to reach Rota. Or perhaps it proved impossible to sail into the inlet, and they were forced to go out into the open sea—to abandon their attempt.

"If they'd been discovered, we would know," says Santos.

The woman nods without replying. She knows the old sailor is right. The stillness means that wherever she may be, the *Culebra* has not yet been spotted. In fact, a little while ago, some of the French batteries at Santa Catalina and Rota shelled the city and the wind from the far shore carried the sound of the guns. The silence now seems absolute, except for the occasional howling of the wind across the bay.

"No easy task, sailing into that inlet," says Santos. "It'll take time."

Lolita nods again, unsure. Anxious. When the fierce gusts blow through the open window she shivers with cold, in spite of the woolen shawl pulled over her robe; her hair is gathered in a silk coif covering and she is wearing leather slippers. She has been awake much of the night, and in the past two hours has not moved from the tower. The last time was when she went downstairs, but her sleep was brief and fitful, leaving Santos on guard with orders to wake her if there was the slightest news. Shortly afterward she was back in the watchtower, demanding the spyglass. Her hands and face are chilled to the bone; she feels exhausted by the long wait, and her eyes are wet with tears from the long hours spent pressed to the eyepiece of the telescope. She carefully scans the black line of the coast from right to left, pausing at the shadowy entrance to the inlet: there is nothing but darkness and silence. The thought that this one attempt might fail, that the *Marco Bruto* and her cargo could be lost forever, fills her with dread.

"I fear there is nothing to be done," she murmurs. "Something must have prevented them reaching their destination."

"Don't say such things." Santos's voice has the age-old calm of seamen accustomed to the inconstancies of fate. "The captain knows his business."

There is a pause. The wind blows in fitful gusts, causing the clothes hung out on the nearby terraces to shudder and flutter like the shrouds of ghosts.

"May I be permitted to smoke, Doña Lolita?"

"Of course."

"I thank thee."

In the brief flare of the tinderbox the manservant uses to light his hand-rolled cigars, Lolita Palma sees the hard lines etched on his face.

Pépé Lobo must be surrounded by such men at this moment, she thinks, by weather-beaten faces chiseled by the sea. It requires no effort for her to picture the corsair—if he has not already abandoned his venture and sailed on—peering into the darkness beyond the bow of the cutter, attentive to the slightest noise other than the wind and the creak of wood and canvas, and the whisper of the leadsman perched on the cathead counting the fathoms beneath the keel, while the whole crew wait, tense and tongue-tied, for the flare of a cannonade that will sweep the deck.

A gust of wind howls across the terraces and whistles through the window of the watchtower. Shivering beneath her shawl, Lolita can feel, as palpable and precise as an open wound, the yawning emptiness of the gestures she did not make, the silence of the words she did not say while the gathering shadows—a few short hours have passed, yet they feel like years—shrouded the face of this man whose very memory causes her to tremble: the white slash of a smile against bronzed skin, the double reflection of his green eyes, pale, distant, staring into the darkness, as the night inexorably took possession of their emotions, of their lives. *Perhaps when all this is over he will return*, she thinks suddenly. *Perhaps I might, perhaps I should . . . Then again, no. Perhaps never. Or yes. Perhaps forever.*

"There!" Santos shouts.

Lolita Palma starts, then looks in the direction he is pointing. She holds her breath and feels her skin prickle. From across the bay, the wind brings a faint, monotonous rumble like distant thunder. In the cove at Rota, small flashes glitter over black waters.

Timbers splinter, cannonfire blazes, men scream: Every time it takes another hit, the *Culebra* shudders as though alive; as though dying. Since the cutter finally managed to swing her bow clear of the brigantine into the lee of the wind, Pépé Lobo has not had time to check how things are going with Ricardo Maraña and his boarding party. Barely had the last man clambered aboard the *Marco Bruto*—it was a miracle the bowsprit did not split during the final, silent approach, though she was sailing into the wind—than Pépé Lobo had to turn his attention to the unlit ship firing at them across the starboard bow. He had not expected to encounter anything moored to leeward of the *Marco Bruto,* and was surprised to realize at the last moment that there was a vessel—but by then it was too late to change course. It was a small armed vessel; perhaps the corsair místico that prowled the bay had recently dropped anchor here. Her one shot rashly revealed her presence, but by this stage, it hardly mattered; Pépé Lobo had more important things to worry about. Having broken her moorings, drifting in the stiff wind, the místico—if it is her—is now a flaming pyre. No sooner had Maraña and his crew of sixteen boarded the *Marco Bruto* than the *Culebra* launched a broadside from her four 6-pound starboard guns, setting her ablaze. The real problem Pépé Lobo notices, as the *Culebra* comes about to leeward, is off the port bow of the brigantine, where he can see the flare of cannonfire from the corsair feluccas anchored nearby. In the darkness Lobo cannot see his own rigging, but in the blaze of the místico still drifting in the wind, and the intermittent flashes from the *Culebra*'s guns, he can just make out the tattered shrouds and the canvas, gybing or tensed above his head: the mainsail is partially ripped, the gaff is broken, only the foresail is still intact. On the deck, amid the tangle of ropes and splintered wood, framed against the harsh glare of the cannonfire, the crew of the cutter are trying to fix braces and broken halyards to keep the ship on course while the cannon crew swab and charge the four starboard guns with a double shot. Pépé Lobo walks along the guns, cajoling, harrying, helping to maneuver the pinch bars securing the limbers.

"Fire! Fire!"

His eyes are streaming from the burnt gunpowder and his shouts are drowned out by the din of combat. They are very close to the enemy felucca, still moored and firing rapidly—three 6-pound guns and a 12-pound carronade on each bow, as Pépé Lobo knows. The carronade fires shrapnel, which at this range has a devastating effect on the deck of the cutter. With every hit, the hull of the *Culebra* shudders, powerful jolts that shake the rigging and the torn shroud lines. Too many men are lying on the deck: those who are dead or wounded and those crouching, terrified, trying to protect themselves from the shrap-

nel and splintered wood whistling past. Lobo is glad he threw the
launch overboard before they sailed into the inlet; if it had been on
deck, the cannonfire would have turned it into razor-sharp slivers, capable of killing anyone nearby.

"If any of you want to get back safely, keep firing!"

The cannons flash, each time recoiling against the gun ropes. The
cutter is beginning to seem short-handed. The boarding party of the
Marco Bruto left him with insufficient hands to man the guns even before the fighting started. Those who are still fighting cough and wipe
their eyes, muttering obscenities as they take the handspikes and slot
the cannons back into the gunports. Lobo joins them, cutting his hands
on the lashing, tugging desperately. Then he dashes back to the stern,
stepping over the wreckage and the fallen bodies. His composure begins to crumble; he has a nebulous sense of losing control, of imminent
disaster. The wind quickly sweeps away the smoke of cannonfire and he
can see the lean shadow of the anchored felucca, and the bright flare of
cannons all along its starboard bow, the flash of muskets. Thank God
she is too close, he thinks suddenly—the batteries on the mainland
won't dare fire for fear of hitting the felucca.

"Starboard helm! Starboard helm! . . . If we hit her, we'll never get
out of here."

One of the helmsmen—or what remains of him, his body is as
hacked and slashed as a butcher's block—is sprawled across the starboard waterway. The Scotsman heaves the helm toward the opposite
bow with all his might. Pépé Lobo tries to help him, but slips on the
deck, slick with blood. As he gets to his feet, a cannonball crashes like
a giant fist into the hull, slashing a long breach like a hatchet-blow in
the deck. Lobo, who has been sent sprawling again, closes his eyes then
opens them a moment later, dazed. In the haze from the guns and the
burning místico, he sees the tiller swinging wildly side to side; under it
the Scotsman is crawling on all fours, his guts spilling out, howling like
an animal. Getting to his feet, the captain shoves him aside and grabs
the helm, but it refuses to respond. The *Culebra* is out of control. In
that moment, a number of things happen: a rocket flare goes up along
the coast, lighting up the inlet; the mainsail of the cutter rips from top

to bottom; the mast topples with the long groan of a tree falling; and as ropes, hoops, pulleys, canvas and splintered wood rain down all around, the side of the *Culebra* shudders as it slams into the enemy felucca and their tattered riggings tangle.

There are no orders left to give. And no one to give them to. Helpless, in the dying light of the flare as it gutters in the sky, Pépé Lobo watches Brasero the bo'sun die as he tries to clear away the sheets, the halyards and sail that have fallen across the cannons: a shrapnel shot blows away half his head. From ship to ship, bow to bow, men shoot each other at point-blank range with muskets, blunderbusses and pistols. Letting go of the helm, Lobo turns to the taffrail chest, takes out the loaded pistol and grabs a cutlass. As he does so, he hears a distant boom; looking over the bow he sees plumes of spray falling back into the sea. The French batteries are firing from the beach. For a moment he wonders why they are trying to hit the *Culebra*, given that it is still attached to the felucca. Then, silhouetted against the faint glow from the blazing místico, he sees the dark shape of the *Marco Bruto* gliding across the water, her mainsail set, her sheets taut, looming next to his crippled ship; in her bow he thinks he can make out the lean, impassive figure of Ricardo Maraña.

Pépé Lobo turns back, detached, to survey what remains of his ship. The utter devastation that greets him somehow restores his calm. He is aware only of the flash of gunfire, the smoke and the noise amid the tangle of canvas, tattered rigging and mutilated bodies, the crack of timbers sundering, the whistle of bullets and shrapnel, the screams and the curses. The mizzen lateen yard from the enemy felucca crashes down on to the cutter, adding to the confusion on deck, where every muzzle flash is reflected on a viscous, red varnish—as though some drunken god is spilling countless buckets of blood.

A carronade blasts shrapnel across the bow, which crackles as the debris hits the companion hatch, raising a cloud of splinters. Feeling suddenly numb with cold, Pépé Lobo looks down in astonishment, putting a hand on his blood-soaked trousers: the blood is warm, sticky, coming in great spurts as though from a bilge pump. *Well, well*, he thinks. *So that is it. A curious way to bail out. So this is how it happens*, he thinks finally, feeling his strength ebb as he props himself against the shattered hatchway. He does not remember Lolita Palma, nor the brigantine that Ricardo Maraña has managed to bring to safety. His only thought, before he collapses, is that there is not a mast left standing on which to raise the white flag.

CHAPTER EIGHTEEN

✺

The fog makes matters difficult for Rogelio Tizón. His hat is wet, and his redingote, buttoned to the throat, is dripping; wiping a hand across his face, he finds his mustaches and whiskers are damp too. Suppressing the urge to smoke, the comisario curses volubly under his breath between yawns. On nights such as this, Cádiz seems half sunken in the sea that surrounds it, as though the line between land and water is blurred. In the gloom, where a fine gray halo of moon reveals the outline of the buildings and street corners, the fog settles in a wet film on the cobbles and the wrought-iron railings and balconies. The city looks like a ghost ship run aground on the reef.

As usual, Tizón has set his trap with care. Despite his earlier failures—this is his third attempt this month, the eighth in total—he has not dropped his guard. Only a single lantern lights this stretch of the wall bounding the Convento de San Francisco, which extends to the corner of the Calle de la Cruz de Madera. There, the swirling mist thickens into murky darkness and shifting shadows. Half an hour ago, the bait moved to the other side, having spent some time on this side of the square. The hunters—six officers in all—are carefully distributed in the surrounding streets. Cadalso is among them; the others are swift young men, each with a loaded pistol and a whistle to call for help should anything occur. The comisario is also carrying his gun— a double-barreled pistol, primed and ready—beneath the flap of his frockcoat.

A little earlier, three explosions rang out near San Juan de Dios and the Puerta de Tierra, but now the silence is absolute. Sheltering in a doorway near the corner of the Consulado Viejo, Rogelio Tizón removes his hat and leans his head against the wall. Standing still in the dark, the damp gnaws at his bones, but he dares not move, for fear that he will attract attention and reveal himself. The lantern on the convent wall casts a faint red glow that is multiplied by the millions of droplets of water suspended in the air. The comisario shifts his weight to his other foot. *I'm too old for all this,* he thinks irritably.

There have been no deaths since the night Rogelio Tizón chased the murderer through the streets, only to lose him. The comisario is not sure why. Perhaps the incident frightened off the killer. Perhaps the comisario's meddling—changing where the bombs fall and supplying bait (tonight's girl is also a young prostitute)—may have altered his modus operandi, his curious plans and calculations. At times, Tizón is tormented by the thought that the murderer may never strike again; the idea fills him with a furious despair. In spite of the time that has gone by and all his futile attempts, the nights spent casting nets that are hauled in empty the following morning, his every instinct tells him that he is on the right path; something in the murderer's twisted disposition overlaps with his own, their paths are constantly crossing and recrossing like the penciled lines on the baleful map of the city only they share. His face gaunt, his eyes feverish from too many vigils, too much coffee, overwrought by this obsession that has become the sole purpose of his job, his life, Rogelio Tizón has, for some time, found himself constantly looking around, sniffing the air like some demented bloodhound in search of subtle signs that are comprehensible only to him and to the murderer. A murderer who might even now be close by, prowling, watching the bait from a distance, careful not to put his head in the trap. His is a cunning, cruel game of cat and mouse. He may even be watching the watchmen, waiting for them to drop their guard. Or perhaps, the policeman sometimes worries, the game has moved to a different level, has become an intellectual challenge—a confrontation between twisted, clever minds. Like players in blindfold chess, who do not need to move physical pieces on a board to play the game. If this is the case, it is only a matter of time before one of them makes an error.

The possibility terrifies Tizón; never in his life has he been so afraid of failing. He knows that things cannot continue as they are indefinitely; there are too many places in the city suitable for these crimes. There is too much chance at work here, and there is nothing to prevent the killer from striking in one location while Tizón is staking out another—to say nothing of the fact that, at any moment, the French artilleryman on the far side of the bay may grow tired of the game and give up.

Footfalls on the wet cobbles. Rogelio Tizón shrinks back into the doorway. Two men wearing richly embroidered jackets and caps pass through the hazy light of the lantern and walk on toward the junction of the Calle de la Cruz de Madera and the Calle del Camino. They look like young dandies and are wearing no topcoats. Tizón cannot see their faces, but he watches until they disappear into the darkness near the spot where, two weeks ago, he stood motionless, keenly aware of the absence of sound, the rarefied air inside one of those imaginary bell jars that the comisario steps into with the profound, perverse satisfaction of someone confirming the existence of a secret space within the city. The geometrical tracery, invisible to others, of a map he shares with the murderer.

Now he thinks he sees a woman moving through the mist—probably the bait, following the instructions he has given her, walking back to this side of the square. She is a girl of seventeen, recruited by Cadalso near La Merced; Tizón does not even know her name. A moment later he sees it is her. She moves slowly, keeping close to the convent wall, as instructed, to ensure she is visible in the light of the lantern, then she turns back into the shadows. The comisario is worried by the casual, practiced manner of her walk. This will not work, he thinks suddenly, as he watches her sinuous curves move through the misty gloom. The girl is too brazen, too blatant. It is like putting a huge hunk of cheese in a rat trap; having prowled the city so often, the murderer is too well versed to fall for such a crude snare. *Once again*, thinks Tizón, *my king is pinned in a corner of the chessboard, as I listen to my enemy's laughter booming through the city streets. I have had enough of vortices, of bombs. I should go home to bed and have done with it. I'm tired. Sick and tired.*

For a moment, he thinks of stepping from his hiding place, lighting a cigar, stretching his legs and shaking off the bitter chill that gnaws at his bones. Only the practiced, long-suffering patience he has learned in his profession holds him back. The girl is now standing beneath the lantern, where she pauses for a moment before turning and walking back. In the thickening fog near the corner of the street, a shadow appears. Tizón, ever vigilant, watches as the lone figure of a man walks along the convent wall toward the girl and, as he draws close, steps aside to let her pass. He is wearing a round hat and a short, dark cape. He passes the girl without looking at her or exchanging a word, and walks on toward the doorway where the policeman is hiding. Just then, before he has drawn level with Tizón, there is a cry from far off, near the Calle de la Cruz de Madera—a hoarse, powerful shout. Tizón is convinced the voice is that of Cadalso. A moment later, he hears the shrill blast of a whistle, then another, and another. Flabbergasted, Tizón looks toward the girl, still framed in the glow from the lantern, staring into the darkness. Tizón is wondering what the hell is happening. Why the shouts, the whistles? Finally, he grabs his cane and emerges from his hiding place. Seeing him, the petrified girl rushes toward him and in that same instant the man about to pass Tizón puts his head down and breaks into a run. For a fleeting second, the comisario stands frozen. Then instinct takes over and he turns to stare at the fleeing figure. Almost instantly he recognizes the loping gait—swift, silent, head bowed—of the man who ran from him on the Cuesta de la Murga. For a moment the comisario is paralyzed by this realization, time enough for the man to dash past him and run down the street into the fog, his hat pressed down on his head, his cape flapping behind him, making him look like some nocturnal bird of prey. Forgeting the girl and the whistle blasts, the policeman takes out his pistol, cocks the double firing pin, frantically aims and squeezes one of the two triggers.

"Murder!" he yells as the shot rings out. "Help! Murder!"

Either the bullet strikes home or the fleeing figure slips on the wet cobbles: Tizón sees him fall on the corner of the Calle de San Francisco then, with astonishing agility, he leaps to his feet again. By now the policeman is only a few paces behind him. The street runs downhill, making matters easier. Unexpectedly, the fleeing man runs right and disappears. Tizón follows but, rounding the corner, he sees only the deserted street, the damp, gray swirling mist. The man cannot possibly have reached the other end of the street, thinks Tizón, as he pauses to catch his breath and consider the situation. As he collects his thoughts, he realizes he is on the upper part of the Calle del Baluarte where it crosses the Calle de San Francisco. The silence is absolute. Tizón takes the whistle from his pocket, brings it to his lips but, after a brief hesitation, decides not to use it just yet. Carefully walking heel to toe so that his boots make no noise, he moves down the middle of the street, wary as a hunter, glancing around him, gripping his pistol in one hand and his cane in the other, deafened by the pounding of his heart in his ears. Walking on, he sees closed doors, deserted porticos—many people leave theirs open at this time of year—and for one bitter, desperate moment he curses under his breath, convinced he has lost the game. One of the last houses, situated on the left near the corner, has a long, cavernous portico like a vestibule with a gate at the far end. Cautiously, Tizón leans against the damp wall, and peers into the darkness. Instantly, a shadow hurls itself at him, knocking him aside, and dashes down the street, but not before Tizón has a chance to fire his pistol a second time at point-blank range—the brief flash is smothered by the folds of the man's cape and he lets out a fierce, desperate, savage howl. Tizón staggers back and falls, injuring his elbow. He scrabbles to his feet and runs after the man, who has already turned the corner; but by the time Tizón reaches the spot he is once again confronted by a deserted street, lit by the misty glow of the moon. Curbing the impulse to keep running, the comisario pauses, takes a deep breath and considers the situation. It is impossible that the man could have reached the next corner, he thinks. The street is too long. Furthermore, a section of it is taken up by the Iglesia del Rosario. This means that, instead of fleeing, the man has taken shelter in another portico, of which there are not many along this stretch of road. It might be a fortuitous hiding place, or maybe he lives nearby in one of these houses. He is almost certainly injured. Perhaps he needs a hiding place where he can inspect the wound, where he can rest and catch his breath—or pass out. Never taking his eyes off the street, the policeman studies the houses, one by one, and tries to imagine what he would do. He knows his men will have heard the shots and will come running. This time he has got him, he thinks. The wolf has sunk his teeth into his prey and is not about to let go. Not while he can corral him in a little more. The first thing is to seal off the area for as long as necessary. Close the net. Let no one out without frisking them from head to foot.

Standing in the swirling fog, Tizón slips the pistol into his pocket, brings the whistle to his lips and gives three long blasts. Then he lights a cigar and waits for his men to arrive. Meanwhile, he mentally reconstructs the sequence of events. Only then does he wonder what could have happened before, in the shadows of the square. Why Cadalso screamed—if it was him—and what prompted the first whistle blasts.

In the small ground-floor parlor, with nautical engravings hanging above the dark-wood dado rail, the faint ticking of the English grandfather clock punctuates the frequent and unsettling silences—pauses filled with shock and revulsion. Sitting in the leather armchair, Lolita Palma twists a handkerchief between her fingers. Her hands lie in the lap of her dark-blue morning dress, trimmed at the waist with buttons of black amber.

"How was she found?"

The policeman—who introduced himself as Comisario Tizón—is sitting stiffly on the sofa, his hat next to him, his cane resting against his knee. His coarsely cut brown redingote is as rumpled as his trousers. His face looks haggard, dark circles ring his reddened eyes, and beneath his whiskers and mustache his chin is unshaven. He has clearly had a grueling night. He is sleepy and exhausted. The strong aquiline nose recalls a bird of prey: a cruel, dangerous, exhausted eagle.

"By chance, in a timber yard . . . One of our men went in to relieve himself and saw her body lying on the ground."

He looks her in the eye as he speaks, but she can tell he is uncomfortable. From time to time he glances at the clock against the wall, as if he has lost his train of thought. He seems keen to keep the conversation brief—a tiresome formality.

"Was she badly . . . mistreated?"

The man makes a vague gesture.

"She was not violated, if that is what you mean. Otherwise . . . well . . . it was not a peaceful end. Death never is . . ."

He trails off, leaving Lolita Palma to imagine the rest. She shudders again, still unable to believe what is happening. In spite of herself, she peers into this abyss of pain and terrifying darkness.

"She was little more than a child," Lolita murmurs, devastated.

She goes on twisting the handkerchief. She is determined not to falter, not to seem weak. Not in front of this man—nor in front of any man. Cousin Toño, who came the moment he heard the news, is upstairs traumatized, slumped in an armchair, weeping like a little boy. With him are Curra Vilches and some of the neighbors.

"Have you caught the man who did this?"

The same vague gesture. The question seems to add to the comisario's uneasiness.

"We are working on it," he says neutrally.

"Is it the man who murdered the other girls? For some months now, there have been rumors—"

"It is too early to tell."

"I heard that a bomb fell almost on the same spot shortly afterward . . . Is it true two people were killed, and another three gravely injured?"

"So it would seem."

"What an unfortunate coincidence."

"Very unfortunate."

Lolita Palma notices that the policeman is looking distractedly at the pictures on the walls, as if eager to change the subject.

"Why did the girl leave the house?" he asks.

Lolita explains briefly: she had been sent on an errand to the apothecary on the Calle Cruz de la Madera. Rosas the steward is ill in bed. He needed some curative and asked Mari Paz to fetch it.

"Alone, at such an hour?"

"It was not very late: ten o'clock or thereabouts. And the apothecary is only three blocks from here . . . out of range of the French shells. This has always been a peaceable area, safe and respectable."

"And no one was worried when she did not return?"

"We did not realize. Dinner had already been served . . . The steward was asleep in his room, and I was upstairs in my office. I was not intending to come downstairs, and I had no need to call her."

She pauses, thinking back over the evening: she in her study upstairs, oblivious to what was happening to the unfortunate girl. Working late into the night on official paperwork relating to the recovery of the *Marco Bruto* and the loss of the *Culebra*. Moving like a soulless automaton, reluctant to think about anything unrelated to the practicalities of the matter. Her eyes dry, her heart calm. And yet from time to time, despite everything, she found herself going over to the window and staring through the potted ferns at the halo of moon in the misty sky. Remembering Pépé Lobo's green eyes. *Admit to me that it is too much to ask.* Those were his words. *If this were any other place in the world, I would . . .*

"This is dreadful," she says. "Horrifying."

The policeman's voice sounds normal: brusque and professional. "Did she have a beau . . . ? Admirers?"

"None that I know of."

"Did she have family here in Cádiz?"

Lolita shakes her head. The girl was from the Isla de Léon, she tells Tizón, from a poor but decent family working on the salt flats. Her father is a good man: Felipe Mojarra. He is one of the company of fusiliers led by Don Cristábal Sánchez de la Campa.

"Does he know what has happened?"

"I sent word to him with my coachman, and a letter asking his superiors to give him leave to come here . . . poor man!"

She falls silent, distraught. Now, finally, her eyes well up with tears, imagining the pain this family is going through. The poor mother— her daughter slaughtered in this terrible fashion, barely seventeen years old.

"It's unbelievable. Unbelievable and horrifying . . . Is it really true, what you told me? That she was tortured before she was killed?"

The policeman says nothing; he simply looks at her blankly. Lolita Palma feels a tear trickle down her cheek.

"My God," she sobs.

She feels ashamed, showing weakness in front of a stranger, but she cannot help it. Her imagination gets the better of her. That poor girl.

"Who could be capable of . . . ?"

She chokes on her words. The dam bursts and she feels hot tears coursing down her face. Embarrassed, the comisario turns away and clears his throat. After a moment, he takes his hat and cane and gets to his feet.

"The truth, señora . . ." he says gently, "is that anyone could."

She stares at him, not understanding. What is he talking about? Who does he mean?

"I hope you find the killer."

Tizón's lips curl into an animal rictus. A gold tooth flashes—a canine.

"If things go as planned, we should catch him very soon."

"And what will happen to this brute?"

The cold, hard gaze seems to go right through Lolita, as though he is staring at some point far away. Some dim, unfathomable place that only he can see.

"Justice," he says, his voice almost a whisper.

A few short steps away, light is streaming from the south; the sky is so pure, so blue that it dazzles. The Calle del Rosario looks utterly different from how it did last night: shimmering whitewash, golden sandstone, pots of geraniums hanging from the balconies. Standing in the sun's glare, sweaty and disheveled, his face bearing the marks of lack of sleep, Rogelio Tizón's assistant hangs his head like a lumbering mastiff.

"I swear to you we are doing everything we can, señor."

"And I swear to you that I will personally kill every last one of you, Cadalso . . . If this man has escaped, I will rip out your eyes and piss in your skulls."

The henchman blinks, knitting his brow, seriously weighing up how much of this threat is hyperbole and how much is serious.

"We have scoured the street, house by house," he says finally. "There's no sign of him. No one knows anything. No one saw anything . . . The only thing we know for certain is that he was wounded. You shot him."

Tizón walks a little way, swinging his cane, livid. There are guards at either end of the street and in the doorways of some of the houses: twenty officers and nightwatchmen spread out around the area, keeping order under the critical eyes of neighbors who peer down from balconies and windows. Cadalso points to a portico near the corner of the street.

"He left a bloody handprint when he leaned here. And another one over there."

"Have you checked the man is not local?"

"We have checked the municipal register and the list of inhabitants name by name." Cadalso nods to the locals leaning out of the windows. "No one around here is injured. And no one went out after ten o'clock last night."

"That's not possible. I cornered the bastard right here, and I didn't move until you and this gang of cretins showed up, blowing your whistles."

Tizón steps over and studies the reddish-brown handprint on the whitewashed doorframe. At least one of his shots hit home, he thinks with grim satisfaction. Clipped the bird's wing with some lead.

"Couldn't he have disappeared in the fog, señor?"

"I already told you he didn't, damn it. I was right behind him—he didn't have time to get to the end of the street."

"Well, we have set up a cordon covering the two blocks to left and right."

"Have you checked the basements?"

Cadalso's sullen pout indicates he is clearly offended at the suggestion. He is, after all, a professional.

"With a fine-tooth comb. We've searched the woodpiles and the coal bunkers."

"And the terraces?"

"All checked, one by one. We still have some officers up there, just in case."

"This is impossible."

"Well then, tell me what to do."

Tizón taps the cobbles with his cane impatiently.

"I'm sure you must have blundered somewhere."

"I'm telling you, señor, we haven't. Take my word for it. We followed your orders to the letter—I saw to it personally." Cadalso scratches his head, bewildered. "If only you had got a look at his face . . ."

"You should have seen him; he walked right in front of your nose. Idiot."

Cadalso bows his head, offended less by the insult than by his boss's lack of faith. Turning his back on his assistant, Rogelio Tizón walks away, studying his surroundings.

"Someone must have slipped up," he mutters, "I'm convinced of it."

Cadalso trails behind, like a faithful puppy following the master who has just whipped him.

"Anything is possible, señor," he finally admits. "But I swear we did the best we could. We sealed off the area last night. He couldn't have got far."

There is an explosion nearby. A bomb has just fallen on the Plaza del Palillero. Cadalso flinches and glances toward the sound and many neighbors disappear from their windows and balconies. Rogelio Tizón does not react, but walks as far as the Iglesia del Rosario. Like many churches in Cádiz, it is not a separate structure, but integrates with the cornices of the adjoining houses. Only the towers stand out, soaring above the vast doorway, which now stands wide open. Last night it was closed. Tizón goes inside, checking the pulpit and the side aisles. At the far end, beneath the altarpiece, the sanctuary light is burning.

"Besides," Cadalso says, catching him up, "if you don't mind my saying, I treated the case as a . . . well . . . a personal matter. The shock

I got when I went into that yard to piss and stumbled on that poor kid . . . Jesus. You heard me screaming to let everyone know. And it was lucky you were close to the suspect. Otherwise he would have escaped again."

Tizón shakes his head in disbelief. With every hour that passes, everything begins to stink a little more of failure. And failure has become an old acquaintance in this case. It is more than the comisario can bear.

"But he escaped again anyway. With or without my help."

Cadalso raises a hand, awkward as always. For a moment, it looks as though he is about to pat the comisario on the shoulder. *If he does,* Tizón thinks, *I'll split his skull with my cane.*

"Don't say that, señor." Seeing his boss's expression, Cadalso leaves his hand hovering in the air. "We'll find him. He can't have got far with a bullet in his side . . . He'll have to go somewhere to take care of the wound. Or to hide."

I don't even have the energy for insults, thinks Tizón. *I'm so sick and tired of this whole case.*

"Somewhere, you say?"

"Exactly."

Further down the street, near the entrance to the church is the grotto known as the Oratory of La Santa Cueva. Beneath the triangular pediment, the door is open.

"Did you check in here too?"

Another offended pout at the thought that Tizón could doubt him. "Of course."

Rogelio Tizón steps into the vestibule and glances around. He is about to go on his way, but just as he is leaving something catches his eye and makes him look again: something to the left of the double staircase leading down to the subterranean chapel. It is as familiar to Tizón as it is to everyone in Cádiz, since it is a part of the traditional statuary of the region. It is an effigy he has been familiar with all his life, or almost. And yet, in this case, it takes on a new, startling quality.

"What is it, señor?"

Rogelio Tizón does not answer. Rooted to the spot, he stares at the glass case that stands at the foot of the stairs on a floor tiled in black and white, just like a chessboard. Inside the case is a statue depicting *Ecce Homo:* Christ in the throes of His passion, between Herod and Pilate. There are hundreds of statues like it in churches around the city, in Andalucía and all over Spain. The version in the Santa Cueva is a particularly expressive example of its kind: lashed to a pillar, His flesh is marked by countless red weals, slashed with bleeding wounds by the whips of His tormentors. The figure conveys a sense of exalted agony, of helplessness and absolute suffering. And suddenly, as though a veil has been torn away, the comisario realizes its significance—what it represents. Founded thirty years ago by a priest of noble ancestry—the late Father Santa, Marqués de Valde-Íñigo—the Santa Cueva is a private subterranean oratory, like a basement, beneath a small chapel of elliptical form. The lower part is dedicated to the ascetic practices of a religious brotherhood well known in Cádiz: wealthy people, people of high social standing, scrupulous in their observance of Catholic orthodoxy. Three times a week, the brothers gather to take the sacrament and practice traditional devotions with extreme rigor. This includes the use of whips. Flagellation to mortify the flesh. To subdue it.

"What's in the cave?" he asks.

An unsettling silence, lasting three seconds precisely. Tizón does not look at his assistant. Instead he stares at the chessboard-patterned floor beneath the statue of Christ.

"The cave?" echoes Cadalso.

"That's what I said. There is a chapel upstairs and a grotto below. That's why it's called the Santa Cueva ... Santa because it is Holy, Cueva because there is a cave. Do you need me to draw you a picture?"

Cadalso shifts his weight from one foot to the other. Embarrassed.

"I thought . . ."

"Out with it, then. What the fuck did you think?"

"The doors downstairs are always locked. That's what the guard said. Only the twenty or so members of the brotherhood have keys. The guard doesn't even have one."

"And?"

"And . . . that's all." Cadalso shrugs evasively. "I thought that no one would have been able to get in there last night. Without a key."

"Unless he was a member of the brotherhood."

Another silence, longer and more awkward this time. Cadalso looks anywhere but at his boss.

"Of course, señor. But they are respectable people. Religious. What I mean is this place is . . ."

". . . private? Holy? Sacrosanct? Above suspicion?"

The assistant's whole body seems about to dissolve into liquid.

"Well, yes, I suppose—"

Tizón raises a finger to silence him. "Listen, Cadalso."

"Yes, señor?"

"Damn you to hell!"

Tizón turns away from his assistant. He feels a shudder run through him, like a silent, long-suppressed sigh. It is almost pleasant. After the initial jolt of surprise, and the subsequent flash of anger, there now comes a determined wolfish snarl, the reaction of a trained bloodhound on finally discovering—or rediscovering—the trail. Suddenly, everything is no longer intuition, but certainty. Descending the stairs under the mournful gaze of the flagellated Christ, the comisario feels his blood pulsing, slowly, powerfully, overcoming his exhaustion. It feels like he has stepped once again into one of the impossible or improbable places where silence becomes absolute and the air seems to hang, suspended. The bell jar, the vortex that leads to the next square of the chessboard that is the city and the bay. He has finally seen the game. And so, rather than rush forward with a shout of triumph or a growl of satisfaction, the comisario moves diagonally across the checkered floor, slowly, soundlessly; he carefully scrutinizes everything, and savors the prickling sensation in the fingers that grip his cane. He moves toward the grotto door. If only, he thinks abruptly, this moment of jubilation would never end.

"If you want, I can have it opened," says Cadalso, trotting behind. "It should only take a minute."

"Shut your trap."

The lock on the door is of a commonplace variety, requiring a large key. Tizón takes out his picklocks and manages to slide back the hasp within a minute. Child's play. With a soft click, the door opens onto a windowless grotto. Tizón has never been here before.

"Fetch a candle from the chapel upstairs," he tells Cadalso.

From below comes a smell of must and damp, and a chill draft which grows colder as Tizón steps further into the cave, his way lit by Cadalso holding a large candle aloft. The shadow of the comisario glides along the walls. Every footfall echoes in the confined space. Unlike the chapel above it, the cave is sparsely decorated, its walls stark and bare. It is here that members of the brotherhood perform their rituals. Above one of the arches, Cadalso's candle picks out a skull and crossbones painted on the ceiling. Beneath it is a dried, brownish stain—a trace of blood.

"Holy Mother of God," cries Cadalso.

The man is huddled in a corner against the back wall of the cave, a dark shapeless mass, softly whimpering and moaning like a hunted animal.

"WITH YOUR PERMISSION, sir."

Simon Desfosseux looks away from the eyepiece of the Dolland telescope, the image of the twin spires of the San Antonio Church still burned on to his retinas: 2,870 *toises*, he cannot reach them, he thinks gloomily. His maximum range is 2,828 *toises*. None of the French shells that have fallen on Cádiz have gone further than this. Nor will they ever, now.

"Go on, Labiche. You can take her."

Assisted by a group of soldiers, the sergeant dismantles the telescope and folds the tripod, packing everything away. The rest of the optical instruments from the observation deck are already stowed on the carts. The Dolland was left until last, so that he might observe the last shots from the Cabezuela. The very last was fired from Fanfan twenty minutes ago. A 100-pound bomb containing a ballast of lead and sand which fell short, barely grazing the city walls. A sad end.

"Any other orders, sir?"

"No, thank you. You can take it away."

The sergeant salutes, and he and his men go back down the ladder with the equipment. Looking through the empty embrasure, Desfosseux sees smoke rising vertically in the waning afternoon light—there is not a breath of wind—over most of the French military posts. All along the line, the imperial troops are dismantling their positions, burning equipment, spiking any field guns they cannot carry and throwing them into the sea. King Joseph's hasty departure from Madrid, and the news that Field Marshal Wellington has marched into the Spanish capital, has put the army in Andalucía in a quandary. The order is to retreat to safety on the far side of the canyon of Despeñaperros. Preparations have begun for the evacuation of Seville; tossing gunpowder reserves from La Cartuja into the river, destroying the foundries, the arsenal and the saltpeter works. The whole of the Premier Corps has retreated northward: pack mules, carts and carriages laden with pillaged booty, convoys of the wounded, the supply corps and Spanish troops loyal to the Emperor, who cannot safely be left behind. Around Cádiz, the orders are to shield the retreat with a constant bombardment from positions in the channel around Chiclana and bastions along the coast from El Puerto de Santa María all the way to Rota. As for the Cabezuela, one small battery of three 8-pound guns will continue to fire at Puntales until the last moment, to keep the enemy occupied. Any artillery that cannot be transported will be thrown into the bay, into the mud along the shore, or left abandoned in the redoubts.

Hsssss. Boom. Hsssss. Boom. Two Spanish shells cleave the air above the observation deck, exploding somewhere near the barracks—where, by now, Lieutenant Bertoldi should have burned all the official documents and useless paperwork. Simon Desfosseux, who ducked when he heard the shells pass overhead, straightens up and looks over for the last time at the enemy fort of Puntales. With the naked eye—it is barely half a mile away—he can make out the stubborn Spanish flag, riddled by shrapnel, that has fluttered there every single day. The garrison is composed of a battalion of Volunteers, experienced artillerymen and a handful of Englishmen manning the upper gun battery. The full name of the stronghold is San Lorenzo de Puntal and, some days ago, during the celebrations for its patron saint, Desfosseux and Maurizio Bertoldi were astonished to see through the spyglass these defenders—who had remained stoic throughout the ceremony, impassive despite being under constant fire from the Cabezuela—cheering and applauding as they hoisted the flag.

Far to his right lies Cádiz. The captain contemplates the white city against the crimson sunset: this landscape which he knows better than he does his own home, his own country, having studied it for so long through his lens and on the lines of a map. Simon Desfosseux dearly hopes he will never have to see it again. Like thousands of other men, he has squandered his life on this bay during the thirty months and twenty days of the siege: mired in tedium and impotence, gradually sinking as if in the filthy mud of some swamp. With no glory, though the word means little to him. No success, no satisfaction and no profit.

Hssss. Boom. Again. And again. The battery of 8-pound guns continues firing at Puntales, and the Spanish fort returns their fire. More enemy shells whistle above the observation deck; the captain ducks again and decides to leave. It is better not to tempt fate, he thinks as he goes down the ladders. It would not be particularly comical to be hit by a cannonball at the last moment. So he mentally bids goodbye to this vista having fired 5,574 artillery shots of various calibers on the city from Cabezuela: that is the figure that appears in his operations ledger, now consigned to gather dust among the military archives. Of this number, only 534 bombs actually reached Cádiz, mostly inert ones filled with sand and lead. All the others fell short and landed in the bay. Nor will the damage he has inflicted on the city win Desfosseux the Légion d'Honneur: half a dozen houses demolished, fifteen or twenty dead and perhaps a hundred wounded. The brusqueness of Marshal Soult and his general staff when Desfosseux was summoned to give a final tally of operations left little room for doubt. No one, he fears, will ever offer him a promotion again.

La Cabezuela is in chaos, as are all the retreating troops. Broken equipment lies everywhere, limbers and gun carriages from the battering train are burning on pyres, onto which is thrown anything that might prove useful to the enemy. Sappers using hatchets, picks and shovels are demolishing everything they can while another squad, under the command of an Officer of Engineers, are laying trails of tar and gunpowder to torch the barracks, or setting powder charges and fuses. The rest of the soldiers, artillerymen and marines, given the ill-disciplined nature of the moment, are roaming about aimlessly, impetuous and insolent; they steal everything they can, loading the carts with equipment and everything they have looted from nearby houses and villages in the past few hours, paying little heed to the marauders raping and killing. The voluminous baggage belonging to the generals, with their beloved Spanish ladies installed in wagons requisitioned from Chiclana and El Puerto, set out for Seville some hours ago under a heavy escort of dragoons; the road to Jerez is heaving with carriages, cavalrymen and a confusion of troops and civilians—the families of French officials, those Spaniards loyal to Bonaparte and collaborators fearful of being left to the tender mercies of their compatriots. No one wants to draw up the rear, to risk falling into the hands of the *guerrilleros*, who already prowl like vicious vermin, ever more daring, fueled by pillage and blood. Only yesterday, twenty-eight sick and wounded Frenchmen, left without an escort between Conil and Vejer, were captured by locals, surrounded by straw bales soaked in oil and burned alive.

As he reaches the foot of the ladder, Simon Desfosseux sees four sappers setting charges around the supports of the observation deck. It is hot and they are sweating profusely in their blue frockcoats with black lapels. Standing a little further off, the Officer of Engineers— a fat lieutenant mopping his neck and brow with a filthy kerchief— watches them as they lay trails of tar and gunpowder.

"Anyone left up there?" he asks Desfosseux as he passes.

"No one," says the captain. "She's all yours."

The officer gives an unconcerned shrug, his eyes watery and expressionless. He did not even bother to salute when he registered Desfosseux's rank. He barks an order. The captain walks away without looking back; he hears the hiss of the fuse being lit and then the crackle of the flames as they rise along the piles and the ladder. When he reaches the redoubt, he finds Mauricio Bertoldi staring back at the tower.

"There go two years of our lives," the lieutenant remarks.

Only now does Desfosseux turn to look. The observation deck is a flaming torch, with a billowing plume of black smoke rising into the air. The citizens of Cádiz are in for a fine light-show tonight, he thinks. Flames and fireworks sweeping from one end of the bay to the other: a farewell celebration, with gunpowder provided by the Emperor.

"How are things here?" he asks.

His adjutant makes a vague gesture, as if the concept of things going well or badly has little to do with what is happening.

"The twenty-five four-pounders we're leaving behind have all been spiked," he says. "Labiche will toss them into the bay as soon as he can . . . Everything else has been burned or cut to pieces."

"What about my baggage?"

"Packed and shipped, as is mine. The carts set off under escort a little while ago."

"Good. Not that we would have much to lose, you and I."

The two officers look at each other. Two sad, complicit smiles. They have been living cheek by jowl for so long now they have no need of words. They leave as impoverished as they arrived—unlike their superior officers, those greedy generals who are carrying off chalices looted from churches and the silver cutlery from the elegant houses where they were billeted.

"What orders should I give the officer manning the eight-pounders?"

"He is to keep firing until everyone has left; we wouldn't want the *manolos* landing too early . . . At midnight he is to spike the cannons and get out of here."

Bertoldi gives a skeptical laugh. "I hope he stands his ground and doesn't take to his heels long before then."

"I hope so too."

A huge explosion, two miles northeast along the coast. A black cloud mushrooms over the Castillo de Santa Catalina.

"They're obviously in a hurry too," says Bertoldi.

Desfosseux peers into the redoubt where the howitzers are stored. The sappers have clearly been here already: the wooden gun limbers have been broken up with hatchets, and the metal carriages dismantled. The thick brass barrels lie on the ground like corpses after a bloody battle.

"As you feared, Captain, we could only take away three field guns. We simply didn't have the transport or the manpower . . . We had to leave everything else."

"How many has Labiche thrown into the bay?"

"Just one. But we don't have the resources to dump the rest of them. The sappers will come by later, put a hefty powder charge in each and plug up the barrel. We should be able to crack them at least."

Desfosseux hops down into the redoubt, between the fascines and the broken blanks, and walks over to the broken field guns. It is somehow moving seeing them like this. Poor Fanfan is here, lying amid the shattered remnants of its gun carriage. With its polished brass, almost nine feet long and one foot in diameter, it looks like a strange dead sea creature stranded on land.

"They're only guns, sir. We'll cast more of them."

"For what? Another Cádiz?"

Struck by a curious wave of melancholy, Simon Desfosseux bends and runs his fingertips over the pitted metal: the foundry stamps, the recent marks of hammer blows to the trunnions. The brass is still intact; not a single crack.

"Good lads," he whispers. "Faithful to the end."

He gets up, feeling like a traitorous leader abandoning his men. The 8-pounders are still firing from the battery below. A Spanish grenade fired from Puntales explodes thirty feet away, forcing him to duck while Bertoldi, with cat-like reflexes, leaps down from the parapet and lands on top of him. Rocks and debris rain down all around. Almost immediately, there are screams from where the bomb fell. Some poor bastards have just been hit, Desfosseux realizes as he and his lieutenant get to their feet, brushing the dirt from their uniforms. Rotten luck, he thinks, taking a hit at this stage given that the military ambulances must be in Jerez by now. The cloud of smoke and dust has not yet cleared when a lieutenant from the engineering corps appears, with several men lugging heavy boxes of equipment and explosives.

"The bastards seem to be enjoying this."

Leaving Fanfan and his brothers to the mercy of the sappers, the captain and his assistant leave the redoubt and cross the footbridge to the barracks, where everything now has begun to burn. The heat from the blaze is unbearable—the leaping flames create a haze, the air rippling in the distance where disorganized lines of cavalrymen, artillerymen and infantrymen, pushing handcarts and carrying packs, merge into a sea of blue, brown and gray that moves slowly along the road to El Puerto. Twelve thousand men in full retreat.

"We've got a little way to go," says Bertoldi, "to get to France."

"I fear we have further still. They say we are at war with Russia."

"Shit."

For the last time, Simon Desfosseux looks back at the unattainable city in the distance, flaring red as the sun sets over the bay. Pray God, he thinks, that strange policeman has finally found what he was looking for.

A GENTLE NIGHT breeze from the east. The air is balmy and almost still. Nor is there any sound, except for the whispered voices of two men standing in the half light of a lantern amid the ruins of the Castillo de Guardiamarinas, next to the gap in the wall that leads to the Calle del Silencio.

"You cannot ask so much of me," says Hipólito Barrull.

Next to him Rogelio Tizón falls silent for a moment.

"I am not asking anything of you," he says finally. "Except for your version of events. Your opinion. You are the only person clear-sighted enough to give me what I need: a rational view that might clarify matters. A scientific paradigm to order what I already know."

"There is not much there to order, in my opinion. It is not always possible . . . There are answers that are simply beyond us. Things it would take us centuries to understand."

"A soap merchant," mutters the comisario under his breath. He is disappointed. And still confused. "An ordinary, accursed soap merchant."

He feels the professor's eyes on him. The flash from the lighthouse reflected in the lenses of his spectacles.

"Why not a soap merchant? That has little to do with anything. This is about sensitivities."

"Well then, tell me what you think."

Barrull looks away. He clearly feels uncomfortable here, a feeling that quickly superseded his initial curiosity. Since he came up from the basement of the *Castillo*, his manner has been different—evasive.

"I spoke to him for scarcely half an hour."

Tizón says nothing; he simply waits. After a moment he sees Barrull look around him at the shadows of the old, abandoned building.

"He is a man obsessed with precision," the professor says finally. "I suspect the fact that his job involves a keen understanding of chemistry has much to do with it . . . He has, in a sense, his own system of weights and measures. Truth be told, he is very much a child of our times, a fully fledged son of the Enlightenment. A quantifying spirit, so to speak. Geometrical."

"Then he is not mad?"

"That word is a double-edged sword, Comisario. A dangerous ragbag of ideas."

"Then give me a better word. Define him for me."

"Would that I could," says the professor. "I understand only the smallest part of the matter. When I say obsessed with precision, I mean careful about details. All the more so if one is blessed with a mathematical mind, which is clearly the case here. This man is endowed with both characteristics. Though he had no formal scientific education, he is a natural mathematician, capable of intuiting constants and understanding the laws that govern a host of different types of data: air, smell, wind, angles . . . You know what I am talking about."

"Why did he kill?"

"Perhaps arrogance had something to do with it . . . rebelliousness, too. And resentment."

"Curious that you should mention resentment. This man had a

daughter . . . she died two years ago during the yellow fever epidemic. She was sixteen."

Barrull looks at him curiously, warily.

Tizón shakes his head, looking to one side then the other, his eyes filled with shadows. ". . . Like my own daughter."

He coldly recalls the long interrogation in the cell of the Guardiamarinas—Cadalso's astonishment when he was ordered to bring the man here rather than the dungeons on the Calle del Mirador; the superficial patching of the wound made by the bullet lodged in the man's right hip; the questioning, and the howls of pain at first; the reaction of Hipólito Barrull when he first brought him down into the ruined basement—his initial horror and consternation. *For ten years you have told me you are my friend, Professor. Now prove it. You have half an hour to plumb the soul of this man before he faces his demons, and mine.*

"Go on, please. Tell me what you think."

Barrull takes a little time to answer, and while he does Tizón thinks of the conversation he overheard earlier while leaning against a basement wall smoking a cigar. In the lamplight the comisario had observed the professor, perched on a rickety chair and talking to the prisoner who lay sprawled on an old straw mattress on the floor, his wrists and ankles shackled, a makeshift bandage wrapped about his hip. The sound of low voices, almost whispers, as the lamp's oily glow shimmered on the soap merchant's greasy skin and glittered in his eyes, the pupils dilated by a drop of laudanum—just one—poured into a glass of water. *I need him lucid and not in too much pain*, Tizón had explained. *Capable of reasoning. Just for a while, so the two of you can talk. After that, I don't care whether or not he suffers.*

"It is clear that this man is rebelling against our prosaic vision of the world," Barrull finally speaks. "To him, making soap is not simply a job, it requires great accuracy: it entails combining the various elements with absolute precision. It calls on his sense of touch, of smell. And the resulting product serves to luster other flesh, other skin—that of young women, mostly . . . the girls who come into his shop every day to ask for this or that."

"That son of a bitch."

"Don't oversimplify, Comisario."

"Are you suggesting that he is an artist as well as a scientist?"

"That is probably how he sees himself. Perhaps that notion saves him from having to think of himself merely as someone who combines substances. Deep down, he may be sensitive. And it is that sensitivity that leads him to kill."

Sensitivity. The word draws a bitter laugh from Tizón.

"The whip of braided wire . . . he had it with him. We found it in the grotto."

"I assume he got the idea from the penitent brotherhood," Barrull says.

"He is not even a true member. In the Santa Cueva, they accept only men of noble birth . . . This man merely assists at ceremonies. He is a sort of acolyte, a servant."

Tizón looks up at the heavens. Above the crumbling walls of the shadowy *Castillo*, the stars are shining, as cold as his own thoughts. Never has he felt more lucid, he thinks; never has he been as clear-sighted about the present and the future.

"How could he anticipate the bombs?"

"He trained himself. He sensed that Cádiz is a special place, shaped by the sea and the wind, and the urban landscape that challenges or channels them. To him, the city is not merely a collection of buildings inhabited by people, it is an agglomeration of air, silences, sounds, temperature, light, smells . . ."

"So we were on the right track?"

"Absolutely. You proved it yourself. Just like this man, you created a singular map composed of just such elements. A secret, parallel city."

There is a long silence, one that the policeman is loathe to break. Eventually, Barrull shifts slightly, anxious.

"Damn it," he says. "This is complicated, Comisario . . . I can scarcely imagine it. I only spoke with the man for half an hour. I am not at all sure that getting myself mixed up in this—"

Tizón raises his hand impatiently, brushing aside these excuses. He does not have time for such luxuries tonight.

"The bombs . . . Tell me how the *before* and *after* came about."

This time the silence is brief, thoughtful. Barrull stands frozen again.

"I can hazard a theory," he says finally. "A simple hypothesis with no scientific basis. When the French field guns began to fire, the complex world of this chemist-soap merchant changed in ways he could not have anticipated. Perhaps at first he feared he might be a victim of one of these shells. Perhaps he visited the bomb sites, drawn to them by the relief of having emerged unscathed. It may be that, having do so over and over, his sense of relief gave way to other feelings."

"The desire to expose himself to danger?" Tizón suggests. "To put himself at risk?"

"It's possible. Perhaps he wanted to position himself at the far end of the trajectory, in the danger zone . . . His instinct, his sensitivity urged him to manipulate these events."

"By killing?"

"Yes. Why not? . . . Consider his position: a human life in places where bombs have exploded but not killed. Compensating for some flaw in science, complementing an imperfect technology using his innate sense of precision. In this way, a death and a point of impact would correspond with absolute exactitude."

"How then was he able to anticipate the bombs?"

The lantern illuminates a strange expression on Barrull's equine face; something akin to a smile.

"You said it yourself, in a way . . . Obsession when combined with extreme sensitivity can produce monsters. And this man's obsession did just that. He deduced that there is no such thing as chance, and he felt an aching need to predict precisely where the next shells would fall. To challenge the illusory bastard son of ignorance."

"And so he began to think?"

Tizón notices Barrull is staring at him curiously, as though surprised by his keen understanding.

"Exactly so. Or that is what I believe—that he simply thought and thought. And with cold precision, his sick mind and his extreme sensibility did the rest. His monstrous crimes became merely . . ."

"Technical?"

The comisario is aware he said this in an authoritative manner. But the professor seems little concerned with his tone; it is the idea that fascinates him.

"Yes, I think so," he says. "Technical, objective . . . He was reasserting the rights of the universe, do you understand?"

"I understand."

And the policeman does understand. He has understood for some time. The distance separating them is being curtailed at a rate that seems astonishing. Even frightening. What were the professor's words? He remembers: *rebelliousness and resentment.* A vision of the world in accordance with the laws of Nature. The human condition and the state of the universe. Ants brushed beneath the foot of a cruel God, oblivious to everything. An avenging hand. A whip of steel.

"He was bringing order out of chaos," Barrull says, "by means of reducing suffering to simple natural laws. Being intimately familiar with the city, the man began to devise a series of auspicious sites throughout the city. It is possible that the sense of smell required by his job helped him in this: his sensitivity to air, to odors. And he began to wonder: given factors such as wind speed and direction, are there specific points more likely to be hit by the French bombs? And so in his mind he mapped out the places where bombs had fallen and attributed to each a probability. In this way, his mental map would have colored sectors representing greater or lesser probability. His mathematical intelligence analyzed these impact points and pinpointed anomalies, curves and trajectories. He identified gaps in the map that had to be filled. By now, there was no turning back. This was probability, not random chance . . . precise mathematics—"

Tizón interrupts him with perverse satisfaction. "Not quite precise," he says. "He made one mistake. No bomb ever fell on the Calle de Laurel."

"That makes our hypothesis all the more likely. It gives him a margin of error, don't you agree?"

The policeman does not answer. He remembers his own nervousness, the fruitless waiting and the temptation to redefine everything. He thinks of the sequence of mistakes he himself made on this chessboard, including the last: the queen's gambit.

"The fact remains," Barrull continues, "that it was in these gaps, waiting for a bomb to fall, that the man killed . . . By now it was no longer a matter of compensating for some flaw in science or technology, nor of using the suffering of others to fill the void left by his dead daughter . . . Over and over, he wanted to confirm that he, a humble artisan, had penetrated the mysteries of the universe."

"Hence the final challenge."

"So I believe. He knew that you were on his trail, and he accepted the challenge. This was why he waited so long before killing again. He was hunting the hunter. And when he believed he was ready, he decided to capture a different pawn to the one you offered him. He succeeded, but misjudged his play by a few short minutes."

Tizón's laugh echoes around the dark walls of the castle, as sinister as the scene itself. "Random chance! Cadalso's desperate need to piss!"

"Exactly. The soap merchant did not factor this into his probabilities."

The two men stand in silence. The air is still, not a breath of wind. The sky is a black curtain dotted with pinpricks.

"I am convinced," Barrull adds after a moment, "that he felt no pleasure when he killed."

"Probably not."

The sound of footsteps. Two shadows appear from the street, emerging through the gap in the wall. One of them, tall and lumbering, steps forward, outlined in the darkness. Tizón recognizes Cadalso.

"Señor?"

"Did you come alone?"

"Yes. As you ordered."

The policeman turns to Hipólito Barrull.

"I'm afraid I must ask you to leave now, Professor . . . I am very grateful, but you have to go."

Barrull looks at him curiously, anxiously. The lantern reflects in the lenses of his glasses. "Who is the other man?"

Tizón hesitates for a second. *What difference does it make now?* he thinks. "The father of the last girl who was murdered."

Barrull takes a step back, seeking out the shelter of the darkness— seeking to distance himself. A knight on a chessboard, thinks Tizón, retreating from an attacking rook.

"What do you intend to do?"

This is one of those questions that, deep down, requires no answer. And Tizón does not bother to give one. He is so calm that, although it is a warm night, his hands feel cold.

"Go," he says. "You were never here. No one knows about this meeting."

Barrull hesitates, then finally steps past Tizón; as he does so, his face is framed in the lamplight, grave, streaked with shadows.

"Take care," he whispers. "These are different times. The Constitution . . . You know. New laws."

"Indeed. New laws."

They shake hands: a contract, one drawn up by Barrull, who stares at Tizón as though for the last time. For a moment he seems about to say something, but in the end he simply shrugs.

"It has been a privilege to help you, Comisario."

"Goodbye, Professor."

Barrull turns on his heel, steps through the breach in the wall, and disappears into the Calle del Silencio. Tizón takes the leather case from his pocket and extracts a cigar as Cadalso and the other shadow step forward. Next to Tizón's henchman the lantern set on the ground reveals a humble man of average height, who takes a few steps before stopping, silent.

"You can go," the comisario tells his assistant.

Cadalso obeys, disappearing through the gap in the wall. Then the comisario turns back to the newcomer. He notices a flash of cold steel tucked into the man's belt.

"He is downstairs," Tizón says.

THE STAIRCASE PLUMMETS like a black spiral into some nightmare. Felipe Mojarra gropes his way blindly, leaning against the dank walls, avoiding the rubble on the steps. From time to time he stops to listen, but he senses only the rarefied air of the hollow into which he is descending. Shock and pain—the passing hours and the habit of living reconcile a man to everything—have now given way to a cold, inexorable desperation, as dark and still as stagnant water. He realizes his mouth is dry, his skin numb, insensible to everything but the slow, powerful throb of the pulse in his wrists and temples. At times, the beating seems to stop for a moment and he feels a sudden emptiness in his chest, as if his lungs and his heart are paralyzed.

Felipe Mojarra takes another step, and another. However often he blinks, however much he closes his eyes against the dark, dizzying, seemingly endless descent, still an image hovers clearly before his eyes: an image of cold, dead, naked flesh laid out on a white marble bench. His own wail of shock still burns in his throat, a hoarse, desperate, defiant howl at the unfathomable nature of what has happened—at the injustice. And then, like a sliver of ice in his gut, the anguish of being unable to recognize in this pale, mutilated corpse—reeking of human entrails, sluiced with water that has pooled on the stone floor of the morgue—the small, warm, sleeping body he once held in his arms. The smell of gentle fever, of dreams. The warm, slender girl he will never again be able to remember as she was.

A light below illuminates the final steps. Felipe Mojarra stops, one hand on the wall, as he waits for his heart to slow, for his pulse to return to normal. He takes a deep breath and then descends the last few steps. He finds himself in a vaulted, empty space, dimly lit by a half-burned tallow candle set into a niche in the wall. In the faint light, he sees a man naked but for a blanket around his shoulders and a soiled bandage wrapped around his hip. Shackled at wrist and ankle, he sits on a straw mattress, his back to the wall, his head drooping onto arms that rest on his knees, as if he is half asleep. Seeing him, Mojarra suddenly feels his legs give way and slowly lowers himself to sit on the bottom step. For a long time, he does not move but sits, staring at the man. At first the other man seems unaware of his presence, but finally he raises his head and looks at the salter. Felipe Mojarra finds himself face-to-face with a stranger: middle-aged, with red hair and freckled skin. His whole body is a mass of bruises. His lower lip is split, and a trickle of dried blood extends to the tip of his chin.

Neither says anything. They stare at each other for a moment, then the man listlessly rests his head upon his arms again. Felipe Mojarra waits for the emptiness of his heart to fill and then struggles to his feet. The warm slender body, he remembers, the smell of a sleeping child. As he opens his knife, there is a soft click from the safety catch and the shackled man looks up.

Rogelio Tizón leans against the wall, smoking. The moon, appearing from behind the ruined battlements atop the tower of the Castillo de Guardiamarinas, casts a milky glow that throws the rubble of the courtyard into sharp relief. The tip of Tizón's cigar, glowing intermittently, is the only thing about him that seems alive; were it not for this point of light, a casual observer would not see the comisario for the shadows, in spite of the lantern that is now guttering out.

The screams stopped some time ago. For almost an hour, Tizón listened with a professional curiosity. Muffled by distance and the thick walls, they came from the stairwell to the basement a few feet away. Some were sharp, short cries; brief, stifled moans. Others were longer: howls of agony that seemed to go on forever, finally faltering when whoever was screaming had expended every ounce of energy and despair. There is no sound now, but still the comisario does not move. He waits.

Slow, uncertain footsteps. A presence nearby. A shadow emerges from the stairwell, moving toward Tizón. Finally it stops next to him.

"It is done," says Felipe Mojarra.

His voice sounds tired. The policeman makes no comment but offers another cigar from his case, patting Mojarra's shoulder to get his attention. It takes a moment before the man reacts. He takes the cigar. Tizón strikes a match on the stone wall and holds the flame close. In the flickering glow, he studies Mojarra's face as he bends to light the cigar: the whiskers framing his hard features, eyes staring into space, still filled with horror—his own and that of the other man. Tizón notices a slight tremble in the damp fingers that smear the cigar with blood.

"I didn't think it was possible to scream with no tongue," Mojarra says finally, exhaling smoke.

He seems genuinely surprised. Rogelio Tizón laughs in the darkness—his habitual dangerous, wolfish laugh, baring his teeth. A flash of gold on one side of his mouth.

"Well, now you know. It's possible."

EPILOGUE

ငာင

Rain is falling over the inlet at Rota. A warm summer drizzle—the sky will clear to the southwest before sunset—its small droplets speckling the glassy waters. There is not a breath of wind. The low, mournful sky is reflected on the bay, framing the distant city like an engraving or a painting in white and gray. At one end of the beach, where the sand is broken by a line of black rocks and dead seaweed, a woman gazes at the wreck of a ship grounded near the shore: shorn of its masts, the blackened timbers are charred and riddled with cannon-fire. The hull, which still offers some sense of its original length, is canted on its side to reveal the keel, the battered deck, a section of the internal frame and cross-timbers, like a skeleton gradually stripped by time and weather.

Before the remains of the *Culebra*, Lolita Palma stands, impassive; the drizzle soaking the mantilla covering her head and shoulders. She is clutching a purse. For some time she has been trying to re-create in her mind the last moments of the vessel that lies before her. Her calm gaze moves across the scene, calculating the distance from land, the proximity of the rocks, the range of the cannons that until very recently stood in the empty embrasures of the forts ringing the inlet. She tries to imagine the darkness, the danger, the din of battle and the blaze of cannonfire. And each time she manages to catch a glimpse, to conjure some image, some concrete moment, she bows her head in grief—astonished, in spite of herself, at the darkness, the terror and lies in the hearts of men. Then she raises her eyes and forces herself to look again. The air smells of damp sand and seaweed. On the steel-gray water, the concentric circles made by each drop of rain ripple out with geometric precision, overlapping with others, covering the surface between the shore and the ravaged hulk of the cutter.

Finally turning her back on the sea, Lolita Palma walks toward Rota. On the left, by the jetty, small boats lie at anchor, their lateen sails hoisted, washed by the rain, hanging from the yardarms like wet laundry. Next to the jetty are the remains of a dismantled bastion— probably one of the gun batteries that protected this stretch of coastline. The walls are still hung with withered garlands of flowers placed there by the people of Cádiz; on the very day the French retreated, beneath a blazing sun, with every church bell in the city tolling victory, they set off across the bay in hundreds of small boats or along the reef road in carriages and on horseback, making a pilgrimage to the abandoned military posts to celebrate their liberation. But the official jubilation was tempered by a barely concealed feeling of frustration that they were witnessing the end of an era marked by market speculation, lucrative rents and exorbitant leases. As cousin Toño, seeing the long faces of some of his friends, succinctly remarked between two bottles of sherry—now finally available in Cádiz without restriction— patriotism is never far from the pocket.

On the far side of the curved ramparts, up the hillside, the streets of Rota still bear the scars of looting and pillaging. The ashen sky, damp air and drizzle underscore the tragic scene: ruined houses, streets filled with rubble, scenes of desperate poverty; people bankrupted by war beg in the doorways or eke out a living in the shells of houses with roofs made of sailcloth or makeshift timbers. Even the railings have disappeared. Like all the villages in the area, Rota was devastated by the last spree of looting, murder and rape that marked the French retreat. And yet many women left with the Imperial Army of their own volition. Of fourteen such women who were traveling in the carriages captured by *guerrilleros* near Jerez, six were shot and eight exposed to public shame, their heads shaven, beneath a sign reading *Gabacho Whores*.

Walking between the parish church—its doors smashed, its interior plundered—and the old castle, Lolita Palma stops for a moment, trying to get her bearings; then, taking the street on her left, she heads for a large mansion that still preserves some of the old white and dark-red rendering that once decorated its brick walls. Santos, her manservant, is standing in the vaulted doorway, smoking, an umbrella tucked under one arm. Seeing his mistress arrive, the old sailor drops his cigar and rushes forward, struggling to open the umbrella, but Lolita waves him away.

"Is he here?"

"Yes, señora."

The interior of the building—a former wine store with blackened barrels still lining the walls—is lit by narrow slits high up on the walls. The ghostly gray light gives the place a mournful atmosphere, made worse by the acrid stench of sick, maimed and filthy bodies that emanates from the hundreds of poor wretches who lie in piteous rows on thin straw mattresses or on blankets laid on the floor.

"It is not a pleasant place," Santos says.

Lolita Palma does not respond. She has removed her mantilla to shake it dry and is holding her breath, not allowing herself to be overcome by the grim scene and the nauseating stench. Seeing her enter, a surgeon's mate in the Royal Armada—a haggard young man wearing a dirty apron over his blue uniform, his jacket sleeves rolled up—comes to meet her, pays his respects and points to a spot at the far end of the ward. Leaving Santos and the surgeon's mate behind, Lolita walks alone as far as the mattress against the end wall, next to which someone has just placed a low wicker chair. On the mattress, a man is lying on his back, draped with a sheet that molds itself to his body. In his ashen face, its gauntness emphasized by a beard that has not been shaved in several days, the eyes are shining with a feverish glow. A thick, ugly purple scar slashes his whiskers, running from the left corner of his mouth to his ear. He no longer looks handsome, thinks Lolita with a surge of pity. He no longer looks like himself.

She sits down on the low chair, holding the bag in her lap, rearranging the folds of her skirt and her damp mantilla. The feverish eyes watched her approach, following her in silence. They are not green now, but seem darker because the pupils are dilated—drugs, probably, to ease the pain. For a moment, the woman turns away, uncomfortable, looking along the body to the hollow in the sheet below the right hip where one leg has been amputated, a hand's-breadth from the groin. For several seconds she stares, fascinated, at this empty space. When finally she looks up again, she notices he has not taken his eyes off her.

"I had so many words prepared," she says eventually. "But none of them will serve me."

No answer, only the dark, intense stare, the feverish glow. Lolita leans over the mattress and as she does a raindrop trickles from her hair across her face.

"I owe you so much, Captain Lobo."

Still the man says nothing, and she studies his face again: pain has drawn his skin taut against his cheekbones and his lips, cracked by fever, are covered in scabs and sores. Including the vicious scar. *Those lips once kissed mine*, she thinks, distraught. *This mouth once barked orders during the battle I witnessed from the far side of the bay*—tiny sparks of cannonfire against the darkness.

"We shall take care of you."

She is conscious of the plural the moment she utters it, and she can tell Pépé Lobo has noticed too. She feels grief surge within her, a desperate, deep-seated sadness. And so the word hovers in the air, an unwelcome intruder between the woman and the man, who is still staring at her. Then she sees the corsair's tormented lips contract. The hint of a smile, she thinks—or perhaps something he is about to say, some word that does not come.

"This is a terrible place. I will try to have you moved from here."

She glances around uneasily. The stench—even he smells, she thinks, unable to stop herself—is nauseating. It seems to cling to her clothing and her skin. She cannot abide it, so she takes her fan from her bag and fans herself. After a moment, she realizes this is the fan with the dragon tree painted on it, the tree they had planned to visit together but never did—the symbol of what could never be, and never was.

"You will live, Captain. You will come through this. There is a lot of . . . Well. There is money waiting for you. You and your men have earned it."

The feverish eyes, which have been staring at the fan, blink suddenly. It is as if, for the corsair, the words *live* and *come through* are not related.

"Me and my men," he whispers. Finally, he speaks, his voice low and hoarse. His dark, dilated pupils stare into space. "Now there's a pretty joke . . ."

Lolita leans toward him, confused. Close up, he smells of defeat, of stale sweat and suffering.

"Don't talk like that. So sadly."

Pépé Lobo shakes his head. Lolita looks at his hands as they lie on the sheet, the pale skin and the long dirty fingernails, the blue swollen veins beneath the surface.

"The surgeon says you are recovering well. You will always have someone to look after you and enough to live on. You will have what you always wanted, a plot of land and a house far from the sea . . . I give you my word."

"Your word," he echoes, almost wistfully.

His butchered mouth finally curls into a smile, she notices. Or rather a pensive, almost indifferent expression.

"I am dead," he says suddenly.

"Don't say such foolish nonsense."

He is no longer looking at her. He turned away some moments ago.

"I was killed in the cove at Rota."

Perhaps he is right, thinks Lolita. A corpse capable of speech would smile exactly as Pépé Lobo is smiling at this moment.

"I am buried on the beach there, with twenty-three of my men."

Lolita turns this way and that, trying to stem the pain that wells in her breast. Moved by her own pity. Suddenly, without wanting to, she finds herself on her feet, covering her head with her mantilla.

"I will see you soon, Captain."

She knows this is not true. She knows it even as, step by step, quickening her pace, she walks back along the ward between the rows of men lying on the ground. She knows it as she steps outside and can finally take a deep breath of cool, damp air. She does not stop, but keeps walking until she comes to the shoreline and stands, staring at the blurred line of the white-gray city in the distance, as rain splashes her face with cold tears.

ACKNOWLEDGMENTS

The Siege is a novel, not a work of history. This makes it possible to take small liberties, adapting a date, a name, a character or an actual event to the needs of the narrative. That aside, I am grateful for the invaluable help of numerous people and institutions, in particular Óscar Lobato, José Manuel Sánchez Ron, José Manuel Guerrero Acosta and Francisco José González, the librarian of the Observatorio de la Armada. The director of the Museo Municipal de Cádiz, the municipal council of San Fernando, and Luisa Martín-Merás of the Museo Naval de Madrid put at my disposal maps and documents which proved extraordinarily useful, and my friends at the Cádiz bookshops Falla and Quorum kept me up to date on everything that has been published in recent years about Cádiz during the French siege and the Constitution of 1812. Juan López Eady, sea captain and hydrographic surveyor, guided me at appropriate moments. Thanks to the expert advice of Esperanza Salas, chief librarian at Unicaja, I was able to discover in the newspapers of 1810–12 some crucial information about ships, fleets and port-related incidents. My old friend, the antiquarian bookseller Luis Bardón, tracked down a number of key works of the period for me. The Cádiz historian Alberto Ramos Santana and his wife, Marieta Cantos, were kind enough to read the book in manuscript, and Iñigo Pastor cast a careful professional eye over Lolita Palma's finances. It is only fair to mention, among others, the specialist work of María Nélida García Fernández, Manuel Bustos Rodríguez, María Jesús Arazola Corvera, María del Carmen Cózar Navarro, Manuel Guillermo Supervielle and Juan Miguel Teijeiro, all of whom were of great help in acquainting me with the mind-set, the mores and the customs of the commercial class of Cádiz at the turn of the nineteenth century. I would also like to thank the city of Cádiz and its inhabitants for their kind hospitality, their assistance and their unfailing warmth.

A P-R

La Navata, December 2009

TRANSLATOR'S ACKNOWLEDGMENTS

There are times when being armed with diligence, persistence and even a copy of the 1836 *Diccionario Técnico Marítimo* are not enough when a translator is faced with a world that is as truly unfamiliar as the high seas during the Napoleonic wars. I would like to offer my heartfelt thanks to historical novelist and maritime historian David Cordingly for his generous help and advice in translating the seafaring passages of the novel; his encyclopedic knowledge of historical vessels, armaments and sailing terms proved invaluable in bringing the novel to life.

FRANK WYNNE

ABOUT THE AUTHOR

ARTURO PÉREZ-REVERTE's bestselling books, including *The Club Dumas*, *The Flanders Panel*, *The Seville Communion*, and the Captain Alatriste series, have been translated into thirty-four languages in fifty countries and have sold millions of copies. Pérez-Reverte was born in 1951 in Cartagena, Spain, and now lives in Madrid, where he was recently elected to the Spanish Royal Academy. A retired war journalist, he covered conflicts in Angola, Bosnia, Croatia, El Salvador, Lebanon, Libya, Nicaragua, Romania, the Persian Gulf, and Sudan, among others. He now writes fiction full-time.

ABOUT THE TYPE

The text of this book was set in Janson, a typeface designed about 1690 by Nicholas Kis (1650–1702), a Hungarian living in Amsterdam, and for many years mistakenly attributed to the Dutch printer Anton Janson. In 1919, the matrices became the property of the Stempel Foundry in Frankfurt. It is an old-style book face of excellent clarity and sharpness. Janson serifs are concave and splayed; the contrast between thick and thin strokes is marked.